THE
MANNINGS

Also by Fred Mustard Stewart:

LADY DARLINGTON
THE METHUSELAH ENZYME
THE MEPHISTO WALTZ

THE MANNINGS

A NOVEL BY

Fred Mustard Stewart

ARBOR HOUSE

NEW YORK

*As always to my wife, Joan, and to the
memory of my mother, who used to tell
me stories of how it used to be*

PART

I

THE ROOTS OF EMPIRE

1900–1905

CHAPTER ONE

IT WAS the first parade of the century. The first big, brass-band, American-flag, Fourth-of-July parade of the new twentieth century, and that's how Elkins, Ohio, was celebrating it. Down the main street of the small town ten miles west of Akron came the high school band, resplendent in its red uniforms and white hats, blaring "Columbia, the Gem of the Ocean." Behind the band marched the local chapter of the Grand Army of the Republic, their uniforms still smelling faintly of mothballs but now freshly pressed, their late-middle-aged legs, trying valiantly but not quite managing to keep in step or in time with the music, their faces—which had been so unlined at Vicksburg and Atlanta thirty-five years before—showing the marks of time's parade. Then, in his buggy drawn by a fine bay, the mayor of Elkins, the Honorable Eugene Pierson, tipping his straw hat to the cheering crowds that lined the street and wishing to God the parade were over so he could beat the blasted Ohio July heat with a cold beer. Sitting beside the mayor, also tipping his straw hat, was the guest speaker of the day, the Honorable Adrian Tutwiler, third-term Congressman from the district and protégé of the powerful Republican boss, Mark Hanna. Congressman Tutwiler, a pleasant-faced thirty-nine-year-old who had been a salesman for the Hanna Coal Company before his ingratiating personality and devotion to the Ohio Republican machine had attracted the attention of Mr. Hanna himself, was up for re-election in November and was spending his summer reminding the voters of his voting record in Congress, which proved his unwavering devotion to *their* best interests.

Behind the mayor and Congressman Tutwiler came the Number One Fire-Eaters, Elkins's proud volunteer firefighters, on their gleaming red wagon. Then a contingent of stern-faced, white-dressed W.C. T.U.-ers carrying sternly worded placards warning against the evils of "Devil Rum." Next, the Odd Fellows; the Grange; the Elks; the

9

Methodist Church Ladies' Volunteer Charity Breakfast League; the
Over the Teacups Club (belles-lettres and the Arts); a float, donated
by the Elkins Bank and Trust Company, featuring a *tableau vivant*
representing America's Manifest Destiny; the China Missionary Society, currently much in the news thanks to the Boxer Rebellion (only
one month before, Christians in Hopei had been massacred by the
Boxers, precipitating the siege of the legations in Peking); another
float, prepared by the Presbyterian Church, this one a tableau representing Christian Virtue Rewarding Democracy with Abundance; and,
finally, one hundred employees of the Rosen Stove Company, Elkins's
largest (and only) industry, which employed half the town's work
force, each employee wearing a straw hat with star-spangled hatband
and carrying a paper Amreican flag. It was a grand parade, everyone
agreed, suitably spectacular to welcome in the new century, the American century bursting with energy, muscle, high hopes, dreams, youth,
not to mention greed and corruption. The "Christian Century," Rev-
erend Sims had designated it in his sermon the previous Sunday. The
"Democratic Century," the Elkins *Star Chronicle* had called it in that
morning's editorial. Congressman Tutwiler was going to call it the
"Century of Unparalleled Wealth and Opportunity" in his speech
later on (there would be no mention that the average factory worker
made less than five hundred dollars a year, and one American out
of eight lived in the slums).

But no one in Elkins was thinking of slums or statistics. Life was
good; the day was gorgeous and hot; the red brick and limestone store-
fronts on Main Street were festooned with bunting and flags; the
band was playing, the parade was exciting, the century was new, and
there was going to be plenty of beer in Matahoochi Park afterward
and, that night, the grand fireworks display.

Mark Manning felt on top of the world. He was twenty-two, tough,
smart, attractive, and had something of a bad reputation. Not that
his beginnings weren't respectable enough: the Mannings had worked
a small farm two miles outside of town for three generations. Mark's
parents, Seymour and Margaret Manning, had been hard-working,
God-fearing Presbyterian Scottish-Irish. Aside from their intelligence
and perseverence, there was nothing in their lives to give a genetic
clue to what eventually would be their son's spectacular career. Margaret Manning had died in childbirth when Mark was four, and
people said this was one reason the boy had grown up "wild," because the father had become so depressed by his wife's death that he
lost all interest in raising his only child and let him run free, not

even forcing him to go to church any more. Mark was always picking fights in school, which his critics in later life were to point to as an early indication of his "ruthless" character. However, some of his more generous contemporaries attributed much of his bad reputation to plain old American love of adventure and a liking for practical jokes, not always appreciated by his victims. No one denied that he was bright and a natural leader, but his teachers deplored the fact that though he claimed he believed in God, he had no true interest in religion, his moral code being more his own than the church's. He was, in short, a "bad 'un" to the town's leading citizens. And when he passed through puberty, he graduated into a full-fledged menace in the eyes of the respectable mothers of the respectable girls—though the daughters were secretly enthralled by his cocksure attitude and mischievous good humor. Most of all, they adored his good looks; and even the church ladies had to admit that he was handsome, though they also said that his looks were proof of his bad character, as if the Devil made his children beautiful. He was six foot two, athletically built, with a full head of red-gold hair that had, it was whispered, been the undoing of the Keys girl. Poor Arabella Keys had fallen for that red-gold hair when Mark was sixteen, and shortly afterward Arabella had begun putting on suspicious weight. The Keys family had abruptly moved to Cleveland, Mr. Keys saying he had been offered an unexpected promotion by the railroad.

When he was eighteen, Mark had gone to Ohio Southern, a small college near the West Virginia border, where he excelled in sports and managed high marks, though the faculty said his "natural leadership abilities" were not channeled into "morally constructive outlets." How old Seymour Manning interpreted these reports was never known, for in the middle of Mark's sophomore year his father contracted pneumonia and died, leaving his son the small farm and a savings account totaling $1,852.36. Mark sold the farm for five thousand dollars cash money, then began adding to his nest egg by traveling through the Midwest during his summer vacations, selling everything from hair oil to back liniment. When just the previous month he had graduated from college, he finally did channel his energies into something "constructive" by buying Bancroft's Bicycle Shop on the corner of Fifth and Main, and though everyone said the young upstart would fail, Mark proceeded to do remarkably well. Now, only a few weeks after setting up in business, people were beginning to change their minds about the "young Manning boy." He seemed finally to be settling down, which was a good thing; and there certainly was no one in town who worked harder at his small business or seemed to believe more wholeheartedly in the Great American Dream, which was, after all, what the Fourth of July was all about, wasn't it? Still, if he *only* would stay away from that Farr girl . . .

The "Farr girl," with whom Mark was watching the parade, was Sheila Farr, the daughter of Maryann Farr, an Irish lady addicted to the grape who owned Farr's Restaurant, next to the Central Ohio Railway tracks. Sheila's morals were considered to be about on a par with those of her mother's clientele—railroad men, bachelors, general lowlife, and Mark Manning. Sheila managed the restaurant, and it was generally assumed she was available. She was attractive, possessed of a fine, voluptuous figure, but the church ladies believed her "cheap." Her face somehow lacked "refinement," and there was a brassy quality about her. Of course, what could one expect from a cashier-waitress in a cheap restaurant on the wrong side of the tracks?

The judgment was too harsh. Sheila behaved outrageously with Mark because he goaded her into it, because she was in love with him, and because she rather enjoyed shocking the stuffy people in town. She wasn't, though, "available" except to Mark, and she had been totally faithful to him for two years. Now, as the float representing Christian Virtue Rewarding Democracy with Abundance went by, Mark leaned down and whispered something in her ear. Sheila gave him a disapproving look but couldn't quite stifle a laugh that brought glares from those standing nearby. After all, everybody knew that Cynthia Barnes, representing a classically gowned Democracy, was cross-eyed and that she did look a bit, well, peculiar as she stared rhapsodically at Beverly Amstuts, representing Christian Virtue. But the tableau was beautiful and sincere, and it wasn't Cynthia's fault she was cross-eyed (particularly with her pince-nez).

The parade passed down Main Street, then turned right onto Elm, the shaded residential street of the town's well-to-do that led out to Matahoochi Park. The crowd followed along, the children running excitedly to keep up or surge ahead, not minding the heat, while their parents moved more slowly, encumbered, as most of them were, with picnic baskets. Elm Street was at least cooler. The noise of the band echoed off the façades of the stately white houses, most girdled with gingerbreaded front porches, on many of which the elder members of Elkins's leading families were either standing or sitting in wicker rockers, sipping lemonade and fanning themselves with paper fans from Jenkins's Funeral Parlor as they watched the show. Crash! Bang! went the cymbals. Tarantara! went the trumpets. What a parade! What a glorious Fourth!

"What a hell of a day to make love," Mark whispered to Sheila as they moved with the crowd down the Elm Street sidewalk.

"Mark!"

"Well, isn't it?"

"Too hot, if you ask me. And knowing you, you won't."

Clang went the fire bell; boom went the big bass drum. Bang, bang, bang, bang, spit a distant string of firecrackers. They passed the biggest house on Elm Street, a brick Victorian mansion bristling with turrets and chimneys, its wide lawn almost hidden from the sidewalk by lilac bushes and a low, wrought-iron fence. Mark looked through the gaps in the hedge as they passed by, getting a flickering view of the tall, lace-curtained windows shielded from the baking sun by striped awnings that drooped over the glass, further concealing the dark rooms within. The house appeared lifeless, but Mark was sure it wasn't. Somewhere in those large, cool parlors she would be sitting before her Bechstein practicing, probably, ignoring the parade and the town as she always did (or was she perhaps afraid of it?). And her father would be—where? In his study, reading the month-old German newspapers the postmaster said came in thick bundles from New York, transported from the Old World at incredible expense by the Nord Deutsche Lloyd steamers? Or reading his beloved Heine? Or reading—what? What did Jews read? Sacred scriptures telling how to kill Jesus? That's what the church ladies whispered, but Mark thought they were nitwits.

Jews were exotics in Ohio and practically nonexistent in small towns, their rarity merely serving to fan the flames of anti-Semitism that already smoldered in the provincial Midwest. But Mark wasn't an anti-Semite. Far from hating Sam Rosen and his daughter, Mark was fascinated by them. Sam Rosen was the richest man in town, the founder and chairman of the Rosen Stove Company, a *millionaire.* He and his daughter stayed aloof from the town, which was the way both the Rosens and the town seemed to prefer it. Mark was determined to do something about that aloofness. The Rosens were not only rich, they were "cultured"—not like the Over the Teacups ladies with their book reports on *The Prisoner of Zenda* and their musicales where the church organist would stumble her way through "The Scarf Dance"—but cultured in a way Mark vaguely connected with Europeans. They were, somehow, Big Time, and Mark wanted very badly to be Big Time. He had surely bought the new century's dream. The question was how to live it. . . .

"Trying to get a peek at Charlotte?" Sheila asked playfully, though there was an edge to her voice.

"And what if I am?"

"I suppose you'd like to add her to your list of conquests, along with yours truly, not to mention Irene Sherbaugh."

Irene Sherbaugh was secretary to the president of the Elkins Bank and Trust, and Sheila was no admirer of Irene Sherbaugh.

Mark laughed. "And what if I would?"

"Bet Charlotte would tell you where to go if you even tried."

"Five dollars?"

"Don't be silly."

"You're afraid you'll lose."

"Not at all. Besides, Jewish girls don't like Christians."

"Bet on it."

Sheila gave him a sour look. Her playful tone was getting more difficult to keep up. She wanted Mark, and whenever he showed interest in other girls—which was too often—she could hardly stand it. Still, in moments of cold honesty, she told herself that Mark was probably too ambitious to marry anyone who couldn't help him, and how could she help him, saddled the way she was with a mother like hers and no money at all? But mostly she pushed aside such thoughts, so that now just the idea of losing Mark to the beautiful Charlotte Rosen was enough to make her frantic. Not, of course, that she thought he had much of a chance. Charlotte had just graduated from some place out East called Wellesley and (it was said) she had a Princeton man for a beau, so why in the world would she be interested in Mark Manning? Besides, Mark didn't even know her! Then why was she afraid of losing him to her? Because she knew he was intrigued by the Rosens, by the Rosens' money, if nothing else. And she would never underestimate Mark Manning's ability to get what he wanted. It was possible she could lose the bet.

The parade passed through the rock-built gate of Matahoochi Park and the crowd swarmed into the grassy acres deeded to the town thirty years before by the now-extinct Elkins family and named after Chief Matahoochi, the chief of the Indian tribe that had inhabited this area in Ohio before the settlers bribed, bought or plain stole it away from them at the beginning of the previous century. The park was situated on the edge of the Matahoochi River, and wooden tables and benches were placed at intervals along the river and under the trees. There was a gaudy white bandstand in the middle of the park, and it was here the parade ended, with the band taking its seats for a well-deserved rest. Everyone else spread out to reserve a shaded piece of turf and listen to the speeches. Picnic baskets were unpacked, blankets spread on the grass by those who couldn't get a wooden table, bottles of homemade pickles were opened along with the crocks of potato salad and baked beans, hams and chickens were sliced and the beer kegs provided free by the town were tapped.

As Sheila laid out the picnic she had prepared, Mark went to check on the bicycle he had donated to the raffle being held to benefit the hospital construction fund. The town had been trying for two years to raise a hundred thousand dollars to build a much-needed hospital, and Mark felt his donation to the raffle would help offset the unfavorable reputation he still had among many of the town's leading citizens. After checking the bicycle, Mark returned to the rear of the bandstand, from which Congressman Tutwiler was making his address. Mark leaned against the white railing and with his straw hat waved away a bumblebee from his head, waiting for the Congressman to run dry.

He had an offer to make Congressman Tutwiler.

In the luxurious main cabin of the yacht *Alberta,* moored in the harbor of Cap Ferrat on the Côte d'Azur, was an old man with a long white beard, unnaturally long fingernails and a huge nose, and portions of whose not altogether savory career would one day find their parallels in the exploits of a young American named Mark Manning. One of the richest men in Europe, he was also one of the most notorious and, in many ways, the most eccentric. An advanced hypochondriac, he eschewed germs by having his table linen boiled daily and by instructing his valet to iron the London *Times* to bake out the microbes. On rainy days, he encased his beard in a Russian leather bag to prevent it from becoming wet and giving him a cold. He was fascinated by his bowels and drank frequent carafes of warm water to keep them moving. Hypersexed throughout his life, he possessed little discrimination in women, having bedded a gamut from ballerinas to prostitutes, including, according to the infamous Mrs. Jeffries, head of a London child prostitute ring, prepubescent virgins. Though intelligent, he was one of the greatest Philistines in an age of unparalleled vulgarity. He detested music, sneered at poetry and literature and had execrable taste in architecture. Though married to a Hapsburg archduchess, though a cousin of Queen Victoria, a brother of the former empress of Mexico and a former father-in-law of the heir to the Austro-Hungarian throne (the Archduke Rudolph who had killed himself and his mistress twelve years before at Mayerling), this man was shunned by Europe's royalty as a moral leper. The butt of vicious political cartoons, diatribes, pamphlets and editorials, he seemed to throw off every scandal and survive every attack, though his subjects (who rarely saw him since he hated the climate of his own country and spent most of his time in the south of France) were beginning to detest him.

The man was Leopold II, king of the Belgians, and absolute monarch as well as personal owner of the immense and ironically named Congo Free State.

Leopold had gained control of the Congo by almost twenty years of intrigue, bribes and lies. He had hired the famous explorer, Stanley, to lead expeditions into the basin, cloaking his true purpose with lofty sounding publicity about ending the Arab slave trade and developing the Congo's natural resources. What was not said was that he wished to develop its resources for his own privy purse, to free himself and his family from dependence on a niggardly parliament. This he proceeded to do, financing his endeavors through stock companies, vaguely defined "loans" from the Belgian government and the sale of franchises. He amassed a great fortune in the process, but lately more and more reports had been filtering out of the Congo hinting at the methods used by the Europeans to extract first the ivory and, more recently, the rubber from the jungle. Stories of a new slave trade, as inhuman as the Arabs' version that had been one of Leopord's excuses for going into Africa, the slaves again being the blacks but this time the masters being the Europeans. Stories of hands and feet being cut off natives who failed to gather their quota of rubber. Stories of the "chicotte": naked blacks tied to stakes and whipped. Stories of one colonial who decorated his flowerbed with severed heads instead of rocks. Stories of crucifixions, mass murders, emasculations; of headless bodies found floating in lakes; of baskets filled with severed black hands. Photographs of smiling black overseers standing next to their pith-helmeted white employers, holding up parts of human bodies. Christian Europe was far from believing the African to be more than subhuman, but even the most callous were shocked by the stories, and public opinion was beginning to wonder if something—exactly what was not yet known—shouldn't be done about the atrocities.

At first Leopold had ignored the bad publicity. It would go away; there were other things the public was more interested in—the Boer War, the troubles in China, the weather. But now as he sat on his yacht reading the latest collection of press clippings assembled by his equerry, he began to wonder if he perhaps shouldn't counter the stories with a publicity campaign of his own. He could hire writers to take trips up the Congo—carefully arranged, "Potemkin Village" trips—to see for themselves how well the Belgians administered their territory, how humanely the natives were, in point of fact, treated. He could develop tourist facilities; offer prominent clergymen special jungle junkets; arrange for his own staged photographs to appear in the European press. It would be expensive, but much less expensive than losing the personal empire on which he had lavished so much money and effort. In the Congo, Leopold was absolute, but at home he was merely a constitutional monarch. And if the Parliament became sufficiently aroused . . . particularly with the growing strength of the Socialists and the damned gossip about his personal morals . . . was it any of *their* business what he did? The press—the *Belgian* press! —had gone so far as to refer to his "obsessive senile passion," defining their own king as "the living symbol of public immorality." Of course, it was probably true. He didn't deny it. Still, it was damned presumptuous.

He thought with amusement of what they would say if they knew of his latest acquisition: a sixteen-year-old tart he had met in a corridor of the Elysée-Palace Hotel in Paris in the company of her ponce, a man named Durrieux. The tart's name was Caroline Lacroix, and she had excited his "senile passion" more than anyone he had met for some time. He squeezed the end of his beard, as was his habit, and contemplated again whether he should make her his mistress. His stupid daughters would be outraged, of course, but they were outraged at everything he did anyway. It would be amusing. Perhaps even give the little bitch a title. *That* would be even more amusing.

Caroline. The Congo. Tourist facilities. Flowerbeds outlined with heads. Publicity. Rubber. The king of the Belgians had much to think about. Particularly rubber. The black gold that was making his profits from ivory look minuscule by comparison. Rubber for raincoats, galoshes, baby nipples, girdles, hot-water bottles, bicycle tires. And lately something new and most promising—automobile tires. The market was growing with unexpected speed, and the Congo, with Brazil, provided the world's supply. And the Congo was his.

The king of the Belgians intended to keep it.

"Congressman, my name is Mark Manning. I own the Manning Bicycle Emporium here in Elkins. I'm going to vote for you in November, and I have a proposition to make to you."

Congressman Tutwiler, who had just come off the bandstand after finishing his speech and was now relaxing with a beer, smiled benignly at the brash young man in the straw hat, though his eyes were suspicious. Congressman Tutwiler was always wary of strangers with propositions.

"Glad to meet you," he said, shaking hands. "And what's the proposition?"

"Well, sir, I'm a great admirer of your kind of politics and I think it's important that the young men in town—the young *businessmen*, like myself—support a man like yourself who's doing so much for American business. So, if it's all right with you, I'd like to try and form a Young Businessmen for Tutwiler Committee here and help get out the vote for you in the election."

The suspicion fell away.

"Why, Mr. Manning, that's a fine idea! And I certainly will appreciate anything you can do for me. And if there's any way I can help you, you be sure and let my office know. Any time."

"Thank you, sir. And there *is* something you can do for me."

Back came the suspicion. "What's that?"

"Well, I'm a kind of part-time salesman for the Rosen Stove Company. And a couple of weeks ago, I was over at Fort Lincoln talking to Captain Wheeling there, and he told me the Fort is considering putting in gas stoves to replace the old coal ranges. Now if a well-known and influential Congressman such as yourself put in a good word for me with the commanding officer, well, I thought there might be a good chance he would give me the order—assuming, of course, that our bid was reasonable."

The Congressman was frowning. "Mr. Manning, I don't do favors like that. And I don't like people who offer to help my campaign expecting to get favors in return. You're not very subtle, young man."

Mark stuck his hands in his pockets. "Well, I guess you're right. Of course, I'd be willing to split the commission with you—say, seventy-thirty. Or donate it to your campaign fund, if you thought that would be more subtle."

"Are you suggesting I'd take a bribe?"

Mark shook his head morosely. "You see, I've done it again. Damn! I guess it's just impossible for me to be subtle with you, Congressman, and I sure don't blame you for getting mad about it. But you see, I happen to know someone who knows Horace Brown pretty well. . . . Do you know Horace Brown?"

The Congressman deflated slightly, a worried look coming into his eyes. "Of course. He's the president of the Elkins Bank and Trust."

"That's the one. Now, this person who knows Horace Brown pretty well told me that Mr. Brown had arranged for you to get an interest-free mortgage so you could buy the McCullough Building on Main Street in return for your arranging to have the Fort Lincoln accounts kept on deposit in Mr. Brown's bank, which Mr. Brown puts out on short-term loans and makes a nice tidy profit off of—"

"For Christ sake, keep your voice down!"

"Oh, no one can hear us, Congressman. I mean, no one will hear us as long as I don't *want* them to hear us. Now about those stoves . . ."

"Who told you about the mortgage?"

"Can't say, Congressman."

"You young son of a bitch, I don't like being blackmailed."

"Congressman, I don't think there's many people that do. But I don't consider this blackmail. It's just a friendly business transaction."

"If I took you to court, a judge would damn well know what it is!"

"But I don't think you're going to take me to court."

The Congressman didn't say anything for a moment. Then: "All right, I'll talk to the colonel. But don't get any ideas about trying this on me again. Mark Hanna's coal company isn't going to be happy if I start selling gas stoves."

"Oh, I'm not greedy, sir. I'll be more than satisfied with just this deal."

The Congressman finished his beer and wiped his mouth with his sleeve.

"How do I know you won't talk about the mortgage?"

"Well, now, you don't, do you? But it'll give you something to think about during those long, dull speeches in Congress. And if it makes you a little nervous, well, politicians shouldn't get too complacent, I always say. They might forget about serving us folks back home who vote for them. And Congressman, believe me, as long as you keep serving me, I'm going to vote for you."

A generous, friendly smile, and then he started back to where he had left Sheila, whistling "Columbia, the Gem of the Ocean."

"You know something?" he said as he rejoined Sheila. "I don't think we're getting very good representation in Congress."

"I couldn't agree more," said Sheila, who was making a ham sandwich. "I thought his speech was all wind, going on like that about the 'American Empire'—who cares if America has an empire? Why do we need one? There are other more important things like . . . Do you want mustard on your sandwich?"

He smiled and nodded, then lay back on the blanket and stared up at the sky, or rather the infrequent patches of blue he could see through the leaves of the maple tree they were camped under. "Oh, I don't know about that. Why shouldn't America have an empire, just like England and France and everyone else? We're as good as they are. Better, probably."

"The reason we shouldn't have an empire is because it causes a lot of trouble. Look at England and that Boer War. What a mess *that* is. I think it's stupid to talk about an empire, and I think it's snobbish to try and be like the English, and you're going to dribble mustard all over yourself if you don't sit up."

"Oh . . . I guess you're right." He sat up, accepted the plate she'd prepared, then took a large bite out of the sandwich.

She poured him a beer, then one for herself. "What were you talking to him about?" she asked.

"Tutwiler? Oh, a little deal, courtesy of your old friend Irene Sherbaugh."

"Irene? What did she have to do with it?"

"Well, Irene's Horace Brown's secretary, as you know, and sometimes she tells me interesting things about some of our leading citizens. Like Congressman Tutwiler."

"Well, it wouldn't surprise me *what* Horace Brown does. What a crook *he* is. Oh Mark, stop it . . ."

He had put down his plate and slipped his arm around her waist. She could feel his hand reaching for her breast.

"*No!* I don't want people saying worse things than they already do about us."

"What do they say about us?" he asked, retracting his hand as he noticed Mayor Pierson's wife staring at them from a nearby picnic table. He smiled at the mayor's wife, who glared back.

"You know what they say about us—or at least what they say about *me*. 'Oh, that Farr girl! Well, no one should be surprised at what *she* does!' I'm getting sick of being 'that Farr girl'."

"What do you want to be?"

She looked at him. "I'd *like* to be Mrs. Mark Manning, but in case that doesn't happen I'd at least like to get out of this town and work at something exciting. Maybe a newspaper or a magazine, be a reporter."

"You? A reporter?"

"I'd like to know why not?"

"Because women aren't reporters, that's why not."

"Oh? Well, you might be interested to know there *are* some women reporters working for magazines in New York and Chicago, and you also might be interested to know that I sent an article to *Independent* and *Collier's Weekly*."

"When?"

"Last month."

"What about?"

"Running a restaurant, naturally. Well, they both turned it down, but at least writing about running a restaurant beats doing it."

"You see?" Mark said. "That's why I don't propose to you. If you were my wife, you'd still be in the kitchen business. And what you really want out of life is to write up murders for the *Police Gazette*."

"Uh huh. You know, Mark, I'm not completely unattractive to the opposite sex, and it's conceivable that other gentlemen might take an interest in me if I weren't always in the company of a certain red-headed gentleman who sometimes thinks he's smarter than he is. And, in case I haven't made myself perfectly clear, I'm not going to wait forever to become Mrs. Mark Manning."

"Sheila?"

"What?"

His look traveled lazily up her blue skirt, over her rounded hips to her white blouse and full breasts. "I think," he said with great seriousness, "that if you ever become a reporter, you will absolutely be the sexiest reporter in all of America."

She sighed. "And you will still have the world's champion one-track mind."

CHAPTER TWO

The doors to the mansion were heavily carved mahogany, the top halves containing leaded stained-glass windows through which Mark received a distorted view of the big entrance hall inside and the butler coming to answer the bell. It was five o'clock that same afternoon, and Mark had come directly to the Rosen house after taking Sheila home from the picnic.

The butler opened the door and gave the young man an appraising look. "Yes?"

"I'd like to see Mr. Rosen, if he's in. My name's Mark Manning. Here's my card."

The butler glanced at the business card that read, "Manning Bicycle Emporium. Mr. Mark Manning, Prop." He didn't seem impressed.

"Tell Mr. Rosen it's about some gas stoves."

The butler held the door open and Mark came into the entrance hall, a blissful twenty degrees cooler than the outside, and watched the butler cross the Persian rug that covered most of the parquet floor and then disappear down a dark hallway. Mark looked around the hall with the dark-walnut-paneled ceiling. He had seen other Victorian entrance halls. The Midwest was full of them, and he'd been over a good part of the Midwest as a salesman. But this was the most impressive one he'd seen. He knew that Samuel Rosen had built the house only ten years before, but somehow it seemed mellow, as if it had been there for decades. The paneled walls had a richness to them, as did the wide, dark wood staircase with the wine runner and the large stained-glass window on the landing through which the sunlight came in ruby reds and pale yellows. To his right were two closed sliding doors that led to the front parlor. Beside them was a large gold-framed portrait of a plump but beautiful woman, Mrs. Rosen. He remembered as a boy, seeing her walking down Main Street by herself shortly after she and old Sam had come to Elkins. That must have been in the Eighties. They had originally come from Hamburg, migrating to New York and then on to Ohio. The stories varied: one version had it that old Sam had been a wealthy merchant in Hamburg who had somehow gotten himself in trouble with the authorities and skipped out of the country. Another said he had been a penniless anarchist who had, again, skipped the country because of the police. Still a third version maintained that he had murdered a Gentile. The truth was that he had emigrated to America to make his fortune, but that was too prosaic for Elkins to accept. Everyone agreed, though, that he had worked a few years for one of the Wall Street banking houses and then, in 1880, he came to Elkins —why Elkins no one knew, except that it was on the railroad—and bought a warehouse which he converted into a factory to make his stoves. He hadn't had much capital to begin with, but he had brains and drive. Within five years the business had grown so that he was able to refinance it through his Wall Street connections, build a new factory on the edge of town, and expand.

It was about then that Mrs. Rosen had died. No one had known her very well. Her English wasn't very good; she had kept to herself, as had her husband, partly because they were Jews—the only Jews in Elkins—and partly because, it was said, she was desperately shy. As her husband became more successful, her seclusion became even more pronounced. Their daughter was taught by a governess imported from Cleveland; later, she was sent east to boarding schools and college, so that even the opportunity to mingle with their neighbors through their children's social functions was not available. Mrs. Rosen had died instantly of a heart attack: the story was that she was pouring coffee at breakfast when she actually fell over dead. Old Sam was the original stone face, so no one could tell whether or not he was grief-stricken by his wife's death. He merely put on a mourning band and became even less communicative than usual. Mrs. Rosen was buried in a Jewish cemetery in Cleveland and the town forgot her. Five years later, Sam built the brick mansion and buried himself in *it*; but the town couldn't forget him. He was too important. And now, as Mark looked at the portrait of the woman with the delicate, almost English, features, he wondered if old Sam did indeed miss his wife.

The butler reappeared and led Mark down the long, dark corridor, lined with even darker etchings and prints, to a heavy door which he opened.

"Mr. Manning, sir."

Mark entered the room, which was a round library, being part of the corner tower of the house. Floor-to-ceiling bookshelves were interrupted with three floor-almost-to-ceiling windows draped with green-velvet curtains. A round rug on the parquet was thick, and the claw feet of the heavy Victorian chairs sank into its piling. Opposite the door was a carved mahogany desk holding a row of finely bound books (one of which Sam had been reading—a slim volume of Heine poems), a silver inkwell and a brass lamp with a round green-glass shade. Behind the desk, peering over the green shade at Mark, was a face with sunken cheeks, a tight, thin mouth, a sharp nose on which perched a gold-framed pince-nez, and two eyes bristling with intelligence. Old Sam might once have been a handsome young man, but now with a head devoid of even a suggestion of hair, he looked like death itself, albeit well dressed, even elegant, and distinctly unhappy at being disturbed. As the butler closed the door, Sam Rosen said, "What do you want?" His German accent was light, but there was no *gemutlichkeit* in it.

"May I sit down?" said Mark.

The death's head nodded. Mark pulled up one of the heavy chairs and took a seat. "How would you like to sell the Army a dozen gas ranges?"

"Who says the Army wants to buy them?"

"I do. I can guarantee the sale."

"How?"

"Connections," followed by the Manning smile.

Silence.

"Who gave you permission to sell my stoves for me?"

"No one. Look, Mr. Rosen, if you don't want the business . . ."

"I didn't say I didn't want it. I do say I don't like people going about selling my stoves without my permission. Particularly people like you."

"Now wait a minute, what's wrong with me?"

"You have a bad reputation. You're no gentleman, and you're immoral with women." Sam leaned back in his chair, folded his hands in front of him. "Otherwise, you're a fine young man."

Mark laughed. "Well, I'll admit I'm not much of a gentleman, and I guess my moral character isn't going to win me the Methodist Church Fellowship Award. But I can be a very lovable fellow when you get to know me."

"I see you are also sarcastic, Mr. Manning. Well, sir, what do you want out of this?"

"A finder's fee. Ten percent."

"Ten percent? A finder's fee is 2 percent!"

"*My* finder's fee is 10 percent."

"Five."

"Ten."

Sam paused a moment, then nodded curtly.

"All right. But this is unorthodox, and I don't like business done in an unorthodox manner. Now who in the Army wants to buy?"

"The colonel at Fort Lincoln. I'll let you know the details Monday." He stood up and reached his hand across the desk. "It's been nice doing business with you, sir. Maybe I can sell some more stoves for you some day."

Sam looked at the hand, then reached out and shook it. "Would you be interested in coming to work for me on a permanent basis?"

"No thanks. I like being my own boss. Besides, you wouldn't want a salesman who's immoral with women, would you?"

Sam looked at him coolly. "If a man has no character with women, then he has no character in business. And in business, character is everything."

"There are some people who say in business success is everything."

"They don't," said Sam, "know what they are talking about."

The two men looked at each other for a moment; then Mark went to the door. He opened it, then turned. "Oh, by the way, what do your stoves sell for?"

"The large professional range, our Model A Ever-Lite, sells for a hundred and twenty dollars."

Mark looked impressed. Twelve ranges at $120 was $1,440, so he had just made $144. Not so bad for an afternoon's work.

"Thank you. And good-bye, Mr. Rosen. It's been a great pleasure to meet you."

Sam said nothing as Mark went out of the room and closed the door. As he walked back down the dark corridor to the entrance hall, he told himself he'd have to remember to buy Irene Sherbaugh a nice present in appreciation for everything she'd done for him.

In the entrance hall he stopped as he heard piano music coming from behind the closed doors of the front parlor. That would be Charlotte, practicing. He looked around. The butler was nowhere in sight. It was the perfect opportunity to meet her, so why not? He straightened his tie, ran his hand over his hair, walked to the doors and slid them apart.

The room was spacious, banked with potted palms and flooded with the afternoon sun, which had been filtered and softened by the lace curtains in front of the windows. The black Bechstein, its top piled with piano scores, was to the left, and the girl playing it had her back to the doors. Now, hearing them open, she stopped playing and half turned around. Mark, still rough around the edges himself, nonetheless had an eye for beauty, an appreciation of style and elegance. This lovely creature who was his age, turning gracefully around on the piano stool, her delicate left hand resting on the keyboard, her exquisite features bathed in the soft yellow light, struck him as the most beautiful woman he had ever seen. He had observed Charlotte Rosen before from a distance as she rode through town in her father's carriage. Now, up close, she was truly breathtaking. She was wearing a white blouse and a light green skirt—very simple, no frills. Her auburn hair was pinned carelessly in a chignon and looked softly untouched, like that of the Gibson Girls. Her skin was delicate and incredibly white. Her nose had a slight sharpness, reminiscent of her father's; otherwise, her face had the near-classic English beauty of her mother's in the portrait. Her eyes were intensely blue and intelligent. She had innate style and the poise of a lady. Someday, Mark knew, he was going to make her his wife.

He cleared his throat. "Excuse me, Miss Rosen, but I heard the Beethoven, and I'm such an admirer of his music that I took the liberty of coming in to congratulate you on your playing."

Her eyebrows raised slightly.

"Oh? You like Beethoven?"

He closed the doors behind him. "I certainly do. Especially the 'Moonlight Sonata.'"

"You liked the way I was playing the 'Moonlight Sonata'?"

"Very much." He approached the piano.

She suppressed a laugh. "I don't often play the 'Moonlight Sonata,' you know. I've heard it so often, I've gotten rather tired of it."

"Well, a person would never know, listening to you. Why, it sounded so fresh, like hearing it for the first time."

"That's interesting. Maybe it *was* the first time you heard it. You see, I was playing Brahms's third piano sonata."

Silence.

"Oh." He shrugged good-naturedly. "Oh well, it was worth a try. My name's Mark Manning and I was just in seeing your father, and I thought I just couldn't pass up this opportunity to meet the lovely Miss Rosen. I'm glad I didn't."

She stood up and extended her hand.

"I'm glad too, Mr. Manning. I've heard a lot about you."

"All bad, I suppose?" he said, taking her soft hand and liking the touch of her skin.

"Not *all*. Would you care to sit down?" She led him over to a horsehair sofa, then sat down in a small chair opposite it. "Perhaps you'd like a lemonade? It's very warm today."

"Yes, it is, but no, thank you. I don't want to put you to any trouble. You know, I'm sure you've heard this from a lot of men, but I'm going to say it anyway. You're really a very beautiful woman."

She smiled slightly. "Why, Mr. Manning, I'm flattered. And I see that you're not the least bit shy."

"That's one thing no one's ever accused me of. And since I've made the plunge, I might as well go the whole way. I'd be very honored if you would allow me to take you out to dinner some evening. Say, tomorrow night?"

She looked as though she were about to laugh at him.

"What's so funny?

"You! You're so formal and polite and respectable! I'm impressed! But what about Sheila Farr?"

"Sheila just happens to be a very good friend."

"Oh, I'm sure. And she's very attractive too, I believe."

"Not half as attractive as you."

She leaned back in the chair, putting her hand to her chin, and inspected him.

"Mr. Manning, you're a real primitive, aren't you?"

"What's that supposed to mean?"

"Oh, just that you think there's not a girl alive that can resist you. Well, you *are* big and strong and, I admit, *quite* good-looking, and for most girls, that's enough."

"But not for you, I suppose. And just what makes you so different? Because you're Jewish?"

She stiffened, and her bantering tone vanished. "I hardly think so," she said coldly.

"Then why hole yourself up in this house when you're in Elkins? Do you think you're too good for the rest of the town?"

"Of course not, and I find you becoming offensive."

"Why? I come in here and compliment you and ask you if you'd like to go to dinner with me, and you call me some kind of an ape. So it seems to me either you must think I'm not good enough for you, or you're afraid I'll say something about your religion. Now it's possible I'm *not* good enough for you—although I don't think so. But I'd certainly never say anything against your religion, because, frankly, it wouldn't be smart and besides it interests me. So why am I so offensive?"

She cooled down. "I'm sorry. Matter of fact, the reason I 'hole myself up' in the house, as you put it, is that my father prefers it that way. He's . . . well, he doesn't like me to mix in with the town because he's afraid of what he calls an incident."

"There'd be no incident, believe me, Miss Rosen. The people in Elkins are pretty narrow-minded, I'll admit that. But no one meeting you could think that you were anything but an extremely charming young lady."

She smiled, this time warmly. "You're a very persuasive young man, Mr. Manning. And *you* don't seem narrow-minded at all. Why?"

"Well, I've been to college and I've traveled around a lot so I'm not exactly a hick. Besides, I think people should be judged for what they really are, not what people say about them. Now take me, for instance. You've probably heard I'm a Wild Man of Borneo type. But if you went out to dinner with me, you might find I've got the soul of a poet."

"A poet? I don't think that's your style, Mr. Manning."

She laughed.

"Why? I'm a very sensitive person." He smiled when he said it.

"Oh really? Well, I'm delighted to hear it. But you strike me as a bit, well, aggressive for a poet."

"Do you have something against aggressive men?"

She hesitated. "Well, yes and no. I admire men who make something of themselves, but I like men to be gentle too. Are you gentle, Mr. Manning? Somehow I don't think so."

"I'm very kind to animals, and I've never been known to strike an elderly woman."

She smiled. "There's a little bit more to being gentle than that. At any rate, I apologize for calling you an ape—though that wasn't exactly what I said. But I'm afraid I'll still have to decline your invitation."

"You just don't like me," he said flatly.

"On the contrary, I like you very much—I think. But you see, I'm engaged to be married."

He looked genuinely astonished and then very disappointed.

"Who to?" It came out almost a growl.

"A gentleman from New York named Sydney Fine. We're to be married next month, and then I'll be moving to New York. So I'm afraid there'd be very little point in my going out to dinner with you, Mr. Manning, and I don't think my fiancé would approve. I hope I haven't disappointed you?"

He got to his feet, looking at the large diamond ring on her finger that he had noticed but hadn't attached any significance to. Then he said quietly, "Yes, I'm disappointed."

"There's lots of other young ladies around who would love to go out with you."

"But I'm not in love with lots of other young ladies, and I think I'm in love with you."

"In 'love'? Oh come now, Mr. Manning, you've only known me ten minutes!"

"That doesn't matter. When I came through those doors and saw you sitting at the piano, I honestly thought you were the most beautiful girl I'd ever seen and I wanted you."

"That's not love."

He shrugged. "Call it anything you want."

"Maybe I misjudged you, Mr. Manning. Maybe you do have the soul of a poet after all, although I find it a bit difficult to accept that you actually believe in love at first sight."

"I didn't before. I do now." He reached out his hand and took hers. "Well, it's my loss," he said quietly, "and I wish you the best of luck. I hope this Mr. Fine makes you very happy."

"Thank you."

He looked into her blue eyes a moment, then released her hand and walked over to the doors. He opened them, and turned. "If it doesn't work out with Mr. Fine," he said, "remember, you still have a dinner invitation from me."

"I'll remember." She smiled.

She watched as he left the room and slid the doors shut.

Mark Manning's visit had, she was quite sure, been at least partly an act. But it was most assuredly a pleasant one. She had to admit, to her surprise, that she was rather sorry to see him go.

CHAPTER THREE

The excitement of the parade and the fireworks was over. It was the fifth of July, and Elkins had returned to its normal sleepy, comfortable routine. At nine-thirty that evening Mark finished repairing George Bailey's bicycle and washed up. Then he closed the garage and went out onto Main Street to walk over to Farr's restaurant.

He was feeling depressed, and the emptiness of the silent streets did little to cheer him up. Having met Charlotte Rosen, he now wanted her more than ever, but Charlotte was moving to New York, out of his reach, which was damn frustrating. Suddenly Elkins seemed a dull one-horse hick town only three generations removed from wilderness. Yes, it was a nice place to live, and maybe later generations would romanticize its idyllic smallness, forgetting that smallness could also be stifling. But one dividend of Mark's summer as a traveling salesman had been to dramatize for him the narrow horizons of his home town. The men his age had little vision or ambition; most of the girls were silly and sort of boring, although Sheila was an exception to this: Sheila had brains. But only the Rosens had any real stature, and now Charlotte was gone, and he was feeling lonely and depressed. He was already beginning to wonder if buying the bicycle shop had been a mistake. He'd had the money, he'd wanted a business and the place was available. Even though he didn't know much about bicycles, he'd bought it and he supposed he was making a go of it. But how much of a "go" could a man make with a bike shop, and in a place like Elkins? He was an intensely competitive and ambitious man, and he wanted the brass ring, which, as he went into Farr's restaurant, he told himself wasn't to be grabbed in Elkins, Ohio.

The place was empty, it being almost closing time, but he knew Sheila would be in the kitchen. He went behind the counter and opened the kitchen door. She was at the sink drying her inevitable dishes. She watched him as he came over, pulled out his wallet, and put five dollars on the counter.

"There's your money," he said.

She continued drying.

"Romeo didn't make a hit with Juliet?"

"She's moving to New York to get married. Got anything in the icebox? I'm starved."

"There's some cold chicken."

He got a drumstick, then leaned against the big zinc-topped table in the middle of the room. The table and everything else in the place was clean; whatever the town might say of Sheila's morals, everyone admitted she kept her mother's restaurant immaculate. As he hungrily tore into the chicken leg she said, "What's wrong? Mad because Miss Rosen didn't tumble?"

"I don't know, I just feel restless."

"You're always restless. Now, if you'd make an honest woman of me, I could keep you from getting bored."

"Come on, Sheila. I'm not in the mood."

She looked at him. "You really are off your feed, aren't you? What is it?"

"Oh, this town, I guess. I don't know, but if I stay here, some day I'll wake up and be seventy-five and my whole life will be gone."

He tossed the chicken bone in the garbage as she put away the last plate. "Mark, that's what I was saying yesterday! We both should get out of here—maybe go to Cleveland or somewhere—"

"How could you go to Cleveland? What would you do with the restaurant?"

"Sell it! I may have to anyway. Mother's getting worse, lying upstairs all day putting away one bottle after the other. I may have to put her in a clinic. . . . But, Mark, why don't you think about it? Seriously. We could both go to Cleveland and you could open a shop there and maybe I could get that job as a reporter—I mean, it's possible, isn't it? And we could help each other! We're certainly getting nowhere here."

"What do you mean, 'help each other'? In other words, get married?"

"Well yes, frankly. Is that so terrible?"

"And you say *I've* got a one-track mind."

"But, Mark, I love you! Oh, I know you're ambitious and you think I'll hold you back somehow because I'm not a lady, whatever that is, but I'll tell you something—you'll never find a woman in your whole life that will care more about you or be more faithful to you. You may not think much of that now but someday you will. At least promise you'll think about it. Together at least, two hicks from Elkins might just be able to get somewhere!"

He looked at her, and for a moment he was actually tempted. He did love her, in a way—her honesty, her earthiness, her body. . . .

"Come here," he said.

She took off her apron and came over to him. He put his arms around her and began kissing her.

"Is your mother asleep?" he whispered.

"She passed out an hour ago."

He released her and went over to the window, where he pulled down the shade. Then he came back and took her in his arms again, pressing her back down onto the zinc-topped table.

"Not in the kitchen, for God's sake!"

"Why not?"

He was unbuttoning the front of her dress, pushing his hand in to caress her lush breasts, the erect nipples.

"Because it's against the health code, if nothing else! Besides, I'm getting tired of you shutting me up with sex every time I try to talk seriously with you!"

He straightened and began unbuckling his belt.

"We can talk seriously later."

"No!" she said angrily, sitting up. "I'm fed up with this arrangement we've got, if you want to call it that. You'll chase Charlotte Rosen and offer her the moon because she's rich and has what you think is class, but all I'm good for is to take to bed—or the kitchen table, in this case! Well, to hell with you, Mark Manning. I'm through with having everyone in town call me a slut just because you're too selfish to—"

He shut her up with a hungry kiss, pulling her off the table and pressing her body against him. She tried to push him away, then subsided as she felt his big hands moving slowly over her back. Damn him, she thought. But she couldn't help herself. Slowly, he eased her back down on the table, then moved on top of her. She drew in her breath sharply as she felt him enter her, then relaxed as the sweet warmth began to engulf her. "Oh, *damn* you," she whispered.

"I love you, Sheila," he whispered at her ear as he moved back and forth inside her.

"Like hell."

But the defiant words were spoken in surrender as he flooded her and she felt the brief, ecstatic release that always made everything else in her life seem so unimportant . . . until it was over and like a punctured balloon her spirits slowly descended back to the reality that was Elkins and that was Mark Manning.

The summer days began to shorten, almost imperceptibly at first and in inverse ratio to the lengthening of the corn stalks, but then more quickly as the corn stalks slowed their growth and topped out in lush pompoms of brown silk. Came then the lovely, lazy days of September, and Mark's bike trade boomed just before school opened. Then the chill days of October, when business braked before the late November surge to Christmas sales.

It was on a rainy November Sunday that Mark was sprawled on his bed in the tiny apartment at the rear of the shop, drinking a beer as he studied a thick hardware catalogue and wondered if he should branch out into the hardware business. The bell in the front of the store jangled and he got up, finishing his beer. As he went out into the showroom, he saw through the glass in the door that it was Sheila —Sheila in a brown traveling skirt beneath her gray raincoat, protecting her hat with an umbrella. It was just past noon, and the rain was now coming down in torrents.

He led her back to the "rathole," which was what he called his small living quarters. The room was piled with dirty laundry, ledgers, empty beer bottles, magazines, and several big posters advertising Shearer bicycles pinned to the cracked walls. He plopped back down on his unmade bed and patted the mattress next to him for her to sit down, which she did. "Where've you been?" he asked. "I haven't seen you for a few days."

"I took Mother to Cleveland. She's gotten much worse lately and Thursday she started seeing bugs everywhere, so I decided she had to get to a hospital and took her to the clinic."

"The D.T.'s again?"

"Yes. This is the third time, and I think it may be the last. The doctors didn't look too optimistic."

"I'm sorry," Mark said. "What are your plans? If she dies, I mean."

"Well, I'm putting the restaurant up for sale because I'll have to keep her near the clinic and it's just too much for me to run the place alone. So I'm going to Cleveland and try something new . . . but there's something else. Do you remember the Keys girl?"

"Do I—" He stopped, catching the implication. "Have *you* . . . ?"

She nodded.

He leaned back against the pillows propped on the wall and stared, his light freckles showing up more prominently as his normally ruddy color left his cheeks.

"I'm trying not to panic," Sheila said. "I'm trying to use my head. I intend to have this child, no matter what happens. The question is, what will *you* do?"

Silence. She stood up from the bed and looked down at him. When she spoke, it was a bitter whisper. *"You bastard . . .* why was I ever stupid enough to fall in love with you?"

"What am I supposed to do?" he said angrily. "Marry you, get tied down raising a family before I've even begun to find out what I'm going to do—"

She left him in mid-sentence, returning to the front of the shop. He got off the bed and ran after her. "Sheila, wait a minute! I'll help you take care of the kid . . . I'll do anything I can, you know that . . ."

She picked up her umbrella and went to the door. Then she turned to him. "I don't want your help. I don't want anything to do with you, and I don't want my child ever to know you were his father. Do you understand?"

"Now, wait a minute. I told you I'd help. After all, he's mine too—"

"No, he's mine, Mark. Remember that, and don't ever try to see me again."

As he watched her through the open doorway, walking down the puddled sidewalk, Mark felt genuinely sorry and not a little ashamed.

But he also felt he had done what he had to do.

CHAPTER FOUR

Charlotte Rosen had gone off to marry a member of a family that was one of the pillars of New York's German-Jewish community. Sydney Fine's grandfather had founded the underwriting house of Herbert Fine & Company in the 1850s; it had prospered during the Civil War; and in the enormous industrial expansion of the postwar years it had grown to become one of the most powerful underwriting firms in the country. Indeed, it had been Herbert Fine & Company that had hired Charlotte's father, Sam, when he arrived in New York from Germany twenty-five years before, and it had been Sydney's father, Herschel, who had arranged the financing that allowed Sam to expand his stove company five years later, thus establishing not only Sam's fortune but the social relationship that had led to Sydney's introduction to Charlotte at a ball at the Fine mansion on Fifth Avenue. The founding Fine had died in 1884. His son, Herschel, had taken over management of the firm and had proved as astute a businessman as his father. The family fortune continued to flourish until, by the turn of the century, it was reckoned to be in the neighborhood of fifty millions.

Herschel had married a Goldmark, another establishment family; they had built a French Renaissance chateau on Fifth Avenue, that glittering street studded with the palaces of the American peerage—Vanderbilts, Oelrichs, Whitneys, Astors; and because both Herschel and his wife Anna had great style and lived *en prince*, they managed to defy the rampant anti-Semitism of the day and straddle both social worlds, much to the dismay of many of their peers, who considered Gentile society something to be shunned, if not actually snubbed.

Sydney Fine, indeed, came from a background that was considered difficult to improve upon, and he seemed an appropriate product of it. Handsome, if thin, with chiseled features and affecting eyes, he possessed intelligence, sensitivity, charm and an impish sense of humor. He loved music, though with a dilettante's enthusiasm (and brevity of attention span), and was filled with such musical incidentals as the fact that Franz Liszt's dying word had been "Tristan," a phenomenon that struck him as mystical. It was music that first brought Sydney and Charlotte together, somewhat in the fashion it had brought Charlotte and Mark together. It was in the music room of the Fine mansion. Charlotte had gone to the Steinway and managed a polished Black Key Étude. Sydney had been dazzled by the virtuosity of this lovely Wellesley girl—after all, many girls "played," but he had never met one who was a truly accomplished pianist. At his insistence she played more: the haunting Aeolian Harp Étude, then an elegantly filigreed Valse Oubliée by Liszt and the exquisite, if short, first of the Schumann Bunte Blätter. Sydney was captivated. Charlotte, in turn, was dazzled by this handsome Fifth Avenue prince, who not only apparently shared her passion for music but also seemed to have, beneath his somewhat arch façade, that gentleness she longed for and so admired in men. They saw increasingly more of each other, sometimes at Princeton or Wellesley but most often in New York, to attend the Metropolitan in the splendor of Sydney's family box, delighting in Mozart or, at the other musical extreme, in Wagner, whom they both adored, managing to overlook the German genius's

notorious anti-Semitism. The erotic music of *Tristan* especially moved
them; and, in fact, when Sydney proposed Charlotte had just finished
playing a piano transcription of the *Tristan* Prelude. It was melodramatic, but it also worked. Charlotte accepted without a moment's
hesitation.

So it had begun all music and romance. Sydney's parents both
adored Charlotte. That Herschel liked her didn't unduly surprise her;
that wonderfully expansive man, of whom Sydney was so in awe,
appreciated most pretty women. Charlotte hardly counted winning
Herschel over as a conquest. But that Sydney's mother liked her too
came as a delightful surprise, for the imposing Anna worshipped
Sydney, and Charlotte was certain that she would never truly welcome a daughter-in-law. However, she did. They were both delighted
by Sydney's choice; and to prove it, they bought the young couple a
handsome townhouse a single block down from their own mansion
on Fifth Avenue. A splendid wedding present indeed. And the wedding itself was spectacular, too, old Sam Rosen putting on a fine show
at the Waldorf that golden summer of 1900.

The wedding night, however, was a disaster.

Charlotte had been almost totally innocent of the facts of life, a
condition not unusual for girls of her era, especially respectable young
ladies. She did know, of course, that *something* happened on the
wedding night, but very little more. And when Sydney and she finally
were alone in their suite aboard the luxurious Cunard liner *Cam-
pania* bound for England and a two-month European honeymoon,
she had the impression he was as nervous as she, the difference being
he knew what was supposed to happen and she didn't. He was tipsy
from champagne, not surprising, considering the quantity of champagne Louis Sherry had provided for the reception and later the
sailing party. But when the ship finally moved away from the pier,
he ordered more champagne and proceeded to get stumbling-down
drunk.

Charlotte was shocked and frightened. Drunkenness was as despised
in her family as it was in her bridegroom's, and she had never seen
Sydney more than slightly expansive on wine. But now he was weaving around the elegant suite, attempting to sing something that
approximated a hodge-podge of Princeton drinking songs and the
"*Libiamo*" from *Traviata* while he shed his clothes. Stumbling onto
a couch, he took off his patent leather shoes and flung one after the
other across the room. He struggled out of his pants and kicked
them into a corner. Then he looked blearily at his bride and demanded, "Why are you just *standing* there? You're supposed to *do*

something. Get undressed," he said, waving in the direction of the bedroom. "We have to . . . have to plight our troth. Have to be man and wife, you know . . ."

She didn't know, but she hurried into the bedroom, changed into a nightgown, then crawled into the bed and waited, as, outside the portholes, the distant lights of Long Island's south shore glided silently by. After a while he stumbled into the bedroom, looked at her with bleeding eyes for what seemed an interminable time. Then he said, "You've never *seen* a man, have you?"

She shook her head, staring at his now inelegantly skinny white body, at the thin line of fine black hair demarking the middle of his bony chest.

As she watched, he wove across the room and, as the huge ship rolled slightly to port, lurched onto the bed, face down in the lace pillowslip. For a while he didn't move and she thought he had fallen asleep. Then he turned his head slightly and whispered, "You've got to help me, Charlotte. You've got to help me."

It wasn't until they were halfway through France that Sydney finally managed something more competent, but by that time Charlotte had come to hate even the idea of intercourse. Mostly because she knew Sydney really disliked it; which embarrassed him and crushed her. To make up for his inadequacy he lavished attention, charm and money on her. They "did" Europe to what was considered the nines. But by the time they returned to their newly refurbished house on Fifth Avenue, Charlotte knew her marriage had been a mistake. She accepted the fact. She still loved Sydney, loved what she thought of as the "day" side of him, the gracious social and intellectual aspect of him. He was capable of such unexpected generosity, such tenderness on occasion, such wonderfully absurd things as proposing to her while she played *Tristan*. She would always love the memory of the handsome young man in the tailcoat and immaculate white shirt with pearl studs leaning on the piano, his eyes shining with excitement as she played the Chopin. But the "night" side of him, the physical, she truly loathed. She was forced to seduce him, and yet she pitied him because she knew he was deeply ashamed. And she was also somewhat frightened, sensing as she did that somewhere inside him there seemed to be a demon struggling to emerge, like one of Michelangelo's slaves, she thought, straining to free itself from the restraining clutches of its marble prison. She wondered about that demon, wondered too if it caused the inadequacy in him. She had heard of a Dr. Freud in Vienna who, it was said, was writing extraordinary books that explained such things. She wanted to read them but didn't, not only because of conventional restraints but also because she was afraid of what she might learn.

So she hated the darkness, and her timidity, but was unable to overcome either of them. Meanwhile, she did everything in her power to be a successful wife. She entertained frequently, which Sydney loved. They became leaders of the younger "set." They went everywhere. They attended concerts, the opera; they gave musicales, where Charlotte, as well as the leading musicians of the day, played; they danced, they dined, they dizzied themselves with activity. To Herschel Fine's delight, his son joined the firm and became a perceptive and hard-working underwriter. Everyone liked them; everyone admired them. The surface of the marriage was perfection. Underneath, it was quite another matter.

In the third year of the marriage, Sydney's mother died, and her death finally seemed to free the demon Charlotte had long sensed was there. Sydney was crushed by the loss of his mother and, at the same time, seemed oddly elated. Charlotte was unable to understand it. A week after the funeral, Sydney told her he was moving out of their bedroom. He was tense when he announced his decision, as if expecting her to object. She didn't, however. It was a relief for her, even though she knew it meant the end of her hopes for children. It was also the beginning of his move out of the rest of her life. They saw less and less of each other. He began staying at his club for dinner, leaving Charlotte to eat alone in the big French dining room. They continued to entertain but he took less pleasure in it, as if his mind was elsewhere. The unexpected tender moments he had formerly displayed were not repeated. He became increasingly irritable with her. She accepted all this stoically enough, but privately she was miserable and she also began to understand the reason he had been strangely elated by his mother's death. It relieved him of the need to be a "family man," eased him out of the obligations of his strict heritage. Charlotte sensed the demon was winning.

She was very lonely and spent hours each day practicing the piano. It was a release, but she needed friendship as well as music. A Mrs. Sinclair provided it. She was an elegant woman in her mid-forties whose husband had recently died, leaving her a fortune. She admired and liked Charlotte, who reciprocated the friendship, and they became if not inseparable at least constant companions, seeing each other almost daily, lunching, shopping, going to matinees. Amelia Sinclair—her rather dowdy Christian name contrasted with her sophisticated personality—was considered a woman of the world. She was at home in European society, as well as that of New York. She was tactful and understanding. She never mentioned Sydney unless Charlotte mentioned him first. But she knew what was happening.

He was drinking heavily now. He would come home late at night and Charlotte would hear him singing to himself, stumbling about in his bedroom as he tried to undress. He never missed going to his office, but the alcohol was undermining his health and turning his personality sour. Somehow they managed to keep up the appearance of their marriage, but by the fifth year the effort was becoming a nearly unbearable strain.

Then there was Richard.

His name was Richard Goldmark, and he was a cousin of Sydney's. He was young, good-looking, witty, rich enough not to work and lazy. Richard had been around for some time, being "family." But at a New Year's party at Sydney's father's house—Herschel, a part of two worlds, celebrated both the Jewish and Gentile holidays—Charlotte began to realize that Richard, like the year 1905, was no longer waiting in the wings. He was very much on stage. He was with Sydney the entire evening. He was polite to Charlotte—charming, even; he always was. But clearly it was Sydney he was interested in, and she knew her husband reciprocated the interest. She began now to be aware that their relationship was more than friendship, but she didn't fully understand it.

Amelia Sinclair, however, did, and explained it a week later when Charlotte asked her, after six sleepness nights of agonizing indecision. She loathed the thought of discussing her marriage, even with such an intimate friend as Amelia. It seemed breaking a trust, yet she had to know and she was certain Amelia could explain. Charlotte listened, dazed, as Amelia spoke. She had never heard of such a thing. But after crying and becoming briefly ill, she forced herself to accept it. She had no choice. She would not hurt her husband. As long as Sydney wanted her for his wife—even if only for social purposes—she had a duty to remain, no matter what he did or what he was.

It was an age of belief in duty, and Charlotte believed.

Later, Mark Manning would be pleased to hear about Sydney and Charlotte's difficulty, but at the moment he was back in a restless routine that would suddenly change and be linked to a story that had begun hundreds of years before in the wilds of South America.

The South American Indians called it *cauchu*, which means "the weeping wood" (from which comes the French word for rubber, *caoutchouc*), and for hundreds of years its milk-white tears had been used by the Indians to fashion bouncing balls for various games, as well as for shoes and protective covers for their poison darts. The Indians respected the big tree, the *Hevea brasiliensis*, as the Europeans would later classify it, its trunk growing up to a dozen feet in circumference, rising to as high as a hundred feet, its roots the home of the poisonous *surucucu* snake during seeding time. They had learned how to cure the latex with the oily smoke of the *urucuri* nut, concentrated by a clay cone above the fire; they would turn the rubber over the smoke as they fashioned layer after layer on their clay molds, using the result to make jars and waterproof covering for their feet. For two and a half centuries the Portuguese and Spanish explorers, surely considered men of greater commercial acumen than the "barbaric" Indians, failed to exhibit the slightest curiosity about this remarkable material. Finally, in the 1700s, a French courtier and friend of Voltaire, a talented dilettante with an appetite for recondite knowledge, made a seven-year journey through the New World. Upon his return to France, Charles Marie de la Condamine published the first scientific information about the rubber tree. Slowly interest developed. In 1759 the government of the Portuguese colony of Para on one of the mouths of the Amazon sent a rubber coat to the king in Lisbon. By 1800, rubber bottles were being sent to the motherland.

Portugal had kept its huge Brazilian colony closed to foreign trade, but Napoleon helped them put an end to this shortsighted policy. In 1808, when the French emperor moved against Portugal, the Portuguese court fled to its colony across the ocean. Moving to Brazil seemed to change the court's view of its trading policies, and the Brazilian ports were soon opened to trade with foreign nations; by the 1820s rubber shoes were being sold in the United States, as were the sixty-to-eighty-pound balls of raw rubber, which became known as "fine hard Para," or simply "Paras."

Then came Charles Goodyear, and neither rubber nor the Amazon was ever to be the same again.

The stage was set for Goodyear in 1802 when coal gas was used for the first time as illumination in England. The new lighting was convenient and cheap, and it quickly became the vogue, with gas companies springing up all over the British Isles. As the use of coal gas spread, the tar and ammonia by-products also became increasingly available and enterprising men began searching for ways to use them. A Scot named Macintosh, for example, found that after separating ammonia in the process of converting the tar by-product into pitch, naptha was produced. He thought the new oil might be a good rubber solvent; and dissolving pieces of caoutchouc in the naptha, he produced a thick solution that he found was excellent for coating fabrics. The new solvent evaporated quickly; and by encasing the rubberized fabric between two layers of cloth, the problem of the rubber becoming sticky in warm weather was partially overcome. And so the first Mackintosh (the *k* being added to the commercial name) was born, and in 1824 Charles Macintosh and Company was formed to manufacture the popular raincoats.

Rubber was also being used for printers' rollers, driving belts, fire hoses, surgical instruments—a variety of uses had been discovered for the elastic, not to mention the use from which it derived its name, erasers. But the problem Macintosh solved for his raincoats continued to plague the material: in winter rubber tended to harden and become brittle, and in summer it became sticky and melted. Suspenders that could melt at body temperature were a definite if amusing problem, and the future of the nascent rubber industry looked perilous until, in February of 1839, a rather seedy-appearing inventor who had spent ten years in and out of debtor's prison wandered into the general store in Woburn, Massachusetts, to show off his latest development in a long line of rubber experiments—a mixture of gum rubber and sulphur. When the onlookers made unflattering remarks, Charles Goodyear angrily waved a fistful of gum in the air. It flew from his fingers and landed on the hot stove. When he scraped it off, he found the rubber had charred like leather, and one of the most celebrated accidents in history had occurred—the discovery of vulcanization (a name concocted four years later in England by a friend of the inventor, Thomas Hancock, who had rediscovered the process on his own).

Goodyear's brainchild was to cause him heartache and lawsuit; even though he finally won legal recognition of his patents, he died in 1860 at the Fifth Avenue Hotel some $200,000 in debt. He had, however, created an industry. In 1839 the price of Para had been five cents a pound; in 1860 it was sixty cents and there were a hundred and fifty rubber factories in America and Europe manufacturing dozens of articles made possible by vulcanization. The Civil War would accelerate the manufacture of rubber goods, and by 1865 raw rubber was averaging a dollar twenty a pound—a doubling of market value in five years.

The burgeoning demand for rubber was bringing pressure on the only source of supply at that time, the enormous Amazon basin serviced by the Amazon River, which in 1850 was opened to steam navigation by the Brazilian emperor. By 1867 the river was opened to foreign steamers, and now ocean liners from London could snake 2,300 miles up river all the way to the Peruvian city of Iquitos. The vast resources of the Amazon basin—hundreds of thousands of square miles inhabited by only a handful of so-called semicivilized or uncivilized Indians—were now available to a world hungry for the "tears" of its rubber trees; and in the nineteenth century's near equation of developed nations' demand plus undeveloped nations' supply equaling exploitation, many human tears—and blood—were shed from the Portuguese Amazon to the ravaged heart of sybaritic King Leopold II's Belgian Congo. . . .

Meanwhile, a Jamestown, New York, physician named Benjamin Franklin Goodrich had left his home town for New York City to seek his fortune in real estate. In one deal he traded land for stock in the Hudson River Rubber Company, a firm of which Goodrich became president after buying out the stockholders. The company didn't prosper; there was too much competition from other rubber companies in New England. Goodrich bought a new factory at Melrose, New York. Again, no luck. Then he received in the mail a pamphlet from the town of Akron, Ohio, giving a boosterish pitch for the establishment of new business in the small community of ten thousand situated on the Pennsylvania and Ohio Canal. Goodrich was tempted, wondering if this might be the answer to the New England competition. He looked; he borrowed; he bought and built, attesting to the power of direct-mail advertising. By 1871, twenty-five workmen were manufacturing rubber hose and wringer rolls in the Goodrich plant in Akron, and the rubber industry had found its new home.

Shortly after Goodrich's journey to the American heartland, a Scottish veterinarian living in Belfast, John Boyd Dunlop, took to brooding over the idea of increasing the speed of bicycle tires by building them around a hollow tube filled with compressed air. Until then, tires had been solid rubber. Now Dunlop made an air-tight tube out of thin rubber, using his baby's nursing-bottle nipple as a valve, cemented it to a wooden wheel, filled it with air and took the contraption out to his backyard and tossed it. It traveled well and bounced back from the fence gate. Compared to the same test made with his son Johnny's solid-rubber tricycle tire, the new tube sailed. Soon Johnny's tricycle was equipped with the air-tube tires; the tricycle performed brilliantly, and the pneumatic tire was born. In 1892 the trotting horse Nancy Hanks drew her pneumatic-tired, bicycle-wheeled sulky to a new world's record, and the pneumatic was launched commercially.

In the same year the U.S. Rubber Company—or, as some more ominously called it, the Rubber Trust—was formed. And in October 1900, the same month Sheila Farr departed for Cleveland carrying Mark Manning's bastard child, the Dow Jones Company issued a pamphlet praising the eight-year-old trust for its discouragement of "injudicious forms of competition," its enhancement of management standards and its "perfection" of the boot-and-shoe branch of the rubber industry. All of which signaled a Wall Street version of the already-familiar American story others would characterize as a ruthless march toward monopoly by an industry now employing more than 150,000 workers producing $75,000,000 worth of goods annually. Monopoly was, indeed, the goal. But for all its financial inventiveness, the Rubber Trust was proving itself to be somewhat shortsighted. In 1900, the very year the automobile was beginning to make its first impact, for better or for worse, on the modern consciousness, the Rubber Trust announced it was going out of the business of manufacturing tires.

A remarkable example of entrepreneurial prescience.

Mark Manning, who sold bicycle tires as well as bicycles, was vaguely aware of all this. He was also aware of the fortunes being made in the rubber business, living as he did only a few miles from Akron. He often considered the notion of starting a tire factory, along with dozens of other ideas over the next five years, ranging from hardware stores to founding a chain of groceries. None of these materialized, nor did he have suitable entree for breaking into the rubber business: he needed a gimmick, something special—what, he had no idea. So he stayed in his shop, slowly increased his business and built a head of frustration while the brass ring remained as elusive as ever.

Meanwhile, though, he did manage a campaign to improve his reputation with the local solons by publicly taking the pledge and forswearing all alcohol, thus bringing joy to the hearts of the good ladies of the W.C.T.U. He considered it a good test of will power, an exercise in self-discipline, and to make the test more strenuous he proceeded to slim down from a somewhat pudgy two hundred ten pounds to a lean hundred sixty-five in a year and a half (he was to vary from a hundred sixty-five to a hundred seventy-five the rest of his life. In fact, he never again drank whiskey except once, years later on his yacht, though he was to develop an oenophile's appreciation of wine and champagne). He further pleased the local mothers, as well as promoted his product, by sponsoring an annual bicycle race for the town's youngsters and awarding to the winner a brand-new, free Shearer (his civic generosity perhaps also being prompted by a sense of guilt over his refusal to take on responsibility for his child conceived with Sheila Farr). A star pitcher in college, he also coached a local baseball team, which made him something of an idol to the town's youngsters (who comprised the principal market for his bicycles). He even went so far as to court the daughter of Horace Brown, the bank president, figuring that if he could learn to ignore the fluttery Miss Brown's imperfect skin and empty cranium he might marry into the town's second-wealthiest family. Miss Brown, as it turned out, was too much to take, but the town's leading citizens approved his brave attempt (*everybody* was trying to find a husband for Elsie Brown). Slowly Mark's reputation as lecher and bully faded, as planned, replaced now by a new image as the town's most promising booster and young businessman. Of course, with Sheila Farr gone and Irene Sherbaugh married, Mark required some relief from the rigors of total respectability, which he found on clandestine trips to Cleveland, where he became a regular customer of Stella Ryan's, the town's leading brothel.

It was on a May morning in 1905 that it finally happened. In later years he almost convinced himself that he personally dreamed up the idea that was to make him one of the richest men in America. Actually, it was purest serendipity.

As the automobile began to be seen more and more frequently— the figure of 8,000 registered cars in America in 1900 had ballooned to 77,000 in 1905—Mark's business had been almost forced into car as well as bike repair, and because the early car tires blew out with merciless regularity, he found himself changing tires for motorists more than he liked. It was not only unprofitable, it was hard work. The clincher tire then in use took its name from its crescent-shaped bead, the foundation portion of the tire holding it onto the rim. The clincher bead stuck out from the sidewall and hooked under a curved-in flange on the rim; to get it off and on required jackscrews, special wrenches, clamps and a good deal of strength.

On this particular May morning he was putting a new tire on a Maxwell belonging to the editor of the Elkins *Star Chronicle*, James

Wharton. He stood by watching Mark sweat at his work. As he did so, he made a casual, and somewhat irritable, observation:

"Why don't they change the damned rims instead of the tires?"

Mark required no double takes as he stared at him with the look of a man being offered the keys to the mint.

"Mr. Rosen, I need a hundred thousand dollars."

The remark was made that afternoon in the office of Sam Rosen, a severely paneled room in the Rosen Stove Company factory on the south side of town. Mark had waited an hour and a half to get the interview; when he was finally ushered into the office by Miss Drew, old Sam's secretary, he sat down in front of the desk and immediately made his request.

Sam looked calmly at the young man he hadn't seen for five years, not since that Fourth of July when Mark sold the twelve stoves for him. Sam Rosen was too smart to be taken in completely by Mark's exercise in respectability, but he had been impressed by the effort and considered Mark a man to be watched even though he remained dubious about his character. He was, at the least, assuredly worth listening to. "Why do you want the money?" he said, in typically direct fashion.

"I want to make automobile tires that are sold with a rim that can be hooked onto the wheel, rim and all. The cars can carry a spare that will already be inflated. If a man has a blowout he can put on the spare without all the strain and time it now takes. Here, I've made a drawing of how it could work." He placed a piece of paper on the desk. Sam took it, looked at it, looked back at Mark.

"There's nothing on the market like this now?" he said in his light German accent.

"That's the point."

"Why are you coming to me instead of a bank?"

"Because I like you, Mr. Rosen." Sam looked skeptical, but Mark pushed ahead. "Now, I figure I'll need a hundred thousand to get started. Actually, I think I could net ten thousand if I sold my business and I've saved five thousand, so I'd only need eighty-five thousand from you. If you'll put up the eighty-five thousand, I'll do the rest and I'll give you forty percent of the stock."

"And if I want more?"

"Then I'll go to Horace Brown."

"What makes you think Horace Brown would lend you that much money?"

"Because Mr. Brown knows a good thing when he sees it. And since it's possible I may become his son-in-law, well, it would keep it all in the family, so to speak. But I wanted to give you the first opportunity . . ."

Sam was aware Mark hadn't seen Elsie Brown for over a year, but he refrained from comment.

"Well?" said Mark.

"I like your idea, young man. You don't have to be a genius to see that the automobile business is growing, and the tire business is growing with it. Moreover, I assume you know something about the tire business from running your bicycle shop. However, changing and patching tires is hardly the same as manufacturing them. Running a business is a most complicated matter—"

"Mr. Rosen, I know all this. Not to be impolite, but are you interested or aren't you?"

The intelligent eyes blinked slowly behind the pince-nez, a fox judging whether or not to move, and if so, in which direction.

Finally, "I'm interested."

Mark relaxed in the chair and grinned.

"I was sure you would be."

But Sam Rosen refused to commit himself.

First, he insisted on seeing Mark's books, checking every aspect of his life that was checkable. Next he made careful inquiries in Akron and Cleveland to find out as much as he could about the rubber business. Then days after Mark had first gone to him—ten days during which Mark averaged less than three hours anxious sleep a night—Sam called him back to his office. "I have bad news," he said. "You know that the clincher-tire patents are held in a pool, and only eight companies are allowed to manufacture them. I'm told by reliable sources that we have no chance of getting a franchise from the pool commissioner in New York."

"Then we'll make straightside tires," said Mark, referring to a type of tire that had a reinforced bead without the protruding crescent-shaped hook of the clincher design. "Straightsides are better anyway. The clincher's on the way out."

"I agree. But most of the auto manufacturers are committed to the clincher, at least for the foreseeable future. If we can't make clinchers, we won't be able to get orders from Ford, Maxwell, Olds, or any of the leading companies. We wouldn't be able to survive without those major orders."

Mark stood up and walked over to a window of the office. He stuck his hands in his pockets and stared out at a horse-drawn dray clattering down the street in front of the factory. While part of his mind was trying to figure a way to save his business before it was even born, another part of his mind noted the dray's wooden wheels, and that rubber tires—even solid rubber tires—were still considered an impossible luxury for trucking and that someday whoever could open the trucking market to tires would make another fortune. But first the baby had to be born, and right now it was in danger of being aborted.

He turned and said, "Then we'll bust the pool, Mr. Rosen. We'll make clincher tires and let them sue. By the time the suit gets to court, clinchers will be obsolete anyway."

He watched the older man's face. Immobile as always. "It's a bad way to start a business. The whole industry may freeze us out as mavericks."

Mark came back to the desk. "We've got the better idea," he said quietly. "The public will buy our idea. So to hell with the industry."

Again a silence. Then Sam nodded. "All right. But I want fifty percent."

"No."

"The risk is great, and I'm putting up most of the money. Fifty percent, or nothing."

Mark took a deep breath. He knew he had pushed as far as he dared. "All right, fifty percent. But the company has my name."

Sam allowed himself a tight smile. "I already have one company named after me. You are welcome to this one."

One week later, on May 28, 1905, the Manning Rubber Company was incorporated under the laws of West Virginia (Ohio at that time imposing double liability on stockholders). One thousand shares of common stock at a hundred dollars par were issued, five hundred to Samuel Rosen, vice-president and secretary, and five hundred to Mark Manning, president. As a corporate symbol, the president chose a spoked, tired wheel upon which was superimposed a huge letter *M*.

PART

II

CHARLOTTE IN LOVE

1905–1907

CHAPTER ONE

THE INVITATION read, "Mr. and Mrs. Sydney Fine Request the Pleasure of Your Company at a Soirée Musicale, at 8 o'clock, May 2, 1905. A buffet supper will be served at 10 o'clock." Charlotte Rosen Fine had given many "soirées musicales" in the five years of her marriage. But this was to be one she would never forget.

It was a warm evening, following afternoon showers. The guests stepped out of their carriages and limousines onto the still-wet sidewalk, dressed in the newest spring fashions. As they entered the handsome townhouse on Fifth Avenue, they were greeted by Charlotte in the drawing room; Sydney, however, wasn't there. "He has a bad cold," Charlotte explained. Actually, she had no idea where he was. He had left that morning for the office, as was usual, and she hadn't seen him since. But he had never failed to be present for one of their parties. She had called his club; he hadn't been seen all day. She had briefly considered calling the police, decided against it. It was premature, and it was unlikely his absence had been caused by an accident. Much more likely he was somewhere drinking, perhaps with Richard Goldmark. When Amelia Sinclair, who knew Charlotte was lying to the other guests about Sydney, offered to call Richard's house for her, Charlotte nervously begged off. If he was there, she didn't want to know about it. Besides, at the moment she had too much on her mind to worry about Sydney being with Richard. She was playing the orchestra part, transcribed for piano, of the Brahms Second Piano Concerto, accompanying the soloist, Hugo Lindenbaum, a famous German pianist. Even the accompaniment of this enormous work was difficult, and Charlotte, like every performer amateur or professional, had her case of nerves. She simply couldn't worry about Sydney. But of course she did.

The guests, about thirty in number, seated themselves on gold ballroom chairs in the drawing room and waited for Herr Lindenbaum and Charlotte to make their appearance at the twin grands at one end of the room. It was an elegant assemblage in an elegant room, in an era when elegance was still a practiced art. Sydney's mother had supervised the decoration of the house in the grand style. The walls were paneled in light wood that was heavily carved in a Grinling Gibbons manner, modified by Louis XVI influence, perhaps creating a bastard style but one that was nevertheless undeniably rich and satisfying. Two enormous mirrors faced each other across the room, reflecting the Waterford chandelier. A rich Oriental rug cushioned the fashionable baby Louis heels of the ladies' shoes as well as the gilded feet of the elaborate and heavy furniture. The room bespoke wealth, security, tradition—perhaps more accurately, a mixture of traditions. It seemed impregnable.

Charlotte appeared with Herr Lindenbaum, the latter walrus-mustached with wild, uncombed hair, imitating Monsieur Paderewski's electric hair style. Charlotte briefly introduced him and the Brahms concerto. There was polite applause, after which the two sat down at their keyboards, facing one another, Charlotte beautiful in a white dress and looking especially delicate as compared to the fierce Herr Lindenbaum. But her tone, as she played the opening theme, was anything but delicate: firm and controlled. Herr Lindenbaum responded on the other piano with the ascending B-flat chord passage, and the concerto was launched.

They played the massive first movement brilliantly, Lindenbaum's German technique mastering the complexities of the music and Charlotte providing skilled accompaniment. Then came the powerful scherzo, followed by the haunting third movement with its gorgeous theme, and finally, the bouncy last movement. The guests stood up and applauded as Charlotte and Herr Lindenbaum took pleased bows. There was a fifteen-minute intermission before the second part of the program, which featured German *Lieder*. Charlotte made her way through congratulating guests to Amelia's side and whispered, "Any sign of him?" Amelia shook her head.

Now that the strain of the concerto was over, Charlotte's thoughts concentrated on her absent husband, her exasperating, once-loved, still partially loved, absent husband.

"What should I *do*?" she whispered.

"Nothing," replied Amelia. "There's nothing to do."

Which was true. Charlotte returned to the piano to introduce the next artist, Madame Angélique Duchamp, a well-known French soprano who was to sing a selection of Schubert *Lieder*. Madame Duchamp, unlike the popular concept of opera singers, was not full-proportioned at all but rather thin and pretty. She positioned herself in the bow of the left piano, Charlotte at the keyboard, and softly began the *Ständchen*. The lovely music coiled around the room, caressing and lulling the audience—which was when it happened.

It started with an echolike falsetto coming from the back of the room. Someone was mimicking Madame Duchamp. There was a stir; Charlotte stopped playing, Madame Duchamp broke off in mid-phrase and everyone turned to the rear. The falsetto voice continued: *". . . in den stillen Hain hernieder, Liebchen, Komm 'zu mir! Flüsternd schlanke Wipfel rauschen in des Mondes Licht . . . in des Mondes Licht . . ."*

Sydney stumbled around the rear chairs, heading down the paneled wall toward the pianos. He was really drunk, and mud was splattered over his evening clothes as if he had either fallen into a puddle or been sprayed by a passing carriage. He gestured with boozy bravura as he sang the "Serenade," mocking Madame Duchamp. Halfway down the wall he stopped and leaned on a bombé chest. The guests were muttering, unsure of what to do. Charlotte had risen from the piano stool and was staring at her husband.

Sydney waved his hand.

"Keep playing! Go on, keep playing. *I'll* sing."

Silence. Richard appeared in the doorway at the rear of the room. He looked composed, sober and distinctly pleased. Charlotte wondered if he had instigated this performance to provoke a final break between Sydney and herself.

"Keep *playing*," Sydney shouted, suddenly angry. "Dammit, when I tell you to do something, you *do* it!"

Charlotte didn't move. One of the men sitting near Sydney got out of his chair and started toward him. Sydney yelled, "Keep away," and the man stopped.

Again, silence. Sydney, still leaning on the chest, surveyed the room, then said, "Isn't it lovely? Lovely Mrs. Sydney Fine, who plays so beautifully! The lovely Fines in their lovely house with lovely furniture and music. Culture! Oh, everybody's so cultured and beautiful. You know what I say to you? I say it's all a bunch of crap—"

The ladies groaned as two other men jumped up and started for him. One, Albert Rosensweig, a former Yale tackle turned stockbroker, grabbed Sydney's arm. "Come on," he said in a low voice, starting to shove him toward the door. "We're putting you to bed."

Sydney wrenched himself free. "Let *go* of me!" Sydney backed against the paneled wall. "I reject *all* of you. And I particularly—

especially—reject *you*." He pointed at Charlotte, who did not move. "I don't want any more, do you understand? I need to be free of all this . . ." He gestured around the room again, seeming to lose his bearings. "All this . . ." His eyes began filling with tears as his anger began to dissipate. His hand dropped to his side and he sagged. He surveyed the room once again, almost like someone taking a last look at his native land. "Free," he said, quietly now, "of all this *damn* beauty."

Beauty? The word, so unexpected, somehow stunned the crowd more than Sydney's outrageous behavior. Free of beauty? Who would want to be free of beauty? Surely a most unnatural idea. And yet one of their own had said it.

Sydney now began to weave his way back to the door. When he got to Richard, his cousin took his arm, flashed a look at Charlotte, and led her husband out of the room.

She remained standing by the piano. For all the shock, for all the maliciousness of it, for all the insult to her, still, oddly, she felt mostly sorrow for her husband. The handsome young prince leaning on the piano listening to Chopin was gone, she knew, forever.

The demon had won.

The first year of the Manning Rubber Company's existence was a time of unceasing activity for its founder and president. A buyer had quickly been found for his bicycle business, and though the nine-thousand-dollar price was a thousand less than Mark had hoped for, the speed of the sale convinced him it was worth the lower price. He moved out of the "rathole" and into a rented room off Clark Street, paying forty-nine dollars a month for a second-floor room in a clean house owned by Mrs. Renfrew, a fat widow lady, who cooked delicious pies and tended to baby her handsome new roomer. Meanwhile, Mark went looking for a factory. Not just any place would do; not only did the factory have to be near a rail line, it also had to have a good supply of water, which the manufacture of rubber products required in enormous amounts. Mark bought an empty brick foundry on the Matahoochi River for $6,000. Four acres of land went with the building, which had a trunk line to the main tracks. The one-story foundry provided 9,000 square feet of floor space, plus room for three small offices. Mark went to Akron and purchased a rubber-washing machine for eight hundred dollars, two boilers costing $20,000, a used generator, two rubber mills for $2,700, two tubing machines, a secondhand vulcanizer, and some used molds. While he was there, he also bought a genius: twenty-nine-year-old Harold Swenson, a strapping Swede who had held down nearly every position in the Goodrich factory and who, Mark had been told, was the best foreman in the business and knew more about making tires than anyone else. Mark went directly to the Goodrich factory, waited for Swenson to appear at the gate (it was easy to spot him; six foot four with almost white hair), took him across the street to buy him a beer, offered to increase his salary of thirty cents an hour to fifty cents, and threw in a bonus of twenty shares of Manning stock with a promise of more in the future. The taciturn Swede listened, sipped his beer. "You're trying to buy me," he said in his singsong Swedish accent.

"You're damned right."

"I don't like to be bought."

Mark sighed, ordered him another beer and a second cup of tea for himself.

"Look, Swede," he said. "I'm primarily a salesman. That's what I do best, but I need a good product to sell. You can give me that product. I'm willing to give you almost complete control of the manufacturing so I'll be free to travel around and sell. Now, you have the choice of staying with Goodrich and being a foreman the rest of your life, or getting in on the ground floor of a little company and growing with it."

"What if you don't grow?"

"Then we all lose. It's a gamble, but it's less gamble for you than for me. Hell, I've got everything I own in this. If we flop, I'm rock bottom. You can always go back to Akron. But I don't think we're going to flop. Anyway," he raised his cup of tea and took a sip, "this is your chance to be something besides a big dumb Swede the rest of your life."

Swenson's eyes narrowed and, before Mark realized what was happening, the man had grabbed his coat and pulled him up out of his chair. A big, white-haired fist smashed into Mark's jaw and he fell over backward, sprawling on the floor. The other customers turned to watch the brawl. Swenson glared down at Mark and said, "No one calls me dumb. Understand?"

Mark got to his feet, rubbing his aching jaw.

"I apologize."

Then a big, red-haired fist sailed through the air and smashed the Swede's jaw. Swenson fell back over his chair and landed on the floor in the midst of broken wood and splinters.

Mark looked down at him.

"And no one," he said, "hits me without getting it back. Now, are we in business, or do you want to fight some more?"

Swenson got to his feet, a look of grudging admiration on his face. "You hit pretty good," he said.

"So do you."

The Swede stuck out his hand and grinned. "Okay. We're in business."

Mark laughed and shook his hand.

The factory began production on June 23, 1905. There was no ceremony. The closest they came to it was the previous afternoon when Mark and Sam and the Swede had watched workmen erect the big sign on the roof that read "The Manning Rubber Co. Inc." with the corporate symbol of the spoked wheel and the big *M* centered immediately above it. The next morning they went to work. Fifteen workmen under the supervision of the Swede; workmen hired at the top price, their goal to turn out forty tires a day. The second hour of operation the generator broke down, causing a six-hour delay while the Swede—the miracle man who knew how to fix anything—crawled all over the machine looking for the trouble. It was hardly an auspicious beginning, but finally the thing was working again, and the first Manning Unique Quick-Changer Tires began coming out of the molds.

With production launched, the job of selling was begun, which wasn't simple. The Rubber Trust, which shortsightedly had gotten out of the automobile tire business five years before, had watched the phenomenal growth of the car business and jumped back in by buying up a number of small tire companies. Firestone and Goodyear were booming too. The competition was stiff, but Mark had a few ideas. He had hired Wilma Amstuts as his secretary, Wilma being the sister of Beverly Amstuts who had represented Christian Virtue on the Presbyterian Church float that Fourth of July five years earlier. Wilma was plain, intelligent, hard-working and honest; in short, she was perfect. Mark dictated a letter to her which was to go out to every car manufacturer in the country (there were almost twenty-two hundred of them), every doctor (doctors drove a lot), every fire company, every trucker, every police department. The letter announced the Manning Quick-Changer Tire, "a revolutionary step forward in tires," as Mark modestly phrased it, a tire that came with a rim enabling "almost instantaneous replacement." The letter offered a set of four four-inch tires *with* rims at sixty-eight dollars; larger sizes were seventy-eight dollars and eighty-six dollars.

No sooner had Wilma begun the laborious job of typing up the hundreds of letters than Mark expanded the list by adding race drivers to it. Auto racing was becoming a mania, in Europe as well as America. A retired businessman in Massachusetts, Charles Glidden, who had made a fortune in the telephone business before selling out to the Bell system, had started long-distance auto tours to promote motoring for the family as a "health-giving recreation." The car was still something of a new toy, motoring was an adventure and the Glidden Tours caught on. The whole country seemed fascinated by the horseless carriage, racing and touring caught the public imagination, cross-country tours were organized and followed with breathless interest. Mark figured that if he could persuade some of the well-known race drivers to use his Quick-Changer the publicity would be the best possible kind of sales promotion. So more letters went out. He didn't get a driver's endorsement, at least at the beginning, but the campaign still proved effective.

Orders began trickling in. In the first month, a hundred and ten sets of tires were sold. The second month, two hundred sets. Mark was spending two-thirds of his time traveling with samples, following up the letters with personal sales pitches in Chicago, Indianapolis, St. Louis, Cleveland, Pittsburgh, New York, and at the same time sounding out local businessmen in the various cities who might be interested in buying dealerships. In the third month the frenzied effort began paying larger dividends. The fire department of Indianapolis ordered three hundred sets of tires, converting all their equipment to Quick-Changers. The Philadelphia fire department followed. Then Mark pulled off a coup. Following up on his thought the day he'd stared out the window of Sam Rosen's office at the tireless dray, he had approached several trucking firms. This infant business was still getting accustomed to the idea of using solid rubber tires, much less Quick-Changer pneumatics. But Mark pounded away with his sermon that trucking was the transportation wave of the future. The railroads didn't make money on short-haul freight—freight transported less than a hundred miles—so the short-haul business was a plum just waiting to be plucked by truckers. The roads were still rutted and bumpy; to transport cargo safely, trucks needed pneumatic tires to soften the bumps, and what pneumatic tire was better and more convenient than the Manning Unique Quick-Changer? Finally the sermon found a convert. Ronald Gerstenmeier, owner of a small trucking business in Chicago, listened, pondered, believed. He ordered two hundred sets of tires. Mark believed that the order, small though it was, would in time be followed by millions.

With the influx of orders, by the sixth month they had to expand. The work force had already quadrupled. A dozen new molds had been ordered, and to make room for them an addition to the factory was built, providing another ten thousand square feet of floor space. The addition was finished by the first anniversary of the company's founding. To celebrate the double occasion, Mark organized a company picnic in Matahoochi Park, which was an event all of them would remember for years to come. The company, being still young and exuberant and small enough for everyone to know each other's name, had a team spirit that in later years old-timers would recall with a nostalgia tinged with bitterness. Men were willing to work overtime to get out tires and fill orders, feeling a personal stake in the success of the enterprise as well as a sense of achievement in accomplishing so much so quickly.

On this day off to celebrate, everyone had a roaring good time. Mark provided enough beer and whiskey to float the Great White Fleet (though he personally stuck by his pledge and drank nothing but iced tea), fireworks, a band, games, contests, and expanding on his promotion for the Fourth of July parade six years before, he contributed a shiny new Maxwell as a "door prize," which was won by Bert Miller, one of the rubber washers. Bert was so drunk when the award came to him that he proceeded to drive the Maxwell axle-deep into the river.

The culmination of the day came when Harold Swenson stood up on a table and proposed a toast to "Mark Manning!"—he was not yet "*Mr.* Manning." No public relations man could have produced the heartfelt roar of approval that came out of some seventy beer-washed throats. Four of the men grabbed Mark, hoisted him on their shoulders, marched him around the park and then, as a finale, threw him into the river. Even Sam Rosen laughed. Bert Miller slumped under a tree and passed out. Wilma Amstuts—faithful Wilma who had come to worship her boss—burst into tears of happiness. As Mark slogged, dripping, out of the mud to grab Harold Swenson and toss him into the river, too, the big, handsome, greedy, ambitious farm boy-turned-pitchman found, rather to his surprise and embarrassment, that he was crying nearly as much as Wilma.

Once, years later, he was to tell his grandson it was the best day of his life.

He wasn't rich yet. Far from it. His salary as president was only five thousand a year, and though business had been excellent, the profits—less than ten thousand dollars but still a profit—had been put back into the company, so there were no dividends. To finance the addition to the plant, Sam Rosen had brought in a millionaire friend of his from Cleveland, Brock Sylvester, who was president of a large Cleveland bank. Sylvester studied the books and sniffed a winner. He invested fifty thousand dollars in return for a directorship, two hundred fifty shares of stock and an option of a thousand shares that could be exercised in 1912 at ninety dollars a share. In addition, Sylvester arranged a loan from his bank for a hundred thousand dollars. It diluted Mark's stock position, which he didn't like, but it gave him capital and he had no choice.

Besides, they were still small fish. Orders were pouring in and the factory was turning out two hundred tires a day, but to become big they needed to land substantial orders from one of the large car manufacturers, and this they hadn't been able to do. It wasn't that the car makers didn't see the advantage of the Quick-Changer; they did. But they knew Manning Rubber had defied the clincher-tire monopoly by making clincher tires without the permission of the pool commissioner in New York. It was common knowledge that the pool was about to begin a lawsuit against Manning Rubber; and the car makers, still insecure in their new-born industry, were afraid of angering the commission and perhaps incurring a law suit themselves by buying from Manning—or, even worse, having the pool commission enjoin its licensed tire makers from selling their products to them. So they weren't buying Manning tires, and Sam Rosen was getting worried. A week after the company picnic, he drove over to the plant and was shown into Mark's office by Wilma.

It was a small office, plainly furnished with a battered wooden desk and a few chairs. A coat stand stood in the corner and, at its foot, the inevitable brass spittoon, a fixture in the tobacco-chewing Midwest (though Mark had a fastidious aversion to spitters and eschewed tobacco his entire life, except for an occasional cigar; in certain of his personal habits he was, ironically, something of a puritan.) On the wall hung a big Manning Rubber Company calendar, flanked by photographs of the factory, of a set of four-inch Quick-Changers, and of Mark shaking the hand of the fire chief of Indianapolis after that worthy had placed his order for Manning tires. Otherwise the room was bare of frills. Mark, in shirtsleeves, got up from his desk chair and shook hands with the courteous deference he'd always taken pains to display to his elder benefactor and partner ever since their first encounter.

Sam sat down in front of the desk, removed his pince-nez and wiped the glass with his handkerchief. He replaced them on his high, thin nose and said, "I'm worried, Mark."

"What about?"

"Orders."

Mark leaned back in his chair. "We got a beauty from Wingate this morning. A hundred sets. And Gerstenmeier in Chicago—"

"No, no," Sam interrupted, waving his finely shaped hand to cut Mark short. "I'm talking about the big boys. You know who I mean."

Mark nodded. He knew.

"They're boycotting us," Sam continued, "and if we don't break the boycott we're in serious trouble. Sylvester thinks the same thing. Now, I'm not too worried about this law suit the pool commission's starting. Our lawyers are smart as theirs, and I think our people will be able to take the suit through sufficient appeals to force a settlement from the commission. But meantime we're missing out on the big orders. And unless we can do something about it, we're going to be out of business. So, what do you intend to do?"

The fox eyes turned on Mark, who decided there was something beautifully direct about old Sam. He never beat around the bush, to say the least. Mark recalled the portrait of the plump woman hanging in the entrance hall of Sam's house, Charlotte's mother. He tried to imagine a young Sam Rosen in love, courting the girl he would marry. It was possible the single-minded passion Sam now expended on business might once have manifested itself romantically. Mark suspected the success and sex drives were probably two sides of the same coin, and if so, Sam must have been a very successful young man with the ladies.

"I'm going to launch a campaign against Bennet," said Mark.

"Why Bennet?"

"Because he's the most successful car maker in the business right now. He could make us if he switched to Quick-Changers. And I'm going to offer him a deal he won't be able to turn down."

Sam shook his head. "Bennet's very tough, but he's also afraid of the pool. He's not going to jeopardize his business for a few dollars saved on tires."

"I think he will," Mark said. "I'm going to Detroit tomorrow, and I think I can sell him."

"What kind of a deal are you going to offer him?"

"I'll sell him tires at fifty dollars a set."

"But we'd be losing money!"

"Not if he buys three thousand sets, and that's what I'm going to ask for. I realize that even with an initial order like that, we'll still lose money, but on the *next* order, we'll break even. And if we can tool up to produce that kind of output on a regular basis, we can cut enough waste in the shop to put us way ahead. And once the Bennet Ariel is using Manning tires, *we'll* be number one."

"You make it sound too easy. Bennet's never bought from you before, and I don't know why you should feel so confident he'll buy from you this time, even with a discount. Furthermore, I hear from Brock Sylvester that Bennet doesn't like you personally."

"Why?"

"He thinks you're too tricky."

"*I'm* tricky? What about him? I've heard about the games he plays with dealers . . ."

"I know," Sam said, holding up his hand. "Frank Bennet likes to appear ethical but he's quite something else in practice. I'm trying to prepare you. It's better to know what he is saying about you behind your back so that you can evaluate what he is saying to your face."

Mark relaxed. "You're right," he said, getting up to come around the desk and accompany Sam to the door. "Maybe I'll quote some Scripture to him to show him how proper I really am."

"Don't make light of the Bible," Sam said. "Bennet is very religious, you know, or at least he pretends to be." He shook his head. "Sometimes I think I'll never understand the Gentile mind. You are a very hypocritical people, you know."

Mark smiled. "Do you think I'm hypocritical?"

His partner looked at him. "Yes," he said. "Oh, I know you pretend to be very pure these days, but I have an idea where you go on your business trips. Now Mark, I have no interest in lecturing you on your private morals, but frequenting houses of prostitution is a bad business. It is bad morally, and it is dangerous. I have much money invested with you and your public reputation and well-being are important to me. Those women may be attractive, but they are also diseased. You should stop seeing them."

"But I'm young, I need women—"

"Get a wife! What do you think wives are for? Get married and settle down and raise a family. People in business don't trust a man who's not settled. Isn't there some young woman you're interested in?"

Mark hesitated. "Yes."

"Well? Why don't you marry her? All you have to do is ask. You are a reasonably good-looking young man with a little money. I see no reason why most women wouldn't be interested in you. Who is this girl?"

"I'd rather not say."

Sam shrugged. "Well, of course, it's none of my business. But I'm telling you to stay out of brothels. Get married, settle down." He opened the door. "And sell Frank Bennet."

Mark accompanied him out to his carriage, for Sam, despite the fact that he was a partner in a company making tires mostly for automobiles, stubbornly clung to the past when it came to his own personal transportation; he claimed cars smelled bad. As he got in his carriage, Mark said casually, "By the way, I was sorry to hear about Charlotte's marriage. Is she . . . divorced?"

Sam shook his head. "It's a bad business. She's still waiting for it to come through. She's moved into the Waldorf."

"I suppose this is none of my business, but was her husband . . . I mean, was there another woman involved?"

Sam looked rather nervous. "Oh no, definitely not."

As he drove away, Sam briefly wondered if Mark might have meant his daughter when he said there was someone he was interested in. Then he dismissed the idea. Charlotte would never marry a Gentile even if she were to fall in love with Mark—which was impossible. Charlotte was too refined for a man such as Mark, a whoremonger with no respect at all for the gentle sex. In any case, he would never allow her to marry him. Not only was Mark a Gentile, he was a thoroughly unprincipled one besides.

Sam could tolerate being Mark's partner in business. But he would *never* be his father-in-law.

CHAPTER TWO

Frank Bennet was, like Mark Manning and many other industrial pacesetters of his day, the son of pious farm parents. But, unlike Mark, uninhibited by parental piety, Frank Bennet was a strict Methodist who read his Bible twice daily, believed work was the ultimate virtue and idle hands the Devil's tools. Tall and lean, with a face that was handsome when he smiled—which was rarely—he was already at thirty-nine a millionaire. He had been a lowly machinist who began tinkering with automobiles eight years before in the stable behind his house; in 1900 he sold his first completed car and was launched into the business. He developed an inexpensive, one-cylinder car that he called the Ariel, which didn't sell particularly well the first few years when cars were still very much the playthings of the rich but which began to catch on as automania spread throughout the country. And in 1905 he sold the astonishing number of 5,000 cars, which made him the leader in the now hotly competitive automobile business. Like Ransom E. Olds, Henry Ford and others, he was getting into mass production; and when Mark arrived in Detroit for his appointment, it was held in Bennet's big office in his brand-new factory on the outskirts of the city, a factory considered the wonder of the industry because it was built around an assembly line that could turn out three times more cars per day than any other company.

Bennet's office, like Bennet, was spare to the point of somberness. The walls were bare of even family photographs—much less such factory photos as were on Mark's wall—but there was one portrait hanging in solitary splendor that left no doubt on whose side Bennet was (and who, by implication, was on Bennet's side as well): an engraving of Jesus Christ, picturing Him as androgynous and sad-eyed in the fashion so beloved by churches of the day. In contrast, Frank Bennet, dressed in a rumpled linen suit, looked formidably out-of-sorts as he shook Mark's hand and gestured to a chair before his big desk.

"I've got a rotten cold," he said, proving his point by pulling a huge handkerchief from his hip pocket and blowing his nose so loudly Mark thought the man's eardrums would pop. "Had it for a week, won't go away," he continued, sniffing loudly as he sat behind his desk. "I catch one every summer. Never fails. I suppose you're going to try and sell me some tires?"

Mark grinned at the man's brusque lack of charm which intimidated most people. "That's right. And this time you're going to buy."

Bennet's rheumy eyes looked skeptically at him. "What makes you think so?"

"My price. Fifty dollars a set if you give me an order for three thousand sets."

"Not interested."

"Of course you're interested. You can't afford not to be. I'll be losing money selling at that price and you know it. But it's also worth it to get your business. No other tire maker will sell at my price, which you also know."

Out came the handkerchief, again the loud honk as he blew his nose. Then, "All right, I'll admit you're underbidding everyone else. I'll also tell you I like your Quick-Changers. They're an improvement, no doubt about it. But I'm not going to buck the clincher-tire pool. They might boycott me and then I'd be completely dependent on you for supply. I wouldn't feel very comfortable being that dependent on the Manning Rubber Company."

"The clincher tires have four, maybe five, more years and they'll be through. You know that as well as I do. You'll have to give me a better argument than that."

"I don't have to give you any argument at all, Manning," he said, pulling out the handkerchief for yet a third time. "You say you want my business. All right, let's hear a real sales argument from you. *You're* selling, not me."

"Fifty dollars!"

"Not worth the risk. Make it forty."

Mark laughed. "That's robbery."

"No, it's being prudent. 'A prudent man foreseeth the evil, and hideth himself; but the simple pass on, and are punished.' Proverbs, 27:12."

Just then Bennet's surprisingly attractive secretary opened the office door and said, "Excuse me, Mr. Bennet. Mrs. Bennet is on the phone."

Bennet nodded, rather unhappily Mark thought, excused himself and picked up the phone. He listened, sniffling and looking unhappier as Mark used the interruption to consider his next move. Bennet was negotiating, and if Mark came down by slow degrees, he would probably get the order at around forty-five dollars. But he couldn't possibly afford that price. The fifty-dollar price had been his rock-bottom figure, the one below which it would be ruinous to the company to sell. He probably should have allowed himself a cushion for bargaining, but he had wanted to come in with as dramatic a price as possible, hoping Bennet would be so overwhelmed he would buy on the spot. Obviously, Bennet hadn't been whelmed at all. And the more Mark thought about it, the angrier he was with himself for his miscalculation, and with Bennet for his unreasonable greediness. Despite the glib Biblical quote, Bennet was in fact holding him up. Angry as he was, Mark took some comfort as he noticed that the automobile industry's tower of piety was getting hot under the collar himself.

"Listen, Mildred," he was saying, trying to keep his voice low, "I've told you a hundred times, *no*. I'm *not* going to Mackinac . . . I don't care if I've got triple pneumonia, I can't go till next week . . ." Out came the handkerchief, this time angrily. Honk, sniff. *"No.* You go with the children today and I'll come up next week. Is that so complicated I have to say it *again?* You *won't* feel silly without a husband . . . sit on the front porch and rock—there's nothing silly about that. Now, I'm in a meeting . . . yes, yes, all right, I promise I'll be there next week. Have a good trip."

He hung up, wrinkled his nose in a half sniff and drummed his fingers irritably. Then he looked up and said in a tone so sour Mark strained not to laugh, " 'It's better to dwell in the wilderness than with a contentious and angry woman.' Proverbs, 21:19. Now, where were we?"

"In the wilderness," replied Mark. "Forty dollars a set is out of the question."

"Then make me an offer."

"I did. Fifty dollars. Not a cent less."

Bennet drummed his fingers. Mark tried to look cool but he was sweating. In the perhaps fifteen seconds of silence that elapsed as Bennet presumably considered the pros and cons of the deal, the younger man knew he was tantalizingly close to his sought-after brass ring. If Bennet said yes, Manning Rubber was surely on its way.

Bennet stood up and extended his hand.

"Sorry," he said. "If you can see your way to coming down, call me. Otherwise, I'm afraid we're still in the wilderness."

Mark took a deep breath, stood up, shook hands and forced a smile.

"You know you've made a mistake," he said, keeping up the front.

"It won't be the first," Bennet said quickly, his eyes on some papers in front of him, his mind on the next order of business. Mark said nothing as he left the office. He was thinking: self-righteous son of a bitch. Pious bastard. I hope your wife puts horns on you all over Mackinac.

He was angry and dejected, but he wasn't about to give up on Bennet. Instead of taking the train back to Cleveland that afternoon as originally planned, he decided to stay over a day on the chance that he would get a new idea about how to approach Bennet, or that something would turn up—the salesman's everlasting, if desperate, optimism. Needing some extra cash to pay for a hotel room —or, as he was contemplating, to spend the night at Lillian's, Detroit's leading brothel (to hell with Sam's advice) he proceeded downtown to the Bank of Detroit to cash a check. As he produced his letter of credit at the teller's window, he noticed a small ceremony taking place in the officer's section of the bank. Several bank officials were presenting a uniformed guard with what appeared to be a check while a few newsmen stood by taking notes and a photographer exploded his flash powder.

"What's going on?" asked Mark.

"Well, we had some real excitement yesterday, sir," said the young teller, delighted to tell the story again. "You see that guard? Well, that's Jim Malloy. Big, ugly guy, isn't he?"

"He's not going to win a beauty prize."

The teller laughed. "Not hardly. Well, yesterday in came these two robbers with guns and masks. It was twenty after ten—I remember because I looked at the clock, don't ask me why. Anyways, there was only a few customers in the bank, and we all put up our hands and they made us lie down on the floor. Then one of 'em come back here and started taking cash out of the drawers into this here laundry bag. Now, I didn't see this part because I was behind the cage here, but apparently the other guy was standing at the door over there keeping an eye on the street making sure no one came in, no cops or anything. So Jim, the guard, was about six or eight feet away from him, and he started crawling up toward him. It was a pretty brave thing to do, let me tell you, because that guy could've put a bullet right through his head easy as plugging a turkey. But old Jim's got guts. Anyways, he got up about two feet before the guy saw him and whispers at him to get back, points his gun at his head. Well, Jim knew that the guy didn't want to shoot unless he had to because the noise would bring the police, so he bluffed him and didn't move. He didn't come any closer, he just didn't move, lay there on his belly like a snake. Then the robber hauls off to kick old Jim right in the face, which Jim was ready for. He grabs the guy's foot and pulls, jerking him right down on the floor. Then, quick as you can say 'spit' Jim's on top of him, knocks him out, grabs his gun and shoots dead the one taking the cash, just like that. Got him right through an eye. Boy! He wasn't a pretty sight, let me tell you."

"And now the bank's giving Jim a bonus?"

"Yeah—fifty bucks. He saved them pretty near fifty thousand, and all they can do is give him fifty simoleons. Excuse me, sir, I didn't mean to be critical of my employers."

Mark was watching the guard, who was shaking hands all around. Finally the ceremony broke up and the guard, who looked about thirty, returned to his post by the door as the reporters began to leave. Mark thanked the teller, took his cash, then walked over to the guard.

"Mr. Malloy, my name's Mark Manning, and I just heard about what you did yesterday. That was very impressive work."

Malloy looked pleased. "Well, I was just doing my job."

"Say, mind if I ask you what they pay you here?"

Malloy looked rather surprised, then shrugged. "Don't mind at all. I get thirty-five dollars a week."

Mark pulled a business card from his wallet and handed it to him. "If you're willing to move to Ohio, I'll pay you seventy-five a week," he said.

"Doing *what?*"

"Being in charge of the security system for my factory. I need a man with guts. Think it over. If you decide to do it, send me a wire. Collect."

He walked out of the bank as Jim Malloy stared at the card.

"Take me to Rawley Road," Mark said that evening as he climbed into a cab. "There's a farmhouse there, about a quarter mile south of the highway—"

"You mean Lillian's," interrupted the cabbie.

Mark cleared his throat and nodded. "I see you've been there before," he said, sinking back in his seat. "Okay, Lillian's."

The cab headed out of town for the country. Lillian's was the premier bordello in Detroit, and with the boom in the automobile business, Lillian's business was booming as well. Lillian, a former English teacher who had decided teaching Wordsworth was not only somewhat boring but was also not likely to provide her with the good things of life, had had the brilliant idea to transplant commercial love to the cornfields, where she could offer her clientele maximum privacy. So she bought an old farmhouse, tarted it up on the inside but left the exterior untouched except for a coat of paint, and discreetly opened her doors to business. Mark had been to Lillian's several times before, and remembered with pleasure the quality of the food as well as the personnel. The place wasn't inexpensive—one hundred dollars for dinner and private room—but it was well worth it. The cab bumped down the gravel drive to the house, a sprawling wooden building put up some thirty years before, with a big covered porch in front, and parked beneath a giant elm. Mark arranged to have the cab pick him up in the morning, then he walked across the lawn to the porch, counting half a dozen cars and carriages parked at the side of the house, a sign that business was good indeed. He rang the doorbell and waited. The door was opened by the proprietress.

Lillian was a handsome woman who dressed quietly and well, with none of the garishness of her professional colleagues. Her manner was genteel—perhaps ludicrously so, considering—and now she smiled pleasantly as she saw who was at the door. "Mr. Manning! How *delightful* to see you! Do come in."

Mark did, giving her cheek a kiss and her fanny a pat, which she pretended to ignore. "How goes the tearoom business?" he asked, hanging his hat on a peg and following her into the lushly decorated parlor.

"Well, for this time of year. Summer's not our best season, you know. People go to their summer cottages, but there are always a few gentlemen come to town. Like you." She smiled prettily. "Now let me see, if I recall correctly, last time you were here Barbara entertained you."

"That's right. Very nice girl."

"Oh, Barbara is *very* sweet. And accomplished! She writes, you know. Poetry. Very nice poetry, very lyric. Though she does have trouble with her spelling. I try to encourage her . . . but I'm afraid Barbara is engaged this evening. We have a very sweet new girl, from Quebec. She's French and *most* charming. Would you like to meet her? I think you'll be enchanted."

"Sounds okay to me."

Lillian gently tugged a bell cord and a maid appeared. "Helen, would you ask Gabrielle to come down to the parlor, please? This gentleman would like to be introduced."

"Yes, Miss Lillian." Helen curtsied and vanished as Mark sat down in a French chair.

"Lillian," he said, "if I didn't know what went on here, I'd think I'd wandered into one of those New York City cotillions."

She smiled demurely. "One must set standards, particularly in *this* business. I don't allow just anyone to come here, you know. If a gentleman doesn't behave properly, I won't let him come back. The tone of the place is *so* important. Ah, *voici Gabrielle! Entre, ma chère.*"

A stunning girl in a pink dress had appeared in the doorway. She was about twenty, and her lovely face with its delicate coloring, her slim figure and the pink bow in her black hair gave her the appearance of a schoolgirl. Lillian led her over to Mark, who stood up like a gentleman.

"Gabrielle, this is Mark," said Lillian, who never used her clients' last names in the presence of her girls. Gabrielle smiled and held out her hand.

"How do you do, Mark?" Her voice was gentle and accented.

"It looks as if I'm doing very damn well," he said, taking her warm hand. "Lillian, the chamber of commerce ought to give you a medal for importing Gabrielle."

"*Isn't* she charming? And so clever with her hands. She does beautiful needlework. Gabrielle, dear, take Mark to the green room. We'll bring dinner up in half an hour. We have some beautiful steaks tonight, and would you like some champagne?"

"Fine," said Mark, who regularly broke his pledge when he went to the tonier brothels that served champagne. He had decided wine was low enough in alcohol to exclude it from his proscription on spirits. Besides, he was developing a taste for champagne.

"We'll send a bottle up right away," said Lillian. "*Amuse-toi bien, ma chère.*" She patted Gabrielle's shoulder and Mark followed the girl out of the room, up the stairs to the second floor, where she led him to the end of the corridor. "That is Lillian's room," she said, pointing to a closed door at the end of the hall. "And this is ours." She smiled, opened the last door before Lillian's and led him into a pleasant room with green-striped wallpaper. There was a small table in the center of the room, and two chairs; along one wall was a big sofa piled with pillows; and in the corner, a four-poster bed. Two big windows with lace curtains looked out over the shade-treed lawn, which a rising moon was beginning softly to illuminate.

"Very nice," Mark said, closing the door. "I had the yellow room last time I was here."

He came over to her and put his hands on her shoulders. She smiled up at him.

"You are very nice looking," she said. "I don't meet too many nice-looking men."

He pulled her gently to him and kissed her, running his hands down her arms. She smelled of lilac. "I think," he said, "this is going to be just what the tired businessman's doctor ordered."

It was. The dinner was memorable, as well, being served at the center table by Helen, who then discreetly left the diners alone. Mark ate with gusto, and the two of them easily finished off the bottle of champagne. When dinner was over, Mark stood up and stretched, then walked around the room a few times before sitting down on the bed and taking his shoes off. "I'm going to take a nap till my dinner's settled," he said. "Never make love on a full stomach, they say. Wake me up in about twenty minutes, please."

"Would you like me to rub your forehead?"

"How about my back?"

She came over to the bed. He took off his shirt and turned over on his stomach. She sat next to him and placed her fingers just below his shoulder blades. Then she started to rub, gently.

"Does it feel good?" she breathed in his ear.

"Mmmm." His eyes were closed, his belly full, his back being rubbed . . .

Honk!

His eyes opened. The sound had come from the next room, muffled, but unmistakably a nose being blown triple *forte*.

"Who's in Lillian's room?"

Gabrielle continued rubbing. "Oh, that's probably Mr. X, Barbara's mystery man. She knows who he is and so does Lillian, but no one else does. He uses Lillian's room because there's an outside stairway."

Honk!

"He certainly must have a bad cold—where are you going?"

Mark was off the bed and going to the door. "Back in a minute," he told her.

He opened the door, went out into the hallway, and opened the door to Lillian's room.

"You're not supposed to go in there—" Gabrielle called, jumping up from the bed.

It was too late. He was in, closing the door, then leaning against it and laughing out loud. A naked Frank Bennet was cringing under the sheets of the bed staring at the intruder. Beside him was a full-blown blonde, also naked, though hardly shocked. She was, however, angry.

"What do you mean, coming in here?" she said. "Just get the hell out!"

Frank Bennet coughed in agony. Mark came over to the bed, as if to inspect. "So this is the wilderness it's better to dwell in than with an angry woman?" he said. "Well, Mr. Bennet, I must say I agree with you. Hello, Barbara. Remember me?"

Barbara stared at large bare shoulders and seemed to remember. "You . . . you won't tell anyone?" Bennet said.

Mark leaned against the wall and folded his arms over his chest. "Well, now, Mr. Bennet, for a man with your religious convictions to so fall from grace, it's obviously my duty to tell *someone* just so they can save your soul. Oh, yes, I definitely think I'd have to tell someone. Your wife, for example."

Bennet sucked in air.

"Of course, my silence can be bought. And you know the price."

"You realize this is blackmail?"

"I surely do. Three thousand sets of Quick-Changers at fifty-three dollars a set—this little shenanigan has just pushed the price up three dollars—and my lips, as they say, are sealed. A deal?"

Bennet slowly nodded his head in a painful "yes."

"Good. Shall we shake?"

Out came the hand from under the sheet. They shook. Then Mark playfully patted Barbara's cheek. "Take good care of him," he said as he headed back to the door. "He's my most important customer. Oh, and, Mr. Bennet—" he paused at the door—"you'd better take something for that cold."

When Mark returned to Gabrielle in the green room, he took her in his arms and hugged her. "Gabrielle, you are definitely my lucky star. My incredibly lucky star! I'm going to make you a very happy woman tonight."

Which he proceeded to do.

CHAPTER THREE

Just above the easternmost bulge of the South American continent into the Atlantic lies the Portuguese-founded Brazilian state of Ceara, its capital the port city of Fortaleza. Regularly, every nine to twelve

years, a *secca,* or drought, comes to Ceara, causing the flat cattle land
of the sertao plains to wither and die. Cattle drop into the red dust
to turn to bone. The flowers die. All normal life that does not leave
dies. And men die, or at least wither like the carrasco bush to become
zombies, unless they too leave Ceara. At the turn of the century,
most men indeed did leave, stumbling out of the drought-stricken
province to make their way up the coast to Belém de Para, the port
on the southern mouth of the gigantic Amazon River. And there,
wandering along the Ver-o-Peso, the old wharf, piled high with the
black oblong balls of smoked *borracha,* rubber, the Cearese would
stumble into a system of exploitation that amounted to slavery, a
system as cruel as that in Leopold's Congo, a system from which the
Cearese could never escape, a system whose product was the raw
material of, among other things, the Manning Quick-Changer tire. It
was also a system that one day would inadvertently bring new prominence and fortune to Mark Manning and his company.

The system began at the doors of the *agencias.* The Cearese would
go to the white-hatted *Senhores* in their steaming offices looking for
work until the *secca* was over and they could return to their *fazenda.*
They would be offered work as a *seringueiro,* or rubber gatherer, and
rosy pictures would be painted of the fortunes to be made on the
estradas, the rubber estates up river. How could the hungry, illit-
terate Cearese get to the *estrada?* The *Senhor* would generously advance ten *milreis* needed to get up river to Santarém, plus a few
extra for a man to go out and get himself liquored up on the potent
cachaça, enough to fog his senses that much more and make him, in
the hung-over morning, even more tractable. A contract was signed
with an X but, of course, not read; the coins handed over. The Cearese
would go off to celebrate, thinking himself the luckiest man in the
world to have ten or twelve *milreis* in his pocket, more cash than
he had probably seen at one time in his entire life. Then in the
morning, hot coffee for the hangover and the trip up the river to
Santarém, where he would report to the *patrão,* the rubber-estate
owner. The *patrão* would advance him the materials he would need
and assign him his *estrada* out of the many in the *patrão's seringal.*
The provisions would include a *machado* knife for cutting through
the jungle, a rifle, ammunition, cans of rice and coffee, *farinha,*
quinine, a little knife, a *machadinho,* for tapping the wild rubber
trees on the *estrada.* Then another contract would be presented and
the *patrão* would announce to the Cearese that he owed him, say,
1,400 *milreis,* to be paid back by the rubber he gathered. The man
might be surprised by the enormous figure, but his illiteracy prevented

him from checking the figures or reading the print, and he would sign, unaware that he would never in a dozen lifetimes collect enough rubber to pay off his debt. And from this moment on he had a considerably foreshortened lifetime. The green hell of the Amazon jungle would see to that.

Now he would go farther up river to his *estrada*—the farther up river, the less likely that the rubber trees had been tapped, and "virgin" trees gave the most rubber. On the banks of one of the *paranhas,* a small tributary of a larger tributary of the seeming unending Amazon, he would build with the help of other *seringueiros* a small shack on stilts. Sometimes he would have a wife to share his loneliness; sometimes he would improvise. Even with a wife, the loneliness was crushing, the work exhausting, the jungle—alive with huge scorpions, snakes, spiders, leeches, ticks and jaguars—an ubiquitous, deadly enemy. And if it weren't the jungle, it was the fever. Or the vicious red-bellied *piranhas.* Or the *patrão.*

The trees gave the most latex before dawn, so the *seringueiro* would need to get out of his hammock early. He would set out to cut through the jungle with his *machado* to the first tree. Each day he would cut the same path through the dense, crawling jungle, and each day the lush jungle would grow back. When he reached his first tree he would hack into the bark as high as he could reach with his *machadinho.* Then, with some clay taken from the bag slung over his shoulder, he would quickly fasten one of the *tihelinhas,* the clay cups, beneath the gash from which the white tears would already be oozing. More gashes, more cups. Then back into the jungle to hack his way to the next tree, which could be as far as two hours away.

Once he had made the initial round of his trees, he would rest briefly; then he would take a large calabash or empty kerosene can and start all over again to collect the latex. If he were fortunate, the clay cups might be half full of the cream. More likely, there would be a thimbleful, and some of the trees didn't bleed at all—perhaps because they had already been overtapped or wounded by the brutal gashes of the *machadinho.* Frustrated, the *seringueiro* would hack the bark again, more deeply, or perhaps light a fire at the roots of the tree to drive the sap up into the trunk. Sometimes a desperate *seringueiro* would cut the tree down and bleed it in a dozen places, but if the *patrão* discovered this he would whip him with tapir hides. Or worse.

The *seringueiro* sucked the rubber trees, and the leeches, worms, maggots, humidity, disease and rot of the jungle sucked him. His food —rat-dropping infested even though he had paid ten times its worth to buy it from the *patrão*—was the staple *farinha* and beans with hot coffee, sometimes varied by fresh meat or fish if the *seringueiro* had the time or energy to trap it, which was rare. No fresh vegetables or fruit—though the soil was rich, the *seringueiro* had no time to raise the vegetables. After the inevitable attacks of fever and dysentery, the man's body needed all its strength to survive; but his diet robbed it of the little strength it had left. He and his wife were already victims of diseases inherited from past generations of undernourished forebears. They would transmit the new miseries with those of the past to the future, a malignant cycle perpetuating itself.

When the *seringueiro* returned from his *estrada* with his calabash of latex, the real work would begin: the smoking of the *barracha*. He or his wife would build a fire of kindling and *urucuri* nuts; they would then place a funneled clay pot over the flames, the white smoke passing through the funnel. The *seringueiro* would dip a paddle in the latex and turn it slowly in the smoke until one layer hardened, after which he would dip again and form the next layer. In this fashion, the *pelas,* the biscuits of rubber, were built up, several months being needed to build a biscuit weighing the required twenty kilos. When the *seringueiro* had what he thought were enough biscuits, he would put them in a canoe and paddle down river to Santarém, where the *patrão* would weigh them on the big scales, the scales that would come to symbolize the key to freedom to the wretched *seringueiro*. Whatever his hopes, there never seemed to be enough rubber to pay off the *patrão*, which meant buying more provisions to return to the jungle. Which meant more credit, more fever, more dysentery, more leeches, more of the endless tracking from tree to gashed tree, more rotted *farinha*, more stinking nights and sweating days, more *cachaça* to blot out the nightmare world he had stumbled into. And somewhere in his mind, fading but still there, the memory of his home in Ceara, the home he kept telling himself he would someday return to.

The deal with Frank Bennet, consummated in a Detroit whorehouse, did indeed put Manning Rubber on the industrial map. To fill the intial order of three thousand tire sets, Mark hired more workers (he also hired Jim Malloy, the daring Detroit bank guard, who wired his acceptance of Mark's job offer and moved to Elkins with his wife and two children to set up what was to become known, in some circles, as the notorious Manning Security Force). Moreover, with Harold

Swenson, Mark was able to streamline the tire-making process so that they could turn out the Bennet order with minimum waste. The tires were delivered on time. Bennet grudgingly admitted he was pleased and ordered five thousand new sets to meet the swelling demand for Bennet Ariels. Mark and Sam were jubilant, since the size of the new order put their Ariel business narrowly into the profit column. And by June 1907, the second anniversary of the company's founding, the two men could report to their Cleveland backer, Brock Sylvester, that they would do well over a million dollars in business that year with a projected profit of almost $80,000. Sylvester was, needless to say, pleased, adding that he had already turned down offers for his Manning Rubber stock at more than twice what he had paid for it. Sam was pleased. Mark was not.

One morning he climbed into the Ariel he had treated himself to and drove over to the Rosen Stove factory, where he picked up Sam. "I want to show you something," he said as the older man, with a look of genuine disapproval on his face at the prospect of riding in a "stinker," got into the car next to Mark, who cranked the engine to life, then headed out of town. "I want to buy Sylvester out," he shouted to Sam as they bumped noisily along the rutted country road.

"Why?" Sam shouted back, holding onto his hat, terrified by the speed and nauseated by the dust and the noise.

"He doesn't give a damn about what we make. All he's interested in is making a profit. One of these days Sylvester is going to accept an offer and sell out his stock to someone—Christ knows who— and leave us stuck with people we won't know who'll try to run the show *their* way. It's no good, Sam. We're growing fast and I'd like to buy him out now—before it's too late. Which is one reason I want more capital. Much more."

Sam began to list reasons why they shouldn't rush things, as Mark knew his conservative partner would. They mustn't overextend; they still owed the hundred thousand to the Cleveland bank; the car business was booming now, but who could tell what would happen six months from now. "Sure," Mark interrupted. "Everyone's going to get sick of cars and go back to horses. Well, I'll take my chances the automobile is here to stay. So are we, if we're smart."

He pulled off the road and parked the car near a cornfield. The two men climbed out and looked around. They were a mile and a half east of town, and the farmland stretched as far as the eye could see—flat and fertile. A tenth of a mile down the road was a dilapi-dated farmhouse, a big red barn in the rear. The man who'd constructed the barn had, as was his custom, signed his handiwork by writing on the roof in dark shingles the date of the barn's construction in huge numerals: 1889.

"Over there's the Matahoochi," said Mark, pointing to a row of trees on the other side of the cornfield. "This is the Madison farm. Four hundred and sixty acres. Bill Madison died last April and his kids have put the place up for sale. I want to buy it."

"Why?"

"To build two new factories."

Sam stared at him. "We've just put on the new addition—"

"I know, and we'll outgrow that by next year. I want to build the most efficient factory in the business, one that can turn out at least a hundred thousand sets of tires a year. I want it to be a clean place with as much air and ventilation as possible, so our men don't have to work all day in a stinking pit the way they do now. I want to build a lab—"

"A what?"

"A research laboratory. I've got my eye on a young chemist in Akron named Melville Benny who's fiddling around with ways to speed up vulcanization. I want to hire him and give him what he needs for his work. I want room for a parking lot, because ten percent of our men are coming to work in their own cars now, and within ten years I'll bet all of them will. I want to build a cafeteria for them so they can get a decent lunch cheap . . ." He stopped and looked at the older man's amazed face. He laughed. "If you think I'm crazy now, wait till you hear about the *second* factory."

"I can wait."

"The second factory will be coordinated with the tire factory, and it's going to make the rims. We're going into the steel business, Sam."

To his surprise, Sam took the news calmly. "Yes, I've been thinking the same thing," he said. "If we made our own rims instead of buying them elsewhere, we could eliminate much delay and save the rim companies' profit. Yes, I like that idea."

Mark was delighted. "Sam, you're a genius!"

"Why? Because I agree with you?"

"That's right. Now, how much do you think something like this would cost?"

"More than we can afford."

"I know that. That's why we need more capital. I'd say to do this right and buy out Sylvester we'd need five million. What do you think?"

"At least that."

"Which means we're going to have to sell some stock. Sam, I'd like you to go with me to New York and introduce me to Herschel Fine. He has the best underwriting house on Wall Street, wouldn't you agree?"

"One of the best, certainly."

"Then will you do it?"

Same looked at him. "Herschel Fine is an important man, you know. He's at the top. Do you think you're ready to deal with a man like that?"

"Don't you?"

There was no doubt in Sam's mind that his young partner was a smart, imaginative entrepreneur. Mark was a fierce worker and had the commercial instincts of a Rothschild. Yet Sam really didn't like or even admire him. The difference between the two men was, for example, illustrated by their attitudes toward Frank Bennet. Mark thought it very funny he had caught Frank in the brothel. Sam, when Mark told him, was shocked—shocked not only that the two men were even in Lillian's, but even more that Mark would use this private knowledge to pressure the Bennet order, just as Sam had discovered that his partner had pressured Adrian Tutwiler to get the order for the twelve stoves from the army seven years previously. Sam was a true Victorian, and he found Mark's methods distinctly improper. He also did nothing to stop the orders—the fruits of such impropriety.

"Yes, I suppose so," Sam finally said. "All right. It's agreed. We'll go to New York and see Herschel Fine."

Mark grabbed Sam's hand and pumped it. Then the two climbed back into the car and started back to town. Halfway there Mark said casually, "By the way, let's stay at the Waldorf, shall we?"

"That's where I always stay."

A moment later Sam realized why Mark had said the Waldorf. Charlotte was living in the Waldorf now. Again he wondered if Mark had intentions toward his daughter, and again he told himself it was unthinkable—he was a Gentile and there was his whoremongering, his lack of moral character. Mark Manning was simply too common for someone like Charlotte.

Sam didn't like to admit it to himself, but he did know that there were those who considered him something of a snob.

Taste, some say, is like smoke: you can see it but you can't touch it. Charlotte had exquisite taste; she also believed that if a sense of personal style wasn't exactly the most important thing in life, it was nonetheless important and contributed to the quality of life. Charlotte's personal style included concealing her heartbreak over her husband's desertion and taking up with Richard Goldmark. She went about the job of putting together the pieces of her life in a new mosaic, and without fuss. The same was true of Herschel Fine. Though Herschel lived in princely style, his morals were solidly bourgeois; in the long years of his marriage he had never been unfaithful to his wife and he frowned on those who considered their philandering a kind of acceptable manly sport. The sanctity of the family, of marriage, were engrained in his tradition. And when his own son exposed himself, almost literally, to society as not only being faithless to his wife but—ten thousand times worse!—cheating with a member of his own sex, Herschel received one of the worst shocks of his lifetime. Indeed, thanks to the *con brio* nature of Sydney's exposure, there was no hope of keeping the scandal private. Herschel, however, maintained his immense dignity, as befitted his place and position, and never allowed anyone to observe his hurt and revulsion. His son merely ceased to exist, becoming a nonperson. Herschel wrote him a note offering him one million dollars if he would exile himself permanently to Europe, the moral junkyard of America's upper classes at the time. To Herschel's credit, the note contained no recriminations. To his discredit, perhaps, it also contained no sense of regret or loss. It was coldly impersonal, a financial transaction, nothing else. Sydney, with a celerity that put some legitimate doubt on the sincerity of his drunken rejection of his gilded world, accepted the money and set sail for France with Richard Goldmark. He never saw his father again.

Society rallied around Herschel. There were private gasps and a few snide asides, of course, but gradually the shock ebbed, Herschel's social and professional peers built a united front, and the incident soon passed into near-forgotten history. Herschel's commanding position in his world was never challenged, and as far as Charlotte was concerned, she had always been the sympathetic victim and her friends generally remained loyal. Herschel, who had always loved his daughter-in-law, now drew even closer to her, and she became almost a daughter to him. He made the arrangements for the divorce and presented her with a settlement as generous as Sydney's—one million dollars. Charlotte had not wanted it but he had insisted. She finally accepted the money and moved into the Waldorf-Astoria, independent but lonely.

The Waldorf Hotel had been built in 1893 on Fifth Avenue at the site of William Waldorf Astor's former mansion. There were two

Astor mansions, in fact, twin buildings, one on the corner of Thirty-third Street, the other on the corner of Thirty-fourth Street (where the Empire State Building now stands). The other Astor house belonged to William's aunt and uncle, William and Caroline Schemmerhorn Astor, and it was said that William and his Aunt Caroline did not get along. Whatever the truth of that rumor, William, dubbed "Wealthy Willie" by the press, had run for Congress and lost, and his defeat had so irritated him that he tore down his house, put up the hotel, renounced his American citizenship and moved to England to become, later, a viscount—certainly one of the classic examples of sour grapes in the annals of American politics. Uncle William and Aunt Caroline were infuriated by Wealthy Willie's building a hotel right next door, and they threatened to tear down *their* house and build a livery stable as revenge.

Meanwhile, the hotel opened in the middle of a depression followed by a panic, and everyone predicted ruin for the elegant establishment. They didn't, however, count on the genius of two men—George Boldt, a German emigrant who became the hotel's first manager, and a young Swiss named Oscar Tschirky, whom Boldt hired away from Delmonico's and who was to become the legendary Oscar of the Waldorf. Boldt and Oscar managed to make the hotel the favorite hostelry of society and its men's bar the favorite watering place of such magnificoes as Bet-a-Million Gates, Diamond Jim Brady and J.P. Morgan himself. The hotel became so successful, in fact, that William and Caroline Astor changed their minds about putting up a livery stable and decided to join the success by tearing down their house and putting up a hotel themselves. This was joined with the Waldorf under the management of Boldt, and the two hotels became the Waldorf-Astoria.

It was into this splendid pile that Charlotte had moved after her Fifth Avenue townhouse was sold, taking a six-room suite on the seventh floor of the northeast corner of the hotel, overlooking the intersection of Fifth Avenue and Thirty-fourth Street. The rooms were large and well designed; Charlotte decorated them with what was, especially for the period, an almost stark simplicity, using only the most choice pieces of furniture, keeping everything light and feminine. The walls of the drawing room were a pale lavender, and although the soot of the city was later to cause Charlotte to wonder at the wisdom of this color notion, the pale lavender room became one of the most famous in New York society of the day for its beauty, as well as for the beauty of its tenant. It was in this room, the afternoon following Mark's expounding of his industrial dream to Sam

Rosen in the Ohio cornfield, that Charlotte was pouring tea for her best friend, Amelia Sinclair, and Amelia's fiancé of less than a week, a banker from the City of London named Sir Bruce Clark. Sir Bruce was actually a Scot from that grayest of all cities, Edinburgh, who as a young man had emigrated south to London to seek employment in the Dickensian world of Victorian England's banks. Hard work, a steel-trap mind, and the fierce ambition only those born poor can ever truly understand had brought him to the top of the financial community in the City, where he held directorships in seven of the most prestigious business enterprises in the entire British Empire. His influence had earned him a knighthood, and his fortune had bought him a Georgian estate in Hampshire. Sir Bruce had surely arrived. Personally he was still unpretentious. At fifty-five, he was a big man with a roundly protruding stomach, a ruddy face and curly steel-gray hair. His manner was direct and no-nonsense, his accent still more Scottish than English, and he was infatuated with Amelia, who treated him with bemused affection.

At the moment Charlotte had casually mentioned that her father and his "partner" were on the way to New York to see Herschel Fine, and Sir Bruce had picked up on the information with surprising interest. "Is that a Mr. Mark Manning?" he asked.

"Why yes," replied Charlotte, then adding to Amelia, "he used to be quite the Peck's Bad Boy of Elkins when he was younger. Very fast with the local girls. It wasn't at all respectable to be seen with him."

"He sounds interesting," Amelia said. "Is he also good-looking?"

Her fiancé was unamused. "Is that a proper question for an engaged woman to be asking in front of her fiancé?"

Amelia smiled coolly. "Bruce, you are so deliciously proprietary, but I should hate to think that getting married to you means undergoing the surveillance you give to your business enterprises. I'm not, you know, a stock or bond."

"Of course not but—"

"In any case, I assure you I wasn't interested for myself, being engaged as I am to the handsomest man in London."

"Well you must be daft if you think *that!*"

"You're handsome to me, anyway," she said. "But of course I was asking for Charlotte's sake. A nice-looking young man who isn't at all respectable might be just what she needs. Don't you agree, Charlotte?"

She thought about this a moment, remembering her first meeting with Mark. She was, in fact, looking forward to seeing him after all these years—anticipating it to a degree that rather surprised her. Still, she wasn't about to let her feelings show.

"I don't think it likely Mr. Manning would be interested in me, Amelia. But he is quite an extraordinary man, as I understand it. I've only met him once, but I confess he made an impression on me." More than an impression, she added to herself.

"Do you think he's also a brave man?" Sir Bruce asked. Both ladies looked at him with surprise.

"Brave? Why ever would you ask that?" said Amelia.

"I have my reasons. How about it, Charlotte, do you think Mr. Mark Manning has nerve?"

"Oh yes, he's well equipped with that quality, I'd say. Somehow I doubt there's much in this world that would frighten Mark Manning."

Sir Bruce looked pleased. "Good. Then, if you'd be so kind, could you arrange for me to meet the gentleman?"

Again the ladies looked confused.

"Bruce," said Amelia, "if there's anything I can't stand it's suspense. Would you kindly tell us why you're so interested to meet Mr. Manning?"

The Scot grinned, pleased at his little mystery.

"Why, it's just that I have a question I'd like to put to the laddie, my dear. There's nothing so mysterious about that, is there?"

CHAPTER FOUR

The wide corridor connecting the Empire Room and the Palm Room of the Waldorf had been designated "Peacock Alley" by society editors; and the next day, after checking into his room, the young president of the Manning Rubber Company headed for the Peacock Alley to observe the show. And indeed it was a show. In 1907 the rich were not diffident about displaying their wealth, and the ladies and gentlemen gliding down the plush carpets or sitting in the gilt chairs, top hats on the men and huge feathered cartwheel hats on the women, were an imposing spectacle. Mark, however, did not feel outclassed or even out of place. He had more than a slight streak of the peacock in himself, had always been something of a natty dresser and so was attracting looks now from more than a few of the ladies.

Suddenly he saw Charlotte, whom he hadn't seen for seven years; he had almost forgotten how beautiful she was. Time and her disastrous marriage had seemed to do nothing but ripen her loveliness, now tinged with a hint of sadness that made it even more appealing. She came over to him and extended her hand.

"Mr. Manning, I was just now at the desk asking if you and father had checked in. How very nice to see you."

"And how nice to see you," he said, his eyes savoring her. She was wearing a beige suit with fawn trim and matching gloves. On her feet, which were just barely visible, he noticed she wore spats.

"I've been shopping," she went on, "and I was afraid you and father might go out before I had a chance to see you. Is he in his room?"

Silence.

"I said, is father up in his room?"

"Oh . . . yes, I guess so. I mean, yes, he was up there a few minutes ago. He called Mr. Fine. He asked us all to dinner tonight. You, too."

"Oh? You'll like Herschel. He's a wonderful person—but don't eat anything before you go to his house. He loves his food, and there'll be tons of it. His chef's one of the best in New York. Shall we go up and say hello to father?

He accompanied her to the fifth floor, hardly able to take his eyes off her. Before opening the door to Sam's room, which was next to the one he had taken, he paused and said, "Do you remember that time back in Elkins when I tried to convince you to go to dinner with me?"

She nodded. "I remember." Then she smiled. "I also remember that you said if things didn't work out with Sydney, your invitation would still hold. Well, I hardly have to tell you things didn't work out, and here I am having dinner with you tonight. So you see, I at least never forget an invitation."

"Well, I was really thinking about tomorrow night. Would you have dinner with me then? Show me some of New York's sights?"

She thought about it a moment, her eyes studying the big man with the handsome face who had come far since their last meeting. She liked what she saw.

"I'd be delighted to," she said.

For years, Mark had discounted his chances of ever marrying Charlotte, though the news of her divorce had rebuilt some of his hopes. Now, as he held the door for her, those hopes were definitely rising.

That night, when he should have been concentrating on business or, more to the point, on Herschel Fine, he found himself fixed on Charlotte instead. Not that there weren't other attractions: Herschel's Fifth Avenue mansion, while French Renaissance on the outside, was Medicean on the inside: heavy, somber, magnificent and strewn in princely profusion with art works mostly dating from the fifteenth and sixteenth centuries. Herschel seemed to identify spiritually with the Medicis, certainly an understandable association for a man who was as much a banker prince as Cosimo had been four hundred years before, and who had amassed an art collection that Lorenzo himself might have envied. Herschel was also a student of the period. He knew it intimately; and when he conducted Mark on a tour of the house, pointing out a rich tapestry here, a Giovanni Bellini there, a pair of silver candlesticks on a heavily carved Florentine chest in that corner, a statue in this corner, he provided commentary that was not merely the cataloguing of a collector but the attentive detail of a lover and connoisseur. An outstanding exception to the predominantly Renaissance character of his collection was a series of Goya etchings depicting the nightmare horrors of war.

While Mark was impressed with everything he saw—art to him had heretofore been a vague abstraction that for some reason attracted some people to dark museums—the Goya etchings made a lasting impression on him. He was dazzled; but after a while Mark found his attention wandering more and more frequently from Carpaccio to Charlotte. How absolutely beautiful she was! How graceful, charming, and intelligent. . . . His mind ran the gamut of encomia, omitting only the sensual. She was most definitely a female—she surely aroused his desire—but somehow she was not sensual. He had the feeling no one had ever really made love to her (which, of course, in a way was quite true). He also noticed the melancholy that seemed to hover in her eyes. It was a fleeting impression, but it was there and it made him feel genuine compassion for her. Whatever had happened with her first husband, it had left her a different woman.

Dinner in the huge and ornate dining room was, as Charlotte had predicted, a feast, for Herschel was typically Edwardian in his love of food. His philosophy, in that blissfully diet-free time, was the more food the merrier. It was not as Lucullan a meal as the one given by his fellow grandee, Randolph Guggenheim, for a pride of Tammany Hall politicos, which had consisted of nine courses and cost the staggering sum of two hundred fifty dollars per plate; but for a Tuesday night supper in warm weather it was most substantial. First, an exquisite pâté. Then, in succession, green-turtle soup, Dover sole with champagne sauce, the customary pause for breath and sherbet. Followed by the big guns: canvasback duck, served with fresh asparagus, and finally fresh fruits, vanilla mousse, bonbons, coffee and cognac. This astonishing quantity of food, expertly served by four footmen under the watchful eye of the butler, was laced with the appropriate wines; and though even Mark, who could be a trencherman on occasion, was out of the race by the duck, his host put it all away with a gusto that was near miraculous considering the fact that though he was a big man with a thick waist he couldn't by any stretch of the imagination be considered fat. As Herschel ate he kept up a flow of conversation that ranged from politics through art to the state of the market, about which he was nervous. "There's a good deal of speculation going on," he said. "Too much, in my opinion. The bubble's going to burst sooner or later, and I would not be surprised if it turns out to be sooner. Mind you, I'm not trying to discourage you about bringing out a stock issue. If your business is solid, and if the capitalization is handled correctly, you should not have any trouble. Nonetheless, I fear the speculators are heading for stormy seas." The way his deep voice went even lower when he said "stormy seas," Mark was glad indeed that he was not a speculator.

"I think you'll find," said Sam modestly, "that our tire enterprise is quite solid."

"Oh, we've been hearing good things about your company," said Herschel. "And persuading Frank Bennet to switch to your tires was quite a coup. By the way, how did you manage it, Mark? From what I've heard of Bennet, he's not at all an easy man to deal with."

"I quoted Scripture to him," Mark said pleasantly. "Bennet's always impressed by people who quote Scripture."

Sam looked as if he would gag at this, but Herschel only smiled.

After the meal, the guests were led into the drawing room overlooking Fifth Avenue. As Herschel engaged Sam in conversation about certain stocks in Sam's portfolio, Mark sat on a sofa next to Charlotte and she said, "There's someone I know who wants to meet you."

"Who?"

"Sir Bruce Clark, who's going to marry my best friend next month. He's an important banker in London and a director of—among other companies—the British Imperial Rubber Company. Whether that has anything to do with why he wants to meet you, I don't know—

he's being very mysterious about the whole thing. Anyway, I'll try to get you two together some time tomorrow."

"Mysterious? I wonder why he's being 'mysterious' about meeting me?"

"I have no idea." The butler passed coffee; as Mark took a cup he said, "Do you like living in a hotel?"

She considered this. "Yes and no. I'd prefer having a home, but there are advantages to living in a hotel when one is alone."

Again, that passing look of melancholy.

"Are you lonely as well as being alone?" he asked quietly.

"I have a lot of friends," she said, looking directly at him. "And I have my music." She paused. "But, yes, I am lonely."

"I probably shouldn't ask this, but I will anyway: do you have any beaux?"

She smiled. "Oh, yes, but none I'm particularly interested in." She paused, then added, laughing slightly, "But I'm not giving up."

She gave him a coquettish look that surprised and delighted him. He smiled. "Good. That makes two of us."

She found herself wondering what it would be like having Mark Manning make love to her. She decided it would probably be exciting, very exciting. It could hardly not be an improvement over Sydney. She had thought many times how cheated she had been so far in that area of her life, having had only one man ever make love to her, and that man attracted only to his own sex. She had not been romantically involved for more than three years now, though there had been numerous opportunities. She had been cautious—perhaps too cautious, she had often thought. And now here was a new—and yet familiar—opportunity. Still, he was in business with her father, so probably she should be even more cautious with him than with the others.

But something inside her told her she wasn't going to be.

———————

The next morning at ten, Sam and Mark were shown into Herschel Fine's office on Pine Street, a few blocks from the Exchange. Herschel's office, while not as Medicean as his house, was nevertheless impressive, with its dark paneled walls, its rich rugs and the big French desk behind which the financier was sitting. Now he stood up, shook their hands, commented on the weather, which was superb, offered them seats in front of the desk, then returned to his chair. They were getting first-class treatment.

"Now then," he said, "what area were you thinking about?"

"Five million," said Mark.

Herschel nodded. "Tell me exactly why you want it."

Mark looked at this imposing, almost regal man, this peer of Harriman, Morgan and Schiff, this Jewish grand duke with an elegant, meticulously trimmed gray beard and mustache that gave him an even more seigneurial look. Wall Street was then already eclipsing London as the financial capital of the world, and the men who controlled Wall Street held immense power. Herschel Fine was one of them, so to sit before him and tell him why one wanted five million dollars was a rather awesome experience. He had been the gracious host the night before and he was being gracious now. But though graciousness was ingrained in the man, Mark had the odd feeling Herschel was holding something back from him.

Nevertheless, he launched into his explanation of the financial position of the company, passing the books he and Sam had brought with them to Herschel as he went over the figures. Then he went on to tell about the two new factories they wanted to build, detailing the advantages of manufacturing their own rims and emphasizing the need for setting up research facilities to keep ahead of the competition by constantly improving their product. When he finished, silence. Finally Herschel said: "It sounds good. Very good. However, there is a problem."

Sam and Mark exchanged looks.

"What is it?" asked Sam.

Herschel leaned forward. "Sam, you must understand that whatever my personal relationship with you may be, and no matter how fond I am of you and Charlotte, when you and Mark are in this office I must deal with you on a strictly business basis."

"Of course. That's understood."

"Knowing you were coming to see me about financing, I had one of my partners thoroughly investigate your company. This is normal procedure with us; I might add that I let Mark go through his presentation because I wanted to check out what we already know. However, I think we know something you don't."

"What?" said Mark suspiciously.

"I learned of it this morning, just before you gentlemen arrived here. Have either of you heard of a man named Riley Baker?"

"I have," said Sam.

"Well, I haven't," said Mark. "Who's Riley Baker?"

"Riley Baker is a man of about fifty, I'd say. He comes from a respectable family—his father was a professor of mathematics at Yale

—and he inherited a bit of money which he began investing in the market. Baker has a genius for figures—I assume he inherited that from his father also—and he has a flair for speculation. He also is without scruples. I happen to be a fan of Sherlock Holmes, and I've come to think of Baker as the Professor Moriarty of Wall Street; he has the great professor's brilliance combined with total lack of morals. His, like Moriarty's, I'm convinced, is a criminal mind. At any rate, in the past fifteen years he has built up a fortune estimated by reliable sources at something around forty millions. He likes to operate in secrecy—he has a house on East Thirty-first Street that also serves as his office—and lately his favorite game has become buying into small companies with growth potential, manipulating the stock, bleeding the company, then selling out." He paused. "This morning I was informed that Riley Baker has bought out Brock Sylvester's holdings in your company."

Mark was stunned. "I *told* you Sylvester would sell out!" he told Sam.

"Apparently, Baker offered him a price he couldn't refuse," continued Herschel. "Unfortunately, your success has begun to attract the sharks, and Baker is something of a killer shark. I do not use the term lightly, by the way. Four years ago, his wife was found stabbed to death in her bedroom, and Baker was charged with the murder. He claimed a burglar had broken into the house. In any case, Baker's private life is malodorous—he has had a succession of mistresses, most of them actresses—and the prosecution tried to prove he had killed his wife during a fight over one of his girls—I don't recall her name. She was a rather well-known singer at the time but she seems to have dropped out of sight since then. At any rate, the prosecution didn't have enough evidence to win the case, and Baker was acquitted. However, no one I know believes he was innocent, and no one with any standing will have anything to do with him. The consequence is that even if we should handle the underwriting of your stock issue, we would have difficulty selling the issue with Baker in the picture. But we won't handle it. Even though this is not your fault, our firm could never consider dealing with a company associated with a man such as Riley Baker."

Mark spread his hands helplessly. "Then what are we supposed to do?"

"I'd suggest trying to buy Baker out immediately. He'll undoubtedly try to hold you up, but for the long-term health of your company I'd say it would be worth almost any price to be rid of him."

"What if he won't sell?" said Sam glumly.

"Then," replied Herschel, "you have a considerable problem. You might try to raise your five million privately and go on with your expansion plans. It's conceivable Baker might not want to do anything as yet; he could sit tight until you become big enough for him to make a real killing. But I would definitely try to buy him out first. If you succeed in that, naturally our firm would be happy to underwrite you. I'm sorry, gentlemen, not only because of my personal relationship with you, Sam, but because I think your company has an excellent future."

"Or *had*," Mark said. "Well, I guess I do agree with you, Mr. Fine. We ought to try and buy him out right now. Could you give me his address? We might as well try to get this over with as fast as possible."

"My secretary will give it to you." Herschel got up from his desk, escorted them out of his office and waited while his secretary looked up the address. Then he shook hands and again expressed his regret before returning to his office. As Mark and Sam left the building to hail a cab, Mark said, "What rotten damn luck. And Sylvester didn't even *tell* us!"

Sam said nothing until a taxi pulled up. Then he turned to Mark. "You go see Baker by yourself. I'll wait for you at the hotel."

"Don't you want to see him?"

Sam shook his head. "No. It's your company. You're the president. I trust your judgment in this matter."

It had not been an exactly triumphant morning, so Mark especially appreciated the vote of confidence.

By the time the taxi delivered him to Riley Baker's brownstone on East Thirty-first Street, between Madison and Fifth Avenues, Mark's temper was full blown. The sell-out by Sylvester had upended his plans, and he was more than ready to strangle both the sell-out, Sylvester, and Baker, the buyer. He rang the bell, fuming as he waited for someone to answer. When an English butler opened the door, Mark snapped, "I want to see Mr. Baker. My name is Mark Manning."

To his surprise, the butler said, "Yes, Mr. Manning. Mr. Baker's been expecting you."

The butler led him through the quietly furnished house to a small breakfast room overlooking a back garden. There, seated at a table in front of the window, was a pleasant-faced man in a red-and-black silk bathrobe spooning a soft-boiled egg from its shell. Opposite him was seated a blonde girl who was perhaps all of twenty. She was quite sensational, and despite Mark's anger, he could not avoid staring at her. She was wearing a blue peignoir and was also scooping a soft-boiled egg from its shell, although without the fastidious technique of Riley Baker. The scene was almost domestic, despite the presence of the blonde, and Baker could not have looked less like a criminal or killer shark. He smiled at Mark.

"Good morning, Mr. Manning. I thought you might be dropping by to see me today, and you haven't disappointed me. Good. I dislike being disappointed. You'll have to pardon our appearance, but it's my habit to rise late." He gestured to the blonde. "This charming lady is Miss Sylvia Wingdale. Sylvia, this is Mr. Mark Manning, the president of the Manning Rubber Company I now have some interest in. Sylvia is an aspiring actress, Mr. Manning, though I guess she isn't quite ready for Shakespeare. She's just now appearing at the Hippodrome in the Shuberts' newest extravaganza, *Pioneer Days*. Sylvia and, I believe, ninety-nine other girls walk down a flight of steps in colorful tights and disappear into the Hippodrome's water tank. You can't imagine how spectacular it is, and no one can figure out why it is the girls don't drown. Would you care for some coffee, Mr. Manning? An egg?"

The butler had pulled up a third chair and Mark sat down. "No thanks."

"Tell Mr. Manning how it is you don't drown, Sylvia," Baker said, buttering a piece of toast.

"There's a tunnel," said Sylvia, who had a high, breathy voice dipped in an honest Brooklyn accent. "The audience can't see it and we walk right in this hole. This hole right in the water. And then we go through the tunnel and come out in the basement. Isn't that *won*derful?"

Mark nodded. "Amazing."

"It's really a *won*derful show, Mr. Manning," Sylvia said, eyeing the handsome newcomer. "You really ought to come see it. You'd surely love the songs."

"That will do, Sylvia," Baker said. "I don't think Mr. Manning came here to discuss the theater. Why don't you go upstairs and get dressed?"

"But I haven't finished breakfast yet."

"Yes, you have *just* finished breakfast."

Sylvia stood up, smiled a full smile at Mark. "*So* nice to meet you, Mr. Manning, and I really *do* hope you come see my show. 'Bye."

She drifted out of the breakfast room as both men watched her. When she had gone, Baker returned to his egg.

"A sweet person," he said. "Very sweet. Like a hummingbird, with a brain to match. I understand you're a connoisseur of women, Mr. Manning. How would you rate Sylvia?"

"I don't rate women, Mr. Baker. I've just been with Herschel Fine—"

"Oh, yes, New York's really a small town at a certain level. Everyone knows what everyone else is doing. Brock Sylvester told me you wanted to raise some new capital to expand. That's a wise move. I believe in expansion. But the eminent Mr. Fine has heard about my being in the picture, am I right? He shook is head in mock indignation. 'Never, sir! My firm will never raise money for a company which is involved with that scoundrel, Riley Baker!' Am I close?"

Mark nodded. "Close."

"So, you're understandably upset, and here you are to try and buy me out. Am I still close?"

"How much will it cost us?"

Baker put down his egg spoon and wiped his mouth with his linen napkin.

"Mr. Manning, I have no desire to sell. I have just bought in. I like your company; I like it very much. I think it has excellent prospects and I have no intention of selling out. I'm in it, you might say, for the long haul." he smiled.

"Look, I won't play games with you. As long as you're in the picture, we can't raise capital. No one will touch us."

"Wall Street. Such hypocrites," Baker said, stirring his coffee. "They sell each other out every day, but when they find someone they consider a genuine villain, they love nothing better than wrapping themselves in a cloak of virtue and becoming insufferably pious. Of course, *I* can raise your money, if you'd like. Easily."

He raised the cup and took a sip.

"On what conditions?"

"No conditions. Interested?"

Mark said nothing.

"You think it over," Baker said. "I know Herschel Fine thinks poorly of me, but you'll find out I'm your friend, if you give yourself the chance. I have nothing but the best interests of our company in mind, believe me. I want to help you. Without sounding immodest, I think you'll find I can be a *very* useful friend."

Mark stood up and looked at the pleasant-faced man with the rich head of gray hair. "I'll think about it."

"You do that."

When Mark returned to the Waldorf he was told at the desk that Sam had gone up to his daughter's suite. Mark took the elevator to the seventh floor and knocked on Charlotte's door. Her plump Irish maid, Stella, let him in. He went through the short entrance foyer to the pale lavender living room, where Charlotte was speaking with her father.

"Did you see him?" Sam asked.

Mark nodded as he sank into a chair.

"What did you think of him?"

"He doesn't look like a killer," Mark replied. "In fact, he could pass for a minister or a schoolteacher. Maybe he *is* Professor Moriarty, I don't know. Of course, most ministers don't have breakfast with gorgeous blonde showgirls a third their age.'

Charlotte laughed. "Well, at least we can *hope* most ministers don't."

"But he's smart?" asked Sam.

"As a whip."

"Will he sell?"

"No. Fine was right; he wants to wait until we get bigger. I told him we couldn't get any bigger with him in the picture because we couldn't raise any capital, at which point he volunteered to raise the five million himself."

"That's out of the question! He's going to cause us enough trouble with a minority position. If he raises capital for us from his contacts, he'll dominate the company, and *we* might as well sell out to him."

"I know. We can't raise money with him, and we can't take his money. Maybe we should just give him the key to the factory."

Same stood up. "You're being too pessimistic. I want to think this over. Tomorrow we can start planning how to approach him. Either of you interested in lunch?"

"Not right now," Mark said. He looked glum, and Charlotte felt for him. She told her father she too wasn't hungry, and Sam left the suite. When they were alone Charlotte said, "You mustn't get too upset about this. I'm sure father will be able to raise the money for you."

"Even if he does, where does that leave me?"

Charlotte sat down next to him. "Right where you are now, doesn't it? President of the company?"

"But only as long as Sam's investors like me. After all, I'm going to end up with less stock than anyone else. It won't be *my* company any longer. It will be theirs, and I'll be working for them."

"But why shouldn't they be satisfied with the way you run the company? Who could do a better job?"

"That's not the point. It's *my* baby, my company, and I want to be in charge of it. Trouble is, I don't have any money. You see, it all comes down to the old adage—to get money you need money. When I think of the preachers who say 'money isn't important,' 'it's harder for a rich man to get into Heaven,' and all that junk, I have to laugh. Money's the *one* thing in this world that lets you do anything —the *one* thing. I should know because I've never had much of it, and look at the bind I'm in now." He stopped a moment, then forced a half-hearted smile. "Well, I don't know why I'm boring you with all my problems. You can't be very interested."

"Of course I'm interested, if for no other reason than it's father's company too. But I'm interested for you as well."

He looked at her. "Why?"

"Because you're in trouble, and I'm an easy mark for people in trouble. Besides," she smiled, "I seem to like men with red hair."

He wanted to kiss her but thought better of it. Time, though, seemed to be on his side, especially since she seemed to be warming up to him by the minute. He would behave cautiously. This time he mustn't lose her.

"I'm glad you're interested for my sake too," he said. "It makes me feel less alone." He stood up. "I'll see you tonight at seven. You haven't forgotten our appointment?"

"Hardly! I've been waiting seven years for this dinner."

He laughed and took her hand in both of his. Again he had a strong desire to pull her to her feet and kiss her, and he suspected she would not have objected, but again he played it cautiously.

"Thank you for being on my side," he said warmly. Then he let go of her hand and left the room.

Outside in the corridor he nearly bumped into a portly man in a tweed suit who was accompanied by a woman in her early fifties. "You must be Mr. Manning," exclaimed Amelia Sinclair. She and

Sir Bruce introduced themselves, the latter explaining that they had just been on their way to see Charlotte about arranging a meeting with Mr. Mark Manning. "And here you are," said the Scottish banker. "Will you allow me to buy you a drink downstairs? I have something I'd very much like to discuss with you. Amelia, please do go on in and talk to Charlotte. I'll be up later."

Sir Bruce took Mark downstairs to the men's bar, where they ensconced themselves in a corner booth. Sir Bruce ordered a whiskey and soda, Mark a sherry. "A sherry?" said Sir Bruce, showing distaste. "Not a fit drink for man or beast. You ought to drink nothing but whiskey, laddie. Whiskey's the only decent drink on the face of this earth, and I don't exclude mother's milk. Sherry? English! Good God!"

"Sir Bruce, I didn't come down here to listen to a lecture on my drinking habits. I happen to like sherry, I never drink hard liquor, and I am in one damned poor frame of mind. So if you don't like what I drink—"

"Ah, you've got a hot temper, I can see! It's that red hair, no doubt. Now calm down, my boy, calm down. You can drink kerosene, for all I care, just so long as I get me whiskey. And here it comes! Just in time, too." The waiter brought the drinks, and Sir Bruce glowed with distinct effulgence as he took his first long sip. "Ahhh . . . fine stuff. Now, Mark—you don't mind if I call you Mark?"

"No."

"And you call me Bruce. Forget the 'Sir' business. Not that I don't like it and pick up when I hear it, but I know it don't sit well with you Yankees. Now, I've been told you came here to New York to see Herschel Fine about a bit of financing? And how has that worked out for you?"

"So far, a disaster. We need to raise five million, but somebody named Riley Baker has bought into the company and now Herschel won't underwrite us because of Baker."

"I've heard of Mr. Baker. Where do you go from here?"

Mark shrugged. "Private financing. Or maybe we don't go anywhere."

"How would you like to go to Peru?"

Mark looked at him. "Why should I want to go to Peru?"

The banker smiled. "For five million dollars, perhaps?" He set down his glass. "Let me tell you my story and you decide. Several years ago a Peruvian came to London looking for money, just as you've come here to New York. In fact, he was looking for approximately the same amount of capital as yourself—a million pounds sterling. Now, this man was not, I suggest, the sort to inspire confidence in a conservative banker such as myself. He's a former hat peddler, with small, rather piggish eyes. . . . Flores definitely didn't appear a good candidate for a major loan; his company, however, turned out to be in excellent shape."

"What company?"

"The Peruvian Amazon Company. Its headquarters are in the town of Iquitos on the Amazon, in the eastern part of Peru, near the Brazilian border. Carlos Innocente Flores is the president of the company, and he controls thousands of acres of jungle to the north of Iquitos—actually, he leases it from the Peruvian government for a pittance of *soles* per acre a year and a division of the royalties."

"How did he manage such a good deal?"

"Easy enough, laddie, when your brother-in-law is a Peruvian senator. Now, Señor Flores was shipping a good deal of rubber out of Iquitos but wanted to expand so as to ship more. A consortium of bankers, including myself, raised the money for him and back he went to Peru. Since then, he's increased his tonnage of rubber exports remarkably, and be damned if the stock hasn't soared on the London Exchange. So our business instincts were justified, you might say. Our moral instincts, on the other hand, couldn't have been worse."

"Why?"

"You've doubtless heard about old King Leopold of the Belgians and the atrocities his men perpetuated on the blacks working his rubber plantations in the Congo? And the consequent uproar in London when the publicity started? Well, laddie, we've invested in another Leopold. The last few years stories have been leaking out of Peru and Brazil about the methods Flores is using to increase his rubber production, and I'm the first to admit it's enough to curl your hair. If the rumors are true, Flores is running a bloody abattoir in the jungle, and he's turned the Peruvian Indians into slaves. *If* the stories are true—but the 'if' is the problem. If we could get some proof of what's going on down there, we'd have grounds to cancel our loans to the company and the government would send in a board of enquiry. But unless we have some sort of proof, we can't just arbitrarily cancel Flores's loans, particularly since his stock is doing so well on the Exchange—the stockholders would howl for our blood. On the other hand, we can't afford to wait until a scandal breaks over our heads. So, as you can see, we're in what you might call a stinkin' dilemma. Waiter, I'll have another whiskey."

"Why don't you send someone down to Iquitos to get the proof? That seems simple enough."

"We have, lad. We've sent four men to Peru. Three of them came back and reported that the rubber gathering stations they saw were reasonably well run and the Indian reasonably well treated—no one suggested they lead a pleasant life in the jungle but there seemed nothing that smacked of atrocity. They suspect, though, that Flores had arranged a sort of Potemkin village stage set, just like old Leopold tried to do in the Congo. What goes on in the jungle in the more distant stations they couldn't tell, because they had no way to get there. And of course there are no telephones or wireless down there—no way to communicate at all—so for that reason alone it was too risky for them to attempt to reach the distant stations by themselves."

"What happened to the fourth man?"

Sir Bruce hesitated, rather nervously. "Well, he *did* try to get to the distant stations. At least, that's what we believe. I'm afraid he's not been heard of since."

"And you think Flores is responsible?"

Sir Bruce shrugged. "Who knows? As I said, there's no communication with civilization down there, except for the two boats a month that go up the Amazon from Belém to Iquitos. Otherwise, the town is totally cut off and Flores runs the place like a private kingdom. If he found out that MacCartney was attempting to get to the outlying stations, well . . ." Again, he shrugged.

Mark took a sip of his sherry. "And why are you telling me all this? You're not thinking of asking *me* to go down there?"

"You're way ahead of me, laddie, way ahead. That's exactly what I'm thinking of askin' you."

Mark laughed. "You must think I'm out of my mind even to consider it."

"Ah," said the Scot, "but you're looking for money, and you're having trouble finding it. And I know full well that when a hungry young man like yourself is looking for capital financin', there's just no telling what outlandish things he might consider doing. We need you, lad—I won't pussyfoot about that. And if you'd be willing to take the risk, go down there and try to get proof for us, why then I'll guarantee to raise you your five million in any way you'd like to have it. You'd be takin' an enormous risk; there's no two ways about that. But at least it's a risk you'd be well paid for, eh?"

Mark eyed him with interest. "But why me? I mean, what makes you think I could succeed where your own men failed?"

"Ah, well, that's easy enough. In the first place, you're an American, and that should throw Captain Wilson off the track."

"Who's Captain Wilson?"

"The captain of the *Lanfranc,* the English boat that regularly sails from Liverpool to Belém and up to Manáos and Iquitos. Now, we have strong suspicions that this Captain Wilson, though he seems to be the pleasantest chap in the world, is in fact on Flores's payroll and passes to Flores a list of all passengers he brings to Iquitos so that the *señor* can keep an eye on who's coming into his little domain, if you follow me. We get this information, by the way, from Mr. Baintree, the British consul in Iquitos, who's the only man out there we can trust. He says he *thinks*—and mind you, again there's no proof—he *thinks* Wilson tips off Flores to potential troublemakers. Now, if *you* go down there—you an obvious American—well, there's a good chance Wilson and Flores might both be fooled. And especially if you said you're in the rubber business, which you are, and that you had always wanted to take a look at how the raw rubber is collected from the trees, and so forth. You see what I mean?"

"Yes, but I *don't* see how that would help me find out what's really going on down there—assuming I agreed to go, which I haven't."

"Ah, as to that, I can only say you've got to rely on your wits. Which is another reason I'm making you the offer. I've heard you're a sharp one, laddie, a man who thinks fast on his feet and isn't scared by much. That's why, when I heard you were coming to New York, I decided I wanted to see you. If you'd do it, we'd most surely be grateful to you—whether you succeeded or not—and I don't need to tell *you* it's good business to have friends in London, where I believe the Manning Company contracts for all its raw rubber, now, do I?"

No, he didn't, Mark thought. And it was also true that having powerful men like Sir Bruce beholden to him would always be an advantage. But still, to walk into a rattlesnake pit like . . .

"And you'd really raise five million dollars for me in any way I wanted it?"

"We raised that much for Flores; why wouldn't we raise it for you? Your company's an excellent prospect, even with Riley Baker involved—he doesn't worry me. My God, compared to Flores, Riley Baker's a minor saint—and I'll raise it through a handful of blue-chip financiers, not spread you too thin. Oh, we'll make it worth your while, Laddie, if you'll help us out of this one."

"Would you raise half of it as a personal loan to me?" asked Mark.

Sir Bruce thought about this. "Well, that might be a little more difficult. . . ."

"If I can get half of the financing as a personal loan, I can be sure of keeping control of a substantial amount of ownership."

"Oh, I see well enough what you're up to." He hesitated, then nodded. "It can be arranged. Not easily, mind you, but for what you're risking for us—"

"*If* I do it."

"Yes, of course."

"I'm not too happy about ending up like your man MacCartney— I'm no hero, Sir Bruce. I'll let you know tomorrow."

"Good. And Mark, if you decide to go . . ."

"Yes?"

The older man shook his hand. "Well, laddie, just be careful, is all. I've taken rather a fancy to you, and I'd surely not like anything, well, unpleasant to happen to you after such a brief acquaintance."

Mark stood up.

"Sir Bruce, I was thinking exactly the same thing."

"He *is* good looking," said Amelia Sinclair to Charlotte. "Very dashing. And you say he has a wicked reputation with the ladies?"

She was sitting on the small white Hepplewhite sofa in front of the Adams mantel in Charlotte's drawing room. Charlotte was seated opposite her, and both women were smoking.

"Very wicked," said Charlotte, exhaling. Amelia had introduced her to smoking, which she had taken up as a mild form of feminist defiance but was now becoming a habit unrelated to her original purpose.

"Did he try anything wicked with you?"

Charlotte laughed. "I'm afraid he didn't have a chance. I only met him once, but he did say he thought he was in love with me."

"That, darling, may only be talk. I'm more interested that he's here and taking you out to dinner tonight. That's encouraging."

"Oh, Amelia, don't be idiotic. Trying to play matchmaker when I hardly know the man!"

"He's young, he's attractive, he's single, he obviously has a future and he's interested in you. You've been living alone in this hotel for much too long for your own good. Furthermore, you seem to like him . . ."

"Oh, I suppose in a way I do, but he does seem rather pushy and

awfully interested in money. And I'm not at all sure I find those
qualities so attractive."

"The whole world is money mad and pushy, and I say more power
to it."

"But I don't like men who are too aggressive."

"I think the only men worth taking an interest in are the aggressive,
ambitious ones. Besides, you're not going to tell me you don't think
Mr. Manning is an improvement over Sydney?"

Charlotte said nothing to this, though she silently agreed with it;
rather, she ground out her cigarette in the porcelain ash tray and
got up to walk over to the window and look out on Fifth Avenue.
Amelia watched her.

"Are you attracted to him?" she asked quietly.

Charlotte didn't answer for a moment, then said, softly, "Yes."

"And if he tries to make love to you? Having seen him, I would say
that is a definite possibility for your very near future."

Charlotte said nothing. Amelia got up and came over to the
window beside her. "You're a normal woman, Charlotte," she said
quietly, "and you need a real man who can love you and give you
children. You've been living in a vacuum ever since Sydney left, and,
darling, you know that nature abhors a vacuum."

Charlotte still said nothing, but Amelia went on. "I think you're
much more interested in Mr. Manning than you want to let on."

Now Charlotte looked at her. "Amelia," she sighed, "you know
me too well."

CHAPTER FIVE

When Mark called for her at seven, she came to the door wearing
a yellow satin wrap trimmed with maribou, and she looked altogether
dazzling. Two diamond stars were in her auburn hair and a string
of magnificent pearls around her bare throat. Her beauty erased all
the problems on his mind. He, too, looked well in his tails and top
hat. Admiration was mutual. They descended to the lobby and took
a cab to Rector's at Forty-third Street and Broadway. Charles Rector
packed in the nabobs and swells not only with his sumptuous cuisine

but with his unqualified willingness to please his customers. On one often-cited occasion, when dining with Diamond Jim Brady and assorted celebrities, mention was made that the talk of Paris was a new dish called *filet de sole. Marguery.* Rector removed his son, George, from Cornell the next day and promptly dispatched him to Paris with instructions not to return until he had the receipe for *sole Marguery*—which George managed to acquire.

On this particular night, the restaurant was as usual packed and Mark and Charlotte were led through the glittering assortment of diners to be seated by the maître d'. After they had ordered dinner and a bottle of champagne, Mark said, "Do you think a man would be a fool if he risked his life for five million dollars?"

"I think a man's foolish to risk his life for anything, unless it's something almost, well—now don't laugh at me—something almost noble. And I don't think five million dollars qualifies, do you?"

He considered this. "It's possible there might be a noble side to this too."

"Mark, what are you talking about?"

"Your friend, Sir Bruce. He wants me to go to Peru to check out certain atrocity rumors for him. If I do, he's willing to raise the five million for me. He also admits I might come back to them in a pine box."

"And you're seriously considering it?"

"Yes, I am."

"But that's insane! Father can raise your five million!"

"I'm not at all sure about that. Besides, Sir Bruce will raise half of it as a personal loan to me, and I know there's no way your father can do that. And, as I said, there's another side to it. I mean, apparently the Indians down there are being treated like animals and I just might be able to help them. Now, wouldn't that make it worthwhile?"

She hesitated. "Not if you were killed doing it." She looked genuinely upset, which pleased him.

"I think you'd really worry about me if I went, wouldn't you?"

"Of course I would!"

"Then that alone might make the trip worth it."

She tried to look cool at this, but she obviously liked the remark. "Mark," she said, "I realize money is important to you, but it's not worth seriously risking your life for."

"Well, there is something else. I told Bruce today I'm no hero, and I'm not, but the idea of going down there into a dangerous situation and trying what no one else has been able to do . . . it does sort of appeal to me. I admit I wouldn't do it without the prospect of the five million, but as it is I'm damned tempted . . ."

"But you see, it really *is* the money, and you're going against good common sense by saying it's in a good cause or that it's the excitement of the adventure— Mark, I know I have money and you don't, so it's easier for me to talk this way, but at least please think about this. . . . After all, I'd hate to lose you after only one dinner."

They laughed and as the waiter served a champagne aperitif he said, "I bet you didn't have this trouble with your husband. Being on Wall Street, growing up with money . . ."

The melancholy was back in her eyes. "Sydney? No, that's one thing you couldn't say about Sydney. Money was hardly his preoccupation." She took a sip of the champagne and added, "Sydney's interests were elsewhere."

"Such as?"

She didn't answer.

"What did happen?" he asked quietly.

She hesitated, unsure whether to tell him. "There was another person."

"She must have been very beautiful even to have competed with you."

"Thank you. But you see, it wasn't a she."

The waiter brought the first course.

It had been the last thing he'd suspected, and now he thought he could understand her melancholy as well as her rather pristine attractiveness. He did indeed feel sudden compassion for her and at the same time his male ego was beginning to preen. He would show her what the love of a good man really was. His vanity and her unfulfilled womanliness were now most promising allies.

After dinner, as they left the restaurant, he took her arm and said, "I've had an idea I bet none of your society boyfriends would ever think of."

"What would that be?"

"A buggy ride through Central Park. Strictly for out-of-towners, I'm sure."

"You know, you're absolutely right. No one has ever asked me, and I'd love it!"

The doorman hailed a cab—not one of the new American Mors

Coupe-Landaulets that had recently been introduced to the city, but the genuine horse-drawn variety already becoming something of an anachronism. Mark gave the driver his instructions, then climbed in after Charlotte. The horse jerked forward and began clattering up Broadway. The theaters were just letting out and Times Square, then becoming the amusement and glamor center of the country, was a most festive sight. Dominating it was the two-year-old triangular Times Building, the tallest building north of Twenty-third Street, a marvel of engineering and considered a triumph of good taste (its cornerstone had been laid by an eleven-year-old Iphigenia Ochs, whose father had bought the *Times* eleven years before). It did not yet sport its electric news-flashing girdle, nor had many of the huge electric advertising signs been put up on the other buildings, but the marquees of the theaters filled the square with light, bathing the handsome Astor Hotel with soft illumination, its hundreds of windows lidded with awnings. The sidewalks milled with the elegant theater crowd that was enjoying a season highlighted by Ada Lewis in *Fascinatating Flora* at the Casino, *Brewster's Millions* at the Hudson, Anna Held in *The Parisian Model* at the Broadway (which was billed as having "many novelties and a spectacular skating scene"), Montgomery and Stone at the Knickerbocker in the long-run hit, *The Red Mill,* and, downtown at the Bijou, the incomparable Nazimova in *Comtesse Coquette.* There were still many theaters below Times Square, stretching down Broadway through the Tenderloin district. But the Tenderloin had become maggoty; crime was flourishing, the notorious "Raine's Law Hotels" were damned as hotbeds of vice, and show business, which some claimed attracted corruption, was moving uptown to cleaner air—and what could be cleaner than a square dominated by the respectable *Times?*

Further up Broadway were the new automobile showrooms, and Mark looked out the cab window as the palaces of the twentieth century's *Wunderkind* passed by. There, elegant thirty-five-horsepower Mathieson touring cars could be bought for $4,500, and a fifty-horsepower touring sedan was priced a thousand dollars higher. You could buy a Bennet Ariel for $1,700 or, at the other end of the scale, the *ne plus ultra:* an elegant fifty-horsepower Rolls-Royce with a three-year guarantee for the princely sum of $8,750 (or higher, of course; the Rolls-Royce Company was entering its most ambitious era in the custom production of super-elegant vehicles for royalty and millionaires). There were also the Great Arrows, the Haynes touring car, the ubiquitous Tillmobile, the Peerless, Baker Electrics, the Columbia—variety and competition flourished.

For the vast majority of the city's population, such expensive caprices were of course mere dreams. The millions of emigrants still pouring in from Russia, middle Europe, and Italy to the Lower East Side ghettos could hardly afford autocars; they shopped for bargains in the pushcarts of Orchard Street. The more established middle classes favored such stores as Bloomingdale's, where they could purchase a shirtwaist for ten dollars at fifteen percent off; or Abraham and Straus, where sugar was for sale at twenty-seven cents the five-pound bag and eyeglasses (in contrast to "spectacles," which were more expensive) went for a dollar and fifty cents; or, the king of them all, Macy's. Saks offered silk suits for ladies marked down from forty-five dollars to twenty-four; and men's summer suits could be had for fourteen fifty. As if in contrast to the mindless frivolity of much of Broadway's fare, the Grape-Nut Company offered to increase brain-power (and thus salaries) with its brain-food breakfast cereal; presumably if one consumed enough Grape-Nuts and increased one's salary sufficiently, one could buy a house in a community such as Garden City, a "country paradise" on Long Island, just being developed; or in Pelham Manor, where lots were available for five hundred dollars. Such places, like the autocar, were an unachievable dream to the poor, a carrot to the middle class, and unthinkably déclassé to the rich and the super-rich living in "Millionairesville," which was what newspapers and guidebooks unsubtly labeled Fifth Avenue. Still, they were a special kind of American dream that made life more bearable to those who could not afford them, and though a show of ambition and pursuit of the dollar might be suspect to Charlotte, poverty was the prison of millions, ambition and money the way out of it. It was wretched to be poor, though still pleasant to be middle class. New York was often dirty, malodorous, corrupt, and dangerous, but it was still a wonderful place in which to live and, for out-of-towners such as Mark, a dazzling place to visit. As the buggy turned into Central Park he said, "You must enjoy living here. I mean, after Elkins, I think I would myself."

"I adore it."

"I suppose you'd never consider going back to Elkins?"

"I've never seriously thought about it. I don't think I would want to, though. I never felt a part of the town. Mother and father sent me East to School, and, well, you remember what you said to me that day. About my staying aloof from the town because I was Jewish."

"But you weren't afraid of it, were you?"

"I don't think so. It's just that it was never home to me as it has been to you. I don't have sentimental ties to it, and my friends are here. So I'd have no reason to go back unless, of course, father needed me."

"Suppose I needed you?"

She didn't answer for a moment. Then, "I think you're beginning to rush me, Mr. Manning."

"Look, Charlotte, I'm only in town a few days. Besides, I'm not any good at flowery language so I'll get right to the point. I'm in love with you. I guess I have been for years—"

"Oh Mark, stop it."

"I was working up to a proposal, you know."

"I know. And I wish you wouldn't."

"Why not?"

"Good Lord, I hardly know you!" Then she smiled. "*You* may believe in love at first sight, but I don't. Or even love at second sight. I think love has to develop over a period of time . . ."

"How long did you know Sydney?"

"That's not fair!"

"It seems fair to me." He took her hand. "I'd give you everything, Charlotte. And that includes what Sydney couldn't."

He took her in his arms and tried to kiss her, but she shoved him away. "Don't bully me!" she said angrily. "Don't *ever* try to bully me."

"I was trying to kiss you—is that a crime?"

"I don't like being mauled."

He leaned back in the corner of the cab. "I think you liked it."

"Oh, God, men always seem to think *that's* the only thing women are interested in."

"It seems to me you've been interested in everything *but* that."

"Oh, shut up."

Silence. The horse's hoofs clip-clopped lazily along the park drive as the lights of the Fifth Avenue mansions sparkled intermittently through the trees. They passed the Bethesda fountain, its waters spilling over the upper shelf below the statue of the angel, then splashing into the big circular basin. Supporting the center column were four figures representing Temperance, Purity, Health and Peace.

"Did you know," said Charlotte, "the allegorical figures in the fountain were designed in Rome by Emma Stebbins of New York and cast in bronze in Munich in 1864?"

"No, I didn't know, I don't care a damn, and when I want a guide-book I'll scrape up the money and buy one."

"I'm *trying* to make polite conversation. Did you hear about the

Metropolitan Museum paying eighteen thousand four hundred for
the Renoir painting of Madame Charpentier and her children? I
believe it's the highest price ever paid for a member of the French
plein-aire school."

"Whatever that is. And I'm surprised at you, putting a price tag
on art."

She smiled, despite herself. She was enjoying the game.

"You really are impossible," she said, "and I think my first impression of you was right: you're a primitive, although a fairly attractive specimen."

"Thanks."

"Then *you* make the conversation, for a change."

"I'd rather make love."

"Shh! The cabbie!"

He took her hand. "Charlotte, you're acting like a damn schoolgirl. Let's go back to the hotel."

"Mark, please."

"I don't have much *time*. You're an adult, a divorced woman, and
I'm no choirboy. Let's go to your suite."

She wanted to. She wanted him.

"You'll tell father," she whispered.

He groaned. "Are you crazy? Why would I tell Sam? Even if you
don't marry me, I'd hardly want to upset him by telling him I went
to bed with his daughter."

She hesitated.

"Mark, I know I'm acting like a schoolgirl, but the truth is, I'm
afraid."

"There's no reason to be. You'll see."

"But don't you understand? I've never really known a man—"

"You mean," he said incredulously, "he never did anything all the
time you were married?"

"No, I don't, but it wasn't the same and—" She stopped, and he
thought she was about to cry. "And I'm terrified, can't you understand? I'm . . . I'm terrified I'll fail both of us."

He took her in his arms and kissed her, gently. He felt her tears on
her cheek.

"Please don't be afraid, darling." He moved her face around and
kissed her mouth. This time there was no resistance and she responded
without reservation. After a moment he called out to the cabbie,
"Take us to the Waldorf."

"Right, captain."

"Fast!"

"Right."

The whip snapped, the lazy clip-clop became a brisk trot as the carriage rolled out of the park and turned down Fifth Avenue.

When it was over, she lay in his arms and thought of *Tristan*. It had been almost like listening to the music, except that it was better. Much better. Charlotte at this moment was happier than ever before in her life.

"You know what?" he said, running his hand softly over her thigh. "You're really something."

"I am?"

"A whiz. I think you've got natural talent."

She punched him lightly in the chest. "You know," she said, "I don't feel even the slightest bit guilty? Isn't that terrible?"

"Terrible." He kissed her again and after a while she said, "We mustn't let father know."

"I told you I wouldn't say anything to him."

"But he's no fool, darling. He'll *know*."

"What if he does?"

"Well, he's very strict . . . I mean about religion. I'm afraid he might not like it."

"Because I'm not Jewish?"

"Yes."

"He hardly ever goes to the synagogue."

"But he's old-fashioned, just the same."

"And you?"

"Obviously not," she laughed. "Look who I'm in bed with. No, I've never been very religious, or even very Jewish. Neither was Sydney. Oh, we went to temple occasionally, but we were fairly casual about the whole thing."

"Then will you do it?" he whispered, kissing her again. "I want you, Charlotte. Now more than ever, I want you to be my wife."

She ran her finger thoughtfully over his shoulder, loving the feel of his body. "Let me think about it."

"How long?"

"Until I know I'm sure. I've made one mistake already. I don't want to make another. But I want you to promise me something."

"What?"

"That you won't go down to Peru."

He stared at the dark ceiling of her bedroom, then said, "I can't promise that."

She let it go then, but she was increasingly aware of how destroyed she indeed would be if, in fact, he should come back from Peru in a pine box.

The next morning Mark came to Sam's room on the Waldorf's fifth floor and told him about Sir Bruce Clark's offer, which he had decided to accept. His older partner stared at him. "Why, you damned fool—"

"Look, Sam, this Clark can get us the best financing—"

"*I* can get it too!" he interrupted, waving a piece of paper. "Look at this list I've made up. Twenty names of top men I'm going to ask a half million apiece from, I'm sure half of them will go with us. We don't need Clark!"

"Even if what you say is true, *I* need Clark—if you raise the money from your friends, I'm still out in the cold. Clark will give me a personal loan of two and a half million, which you *can't* do. Clark will give me a real hold on my company, my future, and that's important to me!"

"And what happens if you get killed down there? What happens to the company? What happens to my investment in the company?"

"I'm impressed by your worry about what happens to *me*," Mark said angrily.

"If you get killed, it's your choice and your own fault! This is a damn-fool, irresponsible, half-wit adventure that I'm amazed you'd even consider. And as a half-owner in this company I'm telling you to forget it. *I'll* handle the financing."

Mark said quietly, "I'm sorry, Sam. But this is my company. It's my whole damn life. I'm going to Peru."

The eyes sparkled with rage. "Don't you realize you have an obligation to me?"

"Yes, I have an obligation to you, and a bigger one to myself." He started for the door. When he reached it he heard Sam say with bitterness, "I was right about you all along."

Mark turned and looked at him. "What do you mean?"

"You simply have no character." His voice was ice.

Mark said nothing. He opened the door and went out into the corridor.

Two days later he boarded a ship for Belém, where he would transfer to the *Lanfranc* for the trip up the Amazon. Sir Bruce, Amelia, and Charlotte came to see him off. Sam did not. After shaking hands with the others, Mark took Charlotte aside.

"Father's furious with you, you know," she said.

"I know."

"He told me you've betrayed him, that he gave you your start and now you won't listen to his advice."

"That's not it at all. The question is whose company is it going to be—mine or his or a bunch of his friends'? It's got to be mine, Charlotte. I've got to make the decisions. And I've decided this is the best thing to do. Can you understand that?"

"Oh, I don't know, Mark. All I do know is that I want you back here safe."

He smiled and kissed her. "That's the nicest thing I've heard this week. This year. Now, for the last time, what about it. When I come back, will you marry me?"

"I think you're out of your mind."

"That's a possibility. Will you?"

She nodded her head as she started to cry. "Yes, you madman," she whispered. "But just please come back."

"Oh, I'll come back," he said. "Bad pennies always show up. It's only men with character who get killed."

"Don't say that, Mark."

"I'm just quoting your beloved father." He kissed her again. "Remember, Charlotte, I love you."

"And I love you, darling."

As she watched him climb the gangway of the dirty freighter, she realized that for the first time in her life she was wonderfully, desperately in love.

And with what she was sure was the most wonderful, desirable man in the world.

PART

DESCENT TO THE NINTH CIRCLE

1907

CHAPTER ONE

THE MONTAÑA of Peru is not, as the name implies, mountain land. Rather it is heavily forested land that starts on the eastern slopes of the Andes and stretches hundreds of miles down and to the east to the Brazilian border. Below it, the Urubamba River, which coils through deep gorges around Macchu Picchu, flows north along the Andes, becoming the Ucayali River, which then snakes through the Montaña twelve hundred miles eastward until it joins the Maranon River and becomes the Amazon. A hundred miles downstream from this juncture is the town of Iquitos, capital of the department of Loreto, which comprises almost all of the Montaña and all of Peru east of the Andes.

It was in Iquitos one blazing day four weeks after Mark Manning left behind his well-loved and newly won fiancée that a small boy, half Spanish and half Yagua Indian—a *cholo*—ran into the main office of the Peruvian Amazon Company, scurried across the dirty tiled floor in his bare feet to the elaborately grilled window of the chief clerk, Señor Delgado, and breathlessly got out in his native Spanish, "The *Lanfranc* is here! It docks in fifteen minutes!" Señor Delgado, a thin nervous man in a white suit, checked his pocket watch. Eleven thirty. The *Lanfranc* was, as usual, on time. The river steamers of the Booth Steamship Company—Messrs. Alfred Booth of Liverpool, to be more accurate—were punctual, clean and efficient; in short, maddeningly English. But Señor Delgado admired the English as much as he chafed at their ill-disguised condescension toward Latins. The English were winners throughout the world, after all; and Señor Delgado admired winners.

"Get the list from Captain Wilson," he told the boy, whose name was Pepe Lopez and whose Spanish father, Hernando Lopez, was a stevedore on the municipal dock. Pepe's brown face and big black eyes stared up at the black-moustached Señor Delgado, who glumly pulled a coin from his pocket and shoved it under the grilled window. "Go!" he snapped. "Little beggar."

Pepe whisked the coin from the counter and was out the door, running down the paved sidewalks and across the unpaved streets with their open drains trickling down the middle until he reached the dock of the town of Iquitos. Here the Amazon was seventy-six feet deep and a mile wide; the bow of the R.M.S. *Lanfranc*, the 6,400 ton flagship of the Booth Line that provided regular monthly service from Liverpool to Iquitos, was heading for the dock, its crew preparing to throw the hawsers over the bow and stern. Pepe's father was one of the men catching the thick ropes and looping them over the bollards, his bare knotted back having been turned by the sun even browner than his son's face (the son to whom he barely nodded "hello," Hernando Lopez having little interest in his *cholo* offspring). The big ship squeaked its starboard side against the dock, then came to a halt, aiming upstream because the current even at the dock was swift (farther out in the river, the current reached six knots and was considered so dangerous that if a person were so unfortunate as to fall out of a boat or canoe, no attempt at rescue was made. It would be a waste of time).

A dozen passengers were lined up along the rail of the *Lanfranc*, watching the docking procedure and taking in the small town that nestled on top of the twenty-foot dirt bank of the giant river. There was not much to see. Iquitos had twenty thousand inhabitants—big for a city in the middle of the jungle—and it was a rubber boom town, like Manáos a thousand miles downstream in Brazil. But unlike Manáos, Iquitos had built no giant opera house that had become one of the wonders of the world. Iquitos was a backwater—one- or two-story buildings with white walls, perhaps a grilled balcony nodding in the direction of a Spanish heritage, but only a nod because Iquitos was a ragtag of European heritages. Here and there were Portuguese tiles; a piece of ironwork from France—the first traders had been French Jews. On the Malecon, the promenade facing the Amazon, vultures resembling turkeys strolled, giving the boat passengers a macabre *frisson*. There were a few mansions built by rubber money, most spectacularly the Casa Encantada of Carlos Innocente Flores.

The main square, the Plaza de Armas, boasted a handsome cathedral, and on one corner of the square was an all-metal building that had been exhibited at a Paris exposition, then brought to the jungle—why, no one was quite sure. In the center of the square was a stone obelisk honoring the Iquitenos youths who had lost their lives in the 1879 War of the Pacific with Chile. On the obelisk was a bronze relief depicting a battle scene between the Peruvians and the Chileans; however, the Italian artisans who made the plaque had misread "Chilean" in their instructions for "Chinese," so the Chileans depicted had incongruously Oriental eyes. No one particularly minded; in some ways, Iquitos was a casual town. Physically, it was almost an island, bounded by the Amazon on the south, the Itaya and Nanay rivers on the east and west, these latter two being almost joined to the north of the town by Lake Quistococha. Psychologically, it was entirely an island, surrounded on all sides by the limitless jungle, its only umbilical cord to the rest of the world being the Amazon.

Three-quarters of the inhabitants were Indians: Yaguas, like Pepe's mother, or Jivaros, living in their palm-thatched houses rising on stilts from the river edge, their sharply peaked roofs built to shed the heavy rains that came every second or third day to break the heat. Fifteen thousand Indians, five thousand whites and semiwhites, most of them Peruvian Spaniards, admixed with a few others such as Mr. Baintree, the British consul. The rest of the inhabitants? Mosquitoes, some with noses an eighth of an inch long that could pierce khaki, flannel or duck. Piums, insects resembling small flies that buried themselves in skin, leaving a small irritating spot with a drop of blood in the center. Blue kingfishers; gorgeous parakeets of all colors; scarlet macaws; yellow parrots; monkeys everywhere—gibbering, jabbering and often ending up in the iron stewpots of the Indians. Under the water of the Amazon, enormous turtles weighing up to two hundred pounds, manatee, paiche, the gamitana and palometa, while skimming the top of the water were huge butterflies of brilliant blue or a thousand other hues. The human population of Iquitos might be varied, but the animal population abounded in such extravagant variety that the newcomer could only marvel at the creative energy of nature. Tapirs; yellow-and-black orioles; tiny blue-eyed ocelots; maned lizards; the jaguar, the puma, the South American tiger, the wild boar and the deer sharing the jungle with the boa, the rattlesnake, the cayman, frogs and countless exotic insects. And the flora! Lianas climbing the trees, orchids and passion flowers of dazzling hue, cotton trees with beautiful umbrella foliage, Brazil-nut trees, cedars and mahogany along with the ayahuasca, the curraine, the cascarilla, which yielded quinine, and the catahuana, which provided a deadly poison.

And dominating everything, the river—the huge, swift, dangerous river, with its islands of bank bitten off by the current, floating imperturbably down river, perhaps to remain intact all the way to the ocean twenty-three hundred miles away. The silver snake of the Amazon coiling through a million square miles of jungle until its mouth gaped at Belém, spewing into the Atlantic. The river up whose slippery banks the porters would scramble for the next ten days, unloading the *Lanfranc*, tugging weights of as much as a hundred and fifty pounds for a few *soles* a day. The river that had brought Mark Manning to one of the world's truly Godforsaken outposts.

As he leaned on the rail of the boat, sapped of all energy by the heat of more than a hundred degrees, he could only envy the bare-breasted Indian women he had seen along the river bank, and the near-naked boys in their canoes, casting with impressive grace their fishing nets, their *atarrayas*. He would have liked to take off his clothes too and jump in the river, except he doubted the prim lady from Edinburgh standing next to him—Miss MacGruder, who was coming to Iquitos to be governess for the British consul's two daughters—would approve. She looked absurdly out of place with her prim white dress and enormous white hat and white parasol. At the moment she was remarking in her high-pitched voice, "I am told a local peculiarity is that there are no stones in Iquitos. No rocks or pebbles of any kind. Don't you find that fascinating, Mr. Manning?"

"Very fascinating," he said.

"One wonders if it is the river that causes it. I mean, no stones. Very odd. I imagine the natives will be a source of interesting study, don't you? So fascinating to see at first hand, as it were, creatures barely removed from the Stone Age." Her eyes riveted on a brawny Yagua near the dock wearing nothing but the usual long straw skirt, his face painted red. Miss MacGruder's glance moved along the muscled arms as she droned on. "One wonders if the Peruvians have tried to civilize them, but I doubt it. The Spaniards are so morally lax. I dare say it's the climate, don't you agree? Heat and humidity tend to enervate one's character as well as one's physical condition. In Edinburgh, I am glad to say, the bracing winds keep one morally as well as physically fit. I am a strong believer in exposure to the cold; it is almost, I am sad to say, a *sine qua non* for the existence of true Christianity. Despite the laudable efforts of the missionaries, I fear they are doomed to eventual disappointment in the tropic climes. Or would you disagree, Mr. Manning?"

"Look!" said Mark, pointing to a monkey that had just swung to the lower branch of a tree near the dock. The monkey was hanging on to a branch with one hand while with the other he was scratching his posterior.

Miss MacGruder's eyebrows lifted as she gave a cutting look to the young American standing next to her and moved down the deck to the gangway. Mark smiled, then picked up his suitcase and prepared to disembark.

Carlos Innocente Flores was not an attractive man: fat, with a pasty face from which peered porcine eyes; a beard always in need of shaving; a drooping black mustache and black hair slicked with aromatic pomades. In his office now, he wore the same white linen suit from the previous several days. His pudgy fingers sported three rings: one a gaudy diamond, one a Ceylon sapphire and the third a gold signet ring with an engraved coat of arms Flores insisted proved his descent from Alonso Perez de Guzman el Bueno, duke of Medina Sidonia and grand admiral of the Spanish Armada—a geneological claim so grotesque that even Doña Maria, Flores's docile wife, raised her hands in despair when her husband expressed it.

Carlos Flores was also no fool. He kept tight rein on his jungle kingdom. And so it was normal procedure for Señor Delgado to enter Flores's huge office a half hour after the docking of the *Lanfranc* and present his employer with a passenger list provided, as Sir Bruce suspected, by Captain Wilson and picked up by Pepe Lopez. In return for this courtesy, Flores passed ten English pounds a month to Captain Wilson. The transaction was kept quiet, Flores telling the captain he considered it "good-will" money for his English friends. Captain Wilson considered it a perquisite of his position.

"Anyone interesting?" said Flores, his tiny eyes running down the dozen names.

"There's the new governess for Mr. Baintree's girls," said Delgado. "And that portrait painter from Rio who is to do Doña Maria's picture."

"Ah, good! Yes, here's his name, Manuel Vargas. He's excellent, Delgado. And *very* fashionable . . . He's painted everyone in Manáos who's important, and half of Rio as well. If he can make my wife look attractive, he'll be worth the three thousand *soles* the portrait is to cost . . . Pour me some beer, Delgado." He pushed his glass across the top of the desk and Delgado quickly opened a fresh bottle of German beer that Flores imported by the case.

"I see we have a German baron," continued Flores, impressed. "Baron Heinrich von Stimme, from Heidelberg University and Berlin. What do you think of that, Delgado? The Almanach de Gotha here in our little town! We should have sent the guard of honor to the dock, if he wasn't drunk, eh, Delgado? Wait a minute, here is someone interesting! Mr. Mark Manning from O-hee-o . . . Where is O-hee-o?"

"I believe it is a part of America, señor. Near California."

"Ah, and Captain Wilson has obliged us with a little note next to his name. 'This gentleman is the president of a rubber company in America—the Manning Rubber Company. He tells me he has come to South America to see how raw rubber is secured. He has visited traders in Belém and Manáos and now would like to meet you. There seems nothing suspicious about him, strikes me as a typical American businessman-tourist, open and somewhat naïf.'" Flores frowned thoughtfully. "What do you think, Delgado? We have never had any Americans here, have we?"

"Not that I can remember, señor."

Flores thought about the visitor from America for a few moments as the slowly turning wooden fan whirred above his head and a chameleon dozed on the window sill. "I think I should have a look at Mr. Manning. "Where is he staying? The Bella Vista, I suppose?"

"I will find out, señor."

"Send the boy over with one of my cards. Present my compliments. Tell him my wife and I would be honored to have him dine with us this evening."

"Yes, Señor Flores."

"Ask the baron to dinner, too. And Vargas, the painter. A baron, a painter and an American business executive all in one night! My wife will be overwhelmed, eh, Delgado?"

"Yes, Señor Flores."

"Arrange for Fosco to take Manning to Orellana in the morning. Tell him to give him the very best tour we have."

"Yes, Señor Flores."

"Now get out."

"Yes, Señor Flores."

Señor Delgado hurriedly bowed his way out of The Presence.

The Bella Vista Hotel was situated directly across the Plaza de Armas from the offices of the Peruvian Amazon Company. Outside, its white walls formed an arched arcade on the first floor that shaded the entrance from sun and rain; above the arcade, a grilled balcony onto which perspiring guests could escape their rooms for a breath of slightly fresher air. Inside, on the first floor, the lobby with four wood-blade fans depending from the paint-flaking ceiling, the plasterers of which had done a clumsy job of imitating a florid French coving, the fans whirring from ten in the morning till four in the afternoon, then again from eight in the evening till midnight, these being the operational hours of the hotel's wheezing electric generator. Scattered about the stone floor were pieces of lobby furniture, the overstuffed Victorian lounge chairs looking as if they provided comfortable housing for roaches. The one charming touch to the place was a number of earthen pots filled with red begonias, which had been placed around the walls and on the stairs. Along the wall opposite the door was the wooden desk behind which stood Señora Dolores Rojas, the plump wife of the Bella Vista's owner. To her right, tucked beneath the stair and partly partitioned from the rest of the lobby by two pillars, was the bar, manned by Señor Edgardo Rojas, a cadaverous man in his forties, with a stoop to his shoulders and a droop to his moustache. Señor Rojas, who chained-smoked Turkish cigarettes and suffered from an ulcer, seemed permanently out of sorts with the world, and when Mark came downstairs from his room to the bar to order a glass of bad red wine, the disgruntled look his host gave him was something less than heartwarming. Mark was too hot to care; the bar was only a little cooler than his room. There was a plate of limp hors d'oeuvres on the bar. Mark picked one up and tasted it.

"Not bad," he said to Rojas. "What is it?"

"Marinated *piranha*," came the heavily accented reply.

Mark washed down his queasiness with more red wine. The bar, which had been empty, began to fill up as local shopkeepers shuttered their stores for lunch and siesta. Mark was joined by the young German he had met on the *Lanfranc*, Baron Heinrich von Stimme. The baron, who had boarded the boat at Manáos, was twenty-one, improbably handsome in a Nordic fashion, with blond brush-cut hair, his face being seamed, however, by the obligatory dueling scar on the cheek. On the boat the baron had been stiff, chilly. Now, however, Mark noticed to his amusement that the young *Meinherr* looked somewhat bilious, and his carefully pressed white suit appeared as wilted as its owner. He took a stool next to Mark, ordered a beer, wiped his forehead with a handkerchief. *"Mein Gott,* what heat! Worse than Manáos."

Pepe Lopez appeared in the lobby, looked around, then made for the bar. When Señor Rojas saw him he let loose an angry volley in

Spanish that Pepe pretended to ignore. With all the importance
a ten-year-old feels when entrusted with adult messages, Pepe stopped
in front of the bar and said in surprisingly good English, "Is Mr.
Manning here?"

"That's me," Mark said.

"Señor Flores sends his compliments."

The boy bowed stiffly, almost comically, as he thrust an engraved
calling card into Mark's hand. Then the ceremony was repeated with
the unhappy Baron von Stimme.

"Dinner," announced Pepe in a loud voice to inform everyone at
the bar of the importance of his trust. "At Casa Encantada at seven
o'clock. Thank you."

With that he shot his hand up to the bar and grabbed a marinated
piranha, then turned to run. Señor Rojas, who had been scowling at
him, grabbed at his wrist, missed, then—as Pepe rushed for the door
—ran around the bar and went after him, surprising everyone with
his burst of energy and speed. Calling out Spanish epithets at the
boy, Rojas managed to catch him. Pepe wriggled to free himself, but
Rojas raised his hand and slapped him so hard the boy was knocked
to the floor.

Silence. Pepe, stunned, tears filling his eyes as a trickle of blood
ran down his chin. Mark got up from the bar and went over to
Rojas.

"That wasn't a nice thing to do, you know?" he said pleasantly.

Rojas shrugged. "Dirty little *cholo,* always stealing from me."

"Uh huh, but I'd say slugging a kid is overdoing it a little. Why
don't you apologize to him?"

Rojas stiffened.

"Me. Apologize to that roach?"

"That's right. Apologize."

"You mind your own business, Yankee—"

The sentence was not finished. Mark hit him in his ulcerous
stomach, causing Rojas to groan with pain as he doubled over. Then
Mark hit him on the chin, sending him sprawling to the floor, where
he lay rubbing his stomach and moaning.

"Murderer!" screamed Señora Rojas, rushing from behind the bar
to kneel beside her husband. *"Asesino!* My poor Edgardo has the
ulcer—"

"He should take better care of himself." Mark turned to help
Pepe up, but the boy had already gotten to his feet. Now, as he
looked wonderingly at Mark, he tried to say something that came

out a mumbled, "Thank you, *señor*," then ran to the door and out of the hotel, not failing before he left to scoop up the piece of marinated *piranha* from the floor and stuff it in his mouth.

Casa Encantada was enchanted only if one's architectural tastes ran to the floridly baroque. Designed two years before by an architect from Lima, it had been built in a style some local irreverent citizens called (in whispers) "Viceroy's Palace Outhouse." Indeed the big house, with its balconies, pedimented doors and windows, niched statues, wrought-iron gas lanterns and classically balustraded roofline might have passed muster as some sort of Beaux-Arts nightmare of a privy built for the gigantic structure in Lima that housed the successors of Pizzaro. The function of Casa Encantada had been to display Flores's new rubber fortune to the world, and in that sense the building admirably achieved its purpose. It shouted his new money; the fact that usually the only living creatures about to be impressed were the Iquitenos and the monkeys and macaws in the gorgeous gardens surrounding the house mattered not at all to Carlos Innocente Flores. He had built the place to impress himself as much as the world.

In fact, the construction of Casa Encantada had changed Flores's life. Much as a decade later the factory workers of Petrograd would move with awe through the Winter Palace, Flores, when he saw what his money had wrought, felt uncomfortable in his grandeur. And while he continued to be something of a grotesque in his office, when he came home evenings to Casa Encantada with its richly vulgar furnishings that might have been—and in the case of two gilt thronelike chairs actually had been—bought from a third-rate touring opera company, his house would intimidate him at least into changing out of the sweat-stained linen suit into something more appropriate for his surroundings. And on evenings when he played host to visiting dignitaries, he would affect a near Cinderellalike transformation—bathing, shaving, trimming his hair and moustache and adorning himself with clean clothes and his best pair of London shoes.

So that evening at seven, when Flores's elegant landau rattled up the driveway of Casa Encantada bearing Mark, Baron von Stimme and the portraitist Manuel Vargas, the guests were greeted by the black butler from Barbados (Flores had imported a number of blacks from that island to work as house servants and overseers), then led into the huge grand *sala* where they were welcomed by a relatively immaculate Flores in a spotless dinner jacket.

His guests were equally well turned out for the occasion. Mark had brought his dinner jacket, and though wearing it in the jungle reminded him of every joke he'd ever heard about the stiff-upper-lip British colonials, the dress suit, he found, was as comfortable as anything else in the heat, which the twenty-foot ceilings and thick stucco walls of the house tended to abate. Baron von Stimme had recovered and looked well in his dinner clothes, very nearly the model of a modern young Junker. Señor Vargas, an ageing Brazilian with long white hair, was dressed in a courtly elegance that seemed a hangover from the lost empire of the last Brazilian emperor.

This trio was introduced to Doña Maria Flores, and if Flores might have passed for some dissolute Hapsburg's pornographer royal, his wife might have stepped out of Tenniel's *Alice in Wonderland* drawings; she was an astonishing lookalike for the howling Duchess. Though docile by nature, she was physically overpowering, a Peruvian Valkyrie squeezed into a black gown, with a heavy-set face frozen in a permanent frown beneath black hair parted across her forehead like an opening curtain. She wore an enormous diamond necklace, and since her English was nonexistent, she would of necessity be mostly silent during dinner, English being the lingua franca for the evening (Flores's English was passable, as was Señor Vargas's, and the baron spoke it excellently). Then Flores's daughter was introduced. Considering her parents, it would have been a miracle if Felicidad Flores had turned out a beauty. Alas, the miracle had not happened. Felicidad at twelve had been fat and dumpy, and now, at eighteen, she was more so, her only saving grace being a lovely complexion, which she had inherited from her mother. She seemed painfully shy, and Mark felt sorry for her. The handsome baron, on the other hand, seemed unaccountably enchanted. He clicked his heels, kissed her hand, then turned to his host and hostess and said gravely, "May I be allowed to congratulate you, Señor and Señora, for raising such a lovely and delicate flower in this most indelicate climate."

Mark would have suspected the baron guilty of a tasteless joke except that the man was so Teutonically humorless and patently sincere. Flores blinked with surprise, followed by a look of undisguised joy. There could be little doubt that no one had ever paid Felicidad such a heartfelt compliment before, certainly no one as apparently eligible to be a son-in-law as the baron. Flores's evening

was off to a most promising start. And as von Stimme proceeded to
a sofa in the corner of the room where, under the stern eye of Felicidad's dueña, Señora Guzman, he talked with Felicidad in earnest
Spanish for the half hour before dinner, Flores could hardly contain
his pleasure.

When they first had entered the Casa Encantada, Mark had had
the feeling his host was giving him a suspicious once-over, and he
hoped very much that his careful attention to Captain Wilson on
the *Lanfranc* coming up the Amazon had paid off in a favorable report from Wilson to Flores. Whether it was this, or Flores's delight
at the baron's interest in his daughter, Mark couldn't be sure but
certainly whatever interest Flores had in his American guest dissipated as his tiny eyes kept darting to the corner sofa, barely able
to believe that this blond Prince Charming could be interested in his
ugly duckling. And Felicidad! Though she had been awkwardly shy
at the beginning, she was melting under the warmth of von Stimme's
attention; and by the time the party had gone in to dinner, only a
blind man could have failed to notice that Felicidad was falling
worshipfully in love. Certainly her dueña Señora Guzman wasn't
missing the signals, and she now whispered to Flores, who brushed
aside her caveat with a wave of his hand. Mark was close enough
to hear him whisper *"Es perfecto!"* to the duenna. Far from worrying about his daughter's safety, he changed the seating at the table,
unsubtly placing von Stimme next to Felicidad.

The romance flourished through dinner, interrupted only by the
eager Flores questioning the baron about his family, his plans for
the future—if he had asked him for his bank statement, Mark
wouldn't have been surprised. Von Stimme handled his answers well,
explaining that his father had been in the diplomatic corps, was
now dead, and that his mother lived alone in the family country
estate outside Neustrelitz in Mecklenburg. He was the only child;
he had not yet decided on a career, though he thought he would
probably end up in the diplomatic corps, like his father, which was one
reason he was touring South America that summer. All this Flores
attentively listened to, beaming as the baron sprinkled his answers
with references to titled friends and relatives, which Flores would
quietly translate into Spanish for the benefit of Doña Maria.

During these exchanges Mark and Manuel Vargas were increasingly ignored, and Mark took the opportunity to reassess his situation. All the way down from New York he had had second thoughts
about his decision to accept Sir Bruce's offer. There was not only
the personal risk involved, there was also his antagonizing Sam

Rosen, which very much concerned him. He kept telling himself it was all worth it to earn a chance to be master in his own house; and as for Sam, well, he had had no illusions about his partner's feeling toward him. Whatever Sam's opinions of Mark's business acumen, he disliked his younger partner and Mark knew it. So perhaps what had happened was for the best—at least it had cleared the air.

By the time he had boarded the *Lanfranc* at Belém and started up the Amazon, his doubts about making the trip had diminished. The river and the jungle intrigued him. It was a gorgeous, primitive world far removed from anything he had known, and he was still young enough to be exhilarated by the new and the adventurous. His first impressions of Iquitos were that it was a sleepy, rather seedy Latin version of a frontier town out West. A little wild, perhaps, but so far there didn't seem to be anything especially menacing about it. And certainly Flores struck him as more third-rate comedian than a first-rate villain, especially hovering as he was over the baron. The man's eyes were shifty, but that hardly established him as a perpetrator of atrocities, and Mark began wondering if Sir Bruce and his fellow bankers hadn't overreacted to the Congo atrocities. As a safety precaution, he had brought along a small hand gun, which he had left in his hotel room. Now he doubted he would ever need it. This house; the plentiful Doña Maria; her daughter and her scowling duenna; the silent black servants; the glib young German; most of all buffoonish Carlos—it all seemed more operatic than dangerous.

He had been seated at the end of the table next to the old artist. Vargas had a gentle, intelligent face and a mind to match; he engaged Mark in a conversation about Peru and the Incas, a subject Mark had studied on the trip from New York, having brought along, courtesy of Sir Bruce, a copy of Prescott's *Conquest of Peru*, a book he was surprised to discover he enjoyed greatly. Vargas, it turned out, was knowledgeable about Incan art and history, and they were now having a good talk about the kidnapping of the Inca, Atahualpa, and the fantastic ransom asked for him; Pizarro's treachery; the fabulous gold Incan statues the Spaniards found outside the temple at Cuzco, including the legendary cornfield of solid gold and the gold sheep watched over by golden shepherds—gold being a religious symbol to the Incas—they called it "sweat of the sun." "We of European descent," said Vargas, "like to think we civilized this continent. But when I read of the sophisticated society the Incas had developed centuries before Columbus, when I see their beautiful artifacts, when I think of the size and wealth of the Tawantinsuyo —that was their name for their empire—do you realize destitution was unknown to them? Think of it! I don't know your politics, Mr. Manning, but the Incan Empire was an historic advertisement for the benefits of a planned economy. When I think of all this and I read of the cruelty of Pizarro and his men—all, by the way, committing their crimes in the name of religion and no doubt believing they were in God's service—when I consider all this, I sometimes wonder if we are not all living in a mad dream, especially to believe *we* are the superior civilization."

"Well," Mark said. "Pizarro was certainly no bargain, as I can tell, but that was almost four hundred years ago. Don't you think the Indians are at least better off now?"

"No."

"But the Incas couldn't even write—"

"They didn't need to. They managed to communicate very well, in fact. For that matter, most of them are still illiterate. No, Mr. Manning, the Incas had developed a just and contented society with an exquisite culture and an interesting, if bloody, religion. I can't be convinced the white man has brought them anything but misery." He glanced down the table at his host, who was still talking with the baron. Then he dropped his voice. "Certainly *that* white man has brought them nothing but misery."

Mark's interest picked up. "In what way?"

Vargas shrugged. "It's not for me to say, but Manáos is filled with stories."

"About the rubber gatherers?"

"Of course. Our genial host, so plump and pleasant, runs a living hell out there in the jungle if the stories are to be believed."

"Do you believe them?"

Vargas started to say something, then changed his mind.

"I have no way of knowing. Except that in Rio they have a saying: 'When the Devil goes to carnival, he comes dressed as a clown.' "

He looked back to the beaming Flores at the end of the table; there was no question whom he meant. Just then, the conversation was interrupted by Doña Maria rising to lead the ladies out of the dining room. Flores's butler passed cognac and cigars. Just as the host's cigar was being lighted by one of his giant houseboys, von Stimme excused himself and left the dining room. "Did you see him?" said Flores. "Did you? *Fantastico!* He couldn't take his eyes off her! And now he's after her, burning to be with her—oh my God, such good fortune! Love at first sight—and with such an Adonis! Such a Don Juan, and a rich baron . . . Gentlemen, you'll drink with me to this romance, eh?"

They raised their glasses and sipped the cognac. "Vargas!" Flores pointed a stubby finger at the portraitist. "You must paint her too! My flower, my delicate—did you hear him call her 'delicate'? I never thought of her as 'delicate,' but of course I'm her poppa, her blind poppa who has never seen her true beauty! But *now*—Vargas, you'll paint her, eh? Paint her before you do my wife—to hell with my wife. Paint Felicidad! I'll buy her a new gown for the picture— you'll do it, eh? I'll pay you 3,500 *soles* for Felicidad, and I'll give a bonus of 400 *soles* if you . . . how do I say it? . . . slim her down a little in the picture, you know? Will you do it?"

Vargas smiled, and it occurred to Mark that even though the old man had probably long since adjusted his pride to taking money from the likes of Flores, it still must hurt a little.

"Of course, *señor*," Vargas said. "I'd be delighted to paint your charming daughter."

"Excellent! Bravo! Oh, what a night, what a beautiful night . . . that this perfection, this baron, should drop into my life like this! Personally I've never liked the Germans much, but *this* one! Hah! A Siegfried! A Siegfried with a title! A *rich* Siegfried with a title! My God, I'm so happy I could cry . . ."

And to Mark's amazement, Flores proceeded to do just that, tears streaming down his cheeks as he went on about "Heinrich," as he began to call him, this paragon who was probably at that very moment proposing to Felicidad underneath a palm tree in his garden. The whole thing seemed like comic opera, from von Stimme's being smitten at first sight to Flores's rhapsodizing about an almost total stranger becoming part of the family. Mark believed he had fallen in love with Charlotte at first sight, but Felicidad Flores was not Charlotte, and Mark was skeptical about Heinrich's instant passion for the girl. On the other hand, he couldn't think of a reason why the baron should bother with such a show if he were insincere.

When Flores led them out of the dining room to rejoin the ladies, he put his hand on Mark's shoulder, asked him if he would like to see one of his collection centers. Mark immediately replied in the affirmative and Flores informed him that his director of public information, Tony Fosco, would call for him at his hotel at eight the next morning and take him down river to Orellana. When Mark thanked him, Flores said it was an honor and privilege. "We are always happy to show what we do—especially to a man like yourself.

It is a difficult business. The Indians are lazy and we must be like stern parents for their own good. Unfortunately some people take advantage of the Indians. You may have heard stories . . . we all have heard them and it's very bad for you and me and the industry we serve. I am proud to say that our *seringueiros* are properly treated. But you shall see for yourself in the morning . . . Ah, there they are on the terrace . . . My God, what an evening! What a beautiful evening!" . . .

On the way back to the hotel in the carriage, Mark politely asked von Stimme if he really found Felicidad so irresistible.

"Not at all. As you can see, she's quite plain. But she is solid, and a man needs a solid woman for a wife."

"Oh? Then you're going to ask her to marry you?"

"That, sir, is my business."

Manuel Vargas's comment about Flores and the Devil wearing the clown's mask alerted Mark to stop playing the role of naif American he had adopted to divert Captain Wilson's suspicions. He was, he suspected, being foolish to discount Flores merely because he happened to be the anxious father of an unattractive daughter who gushed over potential suitors. That night in his steaming quarters at the Bella Vista, his sense of Iquitos began to change as well. Was it the nervousness of some of the shopkeepers he had seen in the hotel at lunch? Or Flores's houseboys, who looked strangely powerful for housework? On reflection, he was less certain he would have no use for the gun he'd brought from New York.

His changing opinion was reinforced the next day by his trip down river to the rubber-gathering station at Orellana. Tony Fosco, "director of public information," was too glib, and the station at Orellana was just a bit too "model" to believe. When Mark was returned to his hotel at four that afternoon, he thanked Fosco, pretending to be impressed by what he had seen, then went up to his room and flopped on his bed (the heat had enervated him, and his stomach was queasy). Now he was convinced that, far from being sleepily innocent, Iquitos and the Peruvian Amazon Company had a distinctly sinister feel about them. There *was* a tension in the town, as if the people knew that somewhere out in the immense jungle that surrounded them was something so monstrous they preferred to ignore it and yet couldn't quite ever force it entirely out of their minds.

The problem was, how to get past the stage set and see the reality? And even if he managed to do that without ending up like Mac-Cartney, how to prove what he saw to the rest of the world? Sir Bruce had been irritatingly vague about this, telling Mark he'd have to rely on his wits. Well, he was trying that, with little results. If he began to ask questions around the town, word would inevitably get back to Flores. He only had nine days before the *Lanfranc* would start its return trip—nine days to achieve what now seemed to be the impossible. Mark had no idea where to begin.

Now his queasy stomach began to impinge, and he realized his troubles were being compounded by the "bug." Mark spent the next four hours trying to get some sleep on his bed and making hurried trips to the Bella Vista's lone bathroom. By ten o'clock, when he finally began to feel better, he had decided Iquitos was fate's (or nature's) way of punishing him for his sins—past, present and future.

It was then that he heard a soft knock on his door. Too weak to get off his bed, he called out, "Come in." The door opened. It was the young Indian boy Señor Rojas had slapped in the lobby. He appeared frightened and quickly closed the door behind him. "Mister Manning, may I please talk to you a moment?"

"Sure. What is it?"

The boy came to the end of the bed and put his hands on the brass footing. "Why did you go to Orellana today?"

"To see the rubber-gathering station."

"What did you think of it?"

"It's a nice place." Mark paused. "Are all the stations like Orellana?"

The boy slowly shook his head.

"I didn't think so."

"Are you a friend of Señor Flores?"

"No. Are you?"

Again the boy shook his head.

"What's your name?"

"Pepe."

"Well, Pepe, what is it you want to know?"

He shrugged. Mark decided to end the game and take a chance on the boy. He had to begin somewhere. He then told him he had come to check on certain stories.

Pepe smiled with relief.

"Are they true?" Mark asked.

"Yes, *señor.*"

Mark hesitated. "Can you help *me* see what's really going on here?"

"Yes, *señor*. That's why I came to see you. But it has to be tonight."

Mark needed no prompting. Miserable and weak as he felt, he knew he had just gotten the opportunity he'd been looking for. He got out of bed, ready to follow Pepe—where, he had no idea.

CHAPTER TWO

After Mark's departure for Brazil, Sam Rosen and Charlotte had accepted an invitation from Herschel Fine to a ten-day round-trip cruise to Newport on his yacht the *Aldebaran*. The *Aldebaran* was a wondrously luxurious toy: two hundred fifty feet in length, with a gleaming white hull trimmed with gold, the sleek yacht had a single stack, two masts, a spearlike bowsprit, trim lines, carried five thousand tons of coal and a crew of twenty; it could make eighteen knots and cross the Atlantic, had cost Herschel the princely sum of $450,000 and required over $20,000 a year for maintenance. Its quarters included a handsome saloon, a dining room, a library with a thousand volumes and staterooms for a dozen guests—all furnished in the standard (for the rich) Louis XVI style. Nothing gave Herschel greater joy than to cruise the then unpolluted waters of Long Island Sound or Narragansett Bay, breathing the sea air, reading the latest Sherlock Holmes adventure, eating the excellent meals prepared by his chef and forgetting the pressures of Wall Street. Charlotte, who had cruised on the *Aldebaran* many times before, loved it almost as much as her former father-in-law.

On their fifth day out, as they lay at anchor off Newport, Charlotte, dressed in a white yachting suit with a boater on her head, was standing by the starboard rail watching a half dozen distant sailboats jockey for position at the start of a race as her father stretched in a deck chair behind her, reading the latest adventures of Buster Brown and Tiger (Sam lately had developed an incongruous interest in the comic strips).

"Father," said Charlotte, "are you still angry at Mark for going to South America?"

Sam looked up from the paper. " 'Angry' is too polite a word," he said.

"Do you still think Mark, as you said, betrayed you?"

"I do. I have always known the man was an opportunist, but this is completely irresponsible behavior!"

"Now, poppa . . ." She came over and took the deck chair next to his, reaching over to hold his hand. She smiled her best smile as she said, "Don't you think you're being a *little* hard on him?"

"No. And why are you defending him?"

"Well . . ." She took a deep breath before the plunge. "I suppose it has to do with Mark asking me to marry him. And even more with my decision to accept."

Sam's face drained. "Charlotte, you're my only child, the dearest person in this world to me. I ask you . . . No, I *beg* you, don't marry this man."

"But why? Really, poppa, you're being terribly unfair to Mark. Just because he didn't take your advice—"

"He's not Jewish!" interrupted her father.

"Oh, I was sure you were going to say that. Really, it makes no difference to me. Perhaps it should, but I love Mark—"

"Love him? How could you love that man? He's totally unprincipled, he's shifty, he's . . ."

"If he's *that* bad," interrupted Charlotte, who was becoming angry, "why are you his partner in business?"

"Because he's smart, because he had a good idea. Oh, yes, he's a man who knows how to make money. But don't be mistaken—I am not proud of my association with him! No, and I certainly do *not* want him for a son-in-law. If you are foolish enough to marry him, then I must say your judgment in chosing husbands is hardly improving with experience."

She looked at him icily. "You have no reason to say such a thing."

"I have plenty of reason. Why, the very first time I met Mark Manning he was involved in something shady. He sold twelve stoves to the army by blackmailing Adrian Tutwiler! He has no principles or ethics, no personal morality—what kind of a husband do you think he'll make? And what kind of a father to your children? Do you think you will ever be able to trust him?"

"I'm not saying he's perfect," she snapped, "but he certainly is *not* corrupt, the way you're making him out to be. I'll even admit there are some things about Mark that make me a bit uneasy—his extreme ambition, for one, and the importance he puts on money—although it's easier for someone like me to be uninterested in money than Mark, who never had any. But what really matters is that I am lonely and I *do* love him."

"He is also a whoremonger!" Sam lowered his voice. "Is *that* the sort of husband you want? He frequents brothels—"

"Oh, Father, for heaven sake, there's hardly a man in the country under sixty who hasn't gone to a brothel. And frankly, it will be a pleasant change to have a husband who prefers women—even prostitutes—to men."

"Keep your voice down! What if he heard you?"

"Herschel's asleep in the stateroom. Father, I believe Mark is in love with me and I'm sure after we're married he'll stop going to those places. I'll make *sure* he stops going to them."

Her father looked at her.

"And what makes you so certain Mark is in love with you?"

"Oh, poppa, how can you explain these things? You *know* it, that's all."

"Did it ever occur to you that he believes if he marries you he will inherit my stock in the Manning Rubber Company some day?"

"Of course, but I don't believe that's why he's marrying me."

"Then you're a fool! And I'll prove it to you when he comes back from Peru—if he ever comes back."

"How?"

"I'll tell him that if he marries you I'll leave my Manning stock to a charitable foundation. Then you'll see how fast Mr. Manning backs off."

Charlotte stood up. "All right, do it," she said quietly. "I think *you'll* be surprised when he tells you to go to hell."

She walked away, leaving her father in a state of mild shock at hearing his daughter curse for the first time in his life, and in a state of severe shock at the prospect of having Mark Manning as his son-in-law.

Pepe Lopez would not leave the hotel with Mark for fear of being spotted. Instead, he told Mark where to go, then hurried out of the room. Mark waited ten minutes before leaving the hotel. He strolled down to the docks, where Pepe stepped out of a shadow and motioned him to a ladder leading down to a canoe. Mark looked at the frail boat unenthusiastically. "Where are we going in that?"

"Down river. The boat is safe, *señor*. Do not worry."

Feeling somewhat ashamed of his nervousness, Mark climbed down the ladder into the canoe and sat on the bottom, squeezing his long

legs into a space obviously not designed for Ohio farmboys. Pepe
hopped in the stern, shoved off, then paddled the canoe into the
river, where the swift current picked it up and whizzed it downstream. Though Mark was gulping as the seemingly fragile boat sped
down the black river, Pepe handled it with quiet dexterity and his
passenger soon began to relax. From the dark bank came a chorus
of croaking frogs, intermingled with the occasional screech of an owl
and other, for Mark, unidentifiable jungle noises; somehow, though,
the jungle no longer seemed quite so menacing. Perhaps, Mark
thought, he was becoming accustomed to it. Or perhaps it was the
growing conviction that the jungle was less dangerous than the men
who exploited it and its inhabitants.

After fifteen minutes on the river, Pepe guided the canoe into the
bank and beached it near a group of high-peaked Indian houses that
loomed in the darkness, only a few showing any illumination.

"This is my mother's village," said Pepe, leading Mark up the river
bank. "Sometimes I live here with her, sometimes in Iquitos with my
father. I go to school in Iquitos," he added with pride. "That is
where I learned English. I speak English, Spanish and Yagua, my
mother's language. No one has ever tried to write down my mother's
language, but someday I would like to try."

"Sounds like a good idea," said Mark, who thought that the boy's
English, though accented, was better than he had remembered from
his first encounter with him at the Bella Vista bar.

"We Yaguas," continued Pepe as they climbed to the houses, "were
the ones who attacked Francisco de Orellana. We Yaguas sometimes
wear straw wigs that come down to the shoulders, and Orellana
thought the warriors were women so he named the river Amazon."

Mark noticed that sometimes the boy referred to his Indian heritage
as "my mother's" and at other times as "we Yaguas," an understandable ambivalence about his Indian blood. In Iquitos, it would not be
something to be proud of, considering the low esteem in which the
Indians were held. But here, in the jungle, in his mother's house,
the boy would not be ashamed.

They entered the first house, which was illuminated by a glass
kerosene lamp. The house consisted of one room whose bamboo walls
reached a little over half the way up to the roofline, the rest of the
space being left open for ventilation. The thatched roof itself, being
peaked so sharply, afforded more air space, so that the room was as
comfortably cool as the Casa Encantada and, despite the fact that it
was built on stilts over the river, not as damp as the Viceroy's Outhouse. A bright-blue-and-yellow parrot perched cheerfully on one

ledge. Below it, an aged woman squatted on the floor staring at the fire that smoldered in the center of the room on top of a large flat stone; she looked up as Mark came in, but though it was undoubt-edly the first time a white man had ever been in the house, she seemed uninterested and her eyes returned to the fire. There was another woman by the fire, stirring a broth in an iron pot wedged between two rocks that held it over the flames. This woman was younger—perhaps thirty, Mark thought, though he knew judging the Indians' ages was tricky and that they usually grew old quickly. She had the straight black hair of the Indians, and over her bare breasts, though not entirely concealing them, was the short straw bib he had seen on both Yagua men and women. She wore a cotton skirt on which she wiped her hands as Pepe came over to her. The boy didn't kiss her, but Mark assumed she was his mother. He said something to her in the Yagua tongue, and she looked cautiously at Mark, who forced an uncertain smile and nodded. Then Pepe motioned to Mark, who came across the room to a pile of straw in the corner. A man was lying on the straw, a thin cotton throw-rug covering him. He was awake, and his face was covered with sweat which, along with his trembling, indicated fever—and a serious case at that, because the man—though young—looked to be nearly dead. He stared at the white man and began mumbling in fear. Pepe said something to him, and he stopped. "This is my mother's brother, Imbitide," Pepe said. "He worked for Señor Flores at La Chorrera. He has worked there for a year and a half now, but La Chorrera is not like what you saw at Orellana. He ran away five days ago. The *jefes* caught him a few miles from here, and today he came here to my mother's house. The *jefes* had done this to him."

He pulled back the cotton throw rug and Mark winced as he looked at the naked body underneath. Savage lash marks covered his shoulders and chest. Two scabbed stumps were where his hands had been cut off above the wrists. The genitalia had been beaten by either a club or rifle butt or a boot.

"Good Christ," Mark whispered.

Pepe replaced the rug, then led Mark back to the fire, where there was a stool.

"My uncle will die before morning," said Pepe as he offered Mark the stool, "which is why it was necessary for you to come tonight. It is a miracle that he got here alive, but it is good that he die soon because he is in great pain. Other men have come here to see what Señor Flores does to the *seringueiros,* but he always takes them to Orellana, like he took you, and everyone is too afraid to tell the truth. But I am not afraid. When my uncle came here today, I decided I would show you the truth because you are a good man—I was sure of that when you hit Señor Rojas because he slapped me. I know a man has to be *shown* the truth to believe it. I hope you now believe it?"

"I believe it," said Mark quietly. "Where is this La Chorrera?"

"A long way to the north, on the Paraná River. It is one of the big collecting centers of the Company."

"Is there a center nearer here? I mean, one where . . ." he nodded toward the corner, "where that goes on?"

"Oh, yes, at Oro Blanco, two days from here. There is a collecting center a few miles upstream from Oro Blanco. Do you want to see it?"

"The more I see, the more I can tell when I go back home. And the better chance we'll have of stopping this."

Pepe looked at his uncle a moment, then turned back to Mark. "I can take you to Oro Blanco, but you must not let Señor Flores know or he will kill both of us."

"And we can't just walk into the collecting center like lost tourists," Mark said. "We need an excuse. . . ."

Silence as he stared across the room at the dying Indian. Then he said to Pepe, "What sort of communication is there between here and Oro Blanco? Does anyone from the office in Iquitos go regularly up to Oro Blanco, or do they send someone down here?"

"Once every two weeks the *Felicidad* takes mail and supplies to Oro Blanco and picks up the rubber. That is all."

"So otherwise they're completely isolated? If we got there and I told them I was someone else—a Mr. Smith, say—there'd be no way for them to check back here to find out if I was telling the truth?"

Pepe thought a moment, then shook his head.

Mark stood up. "Then, Pepe, I think we are in business. Be outside the hotel at noon tomorrow. Okay?"

"Okay," said Pepe seriously, yet enjoying the use of the new word.

"And Pepe," continued Mark, putting his hand on the boy's head, "I'm grateful you showed me the truth. It took real courage. Your uncle should be very proud of you. Just as—" again he looked over at the corner—"you should be very proud of your uncle. Now I think you'd better get me back to Iquitos."

Pepe nodded and led Mark out of the house back down to the river.

It was past midnight when Mark returned to the Bella Vista, and the hotel was in darkness except for a kerosene lamp on the desk. He went upstairs, passed his own room and knocked on the door next to his. After a minute the door was opened by a sleepy-eyed Señor Vargas, wrapped in a bathrobe.

"May I talk to you for a moment?" Mark asked.

The portraitist looked confused, but led Mark into the room, lighted the kerosene lamp and offered his unexpected guest a chair.

"I apologize for waking you up," said Mark, "but I wanted to talk to you about Prescott."

The white-haired artist looked even more confused.

"Prescott," continued Mark, "was almost blind, but without ever seeing Mexico or South America I understand he wrote about it in such a convincing way that he showed it to thousands of people. Now if I could write like Prescott, I wouldn't need a camera. But I can't, so I do need one. You said the other night you thought the white man had brought nothing but misery to the Indians, and you gave the idea you thought Flores wasn't much better than Pizarro. Well, I've just come from seeing one example of what Flores has done, and you can take my word for it—Flores makes Pizarro look like Florence Nightingale."

"I know," Vargas said. "Flores is a pig and a sadist."

"I'm glad we agree," Mark said. "I trust you enough to tell you the reason I'm in Iquitos is to check on the truth of stories about the Peruvian Amazon Company. The best way to show what's really happening here is with a camera. Not a real one—I wouldn't have a chance taking pictures. But you."

"I'm not quite following you, *señor*."

"Have you started Felicidad's portrait yet?"

"No, we're waiting for her dress to be finished."

"Good. What I hope you'll do is tell Flores you want to take a few days off to go into the jungle and sketch the wildlife, the flowers, whatever sounds right. Then you leave Iquitos with your sketchbook and a guide. I'll join you later—if Flores knows I'm with you he'll get suspicious. We'll go together to a rubber-collecting center he has near Oro Blanco. We'll tell the men in charge that we're friends of Flores, and give them the same story we gave him—"

"That I'm making jungle sketches?"

"Yes. I'm your assistant collaborator in doing a book. Flores might even give you a letter of introduction—I don't know but at least try for it. We'd be taking a real chance—that Flores's people would believe us. But you'd actually be making and showing them your sketches. Meanwhile, what I'm hoping is that I can get a look at what they're really doing to the Indians, and that you can sketch that, too. You would give me the cover I need to get into Oro Blanco, and your sketches would be my camera to show what's going on once we get back to the States."

Vargas smiled. "You neglected to add, 'if we get back.' Señor, I'm an old man, a portraitist, not a newspaper sketch artist, certainly not a portrayer of—atrocities."

"Goya did portraits," Mark said, remembering the etchings he had seen in Herschel Fine's house, "but didn't he paint atrocities too?"

"Señor, you are cunning to compare me to such a great master. But I am far from being a Goya. And you must realize I make a good part of my living from men important in the rubber trade. If I were to display or publish sketches of the atrocities, they would ruin me!" He hesitated, then added thoughtfully, "Of course, it might be a *succès de scandale* . . ."

"I'm not going to try and push you into this," Mark said, "though without you I don't know how I'll manage it. And I also want to make it clear that if we are caught, well, God knows what Flores might do. He'd certainly never let us take the sketches out, probably not let *us* out."

Vargas nodded. "But suppose I were to go up with you to Oro Blanco and we succeed in convincing the men up there that I am sketching flora and fauna and you are my assistant or collaborator. When we leave Oro Blanco and come back here, sooner or later Flores is going to hear you were there as well. Wouldn't he find there was something suspicious about that?"

"Yes, but remember there is no communication between Oro Blanco and Iquitos except the company's river launch, the *Felicidad,* which only makes the trip every two weeks. I'll check on its schedule in the morning, but with some luck we should have left Iquitos before it makes its round trip and they can find out about me and where we've been. If not, I figure we can put ourselves in the hands of Mr. Baintree, the British consul. I'm going to introduce myself before we leave and tell him what we're up to. It's risky, I admit, but we at least will take advantage of everything we have to reduce the risk."

"What about Captain Wilson of the *Lanfranc?*"

"I've been told he's on Flores's payroll. By the way, I guess one advantage if you do decide to go with me is you won't have to go on painting Flores's daughter."

"That, sir, would be a blessing, believe me."

"Well, think it over. I have a small gun, which may be some help, but it's still going to be a dangerous trip. I agreed to take this job for certain business advantages. I'm not a particularly brave man, and I'm certainly not anxious to get killed. But after seeing what Flores's deputies did to that Indian tonight . . . well, all I can say is it would be a good feeling to be able to put a stop to what's going on out there. That may not be much of an incentive, but it's all I've got to offer. If you decide not to come, I'll understand." He stood up. "I'd appreciate it if you could give me an answer in the morning."

He shook the old man's hand, then went to the door.

"Señor Manning."

Mark turned; Vargas was standing by his chair, a smile on his face.

"The Devil must have inspired you to mention Goya. When I was young, believe me I had dreams . . ." He shrugged. "Well, they obviously never came true. I am a portrait painter for the rich and fashionable. A good one, mind you, but I have no illusions. A few years after I'm dead, who will remember my portraits or look at them except indolent descendants of their wealthy subjects." He hesitated. "But maybe people would remember *these* sketches."

"Then you'll do it?"

Vargas sighed. "It's insane, but I'll do it."

Even though it was what Mark had hoped for, he was surprised how moved he felt at the man's words and agreement. "Señor Vargas," he said, "I think plenty of people will remember your sketches."

Then he left the room.

"Captain, can you keep a secret?"

It was the next morning and Mark was sitting in the cabin of the *Lanfranc*. Opposite him sat Captain Arnold Wilson, the captain of the Booth Line's flag ship. Captain Wilson was not cast in the same mold as the captains of the great White Star and Cunard liners of the day, men who were by necessity magnificos as well as mariners, as adept at small talk with a duchess as steering through a field of icebergs (or, in the case of the *Titanic*, of course, not steering through). Arnold Wilson was not long on social tone, being a Lancastrian from a lower-middle-class background who had worked his way up from the boiler room. He had all the virtues and vices of his class, being hard-working and responsible, and at the same time smugly intolerant of allegedly un-English behavior. Reeking of rum at ten in the morning was considered distinctly un-English behavior, and as the captain's nose crinkled from the aroma emanating from the bleary-eyed American businessman, his low opinion of Americans in general was strongly confirmed.

"Of course I can keep a secret," he said stiffly, "as long as it involves nothing dishonorable."

"Oh, well," laughed Mark, "then maybe I'd better not tell you."

"See here, Mr. Manning, I'm not accustomed to having my passengers—"

"I know, passengers don't tell the captain their little secrets, but *this* one . . . You know, captain, in Ohio people are very straightlaced. *Very.* It's not easy for someone like me to have some fun and break loose—you know what I mean?" He winked what he hoped was a broad wink at the captain, who stiffened further. "A little fun with the ladies—you know?"

Captain Wilson's face was shading red.

"Mr. Manning, I'm a busy man—"

"Now, now, Captain, hear me out . . . After all, I'm a paying customer, you know, and like they say, the customer's always right. Right? I paid a lot of money to come down here to this deep dark Amazon jungle, and you know why I did it? You can bet not to see *this* town!" He waved drunkenly at Iquitos through the porthole. "No sir. I came down here because I wanted to get away for a while. Get away from all those damn straight-laced, church-going crones. I wanted to go, well, native. You know what I mean? Get a little brown girl and forget the whole damn world! That's why I came down here, and that's exactly what I'm gonna do. But *you've* got to help me . . ."

"Manning, you've behaving like a swine."

"Oh, yes indeed, a real pig; you ought to try it sometime. Well now, here's the set-up—I've found me a cute little Indian diversion and you see, she's got a shack down river a ways and I'm going down there for a couple of days and go native. Yes sir. Got a case of rum, and I'm going to booze it up and love her right into the next county—oops, they don't have counties down here, do they? Well, anyway, that's what I'm going to do and you're going to give me some help. You see, I'm checking out of the hotel and I've told everyone I've got the local tourist bug and am coming back here on the boat till I get over it. That way, that sauerkraut baron won't be on to what I'm up to, or the British consul, or Señor Fatface Flores—wouldn't want *him* telling other people in the rubber business that the president of the Manning Rubber Company of Elkins, Ohio, came down here and had himself an Injun girl—you see what I mean? But I know I can trust *you,* captain, because you're a good understanding fellow, I can tell. And if I bring my bags back on board and then disappear into the night, so to speak, well, you won't tell anyone, will you? You'll just say I'm holed up in my cabin with the bug? You'll do that for me, captain, won't you? Here . . ." He groped for his wallet. "I've got a little appreciation for you . . ."

"Mr. Manning, I do not accept bribes, and I certainly wouldn't accept one from you! Your behavior disgusts me, but be assured I will tell no one what you're actually doing. The last thing I should want anyone to know is that a white man—an Anglo-Saxon at that!— would so much as *touch* one of these filthy Indians, much less indulge in sexual concert—"

"Sexual concert! Oh, I *like* that, captain. We're going to have a concert—"

"Now, sir, you will please get out of here. When and if you ever sober up, I trust you will have the good sense to regret what you're doing. As for me, I shall try to forget what you've told me—not for *your* reputation, believe me, sir, but for mine and the white race that you so disgrace . . ."

Mark, swaying to his feet, assumed a look of drunken insult and weaved to the door of the cabin.

"No need to be unpleasant, captain. You English are so damned snobbish, might do you good to try one of these brownies yourself."

He left the cabin, amused at his act and pleased with the shocked reaction of Captain Wilson. His mouth, however, tasted terrible from the rum he'd gargled, and he could hardly wait to get back to the hotel to brush his teeth.

———————

At one that afternoon he moved from the hotel to his cabin on the *Lanfranc* and promptly retired to his stateroom. At midnight he quietly slipped off the ship, carrying a small valise, and met Pepe at the end of the dock, where once again they got into the canoe and pushed out into the river. Thanks to the swiftness of the current, they reached the small river village of Mazan by dawn. Here, as had been arranged, they met Manuel Vargas and his guide, Pepe's cousin Arrube, a full-blooded Indian, who owned a larger canoe. Leaving Pepe's canoe at Mazan, Arrube, Manuel, Mark and Pepe portaged the canoe over a short track of jungle until they reached the Napo River, a tributary of the Amazon, where they once again put the canoe in the water. There were four paddles, and though Mark told Vargas to conserve his strength, the elderly man insisted on contributing and took up a paddle. They pushed out and headed north for the collection center at Oro Blanco, which Arrube calculated they would reach the following morning. Arrube, who Mark judged was about twenty, spoke no English but passable Spanish, and as they nosed the boat into the current he exchanged a few words with Vargas. Afterward, the artist said to Mark, "Did you check on the river launch?"

"The *Felicidad*? I checked, and so far we're in luck. It made its last trip to Oro Blanco three days ago, so it won't be going back up for another ten days. I also had a talk with Mr. Baintree, who said he'd do his best to give us what he called diplomatic immunity if we thought Flores was after us when we return to Iquitos. The consulate's only been operating here six months but Baintree's not blind to what's going on. He thinks Flores is covering up a hellhole, but his position keeps him from watching him more closely. He also said he doubted he'd have the taste for it anyway. But at least he can try to help us when we get back. But why did you ask about the *Felicidad*?"

"Well, Arrube tells me Oro Blanco is the nearest collection center to Iquitos, besides Orellana, and Arrube also says the *Felicidad* is fast, that it can make Oro Blanco from Iquitos in less than twenty-four hours."

"Then let's hope Flores stays convinced you're only drawing jungle flowers. He did give you a letter of introduction, which is more than I'd hoped for. He probably wouldn't have done that if he'd suspected anything. Although to refuse a sketch artist would have made him look like he had something to hide and he took a calculated risk . . ."

"True," replied Vargas, "but perhaps he's so delirious about the baron wooing Felicidad that even if I told him the truth he would have given me a letter of introduction."

Mark laughed. "It seems the baron is turning out to be our secret ally."

———————————

Unless one was a sadist, the great deal of energy and patience required to torture human beings was an unpleasant business. Certainly Jorge Ruiz, the manager of the collection center at Oro Blanco, had often told himself it was hardly pleasant living in this stinking jungle, constantly besieged by letters from the office in Iquitos demanding ever-increasing rubber production, a production that he, in turn, had to sweat out of the worthless Indians, who were too lazy and stupid to be motivated by anything more sophisticated than brute terror. Consequently, it was necessary to resort to all manner of devices that were disgusting to see. Certainly he, Jorge Ruiz, derived no pleasure from maiming and killing, though he was aware some of his lieutenants did, particularly the niggers from Barbados. El Barbadiano, for instance, that giant black man whom Jorge had seen lift three hundred pounds, El Barbadiano felt definite sexual pleasure from the barbarities; Jorge was sure of it from the look in the giant's eyes, a look of abnormal excitement as he would lay into a man's back with the tapir-hide whip. It was perverse, and Jorge despised it when he saw it in his men, though he never let them know his thoughts; after all, the important matter was to get the job done. He exercised constant vigilance that *he* never felt such excitement, for he knew if he did, it would be a sure sign that the tattered vestiges of his culture were going and the jungle was finally claiming him. And Jorge had "culture." He had come from Caracas, where his father had been a doctor, and he had gone to the University, where he had learned a smattering of English and French. He wasn't like one of the niggers or *racionales* he employed; he was a white man with refinement, a white man who once had had access to the better homes of Caracas. Of course, his father had lost his money and died of drink, forcing Jorge to leave Caracas and come to the Putumayo to try to build his fortune, lured by the stories of the rubber boom. He had not wanted to go to work for Señor Flores —Flores most definitely had no culture—but he paid so well. So it was that the year before he had been sent to this hellhole at Oro Blanco. It was not all that unpleasant a place physically; the *jefe's* quarters were presentable and the jungle had been cleared back from the river so that the heat was at least bearable. There were the long wooden sheds where the *pelas* of rubber were stored, and the huts for the niggers and *racionales*—the Indians who were used as overseers rather than gatherers. The big scales at the weighing station and, of course, the *cepo*—that wasn't so pleasant. He had been told what to expect before he came, and what was expected of him. He hadn't liked the sound of it but he told himself it was the necessities of the business. Still, he didn't like it and he had been fastidious about never personally killing an Indian himself. Well, once, but in self-defense. Some damn-fool Huitoto had gotten drunk and attacked him with a knife during the middle of the night when he was asleep. He was fortunate to have survived the attack. Happily he always kept a gun next to his bed and, happily, the Indian was

so drunk his aim was bad and he stabbed the pillow first, thinking
it was his victim and giving Jorge time enough to grab his pistol
and fire a shot point-blank into the man's heart. The Indian had
been leaning over him, and he just dropped, dead weight suddenly
on him, his heart spurting blood. Jorge remembered uncomfortably
that there *had* been an odd excitement as the hot, sticky blood smeared
his naked chest. It was possible, he realized, that even he could
sink to the level of El Barbadiano, which was why he was sensitive
about the sadistic aspect of the barbarities, as he thought of them,
and took care not to indulge in them himself.

He merely gave the orders.

But now he had a new problem, which was enough to make him
feel older than his thirty-nine years. Ever since ten that morning
when the canoe had tied up at the pier and that ancient artist and
his associate had arrived with their two Indian guides . . . what
was his name? . . . Vargas, and with a letter from Señor Flores himself telling his employees to extend every courtesy to Señor Vargas.
. . . Well, what was he to do? Of course, he could hold off with the
whippings but he had no illusions about the impression the collection center would make on an outsider. For that matter, he had seen
the look on Vargas's face when the indigenous stench reached him
on his way from the pier to his office. Jorge was accustomed to the
smell, which lingered for a while after every *correria,* the slave hunt,
and there had been a particularly bloody one a few days before;
but there was good reason to leave the bodies in the jungle—an
object lesson to the others that they should bloody well produce
more rubber and do as they were told, or face the consequences.

But what to do with the artist and his American friend, who
were sitting on the opposite side of Jorge's desk smiling politely
as he perused the letter from Flores? There was something definitely
odd about the letter. Flores allowing any outsider to wander through
the jungle was strange. And the letter made no mention of the red-
headed American. Only Señor Vargas, and that he wanted to wander
through the jungle with his guides and sketch butterflies and flowers
. . . and why here, at Oro Blanco, of all places? On the other hand,
the artist looked to be a sophisticated old goat. Certainly Señor
Flores would not have given him a letter of introduction if he were
not certain Vargas was safe. Perhaps he was being too nervous. Why
was life always so difficult for him? Such as this past week when at
least a dozen Indians had joined that Yagua runaway from La
Chorrera, and he had been obliged to organize the *correria.* They
had all been found—El Barbadiano was the best slave hunter in the

business—and then . . . well, better not dwell on that, though what El Barbadiano had done to the Yagua was especially cruel, in his opinion. Not the mutilation, his hands and genitals, but leaving him *alive!* My God. But then El Barbadiano was not a well man. He had seen that frenzy in his eyes—the nigger enjoyed it, he did; it was beyond dispute. Thank God he, Jorge, had at least a residue of compassion inherent in his culture.

Anyway, what to do about this old goat of an artist? Let him wander wherever he wanted? But what was the alternative? Hide the *cepo*? Impossible.

Jorge sighed and handed the letter from Flores back across the desk. "Well, *señor*, what may I do to help you?"

"Oh, nothing," replied Vargas. "We only wanted to introduce ourselves. My friend Mr. Smith is also my author-collaborator—he is a well-known naturalist in America, and one of the world's leading lepidopterists . . . butterflies, you know . . ." He smiled.

"I know, *señor*. I went to the University."

"Ah? Indeed. A university man here in the jungle—extraordinary. Well, now, where was I? Oh, yes, butterflies. All we wish is to wander about in the jungle for a day or so to make notes and sketches. We shan't bother you, I hope, though we would appreciate it if you could put us up for the night."

"Of course, and I hope we can entertain you at dinner tonight. You may go where you wish. . . . There is only one matter . . . you may see things that appear cruel—" He hesitated, then shrugged. "Gentlemen, you have put me somewhat on the spot. The fact is, we have just had a *correria* and you will find a few dead Indians. It cannot be helped. We leave them in the jungle to remind the others what to expect if they run away. It is rather cruel, perhaps barbaric, but there you have it—we must be cruel to insure that they work. Naturally, there are some who would not understand, but you gentlemen seem men of the world, and Señor Flores's letter . . ."

Vargas held up his hands. "Please, *señor*, it is not our purpose to interfere with your business."

Jorge smiled with relief. "Good. Well then, gentlemen, I'll leave you to your own pursuits, and if you should want *anything*, please do ask."

They all rose and shook hands.

"*Señor*, you are too kind," said Vargas with elaborate politeness. "A thousand thanks."

Jorge led them out of his office onto the front porch, where he instructed Ife, his *racionale* lieutenant, to give the visitors the privileges of the collection center. Then he went back into his office, relieved to have this new problem at least temporarily resolved. He was already, at ten fifteen in the morning, aching for his second—or was this his third?—brandy of the day.

CHAPTER THREE

Captain Wilson had just come aboard the *Lanfranc* to go to his cabin for lunch when his steward told him that Baron von Stimme was most eager to see him. Captain Wilson sliced into his fish, taken but an hour before out of the Amazon, and said, "Show the baron in."

The young Prussian looked as handsome as usual, but his suit was wrinkled and he hadn't shaved. Captain Wilson noticed the man's nervousness immediately. He looked as though he had seen a ghost. The captain offered him a chair at the table and a gin sling, both of which the young aristocrat readily accepted.

"Captain," he said in a low voice after the steward had served him the drink and left the cabin, "I am in trouble, and I need your help."

"What sort of trouble, baron?"

"Perhaps you've heard that since we arrived in Iquitos last week I have been paying court to Señorita Flores?"

Captain Wilson nodded.

"I may also say with due modesty that I have been quite successful. The *señorita* has fallen in love with me and—"

"Congratulations," interrupted the captain.

"Please, it's little enough to be congratulated about, believe me, sir. My intentions, however, were honorable, which I told Felicidad's father the night before last. Not having too much time here in Iquitos, I have needed to move rather quickly, but this didn't bother Señor Flores. He was delighted. To be blunt, he was delighted at the prospect of acquiring a wealthy German baron for a son-in-law. So I proposed to Felicidad, who accepted, and everyone was overjoyed, until last night . . ."

He gulped more gin, and Captain Wilson noticed his hands were shaking.

"Last night," he continued, "I went to dine at the Casa Encantada.

Señor Flores had invited a number of his friends to celebrate our engagement, and there was much drinking. I became somewhat drunk myself, unusual for me. Felicidad whispered she wished to get away from everyone else and be alone with me. I went out to a corner of the garden and met her there on a bench. She had managed to avoid Señora Guzman . . ."

"Her dueña?"

"Yes. Now to be blunt, captain, Felicidad is not a pretty *Fraulein*. In fact, speaking man to man, she repulses me."

"Then why are you marrying her?"

"I shall get to that . . . Felicidad is what is known as a hot-blooded woman—incredibly hot blooded, I discovered—and she began to make love to me."

"But, baron, it is supposed to be the other way around—"

"But, captain, that I am aware of. Last night, however, suffice to say she was the aggressor, I the unwilling victim. There comes a point, however, when even the most unattractive female arouses, and I, primed with much champagne, in fact became aroused. I made love to her—on the bench in the garden. For purpose of statistics, I can report she was a virgin."

Captain Wilson gave him a cold, prudish look as von Stimme drank more gin. The Prussian's behavior was nearly as un-English as that of the drunken American, Mr. Manning.

Von Stimme continued. "Felicidad was rapturous—in fact, she wished me to do it to her again. Since she was so clearly well disposed toward me, I decided it as good a time as any to tell her the truth about myself—she would have to know sooner or later anyway."

"What do you mean, 'the truth'?"

Von Stimme gave him a rather contemptuous look, as if surprised the man hadn't already guessed.

"I am no baron. I am not rich. I concocted the title, inserted the 'von' in front of my name. Even the dueling scar is self-inflicted."

Captain Wilson looked stunned. "But why would you go to such lengths to—"

"To get a rich wife, of course," said Stimme. "I had read of the rubber boom in Brazil and came over to take advantage of my most negotiable commodity—my looks. Manáos crawls with gigolos. In fact, there was so much competition in Manáos that when I heard of Señor Flores's ugly daugher I decided to come up river and try for her. It was a shock when I saw her—I had no idea she was *that* ugly—but it did make things easier. No male had ever paid romantic attention to her before. A few compliments, a few hand kisses and soulful looks . . . *Mein Gott!* I did not tell her *all* the truth, but I did tell her I was not a baron, nor do I have a *Mark* to my name. Usually such confessional honesty works wonders with a woman. Brings out the motherliness, the protectiveness. But that stupid Felicidad does not *have* any motherliness. Instead of forgiving me, saying it was of no consequence and she loved me all the more for being honest, the stupid *dirne* went into a rage and commenced howling at me, calling me names and trying to hit me. She then ran back into the house and told all to her father."

He paused to drink more gin.

"Flores was already drunk when Felicidad came to tell him I was a cheat, and her hysteria and his alcohol and the news he was not to have a titled son-in-law after all combined to turn him into a monster. He went insane wtih rage, came rushing from the house with his pistols to kill me. He has two houseboys that are his bodyguards, who also pursued me. Believe me, captain, I should be a dead man if I had not circled around the garden and gone back into the house, then run out the front door. I hid in the jungle during the night because I was sure they would go to the Bella Vista to search for me. This morning I made my way down to the river and waited until noon before I came into town. Now I am here, and I beg you to put me under your protection and allow me to stay on the boat until we sail. Otherwise, I don't have a chance. Believe me, Flores will kill me if he can get at me."

He looked fearfully at the captain, who said, "But are you so certain you're not overstating the case? I can believe Señor Flores may have threatened you last night when he was drunk, but this morning I imagine he's decided he was too extreme—"

"No!" interrupted Stimme. "If I had not made love to her, perhaps. But idiot that I was, I did make love to her and she told him, and now he believes her *ruined* and he will *never* be rid of her. When he came out of the house I heard him screaming that he would pay ten thousand *soles* to the man who brought him my testicles. Believe me, captain, Flores is still searching for me. You *must* protect me."

Captain Wilson wiped his mouth with his napkin.

"Of course, there's no question about that. I would do it even if you weren't one of my passengers. Stay aboard, and I'll instruct the crew not to allow anyone aboard whom they don't know. I still believe you're being overly nervous, but nevertheless an ounce of prevention, and so forth. Shall I send one of the stewards to the hotel to fetch your bags?"

"Yes, please. And tell them to determine my bill and I shall send the money."

He stood up and clasped the captain's hand. "Captain, I cannot tell you how relieved I am. I am not a particularly brave man, but I do not believe I am a coward either. However, I know what Flores would do if he were able to get his hands upon me and believe me, sir, it makes me sick to my stomach even to think of it. The man is a butcher, I am sure of it! The stories I heard in Manáos about his rubber gatherers . . . I can believe them now!"

"Perhaps. I still believe you're being a bit too nervous. And of course, in a way you brought this on yourself, you know. Neither your motives nor your behavior was gentlemanly. And to lie about your background . . . Well, I find it difficult to sympathize with that."

"I admit all that. But certainly what I have done does not deserve castration!"

"Don't worry. You'll be safe here."

He escorted Stimme to the cabin door, telling his steward to take him back to his former stateroom. After Stimme had left, he closed the door and stood a moment, reflecting. Then he went to his desk, sat down, and pulled a sheet of paper from the drawer. After writing a short note, he folded the paper and enclosed it in an envelope on which he wrote, "To Señor Flores. Deliver by hand."

"There is no such thing as death," said Manuel Vargas as he sat on the camp stool sketching the fly-and-insect-crawling corpse of the Indian lying in the weeds before him. "The body dies, of course, but the products of the mind live on forever. Plato said ideals were the ultimate reality, but I think it would be more accurate to say that *ideas* are the ultimate reality. And since ideas live forever, then there is no death. But I imagine that's small consolation to this poor fellow before us."

Mark, standing next to Vargas, stared at the corpse. It was the third one they had literally stumbled on after going into the jungle; the man had been dead for some time, and his corpse was rapidly decomposing, the process being hastened by ravenous ants. The jungle, which had proven to be less torrid than Mark had expected —the sun being permanently barred from the jungle floor by the canopy of tall trees—was itself exotically beautiful, though swarming with mosquitoes. It was a primeval world, a Garden of Eden, in a way. Yet it was hardly a paradise. It was permeated with evil, the evil brutality of men when all restraints are removed from their animal natures. Jorge Ruiz, the dissipated manager of the center, might have been a mildly successful clerk in Caracas, but here in the jungle he had become a monster—how much of a monster Mark was only beginning to appreciate. Mark had little doubt that most people operated most of the time on the level of self-interest, including himself, but this sort of monstrous brutality went far beyond the bounds of self-interest or even greed. He did not consider his trip to Iquitos a moral crusade. Moreover, the practical businessman in him marveled at the stupid waste of the operation at Oro Blanco. There had to be a better way of getting the rubber out of the jungle than this. Carlos Innocente Flores, in managing this nightmare world, was showing himself not only to be a vampire but an inept businessman as well.

But more than all the rest, Mark was a human being and the sight of the Indian corpses nauseated him. It would be a sweet feeling to expose these butchers to the world—assuming, of course, Flores didn't become suspicious. He nervously attempted to push that idea out of his mind. Ruiz had looked somewhat suspicious when they first docked that morning, but he apparently had believed Vargas's story —whether it was the plausibility of the story or the letter from Flores or Ruiz's whiskey-soaked wits, Mark was unsure. At any rate, so far they were not bothered, and now as he watched Vargas's skilled hand penciling in the gruesome details of the corpse, he congratulated himself for having had the idea to persuade the artist to accompany him. The sketches would be better than photographs, infinitely more persuasive than words.

"Unfortunately," Vargas went on as he began drawing the Indian's exposed thighbone, "the human mind aspires downward more often than the other direction—the word ought to be 'despires,' though that doesn't sound right. My point is we who are alive are at the same time living in the past. The ideas of our forebears still control us, and what we think will live on after us and affect our descendants. The good minds of the past created beauty that can still touch us. Goya, or de la Tour, to mention two of my heroes. Several months ago in Rio I was at a party and a French pianist sat down after dinner and played a piece I have never been fond of—a Liszt rendition of a song by Schumann called 'Widmund.' I have always thought it pretentious and vulgar, but this man played it as I had never heard before. Suddenly the piece sounded noble, beautiful, and I found myself weeping. Schumann and Liszt have been dead for some years now but their minds had affected me. Whenever that happens, I find myself marveling . . . and I suspect I am going on too much. I apologize . . ."

"Not at all," Mark said, though, in fact, he was a bit glassy-eyed from the old man's garrulous philosophizing. Pepe Lopez, who was also watching the sketch artist, was listening intently, though it was difficult for him to follow.

"But if good minds produce masterpieces," went on Vargas "—I think I would change 'good' to 'first-rate'—second-rate minds produce short-lived trash, third-rate minds produce nothing, which brings us to debased minds. Butchery is surely the art—if you can call it that—of debased minds. Atrocities are *their* museum pieces, and affect us just as the masterworks of the past affect us, and just as *this* atrocity will affect the future—at least it may if we can get these sketches out so the future will know of them."

He drew in the stump of the Indian's right arm, which had been severed just below the shoulder and was now four or five feet away from its former owner. The left arm was not to be seen, perhaps dragged into the jungle by a puma.

"Señor Vargas," said Pepe timidly, "do you mean you hope there will be no more . . ." he hesitated before attacking the word ". . . atrocities?"

"That's correct, Pepe. I like to think the human race learns and betters itself. I know it is a slow process, but one hopes as each generation learns more it becomes better. Someday there will be no more atrocities, and perhaps this sketch will have helped to achieve that moment."

There was a silence, then Pepe said in a dubious voice, "I hope you are right, *señor.*"

Vargas looked up at the boy. "But you doubt it?"

He didn't answer. Vargas sighed and returned to his sketch, beginning now to draw the head, which had rolled several feet from the body after decapitation. It had come to rest face up, eyes closed, mouth gaping as though silenced when about to scream. Mark, surprised at the Indian boy's unexpected cynicism, looked at the head and wondered if that unheard scream would end up a colorful footnote in some future guidebook.

At two in the morning, Carlos Innocente Flores came up the gangway of the *Lanfranc* with his two bodyguards, Billy and Timothy. They were led by the quartermaster to Captain Wilson's cabin. After rapping lightly on the door, the quartermaster returned to his post while the captain admitted Flores to his quarters.

"Ah, my friend," said Flores quietly, "you've done me a great service. He *is* aboard?"

"Yes, number three."

Flores's esurient eyes narrowed as he handed the captain an envelope.

"You have earned it."

Wilson opened the envelope to check its contents, and Flores watched him as he counted the ten thousand *soles*. Satisfied the money was all there, Wilson took a key from his pocket. "This is the master cabin key. Your men can use it to open his door. But they'll have to take him off the ship. You understand that? I can't allow anything to happen on board."

"Of course. What about Mark Manning? There's no chance of his waking, interfering?"

"Manning's not even aboard."

"But I was told he had moved back on the boat because he was sick?"

The captain shook his head. "That was the story he spread to cover up going down river with some bloody Indian girl."

"An Indian?"

"So he said. Americans! Disgusting! Manning's a pig, almost as bad as Stimme. Well, now, here's the key."

Flores took it and looked curiously at the Englishman. "Tell me, my friend, you have helped me before, which I have always appreciated, of course. But this is different. Why are you helping me now?"

The captain's face became hard. "The German is scum. I've seen many of them on this ship—adventurers, gigolos. I've brought them up to Manáos and taken them back to Belém; they come up river hungry, ready to use their bodies like prostitutes, and most of them return bloody broke—which serves them right and proper. But this one is the worst of them all."

Flores smiled, amused by the captain's so conveniently omitting any mention of the 10,000 *soles*. "Well, my friend, you have a fine sense of justice, like a true Englishman. I congratulate you." He left the cabin, closing the door behind him.

"Cabin three," he whispered to Billy, the first Barbadian bodyguard. Billy nodded, took the key, then led Timothy, also Barbadian, down the companionway back out onto the deck. Flores followed more slowly, thinking about what Captain Wilson had told him. Manning seemed so pleasant, so bland, at dinner that night at Casa Encantada, sitting at table chatting with Señor Vargas. He had seemed the typical American businessman, like the ones Flores had met in Lima and Manáos—a mixture of Yankee shrewdness and provincial naïveté. It had never occurred to Flores to question Captain Wilson's initial assessment of why Manning had come to Iquitos —certainly not after he had met Manning. But now he had gone into the jungle with an Indian girl? Some whites were entranced by the natives, of course, but Manning? Somehow it sounded wrong . . .

He stopped. Vargas was a simple, obvious person—a *portrait* painter, barely a man. Why not grant the letter of introduction for sketches of "jungle flora." Manning and Vargas talking together at Casa Encantada. Mother of God, he thought, is it possible? While I have been hunting this bastard German, is it possible those *two* went to Oro Blanco? . . .

Billy and Timothy quietly unlocked the door of cabin three and stepped inside. The light from the passageway spilled through the doorway onto the bunk, where Stimme was asleep, dressed in his pajama bottoms. Swiftly Billy grabbed him, clapping one enormous hand over his mouth as his other hand pulled him off the bed. Timothy grabbed his legs. Stimme was awake now, struggling to free himself from the two bodyguards. Timothy took the pair of pants off the hook on the door while Billy brought the blackjack down on Stimme's skull. The German slumped into unconsciousness. Quickly they pulled his pants on and slipped his arms through a shirt. They jammed his feet into a pair of shoes and carried him out of the cabin down the passageway to the deck. Flores was already on the dock, sitting in his carriage. Billy and Timothy, each on one side of Stimme, smiled at the quartermaster as they hoisted the German onto the gangway.

"Drunk," Billy grinned, winking at the quartermaster, who nodded sleepily.

They hauled Stimme down the gangway to the dock, then pushed him into the carriage. Billy climbed in after him, but Flores leaned out and said to Timothy, "Go wake up Alfonso. Tell him to ready the *Felicidad*. Tell him I will be on board in two hours. We are going up to Oro Blanco."

Timothy nodded and ran up the deserted street as the coachman flicked his whip on the horses' rumps and the carriage rolled away from the dock.

Flores waited until Stimme regained consciousness before castrating him. It was in Flores's office. Flores himself using the knife. Billy had stripped the victim and tied him to a chair. As Stimme awoke and saw what was about to happen to him, he began whimpering with terror, the whimpers turning to screams as Flores proceeded. He lapsed into unconsciousness once again, and Flores instructed Billy to slap him awake. As the bodyguard did so, Flores drank beer, staring at the blood streaming down the naked thighs. When Stimme was awake again, Flores took up the knife and cut him on the cheek first, then a deeper cut on the side, done with an expertise acquired from killing Indians that kept bleeding to a minimum to prolong life and the agony. A half hour later, when he slit the man's throat, Flores felt a new pleasure. He had, after all, never done this to a white man.

When Mark, Vargas, Pepe and Arrube returned to the collection center that afternoon from their expedition into the jungle, they were met by Ife, Ruiz's outsized Indian lieutenant, who asked in bad Spanish to see Vargas's sketchbook. There was a strained moment, then the artist opened the book and showed the pages where he had hastily sketched in flowers, butterflies and birds—the sketches of the coprses he had folded and put in his pocket. They seemed to satisfy the Indian, who looked at the drawings, then nodded. The party walked across the clearing to the low, white, wooden headquarters building, where Jorge Ruiz was stretched in a hammock on the front porch, humming to himself and drunkenly nursing a fresh bottle of brandy.

After greeting him, Mark and Vargas went to the room they had been assigned in the building (Pepe and Arrube had been given hammocks in the hut reserved for the overseers). "Do you think the Indian still suspects anything?" Vargas asked.

"I don't know," Mark said, taking off his sweat-stained shirt to wash himself. "I think Ruiz told him to check the sketches, but he looks happy enough now. We'll see."

When they had changed to fresh clothes, they rejoined Ruiz on the porch. Far from seeming suspicious, the manager was eager to entertain his unexpected guests, as if the sight of white faces was a rare treat he wished to savor, and before dinner he insisted on taking them for a river cruise on the collection center's wheezing steam launch. Ruiz led them in a drunken weave from the headquarters building to the pier jutting out into the river where the antique launch was tied up opposite Arrube's canoe. It had one stack, a small cabin area below deck and an ancient engine fired by wooden logs. The deck area was shaded by a patched striped awning. As two Indians who had already fired the engine stood by the lines, Mark and Vargas climbed aboard behind Ruiz, after which the Indians cast off and aimed the launch into the river. It chugged and belched smoke as they headed upstream; Ruiz, sprawled in a deck chair, invited his guests to partake from the brandy bottle, which they both did.

"What do you think of my little empire?" asked Ruiz, gesturing drunkenly at the tree-lined river bank. "Stinking, isn't it? Nothing but rubber and Indians, Indians and rubber. And all the money goes to that fat bastard, Flores. What an empire!"

He was speaking in Spanish, which Vargas translated to Mark. As they proceeded upstream, Ruiz rattled on, unburdening himself of his many grievances. He had taken this "stinking" job in hopes of getting rich but now he was in debt to the Peruvian Amazon Company, which he hated, and he didn't see any way out of this life he hated and why he didn't just throw over the whole thing he didn't know except that at least he was pretty much in charge here in this forsaken corner of the globe which was some, if not much, consolation. . . . As he paused to catch his breath and drink more brandy, Mark told Vargas to ask him how they got the Indians to work for them. "We bribe them," answered Ruiz. "In Brazil, they hook them with the contract—advance them money they can never pay back. Here we don't bother. We send men to their villages and distribute presents—mirrors, combs, junk. They are so stupid they think they're worth something. Then we tell them if they will bring us *jebe*—rubber—here to Oro Blanco, we will give them more presents. They bring in a little *jebe*, we give them some liquor, let them have a few of the Indian women we keep on hand for them—and for us—and then when they want to go home, we beat them. We take their sisters or their mothers and make them hostages and tell the men to go out in the jungle and bring us more *jebe* or we will kill their relatives. It works; they do it." He laughed. "And if they do not do it, we kill them. You must credit Señor Flores; he has developed a workable system. Of course, I personally do not approve of it . . ." he belched ". . . but it works."

Just then he noticed a crocodile sliding into the river, a sight that brought him to his feet. "Now for some sport, gentlemen!" He lurched to the stern of the vessel, where he opened a metal box that Mark saw was filled with sticks of dynamite. Ruiz took out one and proceeded to light a match and hold it to the wick. "Don't worry," he said drunkenly, "I'm not going to blow *us* up." With that, he hurled the dynamite off the stern at the back of the crocodile. The stick sailed through the air and landed in the water. "Damn," mumbled Ruiz. "The trick is to hit the croc so the thing blows up before the water puts out the wick. Want to try?" His guests demurred, at which point Ruiz tried again, lighting another stick. This one he hurled at two crocodiles on the bank. The ugly creatures stirred slightly as the dynamite landed between them, oblivious to the danger. A loud explosion. The two crocodiles were blown into the air and into pieces which sailed bloodily in all directions. As Mark and Vargas looked on, sickened, Ruiz howled in brandy-soaked pleasure.

A day at Oro Blanco was enough to turn the strongest stomach, and by the time the launch returned them to shore, both Mark and Vargas badly wanted to get out. And yet, Mark whispered to his friend, they had come this far to see the worst; they would have to stick it out a little while longer until they had seen the rest. Vargas wearily agreed. They endured a terrible dinner during which Ruiz rambled on, his conversation now turning to rancid jokes so obscene that Vargas refused to translate them to Mark. Then, mercifully, after dinner their host stumbled off to bed, his brain pickled.

The following morning he emerged on the front porch to join his guests for breakfast, not unnaturally complaining of a vicious hangover. He took a seat at the table and gulped some hot coffee with shaky hands as Mark watched the Indians lining up before the big scales a hundred feet or so from the porch. Ife, the *racionale,* was in charge of the operation, watching the pointer as each Indian silently placed his ball of rubber on the weighing platform. An enormous black man was standing beside the scale holding a curled whip. He was apparently the chief of the barbaric police force, and the manner in which the small Indians cringed as they passed him indicated the terror the man's presence instilled in them. He wore khaki shorts and a matching shirt and heavy boots, and his imposing physique gave him the look of some demon from a Doré engraving of hell, while the dozen near-naked Indians, holding their rubber and waiting in line to weigh it at the scales, might have passed for sinners damned and doomed for eternity to the Ninth Circle.

Ruiz had just begun to spoon his melon when screaming was heard behind the overseers' hut, adding sound effects to the Doré hellscape. The screams continued. Ruiz, annoyed, dispatched one of his Indian houseboys to see what was happening. He quickly returned to inform the manager that one of the men in the *cepo* had gone berserk. Ruiz mumbled something and excused himself; as he got up, Mark prompted Vargas to ask if they could accompany him. Ruiz looked dubious, then shrugged and told them to follow him. He led them across the clearing around the overseers' hut to the edge of the jungle where a small thatched-roof hut had been constructed. "This is the *cepo*," he said. "The *seringueiros* sometimes put rocks in the middle of their *pelas* to make them weigh more on the scales. When we catch them, we put them in here to reflect on their sins." He ducked through the low door, and Mark and Vargas followed him into the hut. It was stifling from human excrement. In the dim light, they could make out six Indians whose hands and feet were locked in crude wooden stocks, their necks manacled with chains attached to a stout post. Two of the Indians' bodies had swollen from disease, and one was screaming, obviously out of his mind. Ruiz glanced at him, shrugged and came back out of the hut, Mark and Vargas accompanying him, relieved to get out of the stench and heat and noise. "*Loco*," said Ruiz philosophically. He issued a curt order to an overseer who nodded; then he started back to the head-quarters building, saying, "I am sorry to have disturbed your break-fast, gentlemen. The Indian has been in there two weeks. I suppose if I were he, I'd go crazy myself."

"What will you to do to him?" asked Vargas.

Ruiz seemed surprised at the question. "Shoot him," he said matter-of-factly. "It is an act of mercy, believe me."

To prove his words, as they started across the clearing a shot rang out and the screaming ended. Mark winced, feeling his disgust boiling over; but he forced himself to disguise it.

"Ask Ruiz," he said to Vargas, "if he isn't afraid the Indians might organize against him."

Ruiz listened to the question, shook his head. "Never. They are too terrified. They know what will happen to them." He stopped and pointed to the giant standing beside the scales. "See that nigger over there? His name is El Barbadiano. The Indians know him well—they say El Barbadiano splits skulls for exercise, and it is the truth. The

Indians are not going to organize, ever. Besides, they are too stupid, too lazy. They don't want to work, they don't see any value in working—they have not worked for centuries, just sat around and lived on breadfruit and laid in their hammocks and copulated. Now we come along and give them some trinkets, put them to work, and they don't like it. That's why we are forced to use such methods on them. That is why I allow El Barbadiano to do what he does."

"But," said Mark, "they must hate the whites and it would seem to me one of them might get the idea they have nothing to lose by trying to fight back."

"But they *have* something to lose—their lives."

"But their lives are miserable! If I were one of them, I'd rather take the gamble—"

"But you're white, superior in intellect. I keep telling you they are stupid. You don't understand the tactics of fear. Fear can paralyze a man, particularly if there is no logic to the fear. The Indians know they will be punished if they cheat on their collecting, or weight the rubber, or kill the rubber trees or try to run away. They know that. But what reduces them to *flan* is the knowledge that they may be punished even if they do *nothing* wrong. Let me show you what I mean."

He led them over to the Indians lined up before the scales and pointed to one of them. "You!" He waved him out of the line. The Indian, who was about seventeen, obeyed, a look of confusion on his face. Ruiz nodded to El Barbadiano, who came over to the Indian, kicked him to the ground, then began to whip him. The move took Mark by surprise.

"For God's sake, stop him!" he said to Ruiz.

"No, it will show you what I am talking about. See the *look* on the others' faces?"

"Christ, man, I believe you! Now tell him to stop!"

Ruiz grinned, as if it were all a game, then called out, "El Barbadiano, show our visitors what you did last week to that run-away!"

El Barbadiano threw down his whip, took hold of the screaming Indian by his ankles, picked him up, and carried him head down over to a tree. He swung him back like a baseball bat, and then with all the power of his huge frame swung the Indian forward and plowed his body and head into the tree trunk. The Indian stopped screaming. His skull had split open.

There are emotions that can be even stronger than fear; and one of them is outrage. Mark was so outraged by what he had seen that he acted impulsively. Ruiz, who had been watching the horrendous object lesson with pleasure, carried a gun in a hip holster—a bigger, more effective gun, Mark saw, than the small handgun he carried under his khaki jacket. Now he slipped his hand over Ruiz's gun and pulled it out, so quickly Ruiz didn't realize it had happened. Mark aimed at El Barbadiano, who was standing about ten feet away still holding the Indian by his ankles, looking at the blood cascading from his skull. Mark fired. El Barbadiano was hit in the chest. He dropped the Indian, astonished, and staggered back. Mark fired again, this bullet severing the jugular in his neck and killing him. Mark saw Ife, the *racionale,* pulling his gun from his holster, and Mark fired at him, hitting him in the stomach. Ife doubled over; Mark fired a second time, hitting the Indian at the top of his head. He dropped to the ground.

Silence now as the Indians stared in disbelief at the corpses of their tormentors. Ruiz was speechless, his bloodshot eyes clouded with fear, his hands trembling. Mark told Vargas, "Manuel, round up Pepe and Arrube and get our stuff. Meet me on the pier. I think we've seen enough of this stinkhole." Startled, Vargas nodded and started toward the overseers' hut. "Wait a minute," Mark said, pulling his own gun from the holster beneath his khaki jacket and tossing it to him. "You may need this." Vargas caught the pistol, stared at it nervously, then ran off. Mark grabbed Ruiz by the arm and pushed the gun in his spine. "Call to the rest of your men to come out," he ordered, jamming the gun hard into the man's back. "*Do* it."

A sweating Ruiz began yelling in Spanish. Two of the overseers had already appeared at the door of their hut, attracted by the shots. Now they came out, uncertainly holding up their hands, as four more emerged from the hut. "Vargas," called Mark, "take their guns and tell them to lie on the ground." Then Mark turned to the Indians at the scale and waved his arms. "Go on!" he shouted. "Run! Go on! *Get out!*" The Indians hesitated, taking still uncomprehending looks at the bodies of Ife and El Barbadiano. Then, as Mark again yelled at them to run, they rushed off, whooping as they disappeared into the jungle.

Ruiz, still trembling, said, "What are you going to do to us?"

"You'll see." He pushed Ruiz ahead of him and started for the overseers' hut. When they reached it, Vargas had been joined by Pepe and Arrube. Mark told them to go to the launch and fire up the engine; then he told Vargas to order the overseers to their feet. When the trembling men, half of them Indian and half black, stood up, Mark marched them behind the hut to the *cepo.* "Tell them to free the Indians," he instructed Vargas. The overseers looked dubiously at Ruiz; Mark shoved the gun into his back again, this time hard enough so that the man groaned with pain. "Tell them," he said. Ruiz obeyed, and one of the overseers entered the tiny hut. A few minutes later the dazed Indians, who had been imprisoned for so long in the abominable hole, stumbled out the door, gasping for air and looking incredulous when they saw their captors being held at gun point. Vargas told them they were free; though they didn't understand Spanish, they understood the message and wasted no time in getting away from their prison.

Mark then ordered Ruiz and his lieutenants inside the *cepo,* where he and Vargas proceeded to place the jailors in their jail, locking their hands and feet into the stocks and chaining their necks to the post. The overseers, terrified, were babbling, and Ruiz cried out in his broken English for mercy. "You can't leave us, we'll die!" Then he turned to Vargas and loosed a stream of Spanish. The artist said to Mark, "They *will* die, you know."

"Tell them we'll send their *seringueiros* back to free them," he said, which, when Vargas translated to Ruiz, put the manager into an even greater frenzy of terror. He continued to scream in Spanish as Mark preceded Vargas out of the hut, carrying a big earthen water pitcher which he took over to the station's water pump to fill. "We really *can't* leave them there," insisted Vargas, following along. "We can, and we're going to," said Mark, "because this is our best insurance that Flores won't get word of what we've done at least until we're halfway back to Rio. We'll leave them enough food and water to last until the *Felicidad* comes up on its regular visit nine days from now. By that time the *Lanfranc* will have sailed with us on it. Go find another pitcher to leave them, and get some food. Not too much— I don't want them to die in the next nine days but I don't want them to be too happy to be alive either."

Vargas hesitated, a dubious look on his face.

"Look, Manuel," said Mark, "it was probably not too smart of me to shoot El Barbadiano, although I really can't say I'm sorry I did it—"

"No, no, you were right to do it. And it was right to free the Indians. But I don't want these men's lives on my conscience, despicable as they are . . ."

"If they die, they'll be on *my* conscience. Now go get them some food."

He started off to carry the pitcher back to the *cepo* as Manuel went to the headquarters building to carry out his assignment. The center seemed eerily deserted now, even the houseboys having fled into the jungle when they saw what had happened. In ten minutes Mark and Vargas had deposited food and water in the *cepo* for the guards, after which they hurried to the pier. Pepe and Arrube had managed to fire the boiler of the launch. Now Mark instructed them to put Arrube's canoe on the larger boat and to shove off, which they did. As the antique launch headed into the river, the four men watched the collection center recede. After the shouting and the gunshots and the excitement, the chugging of the launch's engine seemed quietly peaceful.

"I've never killed a man," Mark said thoughtfully as he leaned on the rail. "Now I've killed two."

"Were you afraid?" asked Pepe, eyeing the American with a new-found respect.

"I was scared to death," Mark told him, and smiled.

"As was I," Vargas said, then added, "you know, ever since coming to this disgusting place, I have asked myself how Ruiz could have seen and been a part of what has been going on here without reacting to it in *some* fashion, to at least have done *something*. Yet he did nothing . . . and he had gone to the University!"

The trip down the Napo River was placid, even idyllic. The launch made four knots, and the current added two more to its speed, so they were making fairly good time. Mark quickly mastered the mechanics of the primitive engine and manned the helm, which was located aft, as Arrube positioned himself in the bow to watch for floating logs or debris, and Pepe rummaged around the boat. Vargas seated himself on the rear deck to draw the scenes that were still vivid in his memory: the *cepo*, El Barbadiano whipping the Indian and then killing him, the look on Ruiz's face as Mark shot his lieutenants. All felt an enormous, unspoken relief to be free of Oro Blanco.

But Pepe and Arrube presented a problem. Even if Mark's plan worked and Flores got no inkling of what had happened until the *Felicidad* made its regularly scheduled trip to Oro Blanco nine days hence, Pepe and Arrube would then be at Flores's mercy. They could not leave Iquitos as Mark and Manuel could, and once Ruiz was freed from the *cepo*, he would identify the two Indians to Flores, at which time both would be as good as dead. Mark had grown fond of the Indian boy who had risked so much in coming to him and whose courage had enabled him to see behind Flores's stage set. He did not intend to leave him to be killed. Thus, a half hour after they had left Oro Blanco, Mark came to a rather surprising decision.

Pepe, while looking around the boat, had come across six rifles and a box of ammunition. Mark showed him how to load the guns, figuring they well might be needed in case of further trouble. Now, as Pepe sat cross-legged on the deck cleaning the rifles with a cloth, Mark said, "How would you like to go to America?"

The boy looked up, confused.

"You and Arrube aren't going to be very popular in Iquitos after this. It occurred to me both of you might like to come to the United States, go to school there. I could make the arrangements and pay the bill . . ."

"But Arrube doesn't speak English, señor," interrupted Pepe. "Besides, he has a wife and three children."

"Well, perhaps we could make other arrangements for him. But how about you?"

Pepe thought a moment, then shook his head.

"Thank you, señor, but I wish to remain in Iquitos."

"But it's not going to be safe for you! And wouldn't you like to see the United States?"

Pepe looked embarrassed. "No, señor."

Mark felt more than a little frustrated. Vargas, who had been listening to this, said, "Mark, America is like another planet to Pepe. Your offer is most generous, but I can understand why Pepe would be afraid to accept it."

"There's no reason for him to be afraid. I'd look after him . . ."

"For how long? The rest of his life?"

Mark considered this, admitting to himself there were practical difficulties.

"Then what are we going to do?"

"I know a wealthy couple outside Rio that has taken an interest in Indian education. They have begun a private school on their ranch for children Pepe's age, and I am sure they would enroll him. What would you say to that, Pepe? Brazil is not as far away as America."

Pepe considered this. "Thank you, señor," he finally said. "I will think about it, please."

Mark decided Pepe definitely had a mind of his own.

Finding a shaded, secluded inlet, they left the river and tied the launch to a tree at two o'clock to go ashore for lunch. As Arrube speared some fish from the river bank, Mark and Vargas collected wood for a fire. They cooked the fish, which was excellent, and washed it down with coffee Pepe had found on the launch and Mark had brewed. After the meal, Pepe and Arrube wandered back to the river bank as Mark and Vargas sat by the small fire they had built and had a second cup of coffee. The inlet, screened as it was from the river by a line of trees and jungle growth, was pleasantly cool, and Mark was feeling relaxed for the first time since they had set out for Oro Blanco. After a while, Vargas said, "I wonder if Pepe is right after all?"

"What do you mean?"

"I wonder if my sketches will make enough public outrage to make Flores stop what he has been doing. Does anyone really care what happens to the Indians? You will go back to America and continue the manufacture of tires. The world will go on buying your tires, as before, whether there is blood in the rubber or not. So perhaps we have been wasting our time . . ."

Mark considered this, then shook his head. "No, now I think you're being too pessimistic. I think the sketches will do a job and at least get rid of Flores."

"I hope you are right."

"And even if this doesn't change the system, the plantations the British have started in Malaya will. This whole set-up down here isn't only cruel—it's inefficient and outmoded. Getting the rubber from wild trees is crazy—no one can depend on the supply and so the prices on the London Exchange fluctuate so much they bring in the speculators. . . . It's a rotten system from bottom to top, and it's just a matter of time before it goes under anyway. I hope we've done our part to push it along."

"But there will always be others such as Flores, won't there? A strong man exploiting the weak and helpless?"

"Isn't that part of human nature?"

"Perhaps," replied Vargas. "But I should like to think a society could be built—like the Incan society—where men behaved as real brothers."

"A socialist society?"

"Perhaps. At least socialism curbs man's greed."

Mark sipped his coffee. "Does it? I wonder. It's easy to make capitalism out as a bad and cruel system when it's run by animals like Flores and Ruiz. And it's easy to blame poverty on the rich, and weakness on the strong. But I doubt either socialism or communism would get rid of greed or the strong exploiting the weak. Politicians and bureaucrats are just as greedy for power as businessmen are for money. The only difference I can see is that politicians and bureaucrats don't give the public much return on their money. At least I give the public a product—and a damn good one—"

Suddenly he saw Pepe and Arrube running down the river bank to the entrance of the inlet, then heading toward them. "Put out the fire!" called Pepe. "A boat comes up the river. It looks like the *Felicidad!*" Mark quickly kicked dirt on the fire, hastily trying to smother it. Then the four hurried onto the launch and went to the port side to watch the river through the protecting trees and undergrowth that separated the inlet from the main stream.

"If it *is* them, what are they doing up here now?" said Vargas, dropping his voice to a near whisper.

"Who knows," Mark whispered back, "unless somehow Flores got word about us. . . ."

They watched through the trees as the trim white bow of the *Felicidad* appeared, moving rapidly from right to left upstream. The *Felicidad* was some fifty feet in overall length, and there were a half dozen men on the deck, most carrying rifles. A few sat on the deck, leaning against the cabin, dozing; others were leaning over the rail staring at the passing jungle.

"If you believe in God," mumbled Vargas, "send Him a message not to let them see us."

"Not a bad idea," whispered Mark. The ship was gliding by quietly and smoothly, the chugging of the engine echoing lazily off the trees lining the river. The two white men and the two Indians waited.

"I think they missed us," Mark said.

Just as the stern of the boat was passing out of sight to the left, one of the men leaning on the rail straightened and pointed in their direction. The boat was out of sight before anyone could tell what was happening, but the four froze, listening for any change in the sound of the boat's engine. After a moment, it came.

"They're turning back," said Mark tensely. "They're going to take a look. Pepe and Arrube, get out of sight with your rifles, don't make any noise, don't fire unless they do first."

Pepe hurried to get the guns. The three of them, armed, stationed themselves out of sight as Mark went to the stern and ducked down behind the fantail bench to wait. In a few moments the bow of the *Felicidad*—and now Mark, peering through a space between two boards in the back of the seat, could see the name painted on the hull—reappeared in view, heading slowly toward the inlet. On the bow were crowded not only the men previously lolling on the deck, but Carlos Innocente Flores himself. He was waving at the wheelhouse now and yelling something. The engine stopped, and the boat glided silently toward the mouth of the inlet. Then as the bow entered the inlet, the engine backwatered, shuddering the boat to a near stop. The *Felicidad,* now fifteen feet from the stern of the launch, inched toward the smaller boat.

Flores yelled something in Spanish. Silence. Then he yelled in English. "Manning, I know you are aboard. I know why you have gone to Oro Blanco and why you have got my launch. Come out now, all of you. It will be your only choice."

Silence. Mark, crouched out of sight, quietly opened the metal box beneath the bench and lifted out two red sticks similar to the ones Ruiz had thrown at the crocodiles. He took a match from his pocket and lighted the wicks. He waited until the sputtering flame was halfway down to the dynamite, then stood and hurled both sticks with all his strength at the *Felicidad.* The men on the deck, momentarily surprised at Mark bobbing up, didn't get off their fire until he had ducked down again. Then as the two sticks bounced off the superstructure back onto the deck, there was yet another second as they stared at the dynamite, followed by one bang, then another, and a final ear-splitting explosion as the *Felicidad's* boiler blew up.

Pepe, Vargas, and Arrube waited nearly two minutes for the debris to stop dropping through the branches of the trees and for the smoke to clear. Then they emerged from their hiding places to join Mark at the stern and stare at the shattered wood and parts of bodies floating in the bloodied water.

"I imagine," said Vargas quietly, "that Señor Flores is presently having a fascinating conversation with God."

"Something tells me God's not very happy with Señor Flores," said Mark.

Pepe, thinking of his uncle, hoped he was right.

Mr. Baintree, the British consul in Iquitos, registered official shock when Mark told him of Flores's demise; unofficially he was delighted. He told Mark and Vargas to board the *Lanfranc,* which was sailing in three days, and say nothing. When the ship had left, he would officially inform the Peruvian Amazon Company that Señor Flores had died in an "unfortunate" boiler explosion and that he, Mr. Baintree, had received word that the manager of the Oro Blanco collection center was a prisoner in his own *cepo*. He would remain officially inscrutable as to how he had found all this out, but the Company, he told Mark, would be leaderless without Flores—he had made all decisions personally, refusing to delegate authority—and the Iquitos police force was something short of Scotland Yard standards of efficiency (besides, the police force, which consisted of two men, was still looking for Baron von Stimme, who had mysteriously disappeared a few days before, and Baintree was certain there was something "sticky" about that). By the time Jorge Ruiz would be able to tell the police that it was Mark who had imprisoned him, the *Lanfranc* would be at Manáos, where it would be up to the Peruvian government to get them back. By then, Mr. Baintree hoped that government would be sufficiently embarrassed by the publication of Vargas's sketches so as not to create more than a perfunctory stir.

Arrube returned to his wife and children, thanking Mark for his offer to send him elsewhere but insisting that he was not afraid to stay in Iquitos now that Flores was dead. Pepe, on the other hand, accepted Vargas's offer to place him in the Rio school. And, after bidding his parents good-bye and forcing himself into a suit Mark insisted on buying him (he was distinctly uncomfortable in European clothes and told Vargas and Mark he thought the white man had much to learn from the Indians about clothing fashions—to which they both laughingly agreed), he came aboard the *Lanfranc* the following morning to sail with Mark and Vargas to Belém. Mark had paid for a first-class cabin for him, and though Captain Wilson had been outraged at the idea of having a "savage" as a passenger on his ship, he was under too much nervous strain to put up more than a token fight—he was beginning to feel haunted by the ghost of "Baron" von Stimme. More to the point, he knew rumors were circulating among his crew that he had made it possible for Flores to take the German off the *Lanfranc,* and Captain Wilson was not looking forward to their return to Liverpool. If the Booth Line conducted an official investigation, Captain Wilson might find himself embarrassed to explain why Señor Flores had come to his cabin the very night Stimme had vanished.

The Captain decided it might be wise not to bank his 10,000 *soles* for a year or two. . . .

CHAPTER FOUR

(Article published in the New York *Herald,* October 6, 1907)

HAIL, THE CONQUERING HERO!

All the world loves a hero, and yesterday New York opened its heart to a new hero, Mr. Mark Manning, of Elkins, Ohio. The youthful Mr. Manning, who also looks the part, docked yesterday at Pier 12 on the *S.S. Southern Cross* from Belém, Brazil, and was met by a crowd of over two hundred people. For the past ten days newspapers all over the world have been headlining the story of Mr. Manning's daring exposé of the so-called Putumayo atrocities perpetrated by the management of the Peruvian Amazon Company of Iquitos, Peru, on its Indian rubber-gatherers at that company's rubber-gathering centers in the vicinity of the Putumayo River. At the risk of his own life, Mr. Manning, in the company of the Brazilian portrait painter Manuel Vargas, managed to penetrate the veil of secrecy the company had woven around its brutal policies and viewed what was actually going on in the Amazon jungle. His account, which was telegraphed to London ten days ago, was released to the British press, and Señor Vargas's sketches of the atrocities will be published this Sunday in the Rotogravure section of the *Herald.* All who have seen them report that the sketches are not only recordings of nightmare horrors reminiscent of the atrocities exposed in the Belgian Congo several years ago by Sir Roger Casement, but also genuine works of art, if "art" is a word that may be applied to such debased subject matter.

Prominent in the group meeting Mr. Manning at the dock were the Deputy Mayor; Sir Bruce and Lady Clark, Sir Bruce being a director of the British Imperial Rubber Company; Mr. Samuel Rosen, also of Elkins, Ohio, President of the Rosen Stove Company and a partner in Mr. Manning's own company, the Manning Rubber Company; Miss Charlotte Rosen, daughter of Mr. Rosen and a well-known figure in New York society; and Mr. Herschel Fine, senior partner of the underwriting firm of Herbert Fine & Co.

After greeting Mr. Manning, the party, led by the Deputy Mayor, drove to City Hall, where Mayor George B. McClellan officially greeted Mr. Manning in the name of all New Yorkers and presented the brave Ohio industrialist with the Key to the City. In a brief speech Mayor McClellan extolled Mr. Manning's courage, comparing his daring to that of none other than our own former Police Commissioner, who, of course, now sits in the White House. His Honor also read to the crowd gathered in front of City Hall congratulatory telegrams from President Roosevelt, His Majesty King Edward VII of Great Britain, and the British Prime Minister, Mr. Herbert Asquith, who has announced the formation of a Parliamentary Board of Enquiry to investigate the South American rubber industry, much of which is financed by British capital. Following this, the party retired to City Hall, where Mayor McClellan hosted a six-course luncheon catered by Louis Sherry.

Last evening, Mr. Manning addressed a gathering of the National Geographic Society, and tonight New York society will have the opportunity of honoring the young hero at a gala ball being given by Mr. Herschel Fine at his Fifth Avenue residence. This event will be covered by this newspaper's Society Editor, Mr. Hanson Mayberry, in tomorrow's editions.

Meanwhile, all New York continues to honor Mr. Manning, whose resourcefulness and courage are an inspiration to all Americans.

Mark was honest—and human—enough to admit that he enjoyed all of it: the gushy newspaper articles, the long-winded speeches, the telegrams, the attention. After the ceremony and lunch at City Hall, Sir Bruce Clark asked Mark to meet him at the men's bar of the Waldorf to give him his check for a well-earned personal loan of two and a half million dollars. While Mark was in Peru, Sir Bruce had married Amelia Sinclair, and they had just returned to New York from a honeymoon trip across the United States, during which he had stopped in Detroit, Chicago and St. Louis and talked to prospective investors in the Manning Rubber Company. He had succeeded in raising the other two and a half million from Elmo Tilden, the successful father of the Tillmobile, one of the fastest-selling automobiles of the day; Ronald Gerstenmeier, the Chicago trucker, who knew and liked Mark and his company; Percival Hutchins, the president of a large Midwest railroad; Raymond Margate, a New England insurance baron; and finally, to Mark's surprise, none other than Frank Bennet, whose bad cold and indiscreet use of a Detroit bordello had in a sense helped launch the Manning Rubber Company. "My God, I never thought *he'd* invest in my company," Mark said.

"Why not? He spoke very highly of you. He says you make the best tires in America and your company is the best in the business."

"And he's one of my best customers, but the way that was managed is another story."

"Maybe so, laddie, but he must think well enough of you and your company to invest a half million dollars in it. You're a rich man now. How does it feel?"

"Rich?" He laughed. "I owe your bank two and a half million dollars plus interest!"

"Ah, but Mark," said the Scot, rolling the *r* in Mark, "ye'll find that the secret of becoming rich is to go in debt—much as it hurts my Scottish heart to admit it. Once you've suckered the rich into loaning you enough money, they have to make you rich to protect their investment and get their money back. My bank has taken a two and a half million dollar gamble on *you,* and they're not about to let you slip through their fingers and go broke. So, as I say, you're rich, laddie. Now tell me, how does it feel?"

Mark thought about it a moment. "Well," he said, "I'd be a hypocrite if I said it didn't feel damn good."

"A hypocrite? You'd be a damned fool!"

Mark Manning not only had won the brass ring, he won the girl as well, because Charlotte lost no time in confirming to him that she would adore being Mrs. Mark Manning. She also warned him that Sam was far from happy about the marriage, but she took care not to tell him about Sam's threat. That was up to Sam after the three of them returned to Charlotte's suite in the Waldorf following Mark's address to the National Geographic Society.

"Well, Mark," Sam said as Mark and Charlotte sat down on a sofa in the lavender living room, "you're a good businessman and a smart one, and for that I don't regret having backed you and the company. I'll also admit you did a brave if foolhardy thing, and I approve the investors Sir Bruce has brought in. But Mark, I warn you, if you marry Charlotte, you make an enemy of me."

"So I hear," replied Mark as Charlotte took his hand. "And I'm sorry you feel that way. Don't you think you're being a little narrow-minded?"

"It's true, I think it wrong for Charlotte to marry a Gentile. But I also believe you are marrying Charlotte to get your hands on my stock in Manning Rubber."

Mark glanced at Charlotte, who said nothing.

"You know I don't play with words," continued Sam, putting his hands in his pockets, "so I will say it clear and direct: if you marry Charlotte—which I cannot prevent you from doing—I shall rewrite my will and leave all my Manning stock to either a charity or to Temple Emmanuel here in New York. I thought," he added, "that you would want to know."

Charlotte nervously watched Mark's face. It was stony. After a moment he said, "Sam, I owe you a lot, and I appreciate what you've done for me. But I happen to love Charlotte. As far as I'm concerned, you can throw your damn Manning stock off the top of the Flatiron Building."

Charlotte let out a little whoop of glee and threw her arms around Mark. "Oh, darling, *thank* you for saying that! See, father? I told you he'd tell you to go to hell, and he did! And frankly, I think you deserve a good kick in the pants for being so mean."

Sam's skull-like face turned glacial.

"Some day, Charlotte," he said curtly, "you're going to wish you had listened to me." Then he turned and walked out of the room.

"He'll get over it," said Charlotte. "Don't worry. And he's not going to rewrite his will, either. He told me he was going to do this, and now that it's out of his system he'll see how silly he's acting. I know father."

"I hope you're right."

"Oh, but darling, you look so grim! Now don't make me think you're after poppa's stock after all!"

"I'm after *you*, Charlotte. But I also hate to lose poppa's stock, which could mean losing control of my company someday. Anyway"— he smiled and took her hand—"I'm just glad to be back and alive. By the way, I missed you."

"Oh, and how I missed you! And Mark, I'm so very proud of you. You did such a marvelous thing down there, and even though I didn't want you to go, I admit I'm glad you did now."

"By the way"—he pulled a small Tiffany box from his jacket pocket and handed it to her—"I bought you something this afternoon." Her eyes sparkled as she opened the box to reveal a small sapphire-and-diamond engagement ring.

"It's beautiful," she said.

"It's not exactly the Hope Diamond, but at least it's the real McCoy. Here, let me put it on."

He slipped the ring on her finger, then took her in his arms and kissed her. "Hello, wife," he whispered.

"Hello, husband," she answered, and after a moment said, "Mark, let's promise we'll always be faithful to each other."

"I promise, darling."

"And no more visiting your shady ladies?"

He released her and looked at her suspiciously. "Why do you say that?"

"Let's say I have my spies." She smiled.

"Name of Sam Rosen, no doubt. Well, I admit nothing, but I promise, anyway."

"In that case, you may kiss me again, knowing that I have purified your soul and uplifted your character, which was surely in dire need of uplift."

"If there's anything I hate," he said, bringing his mouth to hers, "it's a reforming woman . . ."

He was making light of it, but she fully intended to make him keep his word.

PART

IV

DEATH OF A WOBBLY

1913

CHAPTER ONE

B Y THE second decade of the twentieth century America's love affair with the automobile was in the first hot flush of passion. In
1910 car production was 89,110 vehicles; in five years this would multiply tenfold. Nineteen hundred and twelve saw a production of 356,000
cars, bringing total automobile registration to 1,250,000. By 1915, the
automobile industry, which had been nonexistent twenty years before,
was producing 880,480 cars valued at $691,778,000 It was one of the
most phenomenal spurts of economic growth in history, and the effect
on the public mind was jolting. A whole new type of transportation
had been developed, for the motor vehicle was the first free-ranging
form of inland transportation not tied to rails or to rivers—discount-
ing, that is, the faithful horse. The remoteness of America was to
be conquered, and economic and social isolation were beginning to
vanish. Farmers could, for the first time, get their products to market
with ease as well as bring the market's products to their farms. The
death knell of rural America was, if anything, the chugging of the
Tin Lizzie.

Culturally, America was still in Europe's shadow. But America
was maturing fast, and even in the Teens the Liberated Woman was
emerging as a new force in society. If sex were still a taboo, it was
becoming less so, and the young were straining the seams of Victorian
prudery.

All this the movies, which were just beginning to win their mass
audience, would exploit and encourage as Hollywood created its dream
factory that would open up the last American frontier, the imagination. For at the same time the car was introducing the public to the
intoxication of speed, the movies were introducing the intoxication
of living in a fantasy world of adventure and romance. But the movies
were still young—the automobile was king. Automobiles were exciting,
and they were making fortunes for men such as Mark Manning who

had been lucky or quick-witted enough to get in on the ground floor.

Mark was, indeed, rich now, growing richer at a rate that surprised even him. The acquisition of money might have seemed vulgar or immoral to those born with it, but to those born without it, like Mark and Sir Bruce Clark, the piling up of wealth could be almost sensually gratifying, and Mark experienced a special satisfaction when, one morning in 1911, he repaid to Sir Bruce's bank the last installment on the two-and-a-half-million-dollar loan, which he had used to buy stock in his own company, thereby leaving him debt free and a genuine millionaire. By 1913, such was the phenomenal growth of the Manning Rubber Company, Mark was worth close to four million dollars; and though this was the year the income tax was born, the rates were still so low and the purchasing power of the dollar so high that being a millionaire meant being rich.

Mark's fortune was based on his twenty-two percent of the preferred stock of the company and his ten percent of the common. By 1912, the five million that had been invested five years earlier had tripled in value; and Mark, wishing to raise ten million dollars for further expansion, had little difficulty talking the board of directors into "going public."

Herschel Fine had been so impressed by Mark's performance in Peru, as well as the dazzling success of his company, that he overcame his scruples about Riley Baker and agreed to handle the underwriting. He formed a new Ohio corporation that bought out all the shares in the old West Virginia corporation; new preferred stock was issued to Mark, Sam, Riley Baker, Frank Bennet, Elmo Tilden, Ronald Gerstenmeier, Percival Hutchins and Raymond Margate—the previous investors (all of whom were directors). The pie of preferred stock ended up being sliced: Mark, twenty-two percent; Sam, sixteen percent; Baker (who had exercised his stock options—thus increasing his position—but who had otherwise remained surprisingly docile) twelve percent; the other five, ten percent each. Then 100,000 shares of common stock were issued at one hundred dollars par, and the offering was gobbled up by an eager public, which sent the price on the New York Exchange to one hundred twelve in three weeks. Mark went back into debt by borrowing another million dollars, which he used to buy 10,000 shares of the common; he had found that one of the sweetest dividends of being rich was the ability to borrow money with little or no difficulty. There was no fear that actual control of the corporation would pass out of·the preferred stockholders' hands, for between them the directors owned fifty percent of the entire corporation. And Mark had no fear of losing control of the directors. Most of them liked him and trusted his judgment. Riley Baker was still no problem, and even Sam—though his hostility toward his son-in-law, far from dissipating, had increased with the years to the point where they hardly spoke—even Sam consistently voted for Mark's policies.

So by 1913 Mark was in undisputed control of the company he had started eight years before on a comparative shoestring.

He recognized her immediately, though it had been thirteen years since he had seen her.

He had been in Cleveland on business and had gone into a downtown lunch counter for a sandwich when he saw the still attractive woman in the plain summer suit seated at a table with a red-haired, thirteen-year-old boy. They were both sipping sarsaparillas as Mark came up to the woman and extended his hand.

"Hello, Sheila," he said rather tentatively, not expecting a gush of enthusiastic warmth from his bedmate of thirteen years past. She looked up, astonished to see the red-haired man in the Panama suit. Then hostility and apprehension filled her eyes as she glanced quickly at the boy sitting beside her and back to Mark, silently asking Mark not to let the boy know.

Sheila Farr then nodded and said only, "Hello."

Mark withdrew his unshaken hand and continued, "It's been a long time, hasn't it?"

She didn't reply. Instead she said to the boy, "Roger, this is a gentleman from my home town—Mr. Manning."

The boy stood up and turned a sensitive, highly intelligent and freckled face to his unknown father. The noticeable resemblance between the older freckled face and his own had the boy momentarily wondering if this possibly were a relative—red hair *that* color was, after all, rare. He held out his hand. "How do you do, sir," he said gravely.

"How do you do, Roger. Mind if I join you?"

"We're about to leave—" Sheila said hastily, but Mark had already taken the third wire-backed chair at the table, placing his straw hat on the empty fourth one. He smiled pleasantly at the mother of his bastard son, noticing the gold wedding band on her finger.

"It's a real pleasure to see you again, Sheila. You're living in Cleveland now?"

"Yes."

Mark maintained his smile but turned to the boy as possibly a readier source of information. He was enormously curious. "And do you like Cleveland, Roger?"

"It's all right, I guess. I like the lake. Are you the Mr. Manning that owns that Manning Rubber Company?"

"That's right."

The boy looked impressed. "I've read about you in the papers."

"I hope it was flattering."

"Oh, it was, sir."

"Well, it depends on what papers you read—"

"You're married now, aren't you?" interrupted Sheila.

"That's right. I married Charlotte Rosen. You remember her?" And as he asked, he thought of that day on the way to Matahoochi Park when Sheila had made him the bet that he would never make love to Charlotte.

"I could hardly forget her," was the flat reply. "Did you convert, or did she?"

"We both stayed where we were. We're raising the kids in her faith, though."

"Oh? You have children?"

"Four." Five counting this one, he thought. "When they're old enough, they can make up their own minds about what they want to be. They no doubt will anyway, but we thought that was the sensible solution."

"And maybe they'll turn out to be nothing. Children can get that way if their home life is too confused . . . Don't you agree, Mr. Manning?"

"Oh, I agree. But life is confusing, and you can't protect children from that, can you? What does your father do?" he said to Roger.

There was a silence as the boy looked at his mother. Then Sheila said, "My husband is a high-school teacher. He teaches English. Last week he had a heart attack. Roger and I've just come from the hospital."

"I'm very sorry to hear it. I hope it's not serious."

"It's serious enough. Harter's quite a bit older than I—he's fifty-nine—and he had one a couple of years ago. We're worried, naturally."

"The doctors say he'll be all right, though," Roger said with the cheerfulness learned from hours in the hospital waiting room listening to the lies of doctors and nurses. "Didn't they, mom?"

"He may be all right, and he may not," Sheila said with an honesty Mark admired.

"How long have you been married to Harter?" asked Mark.

Again she gave him a "be careful" look with her eyes. "Eleven years. Harter Boine is a fine man and he's been a good father to Roger. As you may or may not remember, Roger's father died when Roger was only six months old."

"Yes, I do remember."

"Did you know my real father?' asked Roger eagerly.

"Not too well. But I believe he was a good man too." He looked at Sheila, who gave him a sour look in return.

"He was a prince," she said, standing up. "Come on, Roger, we have to get home."

The boy reluctantly got to his feet, obviously wanting to stay with Mark, who fascinated him. The idea that his mother actually knew an important man like Mark Manning . . .

"Do we have to go right *now*, mom?"

She took his left hand. "Yes. Say good-bye to Mr. Manning."

The boy stuck out his right hand. "Good-bye, sir."

Mark shook his son's hand, feeling guilt, curiosity and paternal pride as he looked at his handsome and intelligent offspring.

"I hope it's not good-bye, Roger. I hope we can see more of each other. Maybe your mother will bring you down to Elkins one day and—"

"Come on, Roger," Sheila said, jerking him away from the table toward the cash register. She paid the bill, then took her son outside and started with him toward the trolley stop.

"Why wouldn't you let us stay and talk to him a while?" Roger said. "He seemed like a nice man."

"He is *not*."

"Why?"

"Just take my word for it—he's not."

"But he *seemed* nice," persisted the boy, "and the papers say he has one of the best-run businesses in Ohio—"

"The papers say that because he hires a man to take a lot of editors out to dinner so they'll say all those nice things about him."

Roger frowned. "Well, I still wish we could have stayed a little while longer. He seemed pretty nice to me. . . . What did you mean when you said my father was a prince?"

They had stopped at the corner where a streetcar was approaching, its bell dinging merrily.

"Just that—he was a prince, a wonderful man."

A son of a bitch, she thought.

They came from the back reaches of the Austro-Hungarian Empire. They came from Holland, Ireland and Italy. They came from the hills of West Virginia, where hiring agents sent out by the labor-hungry rubber companies lured the poverty-stricken hillbillies with promises of high wages instead of trinkets as was the case with Flores's Peruvian Indians. The word "Akron" was mispronounced in Zagreb and Budapest, but "money" and "boom" were words understood throughout the world as fortune-seeking workers streamed into the Ohio city where the stench from the rubber factories was ignored by men enraptured by the sweet smell of four dollars a day. Akron almost overnight was turned into a Midwestern boom town, as was its satellite, Elkins. Bars and boarding houses sprang up to service the flood of rubber workers, strapping men who needed their muscles for the back-breaking work in the curing pits; hard-drinking men who drowned the soapstone stench of the factory in the beer-and-whiskey aroma of the bar. "Hunyaks," "hunkies," "red necks," "wops"—racial epithets flew, tempers flared and the inevitable bar fights sent Elkins's murder rate soaring from zero in 1900 to twenty-seven in 1912. No one really cared. Money was flowing, and though the work was hard, everyone thought he was getting rich.

The rubber arrived at the Manning Number One plant on railroad cars in two-hundred-fifty-pound oblong blocks packed in jackets of woven straw matting or burlap. The big blocks were cut into smaller pieces by men wielding sharp knives, men trained to keep an eye out for the sticks and stones implanted in the wild rubber by the *seringueiros* to increase its weight. The small chunks were then thrown into a washing mill where forced streams of water removed the dirt. The resulting smooth sheet would be cut into lacy strips that would be hung in the huge dryers. The dry rubber went to the masticator, a mill that would knead and tear the rubber to make it softer and more plastic. Finally the masticated rubber went to the storage room to wait for its transformation into the hundreds of rubber products the Manning plants were now producing—including heels, galoshes, contraceptives, baby nipples, girdles.

But eighty percent of it became tires.

Most people had the vague notion that rubber was poured into molds which were cooked to produce the tires, much the way that, in the adjacent No. Two plant, the steel was poured into molds to make the tire rims. The truth was that the tires were built, and the process required brain as well as brawn. The rubber to be turned into tires was taken from the storage room into the compound room, where the compounder would weigh it and the pigments required for the batch; it would then go to the mill room, where it would be thrown into a rumbling mill. Two rolls, one slower than the other, would shriek the rubber into a smooth sheet as a millman poured in the heated oils and melted waxes that were used as softeners—and then the dry powders, mostly sulphur, which were the tougheners—a tire made only of pure rubber would be useless. With the powders mixed in, the millman would slash the rubber with a knife to insure a uniform mixture; finally he would cut the sheets into slabs for the next step in the process, which involved the big mixer. In later years a giant mixer called the Banbury would be developed, high as a three-story house. But for then the mixer was big enough and its primary purpose was the addition of carbon black, the essential toughening ingredient. When the rubber emerged from the mixer it would be cut on the bias into plies the exact length of a tire circumference, and these plies would go to the tire builder. (In 1916, the discovery that cotton cording—and, later, nylon cording—could be introduced into the rubber as a further strengthener would add another step to the process: a calender mill that would press treated rubber onto sheets of rubber-dipped cord.)

While the rubber was being prepared for the tire builder, the tire foundation was being made in the bead room; the bead was essentially a hoop of steel wire coated with rubber. The beads and the plies would converge at the tire builder, and here the most skilled (and highly paid) man in the factory would create the tire. Formerly this process had had to be done mainly by hand alone. But at the beginning of 1913 a tire-building machine was introduced, which would make the process simpler and, at the same time, cause a major strike. The machine was a revolving collapsible steel drum that the tire builder would operate with foot pedals. He would cement the plies onto the revolving drum one ply at a time, each ply having to be fitted exactly, the final ply stretched over the bead. Next the tread would be put on; finally, the sidewalls. Then the bead would be trimmed with a knife and the drum collapsed. The tire would be pulled off the drum, but it would look more like a rubber barrel than a tire. The whole process was supposed to take no more than four minutes—the requirement that would provoke a strike.

The "green" tire would now move on hooks attached to a moving belt from the tire builder to the curing pit, which was considered the inferno of the factory. It was a hissing, roaring hot hell of a place where rows of molds were kept at temperatures ranging from two hundred thirty to two hundred ninety degrees. The pitmen were the giants of the business—strength was the prerequisite for the job, and stamina was necessary to withstand the heat and the stench—not to mention the dust of the soapstone used to keep the rubber from sticking that was everywhere in the factory. The pitmen would work several pots, or molds, in turn, putting a tire in one, locking it, watching the temperature as he opened the next to take out a cooked tire and hang it on the moving hook. The curing of the tires in the molds was the vulcanization. Air bags would go inside the tire and steam would fill the bags, pushing the rubber into the tread design on the inside of the mold and curing it. When this waffle-iron operation was finished, the tire actually looked like a tire. From the pit to final inspection was, after the fireworks of Dante, a peaceful anticlimax.

It was hard work, stinking and dangerous work. Many hands were caught in the mill rollers, pulling in the arm and, in some cases, the whole body. Fingers were cut off by the flying bias-cutting knives. Heart attacks were induced by the heat of the pit, and no one was sure what the soapstone dust—called "snow" by the men—did to the lungs. But most of the Manning workers agreed that the two new factories opened in 1909 on the site of the old Madison farm by the Matahoochi River were a vast improvement over the rubber factories in Akron. Not only were the buildings airy and light and as well ventilated as rubber factories of the day could be with only their giant fans; the buildings themselves, designed by a young Cleveland architect Mark had discovered named Bill Bixby (with Mark's seemingly unending design alterations), were handsome—and this in a day when the average factory was not far removed from the Gothic horrors of Dickens's England. The structures had clean, pleasing lines and were surrounded by handsome landscaping, and the parking lot, the cafeteria (where the food actually was good), the infirmary and the overall cleanliness of the place were all considered enlightened innovations by even Mark's most hostile critics. More impressive to industry men was the research lab, which constituted an entire, separate wing. Here Mark had installed the latest chemical equipment, sparing no expense, and he had put the young chemist he had found in Akron in charge of the place, giving him a free hand. The chemist, whose name was Melville Benny and who was only twenty-eight,

could hardly believe such an open-handed policy from a manufacturer, most of whom then regarded research as a waste of time
and money. Mark considered it anything but a waste. A salesman at
heart, he knew every step forward, every breakthrough in the manufacturing process, would mean a sales gimmick that would give him
the edge over his lupine competitors. The money he spent for research
was an investment in the future. The only thing he wanted, he told
Melville as he gave him the keys to the lab, was "to be surprised."

The surprises began to come out of Melville Benny's lab even
sooner than Mark had hoped. Melville was an innovator, and he had,
like Mark, the instinct for serendipity which, after all, was at least
partially the result of having a good sniffer. Melville quickly sniffed
out and stumbled on an improved accelerator, a coal-tar derivative,
which, when added to the rubber, hastened the process of vulcanization. This improvement alone more than justified the money spent
on the lab, but Melville was to produce much more in the years to
come. The young chemist, who neither smoked nor drank, was stringbean thin and seemed terrified of women, but, in his specialty, Mark
was sure, he was a winner.

By 1910, at thirty-two, Mark had become the *Wunderkind* of the
rubber industry, a reputation begun three years before after his return from Peru. An impatient skeptic born poor, he had little regard
for tradition, which, in a tradition-bound age, was one of his greatest
assets. His early forays into the trucking business, which were breaks
with tradition, were now paying golden dividends. As trucking
boomed, Manning Rubber's truck-tire division, with its head start,
took a booming position in the business (having the owner of the
Gerstenmeier Truck Company on the board of directors didn't hurt,
of course; Gerstenmeier bought his tires exclusively from Manning).
Nonskid tires, multi-plies, wider treads were all innovations, and
what Mark didn't initiate he quickly imitated, not giving a damn
about his competitors' howls and, in a few cases, patent-infringement
suits. In 1911 he introduced the Manning Jaguar, a nonskid tire,
which Mark backed with a million-dollar advertising campaign built
around the logo of a running jaguar, an idea he decided must have
germinated in Peru. The tire was excellent, but the sales pitch, with
its overtones of speed and ruggedness, was doubtless what made the
tire one of the fastest-selling items on the market. It sold in the
hundreds of thousands and made the company millions. To sell it,
Mark now had more than two hundred dealerships throughout the
United States and Canada, and in 1913 he granted franchises in
Mexico City, Havana, Rio, London, Paris and Berlin. As his products

sold all over the world, as the profits poured back into Elkins swelling
his personal fortune, he had ample reason to conclude that life was
indeed sweet and it was a very good time to be alive.

For those who labored essentially by the sweat of their brow, life
was less sweet and the times were becoming increasingly out of joint.
The unions were in their adolescence, beginning to feel their strength
but still far removed from the clout of their maturity. The mentality
of management was overwhelmingly antiunion, and in this regard
Mark was one-hundred percent management—he despised even the
idea of unions. The company was his, he would control it and he
would brook no interference from what he called the union "sons
of bitches." On the other hand, he did not share the prevailing
management contempt for labor. To the contrary, he went to what
were then considered quasirevolutionary lengths to keep his labor
force of more than five thousand men happy, or at least content. He
paid top wages. More than this, he encouraged his men to buy
shares in the company, arranging a voluntary withholding system from
their pay checks for the purchase of Manning common stock. His
health-care plan was revolutionary and one of the best—as well as
the first—in the industry. In 1912 he bought a two-hundred-acre tract
of land a half mile from Number One and Number Two plants, then
again used architect Bill Bixby, this time to lay out the land in a
pleasant development with half-acre building lots, which he offered
to his employees for two hundred dollars per lot, fifty dollars cash
down and the rest on no-interest time payments. He arranged favorable mortgage rates for Manning employees to build their houses on
the lots, accomplishing this by threatening instant withdrawal of his
company deposits from Akron and Cleveland banks unless they complied. They complied. His pension fund was adequate for the times,
but the efforts he expended on keeping his men happy and his factories relatively clean and pleasant places to work placed him far
ahead of the times.

Most of his workers appreciated these efforts and though there
was the normal amount of grumbling in the factories, Mark was
considered a popular employer. The unions, however, were frustrated by his corporate paternalism; they were having enough trouble
organizing the industry without having so-called enlightened bosses
steal their thunder. In particular, the Industrial Workers of the
World—or the Wobblies, as they were called—hated Mark. The Wobblies were considered the most radical of all the unions and were
even disliked by other unions such as the American Federation of
Labor because they made their organizing appeal to unskilled labor,

which the more exclusive craft unions felt would dilute and impede their own efforts. They had already locked horns with the A.F. of L. at the Firestone plant in Akron when Firestone introduced its new tire-building machine and quietly posted new "speed-up" rates. The reaction had been anything but quiet—the workers complaining they couldn't keep up with the new tire-building schedules and walking out on strike. The Wobblies staged a protest at the factory gates and a general strike was on, the first full-fledged attempt to unionize the rubber industry since the abortive A.F. of L. try in 1902. The A.F. of L. immediately sent its men in to steal the show away from the Wobblies; the resulting internecine union war had weakened the strike effort, which finally had been settled by the management without the unions' participation.

The Wobblies were even weaker at the Manning plants, where the union's sole representative was a rather strange thirty-two-year-old tire builder named Bill Sands. Sands was a wiry man whose slight stature belied his considerable physical strength. He had hair the same color as his name, and a not unpleasant face, though his nose was slightly askew and his eyes, according to many of this co-workers, had a "crazy" look to them. Sands was the son of a Michigan farmer-politician who had been more successful siring children than getting elected to public office. The elder Sands had had fourteen children, of which litter Bill was the runt; and since the father had managed to be elected mayor of his small town only once, the rest of his life being forced to eke out a precarious existence from his farm, money had been too tight to send any of the children to college. Mr. Sands was undaunted by his lack of funds, however, and proceeded to educate his brood himself, joking that there were so many of them they made up a small college by themselves. Mr. Sands, who was widely read, raised his sons up on a heady diet of political philosophers and novelists, mixing in Hegel and Marx with Thackeray and Dickens, so that by the time Bill reached maturity he was far better read than most of his contemporaries but his view of the world tended to be rather lopsided and impractical, though people did admit he was precocious. He played the flute—unusual instrument for a male—well and had a natural flair for cartooning, making more than a few enemies in his home town by circulating caricatures of some of the more pompous locals. He also loved roughing it and would vanish for weeks at a time in the Michigan woods, living off the land—he was an excellent shot—and, as he put it, "communing with nature." None of this was much use for making a living, and after drifting from odd job to odd job through most of his twenties he finally made his way to Elkins, where he got a job in the Manning plants and rapidly worked his way up to the position of tire builder.

In 1910 he attended a Wobbly organizational meeting in Akron, liked what he heard and joined, volunteering to take over the organization of the Manning plants. The Wobbly leaders were skeptical about him but they had no one in Elkins and his enthusiasm was undeniable. Sands had turned out to be a dubious choice. He was not popular with the workers. He was unmarried and apparently not interested in women, and though no one ever doubted the wiry little man's virility, he was definitely not one of the boys. He tried—he would go drinking with them at the local bars but he didn't hold his liquor well and would pass out early in the evening. Before that, he would antagonize everyone by trying to drag them into discussions of Marxian dialectics, which was not the most popular of drinking topics, or he would pull out his silver flute he'd inherited from his Scottish grandmother (it was the *only* thing he had inherited) and start playing Handel sonatas. Neither his talk nor his music was calculated to make him acceptable to the bar faithfuls and he quickly became labeled "Crazy Bill." After three years, Crazy Bill had converted less than a dozen men to the cause.

On the other hand, he did start a small weekly paper that delighted the town. He badgered the Wobbly leadership into buying him a broken-down hand-operated press, which he installed in his garage, and he began turning out, single-handedly and at his own expense, a two-page sheet called the *Sting*. The *Sting* stang. Wisely eschewing dull polemics, Sands used his talents for cartooning and lampooning to take jabs at the Manning management, his favorite targets being Harold Swenson, the Swede who was now Mark's number-two man and executive vice-president of the company, and Jim Malloy, the former Detroit bank guard whom Mark had hired to run his security force. Crazy Bill invented a mythical factory called the Miracle B-B Gun Company and staffed it with mythical executives whom everyone immediately recognized. Harold Swenson, who had a well-known mania for efficiency and who was always touring the plants with a stopwatch trying to shave seconds off every operation, became, in the B-B Gun factory, Mr. Stopwatch, who would appear in the men's room and stand behind the men at the latrine asking "if they please couldn't shave a few seconds off this operation." Crude, but the workers loved it. Nor was Crazy Bill above ethnic humor, knowing that the many immigrants in the plants enjoyed this form of ribbing (as long as it wasn't directed against them); so that

Mr. Stopwatch always spoke in a Swedish accent, and his favorite word was smorgasbord. Jim Malloy, the head cop, became Mr. Ugly; and when Mr. Ugly wasn't prowling around the B-B Gun factory in ludicrous disguises, spying on the employees (it was well known Malloy had at least a dozen spies planted in the factories who kept him informed of what was going on), he was standing in front of a mirror squeezing blackheads, which, in fact, was one of Malloy's favorite pastimes.

With telling accuracy, Crazy Bill had hit on the two most sensitive areas of both these gentlemen. Harold Swenson was sensitive about his Swedish accent, and Jim Malloy about his remarkably ugly face and bad skin. Since neither had the faintest trace of a sense of humor, they both began a campaign with Mark either to force the *Sting* to close down or to fire Bill Sands—or both. Crazy Bill had avoided lampooning Mark, not only because he knew he was popular, but also because he hadn't been able to get a bead on Mark's exploitable weakness. So Mark secretly enjoyed the *Sting* and would take a copy home and roar with laughter at Sands' gibes. Mark also knew that the *Sting* was a valuable safety valve, and that it was better to let the *Sting* take the sting out of whatever gripes his work force might have against management than to suppress it, which would only serve to make Crazy Bill something of a martyr. So he protected Sands, and no matter how vehemently Swenson and Malloy would attack the man, Mark would just as vehemently refuse to do anything about him.

Which was the potentially explosive situation when, in the fall of 1912, Mark and Charlotte decided to build their dream house.

CHAPTER TWO

He had become a millionaire, but during the first five years of his marriage he had not lived like one. He and Charlotte had occupied a roomy but unpretentious white clapboard house on the same street as old Sam's Victorian mansion, a house for which Mark had paid twenty-nine thousand dollars a month after the wedding. It had two parlors, a study, a dining room and kitchen on the ground floor, and six bedrooms and three baths on the second and third floors, all of which were needed when Charlotte began bearing

what for a time became her annual baby. Making up with a venge-
ance for the unproductiveness of her first marriage, she bore a son,
David, in 1909. In 1910 came Ellen; in 1911, Richard; and 1912 saw
the birth of the fourth Manning child, yet a third boy, whom Mark
named Christopher. David, Ellen, Richard and Christopher were
all healthy, bawling babies, all of whom Charlotte and Mark doted
on. But by number four, Charlotte was growing weary of near-
constant pregnancy. She told Mark she wanted no more children,
to which he agreed. She had brought her Irish maid Stella to Elkins
with her, and Stella had become chief nursemaid and head of the
domestic staff, which by 1912 included three maids, a cook and a
full-time laundress—the last of whose skills were especially needed in
those pre-diaper-service days. Between the children, the staff, and
Mark and Charlotte, the house, roomy as it was, was overcrowded.

And so it was hardly surprising when one night in the spring of
1912, as they were finishing dinner, Charlotte said, "Mark, I think
we should build a house for the Manning brood."

He finished his hand-churned peach ice cream. "Do you get the
idea we're being pushed out of this one?"

"Definitely. Besides, I've always wanted to build a house of our
own. Why not now?"

He wiped his mouth, then put down his napkin. "I'll think about
it."

"But darling, what's there to think about? It's not as if we don't
have the money."

He laughed good-naturedly and allowed as how they might be
able to scrape up enough for a little bungalow, but in fact he had
been thinking himself about building a place for some time and
quickly now he and Charlotte began looking for a suitable building
site. They found it a week later: forty-five acres of lovely wooded
land three miles out of town overlooking the Matahoochi River.

Their dream house started out modestly enough but rapidly ballooned to palatial proportions as they both added on their most
private and longed-for desires. Mark, who in his new affluence had
become an oenophile, wanted a fine wine cellar. He also enjoyed
tennis and swimming, so courts and a pool were needed. Charlotte
had developed a fondness for gardening, so she wanted a greenhouse.
There also had to be a music room for her Bechstein, and she fought
strenuously for the inclusion of a pipe organ, a folly she had always
dreamed of but which Mark thought was a bit crazy, though he
finally gave in. They both wanted a big nursery for the children, and
Charlotte desired a ballroom, reminding her husband that he had

become an important man and she fully intended to entertain in a style befitting the wife of an important man. Mark gave in on this as well, because he fully realized that Charlotte missed the ambience and style of life in New York as a member of the Fine family.

Though he began to be apprehensive about the magnitude of the house that was forming in their imaginations, the planning of it was giving such pleasure to Charlotte that he continued to indulge her requests, though he sometimes thought of the Casa Encantada in Iquitos and wondered, with a slight chill, if he were about to emulate the late Señor Flores's *nouveaux* pretensions. Charlotte would not hear of engaging Bill Bixby, Mark's favorite architect. Rather she went to New York and retained one of the most fashionable architects in the east, a man named Franklin Riggs who had trained with Stanford White. Riggs drew up the plans and made the estimates, which came to a staggering total of more than $600,000. Mark gagged, but Charlotte pleaded with him for what had now become almost her obsession. Of course he gave in.

Construction, begun in May 1912, was not completed until the summer of the next year. No one could deny that the Mannings' new house was one of the most beautiful private homes in the entire Midwest. It was built of softly subdued rust brick in a style that was vaguely both Elizabethan and Jacobean but which gave the impression, however eclectic its design, of a warm, rambling, English country home. To begin with, the site was superb. Mark and Charlotte had found a truly beautiful spot, and the view westward over the river from the house's hundred-foot elevation was magnificent. The acreage was wooded and rolling, crisscrossed by charming gullies and soft knolls. The house was positioned at the end of a long drive, which was entered through the woods until a turn was rounded and the woods vanished to be replaced by a smooth lawn surrounding the house. If the light from the sun was soft, the bricks took on a mellow russet color that made the house appear as English as Compton Wynyates. Its slate-shingled roof, rising in one main dramatic peak but because of the size of the house dipping and rising again in many smaller peaks like foothills surrounding a mountain, presented a fascinating interplay of planes interspersed with a dozen brick chimneys, each a masterpiece of the bricklayer's art. There were huge mullioned windows, and hundreds of smaller ones. There was a brick-paved courtyard surrounded on two sides by the house, on the other two by a brick wall.

The house rambled, but it was held together by good design and Franklin Riggs's excellent taste. It contained forty-two rooms, twelve baths, six garages, a greenhouse, a poolhouse and pool to the side, two tennis courts and, a short distance from the main house, a small but delightful brick house for the dignified butler Mark had hired from Kentucky, Peter Bowden, and his family. Yet one was not overwhelmed, for the place was a tasteful creation made possible by wealth rather than a meretricious showpiece such as the Casa Encantada. It seduced with beauty, and most viewers fell in love with it.

Inside, the house seemed to be a world under one roof. A big, two-story entrance hall had a gray-marble floor from which rose a handsome staircase with a Gobelin tapestry on the wall, which Charlotte had bought from Sir Joseph Duveen. At the top of the stair was Charlotte's Folly, the pipe organ (the workings were installed in the basement and the sound came up through vents into the hall). Off the hall was an enormous living room, so enormous—eighty feet long and forty feet wide—that someone joked it was more like the grand saloon of the *Lusitania*. The room had a mullioned window that soared thirty feet to the ceiling and looked out over the lawn, the river a hundred feet below and then beyond to the flat fields stretching to the sunset. The huge window with its simple, straight, white curtains was as dramatic as its view; and it was in front of it, in the long comfortable sofas and club chairs that Charlotte's architect had arranged as an "area," that the Mannings gathered to have their evening cocktails. There also were other "areas"— the room was so large there had to be. The furniture was picked with an eye toward comfort as well as handsomeness—in a house with four children, antiques would have been an invitation to disaster—and the result was, again, English country house. At the end of the room above the big hearth was hung Mark's third-anniversary present to Charlotte, a full-length Sargent portrait of her in a white-satin gown. It was one of Mr. Sargent's better efforts; he had obviously been intrigued by his sitter's warmth and charm as well as her beauty, and he managed to capture it all in the portrait.

Off the living room was a handsome library, and also on the ground floor—in addition to pantries, kitchens, laundry rooms, flower rooms, maids' rooms, silver rooms—were a music room with Charlotte's Bechstein and a locked shelf holding her huge collection of scores; a study-office for Mark; a huge, formal dining room and a smaller family dining room; a billiard room; and a ballroom that filled the entire north wing. On the second floor of this sprawling Ohio chateau were the suites and bathrooms one would expect, but on the third floor in the center section of the house (the only section with a third floor) was an unexpected gem, a delicious fantasy of a

room: a peaked-roof nursery—huge, with candy-striped walls, filled
with every conceivable toy, gimcrack and whatnot to enchant a child,
including a ten-foot-high toy fairy-tale castle, electrically wired and
replete with mirror moat and drawbridge. The nursery was written
up and photographed in countless newspapers and magazines, the
Ladies' Home Journal featuring it in a spread in their September
1913 issue. Mark and Charlotte adored and coddled their children.
It was a wonderful time in which to be a beloved child; it was a
gorgeous time to be a Manning child.

The evening they moved in Mark opened a bottle of champagne
and he and Charlotte, glasses in hand, went out to stand above the
river and watch the sun set.

"Well, do you like it?" he asked, putting his arm around her waist
and kissing her.

"Oh, darling, I adore it. How about you?"

"Well, I'm a bit overwhelmed," he said, grinning, "but I guess I'll
get used to it. Just don't get too near me each month when I make
the mortgage payment."

"Oh, tightwad! You've so much money you don't know what to do
with it; don't you try to fool me. Besides, it's worth every penny and
I intend to fill it up with lots of marvelous people and make it a
happy house for us and the children. And I *don't* mean filling it up
with gloomy Harold Swenson and dear, sweet Leslie Swenson, so you
can just get that idea out of your head right now."

"Yes, dear, whatever you say, dear." This was *her* moment—*her*
territory.

"Now, we have to christen it," she said. "Have you thought of a
name for it?"

"How about 'Dunrovin'?"

"Honestly."

" 'Mortgage Manor'?"

"Oh, Mark, be serious. It has to be something beautiful and romantic, something that sings and has music . . ." She looked around,
searching for inspiration. Then her eyes went down the treed hill to
the river below and its lazy hairpin turn.

"I know," she said. "We'll call it 'River Bend'."

He thought about this. "River Bend? Yes, I like it. Shall we officially
baptize it?"

They clinked their champagne glasses and toasted River Bend,
then finished off the contents of the glass and threw them out and
down the hill. From that moment on the Manning estate would be
known as River Bend.

And it was River Bend that would provide Crazy Bill Sands the target he had so long been looking for.

————————

When she answered her front doorbell that chilly autumn day in 1913, she wondered who the sensationally handsome young man in the camel's hair coat and derby hat was.

"Mrs. Boine?" he said.

"That's right."

"My name is Carter Lang, and I'm representing Mr. Mark Manning. Might I see you for a few minutes?"

Sheila Farr Boine looked suspicious. "What about?"

"Well, it's nothing I want to discuss on your front porch. And it *is* a bit nippy out here."

"Come in." She stood aside as he came into the small living room of her small house. This section of Cleveland was full of small houses, but Sheila's was at least always immaculate, unlike many of her neighbors'. She never had need to apologize for the house not being "picked up," even though it was only ten in the morning. She offered the stranger an overstuffed armchair by the stove and sat down opposite him.

"What does Mark Manning want?" she said, remembering her shock at having bumped into him at the lunch counter six months before.

"First, he asked me to express his condolences over your husband's death." The well-dressed young man had an Eastern accent. She put him down as a phony, although he looked like a smart one . . . probably some toady on the Manning payroll.

"Mark Manning never met my husband, and even if he had, I doubt whether he'd give a damn whether he lived or died. So why don't you cut the baloney and get to the point?"

Carter Lang shrugged and pulled an envelope from his pocket. "Are you working?" he asked.

"That's none of your business."

"Mrs. Boine, you might try to be civil."

"Why?"

"All right, but I'd still like to know if you're working."

She hesitated. "I've just gotten a job as a secretary for a church magazine," she said, a bit less aggressively. "I start next Monday. I've been doing some writing in my free time but nothing's sold, of course. I hope maybe I'll be able to do some editing for the magazine too. Does that answer your question?"

"Yes, thanks. Is your son home?"

"He's in school. What is it you want, Mr. Lang?"

He extended the envelope to her. She took it and read the front, which was addressed, simply, "Sheila Farr Boine." Then she opened it. Inside was a note and a check. The note read, "Sheila: I know what you think of me, but please take this for Roger's education." It was signed, "M.M."

The check, made out to her, was for ten thousand dollars.

She looked at the amount, attempting to hide her shock. Then she looked up at the stranger, who was watching her intently.

"Mr. Manning," he said, "hopes very much that you will take it." She said nothing, and he added, "You *will* take it?"

"Is this," she said quietly, "Mr. Manning's conscience money?"

"I really couldn't say—"

"Well, tell him I'm taking it for Roger, but only on the condition that he never be told where it came from."

"Mr. Manning understands that."

She stood up, stuffing the check into the pocket of her dress.

"And you can tell Mr. Manning I still think he's a son of a bitch."

Carter stood up, thinking that his boss had good taste in women. Charlotte Manning was a beauty with class; this one was a beauty too—a much more sensual beauty than Charlotte. But this one was also tough as nails, which Carter didn't like. He very much preferred Charlotte. . . .

"You *will* tell him that?" she insisted.

"If you want me to."

"I do."

He nodded. Nothing more was said, and Sheila showed the young man out of the house. When he was gone, she pulled out the check and again stared at the figures. She hated taking it because she knew it inevitably would give Mark a claim on Roger.

But she could hardly afford not to.

———

Despite the fact that Charlotte Manning disliked the town of Elkins—or, more accurately, somehow felt out of place in it, missed the social and cultural stimulation of New York—still, she was basically a happy woman. She loved Mark, she worshiped her children and all in all considered her second marriage a success. Especially the physical side of it. Mark was a sensual man who demanded love nightly (and often in the mornings; he had a habit of waking up with "a full head of steam," as he put it). Charlotte was delighted and exhilarated by his lovemaking and his strong body, and her former loathing for even the idea of intercourse had long since vanished. Mark woke up her latent sexuality, and for this alone she would always be grateful to him. There had been a difficult, if perhaps natural, dividend to this: she became intensely jealous of him, and if he so much as looked sidelong at an attractive woman she was sure to take note of it. Fortunately for Charlotte there were few attractive women in Elkins. Moreover, she was certain he had lived up to his promise to her and remained faithful. Even on his many business trips, she felt reasonably confident he didn't stray. He had better not . . . she wanted him all to herself.

She also liked him. He was an intelligent man as well as a fiercely competitive one, and if he exhibited a somewhat philistine indifference to the arts, he was by no means a boor like so many of his fellow tycoons. He kept up with what was happening in the world, being an omniverous reader of newspapers and magazines, and he had perceptive opinions about current events, though she thought his contempt of politicians was somewhat too cynical. He also had an innate sense of style, his flexible mind quickly adapting to each step up in their life style. He always had dressed rather nattily, and though River Bend had developed into something much more grandiose than he had envisioned, once it was completed he loved the place and appreciated the elegance Charlotte had put into it. He was a wonderful father who lavished gifts and affection on his children. He was also a generous husband who took almost childish pleasure in bringing Charlotte presents that ranged from candy bars to diamond bracelets. They traveled together to New York at least twice a year, and on these trips they would indulge themselves with the best restaurants and latest plays. Mark loved the theater, particularly the lavish musical revues of the day. He also was entranced by the movies, and loved spending an afternoon ogling in good humor the Vitagraph Girl or Florence Lawrence. He wasn't so fond of the opera, and Charlotte did not pressure him, going to the performances by herself. He had an easy, dry sense of humor about most things, was usually in a good mood. She enjoyed his company.

He was not, of course, a paragon. She realized he was as much in love with his company as with her, perhaps more so. He was self-centered, and the high ambition that she had worried about from the first still made her nervous. He enjoyed power, and she had no special illusions about what was surely a prime motive for his enlightened treatment of his workers: he coddled them to undercut the hated unions. He was a man who could use people like pawns to achieve his own ends, and though he tended to mask ruthlessness with charm, he could also intimidate with rage when it suited his purpose. His executives for the most part stood in awe of him, the one exception being Harold Swenson, who held a unique position. He was not only Mark's first executive in terms of longevity, but he also knew the factories better than anyone else, including Mark. Mark most needed him, and was always genial to the rather plodding Swede. Besides, Swenson had little personal ambition, being content as Number Two and thereby providing no threat to Mark's supremacy. All the other executives, however, were appropriately wary of Number One, who decidedly was not an easy man to work for.

He was also, at times, not an easy man to be married to. They rarely fought, but he had his moods. Though he was publicly generous to charities and worthwhile causes, privately he was not overly fond of the human race except for his family. If he was no longer the con artist Sam had labeled him, he still, she knew, had the instincts—however exalted the plane might now be—of a manipulator, an operator, and she often marveled at how she could have fallen in love with a man who had so many characteristics she really did not admire.

But she had, and being extremely sensitive to his moods—her own peace of mind was so dependent on them—she was immediately aware something was very much wrong when, one night several weeks after they had moved into River Bend, he came home from the factory in a sulky temper.

"Darling, what in the world is the matter?" she asked as she kissed him.

"The *Sting*'s the matter," he growled. "Crazy Bill's finally gotten around to stinging *me*."

"How?"

"This house," he said, slumping onto a sofa in front of the big west window. "He's been taking pot shots at it for a month or so, but today he really let loose. I've become King Mock and River Bend is my palace where I hold court—he's renamed it Flivver's End, by the way. I'm getting damn fed up with it. Of course Harold and Jim Malloy are laughing—so far they've been his prime targets. They've hammered at me to do something about him but I've always protected him, figuring he was relatively harmless. Now they're saying I don't think the *Sting*'s quite so funny anymore. They're right."

"But Mark, it doesn't sound all that bad. I mean, calling you a king and this place Flivver's End is childish but it's not really vicious."

"No, but calling you Queen Shylock damn well is."

Charlotte stiffened.

"Crazy Bill has gone too far this time and damn it, I'm not going to stand for it!"

"What are you going to do?" she asked quietly. "Fire him?"

"No. I have no legitimate reason to fire him. He does his job well, and I won't fire a man just because he's personally offensive. Malloy wants to rough him up but I told him that was out too. But I *am* going to stop that lousy newspaper of his."

"How?"

He didn't answer her directly. "It's going to be done tonight."

Bill Sands had rented a small house on Fifth Street, and that night —midnight—he was standing in his kitchen playing the flute when he saw the lights go on in his garage. Sticking the flute in his hip pocket, he hurried out the kitchen door and ran to the garage, where he could hear what sounded like somebody banging the place apart. Inside, four men with masks were attacking his press with sledge-hammers. Bill rushed inside and went for the nearest man, who saw him coming and pulled a blackjack from his pocket, crunching it down on his skull. Bill sprawled on the dirt floor, rolling over on his stomach, unconscious.

The man continued to batter the press for several more minutes. When the leader, Manning security chief Jim Malloy, ordered them to leave, he was satisfied the press could never be repaired. As Jim looked down at Crazy Bill, he noticed the silver flute sticking out of his pocket. He reached down and pulled it out, then slowly bent it, until it snapped in two.

Three weeks later, in a bar in Akron, Bill Sands met Eric Lindquist, the I.W.W. organizer for the rubber industry. Taking their beers to a booth, they sat down and Bill told Lindquist his plan. "Manning has invited his directors and their wives for a big party at River Bend the first weekend in November. It'll be a housewarming and directors' meeting combined, and that snooty wife of his will really put on the dog. Now, I'd like to make this a big party for *us*."

"How?" asked Lindquist, a big Dane with a sparkling bald pate.

"Before Jim Malloy put me out of the newspaper business with his strong-arm stuff, I'd been taking potshots at Manning's big estate and his management and I'd been getting some results. You know the trouble I've had with Manning—the men generally like him and he's smart about keeping it that way. But for the first time I got them laughing at him, and there are a lot of people in the plants who resent this palace he's put up. It's just too damn big. All right, the *Sting*'s out of business, but this party Manning's throwing gives us a chance to build up and take advantage of the resentment against him. I'd like to organize a demonstration. I'd like to get together as many workers as we can and march them out to River Bend and let them see the fat cats living it up at their expense. I want them to see the house. And I think we can stir them up—really get them *mad* at Manning."

Lindquist drank some beer, then shook his head. "It wouldn't work. The best you could hope for would be to make Manning look like a self-indulgent pig. Maybe. On the other hand, the men might be fascinated by a big blow-out like that. You just never can tell."

"Not if you're giving it to them about bloated profits from the honest sweat of their labor. You haven't seen River Bend. I've seen it! It really is a damn palace, and when you get men out there who think they're lucky making four bucks a day, when they see how *Manning* lives . . ."

"Bill, you make a big mistake if you think the average American working man resents big money. It's just the opposite—he envies it; he doesn't resent it. Show a pit man a mansion and he doesn't want to blow it up. He'll more likely just sit there and wish it was his."

"It's our job to *make* them resent it."

"We'll never get through the gates," snapped Lindquist, changing the subject when he realized Sands had made a good point. "Which means they won't be able to see the house. And if we did get through, we'd be arrested for trespassing."

"*Let* them arrest us, so much the better! It'll make headlines."

"Bad headlines, make us look like a bunch of housebreakers. No, Bill. It's dangerous, and the likely results aren't worth the risk."

"But they *are* worth it, dammit! Eric, we've got to create incidents! We've got to keep things stirred up! We have to make a show to attract people, convince them . . . Manning's invited all the big shots in the industry and there's going to be reporters—it's a natural! And even if we don't get through the gates, they'll still hear us, they'll know we're there, it'll give us the publicity we need. Sure it's a risk, but I say it's one we've got to take—"

"Bill, you've got a personal vendetta going against Manning because his men busted your press. Our organization has no room for personal feelings—our stakes are too big. We can't risk them in a foolhardy—"

"It's not just the press," interrupted Sands quietly. "Yes, I have a vendetta against him. But what's wrong with a vendetta against the bosses? We're never going to unionize the Manning Company as long as the men like Mark Manning. It's our job to make them *dis-*like him. If he were an obvious bastard it would be a lot simpler, but he's a subtle bastard, damn him, and it makes the job harder. That's why I say we can't pass up any chance to get at him and this party is a chance."

Lindquist stalled for time as he finished his beer. He had to admit much of what Sands said made sense, and though his greater experience tended to make him more cautious, still he didn't want to shut off Sands's enthusiasm. Crazy Bill was far from the best organizer in the business, but he was the *only* one they had in Elkins and Lindquist didn't want to lose him. Besides, it wouldn't look good for his own position if word got around that he was less militant than his own subordinates.

"All right, damn you, it's a crazy idea but we'll try it. Only to the gate though. We don't go inside. We go to the gate and make a ruckus. Christ knows if it'll do any good, but like you say it may get us some attention in the papers, help recruit some new members . . ."

Bill Sands was pleased, but not satisfied. He had won half the battle, at least, and that was something. Maybe with time he'd win it all.

One thing for sure—before he was finished he'd make Mr. Mark Manning pay for what his wreckers had done to his press—and most of all to his flute. Pay, and pay, and pay . . .

Carter Lang, Mark's vice-president in charge of advertising, not only looked like the Arrow Collar Man, he thought like him. At twenty-seven, Carter was improbably handsome with the chiseled profile and square jaw of a matinee idol. The son of a Connecticut clergyman, Carter had gone to Yale, where he had become something of an idol to his classmates. Star quarterback and good student, Carter had epitomized the gentlemanly virtues so admired by his generation, and many of his classmates compared him, only half-kiddingly, to the dime-novel hero, Frank Merriwell. In any case, Carter was a true gentleman, and his attitude toward women was gentlemanly romantic: he liked "ladies"—though on occasion he had been known to indulge himself with New Haven townie girls of a somewhat less than lady-like reputation. However, he always regretted it afterward, telling himself he would have to steel himself against his "baser" nature. Carter was always striving to improve himself.

There was another ring around the Arrow Collar. Carter liked money, of which he and his clergyman father were in short supply, and to boost his finances he had taken to poker in his first year at Yale. By his sophomore year Carter had become one of the sharpest players on campus, and was winning big from his wealthy classmates. In one all-night session he had taken in six hundred dollars, and his winnings for the year, were close to $3,000, which enabled him to dress well and entertain the ladies he so admired. His junior year he did even better, clearing over $3,500. His senior year, however, was a disaster.

Carter's card sense was uncanny, but without the cards even Carter couldn't win; and in the fall of his senior year his luck turned against him. He drew one bad hand after another and quickly went into debt. A professional gambler might have stopped until the odds caught up and his luck turned, but Carter was no professional and, besides, he was accustomed to his poker winnings income. He kept playing, going deeper into debt and giving classmates he had cleaned out so often a chance for revenge. By Christmas, Carter was staggered to realize he owed almost $2,000. It was then that he made the decision he was to regret the rest of his life. Inviting six of his cronies to his room for a final game before the Christmas holidays, Carter's luck seemed to take a dazzling turn for the better. He began winning hand after hand, building up the pots as big as he could, and by ten thirty he was ahead an astonishing nine hundred dollars. It was then that one of the players discovered that the deck was marked, and it took little imagination to figure out who had marked it. He was not turned in to the college officials or the police—that would have been to break the code. But Carter Lang was through. *Everyone* knew he was a "rotter."

He quit Yale, convinced his reputation was forever blackened, and went to New York where for several weeks he lived in a Y.M.C.A. and alternately considered suicide or the Foreign Legion. However, basic good sense finally convinced him he was being overly tragic about the situation, that the world had not yet come to an end for him. Finally he went out to look for a job and landed one as a copy-writer at Tutwiler and Jacobs, advertising being perhaps an appropriate blend of suicide and the Foreign Legion. To his surprise, he found he liked the work. It seemed creative and paid well. In three years he was the Bright Young Man at Tutwiler and Jacobs, by now assigned to the Manning Rubber Company account. Mark was so impressed by Carter's work on the Jaguar tire ad campaign, he offered him a job as head of advertising. Carter wasn't interested until he heard the salary, which was half again what he was making. He then promptly agreed and moved to Elkins, congratulating himself that an ancillary advantage in his move from New York would be the diminished likelihood of bumping into old classmates with long memories.

Being in charge of the Manning Company's advertising was hard work, but even so it did not consume all of Carter's time or interest. He became fascinated by his boss, and managed to make himself indispensable to Mark in as many areas as he could arrange. He convinced Mark that he should cultivate a public image of himself. Because of his role in the exposure of the Putumayo atrocities, Mark was already well known to the public. But it was the age of the muckrakers. In 1904 Ida Tarbell had attacked Rockefeller and the Standard Oil Company, and the following year Upton Sinclair's book on the meatpacking industry had been a prime factor in the passage of the Pure Food and Drug Act. The public was, as always, fascinated by the men who ran America's business empires but they were also being severely critical of them, and Carter convinced Mark it would be well worth the money for Carter at least to wine, dine and flatter important editors when in various cities on company business. Mark agreed, and while many editors were above this sort of patronage, a surprising number weren't and they managed to give Mark Manning and his company a good press.

So Carter was involved in public relations as well as advertising, and Mark had come to trust him with personal chores as well, one of which was delivering the ten thousand dollars to Sheila Farr Boine. And when Mark and Charlotte decided to give the ball at River Bend, Mark put Carter in charge of bringing the out-of-town guests to Elkins. Carter rented a private railroad car and arranged for the guests coming from Chicago, Detroit and New York to board it at Cleveland to be transported in luxury to Elkins. Carter was on hand to greet the guests at the Cleveland station, ushering them into the private car banked with flowers and equipped with two bars, varieties of food and four waiters in attendance. From New York came Riley Baker and his wife of less than a year, the blonde Brooklyn showgirl Mark had met at Baker's breakfast table, Sylvia Wingdale. The new

Mrs. Baker, wrapped in a chinchilla coat, smiled warmly at Carter
Lang (Sylvia smiled warmly at all good-looking men as a matter of
principle, though her husband obviously didn't much approve).
Carter hardly could take his eyes off her as he turned to greet Sir
Bruce and Lady Clark. Amelia Clark favored sable, it being an
unusually cold weekend for early November and looking like snow.
Edna Hutchins, wife of Percival Hutchins, the railroad president, was
wrapped in an alcoholic haze as well as mink, and almost fell on her
face as she entered the private car. Elmo Tilden, manufacturer of
the Tillmobile, was well on his way, too, though it was not yet even
noon. He snapped something at *his* mink-wrapped wife, who looked
furiously at him and proceeded to order a bourbon from one of the
waiters. Frank Bennet came aboard with his wife Mildred, Frank
looking annoyed at Elmo's drunkenness as he sat down in one of the
lounge chairs and commenced reading his pocket Bible.

There was also the elegant and witty society editor for the powerful
New York *Herald*, Hanson Mayberry. Hanson would never have
traveled to the Midwest for a party (no social function west of the
Hudson being worth reporting) if he had not been a good friend of
Charlotte's. However, despite his Manhattan insularity, Hanson was
rather intrigued by this gathering of automotive potentates. They
were a new breed with new money—Elmo Tilden was less than eight
years out of a greasepit and, Hanson thought, looked it—and the
public undeniably was interested in them. It would be a show worth
seeing. And certainly spending a weekend in the same house with Riley
Baker and his new wife (the marriage had created much interest in
New York, Riley's first wife's murder still being remembered) should
be amusing. Hanson didn't like blondes (brunettes at the time being
more fashionable) and he did not like to mingle socially with ex-
showgirls. But Sylvia Baker was so breathy and funnily dumb, Hanson
thought she might be amusing.

A crowd of almost a hundred curious onlookers had gathered at
the Elkins railroad station to see the train's arrival; for, after all, this
was one of the major events in Elkins's history. The crowd was getting
its show as the top-hatted swells and their furred (and, in the case of
Mrs. Hutchins, sotted) wives descended from the Pullman to be led
to the waiting limousines and driven out to River Bend.

"My, don't he do it up big!" whispered Mabel Strunk to her sister,
Martha, referring of course to Mark, whom Mabel remembered teaching in the third grade almost thirty years before. "Who'd have thought
that boy would have turned out so!" She shook her head and marveled
at God's mysterious ways as her sister added, tears in her eyes,

"Wouldn't his mother be proud?" Martha, an unabashed sentimental-
ist, was known to have cried at such moving occasions as the opening
of a new bank branch on the outskirts of town.

But the Strunk sisters were hardly alone in their feelings of awe.
After all, whatever they might have thought of his beginnings, when
he was running nothing more important than a bike shop, Mark
Manning had transformed the town with his success. Elkins, which
had entered the century like a thousand other sleepy one-horse towns,
was now a booming industrial city of forty-eight thousand, growing
each month, its suburban housing developments spreading in all
directions as the Manning Rubber Company and its subsidiaries continued to draw in more and more workers. And now, real society
people from Cleveland and New York were making the trek to
Elkins to pay homage to their own Mark! Hope Baine, the pretty
young society editor of the *Star Chronicle*, was agog at this climactic
moment in Elkins's social history, and she nearly tackled Lady Clark
as she stepped down from the train with Sir Bruce to get a quote for
her column (much to Hanson Mayberry's displeasure; as dean of the
profession of society editors, he frowned on such amateur—hence *outré*
—eagerness). Lady Clark, who looked breathtakingly chic, obliged, to
Hope's great joy. Yes, they had come all the way from London for
the party because she and her husband were such admirers of the
Mannings. Yes, the crossing was rough, but the *Olympic* was a wonderful ship. Oh yes, they had seen Irene and Vernon Castle dance—in
Paris, actually—and they had learned the Castle gavotte and the walk,
as well as the tango. For the party she was wearing a gown designed
by Paul Poiret, the newest and most sensational of the Paris de-
signers, who had introduced such bold new colors to dresses as well
as the exciting new Oriental look, inspired by Bakst's settings for the
Diaghilev Ballet Russe. Of course, Monsieur Poiret's dresses were so
theatrical she only wore them on special occasions, preferring Monsieur Doucet for everyday wear. . . . The latest thing in Paris? The
"leaning backward" look introduced by Forzane, the notorious Swedish *demi-mondaine*. The latest thing in Europe? Amelia thought
a moment, then said with straight face, "sex." Hope Baine wondered
how she could fit *that* into her article.

Hope's boss, an editor, Mr. Wharton, the same gentleman who had
unwittingly started Mark's career eight years before by wondering
why they didn't manufacture the tires in place of the rims, was
mentally composing his editorial for the next day, an editorial that
would be a paean to Mark Manning. "The Golden Dream of Suc-

cess," he decided he would headline it. A bit pretentious perhaps, but he wanted to pull all stops to honor Elkins's favorite son and remind his readers of that basic American truth—that hard work was rewarded by success. (Of course some people might say hard work wasn't *always* rewarded with success, that there were a lot of people who slaved and didn't get much for it, but he wouldn't push that in the editorial. . . . People didn't like to read it and he didn't like to write it, particularly since the Manning Company was one of the paper's biggest advertisers . . .).

One of the *Star Chronicle*'s best reporters was not at the station, however, being more interested in another story developing elsewhere in town. George Forley at forty-two had one of those likeable black Irish faces that hard drinking had creased with networks of wrinkles. Forley knew, as did everyone in town, that the Wobblies were holding a rally that evening at eight o'clock in the Pentecostal Church on Main Street. What he didn't know, but wanted to find out, was the reason for the meeting. He had heard that Eric Lindquist, the bald organizer, had been seen at Bill Sands's house that morning, and he decided to try for an interview with Lindquist. He didn't think he'd have much luck, but it was worth a try.

Pulling up in front of the paint-flaking house on Fifth Street, Forley parked his Ford and walked up to the small front porch and knocked. The door was opened by Lindquist himself, who, when Forley identified himself, said "Come to the meeting this evening and you'll find out what it's all about."

Lindquist's attitude was pleasant enough, and Forley thought that even though he didn't get an interview, the Wobbly definitely wanted him to cover the meeting. He had no intention of missing it.

In 1911 Sam Rosen had suffered a stroke that had left him partially paralyzed and forced him to retire from business. He turned over the management of the Rosen Stove Company to the man he had groomed for the presidency, then retired into the dark rooms of his house on Elm Street to brood over his misfortune and snip at his private nurse, Miss Pringle, from his wheelchair. Charlotte tried everything in her power to make his life comfortable, visiting him at least once a day and often bringing along one or more of the children to see their grandfather, but Mark never came, nor did Sam ever accept any of Charlotte's invitations to come to their home. A curtain of impenetrable silence had dropped between the two former working partners, and much as a saddened and exasperated Charlotte tried to penetrate it, she got absolutely nowhere.

Then, several weeks before the gala house-opening at River Bend, she went to the house on Elm Street to try to persuade him to come at least to this party that was so important to her. As she expected, he at first refused, although she sensed he was rather curious to see her new home that he had heard so much about. He also began attacking Mark for building what he called a *Neuschwanstein*. "It is stupid," he said. "It is one thing to build a comfortable house—*I* built a comfortable house!—but a palace? It is showy and vulgar and will do nothing but create ill-feeling in the town."

"Oh, father," sighed Charlotte impatiently, "can Mark and I ever do *anything* right? In the first place, if anyone's being showy and vulgar, it's me, because I've pushed Mark into expanding the original plans. And in the second place, why shouldn't we have whatever kind of house we want? We can afford it and the children adore the place. What in the world is wrong with that?"

"Too big," grumped her father, not budging an inch.

She started to lose her temper, but, as always, she checked herself. She knew what was really at the bottom of Sam's dislike of her husband. For all his talk of Mark's lack of character, of Mark's non-Jewishness, of this, that, and the other thing, there was an intense jealousy within him, the jealousy of an older man at the end of life for a younger at the peak, the jealousy of a successful man for a man whose success was eclipsing his own, the resentment of a father who had long ago ceased being as important to the daughter he loved as her husband. Sam, after years of being the sun, was now a distant asteroid revolving around a new sun, and he bitterly resented it. So Charlotte held her temper. "*Do* think about coming," she said softly. "It would mean so much to all of us, and I want you to see River Bend."

"None of you really wants me to come. Nobody wants to put up with an old man like me."

"Oh, father, now you're being silly. Why do you think I'm practically begging you to come if I don't want you?"

"*He* doesn't want me to come."

"Mark does. Believe me."

He said nothing for a moment. Then, "I'll think about it."

She smiled and stood up, leaning over to kiss him. She thought his curiosity finally had gotten the better of his sulkiness, and she was right.

Elmo Tilden was a man of no social aspirations at all. He made no bones about the fact that luck, or Providence, or whatever had banged him over the head eight years before and made him a multimillionaire almost overnight. Now that he controlled an automobile manufacturing company employing 15,000 men and enjoying an income of a million a year, his idea of a good time was still what it had been when his income was less than $2,000 a year—namely, to get falling-down drunk. Nevertheless, he enjoyed a good show. He appreciated the private railroad car Mark had put at his guests' disposal, and he thought River Bend was "a real eyeful," as he said to Charlotte, almost knocking her over with his breath. After the houseguests had been shown their rooms, Elmo made his way back downstairs to search out Mark, whom he found alone in his library.

"Mark," said Elmo, closing the door, "got a minute?"

"Of course," replied his host, who, though he didn't appreciate Elmo's drinking habits nevertheless liked the bearish auto tycoon.

"Well now," said Elmo, weaving over to hold onto the back of a chair, "this is just between you and me, but I think it's something you ought to know. That Riley Baker, well, I don't like him. He's too slick, too New York, for my money. But he contacted me a couple of weeks ago and tried to buy me out. Tried to buy out my Manning stock. Offered me a damn good price, too, but I told him no dice. I like you, I like your company and I'm not about to sell. But he's up to something, and I thought I'd better warn you. You'd better watch him. He's a tricky son of a bitch, no doubt about it."

Riley Baker, the Professor Moriarty of Wall Street, as Herschel Fine had described him six years before, had been so pleasant and cooperative as a director of the Manning Company that Mark had begun to doubt Herschel's assertion that the man had a criminal mind. But perhaps he had been wrong. Perhaps Baker, as Herschel had foreseen, had bided his time until the Manning Company was big enough to be really interesting. At any rate, he warmly thanked Elmo, who wove off in search of a drink before lunch. Mark was about to join him when he received a phone call from Jim Malloy. "I've found out what Sands and Lindquist are up to," said the head of the Manning Security Force. "They're going to bring a crowd out to your place tonight."

"What the hell for?"

"To stage a demonstration against you."

Crazy Bill Sands again! He told Malloy not to interfere with him but to plant two dozen armed men at the gates to prevent the crowd from entering and to alert the town's sheriff to the possibility of trouble. He hung up wondering what Crazy Bill really hoped to achieve by this and trying to decide the best way to keep his guests from panicking, if trouble materialized.

Riley Baker and Bill Sands—they were making his housewarming uncomfortably hot.

CHAPTER THREE

Hanson Mayberry was impressed by River Bend, and he was especially impressed by the manner in which Charlotte was managing the big houseparty. Of course when one had a butler, a chauffeur, a chief with three assistants, a housekeeper, a laundress, six maids, four houseboys, and two gardeners it could be argued that only gross incompetence would be the reason not to run a house well. But Hanson knew many women with staffs three times that size who could never have managed a weekend houseparty this large as well as Charlotte. And as the houseguests joined the half-dozen drop-in guests for a two-o'clock lunch in the dining room, Hanson's eyes reviewed the table, reinforcing his conviction, which he had once written in his column, that there were only six women in America who knew how to set a truly elegant table—and Charlotte was one of them.

By necessity it was a long table, yet it did not crowd the big, light-paneled room, and its graceful English lines, echoed in the two dozen chairs, were, if not unusual, still lovely. A choice Watteau and two Copleys—which Hanson remembered having seen in Charlotte's Waldorf suite—beautified three walls, and the view of the snow-dusted lawn through the big windows highlighted the fourth. The guests found their place cards and took their seats, Mrs. Hutchins having sobered up a bit after the train ride but Elmo Tilden looking even more awash than before. Hanson found himself at Charlotte's left. The luncheon service was a charming French country set dating from the Directoire period; the crystal was French, the linen Belgian, the silver a simple shell pattern; and the flowers, massed in three porcelain bowls, were freshly cut from Charlotte's greenhouse. The menu—fresh-fruit compote, lobster bisque, delicate raspberry sherbet followed by magnificent pheasant stuffed with an exquisite chestnut dressing; for dessert, an outrageously tasty vanilla soufflé with a Grand Marnier sauce. Its splendidness was only to be expected from Charlotte, but what surprised Hanson were the wines, never one of Charlotte's strong suits. However, with the bisque came a wonderful Corton-Charlemagne '04, which had been an exceptional year for white wines; with the pheasant, a rhapsodic La Tâche '99, which had been a vintage year for Burgundies; and with the soufflé, a Château d'Yquem 1893, which had been one of the great sauternes of the century and which the intervening twenty years had turned to a mellow amber. This last moved Hanson to ask, *"Where did you get it?"*

"The Château d'Yquem?" said Charlotte casually. "Oh, that's Mark's department, not mine."

Hanson turned to look down the long table where, at the opposite end, his red-haired host was talking with Sylvia Baker. Hanson had assumed Charlotte had married another clod-turned-millionaire. He began to have second thoughts.

"The last time I was sitting at a table with you," Sylvia Baker was saying to Mark, "Riley sent me out of the room. Remember?"

"I remember."

"Now he can't." She giggled. "I'm his wife. And a wife has, by God, her rights."

"And how do you like being Mrs. Riley Baker?"

She took a mouthful of pheasant and chewed thoughtfully before answering, glancing across the table at her husband, who was seated some distance down from her and well out of earshot. "It's all right," she said unenthusiastically. "Of course, it's certainly solved my money problems. He's filthy rich, which is sort of fun. I guess." She scooped up more pheasant.

"He'll be even richer after our directors' lunch meeting when he finds out what our profit's been this year. It's going to be a very nice dividend."

Sylvia shrugged. "That's nice. He thinks your company's awfully good, and I guess it must be. Your *food's* awfully good. Do you cook?"

"No, afraid not."

"Oh, you ought to try. I love to cook. I make the best poached eggs. Maybe I'll cook some for you." The open smile. "Do you like the movies?"

Mark was straining to keep up with her nonsequiturs. "Very much. How about you?"

"I'm crazy about them. I'd just love to make one but Riley says I can't because I'm a lady now." She shrugged again. "I don't feel like a lady, whatever *that* is. Anyway, you see, my problem with my stage career was my voice. I sort of squeak, which didn't help me much with dialogue, and it was a disaster when I sang. But in a movie I wouldn't have to say anything. People could just look at me. Yes, I think I might do better in the movies . . . anyway I'd certainly like to try. But—" She sighed—"I guess I'm stuck being a damn lady; *that* gets sort of boring after a while. You know what I mean?"

Mark noticed Charlotte giving him the eye and decided he should spend less time with Sylvia and more talking with Mildred Bennet on his right. He doubted Charlotte could be jealous of Mildred Bennet.

Eric Lindquist was ready to call it off. After giving in to Crazy Bill's idea, spending union money to rent the Pentecostal Church (the only place in town that would rent to the Wobblies), and after printing the rally notices—now Crazy Bill, four hours before the rally, was arguing that the whole venture would be useless if they didn't force themselves into the Manning estate. When it began snowing at noon, Bill used it as an excuse to start pushing for a "face-to-face showdown," as he called it, with Mark Manning. "That was the whole idea in the first place!" he said as he fetched Eric another beer from his icebox. "To get the people in to *see* the house, *see* the party. Otherwise all they're going to see is a lot of goddamn snowflakes. Half of them will probably catch pneumonia and blame it on us."

"Look, Bill," said Eric patiently, "the minute we walk through those gates we're breaking the law. Now, sometimes it pays to break the law but this isn't one of them. This isn't any big cheese of a show, like a major strike. This is a diversionary tactic to keep things stirred up. And I'm telling you it's not worth it to get ourselves arrested over this thing tonight. Whether you like it or not, most

Americans like to think they're good law-abiding citizens and when they read in the papers that the Wobblies are trespassing on private property, they'll just roast us. And for what? No, forget about going through the gates."

"The law makes Manning a millionaire and lets him get away with smashing *my* property. What kind of law is *that*?"

"I'm not arguing about logic, just tactics. Besides, you know god-damn well the minute he gets the word we're marching out to his place he's going to have the sheriff out there."

"So what?"

"So what!" Eric echoed incredulously. "They've got *guns*! And when you have rifles pointing at you, they make their own damned convincing argument."

Bill took a seat at the kitchen table opposite Lindquist and leaned forward, lowering his voice. "But Eric, what if they *did* shoot? Mightn't that be the best thing that could happen to us?"

"You really *are* crazy!" sputtered Eric.

"No I'm not! If one or two Manning workers were shot down in front of the big man's house by police, the whole country would turn against him—not to mention the rest of his workers. Think about *that*."

"You mean you'd lead innocent, unarmed people out to the Manning place and *try to* get them shot?"

"It would be *worth* it!" said Bill, pounding the table with his fist for emphasis.

"It wouldn't be worth it even if it did turn the men against him —which you have no guarantee it would do. Listen, Bill, I've gone this far with you but I'm not going to stage-manage a massacre. Now, I'm telling you—*I'm* the boss. We go to the gate, no further. And we don't provoke an incident. Understand?"

Bill took a deep breath, then nodded. He knew Lindquist couldn't be budged. Lindquist was too cautious to make the total commit-ment that he, Sands, considered necessary to break the power of the bosses—in particular, popular bosses like Mark Manning. So be it. He couldn't buck the union brass single-handed. But at least he would take along his own gun. Just in case . . .

———

Mark informed his directors at the meeting after lunch that there was the possibility of a Wobbly demonstration that night. "Wob-

blies" and "demonstration" were fighting, literally red-letter words
to Frank Bennet and Elmo Tilden, but Mark assured them there
would be no danger. Afterward, Charlotte took Amelia Clark up
to the nursery to show off her four children to her old friend. On
the way Amelia asked about the Wobblies. "Don't they have a rather
violent reputation?"

"Yes, but I'm sure Mark can handle it," replied Charlotte. "He
doesn't scare easily, you know. By the way, did you happen to hear
what he was talking about to that showgirl?"

"You mean Mrs. Baker?" Amelia laughed. "You're jealous! You
must really be in love."

"Of course I'm jealous. Particularly when he's next to someone
as obvious as Mrs. Baker."

"Well, all I heard them talking about was poached eggs, so I
wouldn't get too nervous."

When they reached the big candy-striped room, it was littered
with old toys and new—tin soldiers by the dozens, toy automobiles,
a big Uncle Sam bank that saluted when you deposited a coin, a
cast-iron Liberty Bell bank, toy drums, dolls, dancing "darkies"
innocently reflecting the unquestioned racism of the day; a tin Felix
the Cat and a bright red slot racer. The room was a warehouse. In
the midst of this profusion the two eldest of the Manning brood,
David and Ellen, were fighting over the controls of their new electric
train while Richard, who was only two, waddled around the room
after one of Charlotte's collies, trying to tug its tail, and Christopher,
the baby, wailed in his crib. David, who was now four, was becoming a strapping boy. As their mother introduced Amelia, David
gravely shook her hand and Ellen, who had inherited her mother's
blue eyes as well as her beauty, executed an earnest if somewhat
awkward curtsy. Amelia was enchanted.

"They're beautiful," she whispered to Charlotte. "Absolutely gorgeous!"

"Would you like to see my train run?" asked David.

"It's mine, too!" said Ellen.

David gave her a disdainful look. "Girls don't know anything about
trains. Besides, father gave it to me."

"He did not!"

"Children," said Charlotte, "the train is for all of you. And David,
you shouldn't be so selfish. Now show Aunt Amelia how it works."

David and Ellen hurried back to the controls of the train and
sent the eight-car wonder zooming around the circular track. "I
think David has a bit of the tyrant in him," whispered Amelia.

"Oh, definitely. But Ellen's worse. Last week he was trying to order her around and she kicked him."

Amelia laughed. "The suffragettes would love her!"

After a while they left the nursery and started downstairs. "You're very happy, aren't you?" said Amelia.

"Very. Of course, Elkins isn't New York, but I have the children and my music, and building this house has been a great joy."

"And you and Mark . . . ?"

"We're fine . . ."

"Well, if anyone is, you're certainly entitled to some happiness." She then added cautiously, "I don't suppose you can guess whom I ran into in Paris two months ago?"

"Sydney?"

Amelia nodded.

"How is he?" asked Charlotte, in a flat tone.

"Well, one would like to report that he's miserable, paying for his sins and so on. But I'm afraid the truth is that he looked quite blooming. He and Richard have a spectacular townhouse on the Île St. Louis and a château in the country. And they're accepted. Well, not by the stuffier circles, but they're very fashionable with the smart set. Odd, isn't it? I wonder what Herschel would think."

"I doubt he'd be very pleased with the news," remarked Charlotte. "Do you remember what Sydney said that day?"

"About rejecting the 'beauty'?"

"Yes. I never have really understood what he meant. I assumed he meant the so-called beauty of our little world there, but obviously he hasn't rejected that in Paris, has he? Living on the Île St. Louis . . . no; I wonder what he meant?"

"I think he meant your beauty, and female beauty in general. But I think there was even more to it than that. It wasn't so much the beautiful, ordered social manners of his world—the families all knowing each other, the family parties, and everything and everybody in their place. I think he wanted to smash it. Partially, of course, because of his socially unacceptable love affair with Richard, but also because there is something new happening and in his fashion he was part of it."

"What?"

"Oh, you know, the new attitude about everything. About life and certainly about sex." She smiled. "That society reporter asked me at the train station what was the latest thing in Europe, and I said 'sex' and she about fainted. It's true, though. Everything is becoming loose. Society seems to be breaking down. Personally I think it's a rather good thing. The old ways *were* getting terribly crusty and dull. The old guard thinks it's all perfectly dreadful, but I confess I find it quite exciting."

"Maybe it's exciting in London and Paris, but it certainly isn't here. And it's hard to see anything changing. Oh, the girls aren't quite so nervous as they used to be, but they're still terribly shy."

"Give them time," replied Amelia. "They'll catch up."

"Yes, I suppose so. And what about you? Are you happy with Bruce?"

"Oh yes. I'll admit that sometimes I think about taking a lover —and there have been opportunities—but I always back down at the last moment. I suppose I'm getting too old for that sort of thing."

Charlotte laughed. "I thought no one ever got *that* old."

"Perhaps not. But what about you? Are you having a wild romance here in tame Elkins?"

"Oh come on, Amelia. You know I'm not the type."

"But, darling," countered Amelia, "we're all the type."

"Not in Elkins. Besides, I love Mark. And even if I didn't, there's no one around who interests me."

"Oh? What about that young Carter Lang? He's sinfully good looking, and I noticed him noticing you during lunch."

"Carter is nice, and he *is* handsome, but if for no other reason he's much too interested in his job to risk it with the boss's wife. They're *all* too interested in their jobs. The men in Elkins are more in love with money than women. And that is one thing I dislike about it here—it's all business. Rubber, tires . . ." She sighed.

They reached the bottom of the big staircase.

"But you *are* happy?" asked Amelia.

"Oh yes," replied Charlotte quickly. "I'm very happy. Really."

The lady, thought Amelia, perhaps doth protest too much.

CHAPTER FOUR

Harold Swenson, the Swede who had become rich through his association with the Manning Rubber Company, had one child, a daughter named Lily, who was now nineteen. To Lily's surprise and delight, she had been invited to the River Bend ball by Carter Lang.

And that night at eight o'clock, Lily's green eyes were wide with wonder as Carter escorted her into the entrance hall of the big house she had heard so much about but had yet to see. There were over a hundred guests, the elite of Cleveland and Akron, the men in their white ties and tails and the women in their egrets and jewels. Mary Tilden, who eight years before had packed her husband's lunch pail and taken in boarders, had now dyed her gray hair black and was sporting at least a quarter of a million dollars worth of diamonds, while Mildred Bennet wore a ruby necklace that had taken, it was rumored, two full days' production of Bennet Ariels to pay for. River Bend itself was underplayed; Charlotte was too wise and tasteful to bejewel it with decorations. Nothing but vases of fresh flowers detracted from the house itself, which was the chief attraction. Two orchestras alternated in the big ballroom—a string ensemble for sedate music, and a marvelous black jazz band Charlotte had imported from Chicago. Music and conversation filled the giant rooms as, outside, the snow drifted down like soft popcorn. As Mildred Bennet had told Charlotte, it was all "just swell." Lily was enchanted.

But not completely. Lily, who attended a fashionable Cleveland boarding school, might have looked like an angel with her incongruously almost white hair she had inherited from her father and pretty face and graceful figure inherited from her mother, but there was more than a little of the devil inside the wrapping. For a girl her age, she seethed with a remarkable quotient of resentment. Being bright, she was acutely conscious of her place in the world, and she knew her family were satellites around the sun of Mark Manning. She was proud of her father's position in the company, but she hated the fact that he was Number Two rather than Number One, and inwardly she cringed with embarrassment at his Swedish accent and immigrant's manners. Harold, like Elmo Tilden, might put on a boiled shirt and white tie, but the honest look of the greasepit was never far off and Lily hated it. Rather, she wished her father were more like Mark Manning. He had come from nowhere, too, but he looked like a real swell as he stood next to his wife, smoothly greeting the guests. Besides, he was so handsome!

As Carter and she passed through the receiving line, Lily curtsied politely when she shook Charlotte's hand. "It was so nice of you to invite me, Mrs. Manning," she said, her envious eyes taking in Charlotte's gorgeous pale yellow satin gown with the white-fox-trimmed overskirt at the knees and the yellow satin turban—Charlotte, like Amelia was a convert to Poiret's Turkish-harem style. "We're delighted you could come, Lily," replied Charlotte, eyeing the lovely girl in the sweet white dress and wondering why her green eyes seemed so cold and, yes, calculating. Lily moved on to Mark, trying to decide whether she should drop her eyes demurely or stare at him boldly. She decided to stare. "Your house is just beautiful, Mr. Manning," she said, looking directly into his eyes and wishing, wildly, that he would kiss her right *there* in the entrance hall in front of the whole crowd. "Why, thank you, Lily,"—he smiled —"and I hope you have a good time tonight."

"Oh, I'm sure I will. Mr. Lang was so nice to invite me." She smiled prettily at Carter next to her. "He's so much older and more sophisticated than I am, I'm truly flattered he asked to be my escort." He also knows I'm the best-looking damn girl in Elkins, she thought.

They passed on into the living room, Carter refraining from comment. This Lily Swenson was pretty and well-mannered, but there was something about her that didn't quite go with the advertisement.

At eight o'clock, just as Lily Swenson was curtsying to Charlotte at the house at River Bend, George Forley was arriving at the Pentecostal Church with Charlie Sill, the *Star Chronicle*'s staff photographer. They both were surprised by the size of the crowd. About fifty men and maybe a half dozen women had braved the fifteen-degree cold and the snow to come to the Wobbly rally. Forley wondered if perhaps the attack on Crazy Bill Sands's press and the subsequent halting of the popular *Sting* had generated more sympathy for Sands than people suspected—and, concurrently, more antipathy toward the Manning management—everyone knew it was Manning's security chief, Jim Malloy, who had smashed the press. At any rate, the crowd listened attentively enough as Lindquist delivered a long harangue about the injustices of the Manning company in general and its blind, obstinate opposition to unionization. Bill Sands then took the pulpit and launched into a philippic about the bad labor practices of the company, the brutality of Jim Malloy and his security force (not failing to recount what had happened in his garage, and holding aloft his broken flute for all to see as a real and symbolic proof). He went on to a peroration about the greed of Mark Manning and his top executives, who were piling up great fortunes while the workers were in effect tossed scraps from the table. Lindquist was a good speaker, well-tuned to his audience's attention span; Bill was not, and the crowd began restless shuffling until Lindquiest whispered in Bill's ear a gentle hint and he finally stopped. Then the cry was raised, "On to River Bend!" The crowd poured out of the church, where torches were passed around and lighted. As hip flasks were pulled out—socialist rhetoric being a less-effective antifreeze than alcohol—the march was on to River Bend.

The town was especially quiet for a Saturday night. A few of the bars seemed to have some activity in them, and some of their patrons came to the windows to watch the marchers pass, but otherwise the residents of Elkins seemed to have shut themselves inside their houses —no doubt partly because of the bad weather but also, Forley thought, out of an instinctive desire to stay out of potential trouble. The police, however, were nowhere in evidence, which somehow was ominous. Neither Forley nor Lindquist nor Sands could understand why there wasn't at least a patrol car trailing the crowd. Men and women trudged through the snow, holding their flickering torches up, some making a few comments but most in silence, as if the ominous quiet had turned them inward to their own thoughts . . . second thoughts? Lindquist sensed this. As they reached the outskirts of town, he started singing Christmas carols. Even though it was weeks before the season, it was an inspired move. Everyone knew the words, the tunes were jolly and the snow seemed Christmasy. Quickly the marchers picked up the familiar melodies, nervousness vanished and fifty-odd voices gave forth with "It Came Upon a Midnight Clear," "Hark the herald angels sing, glory to the newborn King! Peace on earth, good will to me-en, Christ is born in Be-thle-hem! Joy-ful all ye na-tions ri-ise, Join the triumph of the ski-ies . . ."

George Forley was walking directly behind Bill Sands, who had a pint bottle of bourbon in his hip pocket. Now as he pushed up his corduroy coat to pull the bottle out for another swig, George noticed something flash in the torchlight.

> Hark the herald angels sing!
> Glo-ry to the newborn King . . .

At ten after nine, they reached the imposing gates of River Bend and waited. Silence, as the crowd looked at the twenty cars lined up in front of the gates and almost fifty feet in either direction from them, a solid phalanx of Tin Lizzies, Ariels and Tillmobiles. Two of the cars were police cars, and Sheriff Benson—tall, stringy, tough Alvin Benson—was leaning on the hood of one of them, a shotgun drooping through his crooked elbow. Six of his men surrounded him, dressed in sheepskin-lined coats and also carrying shotguns. And there was Jim Malloy with thirty of his men, armed with pistols. The elegant lanterns on top of the brick gateposts glowed warmly through the snowflakes.

Eric Lindquist had been leading the crowd. Now he turned and called, "Look at the welcoming committee! Your police force, whose salaries you pay through your taxes, standing there with shotguns! Do you think if Mark Manning walked up to *your* house and *you* called the police, do you think they'd send out two cars and a half dozen men to protect *you*? Not damn likely!"

Silence. Nobody made a noise or a move. George Forley could see that the crowd was undecided, and scared.

Bill Sands reached in his hip pocket for another swig at the bottle, and this time George saw what it was that had gleamed in the torch-light.

It was the butt of a revolver.

———————————————

Mark and Charlotte were dancing the Maxixe when Charlotte giggled.

"What's so funny?" asked her husband.

"I was just thinking about Mildred Bennet," replied Charlotte, whose favorite pearls rested on her bosom. "She told me she thought the party was 'just swell.' Isn't that a wonderful compliment? I've always wanted to be 'just swell.' "

"You are 'just swell.' That's how I've always thought of you."

"Thanks." She pouted her nose, then gave him a suspicious look. "And what's been going on between you and 'Squeaks'?"

"Me and *who*?"

"Little squeaky Sylvia Baker," said Charlotte, imitating Sylvia's breathy way of talking. "You two were very cozy at lunch, and she told me she thinks you're just 'nifty.' "

"Well, I am 'nifty.' " Mark smiled. " 'Just swell' Charlotte and 'nifty Mark'—that's us. And how about you and Elmo Tilden?"

"Oh, be serious! Isn't he awful? I mean, he's a very nice person, I suppose, but what manners . . . Oh, well . . ." They danced for a while in silence. Then she said, "There's someone else I've got my eye on."

"Who would that be?"

"Little Lily Swenson, except I don't know why I call her 'little.' Something tells me little Lily is getting to be a very big girl. And she just thinks you're the most wonderful thing God ever handed down to us poor mortals."

"Honestly, Charlotte, you've go to do something about that imagination of yours. Lily's about twelve years old—"

"She's a very mature nineteen, and I can tell when other women
have their eyes on my husband. And I take notes in that little diary
in my head. So you just be careful."

He laughed. "All right, I'll be careful."

"Aren't you ever jealous of me?"

"I trust you."

"Maybe you shouldn't. What if I had a love affair? Amelia Clark
thinks I should."

"Charlotte, please . . ."

"Anyway, I told her I'm not the type. But would you be insanely
jealous if I did?"

"I'd do my best."

She decided the badinage was at best a draw, looked around and
noticed her father huddled in his wheelchair at the side of the
room, contemplating the dancers with a scowl. "Weren't you amazed
that father came tonight?"

"Yes, I was, but he seems to be having a fine time, doesn't he?"

"He doesn't look well. He looks thinner than the last time I saw
him."

"I wouldn't worry too much about Sam. As long as I'm around,
he'll keep alive just to spite me."

"Oh, Mark, don't say that."

"Well, it's true, isn't it?"

"Even if it is I don't like to hear it. Oh, there's Carter. I think he
wants to talk to you."

Carter Lang had come around the dance floor and was signaling to
them. They left the floor and joined him.

"There's a policeman in the front hall," he said in a low voice.
"They're out at the gate now."

"What's happening?" Mark asked.

"Apparently not much. Lindquist is trying to make something out
of the fact that the police are there, but the crowd doesn't seem too
interested. In fact a few of them have started back to town. It looks
like it's a flop."

"Has anyone tried to get beyond the police?"

Carter shook his head. "I don't think they ever intended to. Lindquist's no fool."

"I'll go talk to the police. You dance with Charlotte, will you?"

"With pleasure."

As Mark made his way to the door of the ballroom, Carter took

Charlotte out on the dance floor. The band had segued to a slinky tango, and Carter said, "Do you know how?"

"To tango? Of course."

The dancers faced each other, then extended their arms forward and slid out, some of them looking awkward, others doing the dance well. Carter and Charlotte belonged to the latter group.

"Say, you *are* good."

"And so are you, Mr. Lang. Where's Lily?"

"She's dancing with Dan Nyquist, from Cleveland. He's been cutting in on me all evening."

"I can see why. Lily's very pretty."

"Yes, and she knows it, too."

"That's not a very kind thing to say about that sweet young lady."

Carter laughed. " 'Sweet' is not quite the word I'd use to describe Lily."

Charlotte smiled. "I hear you've joined the country club?"

"Well, it's not the most exciting place in the world but there's poker in the winter and golf in the summer."

The tango ended and a fast bunny hug took its place. But before they could begin, Mark returned and they joined him at the edge of the floor.

"I told the police to let them through the gate," he said.

"Why?" asked Charlotte, alarmed.

"You'll see."

"But Mark, don't you think that's dangerous?" Carter asked. "The police said they were drinking, and they've got torches. There's no telling what they might do."

"They won't do anything," Mark said. "They're my men and they respect me. It probably was a mistake to bring the police out here in the first place. Charlotte, please tell the band to keep on playing, then I'd appreciate it if you'd join me in the front hall."

He went back around the dance floor as Carter watched him, wondering if he had lost his mind and at the same time admiring his easy self-confidence. He turned to look at Charlotte, who was talking to the band leader. There was no doubt about it—Mrs. Manning was a truly beautiful woman. And charming, too.

Sam Rosen had become physically senile but his mind was still as alert as it had been all the seventy-odd years of his life, and now as

he sat in his wheelchair at the side of the ballroom watching the
son-in-law he had come to dislike, he wondered if the Wobblies had
actually shown up at the gate and what Mark was doing about it.
The Wobblies at the gate! It was like the Visigoths or the Huns at
the gate. Sam thought the calmly ordered America he had known
since he migrated from Germany so many years ago must be coming
apart. Still, Mark had asked for it, building this *Neuschwanstein* of
a house. Sam was glad he had come to the party, after all; seeing
the place had proved out his worst fears. And now the Wobblies.

"Go see what's happening," he ordered Miss Pringle in his thin
voice.

"Now, Mr. Rosen," replied the nurse in the condescending fashion
he hated, "we know I can't leave you."

"Oh, go *on*! I want to know if the Wobblies are here yet. And stop
saying 'we,' damn it."

"Well, *you* mustn't get excited. If you do, we'll have to go home,
and *you* wouldn't want to do that, now would we?"

Sam, defeated, sank back into his chair. The worst part about old
age was being dependent on nurses. Death was surely preferable to
Miss Pringle.

Riley Baker had overheard the little exchange. Now the pleasant-
faced man, whose graying hair had added a touch of distinction to
his looks, said in a benign voice, "I'll find out what's happening,
Sam."

Sam nodded gratefully, and Riley threaded his way through the
crowd toward the entrance hall. When he returned a few minutes
later, his expression was one of surprise. "They're out in front of
the gates," he whispered to Sam, "and Mark's told the police to let
them in."

Sam looked up at him. "Is he crazy?"

Riley shrugged. "I don't know. It sounds like it, doesn't it?"

"It certainly does! To invite those hooligans in here? Why, it's
dangerous—dangerous and damned irresponsible! That idiot is always
doing something irresponsible . . . *damn* him!"

Riley was surprised by the intensity of the outburst, and he was
not slow to profit by it. "Yes, Mark does have a tendency toward,
well, the unconventional, I suppose you might call it."

"He jeopardized the welfare of our company and my daughter's
happiness—not to mention his own life—when he went down to South
America against my wishes, and now he's exposing all of us to danger
by inviting in these violent radicals—ah, the man's a menace. I've
always known it."

He shook his head, as Riley Baker considered the interesting possibilities in what he had just heard.

The crowd was thinning and Bill Sands was getting nervous. He turned to the photographer, Charlie Sill, and said, "Take some more pictures."

"Of what? There's nothing happening, I don't want to waste the plates."

Frustration came over Sands's face, and George Forley momentarily felt sorry for him. The man really wanted fireworks and he wasn't getting it. Lindquist was still in front of the gates trying to start up a chant, "Union now! Union now!" It wasn't working. Only a half dozen or so had joined in. The rest were standing around rather self-consciously trying to decide whether to join those who had already left for town or to stay for—what? No one quite knew. It seemed the wind had gone out of the demonstration before it had even gotten off the ground, which could make for some ugly frustrations, George Forley knew.

The sheriff moved the two cars out of the way. For a moment both Sands and Linquist could only stare. Then Sands finished his bottle, throwing the empty into a snowbank, and hurried around the crowd to Lindquist's side. "They're letting us in!" he said excitedly.

"I've got eyes," snapped Lindquist, who looked distinctly unhappy.

"Then what are we waiting for? Let's go!"

"How do you know it's not a trap?"

"How could it be? Manning's probably sore as hell and he's about to read the riot act—"

"If he was going to do that he'd come out here to do it. He's not going to bring us all the way to the house just to tell us to get the hell out. Don't be an ass."

"You're afraid," said Sands softly. "You have been all along . . ."

Lindquist turned on him, blazing. "You fool!" he said with quiet intensity. "You damn pigheaded fool! You'll explain away anything to get us face-to-face with Manning. You're obsessed with the man and making your own stupid idea work. How do you know the minute we walk through that gate we won't be arrested for trespassing?"

Just then Sheriff Benson stepped into the headlamps of one of the Model-T police cars and walked out to join the two Wobblies. "Mr. Manning's sent word out," he said; "you're to come up to the house if you want to."

Silence. Lindquist was on the spot and he knew it, but he also knew how to hide it. He smiled and said, "Come on, Sheriff, you don't expect us to believe you're going to let us go up that drive without arresting us?"

The sheriff shrugged. "What am I going to arrest you for? You've been invited in."

He walked back to his car. Lindquist turned to Bill, who looked jubilant. "Well, the bastard's got us now," Lindquist said in a resigned voice. "I hope to hell you're satisfied." With that, he turned and raised his torch, calling to the crowd, "We've been invited in! Manning wants us to come on in so he can say hello! All right, come on, let's go visit the millionaire fat cats who want to show us how the other half lives from our sweat."

Waving the torch in an "excelsior" gesture, he started through the gate as Sands waved the crowd on. Now spirits picked up again. The thirty-odd people remaining surged through the gates onto the drive, intrigued by Mark's invitation and curious to see what now promised to be a real show after such a disappointing prologue. They didn't even seem bothered by the police cars which, after waiting for all of them to pass, now started up, following them at a cautious distance. Jim Malloy's men also fell into line behind the police cars, though they were on foot. As Charlie Sill lugged his tripod and camera over his shoulder through the snow, he said to George Forley, "What the hell do you think Manning's up to?"

"Who knows?" shrugged the reporter. "All I know is so far this thing has been a big fizzle."

As they tramped down the driveway through the dark, snowy woods, someone started singing "God Rest Ye Merry Gentlemen." Everyone picked up the tune, and George Forley commented to Charlie, "Some wild bunch of fanatical revolutionaries, aren't they?"

"Yeah. Real bomb throwers."

Lindquist was thinking the same thing, and was mentally kicking himself for ever getting involved in the moribund demonstration. He had miscalculated the crowd's seriousness, letting himself be carried away by his own rhetoric, and by the need at least to keep Bill Sands from doing something crazy enough to live up to his name. At the Pentecostal Church he had thought he was genuinely charging them up, but now he knew most of them were merely onlookers along for the show. He had been foolish, he decided, to get in this deep, but now the problem was that he was in too deep to get out without losing face, and Bill Sands knew it. Probably, he thought, Mark Manning knew it as well, which was why he was *inviting* them in. His anger at Sands, which had blazed when the man had called him afraid, simmered as he thought of the hell of a fix the man's zeal had gotten him—and the I.W.W.—into. Never trust a true believer, he thought bitterly. Never trust a damn fanatic. The worst part was, he'd told himself the same thing a hundred times before.

> . . . may nothing you dismay!
> For Christ the Lord our Sa-vi-our was born this Christmas day . . .

Bill Sands, on the other hand, was up again, partially from the excitement and partially from the considerable quantity of alcohol he had consumed. What had looked like a disaster outside the gates had miraculously been transformed; they were inside now, going up to the house for a dramatic confrontation. After years of *reading* about the class war in Marx, after years of *talking* dialectics, he was now *living* the Great Confrontation between capital and the proletariat . . . the excitement was intoxicating. The crowd would be outraged by the palatial mansion, the stuffed-shirt capitalist exploiters and their bejeweled wives. And Manning! Manning would be outraged, and every word from him would serve to incite the crowd further. Best of all, he had forced a showdown with Lindquist; now the victory would be his more than Lindquist's, and the thought was sweetly satisfying to Bill Sands.

> Oh, tidings of co-om-fort and joy! Comfort and joy!
> Oh, tidings of co-om-fort and joy!

They emerged from the woods to be confronted by the big house, light spilling from its many windows onto the snow; what looked like at least forty limousines were parked in front of it in the long drive. The crowd stopped and Sands yelled, "There it is, boys! There's the modest little honeymoon cottage Mark Manning built for his wife and his brood, and paid for with your sweat!" There were a few awed whistles, then they started up again, crossing the lawn past the Pierce Arrows, the Panhards, Packards and Peerlesses toward the rambling house. From the north ballroom came the jazzy sound of the ragtime band playing the hit of the previous year, "When the Midnight Choochoo Leaves for Alabam'." The crowd, tired of the carols, picked up the tune. Singing raucously, they surged into the brick courtyard. Then they stopped, everyone looking at the closed front door. The midnight choochoo had reached Alabam' and, again, no one was quite sure what to do.

Eric Lindquist decided to take over. "Mark Manning!"

The others took it up and began chanting, "Mark Manning! Mark Manning!"

"You ready?" George Forley said to Charlie Sill, who set up his camera and was aiming it at the front door. He held his flashpan in his right hand and nodded, "Ready."

The front door opened, and there was Mark Manning in his white tie and tails. Beside him stood Charlotte in her yellow satin and white fox. The crowd shut up as the flash powder exploded. At the many windows giving out onto the courtyard could be seen the party guests, staring through the mullioned panes at the workers outside.

"Good evening," Mark said in a strong, friendly voice. "It's open house at River Bend tonight, so why don't you all come in and have a drink?"

The crowd looked confused. Son of a bitch, thought George Forley. Clever son of a bitch.

Eric Lindquist was thinking the same thing. It took two sides for a confrontation. Manning had indeed drawn them into a trap, and was about to spring it with his civility. Now Lindquist was in the damnable position of having to fire up his people or withdraw in humiliation—which would ruin him and seriously set back the organization after all the national—international—bad publicity that was sure to follow. That idiot Sands . . . Well, now he had no choice. . . .

"We didn't come here for a drink," Lindquist yelled, making sure the crowd got the full force of his words. "We came here to tell you and your fat-cat friends there's hunger in this country—hunger and poverty! People like you, *Mister* Manning, build private palaces and throw parties and ride around in limousines—do you suppose we're going to drink to *that*? We can't be bought off that cheap! You spend a million dollars to build this monument to your vanity"—he gestured widely at the house—"while the men who work for you, the men who make you rich, scrape by on a lousy four bucks a day and aren't allowed the privilege—and I say it's a *right*—to join a union!"

The speech was less than historic in its originality, and Lindquist knew it. He also knew how to deliver it with conviction. It began to work. The crowd was murmuring concurrence.

Mark stuck his hands in his pockets. "Well, now," he said, "in the first place, this house didn't cost any million dollars. And in the second place, I happen to agree with you—it *did* cost too much. You can ask my wife—she'll tell you how I yelled about the bills . . ."

"Don't give us that phony just-folks stuff," interrupted Bill Sands angrily. "You're avoiding the question."

Mark looked at him. "And what's the question?"

"The question is whether it's fair for you to be rich and us to be poor!"

"Are you poor, Bill?"

"Compared to you, I'm a goddamn pauper!"

"And what's your solution for evening it up?"

Everyone was watching Sands now, and Lindquist silently cursed him for derailing the argument as well as stealing the show.

"That Manning Rubber be owned by the workers, instead of by Mark Manning and his already-rich stockholders!" shouted Sands. "That *we* get the gravy, not you, because *we* do the work. That's my solution."

Silence. Mark looked at one of the men standing near Sands.

"How about it, Jim? You go along with that?"

Jim Carruthers, one of the original workers whom Mark knew, shifted uncomfortably.

"Well, I don't know if I'd go along with that, Mr. Manning. That's pretty, well, you know, radical. But I think we should have a union."

"Carruthers, you're a stupid weasel," Sands told him.

"And why don't you just pipe down?" Carruthers answered. "You're making one helluva lot of noise."

"You go to hell!"

Mark raised his hands. "Look, whether I'm right or wrong, or whether it's fair or unfair, I still say, at least come on in and have a drink. *You* may not want to corrupt your pure socialist throat with capitalist booze, Bill, but maybe the rest of your friends figure a drink's a drink—never mind the source. How about it, Jim? It's pretty damned cold out here."

"We want fair treatment, not a damn drink!" yelled Sands. "We want a union."

Mark smiled at him and pointed to another man. "Frank? How about it? I guarantee you can go right on hating me when you leave, but we've got a good buffet spread, too. Plenty for everybody."

Silence. Then Frank rubbed the sleeves of his coat over his mouth and started toward the door.

"I don't know about the rest of them, Mr. Manning," he said, "but I'm freezing my ass off."

There was a roar of laughter. Tossing their torches into the snow, the people thronged to the doorway, squeezing to get in as they pushed Lindquist to one side. Bill Sands was enraged.

"You fools, you idiots! Can't you see you're playing right into his hands?"

"Aw, go to hell."

"Yeah, shut up. We're sick of listening to you."

"Besides, we want to see the house! Damn, look at that staircase? Ain't that something?"

Sands launched himself into the crowd and grabbed a man, pulling him back and shoving him into the snow.

"He hasn't answered the question! He hasn't answered the *question!*"

"It's a dumb question," another man said. "How can he? And quit muscling people around. *You* sure as hell don't own us."

They started pushing through the door again as Charlotte disappeared inside the house. George Forley looked at the guests on the other side of the windows. Some looked apprehensive at this invasion of the workers, others mostly curious. Forley spotted elegant Hanson Mayberry scribbling notes on his pad, and George thought it would be the first time the Wobblies would ever make the society page. And there was old Sam Rosen huddled in his wheelchair with his starched white nurse standing behind him. Forley wondered what Sam must be thinking.

Charlie Sill was taking pictures as fast as he could load his flashpan; by now a third of the crowd had made its way inside the house, and George noticed that Eric Lindquist had taken Sands aside and was talking to him, attempting to calm him down. But Bill looked crazy with rage as well as booze and George felt a surge of compassion for the man. Whatever might be said about his sociology— and George, being basically apolitical, wouldn't take sides—still, he genuinely believed it and there had been the ring of undeniable conviction to what he had said compared to the rather stagey sound of Lindquist's speech. Bill Sands's rage was not only aimed at the Mark Mannings and River Bends of the world, the comfortable rich inside, the unrich outside; it was also directed at the crowd's *lack* of supporting anger. Sands looked as if he would have liked to tear the house down with his bare hands, and everything it represented with it, if for no other reason than to galvanize the others out of their apathy. That he probably wouldn't have known what to build in its place was irrelevant; the honest rage itself was fascinating.

Suddenly Sands was pushing Lindquist away. He pulled the gun out of his pocket and fired it into the air. The explosion shocked everyone still. The men shoving through the door of the house stopped and looked back at the emptying courtyard. Lindquist looked as amazed as everyone else. "For Christ's sake, Bill—"

"Shut up!" Sands yelled. Then he aimed the gun at the men. "Everyone get out of there! We're going back to town."

Silence.

"I said, we're going back! If you're too stupid to understand what Manning's doing to you . . ."

"Bill, give me that gun!" Lindquist started toward him.

Instantly, Sands turned the gun on him. "Stay back."

Lindquist stopped. "Goddamn it, you're doing us more harm than good! Can't you see that—"

"The only thing I see is that Manning's tricked us, and we're getting out of here."

The police were piling from their cars outside the courtyard in answer to the sound of the shot. At the same time Mark pushed his way through the crowd and out of the house. Spotting Sheriff Benson, he yelled, "Put the guns away!" The Sheriff, confused, lowered his shotgun, as did his men. But Jim Malloy, who had joined the sheriff, ducked behind the hood of one of the cars, out of Mark's sight, and aimed his pistol at Bill Sands's head.

Mark looked at Sands and said quietly, "Now, Bill, just what the hell do you think that's going to prove?"

Sands said nothing, aimed the muzzle of his gun at the snow-white, pearl-studded shirtfront of his employer. Mark held out his hand and began walking toward him.

"Give me that thing," he said.

"Don't come any closer"—soft-spoken for the first time.

Mark stopped. "Now, Bill, you know damned well you're not going to shoot me. You say I'm a bastard. Well, all right, you're entitled. But if you shoot me, everyone's going to think you're the bastard, not me. So use your damn common sense and put that thing away."

Bill's heart was pumping, the alcohol and blood rushing through his brain, making his ears ring. Two, then one, then two Mark Mannings blurred his vision.

"You told Jim Malloy to bust up my printing press," he yelled, and he hadn't forgotten—nor forgiven them—for destroying the beautiful flute.

Mark started toward him again.

"Look, Bill, you're drunk . . ."

"Stand back!"

Mark stopped. "What are you trying to prove? You say I didn't answer your question—all right, I was poor once myself, and by the way I made a hell of a lot less money than *you* make. But I made myself some money, and what's wrong with that? Why should I have to apologize for that to you? Isn't that what this country's all about? The chance to make yourself rich? And don't give me the crap that I'm some bloodsucker of an employer—no one's going to buy that." He turned back to the door and shouted, *"Do any of you buy that?"*

The crowd at the door was mesmerized by the gun. Now a murmur of "no"s answered the question. Mark turned back to the gun, aimed at approximately the second pearl stud down from his collar button. "You're flogging a dead horse, Bill. You and Lindquist came out here tonight to try to stir up trouble, and you're not doing it. You know why? Because the people that work for me know I give them a square deal—a damn sight better one than you can. So put that gun away, and we'll forget the whole thing ever happened."

"No."

Mark again held out his hand.

"Give it to me. It's getting cold out here—"

"It's never too cold to hate your kind. You've been exploiting—"

Mark laughed. "You've been reading too much of your own propaganda, Bill. Come on, give me the gun."

Afterwards, nobody was quite sure whether Mark had moved first or Sands had fired first. All they knew for sure was that Sands did fire, and Mark twirled halfway to one side, then fell face down into the snow. The crowd was shocked into silence, then most threw themselves down onto the snow-covered ground as Jim Malloy's pistol fired. Its bullet went into Bill Sands's skull behind his left ear. He slumped to the ground, instantly dead. Now the courtyard swarmed with police and people; Eric Lindquist got to Mark first. "Somebody call an ambulance!" he yelled.

By the time a horrified Charlotte had gotten to his side, Mark had been turned over onto his back and the white shirtfront was soaked with blood. He was barely conscious. He stared up at his wife and tried to say something. Then his eyes closed. She was certain he was dead.

———————————————

When Sands fired at Mark, the guests gathered at the windows inside the house had screamed and run for cover. Miss Pringle had been one of the first to scurry, her panic making her forget her duty to her patient as the answering shot from Jim Malloy's gun rang out. Riley Baker, who had been next to Sam, had grabbed the old man's wheelchair to push him away from the window. As he did so, he saw Sam's face. Old Sam was excited, but certainly not horrified in the manner of the others at what had happened.

In fact, Riley had the definite impression that ancient Sam Rosen was anything but unhappy that his son-in-law had been shot and, for all he knew, killed.

Even amidst all the confusion, Riley Baker's tidy mind was filing away this impression for future use.

Like most of his contemporaries, Carter Lang admired the feminine ideal embodied in the drawings of Mr. Dana Gibson: the lovely young woman, well bred, noble, intelligent, fun, graceful and gracious. But Carter seldom encountered her. Some, like Sheila Farr Boine, won his admiration for their remarkable will to survive despite great hardships; others, like Lily Swenson, struck him as amusingly crafty —neither was even an approximation of the Gibson Girl. However, in the confused hours following the shoot-out in the Manning court-yard, Carter was with Charlotte almost the entire time, and he was overwhelmed with admiration for what he considered the most ele-gant performance under stress he had ever seen. And it was a per-formance; he knew that beneath her calm she was a wife and woman terrified she was about to lose her husband. She never showed it. All through the agonizing ambulance ride to the hospital and the inter-minable wait while the doctors operated, she never gave way to hysteria or fear. Rather, she was calm, dignified and in apparent con-trol of herself. She even refused to blame Sands. "He was drunk," she said to Carter and the Clarks as they waited outside the operating room. "His hatred of Mark was so misguided he couldn't have been in his right mind."

Carter thought she was being overly generous, but he considered it a *beau geste* in any case. It was only when the doctor came out of surgery to tell her that Mark would be all right—that the bullet had missed the vital organs—it was only then that Charlotte's cool façade cracked and she began to cry softly with relief, burying her head in Amelia Clark's shoulder and venting the tension inside her. Quickly, she was again in control of herself. She thanked the doctor, then Amelia, Sir Bruce and Carter drove her back to River Bend.

The next morning, to everyone's amazement, she was up for breakfast. She explained to her guests that Mark was going to be all right, and she thanked them for their forbearance throughout all the upset. As she was doing so, Elmo Tilden waddled into the dining room looking woefully hung over. He sank into his seat and looked down the table at Mark's empty chair. "Where's Mark?"

His wife glared at him. "What do you mean, *where* is he? Don't tell me you don't remember?"

Tilden's puffy face looked confused. "Remember what?"

"If you *perhaps* had stayed reasonably sober, you might have *some* recollection of what happened!"

"All right, you don't have to lecture me in front of everybody. And what *did* happen?"

Hanson Mayberry directed a contemptuous look. "Mark was shot by a Wobbly," he said.

The father of the Tillmobile was finally sober. "You mean he's *dead?*"

"No," Charlotte said. "Fortunately, he's going to be all right."

Elmo shook his head. "Why, that's terrible! You mean one of those people came up here to this house and shot Mark? That's outrageous! They ought to round up every one of those animals and shoot 'em!"

"He *was* shot," said Charlotte, coolly. "He was killed."

"Well, that's the *least* they could have done!" said Elmo. (Presumably the *most* would have been to kill Sands twice.) "They're all animals, revolutionaries, want to ruin everything this country stands for! I'd like to stick every one of 'em in the electric chair and pull the switch myself—"

Charlotte stopped him with a glacial stare. "Mr. Tilden," she said, "the man is dead. I certainly am not happy about what he did, but the man *is* dead, and it is vicious to speak evil of the dead. Let's please not say anything more about it."

Tilden said nothing more, then awkwardly dug into his grapefruit, squirting juice on his shirtfront.

Again, Carter Lang thought Charlotte was being overly generous about the fate of Bill Sands, but he nevertheless admired her extravagantly for it. And the discomfiting thought occurred to him that, for the first time in his life, he might be falling in love.

CHAPTER FIVE

CORRESPONDENCE

1913–1915

Letter from Charlotte Manning to Amelia Clark at the Waldorf-Astoria Hotel, New York City, dated November 16, 1913.

Dear Amelia,

Mark is improving every day, and Dr. Brill thinks he may be able to come home in a few weeks. Thank God! He was in great pain the first week after the operation, but the pain is much less now and Dr. Brill says because of his strong constitution and youth (isn't it ironic that we celebrated his thirty-fifth birthday just two days before the shooting?) he should escape any permanent damage to his health. When I think how close I came to losing him, I still shudder. All I can say is, it was lucky Sands was drunk. If he'd been sober, I doubt my darling would be alive today—I understand the man was an experienced hunter and an excellent shot.

As you know, the reaction in the press has been overwhelmingly critical of the union, but what truly has been gratifying is the mail that has come in. Over 4,000 letters and telegrams in the past ten days! People all over the country have written genuinely touching notes, deploring the shooting and saying their prayers were with both of us. People who remember what Mark did in Peru were especially angry that anyone could attack a man who had already risked his life to help the less fortunate. And the reaction from the workers in our own factories has left no doubt what they think of Mark. They've sent flowers and candy and letters to the hospital, and the men passed a resolution condemning the Wobblies and praising Mark's management —all of which, of course, has been very heartwarming. Mark has been too weak to respond to any of this, but I've been doing my best to answer all the mail personally, though it may take weeks. Carter Lang has been most helpful through all this, and I don't know what I would have done without him in these terrible times. By the way, I was *so* wrong about him. He is a dear, warm person and not at all the usual businessman I had first thought. Now, don't get any of your cunning ideas. We are nothing but friends, but it is such a relief to have some-

one to rely on at a time like this. The poor children, or at least David
and Ellen, were so worried about their poppa, but they're much better
now and I've been very fortunate to find a new nanny for them, a Mrs.
Brent who came over from London eight years ago and was recommended by the Davises, whom she worked for in Connecticut. Mrs.
Brent is a wonder, Carter is a Godsend and Mark is mending—so, all
things considered, perhaps our Christmas is going to be a merry one
after all.

More later—affectionately,

Charlotte

Letter from Riley Baker to Sam Rosen, dated November 17, 1913.

Dear Sam:

I have been reading what the newspapers have been writting about
the shooting incident at River Bend, and while I am delighted by the
almost universal condemnation of the Wobblies—frankly, any antiunion publicity is "good" publicity—still I must in all honesty tell you
that I feel, as a major stockholder in the Manning Company, that
Mark's behavior that evening is, regretfully, more to be condemned
than praised. Remembering your remarks on the subject that evening,
I'm taking the liberty of communicating to you some of my own
thoughts on Mark's management of the company we both have such
a large financial interest in.

No one would deny that Mark is an able and astute businessman.
Moreover, he apparently is a good administrator and surely none of
us has much to complain about concerning dividends. But in corporate
management, one must seek for long-term qualities, qualities that will
insure an "even keel" over the long haul, and in this I think Mark
is somewhat lacking. This, by the way, is not unusual. I know many
men who have had the brilliant qualities needed to found large corporations but who have, in time, become something of an embarrassment to their own companies—it would seem the nervousness, energy,
and imagination necessary to get something going are the very qualities
that tend to get in the way of keeping it rolling smoothly once it's
started. Mark is a clever man, and I can certainly understand the tactic
in taking the demonstrators by surprise and inviting them into his
house. But look what happened! And, as you said that night, look at
the danger he exposed all of us to! How much better it would have
been to take a firm stand and not let the rascals through the gate in
the first place. Not "clever," certainly. But *responsible*. I have the feeling that Mark simply can't resist the grandstand play, that he is something of what theater people call a star performer. He wants his men
to love him, be dazzled by him, not only because he thinks that's one

way to control them, but because it feeds his need for their esteem and affection. He's something like Napoleon in this regard, and while I yield to no one in my admiration of the brilliant Corsican, I certainly would have been unhappy if I had invested in the First Empire. This is what worries me about Mark—will he, like Napoleon (surely another theatrical personality, a star performer if ever there was one), continue to be "brilliant" and "clever" and lead all us Manning stockholders into the financial equivalent of Napoleon's fatal invasion of Russia? I may gloat over my dividends now, but do I hear the 1812 Overture in the distance? Or am I being too nervous? You, as Mark's father-in-law and having known him from the beginning, should be able to answer this better than anyone, which is why I'm taking the liberty of writing this note. Recalling your remarks at River Bend, I feel you may possibly share or at least be understanding of some of my misgivings.

Hoping not to have inconvenienced you in any way, I am,

Sincerely yours,
Riley Baker

Letter from Sam Rosen to Riley Baker in New York, dictated by Sam to his secretary, Miss Childes, dated November 24, 1913.

Dear Riley:

Your most kind and interesting letter has cheered me greatly. I don't get much mail any more—no one seems to take much interest in an old party like me—but it was a double pleasure to read your thoughts on Mark, which, though expressed far more eruditely than I could manage, are not dissimilar from my own. As you commented, the press made Mark the hero of that incident, which is good in that it made the Wobbly the villain of the piece. Yet, as do you, I think Mark behaved with extreme imprudence in letting those people through the gates in the first place. As you said, it may have been a clever idea, but it was more a dangerous one, which was tragically proved by what happened. Mark, I agree, is just too clever—that's always been one of his major faults, in my judgment, and as a director and large stockholder in the corporation you have good reason to be nervous about him. Again, I agree with you as to Mark's capabilities. When I first teamed up with him eight years ago, his drive and energy and imagination were qualities I admired and the company needed. But I never felt he had the solid foundation of character so necessary in a lasting business enterprise; and when he told me he wanted to marry my daughter, my objections to the match were based as much on this lack of character as on Mark not being of her faith—no offense to yourself, of course. Time has not altered my feelings, though in fairness to Mark I must admit Charlotte seems happy enough, and they have produced a healthy crop of grandchildren for me. Still, his behavior that terrible night only reinforced my already serious doubts as to his capacity to run a large corporation.

I wish to thank you again for getting me away from the window during the shooting. I very much appreciate it. Miss Pringle's amazing lack of concern for my welfare at that moment gave me the excuse I have long been looking for to fire her. I now have a younger nurse who's much easier to look at and who, thank heavens, doesn't talk baby talk to me.

Hoping to hear from you again, I am,

Yours most sincerely,

Samuel Rosen

Letter from Charlotte Manning to Amelia Clark in London, dated January 19, 1914.

Dear Amelia,

We all went last night to see Carter's production of *Macbeth* (he's set up an impressive amateur theatrical program since you were last here). Carter was quite dashing as the Thane of Cawdor, though I fear Helen Ferguson, the wife of one of the executives at the plant, was somewhat inadequate as Lady Macbeth. She not only forgot half her lines but kept sneezing—apparently she had a cold and in the sleepwalking scene her sneezes sent the whole audience into gales of laughter. Anyway, Carter was marvelous—he really has a great deal of acting talent—and it was so wonderful for me to have Mark by my side again. He's completely well again, though of course he has a deep scar on his side where the bullet went in (missing his liver by an inch, Dr. Brill told me. My God, how close death is in all our lives), and we're off tomorrow for a six-week cruise in the Caribbean, which should do him a world of good. Luckily for me, Mrs. Brent has turned out to be such a gem I don't have to worry about leaving the children, though I'll miss them, of course, and they are distraught at being separated from their father so soon after getting him home again. But Mark needs the rest and the change of scene.

He doesn't talk much about the "incident," as I call it, but I know he's thought about it a great deal and I'm sad to say it's made him rather bitter—though I suppose that's inevitable. He's always considered his men as part of his family, and he's taken pride in treating them well—so much better than others—so when one of them turns against him, well, it has hurt him deeply. I pointed out that Sands was a rare exception, a man who had a reputation for eccentricity (everyone called him Crazy Bill) but this doesn't seem to soften Mark's bitterness. Perhaps time will restore his old feeling, but meanwhile he's hired a personal bodyguard and has taken to carrying a pistol around—he keeps it in a holster under his coat. Well, again, I suppose this is a natural precaution, but it's not one I welcome. The bodyguard is a young prizefighter named Marvin Senjak. He's a pleasant enough fellow (though not very bright, I'm afraid) who now lives in one of the servant's rooms. He drives for Mark and is never too far away from him and apparently is very loyal. If this eases Mark's mind, I suppose it's a good thing. Mark's hired round-the-clock guards for the house, too, and a contractor to build a ten-foot brick wall around the immediate grounds of the house this spring (no minor undertaking, believe me, since the wall will surround almost ten acres!). Mark says we have to be realistic and take into account the possibility of someone trying to kidnap one of the children, but that seems so remote to me and I loathe the idea of turning my beloved River Bend into a sort of prison with all of us like inmates. But Mark wants it and I don't have the heart to fight him about it, though I do think it's a mistake. Anyway, all of this pales beside my happiness at having him well again.

I was amused at your asking me in your last letter whether I considered myself a "new" woman. Well, I am strongly in favor of the movement to give us poor females the vote, as is Mark, and I think the sooner the country gives us the vote, the better. Moreover, I think many of the leading feminists make excellent points (the magazines seem to have nothing but articles on the "movement" lately). But I think probably I'm basically old-fashioned, if loving one's home and husband and children is "old-fashioned." Still, I wonder if I were twenty now, instead of an old married woman of thirty-five, whether I might not think about making a career of some sort for myself, though there are so few things open for women. It's an interesting thought. Carter thinks I would have made a wonderful actress (he's trying to get me to join his theater group), which makes me laugh. Me, a Duse or Bernhardt?

Well, I must peek in on Stella, who's packing my bags for the trip. I not only look forward to the Caribbean, but the chance to get away from Marvin Senjak. Poor man, he only does his job, but I can't help but think of him as a jailor rather than a protector.

My love to Bruce. Affectionately,

Charlotte

Letter from Sam Rosen to Riley Baker, dated July 15, 1914.

Dear Riley:

I will be looking forward to seeing you in Elkins next week for the directors' meeting, and I hope you will accept my poor hospitality and come here for dinner on the night of the 20th. These past six months I feel I have gotten to know you so much better through our correspondence that I now consider you my friend as well as a business associate, and I am anticipating an evening in your company. I fear I don't see many people socially—I haven't since my poor wife passed away, but lately, because of my paralysis, I've become something of a recluse—so it may not be your idea of a lively evening. However, my cook is good and so I can at least promise you an excellent dinner. As regards what you asked in your last letter, it goes without saying I have not mentioned to either Mark or Charlotte that we have been corresponding. It is none of their business whom I write, or who writes me; and frankly, you pay more attention to me than my own family. So you needn't worry about my saying anything during the meeting (that is, if I go, which I may not be up to).

I was saddened to read about the passing of Herschel Fine. He was a good man, in my opinion, and Wall Street will badly miss him. It brought to mind something regarding you, which I would never consider mentioning if, again, I didn't feel that we have through our letters become sufficiently well acquainted for me to bring it up without embarrassing you. Back in '07, when you bought out Brock Sylvester, you may recall that Mark and I were in New York seeing Herschel about raising some money. At the time, Herschel spoke very unflatteringly of you. Well, not to speak badly of the dead, but I now realize he had made a serious error in judgment about your character. We all make mistakes in life, of course, and I'm sure you've done things in your past you've regretted, as have I. But no one privileged to read your letters, as I have been, could have anything but the highest regard for your intelligence and integrity, and I only deplore that Herschel never had the opportunity to get to know you as I have. I'm certain he would have changed his opinion.

What do you think of this Sarajevo business? Some of the articles I've read seem to indicate Austria might actually start a war over the assassination, but I can't for the life of me think they would be so foolish.

Looking forward to the 20th, I am,

Sincerely yours,

Samuel Rosen

Letter from Charlotte Manning to Amelia Clark in London, dated March 5, 1915.

My dearest Amelia,

How this wretched, terrible war drags on and on, and what awful destruction and bloodshed it's causing! When I think of beautiful Belgium and France being devastated by the Germans, it makes me ashamed that father and mother came from that unfortunate country, though I know that's a silly attitude in many ways. Certainly I'm not going to stop loving Beethoven and Wagner just because the present-day Germans are behaving like beasts. But it is so sad that a nation that has given so many geniuses to civilization should now act like a nation that never heard of the word. But how proud you and Bruce must be of England!

Life here in the States goes on as if nothing were happening, though people talk about the war and wonder if we eventually will get in it. I originally was for neutrality, but I'm coming around to thinking we shouldn't stand by when our old friends need us, and Mark agrees with me. I'm afraid—and it greatly saddens me to tell you this—that that's one of the few things we *are* agreeing about these days. I know my domestic spats can be of little interest to you, and the war must make them seem ridiculously petty; but I am so terribly upset that I must impose on our old friendship and "let off steam" to my dearest friend.

It all began with Carter Lang. No, that's really not true. It began earlier, after the shooting here at River Bend that night, what was it, a year and a half ago. As I told you, when Mark got back from the hospital he hired a bodyguard for himself and guards for the house and built a monstrous brick wall around the property. Well, I said nothing much at the beginning, though he knew I disapproved of it. But after a while the whole thing began to have an effect on me—it's such a closed-in way to live! And while Marvin Senjak is really a nice man and completely devoted to Mark and me and the children, still I just don't like having him lurking about. If he were a servant, I suppose I wouldn't mind. They are more like friends. But he's a bodyguard, and though this may sound melodramatic, and I know he's an employee, still *he* seems somehow in charge of *us*, as though he has power over me and the children and there's nothing we could do about it even if we wanted to. . . . Anyway, I just don't like having him here, I don't like the other guards, and I *hate* the wall!

Well, I suppose it's natural that when one's way of life is rather dramatically altered, one begins seeing everything in a new light; certainly, I began seeing Mark in a new light, as well as our marriage and my life. Mark's passion in life is the Manning Rubber Company and piling up a huge fortune. I'm proud of the company, but it's certainly not a "passion" to me. And while I enjoy and appreciate the money, I just couldn't be less interested in whether Mark has five million or ten. But Mark *is* interested. In the past year his business has grown even faster than before—it's really incredible how big the company is becoming—and he's been gone so much on business trips

I hardly even know if I have a husband most of the time. Well, this is hardly a new complaint for wives of successful and important businessmen, I know, and I don't want to sound ungrateful, but it would help some if we lived in a city where there were a few cultural activities and if River Bend hadn't become such a prison. . . . Most of all, I wish I could fool myself into believing that Mark loves me more than his business. But he doesn't. I think I've always sensed it but lately the realization has made me *very* upset. It was bad enough to lose out to a Richard Goldmark. But to a corporation! Somehow, that's worse. At least Sydney left me for another human being—never mind what kind of a human being he was. But what am I really to Mark, if his true love is his business? I'm just a bedmate (less and less frequently), a mother to *his* children and a glorified housekeeper. Somehow that doesn't seem enough. It even seems rather insulting to me. Maybe I'm more of a "new" woman than I ever thought.

Now you mustn't get the wrong idea. I haven't been burning with unhappiness day in and day out. It's just that I've begun to see myself more clearly, and Mark, too, and our life together. I still love him, of course, and adore the children. But my role in the life here at River Bend is not what I used to think it was.

What made all this more bearable was Carter. Carter has spent much time here at the house during the last year and a half. Mark was grateful to him for helping me to handle the flood of mail that came in after the shooting, and he invited him over for dinner frequently. Mark liked Carter, too, and they often would get up all-night poker games (Carter apparently is a whiz of a cardplayer), which Mark loved. Last summer the three of us were almost like three kids on a long houseparty—Carter was here so much, playing tennis with us, swimming in the pool. Well, it all seemed idyllic and there was no hint of trouble. Then just before Christmas last year, Mark began to change toward Carter. I think someone must have said something to him (and I suspect Marvin Senjak, though I'll probably never know for certain), but he told me he thought it would be better if I stopped having Carter over when he wasn't home. River Bend is hardly a private place, crawling as it is with servants and guards and the children, so I never dreamed anyone could say anything about Carter being here for dinner with me. Obviously, I was wrong. I reluctantly gave in—*very* reluctantly, because, after all, Mark is away so much of the time and Carter relieved the loneliness for me. Carter was hurt, too, I know, though he never said anything.

Then last January Carter—who's been after me to join his theatrical group—asked me to play Barbara in a production of *Major Barbara* he's putting on. I agreed. Well, Mark blew up. He ranted and raved and said it was absolutely unthinkable. I had a position to maintain in Elkins and it was undignified for me to take part in some cheap play. Shaw, cheap? Undignified? I was amazed, and I told him I honestly felt he was being unreasonable. It was the worst fight of our marriage, and I was shattered by it. The upshot was that Mark threatened to fire Carter if I saw any more of him. This absolutely astonished me. It was so vindictive, even vicious! I told him he was out of his mind, that Carter was our dearest friend, that he had absolutely no grounds for the slightest suspicion about Carter and me. And Amelia, this was the truth. Carter is a most attractive young man, but he is a gentleman and I swear to you there has never been any hint of anything even slightly improper in our relationship. We are friends, the closest of friends. We admire each other, we enjoy each other. But there it ends. Besides, Carter has plenty of girlfriends. I am nothing more to him than an older sister, and that is precisely the way we both want it.

But Mark thought differently. He claimed that Carter was in love with me and that he was using our friendship to inveigle his way into the household and my affections, and he was determined to stop it before it was too late. He said he would hold nothing against Carter if I did stop seeing him; but he repeated that if I didn't, he would fire him.

Mark, as you know, is a very strong-willed man, and a very possessive one. And, as it's turned out, a very jealous one as well. At one point I think I might have been flattered by his jealousy, but not this time. Of course, I had no choice. Carter has no money aside from his salary, and I couldn't jeopardize his finances merely to save a friendship that was valuable to me. I declined the offer to be in his play, and invitations to Carter to come to our home stopped abruptly. I haven't seen him for three months. I'm sick about it, because I know how hurt and confused he must be. And I do resent Mark's forcing me into this rude behavior. I'm sure he *must* know how I feel. I've been chilly and irritable ever since. But Mark is so stubborn. Sometimes I think he actually has considered backing down, but his nature won't let him do it. And that's how things stand now—our marriage that was so wonderful for so many years turning sour, me thinking all sorts of bitter thoughts about the husband I do love, Mark away even more of the time, Carter banished . . . In short, I'm miserable.

Well, I'm sure all this has cheered you up immensely, and I apologize for putting my domestic troubles on you. It's been a huge relief to get it off my mind and I hope you'll forgive me. I know things will work out eventually. Most marriages have to go through periods of strain like this, and ours is so fundamentally sound that I'm sure it will weather this little storm. But it has been sad. It's always sad when something that was beautiful and sweet begins to go bad.

My love to Bruce. As always, affectionately,

Charlotte

Letter from Sam Rosen to Riley Baker, dated April 12, 1915.

Dear Riley:

I have gone over the documents with my lawyers, and a copy of the agreement has been mailed to you. I am most satisfied with the arrangement, and I am grateful to you for having suggested it. It resolves so many worries in my mind.

Hoping to hear from you soon, I am,

Yours sincerely,
Samuel Rosen

PART

V

A CORNER IS TURNED;

AND A ZIEGFELD FOLLY

1915

CHAPTER ONE

ON MAY 1, 1915, a crowd of passengers gathered at the Cunard Line pier in New York to board the great liner *Lusitania*. Most of them had seen the notice placed by the Imperial German Government that morning in the shipping columns of papers, a notice warning trans-Atlantic passengers on ships flying the flag of Great Britain or her allies that a state of war existed and that the ships were liable to destruction in the waters adjacent to the British Isles. Few of the passengers had paid much attention to it. They boarded, and the giant ship was nudged into the Hudson by tugs to start its voyage.

There were a few celebrities aboard: Alfred Gwynne Vanderbilt, traveling with his valet; Charles Frohman, the theatrical producer; Elbert Hubbard, author of the best-selling *Message to Garcia;* the Welsh coal tycoon D. A. Thomas and his suffragette daughter, Lady Mackworth. The rest of the passengers were mostly British, including serving girls returning home to visit their families, and others traveling on business. The first great war of the century was almost a year old, so no one was feeling especially festive. No one was particularly nervous, either. After all, the *Lusitania* could outrun any submarine; even with six of her boilers shut down to save coal, she could still make twenty-one knots.

Seven days later, at 2:20 P.M., the commander of the *Unterseeboot-20*, Kapitanleutnant Walther Schwieger, observed the *Lusitania* through his periscope a few miles off the coast of Ireland. At 2:35, he fired a torpedo at a distance of seven hundred meters. Two hundred and ninety pounds of an explosive called trotyl plowed into the huge liner aft of the bridge, causing an enormous explosion. Twenty minutes later, the ship sank in three hundred sixty feet of water. One thousand one hundred ninety-eight passengers were lost.

Kapitanleutnant Schwieger made no attempt to pick up survivors.

Shock waves from the sinking of the *Lusitania* went around the world. The sinking of a *passenger* liner with the resultant death of so many innocents, not to mention Americans, hit the world as an atrocious example of German barbarity. America was roused to a fever pitch of anti-German feeling, one of whose casualties was old Sam Rosen. Sam had for ten days been bedridden by a severe second stroke, and was already close to death. The news of the *Lusitania* and the flood of print about the barbaric Huns crushed him with shame for his native land. Forgotten were the anti-Semitic insults that had sent him from Germany to America half a century before. Now, in his old age, he had nothing but nostalgic remembrances of the Germany of his youth; he was as proud of being a German as of being a Jew. Perhaps more so. And the torpedo that sank the *Lusitania* sank his self-seteem as well.

On May 17 Charlotte was called by Dr. Brill, who told her she had better get over to Sam's house as quickly as possible. Charlotte called Mark at the factory, then got into her Packard and was driven into town to the old house on Elm Street. Oddly, during the drive she didn't think so much about her father—for some time she had been resigned to his death—she thought about her husband, and how he would react to the news. The open hostility between Mark and Sam that had begun at Mark's and Charlotte's marriage had abated somewhat lately as old Sam edged nearer to death, and Charlotte fervently hoped that there might be some sort of reconciliation between them now, at the end. After all, they had started the huge Manning Rubber Company together, and now there were blood ties in common through the four children. She hated to think that her father, whom she loved despite the coolness that had developed between them since her marriage, might pass from life in an atmosphere of unresolved family hostility.

Coming into her father's bedroom, she was flooded with memories of her childhood. The room hadn't changed at all since the house had been built some twenty years before, and the dark Victorian wallpaper, the heavily carved bureau and bed and the framed photographs of relatives long since dead reminded her how quickly time seemed to be passing. Her father was lying on the bed, his face waxen, his eyes shut; he looked already dead, though Dr. Brill told her he was still hanging onto life. She went to the bed and kissed his forehead. His eyes opened and looked at her. They were watery but not unaware; inside the body that was about to stop functioning after eight decades, the mind was still vigorously alive. The second stroke had made it almost impossible for him to speak, but he whispered something and she leaned down closer to hear it. "I love you," were his words, and she fought back the tears.

"I love *you*," she whispered back, forcing a smile. He was too weak to respond, but she hoped her being there at least had comforted him. He closed his eyes again, and she sat down in a chair by the bed to wait with him.

Five minutes later, Mark came in. He took off his hat, came over to the bed, looked at his father-in-law, then leaned down and kissed Charlotte. "I'm sorry . . . " he said. She nodded, and thought, despite everything he really was sorry—for her, and that his long partnership with this man, her father, had ended so bitterly. He pulled up a chair and sat next to Charlotte, holding her hand. Ten minutes passed. Sam's eyes opened, and the eyeballs moved to the side and stared at Mark. His lips started moving and Charlotte got up to lean over and listen. "I want to tell Mark something," he mumbled, and she straightened, motioning to her husband to come to the bed as she moved aside. Mark put his ear down to the old man's lips. When he straightened, Charlotte thought he looked as though he had seen a ghost. He stared down at the dying man and said, "You son of a bitch." Then he walked out of the room.

Charlotte was shocked. She hurried out after him. He was standing at the top of the stairs.

"How dare you say that to my father?" She whispered. "That was a terrible thing to say to a dying man!"

He turned and looked at her, said nothing.

"What did he say?"

"He said that he has left all his stock to the children in trust. And the trustee—with complete voting rights—is Riley Baker. He has *given* my company to Riley Baker." He bit the words with such unrestrained anger she almost forgot her shock at what he had called her father. Then he walked down the stairs and out of the house.

The man who had, with Sam's death, obtained control of twenty-eight percent of the preferred stock of the Manning Rubber Company —the largest single block of stock—lived in a world that, on the top, brushed with New York society and, at the bottom, with the underworld. Riley Baker might not have been the criminal mastermind Herschel Fine had called him, but Herschel's estimate of Riley's character had been more accurate than Sam's rose-tinted appraisal.

To society, Riley presented a fairly respectable façade, though there

were still many who remembered the strange circumstances of his first
wife's death, and there were many more who regarded his second wife,
Sylvia, as little more than a tart adorned in sable. In 1911 Riley had
begun to buy up Manhattan real estate, and one of his first investments had been a baronial apartment building on Fifth Avenue and
Seventy-seventh Street, one of the new giant structures that were beginning to replace the private mansions of the past. Riley had retained
the top three floors for himself and had hired an unsuccessful, if
fashionable, actress named Maude Reid, who had set up one of the
city's first interior decorating businesses, to furnish the triplex for
him. Miss Reid was given carte blanche, and she proceeded to do
the large room, boasting a spectacular view of Central Park, with a
lavishness that took the visitor's breath away (and, incidentally, made
Miss Reid's career). Miss Reid's grandfather had been in the China
trade, so she was familiar with Chinese art and furniture, knowledge
she applied in giving Riley Baker's apartment a predominantly
Oriental motif. Coromandel screens vied with Chinese porcelain
lamps, Chinese objets d'art, Chinese rugs, French chinoiserie and exotic
Buddhas to produce the atmosphere of some Mandarin pleasure
dome. The silk curtains, the silver tea chest wallpaper, the exquisite
scroll paintings inaugurated a China craze among the wealthy in
New York. It was in this rich triplex that Riley and Sylvia began
to entertain at large parties, defying Riley's murky reputation and
Sylvia's squeaky voice and plebian manner in an effort to make a
dent on society—or, more accurately, the new, much looser Manhattan
society that was beginning to replace the old Four Hundred and
which ultimately would evolve into the "café society" of the Thirties
and the "jet set" of the Sixties. If the new society was, like the Four
Hundred, inexorably based on wealth, it was infinitely more casual
about family and ethical standards than its predecessor, which was
fortunate for Riley Baker.

Riley's Wall Street wizardry had made him a fortune now estimated
at fifty millions, and he was becoming known as the Street's leading
bear raider. The bear raid was a sophisticated maneuver based on the
device of the short sale. The brokers kept a floating pool of stock
available—stock in the brokerage house name, dormant stock—that
the bear could borrow and sell on the market, hoping the price of
the borrowed stock would go down rather than up. If it did, the bear
would buy the stock back at the lower price, return the stock to his
broker and pocket his profit, the difference between the price at which
he had sold the borrowed stock and the price at which he had bought
the new stock. Of course, if the stock went up instead of down, the

short trader lost. But Riley rarely lost, because he would organize bear-selling raids that would virtually insure the stock's going down.

A bear raid was a short sale on a grand scale. Sniffing out that a company was in trouble—either from a soft spot in a company report, or an inside tip—Riley would begin to sell the stock short, quietly at first, then bringing in his friends to step up the attack as he spread rumors that the company was in trouble. The bears' short selling would in itself begin to depress the price of the stock. But the rumors would cause a panic, and others would start to sell their stock to get out, causing the price to begin a plunge—which was exactly what Riley desired. When he judged the stock was nearing bottom, he would begin to buy back to replace his short sales; being almost the only buyer available, he of course paid the lowest price. Pocketing his huge profits and returning his borrowed stock, he would very often catch the stock on the upswing by switching positions and becoming a bull. His buying activity had slowed the plunge. Now he would start buying huge chunks of stock. Meanwhile, the company would have been declaiming in outraged releases that the disaster rumors were false, upon which the bargain hunters would start rushing in to buy. Up the stock would climb, and Riley would go along for the ride, selling out as he judged the elevator was about to slow, and thereby banking double profits.

It was a tricky game that could ruin the unwary, but over the years Riley had developed it to a fine art. With huge profits from his speculating, he had bought into legitimate corporations, such as Mark's, though the maneuver by which he had gained control, if not ownership, of old Sam's sixteen percent of Manning preferred stock had cost him nothing more than stationery and postage—altogether a psychological triumph of which he felt justly proud. By 1915, Riley was a director in more than a dozen large corporations, and it was this that especially helped sanitize his heretofore malodorous reputation. After all, directors (like Brutus) were respectable men.

His real-estate investments, which had brought him to Fifth Avenue, had, at the other end of the scale, brought him into contact with the underworld, and it was his acquaintance with some of the leading racketeers of the day that gave Riley almost as much pleasure as his triumphs on the market. In 1913 he had bought a block of tenements in the Italian section of Brooklyn for what he considered a bargain price. The day after the transfer of title, his English butler entered his library on the first floor of the triplex—a luxurious room that Riley used as an office—and informed him in shocked if subdued tones that a Mr. Marucca wished to see him. Mr. Marucca proved to be Giovanni Marucca, or Big Johnnie, as he was known in the trade, a rising figure in the Unione Siciliane, a quasisecret criminal society with ties to the Mafia, which had been founded in the Nineties as a legitimate fraternal organization to promote the interests of Sicilian immigrants but which had quickly been taken over by racketeers. Big Johnnie was a dignified-appearing, heavy-set man in his early forties whose face was jowly but impressive. He introduced himself to Riley and quietly told him that the tenements he had just purchased might legally be his but he would never be able to collect a single day's rent unless he cooperated with the Unione Siciliane. Riley, more intrigued than shocked, asked why. Big Johnnie smiled and spread his hands.

"Because we will kill anyone you send out to collect the rents."

Riley leaned back in his chair. "What's the deal?"

"My man will personally collect the rents and personally deliver them here to you every other week. In cash. For those tenants who might be a little slow in paying, we will give a one-week grace period at five-percent interest. If they still can't pay, we will re-rent the flat, if you understand what I mean."

"I understand."

"We will also protect the building against arson and acts of God, such as dynamite explosions."

Riley looked amused. "I see. And how much is this protection against the good Lord going to cost me?"

"For this service, we ask five percent of the gross rent roll."

Riley thought it over and agreed to the deal. Big Johnnie's man turned out to be a nineteen-year-old Sicilian named Franco Ruggiero, and every two weeks Franco would appear at the elegant triplex with a satchel full of cash—$1,800, minus ninety dollars for the service charge—rent collected from the terrorized suffering tenants in Riley's roach-crawling, vermin-infested buildings. Riley didn't object to the charge. He was still making an unconscionable profit on his investment, and the two percent more he paid the Unione than he would have had to pay a regular collection agency was, he quickly concluded, well worth it for the protection provided. Moreover, he came to be fascinated by Franco. Riley had a snobbish dislike of Italians, or at least of Italian immigrants. Like most New Yorkers of the day, he considered them barely above the level of street dogs. But this Italian was different. Franco was a true study in evil: a Borgia reincarnated in the twentieth century. He had a quick mind, a pleasant manner when he wished, the courage of a tiger and the killer instinct of a provoked cobra. Riley liked him. Moreover, Franco, a darkly handsome man with an athlete's build, was a ladykiller, and Riley soon began paying him bonuses for another, even more personal service. Nature had provided Riley with a ministerial exterior that camouflaged the heart of a satyr—a satyr, however, with flair. Riley craved variety. When he moved to his Fifth Avenue triplex, he also converted his former townhouse on East Thirty-first Street into a private retreat for the collection of erotica that he had assembled over the years with the passion (in degree, of course, not kind) of a dedicated philatelist. On his travels through Europe and the Near East he had ventured into the dingy back reaches of the marketplaces and souks, ferreting out choice editions of the works of de Sade, lavishly illustrated copies of de Musset's *Gamiami*, Moroccan-bound albums of pornographic drawings and photographs and a vast range of artifacts representing the most perverse weeds of the human mind. It was here, surrounded by his exotic stimuli, that Riley was pleased to entertain his retinue of showgirls, shopgirls, prostitutes and, in some carefully selected cases, society matrons. And it was also here that Franco Ruggiero commenced bringing the flowers of Little Italy, lovely girls who had been forced into prostitution by their appalling poverty, and often by the bullying of Franco himself as well. Sometimes Franco would be invited to join the amusements, for Riley's attitude in such matters was, if nothing else, democratic. And the young Sicilian, whose dream it was to become as big a racketeer as Johnny Torrio or Big Jim Colosimo, would need little urging to indulge his lust on the pseudo-Turkish couches that lined the walls or at times by joining Riley in sado-masochistic "playlets" that the host enjoyed as much as the guest.

This, then, was the cruel, corrupt and in many ways brilliant man who had convinced Sam Rosen, through the silken prose of his many letters to the aging invalid, that he was a man of integrity and character, infinitely better equipped to vote the stock of Sam's grandchildren than their father—Sam's own son-in-law and partner, Mark Manning.

Riley considered it the most satisfying corporate raid of his career.

Sam was buried before sundown, in accordance with strict Jewish custom, in the same Cleveland cemetery as his wife. The next morning, Mark left for New York, where he checked into a suite on the ninth floor of the Plaza Hotel, overlooking the intersection of Fifth Avenue and Fifty-ninth Street, the pleasant memorial to General

William Tecumseh Sherman, and, on the Fifth Avenue side, the recently completed Pulitzer Fountain with the graceful statue of Abundance on top. But Mark was in no mood for contemplating the sights. He was deeply angry and depressed at discovering control of the corporation he had nursed from its infancy to maturity suddenly and maliciously, in his view, jeopardized. Moreover, for one of the few times in his life, he genuinely did not know what to do about an important problem. So, after checking into the hotel, he made an appointment with Harrison Lord, senior partner of the distinguished firm of Lord, Rainey and Trimmingham, who was Mark's personal attorney, then hurried downtown to Wall Street where he described the situation to Harrison. Mark's first question was whether Sam's will could be challenged. Harrison's legally cautious answer to this was that they would have to study the will when it was probated, then make a decision. Next question—what should he do in the meantime? Harrison's answer: nothing—wait until Riley Baker made the first move. Mark realized the wisdom of the reply but his anxiety was too great to allow him to sit around twiddling his legally constrained thumbs. Leaving Lord's office, he telephoned Riley Baker for an appointment.

At two that afternoon, Reynolds, the English butler, admitted him into the Temple of Heaven—as an acquaintance had named Riley's Chinese apartment—led him through the foyer and the living room, and finally ushered him into the library-office, where Riley was sitting behind his ormolu French desk. He neither stood up to greet Mark nor extended his hand. He merely looked at him.

"I'm going to challenge the will," Mark said.

Riley opened a drawer and pulled out a copy of a four-page legal document which he pushed across the desk. "You won't have a chance. Sam signed this—*both* our attorneys drew it up—in front of witnesses. It corroborates what's in his will. I'm trustee of his stock, with full control of its voting rights, until all your children have reached the age of twenty-one, at which time the trust is dissolved. There's no way you can change it. Your father-in-law obviously didn't like or trust you. I helped those feelings along, convinced him I was his best friend and best-equipped to watch out for the interests of his grandchildren. He believed me. I like to think his confidence in me at least helped him die a happy man."

Mark glanced through the document. He was no legal expert, but he realized with sinking heart that Baker was no doubt right—it looked unbreakable. He put it back on the desk and said, "I suppose you intend to try and run the company from now on?"

"Why would I do that? The present management is perfectly capable. However, I will reserve the right to make ultimate policy decisions."

"Aren't you forgetting I still control more stock than you?"

"How?"

"Forgetting my common position, I own twenty-two percent of the preferred. Elmo Tilden, Frank Bennet, Ron Gerstenmeier, Percy Hutchins and Ray Margate own ten percent apiece, and they'll vote with me."

"Will they? I think you may be mistaken. Oh, I'll give you Bennet and Gerstenmeier. They're old pals of yours and they'd stick by you. But I won't give you the other three. I'm a director of the Ohio and Central Illinois Railroad and I own about 23,000 shares of its stock. So I think in a showdown between you and me, Percy Hutchins would side with me. After all, the chairman of the Ohio and Central wouldn't want to antagonize one of his directors, would he? So that gives me my twelve percent, Sam's sixteen percent and Percy's ten percent—thirty-eight percent in all.

"Now, let's see who's next. Ray Margate, the respected president of the Providence Insurance Company of America. Well, Ray and I are partners in a real estate development in Flushing, and we are co-owners of a shooting lodge in Ontario. I think Ray would probably see his way to voting with me in case of a showdown—not that I want a showdown or expect one, mind you. I'm assuming you and I will see eye to eye on just about everything. But if there's trouble, I think I could count on Ray. That brings me a total of forty-eight percent, which is getting close to a majority, isn't it?"

Mark said nothing. He knew about Baker's relationship with Hutchins and Margate, and despite his previous boast that their votes were in his pocket, he was aware they were uncertain. The one key figure who could tilt the balance his way—or Baker's—was Elmo Tilden, good old boozing Elmo, who had always been such a staunch friend. Unfortunately, Elmo's company had run into trouble during the past year, trouble many people said could be traced to the company president's advancing alcoholism. So Mark was not totally unprepared for what Baker said next.

"Which brings us to Elmo Tilden. You know he's in trouble?"

"I've heard," replied Mark grimly.

"He came to me two months ago and asked me to help him raise a million dollars as a personal loan. I helped him. Now, Mark, who do you think Elmo owes more to? You or me?"

"Why would he come to you? He doesn't even like you."

Riley shrugged. "Everyone else turned him down. I tried to buy his stock a few years ago, and he first tried to sell me the stock again before he asked for the loan. But I don't need his stock now. I have Sam's."

Mark told himself to remain cool, to bluff confidence he didn't feel. "I'll admit you're in a pretty good position," he said, "but I own 15,000 shares of the common. You don't own any."

"True. But you want to avoid a stock war as much as I do. And even with your common, I'm not sure you could out-vote me."

Silence. Mark shifted in his chair.

"All right, where do we go from here?"

"We go forward, arm in arm, into a glorious future of ever-growing profits and dividends. And to show you my good will, I want you to come to dinner here tonight. I have a very distinguished French general that I want you to meet, General Henri d'Aulnay. You've heard of him?"

"No."

"Not surprising. General d'Aulnay's not exactly a bold warrior. He's risen to his present eminent position on the French general staff by ingeniously avoiding combat duty, by being married to a rich countess and by being one of France's leading anti-Dreyfusards, which of course makes him a hero to the army, if not the Jews. The general arrived in New York yesterday to arrange a loan from certain private bankers, using French gold as collateral. He also wants bids on war material, including 50,000 gas masks. Now, you've been very lax about getting into the war business, Mark, and I consider it the right time for us to do something about that oversight, especially since the war's apparently going to drag on for some time. If you come tonight, I think we can favorably impress the general, which should help us with the contract. By the way, I assume we could make gas masks? They're made of rubber, I'm told, although personally I've never seen one. Anyway, you'll come tonight? Seven o'clock."

It was an order, not an invitation, and Mark was not accustomed to taking orders. However, for the moment he knew Riley had him in checkmate. He stood up and said abruptly, "I'll come."

Riley looked pleased. He also stood up, and this time he offered his hand. "I was sure you'd be reasonable, once we had a talk and clarified our positions. We'll get along fine, you'll see."

Mark looked at the outstretched hand, turned and walked out of the room.

CHAPTER TWO

Sylvia Wingdale Baker seemed one of life's more likely losers who had, without especially trying, won beyond her wildest expectations. That is, if by winning one meant becoming rich, and just now Sylvia wasn't at all sure about that. She had been born in Brooklyn, the daughter of a mailman. Her childhood was content, if drab—her family was neither well off nor poor. Boys had chased her for as long as she could remember, and they liked her, too; Sylvia was breezy and good-natured and totally unself-conscious about her funny, squeaky voice. She went into the theater not because she was burning with ambition to be a star but because she thought the stage might be rather fun and she assumed it was an easy way for someone with a figure like hers to make money. She went out with stage-door johnnies, not because she was promiscuous but because she enjoyed meeting people, enjoyed sex, and again, it was a fairly easy way to pay the rent. Sylvia didn't particularly try at anything, and, as sometimes happens, most everything seemed to fall into her lap anyway.

She certainly hadn't tried to catch Riley Baker as a husband, and when he proposed, she wasn't overly eager to accept. She didn't particularly like him. Oh, he was pleasant enough, but he was a cold fish and not much fun. On the other hand, he was crazy about her, at least he had been at first, and could barely keep his hands off her, although he claimed it was her voice that most intrigued him. After they were married, Sylvia finally figured out why he had really wanted her as a wife—although people assumed she was dumb because she looked and sounded it, she was not without a shrewd intelligence. Riley had married her because it pleased him to thumb his nose at society. Riley was full of contradictions. At the same time he courted society with lavish parties, he took malicious pleasure in snubbing it and its assumptions and conventions by marrying a funny, squeaky ex-showgirl. It was crazy, but Riley, she decided, was a little crazy himself.

At first, being married to a multimillionaire had been fun. Sylvia took girlish delight in the jewels, furs and clothes, and their custom-built Silver Ghost Rolls-Royce limousine was not exactly a deprivation. But after a while it all began to pall. Riley was pleasant enough

to her in front of company, but when they were alone he treated her
with open contempt. Moreover, she had seen the museum of erotica
and knew what went on there, which she thought was not only disgusting but a slap in her face as well. She was also lonely. Riley's
passion for her was quickly diluted as he returned to his merry-go-
round of mistresses. Sylvia, with healthy normal appetites, was still a
little too apprehensive about Riley to look openly for a supplement.
People said, after all, that he had killed his first wife, and though
Sylvia didn't really believe it, she was still careful. Now, though, she
was getting tired of being careful. She missed the theater and her
old life, and as she had told Mark, she wanted to try her luck in the
movies—except that this meant getting a divorce and though Sylvia
was discontented, she was not unhappy enough to take the necessary
initiative. She was something of a drifter and procrastinator. Whenever she'd get mad or fed up, she'd lock herself in her room and
forget her troubles by burying herself in one of the dime novels she
devoured by the gross, or in one of her syrupy-sweet magazine romances. Losing herself in the love affairs of fictional heroines was
much easier than doing something about her own unsatisfactory life.

But when Riley told her that Mark would be coming to their party
for General d'Aulnay, Sylvia's interest in life picked up. She liked
the good-looking tire magnate she had met at breakfast eight years
previously, and she decided he might be somebody worth taking the
initiative for. Besides, luck plus her native cunning had given her
the bait she believed he couldn't resist.

Sylvia loved fashion, and kept up with what had been going on in
Paris, which was—despite the war—still as active as ever socially and
in the fields of design and high fashion. Paquin, Laferrière, Doucet,
Vincent-Lachartrouaille, Reboux, Worth and, of course, Poiret were
the Big Berthas of the fashion world, and women in America and
Europe continued to follow with breathless interest their latest crea-
tions at the same time they perused the ghoulish statistics of war dead.
Fashions had jumped erratically from one period to another, reflecting the nervousness of the times. The hobble skirt had been replaced by Directoire and Empire styles; these in turn were displaced
by a return to the Victorian bustle, while others favored the pipelike
tunic. Lately, the eighteenth century had become the rage, possibly
as an escape from the horrors of the twentieth, and Sylvia had picked
out a Nattier blue taffeta dress with a peg-top skirt, a huge pink rose
at the waist, and a portrait neckline that made her look vaguely like
a Gainsborough duchess posing as a shepherdess. Her blonde hair
was set by her maid in a Grecian bun, and as she went out to greet

her guests, even her husband, who normally paid little attention to what she wore, was impressed. "You know," he said, "if you never opened your mouth, people might actually mistake you for a lady."

Sylvia smiled. "But Riley, I *like* to open my mouth."

"I know," he said, then added, "but try to restrain yourself with the general. Just smile at him, keep him happy for me."

"Oh, I know what you mean." In fact, she knew a good deal more than Riley thought, having picked up her bedroom telephone that morning and accidentally overheard a conversation between her husband and General d'Aulnay. What she heard was the bait she thought would hook Mark Manning. Besides, it was one way to get back at Riley for all his snide remarks, not to mention his playhouse on Thirty-first Street. When she opened her mouth tonight, she was, for once, going to be worth listening to.

There were eight couples for dinner, not including Mark and the general; the guests included a bank president, several prominent stockbrokers, an art dealer, and the senior New York senator, Collins Cartwright, a distinguished Republican rich in seniority who was chairman of the Senate foreign relations committee. Senator Cartwright didn't know Riley personally, but he was aware of his reputation and had been somewhat nervous about coming to his home. However, General d'Aulnay, who had arranged the invitation, apparently liked the famous speculator, and the senator, not wanting to offend the general, had swallowed his misgivings.

"Cocktails" were just making their appearance on the New York scene, and Riley's butler was serving them as Sylvia came over to a rather glum-looking Mark and said, "Did you meet the general?"

Mark said he had.

"Isn't he cute?" She looked across the room at d'Aulnay, who was about sixty and round as a butterball. "I don't think he'd fit in a trench, do you?"

"It would have to be a wide trench."

"Do you want to see the rest of the place? Isn't it something? You know, sometimes I feel like I'm living in a Chinese laundry. A real fancy one, of course. Come on, I'll give you a tour."

She led him out of the living room to the foyer, where there was a small private elevator as well as a stairway to the second floor. Stepping into the elevator, which was lacquered with red and gold Chinese designs, she waited for Mark to enter, then closed the door and pushed the lever. The motor hummed and, after a slight jerk, they started gliding to the second floor.

"Can you keep a secret?" she whispered.

"Sure."

"Promise you'll never let Riley know I told you? He could get awfully mean if he knew."

"I promise. What's the secret?"

"Riley and the general have made a deal. The general will give your company the contract for the gas masks—you know about that?"

"Yes."

"Well, he'll give you the contract if you agree to give him a kickback of $100,000. Isn't it fun to know that generals are crooks just like everyone else? Anyway, Riley's going to make you agree to the kickback. He told the general he can do it because he has more stock than you do, or something like that. Anyway, what *you* don't know is that the general will split his kickback with Riley to pay Riley for making you pay the general in the first place. Now, isn't that about as cute a deal as you ever heard of?"

"I'd say so."

"Oh, Riley's lower than a subway. Anyway, I thought you should know. But *please,* don't let him know I told you!!"

The elevator jerked to a halt and Mark said, "If you're so afraid of Riley finding out, why are you taking this chance in telling me?"

She leaned against the wall and smiled. "Guess."

He looked at her, then slowly shook his head. "That's out of the question."

Sylvia looked amazed.

"I've got a very jealous wife."

She shrugged. "Oh, well, don't you worry, honey. She'll never know."

"You may not believe this, Sylvia, but I love Charlotte and I don't cheat on her."

Sylvia wrinkled her nose. "Oh, come *on.*"

"I'm sorry—in fact, I'm flattered, but I really mean it."

"You mean, I went to all this trouble to help you, and it's for nothing?" she said, angrily punching the elevator lever. "God, wouldn't you *know* I'd pick a Boy Scout to help me!"

"As I said, I appreciate it—"

"Oh, go to hell."

They said nothing more until the elevator descended to the first floor.

Before opening the door, she looked at him curiously. "Do you *really* love your wife that much?"

He nodded.

A look of sadness came into her eyes. "She's a lucky woman." Then she opened the door and stepped out of the Chinese-appointed elevator.

Whatever unadmirable things Mark Manning may have done in his life, there were two things almost sacred to him—his family and his company. Tempting as Sylvia's offer had been, he could not accept it. He had exploded at Charlotte about Carter Lang, and he would not —and had not since his marriage to her—play the hypocrite by doing behind her back what he expected her not to do behind his. Nor would he allow Riley Baker to sully the reputation of his beloved company by a sordid little deal with General d'Aulnay. A tire was not, he realized, a glamorous product, but at least it was an honest one.

Which was all very fine, but how to stop Baker? During the dinner he sat in almost total silence, trying to think of a countermove as he watched the rotund general stuffing his face with a voraciousness that, had they witnessed it, might well have incited rebellion among his hungry *poilus* in the muddy trenches of France. The general and Senator Cartwright were sitting on either side of Sylvia, and both gentlemen seemed attentive to her conversation which centered on the movies, a subject neither of the dignitaries knew much about. At the end of the meal, Riley rose from his chair and proposed a toast to Franco-American friendship. This was followed by the general rising to his feet and launching into a lengthy speech in mangled English concerning the difficulties of the French army, which had been unprepared for the war but which now was catching up with the Germans by the addition to the artillery of as many as 1,000 new field pieces a week. "Still," he said, "we have a great struggle ahead of us. There are many things we need—not only guns but helmets, canteens, bedding—the thousands of things an army needs. We cannot produce them all. Which is why I am here in America now, to try and buy some of the items we in France need but cannot make." He went on to speak of France's assistance to the "heroic American colonies in the heroic American Revolution," of the Statue of Liberty, of the "indissoluble ties" between the "two great democracies"—three attempts were required before he could manage "indissoluble." By the time he sat down to applause, Mark had decided what his countermove to Riley Baker's kickback scheme had to be.

He got to his feet and said, "Ladies and gentlemen, General d'Aulnay. I personally have been profoundly moved by the general's speech, and as president of a company that will soon be manufacturing many of the articles he spoke about, I'd like to make an offer to the French government. General, I understand you're interested in buying 50,000 gas masks."

The general, rather startled, nodded. "That's correct."

"Well, sir, I'm willing to make those gas masks for you at cost. The profit we normally would charge will be the Manning Rubber Company's contribution to the French people, a token of our esteem in your hour of trial."

The guests mumbled and applauded enthusiastically as the general and Riley exchanged uneasy glances. The general then forced a nervous smile. "That is very generous of you, Mr. Manning. And speaking unofficially, I would say that my government would be pleased to accept."

More applause and, this time, cheers. Riley Baker looked unhappy, though he too was forcing a smile. Mark held up his hands for silence.

"Then, general, as far as I'm concerned, we have a deal. However, I've been reading a lot of stories in the papers about war profiteering." He glanced at Riley. "Now, personally, I think anyone who would try to make an illegal dollar out of this war has to be the bottom of the barrel. But let's be frank—there are a lot of businessmen more interested in profits than the great principles this bloody war is being fought for." He turned to Senator Cartwright. "I'm also aware that there might be quite a few people who might think that a businessman like myself wouldn't offer to manufacture these gas masks at cost unless there were some hidden clauses tucked away in the fine print of the deal. So to prove to everyone that we mean this to be a gift to the French people and not to ourselves, I would like to ask the senator to have his staff check over all the contracts, just to be sure everything is absolutely aboveboard. Senator, I know you're a busy man, but would you be willing to do this for us?"

Everyone looked at the senator, who nodded.

"I'd be glad to, Mr. Manning. I only wish there were more businessmen like yourself."

"Thank you, sir," said Mark, who then raised his wine glass. "Then I'll propose a toast to the honesty of the American businessman, who now and then probably could stand a few kicks in the pants." The guests hear-hear-ed and drank, as Riley Baker's eyes turned stony cold. Mark smiled at him and sat down.

For the first time since Sam died, he actually felt good.

"I'd like to see you for a moment," said Riley quietly as the guests were leaving. Mark nodded and followed him into his office, where he closed the door. Riley walked slowly over to his desk and sat down. Mark watched him.

"I think you might have discussed this with me first," Riley finally said.

"Why? I'm still the chief executive officer. I make the decisions and it seemed to me a good gesture to make to the general—particularly with Senator Cartwright there."

He crossed his arms casually and looked at Riley.

"You don't seem to understand the general's position," Riley said. "He let me know that he expects a certain fee for awarding the contract. Now, of course, you've put him on the spot. I mean, with Senator Cartwright's staff checking all the papers, it's going to be hell for us to oblige the general."

"I'm afraid I'm not following you. What kind of fee?"

"You know damned well what I mean. A kickback. One hundred thousand dollars. The general is very upset, and he let me know before he left that he still expects his money."

Mark shook his head. "The honorable general's already accepted my offer in front of Senator Cartwright. He can't back out now, especially after I announce it to the newspapers, which I intend to do in the morning. Now let's get one thing straight—you said you wanted to avoid a showdown with me. All right, this is the way to do it. It's still *my* company and *I'm* running it my way, and my way means no kickbacks. If you don't like that policy, then you're going to have to get rid of me. Maybe you control enough stock to do it, maybe you don't. Meanwhile, I'm running the show."

The two men eyed each other for a moment. Then Riley said, "We'll see for how long."

Carter Lang ran his hand slowly over Lily Swenson's soft, beautifully molded right breast, then leaned down and kissed it. They were lying in his bed in the darkened bedroom of his bachelor quarters near the Elkins Country Club, and though this was hardly the first time he had made love to Lily, he was still feeling some guilt.

After he had, so to speak, been turned out of River Bend, he had drifted into taking out Lily again. He still didn't particularly like her—she was now twenty-one and had been "finished" by the school in Cleveland—but Carter, at twenty-nine, was getting too old to resist his baser instincts, as he still thought of them, and when Lily showed such surprisingly little resistance to her own, well, it was almost inevitable that they would become intimate. But Carter could not get over Charlotte, even though he had told himself over and over that he had to get the lovely older woman out of his mind, that to be in love with the wife of his boss was certifiably mad, that the coolness Mark had shown toward him lately was as much a hint of his danger as the abrupt cessation of invitations to River Bend.

Which left Lily.

"Carter?" she whispered.

"What?"

"Do you love me?"

Carter stopped his attentions to her breast.

"I think so, Lily."

"I love you, Carter. I think you're the most beautiful man I've ever known. Now tell me you love me, darling. Please . . ."

He tried to sit up but she reached her arms around his bare back and pulled him back down on top of her, placing a hungry kiss on his mouth.

"*Tell* me . . ."

The phone rang. Carter, with an inward sigh of relief, disentangled himself from Lily's arms, sat up, turned on the bed lamp and answered the phone.

"Carter," said the familiar voice, "this is Charlotte. Are you . . . do you have a minute to talk?"

Carter looked at Lily and said, "Yes."

"I want to see you. Could you meet me at my father's house tomorrow morning? About ten? It's the large brick place on Elm Street. Do you know it?"

"Yes. I'll be there."

"Good." She hesitated, then said, "I'll be looking forward to seeing you."

She hung up. Carter put the phone back on the hook.

"Who was that?" asked Lily, stretching lazily, her light-blonde hair spilling over the pillow like an aureole.

"Oh, one of the men in my office." He wondered why he automatically lied.

"You still haven't told me you love me."

Carter got out of bed and began to dress. "Come on," he said. "I'm going to take you home."

Lily frowned slightly, then gave in. She had plenty of time, after all, and she was fully confident she would win out in the long run.

Lily intended to be his wife, sooner or later.

And sooner would be better.

CHAPTER THREE

On certain mercifully rare days when the wind shifted around to the east, the stench from the Manning factories would blow back onto the town of Elkins, causing thousands of noses to wrinkle distastefully at the acrid rubber smell and people to mutter it was fortunate the factories weren't to the west of town, where the prevailing winds came from.

The winds were at their worst the next morning as Carter bathed and shaved in preparation for his mysterious meeting with Charlotte Manning. It was the last Saturday of May, but spring was not yet in the air and the sun could barely be seen through the heavy, smoky haze. Carter, far too excited about his rendezvous to mind, kept asking himself why Charlotte, after months of silence, would suddenly call him late at night and ask him to meet her under conditions that seemed vaguely clandestine. Why hadn't she asked him to come to River Bend? After all, Mark was in New York. He hurried down the kitchen stairs from his second-floor apartment to the basement garage, where he kept his new V-radiator, six-cylinder Pathfinder, hardly able to wait to find out.

He drove into town, where the traffic was heavy as the Saturday-morning shoppers clogged the streets. Four years before, the town of Elkins had sold a bond issue to raise two million dollars for an ambitious civic project. Unlike most Midwestern towns, Elkins had never had a courthouse square, and the town fathers in 1911 had decided to remedy this. Two city blocks were purchased, their buildings razed and a large square laid out. In the center, a handsome, if unoriginal, courthouse was erected. It was built of limestone and designed in the classic Roman style, replete with Corinthian columns and statues of blindfolded Justice holding sword and scales. Elm trees were planted along the sidewalks, and the buildings around the square became the prime commercial properties in town, which accelerated an already-apparent shift in housing patterns. The old

residential areas near the square and the heart of the city were beginning to decline as business moved in and the well-to-do began
to move out toward the new suburbs. Thus Elm Street, which fifteen years before—when Mark and Sheila Farr had followed the
Fourth of July parade to Matahoochi Park—had been *the* street to
live on, was now becoming slightly shabby. The big, old gingerbreaded homes were either being converted into tourist homes or
boarding houses, or, in one case, a nursing home. And as Carter
pulled into the driveway of the old Rosen house, still the grandest
house on the street, he wondered what would happen to it now that
its owner was dead and his only surviving child was living miles
outside town in River Bend.

He went up to the door and rang the bell. After a moment, the
door was opened by Charlotte. It seemed years since he had seen
her, though it had actually been a little more than five months,
and he was struck as if for the first time by her gentle beauty. She
was wearing a black dress; her sleeves were turned up. Her auburn
hair was loosely pinned in the soft way he remembered so well.
Her face, however, looked somehow different . . . tired, and there
was a faint darkness beneath her eyes.

She smiled and held out her hand. "Carter," she said, "it's so good
to see you. Come in."

He went into the entrance hall as she closed the front door,
then led him into the front parlor, where most of the furniture
was draped with white sheets. "I've been going through everything
in the house," she said, "which has been a tremendous job since
father seems to have kept everything." She removed a sheet from a
horsehair sofa and sat down, motioning Carter to sit next to her.
"I'm putting the house up for sale next week," she went on. "I've
already been approached by the Elks. I rather hate to think of it
becoming a lodge, or whatever they call it, but I suppose no one
else would want it. It's really not that old a house, you know, but
it's already become a bit of a relic."

She stopped, and there was an awkward pause.

"Why did you want to see me?" Carter asked.

She turned her blue eyes on him, and now they seemed truly sad.
"I've missed you," she said.

He felt nervous, tense. "Why haven't you asked me to River Bend?"

"I can't. It's not that I haven't wanted to, but Mark threatened
to fire you if I saw you again and I couldn't risk that. I thought if
you came here instead of River Bend no one would know and it's

the first opportunity I've had to tell you . . . well, to let you know why I haven't invited you over for so long."

It occurred to Carter that she could have told him all this on the phone, but that she wanted to see him, to tell him face to face —this pleased him immensely. "I figured it was something like that," he said.

"Oh, Carter, Mark's so *wrong*. He's so jealous and he has no good reason to be. You're my dearest friend in Elkins—practically my only friend, as far as that goes—and I'm so furious at him for taking this silly attitude." She sighed. "I'm angry at him for other reasons, too . . ." She hesitated a moment, looked about the room and the white sheets that made it seem even more ghost-filled than it already was to her. Finally she pointed to a corner. "My piano was once there," she said. "I used to practice for hours in this room. This was where Mark and I first met, you know."

"I didn't know."

"Of course you wouldn't. How silly of me. But it was fifteen years ago this July. Mark had come in to make a business arrangement with father about selling some stoves to the army. Then he came into this room. I'll never forget. He was very bold and very hand-some, and he told me he was in love with me." She smiled. "I think he really believed it. Maybe he was in love with me, I don't know. I'm still not sure to this day."

"Whether he loves you?"

She nodded. "Oh, I think he does, in his way. Father thought he was after his stock in the company, but I believed father was just being—well, father. The suspicious businessman. Then this week, when father died, Mark and I both received a shock."

"What?"

"Father didn't leave me his stock. He left it to the children in trust, and made Riley Baker the trustee. That's why Mark's in New York now. In a way I feel very sorry for him. Father had threatened to leave his stock to someone else if Mark married me, but neither of us thought he really would, and I know Mark counted on my inheriting it. I'm not quite so sure what he's going to think of me now."

"I don't understand."

"He was furious at father. Furious. He actually swore at him— while he was dying!—stormed out of the room and he hardly said a word to me all during the funeral. Wouldn't it be ironic if father had been right all along? That what Mark really wanted was not me but that precious stock in the Manning Rubber Company?"

"Is that what you believe?"

She stood up and went over to one of the lace-curtained windows to stare out at the lilac bushes bordering Elm Street. They were in full bloom, heavy with white and purple blossoms, their sweet smell in a losing contest with the stench from the factories.

"I don't know what to think," she said quietly, "I'm just confused. My first marriage was a mistake and I'd hate to think my second one finally was too." She turned and smiled at him. "At any rate, it's made me feel much better talking to you about it and I do appreciate your listening, Carter."

It was the opening he'd dreamed of for over a year and a half but had thought would never come. Now he wondered if he had the nerve to take advantage of it. He decided he had to try.

"Does this mean that we're never to see each other again? Because you feel Mark will fire me if we do?"

"I'm afraid so."

"Suppose I told you I don't care if he fires me?"

She looked startled, then shook her head. "Well, I care . . ."

"And suppose I told you . . . that I'm in love with you?"

She smiled. "There must be something about this room that makes me irresistible. Carter, you don't love me and we don't want to make things worse than they are by deceiving ourselves . . . and Mark. I'm an old married woman, and you're a young bachelor with a marvelous future—"

"You're not that old and I'm not that young, and I *do* happen to love you. I've been in love with you since—well, I guess since that night the Wobblies came out to River Bend. I never thought I'd have the nerve to tell you, but now I have and it's the truth. I love you, Charlotte. All last summer when I was at your house playing the role of family friend I was really thinking how much I wanted to make love to you—to have you to myself. So if Mark was jealous of me, he had damn good reason to be."

Silence. Finally Charlotte said, "Carter, I think you'd better leave now. Let's both try to forget what you've just said—"

He stood up and came around the sofa.

"Why? Are you that afraid?"

Her eyes widened. "Yes."

"Of whom? Mark, or me?"

"I'm not sure. Perhaps both. Perhaps I'm afraid of myself, I don't know. But I do think we must stop this now."

He leaned on the back of the sofa. "Has Mark been faithful to you?"

"You have no right to ask that."

"I'm asking anyway."

She hesitated. "I think so . . . yes."

"But you're not sure, are you? And you've just told me you're not sure why he married you."

"Oh, Carter, stop it! I don't like this. I don't like what you're trying to do. Now please *go*."

"No, I won't," he said softly. "Charlotte, this is the one chance I've got—the *one* chance. You're suddenly realizing you don't know very much about your husband, after all. Well, I'm going to show you how little you do know. Did you ever hear of the Wooster School?"

"Yes . . . it's over in Hayesville, I think, about fifteen miles from here. Why?"

"Do you know anyone enrolled there?"

She looked confused. "Of course not. Carter, I've no idea what you're talking about."

"Will you drive over to the school with me? Now?"

"But why?"

"There's someone there you should meet. Will you come? It won't be a wasted trip, I can guarantee that."

She thought a moment, giving him a curious look. Then she rolled down her sleeves.

"I'll get my hat," she said, starting across the room.

Sylvia Baker's bedroom had been spared the relentless Chinese motif of Maude Reid, who had decorated the room with French furniture rather than Chinese, but Sylvia had managed to put her own stamp on the place. To Riley's displeasure, his wife had adorned the walls of her blue room with theatrical posters of her favorite stars, including Pearl White, Ethel Barrymore, William S. Hart, Maxine Talbot, and Francis X. Bushman, and nothing Riley could say would persuade her to take them down. "I love 'em," she once yelled as he tried to tear down William S. Hart, saying it was common and childish of her to have the picture of a *cowboy* in her bedroom. "*You're* a fine one to talk about being *common*," she had snapped back. "What about all those *disgusting* books you've got over at Thirty-first Street? Not to mention that *moving* statue of the naked man and woman making love! Talk about common!"

Riley had given it up and retreated rather quickly on that occasion.

But on the night of the party for General d'Aulnay, after Mark had left and the servants had retired, Riley came back to his wife's bedroom, entering it from the small sitting room that separated hers from his. Sylvia was sitting at her vanity, brushing her hair. She was wearing a blue chiffon peignoir, and Riley looked down at her soft shoulders as he came up behind her, then put his hands on her shoulders, near her neck.

"What are you doing?" she said. "Get out of the way, I can't brush my hair with you on top of me—"

He grabbed the silver-backed brush and wrenched it from her hand. "Hey—!"

He threw it on the dresser, grabbed her blonde hair and yanked her head back.

"You told him, didn't you?"

"Told who what?"

"You told Manning about my deal with the general. I don't know how the hell you found out about it, but you told him . . ."

"I don't know what you're talking about—"

She screamed as he slapped her. Once. Twice. Three times. She tried to stop his hand, she tried to kick him. He pushed her chair over and she fell to the carpeted floor. She was sobbing and screaming at the same time as Riley pulled back his pointed, patent leather evening pump adorned with a tiny black bow and kicked it into her stomach. She groaned and doubled up into a fetal position, holding her stomach with her hands. He looked down at her. "If you ever again tell Manning or anybody else my business, it will be your worst —and last—mistake." He then proceeded to tear down, crumple and throw at her the posters of William S. Hart, Francis X. Bushman, John Barrymore, Maxine Talbot, Elmo Lincoln . . . Sylvia lay silent on the carpet, no longer daring even to make a sound. When Riley had removed the last poster, he went to the door, turned and looked down at her.

"Pleasant dreams," he said as he left the room, closing the door after him.

Charlotte Manning sat next to Carter Lang in the front seat of his Pathfinder, holding onto her hat as they bumped over the ruts and holes in the country road leading south from Elkins. She wondered what it was he had in mind, but Carter said nothing. Finally, a half hour after leaving the outskirts of the town, they approached a white horse fence surrounding what at first glance looked to be a large farm. When they reached the main gate, a neat sign read THE WOOSTER SCHOOL. They turned into the drive and headed for a large brick complex. A few cars were parked in front of it, and a number of boys in blue blazers were idling on the lawn. Carter parked the car, got out and when told by one of the boys that Roger Boine was playing baseball, led Charlotte across the small campus to one of the fields, where a baseball diamond was laid out and a game was in progress.

"Who is Roger Boine?" asked Charlotte, more bewildered than ever.

"You're going to meet him," was the reply, and she thought Carter sounded grim. He spotted Roger, who was waiting his turn at bat, and motioned to him. The red-haired fifteen-year-old hurried over and shook Carter's hand, glancing curiously at Charlotte.

"Hi, Mr. Lang," he said. "How are you?"

"Fine, Roger. How's the game?"

"Not so good. We're all tied in the fifth inning. Where's Mr. Manning?"

"He couldn't make it. But I brought someone else who wanted to meet you. This is Miss Thornton."

Charlotte looked even more bewildered at the pseudonym, but as she shook the boy's hand, looking at his face and the telltale red hair, she began to understand.

"How do you do, Roger?"

"How do you do, ma'am. Can you stay for the rest of the game?"

"I'm afraid not, Roger," Carter said. "We were just passing by and thought we'd drop in to say hello. How's your mother?"

"Oh, she's fine. She's coming down from Cleveland two weekends from now. That's when school lets out for the summer. She thinks she's got a summer job lined up for me on the magazine. I guess it doesn't pay much, but it should be interesting."

"That's good. How are your grades?"

"Hey, I got a B plus in math, and an A in biology! How's that?"

"That's pretty darned good."

One of his teammates yelled that he was next up to bat, and Roger hastily shook hands again. "Guess I've got to go. Say hello to Mr. Manning. And, uh, sure glad to meet you, Miss Thornton."

He hurried back to the game as Carter and Charlotte walked back to the car. "Who's his mother?" asked Charlotte quietly.

"A woman named Sheila Farr Boine. She was originally from Elkins."

"I remember her." Her tone was flat.

"She went to Cleveland and married a school teacher who died a couple of years ago. Mark took over the education of the kid. He's been in this school for two years and every once in a while I drive Mark down to see him. The kid doesn't know—at least I don't think he does. But he likes Mark. He's very bright, and Mark thinks he may have quite a future."

"What's the mother doing now?"

"She worked for a church magazine for a while, then she and this young man—a Calvin Harrington—started a magazine of their own that I hear is doing quite well. It's one of those women's magazines— you know, recipes, furnishings, stuff like that—and their special approach is to use a lot of photography in layouts. It's called the *American Woman*, which is where Roger's got the summer job."

They reached the car, and he helped her in. Then he cranked the engine, got in beside her, and started back to Elkins. She said nothing for a while. Then: "He looks amazingly like his father."

"He's, as they say, the spitting image."

"You know, what irritates me," Charlotte continued, "isn't that Mark has an illegitimate son that he's educating—in fact I think it's admirable that he *is* doing something for the boy. But what hurts is that he told you but never me. It makes me feel rather inferior, as if I weren't worthy of his complete trust. And of course, I suppose it also makes me wonder what else he may not have told me."

Carter passed a horse-drawn wagon.

"But, Carter," she went on, "you simply mustn't rush to any conclusions about Mark and myself. I'm touched and flattered that you *think* you're in love with me—"

"I don't *think* it. I *am* in love with you, and I want more than anything to prove it to you."

"That's out of the question. Carter, if for no other reason, I have the children to consider . . . and I am *not* going to cheat on my husband—"

"Oh, Charlotte, for God's sake, you're talking conventional nonsense—'I have to be a mother and a wife first'—but what about your first obligation to yourself and your own needs and feelings? What you really should be asking yourself isn't, 'Should I be faithful to Mark?'; it's 'Do I love Carter?' And if you do love me, then that should be your *first* consideration."

He stopped the car and put on the brake. The road was bordered by two cornfields. No one was in sight. He turned to Charlotte, took her in his arms and kissed her. She was taken by surprise—or was she?— but at first she did not put up any resistance. He whispered in her ear, "Please, Charlotte . . ."

She pushed him gently away. "You know it's an impossible situation, Carter. Now please take me back to town."

He angrily released the brake and started the car.

"*You're* the one that's impossible."

She said nothing. She was thinking, however, and rather nervously, how pleasant his mouth had felt against hers.

CHAPTER FOUR

If any one building might be said to symbolize the social history of New York during the first half of the twentieth century, it probably would be the Plaza Hotel. Opened on October 1, 1907, designed by Henry Hardenbergh, the same man who had designed the Waldorf and Astoria hotels as well as the Dakota apartments on Central Park West, the Plaza had as it's first registered guest Alfred Gwynne Vanderbilt, the same man who, eight years later, died on the *Lusitania*. Mr. Vanderbilt was the perfect first guest for a hotel built with Vanderbiltean opulence and whose neighbor was the gigantic Vanderbilt mansion that stood on Fifth Avenue and Fifty-eighth Street, the present location of Bergdorf Goodman. The builders spared no expense: W. & J. Sloane had provided magnificent handwoven Savonnerie rugs; 1,650 crystal chandeliers were installed; the Oak Lounge was paneled with the same British oak used for the tomb of Edward the Confessor in Westminster Abbey. Ten elevators, five grand staircases made of marble, a water-filtering system to supply 1,500,000 gallons a day for the eight hundred rooms, an ice-making machine that could produce fifteen tons a day . . . the public gasped at the details of this eighteen-story pseudo-French Renaissance château. There was even a garbage destroyer so sophisticated it could detect and separate silverware thrown in by mistake! Breathless newspaper articles calculated that the permanent tenants who then constituted ninety percent of the guests, represented a combined worth of $387,-000,000, and owned, among them, a total of two hundred automobiles, worth $1,200,000.

The suite Mark had rented in the spring of 1915 was on the ninth floor and consisted of a large living room, a bedroom, and a commodious bathroom. The morning after the party for General d'Aulnay,

Mark was shaving in the bathroom when he heard a knock on the door of the living room. Putting down his razor, he went through the bedroom, throwing on a bathrobe, then into the living room to open the door. Standing in the hall was a heavily veiled woman in a green suit. He recognized her as Sylvia Baker.

"Good morning," he said. She didn't reply but hurried by him into the suite. He closed the door. "Is something the matter?"

In reply, she removed her veiled hat and pointed to an ugly bruise on her right cheek. "See that?" she said. "That's what I got for helping you. Not to mention a kick in the stomach that it's a wonder didn't send me to the hospital."

"Riley *kicked* you in the stomach?"

"He sure as hell did, the bastard!"

"Well, look, I didn't tell him anything."

"Oh, I know." She sighed, sitting down in a chair. "He figured it out for himself. He probably would have beaten me up even if he hadn't been sure, just to scare me. Well, I'm through. I've had it over the ears with him. I'm getting a lawyer and I'm going to slap him with a divorce suit that'll make his teeth rattle. And have I got the goods on poppa! Just wait till I tell the judge about the little dollhouse on Thirty-first Street, and the games daddy plays *there*! Oh, yes, believe me, daddy Riley is going to pay for his kicks, and where it hurts him most, in his pocketbook." She looked at Mark's bare legs and lowered her voice. "Say, I'm not interrupting anything, am I? I mean, is there anyone in there?" She nodded toward the bedroom.

Mark laughed. "No. Remember me? I'm Mr. Pure."

"Oh, yeah. Well, anyway, the reason I wanted to see you is, could you maybe loan me some money? I just walked out cold this morning, and I've taken a suite here at the hotel—right down the hall, in fact— and I only have ten dollars on me and Riley never let me have a checking account or anything. So I'm broke until the divorce goes through. I really need some cash."

"I can lend you as much as you want," Mark replied. "How about ten thousand dollars?"

She looked surprised. "I don't need *that* much. Five ought to do."

"You sure?"

She nodded.

He went back into his bedroom, wrote her a check for five thousand, brought it back out and gave it to her. She smiled gratefully as she stood up. "I appreciate this. Thanks a lot."

"Don't mention it, and since we're neighbors, how about having dinner with me tonight? Here, in my suite. I don't think it would be a good idea for us to be seen together downstairs. You don't want Riley having evidence against *you*."

She thought about this, looking around the suite. "Well," she said, "you've got a point. And certainly no one could think anything could go in here with Mr. Pure." She laughed. "Oh, well, what time?"

"Seven."

She nodded, tucked the check in her purse, and left the room.

———————

"Do you want to do me a favor?"

"Sure. What?"

"Tell me everything you know about Riley's business."

They were seated opposite each other at a small table in Mark's living room that evening. Sylvia had a huge white napkin tied in front of her purple dress, and was tackling a lobster claw with her steel claw-crackers.

"Well, he's pretty secretive. He doesn't tell me hardly anything. Of course, I find out some things . . ."

"You found out about his deal with General d'Aulnay."

"That was an accident. I picked up the phone just when Riley was talking to him. But I know some other things. Sometimes, when he's really excited about something he goes on about it at dinner, although he's usually very careful. Even he needs to let it out sometimes, though, and I'm the one who's been around. Besides, as everybody knows, I'm so dumb it doesn't make any difference. At least, that's what he *used* to think. . . . Say, this lobster's fantastic."

CRACK! She finally broke the claw open and proceeded to spear out the delicate white meat, which she dipped in the melted butter.

"Tell me something he's been excited about recently," prompted Mark.

"Let's see, oh, I don't know—there's a steel company he's interested in. . . . You know, I don't like to talk business during dinner."

"What would you rather talk about?"

She put the fork in her mouth and slid the lobster meat off the tines between her white teeth.

"The kind of thing that any real man should be interested in when he's alone with a poor, deserted female like me."

"You never give up, do you?"

"Huh uh."

"Look, Sylvia, you know damn well I'd like to, and I'm telling you I'm not going to."

She stuck out her tongue at him.

"And as far as being poor and deserted, a girl that looks like you isn't going to be deserted for very long, and when you get done with Riley you're going to be a long way from poor—so let's forget it and get back to the business of Riley's business, which is what I'm really interested in and frankly, why I asked you here. Riley's got me over a barrel. Maybe you've heard something somewhere that would give me an opening—a clue to anything that might help me get back at him."

Her eyes sparkled. "You want to get him as much as I do, don't you?"

"More." He said the word with icy finality. "Now tell me about this steel company. Do you remember the name of it?"

She thought as she held another forkful of butter-drenched lobster before her mouth, then took a bite.

"Henderson, I think. The Henderson Steel Company. Yes, that was it. I never heard of it, did you?"

Mark was interested. "Yes. It's a medium-size company. The founder died last week—Stanley Henderson was his name, an old geezer living in Chicago. What did Riley say he was going to do with the Henderson Steel Company?"

"Oh, I suppose he'll raid the stock," she replied, shrugging. "I hear that's what he does with most of the companies he gets interested in."

"You're right—it's a set-up now that old man Henderson has died! Wait a minute, where's the paper—?" He got up from the table and hurried into the bedroom, where he found the afternoon newspaper. Turning to the stock market page, he ran down the columns searching for Henderson Steel, then came back into the living room with the paper. "Henderson went down a point today. Seven thousand shares traded. That's a lot for a sleeper. I'd say Riley's already started his raid."

"But what good does that do you?" asked Sylvia, wiping her fingers on her enormous napkin as she finished her lobster.

"Well," he said, "it just might give me the chance to pin that bastard right smack to the wall."

Two days later he was in Frank Bennet's Detroit office, asking the car magnate for a loan of ten million dollars.

"Ten *million*? What do you want that much for?"

"To corner the market in Henderson Steel common stock. Frank, I've got to get Riley Baker out of my company or I might as well quit and go fishing the rest of my life. Riley's got the voting rights of my children's stock, he's got his own stock, he's got Hutchins and Margate and Tilden in his pocket. In a squeeze he can outvote you and me and Gerstenmeier. I've *got* to get him out before he ruins the company. He's out for my blood. I blew the whistle on a kickback deal between him and General d'Aulnay. Now here's the situation: I've found out from Riley's wife that he's going to try a bear raid on Henderson Steel—he's already started selling Henderson stock short. The stock's down three points in the past week; Riley's starting soft, slow. All right, I want to buy all this stock Riley's selling short. I want to do it through my broker, Jimmie Page, and I don't want Riley to have any idea I'm behind the buying."

"Hold on, don't you realize cornering a stock is damn risky business?"

"Of course I realize it, but that doesn't mean I can't do it."

"I think you're crazy even to consider it."

"Maybe. Anyway, there are about three hundred thousand shares of Henderson stock held privately that are available for purchase. The rest—two hundred thousand shares—is tied up in old man Henderson's estate and frozen. All right. If I can buy up all that stock—three hundred thousand shares—while Riley Baker's selling the stock short to drive the price down, when I've cornered the market, Riley's going to have to come to me and *crawl*. Because he has to replace the stock he's borrowed to sell short or go to jail—and there won't be anyone else he can buy from except me. And Frank, I can put any price I want to on that stock. *I* will be the market! I can break Baker, and goddammit, I *will*, too!"

"What's Henderson selling for now?"

"It closed at forty yesterday, but like I said, it's down three points already. I figure Baker wants to drive it down to about twenty before he gets out. All right, I figure I'll need ten million to corner the market, assuming the average price I'll have to pay for the stock is around thirty—three hundred thousand shares at thirty would be nine million, but I'd like a million for cushion. Now, my Manning stock is currently worth about eight million, but I'm willing to put that up as collateral. My house and my insurance polices are worth about another million, and I'll put them up too. It doesn't add up to ten, but it comes close. How about it? You can charge me the current bank rates—five percent."

Bennet stared at him. "But Mark, if you don't corner the stock—what if Baker gets wind of what you're up to—you could lose millions! Hell, you could be wiped out."

"I know," he said. "I could get stuck with a load of Henderson stock that no one wants to buy—at least not at the price I paid for it. But, Frank, it's the only way I know to get rid of Riley Baker. And I'm willing to take the risk. Are you willing to lend me the money?"

Frank Bennet thought a moment, then nodded. "Yes. *I* really can't lose. Your Manning stock is gilt-edged, in my book. I still think you're crazy, though."

Mark smiled and shook his hand.

"Frank, people have been calling me crazy most of my life. Right now I'm beginning to think it's kind of a compliment."

Mark had sent Charlotte a letter from the Plaza saying he might be delayed in New York for as long as a month. This news had depressed her, but nothing as compared to the letter she received from her old friend Hanson Mayberry four days later. Hanson, society editor for the *Herald,* whom Charlotte hadn't seen since the night of the so-called Wobbly Ball a year and a half before, wrote:

Dear Charlotte:

Even though I make my bread and butter from gossip, I generally don't like it when it involves people I genuinely like and admire, as I do you. However, hearing gossip can often be less painful than not hearing it, and so I've decided to pass on to you an item I learned from one of my sources at the Plaza Hotel.

That ex-showgirl, Sylvia Baker, has taken a suite at the Plaza, on the ninth floor, just two rooms away from Mark's. She had dinner with him in his suite the first night she moved into the hotel, and she cashed a check from your husband at the hotel desk for $5,000. Perhaps you know about this already, and perhaps there is a perfectly innocent explanation for it, but I thought because of our old and very dear friendship that I should pass this on for what it's worth—which, of course, may be absolutely nothing. Still, the $5,000 check *does* seem curious.

Hoping you will accept this in the helpful spirit intended, and *not* take it as inexcusable meddling, I am,

Fondly,

Hanson

Her first reaction was one of shock. Then she carefully folded the letter, placed it in a drawer of her escritoire and proceeded to get absolutely furious. She very nearly picked up a vase and threw it across the room, but she managed to restrain her anger, which was quickly replaced by a wave of depression. People seemed so faithless—husbands and wives, pledges of honesty, marriage vows—the rules people were supposed to live by apparently were rules meant to be broken. She had been naïve to think Mark would be the exception. She remembered bitterly her assured words to Carter Lang that she believed Mark had stayed faithful to her since their marriage. She believed it because she needed to believe it—not because it was plausible or necessarily so. Not nearly as plausible as Mark combining business and pleasure with Sylvia Baker. She knew Mark's anger at her father leaving control of his Manning stock to Riley Baker . . . Sylvia no doubt could be a useful ally for Mark against Riley if she were on his side—in more ways than one.

Maybe the fault was in her; both her husbands, after all, had strayed, each in his own way and for his own purpose, but nonetheless she had failed to hold them . . . so maybe it was her fault. Or maybe it was the fault of marriage itself. Maybe people simply weren't meant to be forever faithful to a single person. She didn't know. She felt terrible for the children and for herself and, yes, for Mark too. But most of all, she felt tired and somehow defeated. She needed to stop thinking. She was at least entitled to cry on someone's shoulder.

And the shoulder she wanted was Carter Lang's.

A week passed, a slow, empty week in which her depression grew. She received a post card from Mark from Detroit, then another again from New York. Post cards. He always sent post cards and she hated them. Sometimes she felt she was married to a post card.

She thought often about Carter, though she tried to keep him out of her mind. She knew the more she thought about him the better he would seem and the more dangerously weak her resistance would become. So she tried not to think about him at all. She failed.

Carter's theatrical group, the Elkins Little Players, was doing Ibsen's *A Doll's House* at the Episcopal Church Community House. Carter was playing Helmer, and Lily Swenson had landed, so to speak, the role of Nora. On opening night Lily's proud parents, Harold and Leslie Swenson, were giving a cast party at their new house, and

Leslie Swenson had invited Charlotte to attend the play with them and
afterward the party. Harold and Leslie picked her up at River Bend to
drive her to the Community House, a plain stone structure attached
to the Episcopal Church, which could seat as many as three hundred
people. It was a warm June evening, and the house was full as Charlotte and the Swensons made their way to their seats.

Ibsen was perhaps not the most likely playwright to attract a midwest factory town audience, but there was a growing interest in culture
in Elkins and Carter had been able to sell out the five performances
a week in advance. The mayor was there with his wife; the high school
principal as well as half the faculty. Melville Benny was there with
the pretty, if mousy, woman he had finally married in 1913, confound-
ing predictions by colleagues of the brilliant head of the Manning
Research Division that the skinny, teetotaling chemist was too terrified of women ever to marry. Everyone looked very intense and
determined to enjoy the play, no matter if they were bored, because
Ibsen was "uplifting." And almost everyone was more than a little
surprised to find that as the drama began to unfold they were not at
all bored.

Charlotte was fascinated. She hadn't seen the play for years and
had forgotten its cumulative power as well as the fire of Nora. To her
surprise as well as everyone else's, Lily Swenson gave a magnificent
performance. She began the play as the coquettish, rather childish
housewife, but slowly, as scene followed scene, the strong, almost
revolutionary, Nora emerged until, at the final shattering scene when
she walked out on her husband and her children and her whole way of
life, Charlotte found herself trembling with the power of the performance as well as the effect on her of Ibsen's ideas. She had never
dreamed that pretty young Lily had such strength in her—no actress
could have simulated such power unless she had at least some of it
latent within her, and Charlotte was impressed and somewhat awed.
Lily was a *woman* to watch. Also, she had forgotten the potency of
Ibsen's ideas; and when she heard Lily delivering Nora's complaints
about her marriage with Helmer, she was amazed how closely they
paralleled her own unspoken complaints about her marriage with
Mark.

Carter Lang was fed up with the Mannings—Charlotte as well as
Mark. His romantic passion for the Gibson Girl he imagined he saw

in Charlotte had heated into something much closer to simple lust for Charlotte. And that, after her rejection, had lately been replaced by an angry sullenness. Mark, he felt, had been unfair to threaten to fire him if he saw Charlotte, and he thought Charlotte had lacked courage to give in to her husband's demands so meekly—never mind her excuse that in part she was protecting his job. Carter decided it was really very simple—Charlotte rejected him, Charlotte therefore really didn't give a damn about him. The torch he had carried so long for his employer's wife was beginning to sputter.

When he arrived at the Swenson's new home after the play and saw Charlotte, he pointedly ignored her. Charlotte was conscious of the snub and hurt by it. Her defense was to ignore *him*. She also lavished praise on Lily for her performance; when Lily's father, Harold, offered to take her on a tour of the new house, she quickly accepted, following him through the two floors of the Colonial structure the wealthy exforeman had built on ten acres of land near River Bend. The tour over, she told Harold she loved his house, then went out on the rear brick terrace overlooking the Matahoochi River and sat down on the stone balustrade. Lighting a cigarette with a small gold lighter Mark had bought her at Cartier the previous Christmas, she breathed out the smoke and watched it curl up through the darkness toward the half-moon that hung above the dark weeping willow. It was a gorgeous night. Frogs were croaking by the river bank, crickets were chirping on the lawn. Through the open French doors came the chatter of the guests, which in blend sounded not all that dissimilar from the frogs and the crickets.

Carter came out on the terrace and saw her. He considered snubbing her again but then thought better of it. One snub had a certain value. Two became an insult.

"Did you like the play?" he said, joining her at the balustrade.

"Very much. And Lily was a miracle."

"She was good, wasn't she?" he said, sitting down next to her and lighting a cigarette of his own. "How about me?"

"Oh, you're always good, but Lily's performance was the real surprise."

"Yes, she's full of surprises," he said.

There was an awkward pause, than Charlotte said, "You were avoiding me when I came here tonight, weren't you?"

"You were avoiding me."

Charlotte smiled and flicked her cigarette ash over the balustrade into a flower bed.

"So two old friends became enemies. Isn't that rather silly?"

"No, it isn't. Charlotte, I don't want to be your enemy, but I don't want to be just your friend either. Under the circumstances it would seem to make more sense to ignore you. Frankly, life's too short."

"For what?"

"For wasting time on an impossible situation. And I suppose you were right—it is impossible."

"That doesn't sound very generous, Carter."

"I'm getting less generous as I get closer to thirty."

She reached over and put her hand on his. "Oh, don't get cynical like everyone else," she said softly. "Please don't do that. You've always been so warm. Now don't turn cold because I've, well, treated you in a way you think inconsiderate. Do you think I'm happy the way this has turned out?"

"I have no idea."

"Well, I'm not." She withdrew her hand. "When I was watching the play tonight I was amazed how many similarities there were between Nora and Helmer and Mark and myself. When Nora told her husband they had never—what were the words?—'sat down in earnest together to get to the bottom of things' I went cold all over. Mark and I have never done that either. And she said she was tired of being his doll, his toy, and that she had borne three children to a stranger . . . well, I'm Mark's doll and I've borne him *four* children and he's *still* a stranger to me in so many ways. There's not that complete frankness between us, that *total* honesty I always assumed love was supposed to have. Maybe marriages just don't work out that way, I don't know. Mine certainly don't seem to. I suppose after two less-than-honest husbands I should begin to redefine love."

Carter caught the dry edge in her voice. And its promise for him . . . ?

"What's happened?" he asked.

"Oh, nothing. But don't you see, Carter, I'm stuck. Part of me is very old-fashioned. Part of me thinks conventionally, as you called it. A wife is a wife and stays loyal and faithful no matter *what* her husband does. But there's another part of me that wants to rebel against the whole system of marriage, just the way Nora rebelled. Not that I'd ever do what she did, but . . . well, I think what I'm trying to say is, don't be so hard on me. Try to understand me a little. And if I've hurt you, it's unintentional. I don't really know myself well enough— or what I *want* well enough—to be able to give myself to what you want. At least, I don't think I can. Does that make *any* sense to you?"

"It makes some sense . . ."

"Good, because the last thing I want is for us actually to dislike each other."

He waited a moment, puffing nervously on his cigarette. Then he said, softly, "Will you try my way? Once?"

Silence.

"Will you come to my place tonight?"

She watched the end of his cigarette glow in the darkness. She thought of her children. She thought of Mark. She thought of Sylvia Baker.

"All right," she whispered, "I'll try your way."

As she said it she felt a shudder of apprehension. But there was anticipation in it too.

Lily Swenson was feeling triumphant. Her performance had created that electricity with the audience that even she, an amateur, knew meant success. It flattered her and gave her a sweet taste of power. The party her parents had given had carried on and even extended the triumph as everyone—even Mrs. Mark Manning herself—had congratulated her. And then, as the party started to break up and the guests began leaving, her sense of triumph also began breaking up and leaving her. For rather than staying or, far better, taking her to his apartment to make love, Carter had merely said good night, telling her he was tired and was dropping off Mrs. Manning at River Bend on his way home.

"But Carter," she said in a low, tight voice, glancing nervously at her parents standing next to her and talking to Charlotte, "you said we could . . . you *know*."

"I'm tired," he repeated shortly. "I'll see you tomorrow night."

With that he shook her hand, said good-bye to her parents and went out the front door to help Charlotte down the steps and into his Pathfinder. Lily stood at the door beneath the tall colonial portico watching the car and wondering why Mrs. Manning had looked so— what? Pale? Nervous? Yes, that was it. Why had she looked so nervous when she left the house with Carter?

An incredible thought occurred to her, which she just as quickly dismissed as impossible.

Or was it?

The Elkins Country Club had been founded in 1910 by a group of Manning executives under Harold Swenson whose bank accounts were bulging and who wanted a place to drink and play golf. Over five hundred memberships were subscribed; a ninety-acre farm was bought outside town; a clubhouse was built solidly out of stucco, timbers and rock, giving it the rambling Michigan shooting-lodge appearance that was a fad at the time. Tennis courts and a golf course were constructed. The grounds and the golf course were extremely attractive, so that it was a pleasant enough place despite the homeliness of the clubhouse. And social life for Elkins's upper strata would henceforth center in the "club," as everyone called it, with the one exception of the king himself—Mark Manning. Mark refused to join because of the club's restrictive membership policy. And though the membership committee would instantly have waived its restrictions to admit Charlotte—she wasn't really *Jewish*—Mark had told them to go to hell. It was just as well, the members privately agreed. It would have been difficult to let your hair down at the club with Number One there, his eyes on you, waiting for you to take that one extra drink that might embarrass the company.

In 1912 an enterprising realtor had bought six acres from the club and put up twenty "swank" apartments near the golf course. The apartment complex, which consisted of five separate, pseudo-Tudor buildings containing four apartments each, was called Hampton Court (the developer was not modest in his pretensions) and each separate building was named, rather ominously, after one of Henry VIII's wives (the developer hoped to build a sixth unit later on for Catherine Parr). It was in Ann Boleyn House that Carter had rented the east apartment on the second floor, and it was into the garage of Ann Boleyn House that Carter drove his Pathfinder that night, with a tense Charlotte sitting beside him. Carter wished he could think of something to say to relax her, as well as himself, but all he could manage was "We're here," as he got out of the car and hurried around to help Charlotte step down to the concrete garage floor. He led her over to the door that opened to the back stairs of his apartment. Unlocking it, he went in and turned on the light, then waited as Charlotte came in and started up the stairs. He locked the door, followed her up the stairs to the kitchen, where again he turned on the lights. They went through the small dining room to the big living room that overlooked the seventeenth and eighteenth fairways. The view was lovely, particularly at night with the lights of the distant clubhouse twinkling beside the eighteenth green. Charlotte had only a glimpse of it, however, before he drew the curtains.

She looked around the room, which was furnished comfortably with leather chairs, solid, handsome tables piled with magazines, an inlaid victrola cabinet, a big pillow-piled couch, a brass telescope on a tripod, and a wall of books. Then she said, "It's odd. I've often wondered what your apartment would look like, but it's not at all what I imagined."

"What did you imagine?"

"Oh, what any woman thinks a handsome bachelor's place would be—very seductive and exotic. What's the telescope for? To spy on the country club?"

He laughed. "My secret is out. I watch all the pretty girls playing tennis. Also astronomy happens to be one of my hobbies. I like to look at the stars. Would you like a drink?"

"Perhaps a sherry."

As he fixed the drinks, she sat on the edge of a chair and watched him. He was so incredibly good-looking, she supposed there were a lot of women who gladly would have changed places with her. Nor was she unresponsive. It was just that she felt she was destroying something inside her by coming to the apartment—her self-respect.

He brought her the sherry. "Why don't you smile a little? I'm not going to bite."

She forced a smile. "How's that?"

"Radiant." He laughed, sitting next to her. "Don't worry, Charlotte, I'm just as nervous as you are."

"Are you really?" she asked, almost hopefully.

"Yes, really. Matter of fact, I'm scared to death."

"Oh, Carter, I feel terribly out of place here . . ."

He took her hand and kissed it. "Don't."

"I'll try," she said dubiously. "Well, what are we supposed to talk about? I haven't been seduced lately. I'm afraid I'm pretty rusty on technique—oh, God, Carter, I'm sorry . . . that sounds so brittle and I don't mean to but—"

"Just relax, don't force anything. I want to enjoy being with you, and I hope you'll enjoy being with me."

"I'm really enjoying myself," she said. "I'm so nervous I can hardly hold this glass."

"But why? There's nothing wrong with two people being together when they feel what we do for each other."

"If there's nothing wrong with it, why did you just say *you* were scared to death?"

"Look, Charlotte, I admit it's easy to say there's nothing wrong with it and we're both bound to feel a little guilty . . . except, did you ever wonder if maybe it's wrong to feel guilty?"

She thought briefly of Sylvia Baker and Mark—forced the thought from her mind. "Carter, you *are* the ultimate Yalie. That's a collegiate rationale if I've ever heard one. But I'm afraid I'm a terrible flop in the role of a fallen woman. Sitting here, waiting for you to pounce—"

"I'm not going to pounce."

"Well, you have to do something sometime . . . I don't imagine you asked me here because of my brilliant conversational talents . . . and all I can think about is the children and how I'm terrified of hurting them . . . I can't *help* it if that sounds conventional. I just don't want to get involved with something that's—well, doomed. I know that sounds terribly melodramatic but it *is* doomed. You know that as well as I. Elkins is too small a town; someone's bound to find out. Oh, that's only part of it. Mostly it's *wrong*. It's wrong for *me*—never mind what Mark might do or maybe has done."

He pulled her to him and kissed her. She felt the strength and warmth of his body, and she wanted him. "You know it's not wrong," he whispered. "You know it's right because we love each other. You damn well *know* it!"

"I *don't* know it," she replied, pushing him away, gently. "And that argument has been used for five thousand years . . ."

"I'm not interested in arguments. I'm in love. Your problem is you talk too much." He pulled her back against him and kissed her again.

He was probably right, she thought, but she also knew she wasn't going to change.

"Carter?"

"What?"

"You'd better take me home."

He let go of her.

"It's not going to work. I'm too tense and too afraid and too guilty. It's just not going to work."

"It will," he insisted angrily. "If you'd just let go—"

"I can't!"

"We're in love!"

"What kind of love sneaks through garages?" she asked quietly. "Take me home, Carter. Please. Before we really do get to hate each other."

"Dammit, I won't! My God, I've had to fight and wait forever to get you this far. I want you, Charlotte, I *love* you!"

"Do you?" she said, standing up. "All you really seem interested in is getting me into bed."

"But that's part of love!"

"Oh Carter, don't be a child. I may not be any expert on the subject, and I may have had two husbands who have cheated on me, but

I'm not going to take a lover who thinks the same way they do. There has got to be more to love than just going to bed! There's got to be some responsibility, some trust, some faith! Good God, do you think I'd be here if all I wanted was sex? I get plenty of that from Mark. What I thought I might get from you was some warmth and understanding and friendship, not this sophomoric free-for-all as if I were some sweet young thing from Vassar. Oh, that's not really fair to you, and I'm not trying to put the blame on you. I should never have come here. I should have stopped this whole thing weeks ago. But I didn't. I tried, but I wasn't strong enough. Well, now I am and I really must insist you take me home."

Suddenly he grabbed her hand and yanked her back down onto the sofa. He began kissing her furiously as she struggled to get loose but couldn't. He began taking off the jacket of her dress with one hand while the other held her against him.

"Carter—!"

The sleeve ripped at the shoulder as he tore the jacket off. He threw it onto the floor, then grabbed her blouse and ripped it open. She slapped him, but it did no good. She slapped him again; now he grabbed both her wrists and pushed her back down onto the sofa.

"Carter, don't! For God's sake, don't . . ."

He moved on top of her, pinioning her as he pressed his mouth against hers. She could feel his hands trying to loosen her corset. She was pounding at his head with her fists, trying to hold off hysteria. Finally she pushed her right knee up into his groin. He groaned with pain and rolled off her. She pulled herself away from him and got off the sofa. She was trembling and her face was wet with sweat. She pulled her blouse together, then stumbled across the room to retrieve her jacket. He managed to sit up on the edge of the sofa. He looked up at her, his eyes red, his face twisted with shame.

"I'm sorry," he whispered. "I'm sorry."

She felt no anger toward him. Rather, she felt pity; and shame for herself. If it were possible for an attempted rape to be justified, she thought this was the one.

"We'll forget it ever happened," she said.

"Can you?"

"Yes. We both can."

He nodded numbly and got to his feet, wiping his face with his sleeve. Then he forced a smile. "God, the romantic Carter Lang! The Casanova of the country club set." He looked at her morosely. "I wanted to hurt you. The one woman I've ever really loved in my whole damned life and I wanted to hurt you."

She came over and briefly put her hand on his arm. Then she said, "Will you take me home now?"

When they drove out of the garage in the Pathfinder, they nearly rammed into a Bennet Ariel that had just turned into the driveway.

"Christ, it's Lily!" muttered Carter.

Charlotte froze as she saw Lily Swenson climbing out of her car. The young girl hurried over to the Pathfinder, looked in at Carter and Charlotte. Lily said nothing. She just looked, those big green eyes taking in the torn sleeve, the rip in the blouse, everything. The eyes looked, Charlotte thought, deadly. Then Lily reached through the window and handed to Carter a small gift-wrapped package. "I forgot to give you this at the house," she said. "It's my opening-night present to you." Carter took the package and mumbled something that sounded like "thank you." Lily looked once more at Charlotte, then walked back to her car and climbed in. They waited for her to turn around and head out the driveway before doing the same themselves. As they headed for River Bend, Carter said, "Don't worry. She won't say anything. I can guarantee it."

Charlotte said nothing.

"I know Lily. She's got a sort of crush on me, but she'd never do anything that wasn't right—believe me."

"I thought," said Charlotte, "you said Lily was full of surprises?"

"Well, she is, but she won't say anything. Believe me."

"You've said that twice, Carter."

When Lily arrived home, she kissed her mother good night—Leslie Swenson was supervising the servants as they finished straightening the house after the party—then went up to her bedroom and undressed. The room was frilly. White curtains with girlish flounces on the borders, making them look like bouncy crinolines. White, childish furniture with a four-poster bed topped by a canopy with yet more flounces. Lily hated the room. It was so girlish, so immature, and she had fought with her mother over its decoration—a battle she had lost. She looked at herself in the full-length mirror. She was still wearing her slip, but now she pulled it off and examined her nude reflection. Those fresh, ripe breasts weren't girlish nor immature, nor were those slim hips and long tapered legs. She ran her hands slowly down her sides over her hips, then went over to the window seat. Lily's room looked out over the Matahoochi River, which the moonlight glittered off like silver sequins. Lily loved the view. She looked at the river and thought about Carter and Mrs. Manning.

Mrs. Manning. Lovely, gracious, queenly Mrs. Manning, the king's wife! Caesar's wife was supposed to be above suspicion, and now she, Lily Swenson, twenty-one years old, had stumbled onto Caesar's wife's dirty little secret. When she remembered all the years of resentment of the Mannings's supreme position in the town, her jealousy of River Bend, her feelings of love and hate toward the, to her, almost legendary Mark Manning, seeing now that the gods indeed had feet of clay gave her a delicious sensation. Not that she would use her knowledge against the Mannings. Not exactly, anyway . . . What she wanted right now was Carter Lang, and no girlish flounces were likely to stand in her way.

When it was a matter of getting what she wanted, Lily Swenson was prepared to be all woman.

Jimmie Page, Mark Manning's stockbroker, was a pleasure-loving man of fifty-one with an expansive personality and an expanding waistline. He was also one of the sharpest brokers on Wall Street. Jimmie had handled only one other corner in his career, and when Mark set out to corner the stock in Henderson Steel, Jimmie was exhilarated, not only by the handsome commissions the corner would generate for him but by the excitement and drama inherent in the rare attempt to buy up all the stock in a single company. Mark and Jimmie met daily, sometimes two or three times a day. On the tenth day after launching the corner, they met for lunch at Luchow's on East Fourteenth Street, where Jimmie gave Mark a progress report. "So far we've bought 167,250 shares," he said, checking a card covered with penciled notations, "and we've been damned lucky at getting good prices. I figure the average price we've paid to date is thirty-four a share."

"What's the last quotation?" asked Mark.

"It was twenty-nine and an eighth a half hour ago. I wouldn't be surprised if it closed at twenty-eight today. Riley's rumor mill is at work, and there's a good deal of bad talk going on about Henderson Steel, which works to our advantage, of course, because people are eager to sell."

"And it helps Riley, who wants to depress the stock."

"Right."

"Do you think he's gotten suspicious about us yet?"

"If so, he hasn't shown it. He's still selling Henderson short. He went short 10,000 more shares this morning."

"Good. How far is he in now?"

"Well, my best estimate is he's short 100,000 shares. It's one of the biggest raids he's ever tried."

The waiter took their order, then Jimmie lifted another card from his bulging wallet. This one had a list of fifteen names on it, seven of which had checkmarks beside them. "Okay," he said, "here we go on our fifteen biggest stockholders. We've managed to buy out seven so far, right?"

"Right."

"Now, I think Mrs. Wiggins is softening. She's old man Henderson's niece and owns 25,000 shares. I'd already offered her thirty-five a share so we're stuck with that price. And now that the stock's really beginning to slide, our offer is looking awfully good to her. Anyway, she called me this morning and I'm meeting her at two this afternoon. I've got a check made out to her for $875,000, which should finish her off. And which brings us to Maxine Talbot—the great Maxine, queen of the Great White Way. You ever seen her?"

"I saw the Ziegfeld Follies of 1914 last year, but I haven't seen the new one yet. I hear she's one fantastic-looking woman."

"Well, wait till you see her in the rosy flesh. I went to see her yesterday afternoon; I'd offered her 30 for her 15,000 shares and she told me —I use her words—shove it. Miss Talbot, by the way, uses the colorful language of the West Side docks. So then I bumped the offer to thirty-one and she told me what I could do with *that*. I hate to go any higher with her and yet we've got to buy her out—she simply has too much stock. When we spring the trapdoor, Riley's going to be at her doorstep in minutes to get hold of her 15,000 shares. I was thinking maybe you should go see her."

"But what can I do that you can't?"

Jimmie grinned. "Let me put it this way, Mark. I'm fifty-one, and I'm fat. You're thirty-six, trim and good-looking. Get the picture?"

Mark got it.

The morning after the opening night of *A Doll's House*, Lily Swenson put on a new blue-linen suit her mother had bought her in Cleveland, then went downstairs for breakfast. After coffee, she asked her father if she could drive with him to the factory. Harold Swenson expressed surprise at this, but she told him she'd explain in the car —it was "private." They got into the Packard and started for Plant One, where the executive suite was located.

"Now, what's the big secret?" Harold asked in his singsong Swedish accent as he drove the heavy car down the newly paved River Road.

"What do you think of Carter Lang?" asked his daughter, who sat next to him—she wished her father employed a chauffeur, like Mark Manning did. Chauffeurs made a man look important.

"Carter? I like him very much. He's a fine young man."

"Would you like him as a son-in-law?"

Harold shot her a look. "Lily, what's been going on?"

"Oh, nothing. I mean, nothing bad, so you don't have to get upset. Except I think Carter's about to ask me to marry him, and I wanted to be sure you'd approve."

"Are you in love with him?"

She smiled.

"I'm *crazy* about him. And he's got such a good job and makes a terrific salary—there's really no reason why we couldn't get married, is there? After all, I'm twenty-one and there's no one else in Elkins I'm even remotely interested in. Carter's so wonderful! He's so mature and intelligent and good-looking—you really would like me to marry him, wouldn't you?"

"Well, I guess so. I'm not sure I like the idea of my little girl getting married at all . . ."

"I'm not a little girl any more," she said cooly.

Harold looked at her. "No, I guess you're not. Well, I can't think of a better husband for you than Carter."

"Oh, daddy, thanks!" She leaned over and kissed his cheek. Then she sat back and folded her hands in her lap. There was a small smile on her face. As her father glanced at her, it occurred to him that perhaps there was also a trace of smugness about it.

"Lily," he said, "you really haven't done anything wrong with Carter, have you?"

"Oh, no, he's been a perfect gentleman."

"Are you going to see him this morning? Is that why you want to go to the factory?"

"That's right. He asked me to lunch today."

"But lunch isn't for four hours yet!"

"Well, I wanted to tell him something first, you see. Something private. He'll loan me his car to drive home in. Then I'll pick him up for lunch."

Harold Swenson shook his head. "Well, it sounds like an odd way to be courted. But I guess everything's changing these days."

"Oh, everything's definitely changing. And it's definitely changing for the better, in my opinion."

The executive suite in Plant One was entered through a handsome paneled reception room containing display cases filled with the leading Manning products. A door led to a wide corridor off which were the offices of the top executives and at the end of which was Mark's office, guarded by Wilma Amstuts. Harold's office was to the right of Mark's, in the place of honor. Carter was quite a way down the corridor from Harold's, reflecting his junior status in the overall scheme of things. Lily, having been in her father's office many times, knew most of the executive secretaries so that when she came into Carter's outer office, his secretary, Edna Wrigley, smiled as she recognized Harold Swenson's daughter. "Good morning, Lily," she said. "What a pretty suit."

"Thank you, Edna. I wondered if Mr. Lang is in yet?"

"Yes, he got here about five minutes ago."

"Would you ask him if I could see him?"

Edna looked a bit surprised. "Of course. Just a minute." She got up, went into the inner office, then reappeared. "Go right in," she said, holding the door.

"Thank you."

Lily went into the office, where Carter was standing behind his desk. Edna closed the door. Lily smiled at Carter, who smiled back, apprehensively. "Hello, Lily."

"May I sit down?"

"Please."

She took a chair in front of the desk as he sat down and looked at her. "I'm afraid I'm pretty busy this morning, Lily, so I'll have to ask you to make it brief."

"Oh, of course. Actually, we can talk at lunch, if you'd rather."

"I'm not following you."

"I thought it would be nice if you took me to lunch at the club."

Silence except for the ticking of a clock on Carter's desk. "All right, Lily, what's this about?"

"I just think you and I have a lot to talk about."

He got up and came around the desk, sitting on the edge of it.

"Lily, if that sly mind of yours is thinking what I think it is, then I should warn you right off that you're heading for a lot of trouble."

"What do you think my sly mind is thinking, Carter?"

"That there was something wrong going on last night between Mrs. Manning and myself."

"I didn't say that. Of course, other people might think it. It *was* odd—I mean, her torn sleeve, and everything."

"Lily, blackmail is a dirty game, and people that play it get dirty. I think you'd better cut this out right now."

"I haven't said *anything!* You're doing all the talking. All I want is for you to take me to lunch—pay some attention to *me,* for a change, instead of her. You're the one who's playing the dirty game. Mrs. Manning is years older than you, she's married, she has children—"

"Lily, stop it!"

"No I won't! I love you, Carter. I've loved you for I don't know how long and all you care about is getting me into bed . . . if my father ever—" She stopped to pull a handkerchief from her purse, then turned half around, holding the handkerchief to her dry eyes.

Oh, Christ, thought Carter. Oh, Christ . . . "All right. Look, I'll take you to lunch, we'll talk the whole thing over . . . except just don't make a scene *here,* for God's sake . . . Now you'd better go."

She stood up. "What time will you be at the club?"

"Twelve thirty. I'll make a reservation."

"I *knew* you'd understand," she said, then she went to the door. "Oh . . . I came over in daddy's car. I wonder if I could borrow yours to go home in? I could pick you up at noon and we could drive to the club together."

Carter closed his eyes with frustration, then nodded. "All *right.*" He went over to her, taking his car keys from his pocket and handing them to her. She took them and smiled. "You're a wonderful man, Carter," she said. "Much too wonderful to get involved with an old married woman. Whose husband, for heaven's sake, is your *boss.* Are you going to open the door for me?"

Carter opened the door.

Maxine Talbot, the star of the last three Ziegfeld Follies, lived in a little house on Grove Court, which was a small enclave of private houses in the west section of Greenwich Village. The court was entered from the street by an iron gate, and as Mark walked into the courtyard he thought the charming nineteenth-century houses surrounding it gave the place the feel of a small town rather than a corner of one of the biggest cities in the world. Maxine's house was painted a cheerful yellow, with geranium-filled flowerboxes under-lining the windows in red. He rang the bell, which was answered by a remarkably tall woman in a green silk robe splashed with huge flowers.

"Mr. Manning? Come in. I'm Maxine Talbot."

He entered the tiny entrance hall, trying not to gawk at the star, who was without a doubt the most striking woman he had ever seen. It wasn't that she was beautiful; in fact, taken separately, some of her features were far from perfect. Her mouth was too big; her lower lip was too full. Her face was oddly shaped, round, yet with cheek-bones so high that they gave her enormous brown eyes an almost Oriental caste. Her nose was small, sharp, distinctly unpatrician. Yet taken together, the result was a kind of savage, offbeat, primitive beauty, an effect Maxine played up by wearing her jet-black hair in two round buns, one over each ear. Her skin was almost tawny. Her neck was long and graceful, her body magnificent. The silk robe was barely parted, but Mark remembered her legs from a tableau in the Follies in which she had appeared as Cleopatra in a shocking costume, revealing legs long and beautifully shaped, leading the hungry eye up her splendid torso to sumptuous breasts.

"Are you the Manning Rubber Company Manning?" she asked, leading him into a small, cozily furnished living room.

"That's right."

"And why would Mr. Manning Rubber Company Manning be so interested in buying my Henderson Steel stock? Take a seat any-where."

Her voice was throaty, her manner casual. Mark liked her im-mediately.

"I think it's a good investment," he said, sitting down in a com-fortable armchair in front of a window looking out on Grove Court.

"Why? The stock's been going down and yet your broker and now you personally are trying to buy it from me. Mr. Manning, I smell a rat."

Mark smiled. "All right, suppose you're right? But it doesn't happen to concern you. All that should matter to you is that I'm willing—all right, anxious—to offer you thirty-two dollars a share for your fifteen thousand shares. You should be smart enough to take ad-vantage of it—and me."

"It's come up a dollar since yesterday."

"Yes, and that's it. I've leveled with you. I'm offering you a good price and profit." He pulled a checkbook and a pen from his jacket pocket. "Shall I write a check? It comes to four hundred and eighty thousand."

She eyed the checkbook.

"That's a lot of money."

"Isn't it?"

He took the cap from his pen and began writing.

"When I was a kid on Mulberry Street," she said, "I didn't think there was that much money in the whole world."

"Where's Mulberry Street?"

"Little Italy. I'm Italian. Maxine Talbot's just a stage name."

He finished writing and detached the check, offering it to her. She took it and looked at it.

"I'll think it over."

Mark stood up. "Take your time. And while you're thinking, keep the check. I'm staying at the Plaza."

She looked him over, right up to his red hair, then back and level with his eyes.

"I'll give you a call," she said. Then she folded the check, stuck it in her pocket and led him back to the door. As she opened it, he nodded toward the pocket she'd put the check in.

"Don't lose it," he said.

"Don't you worry about that, Mr. Manning. Money is one thing I never lose. Everything else" she smiled, "I lost years ago."

When he walked into the living room of his suite, he was surprised to find his wife waiting for him.

"Charlotte! What in the world are you doing here?"

He came over and kissed her, then he straightened and looked at her. "That wasn't exactly your most loving kiss," he said.

"It wasn't intended to be. I took the train in from Cleveland last night and I'm going back tomorrow afternoon. I trust it won't inconvenience you to put me up here for the night?"

"*Inconvenience* me?"

"Or perhaps Mrs. Baker?"

He looked at her. "Mrs. Baker doesn't sleep here, if that's what you're suggesting."

"I'm told otherwise."

"From whom?"

"I'm afraid, Mark, that's my business."

"Charlotte, what the hell is this? I haven't done a thing with Sylvia Baker! Not a goddamn thing! I've never cheated on you—not once—and I defy whoever told you this piece of garbage to prove I've done anything with Sylvia Baker! My God, she calls me Mr. Pure because I *won't* do anything with her! Yes, she wants me to— I'll admit that, but I haven't—"

"Oh Mark, don't lie. Don't make it worse by lying. . . ."

"It's not a lie, damn it." He went to the telephone and picking up the receiver, said, "Give me Mrs. Baker's suite," to the operator. "I'll prove it to you! You ask her yourself!"

"You know I'm not going to do that so you might as well hang up. Besides, I didn't come all the way to New York to fight over Sylvia Baker."

He hung up and said, "Then why did you come?"

"It's Carter Lang."

"What about him?"

"He's marrying Lily Swenson. She's blackmailing him into it. It's a cheap, terrible thing and I'm sick about it. I'm afraid it's going to ruin Carter's life—he really doesn't like Lily. And the truth is, the whole mess is probably my fault."

"*Your* fault?"

She nodded. "Mark, you're not going to like what you're going to hear now any more than I liked hearing about Sylvia Baker. But I'm going to tell you anyway. For the first time in our marriage we're going to be truthful with each other."

He sat down slowly.

"Carter's in love with me. He has been for some time—you were right about that. I didn't realize how strongly he felt until he took me down to the Wooster School and introduced me to Roger Boine."

"Why, that bastard! He had no right—!"

"Oh, I've been finding out a good deal about my husband lately. I think what bothered me most about Roger Boine was that again you couldn't confide in me—tell me the truth. I'd hardly hold it against you that you've been taking care of your illegitimate child's schooling —although Carter apparently thought I would."

"I'll fire him!"

"No you won't! If you do, I'll divorce you, Mark. And I mean it."

"What is this, Charlotte?" he said softly. "Why are you defending Carter? What went on that Lily's blackmailing him about?"

She straightened slightly. "Last week, I went to Carter's apartment. Alone."

"*Why?*"

She looked at him coolly. "For one thing, I wanted to get back at you for what you've been doing here with Sylvia Baker."

"But I haven't been doing anything!" He was shouting now.

"Please! Keep your voice down, and for once let me do the talking. Anyway, you may be amused to hear that once I got there, I couldn't go through with it. Carter, however, was insistent and . . . well, he tried to force himself on me. Not that I can really blame him . . ."

"You mean, he tried to *rape* you?"

"Yes, but—"

"Jesus, I'll kill him!"

"No you won't. I just told you, he was provoked. Anyway, my sleeve was torn and when we got outside, there was Lily. She saw the sleeve, jumped to the obvious, if false, conclusion, and the next day marched into Carter's office and began to pressure him. Carter's miserable about the whole thing but to save my reputation—as well as his job—he's going to marry Lily. Which is the reason I've come to New York—to tell you so it won't matter if *she* tells you. And to ask you to talk to Harold Swenson, because I think you can pressure Harold into persuading Lily to back down. So now you know the entire, sordid little mess. I'm *not* trying to say I behaved honorably or nobly or to take any special credit for not going to bed with Carter —it might have been more honorable if I had."

He didn't say anything for a moment as he tried to bring his temper under rein. Then he said quietly, "Can you tell me the real reason why you came so close?"

She hesitated. "Because I was lonely and tired of living down your suspicions. And because I was hurt by you—"

"But, Charlotte, I swear to you I have had *nothing* to do with Sylvia Baker!"

She sighed. "It's not just Sylvia, Mark—don't you understand that? You asked for the real reason . . . all right, it's our whole marriage, it's us, it's . . ." She hesitated. "It's most of all the Manning Rubber Company."

"And what's that got to do with it?"

"Everything, I'm afraid, in the long run. Mark, I understand it's your life and your great love. It's also my great rival, and I'm beginning to hate it—especially since I don't think I can ever win. I was so furious at you for what you said to father when he was dying—"

"Didn't it occur to you to be furious at Sam for what he did to me?"

"Yes, but you're missing the point. I don't think what he did was admirable and I don't blame you for being angry at him—it's your *reason* and its importance to you that really worried me and still does, more than ever. I began to wonder if he had been right all along —that what you most wanted from me was his Manning stock, which didn't mean I didn't believe you loved me, but that I had to face the truth: I was and am married to only half of you, because the rest of you is married and in love with the Manning Rubber Company."

"Charlotte, excuse me, but I think that's all a bunch of baloney. Every wife of every successful businessman in America could say the same thing about her husband—"

"But that's just it, Mark!" she interrupted. "That's exactly it. If you're most in love with your business, then what am I? A sort of legalized mistress? A housekeeper, a nurse for the children and hope-fully a social asset. I don't want to sound selfish but that's just not enough, Mark. I'm a human being, too, with some brains and talent. I'm a person on my own, too. It's not that I don't love you. And I adore the children—you know that. But I can't help resenting being so far down in your scale of things—and that's why I went to Carter's that night. It was my small, admittedly feeble and perhaps foolish act of rebellion against being Mrs. Mark Manning instead of Charlotte Rosen Manning."

For a moment he said nothing, then quietly, "But you're both, and you ought to accept the fact. If I were a bad husband to you, Charl-otte, then you might have some legitimate reason to say these things. But I think I've been a pretty good husband—especially considering my lurid past. And for you to jeopardize our life in Elkins as well as our family by going to Carter Lang's apartment is, to me, incredible."

"And *there's* the difference again," she said. "It's all very well for you to go to bed with Sylvia Baker—"

"Which, for the umpteenth time, I haven't done!"

"—but if I so much as think about having an affair with a man, I'm a fallen woman, a betrayer of my family and a terrible mother. You see? We're not equal."

"And just who ever said we're *supposed* to be?"

"*I* do!"

"Well, we're not and I say you were wrong to go to Carter's, even if you really believed I'd been having an affair with Sylvia Baker. Don't worry, I won't fire Carter, because I know that would only push you closer to him. But I am *not* going to put any pressure on Harold Swenson to call off Lily from your precious Carter. I hope he does marry Lily, and I hope she makes his marriage one living hell—just the way you're beginning to do with our marriage with all your crazy new ideas." He got up, started toward the door, then turned and pointed a finger at her. "You know, when I think of the chances I've had to cheat on you . . . when I think of the struggle I've gone through to build up this company that you now say you're beginning to hate, the fight I'm in right *now* when I've got every penny I own on the line trying to get Riley Baker off my back—who, by the way, was put there by your father . . . Damn it, Charlotte, I've loved you and respected you. And now to have you come here with all these cheap, ridiculous complaints about me and our marriage . . . well, all I can say is that I'm afraid you're becoming a very spoiled and selfish and foolish woman."

He went to the door.

"Where are you going?" There was shock in her voice.

"I'm going to make love to Sylvia Baker, if you want to know the truth. Because by God, if I'm going to be tried, accused and convicted of adultery, I'm at least going to *enjoy* it!"

"Mark—"

It was too late. He had already slammed out of the suite.

Sylvia Baker was sitting up in bed reading the *Ladies' Home Journal* when she heard the bell. She got up, put on a peignoir and went through the living room to answer the door.

"Oh, hello," she said, standing back as Mark pushed by her into the room, then closed the door.

"Are you alone?" he asked.

"Not any more."

He took her in his arms, kissed her and began rubbing and kneading her back with his strong hands. It was clear to her that he was at the boiling point, which displeased her not at all. Then he abruptly released her, grabbed her hand and led her into the bedroom. "Get undressed and into that bed," he ordered, taking off his jacket and unloosening his tie.

She obeyed, asking only, "Gee, what did you have for lunch? It really put the beans in you!"

He didn't answer. Lying next to her in bed now, he took her in his arms and kissed her as he hooked his right leg half over her thighs. His hands were caressing her breasts as his tongue probed her mouth. Then, slowly, he eased her over onto her back and himself on top of her. She gasped as he entered her.

"God, you are huge!" she whispered.

He said nothing as he began to thrust, his rage and frustration filling her as he sought to relieve himself.

When he was finished, he lay on his back and stared at the ceiling. Now, of course, he *had* betrayed her, the trust was irrevocably broken . . . who was to say who was more responsible . . . ?

True, it gave him a new freedom, yet he felt saddened to have it.

Charlotte Manning had never truly understood that her husband had indeed—however improbably—fallen in love with her that day, fifteen years ago, when he had come into the Rosen front parlor and seen her sitting at the Bechstein. . . .

Two days later Charlotte arrived in the Cleveland station, where she was met by Marvin Senjak. The uniformed chauffeur, a pleasant-looking, well-built man in his early thirties, tipped his cap and welcomed her in the polite manner he always displayed to his employer's wife—a manner that inhibited Charlotte in her desire to display her dislike and distrust of the man. He transferred her luggage from the Pullman to the big black Packard, helped Charlotte into the back seat, then got in front and began the drive to Elkins.

Charlotte watched the passing landscape and reflected on what had taken place at the Plaza. She conceded that Mark had been at least partially right and that her plaints might well have sounded trivial to a man fighting for his corporate life. Still, they were none the less real to her, and as the car pulled through the big gates of River Bend and she saw the huge brick wall once again, she felt as if she were re-entering her strange prison after an abortive escape attempt.

What *was* the answer? Compromise? But she wasn't sure it was really an answer; perhaps it was merely an avoidance.

Perhaps there was no answer.

The car pulled up in front of the big brick house and Peter, the butler, helped her out. She went directly to the nursery, where Mrs. Brent, the inestimable British nanny, greeted her along with David and Ellen, Richard and Christopher being asleep. As she hugged her beloved, beautiful children and felt the elegant warmth of her house, she reminded herself she also had much to be thankful for . . .

Leaving the children, she went to her bedroom and called Carter at his office.

"Carter, can you talk?" she said quietly.

"Yes, I'm alone. Why did you go to New York?"

"To tell Mark what Lily's done."

"My God, you *told* him?"

"Yes, and it wasn't an especially attractive moment, believe me.

He was furious at both of us. He's not going to do anything about you though—I made him promise that—and besides, as he said, it would make things even more difficult in our marriage. So at least he *knows* and Lily won't be able to pressure you any more. Oh, Carter, when I think of that cheap little blackmailer I want to strangle her!"

He didn't say anything for a moment, and when he spoke he sounded depressed. "Thank you, Charlotte, for trying to help me. But I'm going to marry Lily anyway."

"Why?"

"She thinks she's pregnant."

"Oh, Carter, that's the oldest . . . *don't* let her use *that* on you."

"I know, and I suspect she may be lying, but I'm going to marry her anyway. For one thing, her doting father will surely fire me if I don't—and even worse, blackball me in the entire industry so I'll never get another job. Don't forget, he's a big man on his own, and Mark would back him up. Besides, it's finished with us—we can't even be friends the same way . . ."

"That's not so. I told you we can and should both forget that night."

"But I can't." He hesitated. "And there's another, practical side to all this. Nothing's ever going to happen between us. I'm getting sick of being a bachelor. Lily's a good-looking woman, her father's an important man in the company who can be as helpful toward a son-in-law as he wants . . . as helpful as he can be vindictive if I *don't* marry Lily . . ."

"But you don't love her! You'll be miserable with her."

"Charlotte, I appreciate your trying to help me . . ."

"Well, if you are really determined to marry her, I want to wish you luck."

"I expect I'll need it."

"And Carter?"

"Yes?"

She paused. "I'll always," she said softly, "feel honored that you were in love with me. Because I believe you were telling the truth about that."

He said nothing except, "Thank you for saying that."

The naked woman was spread on the couch in the Turkish alcove, her arms reaching up to welcome the man bending over her. With odd, slightly jerky movements, the man lowered himself on top of the woman, whose arms jerkily embraced him. They commenced to make love.

"Christ, it's almost real!" said Franco Ruggiero, pushing a button and stopping the process. He pushed another button, and the two life-sized mannequins reversed themselves, the woman opening her arms to release the man, who backed away and straightened until he was again standing beside her couch in the starting position.

"Yes, it's remarkably lifelike," said Riley Baker. The two men were in the second floor room of Riley's East Thirty-first Street townhouse, the temple of his erotica. The love machine had been in a Bronx electric shop for more than a year, being repaired and wired for electricity, and it had only recently been returned to Riley —needless to say in an unmarked crate. So it was Franco's first viewing of the elaborate, obscene toy, and the young Sicilian's eyes were staring. "It was made," continued Riley, "by a Viennese civil servant whose official life was one of unimpeachable rectitude—a customs inspector—but whose unofficial life was dedicated to the construction of these remarkably intricate moving statues. He was a genius, in my opinion. This particular creation—the prize of his production —cost me the equivalent of ten thousand dollars. I think it's worth it, don't you?

"Yeah," said Franco, pushing the button that restarted the automata in motion. "It's almost *better* than the real thing!"

Riley laughed. "Franco, you have the soul of a true pornographer, which no doubt is one reason I find you tolerable. How's your brandy?"

"Oh, fine." In fact, his snifter was almost empty, but he was too absorbed in the love machine to notice. Riley went over to a recessed bar to get a refill. The room was a parody of a Turkish harem; Riley understood that, but that was also part of his amusement . . . the bizarrely patterned fabric that covered the walls and was gathered at the ceiling as if in a tent. The Turkish couches, the intricately carved, inlaid coffee tables; the pierced iron lanterns; the water pipes; the ubiquitous pillows—it was all rather like a movie set, which pleased Riley. But the two huge, glass-fronted, padlocked bookcases filled with his priceless albums, not to mention the love machine in the alcove at the end of the room—that one wouldn't find in a movie set, after all. All that was unique.

A young girl came through a curtained door and looked uncertainly around the room. She was about twenty, with long, brown hair, and she had on a Turkish harem outfit—baggy silver pants, bare midriff, a blue-and-silver jacket and a gossamer veil. She seemed ill at ease. "And here's Christina!" said Riley. "Where's Christina from, Franco?"

Franco turned away from the love machine and eyed the girl he'd brought to the weird townhouse a half hour earlier.

"Mott Street. Her old man works in a bakery. She's not too long in the brains department."

Riley had picked up a riding crop and was now slowly circling the girl. "Brains aren't precisely what we're looking for tonight, are they? How does the costume fit?"

"All right," the girl said. She sounded nervous.

"Did Franco explain what we do here?"

She nodded.

"Good. You won't be hurt, of course. Nothing permanent. But there will be some pain. After all, that's what you're being paid for. You understand that?"

"Yes."

Riley stopped in front of her, tapping the riding crop on the palm of his hand. "But that comes later. First, we like to be more traditionally entertained. We think of ourselves as a branch of the arts here. Pantomime, the dance and so forth. You saw our collection of costumes?"

The girl was watching the riding crop.

"Do you dance?" continued Riley.

"Not very well."

Riley put the end of the riding crop on her bare navel and pushed it slightly.

"Why don't you give us your interpretation of a Turkish belly dance? That should be interesting."

"I don't *have* any interpretation of a Turkish belly dance."

"Hey, you—do what you're told, for Christ sake," Franco said.

"But I don't know how!"

"Then make something up, *stupida!*"

The girl put her hands above her head, then started wriggling her hips. Riley sat down on a couch, smiling with pleasure as he watched her, all the while softly tapping the riding crop on the palm of his left hand.

An hour later, Riley counted seven ten-dollar bills into Franco's hand. "Four for you, three for the girl. And of course, she won't talk?"

"Nah. They're dumb, but they're not *that* dumb. You liked her?"

"Very nice. She had a certain . . . style."

"Good." Franco folded the money and stuck it in his pocket. Such an easy way to pick up extra cash, even if the old guy was weird. So what? He'd seen plenty weirder birds than this one around.

As he started for the door he remembered something. "Oh, by the way, Mr. Baker, aren't you a director of the Manning Rubber Company?"

Riley looked up. "Yes. Why?"

"Well, I happen to know Maxine Talbot—"

"*You*"—incredulously—"know Maxine Talbot?"

"Yeah, I've known her since I was a kid. My older sister used to be her best friend when they was kids. And, uh, you know, she thinks I'm good-looking."

Riley looked impressed. "You're going up in the world, Franco. My congratulations. I don't suppose we could hope to entice Miss Talbot here one night?"

Franco laughed. "No, sir, I don't think so. Anyway, I was down at her place in the Village couple of days ago and she was celebrating. Showed me this check made out to her for $480,000—"

"What?"

"Four hundred and eighty thousand! And it was signed by this bigshot you must know. Mark Manning."

Riley tensed. "Wait a minute, did she by any chance sell him her Henderson Steel stock?"

"Yeah, I think that was it. Yeah, she said it was a steel-company stock and she'd been nervous because the price is going down. Anyway, I thought it was funny that this Manning guy would—"

"Sylvia!" Riley said, mostly to himself. "It was that bitch, Sylvia. She must have told him *that*, too . . . Christ. . . ."

His face was chalk white as he ran past a surprised Franco to the door, then rushed into the hall, down the stairs to the first floor, where he ran into his small library. Grabbing the phone off the cradle, he banged frantically for the operator. When she came on, he gave her the number of his broker, Anselm Wittredge. As the phone rang, he squirmed nervously. Anselm's butler finally answered, and Riley managed to say, "Get Mr. Wittredge!! This is Riley Baker! Tell him it's important!"

"Yes sir."

Another interminable wait. Franco stuck his face in the door and said, "Are you all right, Mr. Baker?"

Riley nodded curtly. "Yes, I'm all right. . . . Hello? Anselm? Riley. Who's been buying the Henderson stock?"

Franco watched the older man's face as he closed his eyes.

"They're all fronts for Jimmie Page! Manning's trying to corner me, the son of a bitch. All right, listen. Tomorrow, go into the market and buy all the Henderson you can lay your hands on. Pay anything —understand? Anything! Why? You idiot, I'm 123,000 shares short! If I can't replace that stock, Manning can ruin me! And get a list of the major stockholders in the company—it's in their last annual report. Manning's already six jumps ahead of us, but we may be able to get a few of the big ones—and for God's sake, buy me stock tomorrow! Understand? I don't care if you have to pay forty. *Buy me stock!"*

He slammed down the phone and stood motionless by the desk a moment, trying to pull himself together. Then he looked up at Franco, who was still watching him.

"Is there anything I can do, Mr. Baker?"

"There may well be, Franco," he said. "There may well be."

CHAPTER FIVE

The pinpoint spotlight hit her face, then irised out until the whole glorious figure was bathed in white light against the jet black background. And then Maxine Talbot began to sing. The song was Irving Berlin's newest hit, "The Girl on the Magazine Cover," but Maxine's singing style was as old as Eve. "The costume cost two thousand dollars!" whispered an awe-struck woman to her husband, who was sitting next to Mark in the seventh row. The dress was a silver-spangled gown with a long train that was wrapped—or rather draped—around the black pedestal on which Maxine was standing. The dress was like a second skin: the neck and the throat were bare, the breasts translucently covered, and enough of those astonishing legs were showing to give the audience its full money's worth. On Maxine's head was one of those fantastic headpieces Ziegfeld was famous for: a silver headband holding three towering white plumes that shot five feet into the air from her forehead, a great fountain of feathers that cascaded back down halfway before stopping. Each time Maxine moved—and she moved only slightly—the spangles would glitter in the spotlight back at the audience, so that she seemed like some incredible, magnificent diamond bird. Even if the song had been awful, even if Maxine had been a mute, the audience still would have stared at this wonderful apparition, this Ziegfeldian abstraction of glamor and sex and femininity.

After the first chorus, the orchestra reprised the number as a series of *tableaux vivants* were illuminated around and above Maxine, each *tableau* representing the cover of a popular magazine and each cover featuring a glorious girl. And they *were* glorious: Dolores, the statuesque "girl who never smiled"; Ann Pennington, the "million-aire's favorite"; Olive Thomas; pert Marilyn Miller; and exotically lovely Fanny Brice.

But Mark hardly noticed the others. He was staring at Maxine Talbot, and he was not thinking about home, children, wife or position in Elkins. These at least temporarily faded before the more urgent thoughts concerning Maxine Talbot's legs.

On the way downtown after the show, Mark took out a small package from his jacket pocket and gave it to Maxine. "For you," he said. "For selling me your stock."

"You paid for the stock—you don't have to give me a present too. Of course," she added, untying the blue ribbon, "I'll take it."

The box was from Tiffany's. Inside was a large diamond brooch in the shape of three feathers springing from a diamond headband.

"It's my headpiece!" she exclaimed, delighted.

"That's right. I told them to design it for Maxine Talbot, and it seems they did."

"God, I love it!" She held it up to her green dress and pinned it on. Then she kissed Mark. "One nice thing about millionaires," she said, "is that they're so goddamn rich."

They ate dinner at Maxine's favorite restaurant, Gino's on Bleeker Street, a few blocks southwest of Washington Square. Gino's was a superlative Italian restaurant inhabiting the bottom floor of an aging four-story house as well as a spacious garden in back, and it was to the garden that a beaming Gino led his most famous customer and her handsome, top-hatted escort. "Underneath the tree, okay?" he said, giving them a table under a huge ailanthus tree, one of those miracles of nature that thrive on city air and concrete. They sat down and Mark ordered a bottle of Soave.

"I love this place," Maxine said, looking up at the back of the house. The garden was hung with multicolored Japanese lanterns, and it held a dozen tables, most of which were occupied. "You know, it's my secret dream to own a restaurant just like this. Wouldn't that be fun? Besides, I'm a great cook. Someday I'll cook you my cannelloni—you'll never touch anything else. So . . . tell me about yourself. Where's your wife?"

"She went back last week."

"And wouldn't she be upset if she knew you were taking me out to dinner? Not to mention buying me diamond pins?"

"Yes, she'd be upset." He picked up a spoon and looked at his distorted reflection in its hollow. "We had a fight," he went on. "A really bad one after almost eight years of happy marriage and four kids. I think she was wrong and I was right, and she probably is thinking just the opposite. Maybe we can fix it up again, I don't know. But, meanwhile—" He stopped.

"Meanwhile, you're taking me out to dinner?" she prompted.

He nodded. "I love Charlotte, and I love my children." He put the spoon back on the table and looked at her. "But I'm taking you out to dinner."

"Listen," she said, "you don't have to make excuses to me. I've been married once, and that was enough. The important thing is to stay free. Children are nice, and sometime I'd like to have a couple. But meanwhile, she travels fastest who travels alone, or something like that . . . oh good, here's the wine. I'm so glad you like wine too—most men are always pouring down whiskey, which makes them smell."

The waiter served the wine and took their orders. When he'd left, Maxine said, "Now, are you going to tell me the truth?"

"About what?"

"About why you were so crazy to buy my stock."

"Oh, that. Sure. I've cornered the market."

She looked amazed. "You're kidding."

"No, I really have. I own all but 3,000 shares of the available stock in the Henderson Steel Company, and that 3,000 belongs to an orphanage outside Cincinnati that won't sell to anyone."

"That's the wildest thing I've ever heard of! And you're so casual about it! God, how rich *are* you?"

He smiled. "Not all that rich, right now. But tomorrow I'm going to be, shall we say, filthy?"

"What happens tomorrow?"

"Well, there's a gentleman named Riley Baker—"

"Oh, *him!*"

"Do you know him?"

"No, but a friend of mine sort of works for him, which is a polite way of saying he pimps for him, but let's not get into that. Anyway, go on. What about Riley?"

"Well, he has to get his hands on 123,000 shares of Henderson stock by noon Saturday. That's the deadline the board of governors of the Stock Exchange have set for his returning the stock he's borrowed, and if he can't come up with it, he goes to jail. I'm the only one in the country who has any Henderson stock. So tomorrow he comes to me to try and buy 123,000 of my shares."

"And will you sell?"

"You bet. But the price is going to be *very* high."

"How high?"

"High enough to ruin him."

"Ruin Riley Baker? But he's worth millions!"

"He won't be after tomorrow."

She gave him a searching look. "Something tells me you're a very tough customer."

He picked up his wine glass. "Tough enough, I guess. Particularly with people I don't like."

"Well, I hope you like me."

He took a sip of the cool white wine. "After dinner, I'd like to show you just how much."

She smiled. "I think that could be arranged."

Making love to Maxine Talbot was like the realization of every schoolboy's sexual fantasy, and though Mark's sex life was active enough to preclude the need for much fantasizing, he had his dreams as well, and making love to Maxine was being awake in one of them. Her body was so firm and lithe and sweet-smelling that a few minutes after their first time he was able again. Maxine was happy to comply. She enjoyed and liked this handsome millionaire and was as attracted to his goldish-red-haired, muscular body as he was to all the tawny, impeccable length of her. After their second session, Mark relaxed on the enormous bed, staring up at the ceiling.

"You know something?"

"What?"

"I think I may be falling in love with you."

She laughed. "You know something?" she echoed.

"What?"

"Welcome to the group."

He looked over at her as she sat up and stretched.

"You have competition, Mr. Mark Manning. I told you . . . I like to have lots of friends and no entanglements. That's Maxine Talbot's formula for a long and happy life." She got out of bed and yawned. "Now how about a nice healthy cup of tea before we call it a night? You stay put and I'll bring you a cup."

As she went downstairs to the kitchen, Mark lay back in the bed, reflecting unhappily about the competition.

———

At precisely noon the following day a grim-faced Riley Baker and his unctuous broker, Anselm Wittredge, knocked on the door of Mark's Plaza suite. Jimmie Page ushered them into the living room, where a chubby gentleman named Howard St. Clair rose to greet them. Mr. St. Clair was representing the board of governors of the Exchange and moderating the meeting. Mark then came into the room, nodded curtly at Riley Baker and sat down, as did the others. The atmosphere was fit for an execution.

Mr. St. Clair cleared his throat. "Gentlemen, since we all know why we are here, shall we get right to the point? Mr. Manning, Mr. Baker wants to buy 123,000 shares of your Henderson Steel common. The question is, at what price will you sell the stock?"

Baker's eyes met Mark's. There was a short silence. Then Mark said, "One thousand dollars a share."

Anselm Wittredge jumped out of his chair. "That's outrageous! That's extortion! It's out of the question."

Mark turned to Mr. St. Clair and said, "Mr. St. Clair, I believe I'm correct when I say I can put any price on the stock I choose?"

St. Clair nodded.

Mark turned back to Baker. "One thousand dollars a share."

Riley put his hand on his broker's arm, restraining him. Wittredge sat back down.

"Mr. Manning realizes, of course," said Riley, "that his price is a joke, and that even if I could raise $123,000,000—which I can't—I would rather go to jail than pay such a ridiculous sum. Now, the question is, what price will Mr. Manning *settle* for? And to sweeten the pot, I'm offering to sign over to Mr. Manning my trusteeship of his children's stock in the Manning Rubber Company, and I'm willing in effect to *give* him my Manning Rubber stock at the nominal valuation of one hundred dollars a share. Now, what is Mr. Manning's realistic price?"

Mark considered this. Despite his remark to Maxine at Gino's, he actually didn't want to ruin Riley Baker, if for no other reason than that he wanted to leave Riley something for Sylvia to get as a divorce settlement, but also because, after all, Riley was a close friend of several of his directors. So the challenge was to gouge Riley without destroying him. He estimated his worth at fifty million. Realistically, he thought he could get half of that along with the Manning stock. Riley wouldn't like giving up twenty-five million dollars, obviously, but Mark figured that was the point above which he would choose jail. So he said, "If Mr. Baker gives me his present stock holdings in my company, signs over his trusteeship of my children's stock and resigns his directorship in my company, then I am willing to sell him 123,000 shares of Henderson Steel common at two hundred dollars a share."

Silence. Riley was pale. Anselm Wittredge said, "But that's still incredible! That's $24,600,000! It's out of the question."

"I won't go lower," replied Mark quietly.

Everyone watched Riley Baker. His face was a mask. A half minute. A minute. "I accept," he said, stood up, and walked out of the room. Anselm Wittredge looked confused, then hurried out after him. St. Clair told Mark he would arrange the official transfer of the stock at his office that coming Saturday. Then he left.

Jimmie Page sighed with relief. "Well, that's that. Riley looked like he was about to pop, didn't he? Well, Mark, what's it feel like to be a *very* rich man?"

"Very nice," Mark said. "But it feels even better to be boss in my own house."

Riley Baker didn't attend the Saturday meeting. He sent Anselm Wittredge, who presented Mark with a letter from Riley resigning his directorship in the company and his trusteeship of Mark's children's stock; all Riley's Manning Rubber preferred stock signed over to Mark; and a cashier's check made out to Mark for $24,600,000. In return, he received the 123,000 shares of Henderson Steel stock.

After the meeting, Mark took Jimmie Page to a victory lunch. He had good reason to celebrate. After returning the ten million dollars, along with the five percent interest charge, to Frank Bennet, he was still more than fourteen million dollars richer in cash and he still owned 174,000 shares of Henderson Steel. The problem was that it would take some time for a true value of the stock to emerge, since there was no market in it. Mark instructed Jimmie to start selling off small chunks of the stock until there was enough in circulation to establish a floor price.

But as he had indicated earlier, all this, while gratifying, was secondary to the pleasure he took from his new position in his own company. He now owned, outright, thirty-four percent of the preferred stock and he voted his children's sixteen percent. Taken together he finally controlled fifty percent of the stock.

He would be thirty-seven in November. He was now worth, with his new stock and cash, approximately thirty-five million dollars. He owned and controlled fifty percent of what was emerging to be one of the country's industrial giants. He had defeated one of Wall Street's slickest operators at his own game. His name, like Henry Ford's and Harvey Firestone's, was becoming known throughout the world.

Mark Manning, indeed, had much to celebrate.

It was a drizzly night, unusually chilly for June, and as Mark left Maxine Talbot's house at quarter past two the next morning, he turned up his raincoat collar and wished he'd brought an umbrella. He splashed his way across Grove Court to the little iron gate that led out to Grove Street, the spray from his feet shattering his reflection in the puddles of surrounding night lights into a myriad glistening shards. Grove Street was empty, and a foghorn from the not-too-distant Hudson River reinforced the feeling of desolation. The Village was asleep.

He walked to the east to find a cab to take him uptown. He hadn't gone more than ten feet from the iron gate when he passed a recessed doorway and saw from the corner of his eye—or perhaps sensed, it happened so fast—someone standing in the dark entranceway. He instinctively raised his right arm as he glimpsed the man diving at him, a six-inch knife in his hand. Mark's arm deflected the knife, which was aimed at his neck but grazed his shoulder instead. An instant later, Mark had turned to the right and was grappling with his assailant, trying to prevent the man from slashing at him again with the knife. It was too dark to see much of his face—he was wearing a cloth cap and a black turtleneck sweater—but Mark was fairly certain he was young. The streetlight at the distant corner did flash off the knifeblade, so that Mark could see it poised above his face, about to thrust into his eye if Mark's hands on the man's wrists should lose or relax their grip. They were both strong, and for a while they Indian-wrestled with the knife arm, almost motionless as their two sets of muscles strained for mastery. Then suddenly Mark's left hand let go of the man's left wrist and chopped down on his right. The man grunted and dropped the knife on the sidewalk. Mark pushed him up against a brick wall; the man plowed a fist into Mark's stomach, causing him to double over with pain. The stranger ran for the knife. Mark was after him. As the man stooped to pick up the knife, Mark grabbed his collar, jerked him around and smashed his fist into his nose. The other stumbled backward and fell over a fire hydrant, doing a somersault and landing on his back in the water-filled gutter. Mark scooped up the knife while his assailant scrambled to his feet and started running for the corner. Mark began to chase him but stopped as the pain in his stomach became worse. He leaned against the brick wall and put his hand under his jacket. His shirt was wet with blood, and it occurred to him the man had hit the same area Bill Sands's bullet had entered. He made his way back to Maxine's house. She let him in, put a cold wet towel over the bleeding area and called a doctor as Mark told her what had happened and showed her the knife. She looked at the weapon, and at two initials crudely scratched in the handle, F. R.

"I wonder," she said, "if those might just happen to stand for Franco Ruggiero."

"Who's he?"

"A kid I've known for years. His sister used to be my best friend. Franco's the one I told you about who pimps for Riley Baker. Did you get a look at his face?"

"Not much of one. He was young, though—I'd say about twenty."

"That's got to be Franco. Do you think Baker hired him to kill you?"

"It wouldn't surprise me. It's about all he had left to fight with."

"He's still alive?" Riley Baker said an hour later as he let Franco into the front door of the East Thirty-first Street house. "What happened?"

"He saw me before I got a chance to finish him. He was a lot stronger than I thought. We fought, I fell over a damn fire hydrant—"

"A fire hydrant? You stupid dago, can't you do anything right?"

Franco said nothing, but his dark eyes reflected the insult. He followed Riley into his office, where the older man closed the curtains in front of the windows facing the street. He took a small oil painting off its hook on the wall above the desk. Behind the painting was a small wall safe. Franco watched as Riley twirled the dial. The safe door clicked and swung open; Riley reached in, removed a manila envelope. He took out two twenty-dollar bills, which he tossed on the desk.

Franco looked at the money. "The price was a thousand."

"That was for a completed job. You're damn lucky I pay you a red cent, and the only reason I'm giving you this much is for what we'll call termination pay. I'm selling this house and my collection upstairs because I need the money, thanks to Mr. Manning. I won't need your services anymore, and I'm reporting to Big Johnnie that you are one lousy wop killer."

As he turned to put the envelope back in the safe, Franco moved quietly around the desk behind him. Taking the telephone cord in both hands, he looped it over Riley's head and around his throat, then twisted it with all his strength. As Riley struggled to free himself from the cord, Franco whispered in his ear, "I'd beat you up first, you sick son of a bitch, except I think you'd like it too much."

Franco gave one last twisting jerk on the phone cord to make sure, then released the body, which crumpled to the floor.

He picked up the phone, which had been knocked over in the struggle. The distant voice of the operator was saying, "Is anything the matter, sir?"

Franco answered, "Everything's fine. Thank you."

He hung up the phone and picked up the manila envelope, taking out a sheaf of bank notes—the full thousand dollars Riley would have paid him if he'd been successful in his attempt on Mark's life. Franco pocketed the money, replaced the envelope in the wall safe, closed the door and twirled the dial. Then, remembering he'd recently heard about police beginning to use fingerprints to identify people, he pulled out a handkerchief and quickly wiped the safe and the dial. He rehung the oil painting over the safe, wiped the frame and the phone, and satisfied he had outwitted modern criminology, stepped over Riley's body and walked out of the library, closing the door behind him, and to the front door.

Thirty-first Street was empty as he slipped out of the house into the rain, and walked downtown to the Union Square subway station.

Riley's body was not discovered for two days, and the murder was never officially solved. Neither Mark nor Maxine had told the police of Franco's attack on Grove Street, Mark not wishing the publicity (after all, what was he *doing* on Grove Street with the famous Miss Talbot, the police would be certain to ask, and his associates—and all Elkins—would be certain to know). But the discovery of Riley's body put them in a rather awkward position. It was possible the police might think to question the man who so recently and so spectacularly had taken away half of Riley's fortune, in which case Mark, to establish his alibi, would have been obliged to tell about the attack in Grove Street and why he hadn't reported the incident at the time. Fortunately, Riley's already unsavory and reputedly violent history and associates and the very late hour all pointed more immediately and conveniently to foul play against a disreputable character by person or persons unknown.

Mark decided it was a good time to go home to Elkins to begin mending fences with his wife. Though he hated to leave Maxine, the second night after the discovery of the body he kissed her good-bye, checked out of the Plaza and took the train back to Cleveland. He had, however, every intention of returning as soon as was possible, because by now he had to admit to himself he was not only in love with Maxine Talbot, he was becoming dependent on her for his happiness as well. He wasn't sure what he would tell Charlotte, but he thought he would tell her nothing. At least for the time being. . . .

Sylvia Wingdale Baker inherited her husband's still-extensive estate and to her surprised delight became a very young and very rich widow. She moved to Los Angeles, where she tried to buy her way into the movies, marrying a young stuntman in the process. She made three feature films, none of which was successful, although she did have great fun doing them and enjoyed the company of several attentive directors and producers. (On March 12, 1924, while driving home from a party in her Duesenberg, her short but not so unhappy life ended in a head-on collision with an ice truck on one of the descending curves of Sunset Boulevard.)

CHAPTER SIX

Letter from Charlotte Manning to Amelia Clark in London, dated July 23, 1915.

Dear Amelia:

I apologize for being a dilatory correspondent, but frankly for the last month I've been in a wretched mood—I suppose I've been going through a time of adjustment. I told you about my troubles with Mark over Carter Lang and my going to New York to try to persuade Mark to save or at least protect Carter from Lily. Well, it didn't work. I'm afraid I didn't handle it very adroitly and there was an awful scene between us at the Plaza. I told him what had happened and let him know what I thought of his adventure with Sylvia Baker—or what I believed was his adventure with her. After all, a good friend did tell me, somebody with no possible ulterior motive, and it made sense that Mark might have done it because of his trouble with Riley Baker and Sylvia's usefulness . . . well, whether he had or hadn't been doing anything with her up till then—he strongly denied it—the upshot was he stormed out of the room and proceeded to go down the hall to Sylvia's room, telling me that he intended to live up to my accusations of adultery.

Well, having failed in my mission and apparently messed up things to a fare-thee-well, I returned to Elkins feeling terribly low, as you can imagine. In the time before Mark came home I tried to figure out what was the best way to proceed with him—what sort of relationship we were going to have in the future. When Mark did come home, two weeks later, he was acting a bit sheepish. I said nothing about what had happened for a while, hoping he might bring it up. Since he didn't, on his second night home I decided to bring it out in the open and we had a long talk.

I'm glad to say we both managed to control our tempers. I asked him if he still felt any love for me. He said he did—I tend to believe him—and *then* he admitted there was someone else in his life. He said he thought I was right about at least one thing, that we should stop deceiving and accusing each other and tell the truth, that it was probably less hurtful than all the suspicions that came out of rumor and gossip, such as my believing that he'd been having an affair with Sylvia (by the way, wasn't that awful what happened to Riley Baker? I guess his violent past finally caught up with him).

Anyway, I still assumed he meant Sylvia but to my surprise it turned out to be Maxine Talbot, the Follies star. At least I have glamorous competition! He said that he was in love with Maxine but that he didn't want to break up our marriage. For the children's sake and for our sake as well. I told him that for my part, I still felt as I'd said in New York. I felt dissatisfied with my life and I didn't like the idea of sharing my husband with another woman. But since I didn't have any real alternative to my present life and since, of course, it's so vitally important to the children that they have a home and an *intact* family during these important formative years of their lives, well, I had no intention of leaving him.

And then I surprised myself. I told him I realized that marriage wasn't a form of mutual slavery (after all, I had to be consistent with what I'd said in New York, even if I didn't want to) and I didn't want him to feel caught and miserable either, and that if he wanted to have his fling with Miss Talbot, well, I would try to look the other way as long as he at least kept it discreet. He seemed surprised and pleased by this, as well he might, since he's getting his cake and eating it too. But what's the alternative? Continual scenes? Dishonesty? Divorce? The alternatives are worse so we've made what I believe is called an arrangement. It's civilized, very continental and I suppose very sophisticated. It has everything except that elusive ingredient called true love. Maybe it's gone out of fashion. We hold up the family and marital fidelity, but then we violate them and pretend their sanctity. Well, at least Mark and I can't be accused of that hypocrisy . . .

Speaking of hypocrisy, yesterday we went to Carter's wedding and the hypocrisy was so thick *there* you could cut it with a knife. Sweet Lily has been playing the blushing bride for weeks now, picking her trousseau, going through endless showers and what not, and yesterday at the church she looked so lovely and virginal in her white-satin gown and enormous veil. What a charade! And how unhappy poor Carter looked, though he tried to put up a brave front. I'm sorry to sound so ungenerous, but she is a little weasel. How I dislike her! And what a smug look she gave me in the church, as if to say, "Look who won the prize!" I'm afraid I've nothing good to say about her except that she *is* a superlative actress. Otherwise, I fear the new Mrs. Lang is a heartless you-know-what of the first rank. They've gone to Bermuda for their honeymoon . . .

Oh, Amelia, why can't I just shrug off all these things? Heaven knows I'm not exactly an innocent and have seen more than my fair share of hypocrisy in life—why can't I accept it? After all, that's how so much of society seems to be. Well, I can't. It still *hurts*. Somewhere, somehow, Mark and I lost our own deep love, and even though our arrangement may be the *wise* solution, I'm not sure for me that it's going to be tolerable in the long run.

Sorry to sound so unrelievedly gloomy, but I warned you I was feeling wretched.

Fondly,
Charlotte

INTERLUDE

1917–1918

War. And soon in Russia, Germany and Austro-Hungary—revolution. On April 2, 1917, President Wilson called for a declaration of war against Germany. America was in it—a mud-slogged stalemate that had taken millions of lives, savaged the continent of Europe and was destroying Europe's primacy in the world. The country had been divided on the wisdom of getting into the war, but once in there was a burst of enthusiasm and patriotism that was exciting and praiseworthy except for its darker side, which was the "America for Americans" mania that gripped the nation, forcing hyphenated-Americans, or immigrants, to squeeze into a psychological mold to conform to the native-born image. Alien and sedition laws were passed by Congress, which imposed stiff penalties for criticizing the government or the flag; these laws were responsible for imprisoning, among others, the socialist Eugene Debs, Big Bill Haywood of the Industrial Workers of the World, as well as five hundred other Wobblies. But the country wasn't interested in the plight of Wobblies or socialists; the country was on a holy crusade to make the world safe for democracy —for many, another way of saying to make the world just like America.

Millions registered for the draft. The country Hooverized as food administrator Herbert Hoover launched a program of voluntary food rationing. People collected peach pits for gas-mask filters and donated old books for the boys' amusement and, perhaps, uplift as well (though the boys probably would have preferred something more relaxing, such as Riley Baker's collection of erotica). Women took men's jobs so that the men could fight the Huns, and the sight of women mechanics working on automobile engines became commonplace. Liberty Bond drives raised millions, and show business and society celebrities pitched in at rallies to lure dollars out of wallets —$17,000,000,000 in all. The Yanks were going to lick the Kaiser to the tune of "Over There"; and the country, despite its jingoistic fervor—or perhaps because of it—generally performed admirably. Mark Manning, who was as swept up in the patriotic hysteria as everyone else, performed well, too. Whatever reservations he might have had about the capitalist system years before in Peru had long since vanished. The problems there were abuses of the system—not the system itself. The free-enterprise society worked gloriously well; after all, where else but in America could the son of a poor farmer, like himself, have risen to such improbable heights of wealth and power?

At the outbreak of war, Mark tried to enlist, only to be told by officials in Washington that he was needed in Elkins to run the company. Manning Rubber was now making as much for the Government as it was for the public. Dirigibles and tires—tires by the hundreds of thousands for trucks and airplanes—gas masks, gaskets and the rubber products were only part of what the company was producing. The vastly enlarged steel works were manufacturing steel items for the Government as well, in particular steel helmets. The work was grueling, and night shifts were put in at the factories for the first time as hundreds of new workers poured into Elkins, creating an acute housing shortage that was partially relieved by the erection of temporary housing near Plant One—housing that became known as Manningville (a giant step down from the pleasant Manning Acres, but necessary). Elkins's workers enjoyed bulging pay envelopes, and on Saturday nights bar brawls became so frequent the police ignored them. Saturday was the time to forget the work and the war, but for Manning executives even Saturdays were often work days, and many a Saturday night found the lights in the executive suite still burning past midnight.

Mark was driving them with a whip hand, amazing everyone with his energy, his knowledge of everything going on and his grasp of detail. And Charlotte was almost as busy as her husband. She took over the local Red Cross chapter, and four times a week her elegant mansion at River Bend was filled with dozens of women rolling bandages, knitting sweaters and making up packages for the boys "over there" (though it had been remarked by a returning veteran that no one had actually ever *seen* a boy over there wearing a sweater). Charlotte was also on the Greater Cleveland Liberty Bond Drive Committee and spent at least one day a week in Cleveland working for that organization. Mark was generous in his praise for her efforts, and helped her bond drive in princely fashion by purchasing $1,000,-000 worth of Liberty Bonds. Charlotte, not to be outdone, bought $100,000 worth of bonds for each of the four children—for Charlotte was wealthy in her own right now, having inherited Sam's Rosen Stove stock, which was worth an estimated $4,000,000. The town, the state and the country cheered this patriotic couple, and the large family at River Bend was looked on by the general public as a glowing tribute to the blessings of marital fidelity and family life.

What the general public didn't know was that it was nearly a year now since Charlotte had moved into her own suite of rooms on the second floor of River Bend and that she had had no physical relations with her husband since that time. The marriage had become a façade, much like her first marriage. And Mark was spending more and more of his time—as much as he could manage—in New York with Maxine Talbot. Charlotte forced herself to go along, though she couldn't—as she'd predicted to Amelia—really bring herself to accept it. The four children, they felt confident, had no idea there was a serious rift between their parents, and Mark and Charlotte were determined to keep it that way.

The public continued to treat Mark as a hero. In a nation-wide poll conducted in 1917 by the *Saturday Evening Post,* seeking the "Ten Most-Respected Business Leaders in America," Mark ranked eighth—his gesture to the French on the gas-mask contract, his purchase of the $1,000,000 worth of Liberty Bonds and the revived memory of his trip to the Putumayo all being cited in the article. Moreover, he photographed well and was still youthfully handsome, so that to many Americans he almost embodied the dream of rags-to-riches success. And if the rags part was not exactly accurate, no one could deny the accuracy of the riches. In another article, in the *Wall Street Journal* in 1917, Mark Manning was listed as one of the hundred richest men in America, the enormous war profits of his company having ballooned his fortune past the $60,000,000 mark in a mere two years. In October 1917 the entire financial structure of the corporation was reorganized, and both the preferred and common stock were split three to one. The result was that Mark ended up with 600,000 shares of preferred, which, at the new price of fifty dollars a share, totaled $30,000,000 and almost 800,000 shares of the common, which at the new price of twenty dollars a share, totaled $16,000,000. Even after splitting the stock, the new dividends were averaging $3.00 a year per share, so that his income from his dividends alone amounted to more than $4,000,000. Almost all of this he was investing, living off his other source of income, mainly his Henderson Steel stock and his $250,000 salary as president of the company.

So Mark was a very rich man, and as with very rich men, the sheer force of his capital was making him richer every day. Nor, like most very rich men, did his desire to increase his fortune abate with the agglomeration of wealth. He was investing in real estate, oil, blue-chip stocks—the conventionally safe investments. But he was also taking fliers, some of which failed, but one of which was to succeed spectacularly. One day at lunch, Melville Benny, the head of the research division of the company, who had by now become one of its ranking vice-presidents, casually mentioned to Mark that he had a friend who wanted to manufacture radios and was looking for capital. Mark was interested. He met the man, a ham operator in Columbus named Calhoun Robinson, and he invested $10,000 in the company, which was called the Acme Radio Corporation. Acme went nowhere for a few years, but Mark had faith in Robinson and his idea. He ended up putting $30,000 more into Acme, money his accountant, Gus Nelson, told him was going down "the proverbial drain." (It wasn't until the early Twenties, when the radio craze would sweep the country, that Mark would have the last laugh with the enormous success of Acme. He had, it seemed, the Midas touch.)

Letter from Charlotte Manning to Amelia Clark in London, dated November 6, 1917.

Dear Amelia:

Mark so appreciated your and Bruce's birthday present, and he's sending you a note separately, thanking you both. We had a big family party for him yesterday, and though I don't think he was all that happy about turning thirty-nine, he seemed to have a good time, although there was an unfortunate incident, about which more later.

You asked me in your last letter how Mark has taken his enormous success. Believe me, it was an interesting question to me too, since I have to live with it. I'm beginning to think great material success carries its own kind of defeat. Somehow the more a man becomes a worldly success, the less of a human being he seems to become, or at least have time to be. I'm afraid this is happening to Mark. Oh, it's all very subtle and I think if you met him now you'd hardly notice a change since you saw him last . . . what was it, four years ago? He still can be enormously charming. But I notice the difference. He's become harder, almost arrogant, much less tolerant of the rest of us not so exceptional human beings. Not, of course, that Mark was ever particularly soft. As long as I've known him he's been strong and resourceful and clever, which are qualities I admire. But strong can become heartless, resourceful can become self-centered and clever can become shrewd

—and I see all these surfacing in him too. Remember, years ago at the Waldorf, when I told you his ambition frightened me? And you said the only men worth bothering with were the ambitious ones? Well, perhaps you were right, I don't know. But I think Mark's ambition is running away with him. I almost feel sorry for him.

And of course this double life of his . . . here in Elkins he poses as the *pater familias*, the pillar of the community and the upholder of all virtues. And then he's off to New York into the arms of darling Maxine, giving the lie to all those virtues. At least when he was a young man here in Elkins running his little bicycle shop and going to bed with all the available girls in town, he didn't *pretend*, or if he did, he at least didn't pretend to himself. Of course, I *told* him to be discreet and he *was* honest with me, but I simply can't get used to this and I'm afraid my complaints are getting less and less ladylike all the time.

It's his relationship with the children, though, that shows the change most vividly to me. I shouldn't say the children . . . Ellen, Richard and Christopher he's always adored and he still does—particularly Christopher, who's four now and turning into an irresistible hellion. But David, our oldest! Poor David lately seems to bring out the least lovable side in his father. It's going from bad to worse and driving me to distraction.

David's almost nine, and he has developed into an extremely shy, introspective and sensitive boy. You'll pardon a mother's bias when I say that he is a brilliant child, but he is. As you know, wisely or un- wisely, Mark decided to hire a tutor to teach the children here at River Bend after the Wobbly incident four years ago. He was so afraid of their being kidnaped. Well, we've had two young men since then, both of them excellent, and John Chandler, the current tutor, bears out what his predecessor said, namely, that David is extraordi- narily bright and is almost two years ahead of his age group. I'm sure this is going to present problems next year when we plan to enter him in a boarding school in Cleveland, but it *is* still gratifying to hear, needless to say.

Now David, as you might imagine, is rather bookish. He reads omni- vorously (he's just finished *Candide* and is going deeper into other Voltaire—and he's only eight!). He's not good at sports, he doesn't even particularly like them. Mark was a natural athlete, and I gather some- thing of a star pitcher during his college days. He's also a slambang tennis player (who *always* wins, damn him!) and last summer he started to teach David. Well, the poor boy was a total dud; but Mark, instead of realizing he was a hopeless case, took it as a personal challenge, of all things, and proceeded to drag David out to the court every morn- ing before breakfast for an hour's drill. David hated it. And instead of practicing in the afternoon, as his father told him to do, David would stay indoors and read so that of course he didn't improve, which got Mark even angrier. And then when Mark found out David had lied to him, well, to put it bluntly, Mark was simply vicious to him. He gave him a real thrashing—that I didn't mind so much because David *shouldn't* have lied. But much worse, Mark turned cold to him, very cold, and he accused me of turning him into a momma's boy, which of course got *me* started. The result is that there's been a total estrangement between Mark and David, and that makes me sick. I know Mark would never have been so unfeeling before—at least he has always been fond of the children—but it's part of his being so full of himself lately that he expects his children to live up to his own grand view of himself. The fact that he thinks his oldest son is, as he claims, a sissy—which I honestly don't believe is true—has infuriated him and, of course, it's David that's taken the brunt of it.

Well, the boy's defense has been to become almost a mute around his father for fear of saying something wrong, while at the same time he almost pitifully hopes for some crumb of recognition or affection from Mark, which he doesn't get. And yesterday, the worst happened. I had told the children either to save up their allowance to buy their father a birthday present or to make something themselves, which they all agreed to do. And I knew that David was working very hard on his present, which he was keeping a secret even from me. I knew he had high hopes that it would please Mark, or at least break this awful deadlock between them.

The children usually eat with Mrs. Brent and John Chandler, but for the big occasion we had them all in the dining room for dinner with us, and after Mark blew out the candles on his cake the children all brought up their presents, starting with Christopher. Christopher had found three old tennis balls near the court that he'd wrapped up. Mark absolutely roared with laughter and was delighted. Richard gave him a bushel basket of peach pits he had collected to be used at the factory for the gas-mask filters. Mark was very impressed. Ellen had saved her money to buy him a necktie, and Mark acted thrilled. Then it came David's turn, and we all held our breath.

He was sitting next to me at my end of the table, and I could tell he was nervous. He's a very slender boy, getting to be tall, with my hair and—my bias again!—I think he's going to be very handsome in a sensitive way. Well, he stood up and said, "Father, I've written a poem for you." Dead silence. Mark, at the other end of the table, looked nonplussed. "A *poem*?" he said, almost as if David were joking. David knew immediately he had done the wrong thing again. I took his hand and smiled and said what a wonderful idea and we were all eager to hear it—though my heart was in my shoes. Well, to David's credit, and though he realized he had again struck out with the great man, he was determined to go through with it. He took a piece of paper from his pocket and unfolded it—his hands were shaking so badly I was afraid he'd rip the paper. Then he began reciting, in a thin, quivering voice that broke my heart. It went something like this:

> "Happy Birthday, dear Father,
> From your son who loves you very much.
> From your son who hopes, someday,
> That he may get out of Dutch.
>
> From your son who's not much of a menace
> At football or at tennis,
> But who might turn out to be a whizz
> If people loved him for what he is."

Dead silence. David folded the poem, stuck it in his pocket and sat down. I confess there were tears in my eyes and I leaned over and kissed him and said it was a beautiful poem, or something like that, and tried to signal Mark to say *something*. Which, unfortunately, he did. "David, that's all very interesting, and just what is it you're going to be a whiz at?" At which point, David said, "I don't know, sir." And Mark said, "Writing poems?" To which, to my surprise, David retorted, "Would you be ashamed of me if that's what I was good at, sir?" And Mark—he later apologized but by that time it was too late —answered, "Yes." David, of course, was destroyed, the party was ruined, I was furious at Mark and heartbroken for David and amazed that any father could be so insensitive to his son.

You ask, Amelia, what I think success has done to Mark? I think, if you'll forgive my language, that it has turned him into a heartless bastard.

All my love,
Charlotte

It all depended on the point of view. To Maxine Talbot, who had been raised in the tenement poverty of New York's Little Italy, Mark's strength was admirable and his success dazzlingly exciting, and when he told her that he was fighting a losing battle with Charlotte to save his oldest son from being overprotected and smothered to death with mother love, Maxine sided with him, although she suggested that ultimately the only way to "save" David was to get him out of River Bend, with which Mark agreed. Instead of sending David to school in Cleveland, where he would still be close to Charlotte and inevitably tied to her apronstrings, Mark decided that he would send him as far from Elkins as possible. He began to make inquiries about schools in California.

Nor did Maxine think Mark was heartless. On the contrary, his heart was almost embarrassingly visible whenever he was around her. He was an ardent and a generous lover—during the two years they had been together he'd given her an emerald-and-diamond bracelet, a Russian sable coat, a mink coat and a completely new kitchen for her house. Moreover he was great fun to be with and wasn't at all like her idea of sugar-daddy business tycoons, which ran to the cliché of ruthless old fogies. Mark struck her as a kind man, and he certainly wasn't an old fogy. He got a great kick out of life and shared many of her enthusiasms, which included walking around Manhattan, wandering through offbeat shops, days in the country or at Coney Island and all-day movie orgies. She was observant enough to realize that his success had given him a certain air of properness, but that was only on the surface and he was too human by her lights to be fossilized into some Establishment mold. To his wife, this was seen as hypocrisy. To his mistress, it seemed refreshingly unstuffy. The truth was that Mark was a little of both proper bourgeois and fun-loving roué. It was, however, the former trait that was to cause the one real conflict between himself and Maxine.

It was a simple enough matter. He wanted her all to himself, and —as she'd warned him from the start—she refused to give up her "friends." These were a grab bag of show-business colleagues, artists, carousers and businessmen—the last requiring a great deal of money to win her friendhip because Maxine had a bohemian dislike of businessmen in general. Of all her lovers, Mark was her favorite, even though, paradoxically, he was a businessman. Often, though, he had to wait in line. He might arrive in New York and call her to find that she was busy until the next day. He didn't like it, but he put up with it. As time passed, however, he became increasingly annoyed at having to share her with others, became more determined to possess her outright—to "own" her, as she irritably remarked one night when he had bitterly complained about her having spent the previous day with a "good friend"—Maxine never lied. "I told you in the beginning that I don't like entanglements," she snapped, "and you're trying to entangle me, for Christ sake! You've already got one marriage. Do you want *two?*"

"No! But—"

"But you want to tie me down as if I were your wife, Mark, and it's *not* going to work with me. What, for example, am I supposed to do when you're not in New York?"

He had, of course, no compelling answer.

Then one day in April of 1918 he had an inspiration. He took her to Gino's for lunch and, after ordering, said to her, "All right, I've got a deal to propose to you."

"What sort of deal?"

"You're always saying you want to run a restaurant just like this one. Okay. Gino has arthritis and he's moving to Florida. Suppose I bought you this place?"

"Oh, *Mark* . . ."

"You could run it. It would give you something to do and keep you out of trouble." He emphasized the last words. "What do you think?"

She looked around the main dining room with eyes that were already becoming proprietary.

"Oh, temptation, temptation! God, wouldn't it be fun? And you know what I'd do? I'd turn it into a supper club and put on little revues . . . we could build a small stage over against that wall and I could sing . . ."

"Then you want to do it?"

She turned back to him. "Are you kidding? I'd love to!"

"Then you'd better hear the rest of the deal. You give up everyone else. I become number one and *only*."

She sighed. "You are persistent, aren't you?"

"Well?"

She took a deep breath. "All right, it's a *deal*. You win, damn you. Here I go, and I know I'm going to regret it, but you win."

He smiled and took her hand.

"Is it all that hard to do?"

"No, of course not, Mark. I guess"—she laughed—"I'm getting soft. Maybe you've beaten me down into respectability. Wouldn't that be awful?"

He laughed. "Well, I don't think we're *too* respectable yet. Shall we go talk to Gino?"

The Golden Slipper Club opened on October 3, 1918, seven months after Mark and Maxine's "deal," and just over a month before the Armistice.

One early June morning in 1918 a telegram was delivered to the pleasant home of Lily Swenson Lang in Elkins, Ohio. The telegram informed her that her husband, Captain Carter Lang, had been killed in the battle of Château-Thierry in France. Lily cried her heart out, and this time the tears were genuine. She had loved Carter, even though she knew he had never loved her—had never, in fact, forgiven her for meaning to pressure him into marrying her. Which, perhaps, she decided, was why he had joined the army immediately after war had been declared. No wonder he had seemed almost glad to be leaving her and Elkins. And now he was dead, and she was a widow at twenty-four. Carter. Beautiful Carter. Dead. She wandered through the rooms of the charming house they had built two years before, the house they had really never lived in. Empty. No children. And now no husband. Empty.

She went into the kitchen, opened a bottle of bourbon, poured herself a drink and downed it fast and neat. Next she picked up the phone and called River Bend. She was still crying—and getting tight—when the Manning butler answered the phone. She asked for Charlotte.

"He's dead. Carter's *dead*. Are you satisfied now? I can't have him any more. Are you glad he's dead?" Silence. "*Answer* me!"

All Lily heard was the click on the other end of the line as Charlotte hung up.

PART

VI

THE TWENTIES ROAR

1921–1922

CHAPTER ONE

IT HAD been a great success from the moment it opened its doors. The food was excellent, the revues—Maxine called them "Village Frolics"—were satiric and funny. The upstairs rooms with their privacy and the gaming rooms, where stud poker, "African golf" (dice) and backgammon games were generally under way, all caught on with the uptown crowd, which fought to buy memberships in the Golden Slipper, proudly sporting their little golden-slipper membership watchfob charms. That the establishment was owned by the great Follies star Maxine Talbot added, of course, to the cachet. Maxine was on the premises every night after her show, and often she would get up on the tiny stage herself and sing a number, to the delight of the crowd, and bringing down the house with her famous torchy rendition of "Kiss Me Again." The air was thick with smoke, booze flowed, and the white-tie crowd with its chic women—few of them wives—squeezed around the tiny tables. Outside, only the flashing electric sign shaped like a slipper advertised the place, but word-of-mouth brought in the crowds.

Then on midnight of January 16, 1920, the Volstead Act brought Prohibition, and Maxine closed the Golden Slipper for a month to take stock. The initial reaction to the "noble experiment" was acceptance by the majority of the public, amusement at the novelty of it by the minority, and chagrin by the hard drinkers, who had been stocking up for months but still wondered where, eventually, their next drink would come from. The novelty quickly wore off, however, and as the private stocks began to dry up the public took to looking for ways to get around what was rapidly becoming regarded as a nuisance. Speakeasies began opening all over the country, and the mobs, somewhat reluctant at first to become involved in the alcohol traffic, overcame their reluctance as the prospects of fantastic profits emerged.

By mid-1920, the Golden Slipper had reopened, albeit without the flashing electric sign outside—now no sign at all differentiated the apparently drab house from the others on the street, or the Italian bakery shop next door or the dingy pharmacy on the corner. But the crowds still came, holding up their golden-slipper charms at the peephole for the bouncer's inspection, then being admitted into the inner sanctum where White Rock set-ups cost $1.50, ten Camel cigarettes in a fancy package cost $1, and where, if you hadn't brought your own bottle, as was recommended, a bottle of bad Scotch could be bought for $15. Even sidecars, pink ladies, and Alexanders for the ladies, or gin and Frenches, Ramos fizzes or a Tom and Jerry— one could buy the fancier cocktails, and their quality was passable, the cocktail mixes tending to disguise the unreliable gin or rum. But no one cared if the booze was iffy. No one minded the two raids that closed the club twice for twenty-four hours. The Golden Slipper opened again, the crowds kept coming and the hilarity seemed, if anything, to be heightened by the sense of illegality and derring-do imposed by the strictures of the Volstead Act. If Park Avenue was squeezed at table next to a racketeer and his broad, why, that too was fun, and novel. Prohibition might not be proving to be a noble experiment in temperance, but surely it was proving to be an interesting experiment in democracy. The classes were mixing like gin and vermouth in the common search for drink; and if the mixtures might result in an occasional fight or hangover, it also produced a most exhilarating intoxication.

The success of the Golden Slipper especially delighted Mark because it made Maxine so happy. Also more accessible, because she had lived up to her part of the deal. As far as he could tell, the club had replaced the other men in her life. When he was in New York he spent nearly every night at the place, sitting at his small table next to the stage, watching the show and drinking his private stock of champagne (he had ordered fifty cases of Pol Roger before the Volstead Act went into effect, and fifty cases of assorted wines, part of which he kept in his cellar at River Bend, the rest in the cellar of the Golden Slipper), roaring with laughter at the jibes of Billie Ogden, Maxine's young house comic, and glowing with pleasure when Maxine would get up to sing. The only problem was that he wasn't in New York as much as he'd like. The pressure of business, far from diminishing with the Armistice, had increased after the war and he was forced to spend more and more time in Elkins.

At first the pressure was boom time. As the euphoria of victory dissipated, America went on a buying spree, and the factories that had been turning out war materiel retooled for peacetime products. Cars, trucks and tractors came off the assembly lines in huge quantities. And each one of them required tires. Mark placed huge orders with the London rubber brokers, but he was also buying cotton because of a new element that had been introduced into tires—cotton cording for toughening. To secure cotton at the lowest price, he purchased in 1920 a 50,000-acre cotton plantation in Texas. That year also saw the beginning of construction of an immense Canadian plant outside Montreal to supply the burgeoning Canadian market. All this, of course, required new capital, and Mark found himself returning to Wall Street for new funding—which now, with the gigantic resources of his company, was a much simpler job than it had been fifteen years previously. He was also a frequent visitor to Washington, where he was one of the principal backers of the new highway lobby, in 1920 considered a vital force for good as it pushed Congress to replace the rutted country roads of the past with paved highways.

The boom, however, was short-lived. Prices began to soar after the Armistice, and people began to complain bitterly about "the high cost of living." Inflation spiraled; and in the middle of 1920 the public struck back by drastically reducing its buying. Mark's company owed millions to the rubber brokers, and now suddenly the bottom had dropped out of the tire market. The country had collapsed into a genuine depression in 1921. Thousands of workers were being laid off. The unemployed obviously could not buy cars, and inventories of unsold and apparently unsalable tires ominously mounted. Mark was nervous but he refused to panic. He cut the dividend from $4.50 in 1920 to $1 in 1921, a cut that came principally out of his own pocket, inasmuch as he was the majority shareholder. He instituted draconian efficiency measures in the plants. Most spectacularly, he slashed the price of all his products by twenty percent and launched a $3,000,000 national advertising campaign to inform the public of the bargain. His executives were fearful; the price cut would be ruinous. But as the price of raw rubber plummeted, thanks to the depression and despite the screams of the planters, impressive savings accrued to manufacturers such as Manning. Finally the depression eased and the public once again started buying. And lured by Mark's ads and the twenty-percent price cut, they bought Manning tires over all others. By the end of 1921, the company was clearly out of the woods.

On October 1 an exhausted but jubilant Mark climbed into his new, light-blue Rolls Royce with Charlotte to be driven to Cleveland, there to catch the train to New York for a well-deserved vacation. Charlotte was taking a vacation too, although not one she was sharing with her husband. He was going, as she well knew, to the Golden

Slipper and Maxine. Charlotte had booked the Gainsborough Suite on the *Aquitania* to sail to England, and thereafter she would stay for a month in France. She had not mentioned it to Mark, but one reason she was going to France was to visit a grave.

The night of October 3 was a big one at the Golden Slipper. It was not only the third anniversary of the club's opening, it was also the première of a new revue. To celebrate the double event, Maxine decided to throw a private party. Not only were many of the club members who were personal friends of Maxine's invited, but non-members as well, including such Broadway luminaries as Mr. Ziegfeld and Billie Burke, John Shubert, Marion Davies with the jealously watchful Mr. Hearst, Clifton Webb, Mae Murray, who was going to Hollywood, George Gershwin and John Barrymore. There was Frank Crowninshield, the editor of *Vanity Fair*, and a retinue of young writers and reporters thrilled to be invited to such a glamorous event and even more thrilled to have access to so much free hooch. There was Larry Fay, the man in and out of so many enterprises, some legitimate, some not; Edythe Baker and Billy Reardon, the dance sensation at the Lido; Otto Baumgarten of the Crillon on Forty-eighth Street; Don Dickerman, owner of such Village hot spots as the Blue Horse and the Pirate's Den; and Barney Gallant, owner of the famous Greenwich Village Inn, who was about to open the Club Gallant at 40 Washington Square South. Society was there in force, Maxine spotting a genuine Vanderbilt, and the arts were represented by such diverse figures as Maxfield Parrish, George Plank, Maxwell Bodenheim and Joseph Urban, the set designer. Maxine had hired Ted Lewis and his band to play before and after the show, and the show itself, which featured the Harlem sensation Babie Cindy Williams, was a roaring success.

Babie Cindy, a tiny girl barely five feet tall, tapped out on stage with big pink bows on her shoes and in her hair, and sang in baby talk a risqué song entitled "Ripe Bananas." The finale of the show represented Maxine's most ambitious effort as an impresario, and reflected the influence of her connection with the Follies. She hired twelve models to form a tableau representing the twelve signs of the Zodiac; when the lights came up, the audience gasped to see the twelve gorgeous girls, standing on rising wooden boxes, each wearing an enormous Ziegfeldian hat representing one of the Zodiacal signs

—and nothing else. "Hotcha!" yelled one of the less restrained young writers, and the crowd whooped and howled in agreement. Then blackout and the show was over. Ted Lewis struck up a jazz tune, the buffet was served and bubbly flowed.

After the buffet Maxine told Mark that there was someone up-stairs who wanted to meet him. Leading her lover to the second floor, she opened the door to one of the gambling rooms. There, seated by himself at a round poker table, was a man in his late forties dressed in a well-cut tuxedo with a neat wing collar. He had a sharp-featured —if jowly—face with a prominent nose, very white skin and thick black eyebrows, beneath which were eyes as alive as his expression was bland. A bottle of Johnny Walker was in front of him on the table, as well as an ice bucket, a soda siphon and three glasses, one of which was half filled with scotch. He was smoking a cigar and he had a curious diamond ring on the little finger of his left hand—a circular cluster of small diamonds that seemed deceptively dainty for such a heavy-set man. He also wore diamond cufflinks and diamond studs. As Maxine closed the door, the man got up.

"Mark, this is Big Johnnie Marucca," said Maxine casually. "He's my bootlegger, and about everyone else's who's doing business south of Forty-second Street."

The man had extended his hand, but Mark merely looked at him, refusing to shake. Then he turned to Maxine.

"I told you I didn't want to know anything about where you got the hooch," he said irritably.

"Oh come on, darling, don't be such a prude. Big Johnnie's a very important man in his business, just as you are in yours. He wants to meet you. He even thinks he can help you."

Mark turned to the man, who was watching them from the other side of the poker table, taking an occasional puff on his cigar.

"How can you help me?" asked Mark, curiosity getting the better of his scruples about meeting a bona fide racketeer.

"If you'll sit down and have a drink with me," said Big Johnnie pleasantly, "I'll be pleased to tell you."

Mark hesitated, then sat down, as did Big Johnnie, who said to Maxine, "You too, Miss Talbot, if you're not busy."

"I wouldn't miss this for the world," Maxine said, taking the seat next to Mark. "Big business meets the rackets! It's a historic moment."

"Maxine, shut the hell up," Mark said. She laughed.

"A scotch?" asked Big Johnnie, pointing to the bottle. "It's the real thing."

Mark shook his head. "I never drink hard stuff. Just wine."

Big Johnnie smiled slightly as he poured some scotch for Maxine. "It's a good thing for my business there aren't more people like you." He squirted some soda into the scotch, then passed the glass to Maxine as Mark drummed his finger impatiently on the green-felt tabletop. Finally he said in a voice that had only a light Italian accent, "Now, Mr. Manning, the area I think I can be of help to you is the area of your labor relations."

"I don't need help with my labor relations. I don't have any trouble with my men."

Big Johnnie took a slow drag on his cigar, tapped the ash in a dish.

"Maybe not now. But you have had, and I'd lay you eight to five you will in the future. There's a lot of labor unrest in the country, Mr. Manning. Oh, I know that right now when we're coming out of a depression the men are anxious for work. But you can't head off the unions forever. Sooner or later organizers are going to hit your company—"

"I have my own ways to deal with them."

"Yes, I know. Company spies. All the big companies have them. But spies aren't enough, Mr. Manning. They can tell you what the organizers are up to, and which of your men are likely to go over. But that's about all they can do. Now, my organization has been doing pretty well lately—*very* well—and we're looking to branch out into new operations. What we're going to offer to a few of the biggest manufacturers in the country—men who we think might be interested in our services—is a package deal. A security service, you might call it."

"And you think I might be interested?"

"Frankly, yes."

"Why?"

"You have a reputation for being antiunion, also a man interested in practical results. There was that incident at your house eight years ago, when one of your men shot you. We believe you'd be interested."

"I see. Go on."

"We put some of our men in your factories as line workers. No one knows who they are except you—that way you have direct, personal control without interference from any of your directors or executives. Our men give you a confidential monthly report on *everyone*—including your company spies, including your executives, as far as that goes, if you want it."

He paused, waiting for Mark's reaction.

"Go on," Mark said.

"That's the information part of our services. We also offer an action part. If outside elements infiltrate the plant—in other words, union organizers—we take measures against them."

"What sort of measures?"

Big Johnnie tapped his ash. "It depends on what's required. Threats. Rough stuff. If necessary . . ." He spread his hands. "The men will get the message. And it would all be done with no personal risk to you. It's the surest way to keep the unions out. To keep control."

Mark shifted in his seat. "I've seen tactics like yours used on men before," he said.

"Where would that be?"

"In South America. With the rubber workers. I didn't like it."

"Force is never pleasant, Mr. Manning. That's the point of it."

"Obviously. I don't want anything to do with it. My men are well paid and well off. I don't need to hire private thugs to keep them in line. In fact"—he looked at Maxine sitting next to him—"I think it's pretty goddamn presumptuous of both of you to think I'd even consider such an idea."

Maxine looked more than a little upset by this. Big Johnnie didn't. He put out his cigar and stood up.

"Well, perhaps I misjudged you, Mr. Manning. At any rate, now you know about our service. If you change your mind later on"—he pulled a card from his wallet and placed it on the table—"here's where you can reach me." Replacing his wallet in his inside jacket pocket, he again extended his hand to Mark. Mark looked at him. A trace of annoyance was in Big Johnnie's eyes as he retracted his hand. Looking at Maxine, he said, "A very nice party, Miss Talbot." Then he walked out of the room, closing the door behind him.

Maxine was ashen. "For Christ sake, do you know who that man *is*? No one snubs Big Johnnie! President Harding doesn't snub him! And you wouldn't even shake his hand!"

"Why should I shake hands with a crook?"

"Darling, he's *more* than a crook—"

"I've told you I don't want scum in this club—and I sure as hell don't want to *meet* them."

"You just don't keep Big Johnnie away from a place he wants to be—don't you understand that? Don't be stupid! He's not only my bootlegger, I pay him protection."

Mark looked surprised. "Protection? You mean you pay him money—"

"Of course! How do you think I keep from being raided? Everyone pays Big Johnnie. That's the way the system works."

She nervously pulled a cigarette and a long black-lacquered holder from her bag, fitted the cigarette into the holder and lighted it. As she exhaled, Mark said more gently, "You're afraid of him, aren't you?"

"Anyone who isn't has grapes for brains. That's why when he asked to meet you . . ." She shrugged. "I'm sorry, I didn't have any choice."

"Why didn't you tell me about him before?"

"Because you've told me all along you don't want to know anything about people like him. Pure Mark Manning must have nothing to do with racketeers. Oh no, it would besmirch his reputation. Well, now you know. This business is married to the rackets. Big Johnnie protects clubs from the police and from other hoods and from himself. You can't get around it. Now he apparently wants to branch out and protect big business."

Mark thought a moment. "What other hoods?"

"Well, our old friend Franco Ruggiero, for one. Franco used to work for Big Johnnie, now he's trying to muscle in on his territory. If I didn't pay protection to Big Johnnie, I'd have Franco at my door in two minutes. At least Big Johnnie doesn't jump out of doorways and try to stab you—at least, he hasn't tried it *yet*."

"Well, I don't like paying these people any protection. On the other hand, I don't suppose there's any way to avoid it. But the Manning Company is certainly not going to start hiring them."

"Darling, that's *your* business," she said, getting up and giving him a kiss. "Anyway, I have to get downstairs. Coming?"

"In a minute."

She left him alone in the room. He sat for a moment, looking thoughtfully at Big Johnnie's card.

Then he picked it up, took out his wallet and inserted the card inside.

CHAPTER TWO

She stood in front of the grave and thought of his death, and her life.

The cemetery was near the battlefield just east of the small town of Château-Thierry, which straddled the lovely Marne River fifty-six miles to the east of Paris. Charlotte had driven out from Paris that morning in a rented car. Now as she stood in front of the wooden cross marked "Carter Hughes Lang, Capt. U.S. Army, Aug. 13, 1886–June 1, 1918," the late October wind swept across the adjacent wheatfields, causing her to wrap her mink coat more snugly around her. The graves were temporary; a permanent cemetery was being prepared nearby for the victims of the Belleau Wood and Château-Thierry battles. But there was something more poignant about these rows and rows of temporary crosses, she thought. This was where he had been buried—what was it . . . a few days after the battle when the medics cleaned up the litter of war? And the very crudity of the wooden crosses seemed to convey the reality of the death more acutely than the later, neater graves ever could. Thirty-two years old. He had been twenty-nine that night six years before when she had gone to his apartment. Twenty-nine and beautiful. Now what was left of him after three years in the cold soil? No one had bothered to plant grass on the graves—grass would come later in the permanent cemetery—and chickweed and crabgrass had sprung up from the dirt instead, weeds that the frost had killed. She had placed a bunch of yellow mums in a crude vase by the cross, but they would not last long. Probably the wind would blow them over.

She felt guilty for his death. She knew it was far-fetched, and yet if she hadn't gone to his apartment—or if she at least had followed her impulses and let him make love to her—Lily Swenson would not have seen the torn sleeve, and would not have tried to pressure Carter into marrying her . . . or enlisted her father in that effort. A dispirited and rejected—by her, Charlotte—Carter had capitulated and married a woman he never loved . . . and when the war came had rushed off to enlist . . . oh, it was probably foolish, all these guilty speculations and ifs . . . The fact was, he was dead at thirty-two. He had hardly been a perfect man, but she believed he had genuinely loved her and she had turned him away, been at least partly responsible for the sequence of events that brought him to the grave.

How miserable—yes, and jealous—she had been at the wedding, watching that damnable Lily, seeming so innocent and demure in her white bridal gown as she stood next to him in front of the altar. And Lily knew how she felt. That was why she had phoned her first after learning of Carter's death. Lily, even in her perhaps genuine sorrow, had the killer instinct, and her first impulse had been to lash out at the other person the news would hurt the most.

But what was the difference now? Carter was dead, and Lily was drinking and becoming the talk of the country club. And she? She was alone in River Bend. She didn't even have the children now. Her beloved David, after having spent three years in a small California school (and how it had broken her heart to lose him, and how she had fought with Mark over the California school) had entered Lawrenceville that fall, and the others were in schools in Cleveland. So she was now truly alone in River Bend with the servants, and Mark. Mark with his glamorous mistress in New York and his burgeoning millions. Mark who she felt had been waiting for the propitious time to destroy Carter until a German soldier had done it for him. Mark, whom she was finally coming to despise. How stupid she felt she had been to let him make a fool of her with that Maxine! Oh, yes, he was still decent to her, when they weren't arguing about the children, but it was clearly Maxine he loved, not her. He had hardly opposed the separate-bedrooms arrangement, which deprived her of his lovemaking as he had already deprived her of his love. She was forty-three years old. She was lonely and alone. At least she might have had a moment of love with Carter—

"Was he your husband?" said a voice next to her.

She turned to see a tall man in a Chesterfield coat and gray fedora standing next to her. He had a remarkably long face with an aquiline nose that was distinguished rather than handsome. The touches of gray in his sideburns led her to judge he was about fifty.

"No," she said.

"It couldn't have been your son. You are too young to have had a son in the war."

Despite her depressed mood, she responded to the compliment.

"Thank you. And you're right, he wasn't my son. He was just a friend."

"A friend." That was all she had kept insisting she wanted him to be. He could have been so much more.

"Have you seen the battlefield?" the stranger went on.

She shuddered slightly. "I don't want to. I think battlefields make bad tourist attractions."

"You are right, of course. But I'm afraid that is what it will end up being." He was a Frenchman who spoke near-perfect English— with even a slight English accent. "There are still unexploded shells there. Last summer a little girl was killed by one. She was playing in the field and—"

He stopped, as if sensing she didn't want to hear more about death. "I'm sorry. I'm being rather ghoulish and you want to be alone."

"Oh, no! I was about to go. My car's over there."

"I'll walk over with you, if you don't mind."

"Please do."

They started toward the road.

"You are an American?"

"Do I look it?"

"Yes. But actually it's only Americans who come here these days. It's an American cemetery, and the local people don't like to be reminded of the war . . . they call these fields 'les champs sanglants,' 'the bloody fields.' It's an apt name."

"Then why are you here?"

He stopped by a grave six down from Carter's.

"This American sergeant," he said, pointing to the cross. "He tried to save my wife's life. And my two daughters'. My home is not far from here, overlooking the Marne. That June, three years ago, I was with Foch's staff in Paris. The Germans had been near my home but they hadn't occupied it. I foolishly thought my family was safe. Then the battle started and this American sergeant—his name was Corvici, he was an Italian boy from Philadelphia—stopped by my home in a truck and offered to drive them to safety. They accepted. They started out in the truck—" He paused. "A shell hit the truck. They were all killed."

There was an awkward silence.

"I'm sorry," said Charlotte.

He nodded. "So I occasionally come by here to bring a few flowers. And I periodically write the boy's parents to tell them—well, to let them know someone else also cares." He looked around the cemetery as the wind gusted. "I have a friend who's a writer," he continued. "He tells me he "dries up'—I think that's the phrase. He can't think what to write about. I tell him to come here. Every grave is a novel."

He turned back to her and smiled. "Are you returning to Paris now?"

"Yes."

"I have a very fine chef who's been with me since I was a child. Would you care to have lunch with me? I could show you some of the countryside before you leave. It's very beautiful, in spite of the battlefields."

She thought a moment, then smiled. "I'd be delighted."

"Good. We can go in my car, and your driver can follow us. I think you'll enjoy seeing my home. It's quite old and has an interesting history. By the way, my name is Maurice de Sibour."

"And I'm Charlotte Manning."

"You are . . . Mrs. Manning?"

"Yes, I'm married."

"Then I hope your husband is with you?"

She suppressed a smile at his elaborately polite way of saying the opposite of what he was thinking.

"My husband is back in the States."

"Ah, I see."

As he helped her into the front seat of his shiny Bugatti, she took a look back at the cemetery. The crosses stood row on row, lonely and windswept and already a little forgotten.

The wind had knocked over the vase of mums.

The building that Maurice had modestly described as "home" was a sixteenth-century château situated on the north bank of the Marne on a gently sloping hill, the upper part of which was covered with grape vines. The moment Charlotte saw the vines, she connected them with the fact that they were in the champagne country near Rheims, as well as with the name of her host.

"Are you de Sibour champagne?" she asked.

He looked pleased. "That's right. I hope you approve our product?"

"I love it! It's a marvelous champagne. My husband always used to have at least a case in his cellar until Prohibition."

Maurice winced. "Prohibition is an ugly word to us wine producers."

She laughed. "It's an uglier word to us wine consumers. But how beautiful your place is! It's perfect. And the view!"

He had stopped the car before the front door of the château, from which pleasant gardens, now denuded by frost, sloped down to the river's edge a few hundred feet away. He helped her out, and she stood a moment admiring the view and then the château itself. It was not overly large, but rather a beautifully proportioned gem of a building made of light stone. There were two floors, although a large circular tower at the west corner of the façade and a smaller one at the east corner rose to a third floor; the windows in the towers were narrowly pointed in the Gothic style and outlined with handsome stone tracery. Otherwise, the building was devoid of ornamentation, its flamboyant peaked roof bristling with stone chimneys being the only other deviation from a handsome simplicity. It was solid without being heavy, formal and at the same time relaxed. Charlotte fell in love with it at first sight.

Her host led her inside to a large entrance hall with a stone floor, where an aged family retainer named Gaspard greeted them. Maurice told him there would be a guest for lunch; then he said to Charlotte,

"Would you like to see the caves before we dine? They're connected to the house and it's rather interesting if you've never seen champagne being prepared."

"I'd like to very much."

"Then you'd better leave your coat on. It's chilly in the tunnels." They headed to the rear of the house as Maurice continued, "The soil in the champagne district is chalky, and the Romans dug chalk mines, which was convenient for us because they make excellent storage rooms for the wine. The hill behind the château contains one of them. As far as we know, grapes have been grown on top of the hill since the Romans, but of course, champagne as we know it today wasn't developed until the early 1700's when Dom Perignon, who was the cellar master of the Benedictine Abbey at Hautvillers near here, 'put the bubbles into champagne,' as they say, which isn't exactly true. All he truly did was begin to use a cork wired to the bottle to keep the bubbles from escaping. Even so, it was a magnificent accomplishment, and I would be the last to denigrate the venerable Dom. Here are the steps to the caves."

He opened a heavy wooden door and led Charlotte down a stone stair to a tunnel that was, in fact, quite cold. They walked through the tunnel a short way until they reached another wooden door, which he opened. "We're now in the hill," he said. She stepped into another long tunnel illuminated by naked light bulbs from the ceiling. The tunnel was lined with tilted wooden racks into which rows of champagne bottles were inserted head down. A short distance away from them Charlotte could see a white-haired man moving slowly past the racks twisting each bottle slightly, two bottles at a time. "The grape we use," Maurice said, "is the Pinot *noir,* which is red on the inside and almost velvet black on the outside. At harvest time our especially trained women inspect each bunch of grapes, cutting away any that are green or in any way damaged—the process is called *épluchage.* Then only the best grapes are put into our willow baskets and taken immediately to be pressed. It's the first pressing, the *tête de cuvée,* that we make our best champagne from. A few weeks later, when the fermentation has subsided, the wine is taken to the blending rooms, where our blenders mix the different lots to make our own particular personality of champagne. Then it goes into the bottles with a dose of sugar, which starts the second fermentation and releases the bubbles. This takes from two to four years. That gentleman you see further down the tunnel is Pierre, one of our *remuers.*"

"And what is that?"

"The second fermentation throws a sediment in the wine so we put the bottles in these wooden racks, *pupitres,* we call them, and every day Pierre twists each bottle a little to the left and a little to the right, then tilts it a little bit further down until eventually they're upside down. That's called *remuage.* In this way the sediment ends up at the top of the bottle so we can remove it. And removing it is the trickiest part of all."

They had reached Pierre, to whom Maurice introduced his guest, adding that Pierre could turn almost 30,000 bottles a day, a fact that duly impressed Charlotte, to the old man's delight. Then Maurice led her to the end of the tunnel into a large room where a man about the same age as Pierre was standing in front of several vats. "This is where *dégorgement* takes place," said Maurice. "To get rid of the sediment that has collected in the top of the bottle, Georges dips the neck in a freezing brine solution, which creates a small plug of ice in the bottle. Then he takes out the cork, and the ice and the sediment burst out. The trick, of course, is not to lose the wine, and it takes an expert like Georges to do it well." He introduced Georges to Charlotte, speaking in French, and asked the *dégorgeur* to give her a demonstration of his art, which he did. "You see," said Maurice, "when the cork is out and the sediment gone, he puts another small dosage back in the wine—this time, sugar soaked in wine and brandy for flavor. But not much. Our champagne must be dry. The sweet champagnes are . . ." he made a very Gallic expression, indicating his contempt for sweet champagnes, which brought a smile to Charlotte's face. "The bottles are next recorked and, *voilà,* one has champagne. Speaking of which, here I'm dragging you through these icy caverns when what you must really want is to taste our product."

"But it's been fascinating."

"And I am hungry," he countered with a smile. He led her back through the tunnels into the château, where they removed their coats and warmed themselves before a fire crackling in an enormous Renaissance stone fireplace in the salon. The château, she found, was strewn with eighteenth- and nineteenth-century furniture, some of which was quite beautiful, some not so beautiful, but all of which seemed to Charlotte to be definitely right; everything seemed to be part of the family, and the overall effect was one of comfortable elegance. There were dozens of silver-framed photographs covering the tables and piano; some were of notables in the near past or present, but most were family members. Maurice informed her his family was "huge," with innumerable cousins, nephews and aunts. "Which makes it all the more difficult," he added, "for me to be alone." Across the room from the fireplace was a large oil portrait of a lovely woman dressed in the prewar style of ten years previously, standing in a garden with two beautiful little girls dressed in white. "My wife and daughters," he said.

A champagne apéritif was brought in by Gaspard; the beautiful golden liquid was served in a delicate tulip glass with a dry biscuit, and as they sipped it Maurice's expression changed to one of supreme contentment.

"My family has owned this hill for four centuries," he said, "and we have been making wine all that time. We pamper and love our champagne and go to a great deal of trouble to keep it as excellent as we can. Whenever I sip it, I am convinced it's worth all the trouble. I could really never be an atheist, because who could not believe in God when one tastes champagne?"

"That's an unusual theological argument," said Charlotte.

"But a good one."

As she sipped the wine before the crackling fire, a wonderful feeling of well-being filled her as well. She liked Maurice de Sibour enormously. She liked the pride he took in his champagne, the easygoing relationship he had with his workers, his lovely château in the lovely countryside—it all seemed of a piece and somehow right. The patina of time was on everything, and it gave everything a mellowness that she had never encountered in her own country.

"Now," he said, "tell me something about yourself. No, first let me guess. You are from New York?"

"Wrong. Only half wrong, really. I used to live there. But I was born in Ohio, which is where I live now."

"Ohio? That's in the West?"

"Well, the Midwest."

"I see. And your husband? He is a very fortunate person to have won such a woman as yourself."

She stared into the champagne. "My husband is a manufacturer," she said.

"Of what?"

"Tires, mainly."

"*Manning* tires? Your husband is *Mark Manning*?"

"That's right."

Her host laughed.

"What's so funny?" she asked, rather taken aback.

"It's just that when one runs into a very beautiful woman in a cemetery, one doesn't expect she will turn out to be the wife of one of those famous American tycoons. Your husband is very well known

in France. Why, he gave us all those gas masks! I had a Manning gas
mask myself during the war. Believe me, it is a great honor to be
able to entertain the wife of a man to whom France owes such a
debt of gratitude."

Charlotte smiled halfheartedly. "You're very kind. But my husband
didn't exactly give those gas masks to France."

"But he took no profit off them. We all read about it in the papers
at the time. It was a magnificent gesture."

"It was also good business," she said quietly, hoping she did not
sound tastelessly critical.

Maurice, missing none of the overtones, subtly shifted the conversation to himself. During lunch, held in the charming dining room
which like the salon looked out over the river and the hills beyond,
he told her about his youth, his education in English schools (which
explained the English accent) and his war experiences. What emerged
was a portrait of a man well connected in French society, who spent
part of the year in Paris but much preferred the quiet life of the
country, who enjoyed hunting and fishing as a pastime but also enjoyed the company of intellectuals and who also wrote in his spare
time.

"What do you write?" asked Charlotte.

"Very bad short stories and, occasionally, terrible poetry. But I've
had several *romans policiers* published under a pseudonym. You see,
my intellectual friends would look down their noses at me if they knew
I wrote detective stories."

"But I don't see why! I love detective stories."

"So do I. But they're usually not considered literature." He smiled.
"I'll lend you one, if you'd like to read it—that is, if you read French?"

"I can with a dictionary. And I'd love to read it. What's the name
of it?"

"Well, in English it would be something like . . . let's see—*The
Scratch of the Cat,* though that doesn't sound so good, does it?"

"It sounds terribly scary! Who's the cat?"

"A jewel thief at Monte Carlo. He robs the *salons privés* in a rather
ingenious way."

"I'm dying to read it. But what an accomplished man you are! A
champagne producer and an author too!"

"A very good champagne producer," he said, "but not a very good
author. Would you care for some coffee?"

They returned to the salon for a demitasse served in exquisite cups.
After talking for almost an hour, Charlotte checked her watch to find
to her astonishment that it was already four o'clock. "I didn't realize

it was so late," she said, getting up. "Which shows what a good time I've had. But I must be getting back to Paris." As Gaspard brought her coat, Maurice fetched a copy of his book which he gave her. Then he escorted her out to her car.

"Where are you staying in Paris?"

"At the Ritz. I'll be there for the next two weeks."

"Do you have many friends in Paris?"

"Hardly any at all."

"I'd consider it an honor if you'd let me be your friend. I'm coming into town this Friday, and I know the absolutely best restaurant in Paris. I'd very much like to take you to dine there."

She extended her hand and said, very warmly, "And I'd like very much to go."

He looked delighted. "Good. Then—as you Americans say—it's a date?"

"It's a date."

He kissed her gloved hand, which she liked, then helped her into the car.

As the car drove out the driveway, she looked back. He was standing in front of the entrance to the château watching her. She wondered if at last, at the age of forty-three, it was possible . . .

CHAPTER THREE

On the night of November 6, 1921, six boats rendezvoused five miles off the coast of northern New Jersey, two safe miles past the three-mile limit and a mile to the east of the normal shipping lanes. Three of the boats were Newfoundland fishing trawlers; the other three were American: one, the *Lady Luck,* a hundred-foot private yacht out of Perth Amboy; the other two, trawlers. From 11 P.M. until 2:30 A.M. the Canadian boats transferred their cargo to the Americans with a great deal of difficulty, the sea being choppy and the boats wallowing in the deep swells. The cargo—two thousand cases of Scotch and Canadian whiskey. It was the largest single transfer of illicit whiskey up to that date.

On board the *Lady Luck,* in charge of the operation, was Carlo Marucca, Big Johnnie's cousin. Carlo was somewhat bilious from the pitching of the boat, and several times he yelled at the other men in the cabin who had started to light foul-smelling cigars. He still, though, was in control of himself and the others. All three of the American boats had aboard members of the Marucca gang. Most of them were armed, some with machine-guns. The rest were doing the actual work of hauling the heavy cases of whiskey, transferred from the Canadian boats by highline, onto the decks of the American boats. It was hard work, made harder by the rough seas and the tension imposed by the possible appearance at any moment of a Coast Guard cutter. None appeared, however, and at 2:35, after all the cases had been checked and stowed and the money paid to the "Canook," as the commander of the Canadian flotilla was known to Marucca, Carlo gave the order to start for Asbury Park.

There, several miles south of the beach resort, Carlo had taken a year's lease on a summer home the previous spring. It was a rambling, late-Victorian house, which had been picked because of its isolation, its nearest neighbor being three-quarters of a mile down the beach. Carlo had repaired the rotting pier protected from the ocean by a rock jetty, and built, to his landlord's delight, a sturdy boathouse. Carlo's family—his wife and six children—had taken residence in the house the previous summer and established themselves as pleasant, law-abiding summer people. The chief objective was to use the place in the winter, when the area was practically deserted, as a drop for booze, and so far the plan had worked admirably. In the two months since the closing of the house at the end of the summer season, Carlo had made six runs, bringing in over 5,000 cases of illegal booze, off-loading them in the boathouse, then bringing them under cover of darkness up to the house, where they were stored in the basement to be picked up later by truck and delivered into Manhattan. There, a portion of the haul was sold to speakeasies at an average price of $150 a case. The rest, most of the lot, was taken to a "lab" in the basement of an upper-West Side garage owned by Big Johnnie, where the whiskey was diluted by as much as 70 percent, then spiked with rotgut and rebottled under the good labels. This concoction was sold on a varying scale from as little as $12 a case for the worst quality to a top of $85 for the least objectionable. Thus, on the six runs, which handled 5,000 cases, bought at an average price of forty dollars a case, there had been an investment of $200,000. The 5,000 cases, diluted, produced 8,000 cases which sold at an average price of seventy dollars, grossing $560,000. Deducting expenses and operating costs of $50,000, the net profit to the Marucca gang for the six runs was a little over a quarter of a million dollars.

A pretty good return for a summer home and a boathouse.

The boats anchored a tenth of a mile off the jetty at 3:45. Lifeboats were lowered and the laborious transfer of the whiskey from the trawlers to the boathouse was begun, the task complicated by the bad seas. But Carlo had trained his men well in boathandling, having brought groups of them the previous summer as guests to the house, where, under the command of a retired Coast Guard petty officer Carlo had hired in a burst of audacity, the burly racketeers from the Lower East Side, garbed in jaunty resort wear, had labored in the surf learning how to handle small boats. The retired petty officer was told it was part of a program to give young city slum dwellers healthy exercise and salt air. If he had any suspicions, they were silenced by his salary of five hundred dollars. His training had paid off. The men knew their business. Swiftly and expertly, the boats bobbed and dipped their way back and forth between the trawlers and the *Lady Luck* and the jetty. By 6:45 the transfer was completed, and the trawlers set out to sea. Carlo made the last trip in himself, sending the *Lady Luck* back to Perth Amboy under the command of Mario Sanducci, one of his lieutenants. And by 7:00, when the sky was becoming light, the last case was locked in the basement of the house and the eight exhausted men who had not gone back on the *Lady Luck* were resting in the kitchen.

Two cars had been parked at the entrance to the driveway all night, the drivers serving as guards. Now Carlo dispatched Joe Granelli to walk down the drive and tell the cars to pick them up. Ten minutes later, the cars were heard approaching the house and Carlo sent his men outside while he locked up. He had just locked the front door when he heard the chatter of machine-guns and the screams. He knew what was happening. He saw two of his men run back into the kitchen and slam the door. The bullets ripped through the wood, and the men twisted in a bloody frieze of death. Carlo's machine-gun was on the kitchen table; now he ran back into the kitchen, took up the gun and raced around the stove to the basement door, planning to escape into the cellar, where he might have a chance. He heard the front door split open. He turned and sprayed the living room with bullets. Three men slammed back against the wall, blood gushing from their faces and chests, as they slumped to the floor. Carlo continued firing; two men outside the front door dropped. He slammed shut the door between the kitchen and the living room and wedged a chair under the doorknob. He ran back to the basement door, fumbling with his key ring, trying to find the key to the padlock as he cursed with fear and rage. Then, realizing he was being stupid, he threw down the key ring, aimed his gun at the padlock and blasted it off with a short burst of fire.

From the corner of his eye he saw the figure at the window above the sink. Instinctively he ducked, at the same time turning to bring his machine-gun up. There was a shot, the sound of shattering glass. A bullet smashed into Carlo's nose. He slumped on top of his gun.

Silence.

The back door was broken open, and three men came into the kitchen. They were dressed in dark suits, wide-brimmed hats and dark-blue overcoats. One of them, a handsome six-footer, walked over and looked down at Carlo. He kicked Carlo in his crotch.

The corpse of Carlo made no response.

Franco Ruggiero turned to his men. "Okay, bring up the moving van and let's load this stuff."

Because of the isolation of the house, the bodies weren't found for five days. Then the "Asbury Park Massacre," as the papers called it, took over the headlines. Police learned from informers that the Marucca gang was blaming it on its rivals, Franco Ruggiero's mob, and the fledgling *Daily News*, a mere two years old, plastered its front page with a huge photo of Franco taken the year before as he was coming out of a speakeasy. As Mark, propped up in Maxine's bed, stared at the picture of the grinning and darkly handsome man dressed in an impeccable tuxedo, all he could say was, "trouble."

"What's wrong?" mumbled a sleepy Maxine, snuggling next to him.

"Franco Ruggiero has just murdered Big Johnnie's cousin and eight of his hoods. That's what's wrong."

Maxine sat up and looked at the front page. "Isn't it strange, I'd forgotten how good-looking he is."

He ignored her and handed over the paper. She glanced at the lead paragraph of the article.

"Big Johnnie must be burning," she said.

"From what you've told me about the rackets, I'd say Big Johnnie's going to pay him back."

"Probably." She continued reading the article as Mark watched her. Then he reached his hand over and put it on her breast.

"Don't," she said. "I want to read the article . . ."

He jerked the paper out of her hands, throwing it on the floor. "Damn you!" she said, trying to reach for it. He grabbed her and pulled her over to him, kissing her as her breasts rubbed against his chest. "The morning certainly seems to be your special time," she said, feeling his erection against her thigh.

"I'm glad you've noticed."

He pulled the sheet down, moved on top of her and made love to her as she moaned delightedly, feeling herself alive with his warm semen.

When it was over they lay in each other's arms, and after a moment he said, "What's for breakfast, my love?"

"God, you're just one appetite after another, aren't you?"

He laughed. "Could be."

She lay in the bed a while, staring at the ceiling. Then: "Mark?"

"What?"

"Are you ready for a surprise?"

He sat up and looked at her. "You haven't anything for breakfast."

"Not exactly. You see, I missed my period last week. I went to a doctor. It seems I'm pregnant."

Silence.

"And since you're the only one around these days—remember, that's the way *you* wanted it—well, it seems you're the lucky father-to-be. Do you mind?"

He thought about it. "No. In fact, I'm delighted. But what about you?"

She sat up and said thoughtfully, "Well, I'd have to get out of my contract with Ziegfeld, and there is the matter of our not being married." Then she smiled. "But Mark, I want to have it. I'm thirty-two years old and it's time I have a child. I'm *going* to have it."

He kissed her warmly and said, "I'm glad, Maxine. I really am. And he'll never have to worry about anything. I may not be able to give him my name, but I can give him everything else."

"Don't be so sure it's a 'he.' But you surprise me. I thought you'd hit the ceiling when I told you."

"Why?"

"Well, Charlotte, and your proper reputation and all that."

"Maxine, I want to have a child with you. And while I'm not proud to say it, this isn't a first—"

"There have been *others*?"

"One other. A very fine boy who's twenty-one now. I'm putting him through Amherst."

She looked genuinely surprised. "And the mother? Was she as pleasant about the whole thing as I am?"

"Not exactly. In fact, she hates me . . . I wish I could marry you, Maxine. I've been happier with you than anyone else but I still feel an obligation to Charlotte, no matter what she thinks of me—which, as you know, isn't much. And I admit I don't want to break up our home, at least while the kids are still so young. Can you understand that?"

"Of course, I understand it. I never expected you to divorce Charlotte. For that matter, I'm not all that interested in getting married, and I'm certainly not going to panic because I'm pregnant. I'll just retire from the limelight a while. I like my life just as it is, and the addition of our child is going to make it that much better. And as for whatever problems he may have about not being strictly legitimate, well, he'll make up for it by having such marvelous parents."

He leaned over and kissed her again. "You know," he said, "you're a wonderful woman."

She smiled.

"I know."

He had to return to Elkins the next day, and when he arrived at River Bend he was greeted by an empty house and a letter from Paris in which Charlotte informed him she had decided to spend another ten days in France. She was having some special fittings, she said.

It struck him as rather odd since she had wanted to return on the *Aquitania* and this would necessitate her taking another ship, but he dismissed it from his mind, his thoughts being filled with Maxine, his new child, and, as always, business. But a week later another letter came, informing him she was not leaving until December 12, and now he knew something unusual had happened. He had, after all, perpetrated the same devices on Charlotte in the past—he recognized the signs. The more he thought about it, the more certain he became that there was something she wasn't telling him, and the something, he knew, was that she had met another man.

He had known it would happen sooner or later. Charlotte was not a sensuous woman but she had had a passion of sorts for Carter Lang, and she hardly had made a secret of her dissatisfaction with her life. He didn't try to deny his own responsibility—how could he blame her for being unhappy with a husband who spent a fourth of his time with another woman in another city? And yet, irrationally, now that he thought Charlotte had met someone else, he grew inordinately jealous of the unknown rival, as he once had been over Carter. Suddenly it was wrong for her to "betray" her husband, even if her husband were living almost openly with another woman. After all, she was a *mother,* and hadn't he always gone to the most extreme lengths to keep the family together, even to the point of not contemplating a divorce to marry Maxine, the woman he loved and who was bearing his child? Charlotte wasn't playing the game fairly, not as she'd agreed . . . Women were supposed to be loyal.

Moreover, he *wanted* her. She was his, his *wife.* Without Charlotte, River Bend would be a huge shell. He loved the part of his life River Bend represented as much as he loved the part Maxine represented. He liked, in a word, having his cake and eating it too—he was accustomed to it. He missed his children, who were all away at school. He felt nostalgic about old good times with the family. He became anxious about the effect on the children if Charlotte decided to leave, not to mention the effect on himself.

He contemplated going to Paris to find out what exactly was going on, but he dismissed this as being too awkward. It was more important to put her on the defensive, but it had to be done more subtly, at least in a way she would never expect.

Then one night, as he sat alone at dinner, the idea occurred to him. Hurrying into his study, he placed a call to the headmaster of the Wooster School, Dr. Graham Warner. He had gotten to know Dr. Warner when he had placed Roger in the school, and he admired the man as an excellent educator—admired him so much, in fact, that he had given $25,000 to the school to complete a new gymnasium.

Now it was time for Dr. Warner to return the favor.

Maxine Talbot was about to go upstairs to bed when she heard a knock on the front door of her house in Grove Court. Standing outside was Franco Ruggiero in a camel's hair coat.

"Hello, Maxine," he said. "Mind if I come in?"

Rather uncertainly she stood aside as he came into the house, taking off his coat as she closed the door.

"I haven't seen you for a long time," he said, hanging the coat on a Victorian brass coatstand. "How've you been?"

"Fine," she said, going into the living room. "How's Rose?"

Rose was Franco's older sister, whom Maxine had known since childhood.

"Oh, she's fine," he said, following her into the living room. "She's out in California now, in San Francisco. She's married and has four kids."

"How about you, Franco? Are you married?"

He grinned. "Nah. Not yet. I'm too young to die. Mind if I make a drink?"

"Help yourself."

She sat down as he made a scotch highball.

"How's your boyfriend?"

"All right. Mostly because no one's been jumping out of doorways lately trying to carve him."

Franco laughed. "Oh? He remembers that?"

"It would be hard to forget. It was you, wasn't it?"

"Of course not." He smiled pleasantly and sat down. "I don't do stuff like that. You know I'm a very classy guy these days."

"So I read in the papers. And you go to classy resorts, too, like Asbury Park."

He looked at her and grinned. "That wasn't me. The papers got mixed up. I was in Washington, D.C., that night. Ask the cops—they already checked me out."

"Sure, Franco. I believe you."

"You know, Maxine, you're one gorgeous dame. Also smart. You know, I think I've had it for you ever since I was ten. No kidding. You ought to let me take you out some time and prove it."

She laughed. "That's a real classy line you got there, Franco. Subtle, too."

"That's me. Subtle. Smooth. Like good scotch."

"Come on, Franco, what do you really want?"

He took a drink of scotch, set the glass down.

"The Golden Slipper. Its business, I mean. We can do a better job for you and your friend than Big Johnnie."

"Look, Franco, I've always put up with you because of Rose, and I try to ignore what I read in the papers—which isn't so easy. But don't try this stuff on me. You know I'm Big Johnnie's client, and you know he's not going to let me fire him—nobody fires Big Johnnie Marucca, as you also damn well know."

"You're wrong, Maxine. We're taking over Big Johnnie's territory, and I figured I'd start with you, seeing as we're old pals." He leaned forward. "And because we are old pals, Maxine, I'm willing to give you an option—*sell* me the Golden Slipper."

"Sell it? But I don't *want* to sell it!"

"I'll give you a good price, and I'll pay cash. Think about it."

"But what do you want to own it for?"

"Because it's a good, legit business. Because it's one of the best clubs in town. I'll give you $200,000 cash for the house and the club. Deal?"

"No, no deal. I happen to love the Golden Slipper, I get a kick out of running it and I have no intention of selling—and that's final."

Franco finished his highball, then stood up.

"You think it over, Maxine. I give you a choice—sell me the club, or give me your business. You're lucky. I don't give most people a choice." He walked back to the entrance hall, then stopped at the door and looked at her. "And if you know what's good for you, Maxine, you won't tell Big Johnnie I've been here to see you. Understand?"

She got out of her chair. "Now look, *no* one threatens Maxine Talbot!"

He looked at her and said, "Franco Ruggiero threatens Maxine Talbot. You think about it. I'll see you in a week."

CHAPTER FOUR

Charlotte Manning had never been so happy in her life. All the scars of the past—Sydney's defection with Richard Goldmark, her increasingly unhappy marriage with Mark—all had been forgotten in the wonder of her love for Maurice de Sibour. And wonder of wonders, he was in love with her! This incredibly attractive man, this paragon of everything she admired, this warm, charming, intelligent man was as hopelessly in love with her as she with him, and her month in Paris, alternating with long wonderful weekends at La Colline-sur-Marne, his château, had been closer to heaven than she had ever thought possible this side of the grave.

He had made love to her; at first she had submitted guiltily, but then blissfully. She didn't care any more; it was too good not to be right. She felt completely fulfilled, not only sexually and romantically but in every way. Maurice and she happened to be that rarity— kindred souls. When he asked her to marry him, she didn't hesitate in saying yes. She no longer felt any obligation to Mark; that had been ended by his affair with Maxine. And the children? Well, the divorce would hurt them; there was no way around that. Yet others had

divorced, and the children had survived—many others, more all the
time. They were growing up now anyway, and spending most of their
time in boarding schools. She knew Mark loved them—though David
was his least-favorite of the four, and things had even gotten better
with David since the boy had gone away to school. Mark had begun
to show a greater respect for him, particularly when his grades were
so spectacular—so she would not try to take complete custody of them;
that would be unfair. He could have them part of the time, and she
the rest of the time. That wouldn't be so bad, and what a wonderful
opportunity for them to get to know this wonderful country of France.
And could anyone ask for a better stepfather than Maurice?

But beyond all these considerations, which she admitted to herself
were tinged with self-justification, was her obligation to *herself*. Her
life was half over, and now that she had found fulfillment with
Maurice, nothing was going to stand in her way. She wouldn't be a
Nora Helmer; she wouldn't abandon her children, walk out of their
lives—she would never do that. But she *was* going to make a new
life for herself. And she told Maurice when she boarded the ship at
Le Havre that she would be back in France within three months—
or as soon as the divorce could be completed.

The crossing was stormy, and they arrived in New York a day late.
She called Mark in Elkins and told him which train she was taking.
He sounded pleased to hear her voice, told her he had missed her—
she refrained from comment—and said he would meet her at the
Cleveland train station, which he did, with Marvin Senjak, who supervised the transfer of her trunks and bags as Mark kissed her and
led her through the station to the parking lot. "I've got a surprise
for you," he said cheerfully.

Charlotte, who had a surprise for him, was feeling anything but
cheerful. Despite all her determination, she was not looking forward
to telling him she wanted a divorce. This wasn't a pleasant piece of
news under the best of conditions, and Mark's temper promised to
make it something less than that. With rather strained enthusiasm
she said, "Really?" wanting to keep things pleasant until she got home.
"What is it?"

"I bought you a new car as a welcome-home present."

Her heart sank as he pointed out the enormous blue sedan standing
regally in front of the station, surrounded by admiring onlookers.
The last thing she wanted was to feel obligated to him.

"Do you like it? Isn't it a beauty? Fred Duesenberg started making
this Model A last year in Indianapolis and he tells me it's one of
his best. Of course, that might be a sales pitch, but Marvin and I

have tried it out on a straightaway and it's really something! It's got an eight-cylinder engine and hydraulically operated front-wheel brakes, and it can do eighty-five without even squeaking—not that you ever drive that fast, I hope. Anyway, it's yours." The onlookers stepped aside as he brought Charlotte up and patted the front fender. "Do you like it? Look, I even had your initials painted on the door. C.R.M. How's that for ostentation?"

She could only say it was beautiful, which it was. But she was even more wary now. Mark, who once had always brought her gifts, from diamond bracelets to candy bars, had been much less generous since their marriage had cooled. Maxine, she knew, was receiving the largesse. And now, a $12,000 automobile out of the blue? She realized he must have guessed something, and in his usual fashion was launching an offense as the best defense. On the drive back to River Bend she sat next to him in the back seat, alternating between flashes of anger at his tactics and apprehension at the oncoming scene. He, on the other hand, chatted away as if nothing were the matter, telling her the children were all home from school now for the Christmas holiday, how they were all looking forward to seeing her and how he hoped this would be their best Christmas yet. . . . Stop it! she wanted to shout, and said nothing.

As the big blue car rolled through the wrought-iron gates of the estate, she felt even worse. How simple everything had seemed in France! But here in Elkins, where she was born, where she had so many memories, pleasant and unpleasant, things were much less clear.

And River Bend! There it was, looming at the end of the drive beneath the metallic winter sky, the house she had planned with such love, the place where she had spent almost ten years of her life. She suddenly felt a twinge of fear: would she be strong enough to break away after all? Was she possibly wrong about Mark? For all of his faults, for all his self-centeredness, despite Maxine, was she perhaps being too harsh with him? She remembered the early years of their marriage, when she had been so in love with him. Had she been wrong then? And the children. Always the children. Was she the one who was being self-centered to break up their family because she had fallen in love with a French champagne-maker? The dream suddenly seemed like a nightmare. And as Mark helped her out of the car, he commented on how pale she looked.

"Are you feeling all right?" he asked.

She nodded and forced a smile as Peter, the butler, came out to greet her. And then there were the children piling out of the front door shouting "Mummy! Mummy!" as they swarmed around her, hugging and kissing her, all except David, who was now twelve and in the ungainly stage and who had become sternly undemonstrative in order to appear more manly and adult. He gravely shook his mother's hand, but she kissed him and found herself crying.

They went into the house, where Mark said, "Now, the children have a surprise for you."

She dried her eyes and tried to look delighted.

"What is it?"

"It's really not *our* surprise," said Ellen. "It's father's idea."

"Ellen, you weren't supposed to say that," said Mark. "But anyway, come into the living room to see what it is. But first you have to close your eyes. David, take your mother's hand and lead her."

David obeyed, and Charlotte closed her eyes, wondering what was coming next, following her son across the hall into the living room. They stopped inside the door.

"Don't open your eyes yet," said Mark.

She didn't. She heard a rustling sound, like a number of people shifting in their chairs. The sound of a tapping stick. Then, to her wonderment, the room filled with the soft opening strains of Mozart's Fortieth Symphony. She blinked open her eyes and stared. The huge room had been cleared of its furniture, and about fifty musicians in white tie and tails were seated in folding chairs. In front of them, conducting the symphony, was a young man with a baton. "It belongs to you," whispered Mark, nodding toward the orchsetra. "It's called the Manning Symphony, and it's *yours.*"

She looked back at the orchestra, most of whose members were young, probably fresh out of music school. However, the quality of the music was remarkably good. The children were watching their mother, waiting for her reaction, excited at being in on the big secret.

"Mine?" she finally said incredulously. "What am I to do with a symphony?"

"It's for the town, really," replied her husband. "I thought it was time Elkins got a little culture—you always said so and you were right—so I called Dr. Warner at the Wooster School, who knows all about music and told him I wanted to fund a symphony. He got this bunch together on quick notice, and here they are. I'm going to build them a concert hall in town, and we'll have music scholarships for talented kids, and the whole thing will be under your direction. You love music so much, I thought you'd get a kick out of it. . . ."

He stopped. She seemed, unbelievably by his lights, to be furious.

She glared at him a moment, then turned and walked out of the room.

"Daddy, what's wrong with mummy?" whispered Ellen.

"I think," said Mark, "that your mummy didn't like her surprise."

He turned to watch the orchestra, his face burning.

They played only the first movement of the symphony, to which Mark, the children and the entire staff of the house listened. Then Mark thanked the musicians and Sylvius Lazlo, the young Czech conductor, telling them that Mrs. Manning had been delighted but was tired from her long trip. Drinks and a small buffet were served the orchestra members as planned, Mark being determined to make everything go off smoothly despite Charlotte's absence. He gave them a pep talk, showed a rendering of the concert hall he planned to build for them—a handsome, Greek-style building designed by Bill Bixby—and said that he hoped the orchestra would be the beginning of "a new birth of interest in the arts" in Ohio, "which, God knows, could stand some," he added, eliciting appreciative laughter from the audience. Whatever doubts the musicians might have had about their welcome after the disappearance of the guest of honor were dispelled by Mark's cheerful hospitality. And when they got aboard the two chartered buses for the trip back to Cleveland, from where most of them had been recruited, the morale of the fledgling symphony couldn't have been higher. Sylvius Lazlo, who until now had achieved only assistant conductorships, was in seventh heaven. Like Haydn, he had found his Prince Esterhazy; his future looked wonderfully bright and secure.

The musicians finally gone, Mark went up to Charlotte's bedroom and knocked on the door. Not waiting for an answer, he opened the door and went in. She was lying across her big, four-poster bed and he knew she had been crying. He came over and sat down beside her. "Charlotte, what's wrong?"

She sat up and looked at him. Her eyes were red and her hair disarrayed, flowing loosely around her.

"Can't you guess what's wrong?" she said softly, but her tone was tinged with anger.

"All I know is you behaved rudely, which is something I've never seen you do."

"Yes, Mark, I behaved rudely. The terrible, rude Mrs. Manning whose loving husband prepared a marvelous surprise for her—such a thoughtful, civic-minded surprise—and she stalks right out of the room . . . Except please at least credit me with enough intelligence to see through your impressive production. A symphony orchestra! As if you ever really cared about music or about bringing *culture* to Elkins. The whole thing was a maneuver to put me on the spot—an obvious *trick,* and you know it." She stood up from the bed. "Oh, God, Mark, I suppose I should be flattered. It was at least a stylish trick and so beautifully clever! The Duesenberg was grand but obvious—any rich husband could have managed that. But an entire symphony orchestra . . . You *know* the one thing I adore most in this world is music, so you give me a whole orchestra, a private toy for me to play with, to bring culture and enlightenment to the poor uncultured rubber workers of backwater Elkins, Ohio. Well, I'm sorry, Mark. It's too late. I don't want any of it—nor anything else your money can buy. I'm *not* for sale!"

After a moment he said, "Who is it, Charlotte? Who have you fallen in love with?"

She looked at him. "A wonderful man. Maurice de Sibour. I love him and I intend to marry him, Mark. So, please, no more of your tricks, because this time I'm going to be as selfish about happiness as you've been. I've got a lawyer—I talked with him yesterday in New York. He knows about Maxine and he tells me there's not a judge in the world who won't give me a divorce if I want it. And, Mark, I want it."

"Don't worry, I understand my legal position—or rather the lack of it. I'm not so sure I understand you, or why you feel the way you do about me."

She didn't answer for a moment, then she said, "Mark, I certainly don't hate you. But I also don't love you any more. I did, once. You always dazzled me, and in a way I loved being dazzled. I loved you. That night Bill Sands shot you, I thought it was the end of the world."

"And now?"

"I told you, Mark. But if you're asking how did it happen, I'm not sure I really know. I've thought about it often enough. I know most women would give their eye teeth to have you. You're attractive, you can be charming when you want, and God knows you're certainly successful . . ."

"And Maurice? What are his sterling, superior qualities?"

"Mark, I suppose this kind of talk is inevitable, but I wish we could end this without recriminations and pointless comparisons. I don't want to hurt you, and I don't want to be hurt by you any more."

"Fine, but I'd still appreciate an answer."

"All right, if you insist. It's a special sort of warmth," she said. "And a gentleness, and a code to live by . . . I know that sounds old-fashioned—"

"In other words," he said, fighting his anger, "he's a gentleman and I'm not?"

"Yes, I suppose in a way that's it. But I told you, I don't want—"

"A gentleman," he said contemptuously, getting up from the bed. "A warm, gentle gentleman who had everything handed to him on a goddamn silver platter. Oh, I know about Maurice de Sibour. He makes good champagne—it's not Louis Roederer or Pol Roger or Dom Perignon—but it's good. I've even seen pictures of his château, and that's very nice too. He really slaved his tail off to get it, didn't he? Well, I don't make 'good' tires, Charlotte. I make the *best* tires. And I built *my* château by myself—"

"Oh, Mark," she interrupted with exasperation. "Is that all there is to life? Building up a huge company, making money, seeing your name on tires all over the world? Your ego, Mark, runneth over. And since you insist on comparisons, you *didn't* do it all by yourself. You had just a little bit of help from my father!"

"Your father never even thought about getting into the rubber business till I came to him! Christ, he didn't even *like* automobiles! He thought they smelled bad and were a goddamn *fad! I* made this company! I fought for it, connived for it, risked my damn life for it—which your father thought was irresponsibly risking his precious investment—never mind my life. You're damned right I'm no gentleman. No *gentleman* could have done what I've done—hell, I agree, no gentleman *would* have done it. You may not think much of me or my life, but there's not one thing I've done that I'm ashamed of!"

"Including Maxine?"

"Yes, especially including Maxine. She happens to *like* me."

"Mark, I wish we could stop this. You're a self-sufficient man, a man dedicated to success. You rarely if ever have a moment of doubt or insecurity; you know almost instantly how to solve everything. I'm *not* saying that's bad or wrong. I'm just saying it's not really for me. Maybe you're simply *too* strong for me. I need a real man, but also a man who needs me—"

"I need you!"

"No, don't fool yourself. You need a woman's body to satisfy your appetite. You're in love with yourself, with your company that's a reflection of you, and you're in love with power . . . Mark, I repeat, why should we fight and insult and hurt each other? Does it make any sense? Let's just let go of each other and be done with it."

He started to answer, then changed his mind. She was right. As much as he hated to lose her, he knew it was useless to try to hang on to her—useless and probably wrong.

"All right," he said quietly. "The end. Amen. What about the kids?"

"I think we should share them equally. You can have them half the year, and I'll have them the other half. I think that's the fairest way."

"I appreciate that, Charlotte."

"And as far as a settlement goes, I don't need any money. I'd like to take a few personal things and my piano. The rest should stay here, for you and the children."

They looked at each other awkwardly. Then he forced a weak smile. "Well, what do people say to each other after fourteen years?"

"For one thing, it would be nice if they could say good luck."

"Yes, well, that shouldn't be so hard. And I do wish you good luck, Charlotte."

"And I wish the same to you, Mark. I also think it would be nice if you would kiss me."

He leaned down to kiss her as, in an unexpected gesture, she put her hand on his cheek.

"Don't think badly of me, Mark," she whispered. "For all the harsh things I've said to you, I did love you once . . . and we had so many beautiful times together. I'll always remember them. And thank you for them."

"And you know I could never think badly of you, Charlotte, no matter what you've said or how angry I've gotten at you. After all, you haven't always been wrong," he said, and smiled slightly.

"Do you remember the first time we met? At father's house?"

"I remember."

"I was playing the piano and you came into the room and I said you were a primitive . . . But I thought you were terribly dashing. I still do."

"And I thought you were the most beautiful girl in the world. And I still do."

At half past midnight on the morning of January 14, 1922, Maxine Talbot was driven to the entrance of Grove Court in her new blue Duesenberg by her new black chauffeur, Walter, who got out of the front seat to open the door for his employer. Maxine stepped out of the car given her by Mark two weeks before (he had had the c.r.m. initials on the doors painted out and replaced with m.t.). She was wrapped in the sable coat Mark had given her. And though she was worn out after her final performance for Mr. Ziegfeld (who had not been happy about his star's quitting but who had bowed to the inevitable), and though she was in her third month of pregnancy, she still looked exotically beautiful. She felt beautiful too. When Mark had given her the Duesenberg, he had told her that he and Charlotte were getting a divorce. And he had asked her to marry him. It had come as a shock—she had never believed Mark would actually divorce his wife. Never mind her earlier insistence that she had no desire to marry, when Mark proposed, she accepted. She loved him, and even her fierce independence did not blind her to the difficulties of bearing and raising an illegitimate child, and she fully intended to bear and raise Mark Manning's child—a child by the only man she had ever loved. So they were engaged, with Mark's proviso that she keep it secret until the divorce was completed.

All, however, was not smooth sailing between them. When Maxine told Mark about her visit from Franco Ruggiero, Mark had become alarmed and told her to accept Franco's offer for the Golden Slipper. Maxine had refused, nor would she agree to move to Elkins permanently, telling Mark she wanted to keep her house in New York. Mark said she was trying to hang onto as much of her old life as possible. She agreed but said she could go just so far, that she loved him, but if he insisted on having it all his way the engagement was off. He gave in but personally hired Walter to act as a bodyguard for her as well as a chauffeur. Mark remembered the viciousness of the knife attack on him six years before, and he had made Maxine swear that she wouldn't go out without Walter, to which she had agreed.

So now it was Walter who accompanied her into Grove Court and walked her to her door, where she fished her key from her purse and let herself in, bidding Walter good night. She hung her sable in the coat closet, turned off the downstairs lights and went up to the second floor. It was then that she sensed something was wrong. She had not left her bedroom light on, and yet she could see it shining under the door. She could also smell cigarette smoke.

She opened the door. The naked man sitting up in her bed was reading a newspaper, which he now put down.

"Hello, Maxine," said Franco.

She slammed the door.

"What the hell do you think you're doing?"

"Waiting for you." He smiled, crossing his muscled arms over his broad chest, which was matted with black curly hair. "You know, this is an awfully easy house to break into. Your kitchen window wasn't even locked."

"Now *look,* Franco, I'm tired and I'm in no mood for games. You can get out of my bed and get out of here before I call the cops and tell them big Franco Ruggiero has stooped to housebreaking."

He reached over to the bedtable and held up the phone cord. "You're not going to call anyone, because if you try, I'll have to pull out the cord. Now, why don't you get comfortable and relax. I've been waiting a long time for this."

She looked at the phone cord, and her anger began to be replaced by fear. "What do you want, Franco?"

He dropped the phone cord and patted the bed next to him.

"I'm not going to do it."

"Why? Afraid your sugar daddy will find out?"

"No. Because I don't want anything to do with you. Now for the last time, get out of here."

He scratched his hairy chest thoughtfully.

"You come to a decision yet? About the Golden Slipper?"

"Yes. I'm not selling, and everything stays just as it is."

"You'd better think twice about that, baby."

"I'm not your goddamn baby, and I'm not thinking twice about it! Now, get *out* of here! I mean it!"

"Well," he said, "since you're not going to be cooperative . . ." Suddenly he had grabbed her and was pulling her onto the bed as she tried to hit him with her fists.

"Franco, what the hell do you think you're doing—"

"I'm going to rape you, baby, and then I'm going to ask you once more if you'll give me your business. And then if you say no, I'm going to kill you."

"Franco, please . . . I *can't* give you the business . . . Big Johnnie would stop the booze . . . he'd kill me—"

"*I've* got Big Johnnie's booze now. And when I give you protection, you won't have to worry about that has-been."

"You're bluffing," she said, trying to brazen it out. "You think you can scare me—you go to hell. I don't scare that easily."

He smashed his fist into her right eye. "Bluffing? You want more? You want me to rape you right through this mattress into the basement?"

"Franco—oh God, please, I'm pregnant—"

"Bullshit."

"I *am!* For God's sake, do you want to kill my child?"

He put his hand on her belly and felt the slight bulge. His touch nearly made her throw up.

"It does *happen,* you know. And unless you've turned into a complete animal—"

"Oh, I agree, only an animal would attack a pregnant lady. And I'm certainly not an animal. However, I know someone who is. Hey, Mike!" He called toward the bathroom. "Come on in here."

The bathroom door opened and a fat man in a rumpled brown suit moved into the room. He had a blank expression on his face.

"Come over here, Mike," said Franco.

Mike obeyed, staring down at his feet.

"Maxine, meet Mike. Mike, this is Maxine Talbot, the famous Follies star. You ever go to the Follies, Mike?"

Mike shook his head.

"Mike's not a big theater-goer. He's too dumb even to understand the Follies. But Mike's a good boy, does like he's told. Would you like to screw a Follies star, Mike?"

"Franco!"

"Shut up." He pushed her back down onto the bed. "Hey, Mike, show Maxine your wrists. Go on."

Mike's blank expression colored red.

"Ah, Franco, I don't want her to know *that*—"

"But *I* want her to know. Go on."

Mike pulled up the sleeves of his coat, showing his pinkish-spotted inner wrists to Maxine.

"See the spots?" said Franco. "In case you think they're measles, you're wrong. It's worse, sweetheart, much worse. Mike's got a nice case of v.d. he tells me he picked up on Fourteenth Street, and the doc says those pink spots show he's into the second stage. Now, Maxine, I've heard this stuff is very unhealthy for a pregnant woman, does bad things to her baby—"

"Stop it!!"

"Like the baby's born without any nose, or only three fingers—"

"Stop it, stop it! You can have the goddamn business! Just get that horrible man out of here—*please!*"

She was on the edge of hysteria. Franco signaled to Mike, who left the room. Then Franco leaned close to her face and took her chin in his hand. "You know what'll happen if you doublecross me?"

She nodded, the tears running down her cheeks. Her right eye was already turning black and blue.

"I'll kill you, Maxine, if you doublecross me. I'll kill you. And then I'll turn Mike loose on your corpse. You understand?"

She nodded.

"Say, 'Yes, Franco. I understand.' "

"Yes, Franco. I understand."

"That's better."

He let go of her chin, then got dressed. "You'll like being my client. I'll give you better booze than Big Johnnie, and my prices are right in line with his. And because you're an old friend, I'll give you a break on the protection. Thousand a week."

"I pay Big Johnnie eight hundred!"

"Cost of living's going up, and I give better protection. I protect you from Mike—get the picture?"

She said nothing.

"Don't worry, Maxine. I'll take good care of you. After all, we're old pals, aren't we? I may have roughed you up a little tonight, but now that we're on the same side, don't worry about a thing. Maybe after a while you may even take me up on my offer, how about that?"

She still said nothing.

"I'm making a lot of dough now, baby. A lot. I can give you anything your bigshot can. Think about it."

Still silence.

"Are you listening?"

"Yes, Franco."

"That's better. You think about it?"

"Yes, Franco."

"Good." He got up and stood in front of the mirror to adjust his tie. "This Manning guy, is that his kid you're carrying?"

"Yes."

He finished with his tie, then went to the chair and picked up his coat. As he put it on he said, "Maybe you'll introduce us some time. Formally, I mean." He came over to the bed and looked at her. "Come now, it isn't as bad as all that. Besides, we're together now. We ought to go out and celebrate. Want to come with us? We're going over to a club in Weehawken."

"No thanks."

He shrugged, pinched her chin playfully, then left the room.

She waited by the bed, trembling, until she heard the front door slam. She waited a moment, then hurried around the bed to the phone. She gave the operator Big Johnnie's number. The rings seemed interminable. Finally Mrs. Marucca answered. Maxine asked for her husband.

"He's asleep."

"Wake him up. It's important."

"Wait a minute."

She could hear muffled voices on the other end. Big Johnnie came on.

"What's the matter?" he said sleepily.

"It's Maxine Talbot. Franco Ruggiero was just here."

"Where? At the club?"

"No, my house. He got in the window and scared the hell out of me, threatened to kill me if I didn't switch my business to him. He's just left, so if you want to send someone after him—"

"You any idea where he's headed?"

"He'll be at the Weehawken Ferry at Cortland Street. He's missed the one o'clock so he'll have to wait till one thirty for the next one. Send someone to kill the bastard."

She slammed down the receiver and got up from the bed. As she did so, the bedroom door quietly opened. She turned around. Franco was standing in the doorway. Mike was behind him.

"That was a dumb thing to do, Maxine," he said, coming into the room and pulling a gun from his coat. "Really dumb. Also not very friendly."

"I didn't do anything . . ."

"I listened on the phone downstairs. I thought you might call Big Johnnie. That's why I slipped you that business about going to Weehawken. Only rubes go to Weehawken, baby, and Franco's no rube."

He fired the gun twice, hitting her both times in the chest and killing her instantly. She slumped onto the bed, then slid off onto the floor. Franco walked over and took a look at her, then said to Mike, "Let's get out of here."

Mark was enraged, sickened and dumbfounded by the news of Maxine's brutal murder. How anyone could put a bullet into Maxine was incomprehensible to him. He was no stranger to violence; it had dogged his life ever since the Putumayo. But to kill a beautiful woman like Maxine who was carrying a child . . . that was barbarism beyond all belief. As he boarded the first train to New York to attend the funeral and help Maxine's widowed mother in her bereavement, he swore he would see Maxine's murderer in the electric chair. And he had no doubts who the murderer was. According to the papers, the police still had no suspect. Mark knew it was Franco.

When he got to New York and contacted the detective in charge of the case, a man named Mooney, he found to his rage that the police could do nothing to Franco, even after he told them about Franco's threat to Maxine. "Sure, it's possible he killed her," said Mooney. "It wouldn't surprise me. But we can't prove it. At least there's nothing in the house that connects Franco to the murder. One of the other residents in Grove Court saw two men running out of the house after the shots, but he was looking down on them from a second-story window and never saw their faces. So he can't identify them. But we'll bring Franco in for questioning and let you know."

Mark went to the Plaza and waited till late that afternoon, when he got a phone call from Mooney. "Sorry, Mr. Manning, but Franco's got an alibi. The night Miss Talbot was killed, Franco was in Washington, D.C. He's got two witnesses to prove it."

"I don't believe it!"

"Neither do we. He gave us the same business after the Asbury Park killings, but that doesn't help us any. The fact is Franco's smart. We know the witnesses are bought, or scared to death, or both. But there's not a thing we can do about it. He's got his alibi and so far it looks like it's going to stand up."

Mark, disgusted, hung up. He knew what he had to do, but it also meant overcoming his deep prejudice against associating with the underworld, as well as his justifiable concern about word getting around that the industrialist Mark Manning was dealing with racketeers. He decided he had no choice.

Pulling the card out of his wallet, he placed a call to Big Johnnie Marucca.

CHAPTER FIVE

The house was in the Dyker Heights section of Brooklyn, nearly indistinguishable from the dozen other houses like it on the tree-lined street—brick, homey, front porch, small front yard, the quintessence of middle-class respectability.

He was briefly inspected through a curtained window next to

the door by a burly man who Mark assumed was some sort of guard. Then the door was opened by a middle-aged man who appeared as mild mannered as the guard had seemed menacing.

"Mr. Manning?"

"That's right."

"Mr. Marucca's expecting you."

He was ushered into a narrow hall papered with bright-red roses; a Victorian coat-hanger latticed the left side. Mark gave his coat to the man, who introduced himself as Mario Lucarelli, "Mr. Marucca's accountant"; then he was led into the living room, where Big Johnnie was standing in front of the fireplace. He was dressed in a neat business suit, and as Mark entered the room the man looked at him without moving toward him. Mark remembered his previous encounter with Big Johnnie at the Golden Slipper. Realizing his dignity had been wounded by his refusal to shake hands, Mark sensed he would get nowhere unless he quickly repaired the damage. The man, after all, had his pride.

He came forward and held out his hand.

"Mr. Marucca," he said, "I appreciate your taking the time to see me."

It was an inspired move. Big Johnnie looked surprised. A smile creased his impassive face, and he shook Mark's hand warmly.

"No trouble, Mr. Manning, no trouble at all. I'm honored to have you in my house. Mario, some wine! I understand Mr. Manning likes his wine—I hope you like Italian wine?"

"Very much."

"Good. Here, take this chair. Make yourself comfortable."

Mr. Lucarelli had brought a cut-glass decanter filled with Verdicchio from an old-fashioned sideboard, and now he filled two glasses, giving one each to Mark and Big Johnnie. Then he quietly excused himself, leaving the room and sliding shut the heavy dark-wood doors.

"Mario's a good man," said Big Johnnie, taking a seat opposite Mark. "Been with me twelve years. It's very important to have a good accountant in business, you agree?"

"Very important. My accountant runs my life."

Big Johnnie smiled. "Well, your health." He raised his glass, as did Mark. The two men drank.

"Now," said Big Johnnie, "you've come to see me about Miss Talbot."

"That's right. I think we have a common problem, Mr. Marucca. I've talked to the police. They're convinced this Franco Ruggiero murdered Maxine, but they can't do anything about it because he's got an alibi. Now, I don't intend to let Franco get away with what he's done. You see, Miss Talbot was carrying my child, and we were going to be married."

Big Johnnie leaned over and patted Mark's sleeve.

"Ah, I had no idea. No idea at all. My profoundest sympathy, Mr. Manning."

"Thank you. The reason I contacted you was that it occurred to me that we might be able to help each other."

"I see." He ran his index finger over his lips rather daintily. "Well, Mr. Manning, I can tell you something the police would like to know. Miss Talbot called me the night she was killed. She told me Ruggiero had been to see her and had tried to put pressure on her to give him her business. She must have called me right after he left, because she said he'd gone to the Weehawken ferry and we could catch up with him there. Her last words to me were 'Kill the bastard.' Now, what happened after that I can only guess. But I imagine Ruggiero somehow overheard the phone call—maybe he hadn't left the house—came back and killed her. He's an animal, you know. What we Sicilians call a *delinquente*. He is drunk with the thrill of killing, which we disapprove of. He's dangerous, and he must be . . ." He made a slight gesture that left no doubt as to his meaning.

"We're agreed on that," said Mark. "But why don't you tell the police about Maxine's phone call? That would break Franco's alibi and put him in the chair where the bastard belongs."

There was a heavy silence, and Mark realized he'd said the wrong thing.

"It would mean my taking the witness stand," said the older man quietly. "Besides, we prefer to handle these matters ourselves."

"I see." Mark sipped some more of the excellent wine.

"I hope you understand, Mr. Manning?" continued Big Johnnie, sounding almost anxious not to offend his guest.

"Oh, certainly."

"He killed my cousin, Mr. Manning. *We* will take care of him."

"When?"

"That's another matter." The older man leaned back in his over-stuffed armchair. "Franco's a fox. He's not an easy man to get to. He's got himself a farm upstate, near Katonah. He has men with him, and guns and ammunition. It won't be easy. But sooner or later he will pay. You have my word on that, Mr. Manning, and I assure you I do not give my word lightly."

"But Mr. Marucca—and believe me, I wouldn't presume to tell you how to run your business—but it seems to me you have a real problem in getting at Franco. After all, it's been several months since the Asbury Park business—"

"Mr. Manning, when I say we'll take care of Franco, he's good as dead."

Big Johnnie was annoyed, but Mark felt he had to press. "I believe you; but right now he's very much alive and apparently inaccessible. Now if, as you say, he's a fox, then maybe what's needed is someone to smoke him out of his foxhole."

Big Johnnie looked interested. "What do you mean?"

"Franco knows you're after him, and I assume he knows most of your . . . associates. So it will be difficult for any of you to smoke him out. Correct?"

"Difficult, not impossible."

"However, he wouldn't necessarily be so careful about me."

"You? No, perhaps not. On the other hand, he knows you were Miss Talbot's friend, doesn't he?"

"Yes. But if I use the right bait, I think there's a good chance he might try to contact me."

"And what is the bait?"

"The Golden Slipper. Maxine's mother, whom I've talked to, has agreed to sell the club and to let me handle the sale. Now, not long before he killed Maxine, Franco tried to buy the Golden Slipper from her. He threatened her then. He obviously would take some risks to get something he wants so badly."

"How do you know all this?"

"She told me. I think if I run ads in the papers there's a good chance Franco might answer one of them. Of course, maybe he won't, but I think it's worth trying."

Big Johnnie nodded. "In other words, he makes contact with you, and you with us?"

"Exactly."

"But would you be willing to go to wherever we decided? Franco's no fool. If he saw you weren't there personally, he'd never go in."

"Why wouldn't I be willing?"

"It would be dangerous."

"I carry a gun. And Franco killed Maxine. I *want* to be there."

"What about the publicity?"

"I assume you know how to do these things discreetly. Naturally, I don't want my name involved. You'll have to give me your word on that. I'm willing to take the risk, but I insist on no publicity."

"I understand. I'm in somewhat the same position, after all. You have my word." Then he added, "Mr. Manning, my first impressoin of you was not a good one. I now see I was wrong. You are not only a businessman. You are a man."

"Then it's a deal?"

Big Johnnie extended his hand and they shook. Mark got up, saying, "When Franco hears the price I'm putting on the Golden Slipper, I don't think he'll pass it up. His price, that is. Anyone else who calls will find the price too stiff. For Franco, it's going to be bargain day."

Big Johnnie escorted him to the door. "Good! Very good!" He pulled apart the sliding doors. "Mr. Manning, if this works out, I will be in your debt. And Big Johnnie Marucca never welches on a debt."

Mark smiled as he shook his hand again. "And maybe someday I'll give you a call to collect."

The ads were run in all the metropolitan papers, listing the Plaza number and Mark's suite. For the first ten days the response was disappointing. The few people who called who seemed legitimately interested in the property quickly backed away when Mark announced the price of $250,000. It was, of course, a calculated risk—if one of the callers had been a front man for Franco, then the whole plan would collapse. But Mark took the gamble, hoping that a name or an accent on the other end of the line would signal to him that he was speaking either to Franco or one of his representatives. And he waited.

Meanwhile, he received a note from Charlotte, who was also in New York awaiting the final divorce settlement. She expressed horror about Maxine, which touched Mark deeply. It was typically gracious of Charlotte, who, despite their marital rows, had always retained the instincts of a lady. Mark felt a longing to see his soon-to-be exwife, so much so that he toyed with the notion of calling her and asking her to dinner, then rejected the notion, realizing it was pointless, that it was best not to risk further acrimony in a situation that was truly over. Better to have memories of the best and avoid the realities of the worst.

And there was another, unrelated reason. He was going to Washington. As a young man, Mark's view on politicians was that they all were a pack of rascals (beginning with Congressman Tutwiler, who in a sense had given him his start). However, he had come to admire Woodrow Wilson, for whom he had voted in the 1916 election. At the end of the war, during the Red scare of 1919, Mark, alarmed by the much publicized implications of a Bolshevik take-over in America, had become more conservative politically. And when at the 1920 convention Warren Harding from Marion, Ohio, had received the Republican nomination for President, Mark switched his allegiance to Harding and donated $50,000 to his campaign chest. Not that he thought much of the former editor; he had met Harding several times and had not been impressed. But having in the White House a man from Ohio favorably inclined to big business held obvious advantages to a big businessman from Ohio. Mark climbed aboard the bandwagon. His contribution had opened all the right doors in Washington, helping him in his efforts with the highway lobby. Now he was going to Washington for another reason, one that dealt with the very basis of his business and his fortune—rubber. . . .

In 1876 a young Englishman named Henry Wickham had managed to take out of Brazil 70,000 seeds of the tree called *Hevea brasiliensis.* Until that time no attempt had ever been made to plant and cultivate the rubber trees, the rubber kings of the Amazon being content to steal the raw material of their black gold from the wild trees in the jungle. Nor had the *Hevea,* the most superior of the several rubber-producing trees, ever been grown outside the Amazon basin, a condition with which the Brazilian rubber traders were more than content, giving them as it did a monopoly that they tried to preserve by forbidding exportation of *Hevea* seeds. Wickham, shocked, as was Mark years later, by the barbaric and chaotic methods of gathering wild rubber, and further aware of the economic potential of planting the trees, determined to get around the embargo. By some luck and judicious bribing of the appropriate Brazilian officials, he managed to get the seeds out of the country and across the ocean to London, where they were planted in Kew Gardens. The seeds that germinated were later transferred to Ceylon and thence to India, Malaysia, French Indo-China and the Dutch East Indies. By 1900, plantation rubber was beginning to make a dent in the wild-rubber monopoly. And by 1910, the production of plantation rubber was so great that it had killed the wild-rubber market forever, bringing an end to the fabulous rubber boom along the Amazon and turning into paupers the Brazilian rubber barons, who had been too greedy and shortsighted to take the trouble and expense to found their own plantations.

Not only were the plantations able to provide easy access to the trees and controlled growing conditions, but the planters—notably the Dutch—were able to improve the quality of the trees, principally by a method called bud grafting. Seeds of the best latex-producing

trees were planted. When the seedling was a year old, a small flap
was slit in the bark of the tree near the ground, under which a bud
cut from a "champion" or high-yielding tree was grafted. When the
bud had grown into the seedling and was sending out a shoot of its
own, the original trunk of the seedling would be cut off and the new,
bud-grafted tree would grow. In this way the quality of the trees was
continually improved, and the latex production increased to the point
where an acre of grafted trees could yield about 1,500 pounds of
rubber a year, or enough for about a hundred fifty car tires.

However, the order that was introduced into rubber production
by the plantations was offset by the chaos of the rubber market.
Prices fluctuated almost as greatly as they had in the days of wild
rubber, and the depression of 1921 had nearly ruined the planters by
knocking the bottom out of rubber prices, which had plummeted to
a low of fourteen cents a pound. To counteract this, the British
planters, especially in Malaysia, were bringing enormous pressure on
the Colonial Office in London—then headed by Winston Churchill—
to impose a quota system on rubber production that would stabilize the
price of raw rubber. Mark had been receiving cables from Sir Bruce
Clark in London that a government committee headed by Sir James
Stevenson was working to set up just such a system. Mark knew that
a quota system would force rubber products to remain at an artificially
high price and hurt sales. He was also sick and tired of being at the
mercy of foreign planters and rubber brokers half a world away. So
when he received an invitation at his Plaza suite to attend a White
House dinner being given by President and Mrs. Harding—that
battle-axe of a woman known as "the Duchess"—for business leaders
(which meant, Mark knew, that the hat was going to be passed to
build up the Republican campaign funds for the upcoming Con-
gressional elections), he accepted and took the train for Washington.
It was time to bring pressure on the Government to bring pressure
on the British to prevent the quota system.

Even more important, it was time to renew relationships at the
White House and the State Department. He would need all the
friends he could find in Washington to back him in a project he had
in mind.

For Mark intended to buy a country.

When he returned to the Plaza from Washington three days later
(after pledging $25,000 to the Republicans), he was given a list of

the eight names who had called while he was away. The one name that stood out was a Mr. Morello from Katonah, which was where Franco had his farm. (As Mark suspected, Franco's confidence that he was in the clear about Maxine's death, together with his strong desire to own the Golden Slipper, allowed him the openness of responding with minimum camouflage. And as for worrying that Mark might be dangerous as the vindictive boy friend, all he'd done when Maxine reported threats was to hire a chauffeur for her . . . besides, Franco would no doubt figure, even tough businessmen didn't kill anybody). So when Mark returned the call from Katonah, he wasn't surprised that Mr. Morello had an Italian accent.

"I was calling about the ad for the Golden Slipper club," said Mr. Morello. "Is it still on the market?"

"Yes, it is."

"How much are you asking?"

"One hundred and fifty thousand dollars."

A bargain, which fact Mr. Morello considered.

"Why aren't you selling through a broker?" he asked.

"Why should I pay a commission?"

"Are you Mr. Manning?"

"That's right. I'm handling the sale for Miss Talbot's estate."

"I see. Well, I'd like to take a look at the place."

"Fine. What time would suit you?"

"How about tomorrow noon?"

"I'll be there. You have the address?"

"Sure."

"I'll see you at noon tomorrow."

"Oh . . . uh, Mr. Manning?"

"Yes?"

"I may send an associate of mine. A Mr. Canova."

"All right."

Mr. Morello hung up.

Mark immediately placed a call to Big Johnnie and repeated the conversation.

"You say Morello had an Italian accent?"

"Yes."

"Then it wasn't Franco. His accent's all Brooklyn. It was probably Sal Carruci, his second in command. He may send Carruci to check you out and handle the deal."

"But Carruci, if that's who it was, said he might send a Mr. Canova, and that sounds like Franco wanting to take a close look at the place personally before putting down his money."

"Maybe. Have you ever met Franco?"

"I've been attacked by him with a knife, which wasn't the most pleasant way to meet the bastard, but I feel we've been introduced. I didn't get too good a look at him, though, if that's why you asked."

"But you're seen pictures of him?"

"Yes."

"That's the trouble—Franco may worry you'll recognize him. On the other hand, like you say, he may want to look the place over. Really look it over."

"What do you suggest?"

"Can you get me a key to the club this afternoon?"

"Yes."

"Then I'll have my men upstairs. They can watch from the windows, and if it is Franco, when he gets out of his car they can hit him."

"No, that's no good. At noon there are too many people on the sidewalk. Besides, I don't want to be involved with a street shooting. My name would be on every front page in the country! Wait till he gets inside the club. Then you can kill him and get the body out the back door and leave me out of it."

"And *that's* no good," countered Big Johnnie. "Franco's not going to go in the club alone—at least I'd be surprised if he did. He'll either have Carruci or Mike or one of his boys with him and that means there'll be shooting and you'd be caught in the middle of it. Do you want that?"

Mark hesitated, the memory of Bill Sands's bullet biting into his stomach. "No, I don't want that, but I don't see any other way, do you?"

It occurred to Mark that he should have felt it somewhat bizarre to be discussing possible ways of murdering a man less than twenty-four hours after dining in the White House. On the contrary, he found it exhilarating. Nor did he any longer feel any compunction about arranging with a criminal that most criminal of all crimes, a murder. Franco's guilt was unquestioned, and the law was helpless. It was almost his duty as a good citizen to take justice into his own hands—or so he told himself. The only real problem was doing it without getting his name in the papers.

Big Johnnie said, "Well, maybe we shouldn't do it in the club at all. Let Franco take a look around the place. Make it all business so he won't suspect anything. I'll have someone on the street watching him go in and out. When he gets back in his car, we follow him and take care of him when he heads out of town."

"Won't he know he's being followed?"

"Maybe. That's our problem. All you do is show him around the club. That way you'll be out of it. Okay?"

Mark hesitated. He wanted to be in on the kill of Franco Ruggiero. Mostly, of course, it was his hatred of the man, but there was also a curiosity to see the killing take place, a bloodlust he was reluctant to admit he felt but which was nevertheless there. Still, the complications and the danger outweighed any other consideration. He gave in.

The car pulled up in front of the Golden Slipper punctually at noon, fitting well the publicly established image of the underworld, a black Buick sedan with a rounded radiator grill. Two men were seated in the back, and Mike was driving. One of the men in the back got out and went to the door of the club as the Buick moved away from the curb and down the pushcart-filled street.

The man who shook hands with Mark at the club door introduced himself as Mr. Morello, a wiry little man with tight features, dressed in a pin-stripe suit and a Borsalino hat—he seemed to Mark the quintessence of hood-dom. He also seemed in a hurry to get inside the club and off the crowded sidewalk. Mark led him into the empty club and closed the door.

"Mind if I look around?" said Mr. Morello, his eyes moving around the table-filled room.

"Go ahead."

Mr. Morello then proceeded to search the entire house, not failing to check the kitchen, the basement (which Mark had to unlock), the rear alley, the upstairs rooms—he missed nothing. Finally satisfied the house was, in fact, empty, he returned to the front door, where he said to Mark, "My associate, Mr. Canova, would like to take a look."

"Fine."

Mr. Morello went back outside and waited until the Buick reappeared at the end of the block. It pulled up in front of the club, double-parking as Mr. Morello got into the back seat. A moment later Mr. Canova got out the other side and walked around the car to the curb. He came up to the door.

"Mr. Manning?"

"That's right."

"I'm Joe Canova."

They shook hands, and Mark led Franco Ruggiero into the club and closed the door.

"It's a nice place," Franco said, walking around the main room, poking his head behind the open stage curtains. "A nice place. Maxine Talbot had a real winner here. I've been here a couple of times when she was still running it—as a customer, I mean. It's hard to get a good idea about the layout of a place when it's jammed with people, you understand? Anyway, Maxine was quite a woman."

"I take it you knew her personally?"

"Oh sure, I'd met her a couple of times. Too bad she got knocked off. They have any idea who did it?"

"They think it was her bootlegger," replied Mark, following him up the stairs to the second floor. "But they haven't got any proof."

"Who was her bootlegger?"

"A man named Marucca. I don't know much about it. I was a close friend of Miss Talbot's but I didn't pry into the way she ran the club. Naturally, it wouldn't be wise for me to be mixed up with racketeers. People might not want to buy tires from a man who knew people in the underworld."

Franco pretended a surprised look. He was enjoying the game. "Don't tell me you're *the* Manning of Manning tires?"

"That's right."

"Well, I'm impressed. You make a good product, there, Mr. Manning."

"Thank you. What business are you in, Mr. Canova?"

"You mean you really don't know who I am?"

"Should I?"

"You've never seen my picture in the papers?"

"I live in Ohio, Mr. Canova."

Franco leaned close to him. "I'm Franco Ruggiero. Don't tell me Maxine never mentioned my name to you?"

"Why yes, she did! She said you were a bootlegger who tried to buy the club from her—"

"That's right."

Now Mark decided he should sound angry. "Well, what do you mean by using a phony name?"

"Look, Mr. Manning, I have to be very careful these days. There are a lot of people who don't like me. That's the reason I sent my friend in here first, to make sure this wasn't a set-up, you know what I mean? But a good, solid businessman like you from Ohio? I guess I can trust a man like you. Besides, I've been curious to meet you. You're a pretty important man and I like to know important men. I bet you're worth plenty. How much you think I'm worth?"

"Oh, a hundred thousand?"

Franco looked insulted. "That's peanuts. I'm worth one million bucks. One million! And I made it all myself, too. Just like I hear you did. Came right out of a tenement, didn't have any education, now I'm worth a million bucks. If I buy this place, I'll pay for it in cash. What do you think of that?"

"I think that's impressive."

Why not? thought Mark as Franco wandered through the empty gambling rooms. Why *not* . . . ?

"Maxine had a real class joint here," Franco said, running his finger over the felt poker table tops and admiring the backgammon tables. "Real class. Why are you letting it go so cheap? You could get more for it."

"I'm anxious to get rid of it."

"Why? Because a big important millionaire like you doesn't like to be mixed up with a speak?"

"That partly, and the fact that Maxine's mother is very upset and wants it settled quickly."

"It's nice of you to handle the sale for her."

"I'm a very decent person."

Franco grinned. "Yeah, I'll bet. That's how you got so rich, huh?"

He laughed and started up to the next floor. Mark followed, thinking how much this animal deserved to die . . . trying to buy Maxine's club after murdering her . . . it would give him such pleasure to do it personally . . . But that would be crazy. Let Big Johnnie do it.

"You know,' Franco went on, "my old man came to this country in ninety eight and he didn't have a pot. Came from Catania, my family'd been crapped on there for centuries. And now I'm worth a million bucks and I'm buying my poppa and momma a place out on Long Island where they can grow old and watch the seagulls."

"You're a decent man too, Mr. Ruggiero."

"You bet, long as it doesn't cost too much, know what I mean?"

"I think so."

"Well, the upstairs looks okay. The furniture goes with the place?"

"That's right. The poker tables alone are worth three thousand."

"I can believe it. Nice stuff. I want to see the kitchen. If I buy this place I want to serve good food. Most of the speaks are full of roaches, but Maxine kept this place clean and her food was good. I'd want to keep it the same."

Mark led him back downstairs. It was out of the quesiton . . . Of course it was lucky that Carruci and the driver were in the car . . . but they'd hear the shot and come in and kill him . . . and even if they didn't there'd be a mess with the police . . . unless of course he could fix it so they wouldn't suspect, which he might be able to do . . . God, how he'd love to kill this miserable bastard. . . .

"Have you ever killed anyone, Mr. Ruggiero?"

Franco turned, startled.

"Why?"

"Well, it's just that I've never met anyone connected with the rackets, and it's an interesting experience."

"Oh." He looked relieved. "That's tabloid stuff. They like to print crazy stories about the bootleggers. You know, sensational stuff. Nah, we just fill a public need, that's all. People want hooch and we get it to them and make a nice profit."

"Don't you even carry a gun?"

"Oh, maybe sometimes for self-defense. There's a lot of dangerous people walking around this city, you know. A lot of nuts. Is this the kitchen in here?"

"That's right."

Mark pushed open the kitchen door and Franco entered the gleaming room.

"Nice. Well equipped."

"Maxine put in a lot of new equipment when she opened the club."

"I can tell. And she kept it up. Very nice."

But what if Big Johnnie didn't get him? What if he gets Big Johnnie instead? Franco obviously didn't suspect anything was wrong . . . It would be easy, so easy . . . And it would be *sure* . . . A man should take his own revenge, not assign it to others . . . and it would be so easy here in the kitchen, so easy. . . .

"A nice, big refrigerator," said Franco admiringly as he opened one of the two heavy wooden doors and peered in. "Does this thing break down much? I hear these new electric jobs are pretty unreliable."

"As far as I know, they didn't have any trouble with it."

"Huh. Sure beats hell out of the old iceboxes, doesn't it? I can remember when I was a kid hauling blocks of ice up to our place on the third floor. The iceman wouldn't do it himself, the bastard. He said the climb was too much for his heart. If we'd tipped him a quarter, he'd have done it. But who had a quarter?"

His back was to Mark as he closed the refrigerator doors and Mark took a butcher knife from a rack above the stove and tucked it through his belt, covered up by his coat.

"Dishes and glassware go with the place?"

"Of course."

"How about the wines? I know Maxine had a cellar."

The cellar, Mark thought. Perfect. Even better than the kitchen . . . "Well, I have about a case of champagne left down there that doesn't go. But the rest of it I'll throw in."

"Can I take a look?"

"Sure. That door over there."

Franco went to the cellar door. "It's locked."

"I unlocked it for your friend," said Mark, coming over to the door, "and then I guess I locked it again."

Franco watched as Mark unlocked the padlock, thinking of Carlo Marucca in the house in Asbury Park, of how he'd shot him as he was trying to unlock the cellar door. Something else reminded him of Carlo. Was it that this jerk businessman looked nervous all of a sudden? For an instant he tensed with suspicion, then relaxed. What was he worrying about? Carruci had checked the place out, and Manning wasn't exactly the type . . . a *businessman,* for Christ sake.

Mark turned on the light switch at the top of the stairs.

"You nervous about something?" said Franco.

Mark forced a smile. "Not that I know of."

Franco laughed. "Look, relax. I won't bite you. Hell, I like you!" He slapped Mark's back.

"I like you too, Mr. Ruggiero."

"Call me Franco. You know something? That Maxine Talbot was one fine-looking woman. It was a shame what they did to her."

"Yes, it was. And she was carrying my child, too."

Franco momentarily looked worried. "Yeah, I heard. I'm sorry about that, a real damn shame."

He started down the cellar steps. "Nice basement," he said as he reached the bottom and looked around. "How's the furnace?"

"In good shape. I think Maxine told me the coal bill runs about a hundred dollars a year."

"That's not bad. Is this the wine cellar over here?"

"That's right. Watch out for that beam."

Franco ducked his head as he went across the cracked cement floor to an alcove lined with wine racks.

"I told Maxine she should have put a door on this to control the temperature," said Mark, coming up behind him. "But she didn't want to invest the money. Having the furnace this near is bad for the wines."

"I see. Looks like she has about ten to twelve cases here. Is any of it good?"

"Some. Most of it's mediocre, but she made a nice profit."

"There's a *very* nice profit in booze—"

Franco had just turned as he saw the knife coming toward him, its blade flashing as it caught the reflection of the ceiling bulb. Involuntarily he sucked in his stomach as the blade entered and went in up to the hilt.

He stumbled back against the wine rack, reaching for his gun. Mark's left hand grabbed his wrist as his right hand pulled the dripping blade free.

"That was for Maxine," he said, "and this is for my son."

Franco cringed, trying to grab Mark's arm, but he was already passing out from the pain. The knife plunged through his white silk shirt, ripped through the hairy chest skin and penetrated his heart. He slid down the wine rack, knocking several bottles to the floor as he slumped onto the cement.

Mark pulled the knife out of his heart and stared at the blood coming from the wound. He was trembling, but he also felt elated, satisfied. He leaned down and wiped the knifeblade on the tail of Franco's jacket. Backing out of the narrow alcove, he took a last look at the corpse sprawled on the floor, its mouth slightly open. Then he hurried back upstairs to the kitchen. He went to the sink and washed the knife, drying it thoroughly with a towel, rubbing the handle, then replacing it in its rack and washing the blood down the drain. He hurried out of the kitchen, through the empty main room to the front door. Opening it, he went out onto the crowded sidewalk. There was the Buick, parked in front of the bakery next door. He ran over to it and opened the back door. "Somebody was in the basement!"—he didn't have much trouble feigning shock—"some man with a knife—he stabbed Mr. Canova . . ."

Sal Carruci pushed Mark out of the way as he leapt out of the car, Mike right behind him, mumbling, "Big Johnnie—"

They ran toward the club.

"Shall I call the police?" said Mark, pushing his way through the startled pedestrians as he ran after them.

"No!" Carruci said. "You stupid?"

"But he's been murdered!"

"Shut up!" Mike said, shoving him away from the door as Carruci ran inside.

Mark went to the door and called after the two men, who were running now toward the kitchen. "He went out the back door into the alley!"

They didn't bother to thank him.

Mark closed the door and pushed his way through the crowd that was gathering in front of the club. "What happened?" asked an elderly woman. "Nothing," Mark said. "An accident." He made his way to the curb and hailed a cab to the Plaza Hotel.

By the time the cab reached Sixth Avenue, Mark's nerves were beginning to calm. Why should he feel upset at all? He had done the right thing. The *only* thing to do. He had gotten rid of a murderous roach. He had beaten the underworld at its own game, just as he had once beaten Wall Street at its own game.

As the cab sped toward the Plaza, he leaned back in the seat. He felt astonishingly good.

"You're really something, Mr. Manning," said Big Johnnie on the phone a half hour later.

"Well, it had to be done, and I had an opportunity too good to pass up. No one will ever know except you, and it's to both our advantage to keep it that way."

"Don't worry about that. I don't want people saying Big Johnnie Marucca had to get a Midwest businessman to do his work for him. It could be very bad for *my* business. No, the secret's ours, Mr. Manning, don't you worry about that. And I can understand why you did it—I'd understand better if you were Sicilian. But a nice Protestant gentleman, I didn't think you boys operated that way."

Mark smiled. "History says different, Mr. Marucca."

"Anyway, I'd like to thank you properly, even if it was *our* job."

"You're welcome to take the credit, Mr. Marucca."

"We intend to. But I'd like to have you over for dinner. Mrs. Marucca and I would be honored—"

"Thank you, but I'm sailing tomorrow night for London."

"Lunch?"

"No, I have some things to wrap up tomorrow. I'm turning over the sale of the club to a broker—I've had enough of the real-estate business—"

"You're not worried about the police? They're not going to do a thing, believe me. They're glad to get rid of Franco."

"I'm not worried about the police. This is a business trip I've been planning for some time. I want to visit my European dealers, and then I'm going to Africa."

"It's none of my business, but Africa? What are you going to do there?"

"Some sightseeing, and then some shopping."

"Well, it's been a pleasure dealing with you, Mr. Manning. And I hope you'll always feel free to call on me in the future. You've earned my gratitude, and like I told you, I never forget a debt."

PART

VII

THE KING BUILDS HIS KINGDOM

1925–1927

CHAPTER ONE

MONEY. SUDDENLY, everyone seemed to have it except the poor, and they were ignored. Everyone was playing the stock market, and it became chic for women to toss off the latest stock prices at cocktail parties. The great boom of the Twenties was in its full flood, and there were few people who didn't believe they were either better off than they had been before, or would be better off than they were now. (Booms create their own psychology just as busts do, and the mood in the Twenties was heady with optimism.)

It has been said that the twentieth century was not born until its third decade, which may be only partially true. The war was a historic watershed, but many of the attitudes, ideas and trends that are associated with the Twenties had existed in the prewar era: the independence of women, the revolt against Victorian prudery, jazz, urbanization. It is sure, however, that the look of the twentieth century—or, perhaps more accurately, its style—was born in the Twenties. Short skirts and dictators, dance fads and gang wars, a healthy hedonism and psychoanalysis—these became the hallmarks of the century, and they were popularized in the Twenties. The influence of the movies and the automobile on the public's consciousness was now enormous; but two other developments were changing American life almost as fundamentally.

One was radio. In the autumn of 1920 station KDKA in Pittsburgh began the first regular commercial broadcasts, and a radio craze swept the nation. At first, it was the simple crystal set, but this was quickly replaced by more sophisticated products, and by 1925 the country was spending $430,000,000 on radios and the whole nation was tuning in on the Clicquot Club Eskimos, the Eveready Batteries Symphony, the Dutch Masters Minstrels and the Manning Rubber Symphony—for Mark, who was profiting enormously from the radio mania by his investment in Acme Radio (an investment now worth

$30,000,000), had also decided to exploit the medium's advertising potential by sponsoring the symphony orchestra he had assembled as a surprise for Charlotte. It might not have served its intended purpose with Charlotte, but it gave birth to the Manning Music Hour, which not only pleased music-lovers around the country and sold Mark's myriad products, but also made Sylvius Lazlo a household name—in fact, to many a youngster of the day, the Czech conductor's name became synonymous with "long-hair" music. The impact of radio on the nation's mentality was enormous. Here was instant news and instant sensation, deliverable into the privacy of the home. And of course instant sales. The grip on the nation's collective mind that radio was able to make was not to be exceeded until the advent of television.

The other revolutionary force was installment buying. To a nation where the idea of thrift was firmly entrenched and where debt was considered a disgrace if not a sin, the idea of "enjoy now, pay later" was radically new. Yet it caught on. By 1929, time purchases had quintupled from 1920, amounting to six billion dollars. Everyone was buying everything on time: cars, homes, pianos, rugs, furniture, refrigerators, vacuum cleaners. Debt became respectable, and the enormous surge of buying made possible by this change of attitude helped fuel the business bonfire.

Automobiles shattered isolation, the movies packaged sin and excitement, radio invaded the home, time purchases reversed the time-honored concepts of home economics. Was it any wonder that the older generation was baffled by this brave new, weird new world? This new world of chain stores, chain letters and chain gangs? Where Paradise was Loew's Paradise in the Bronx, in which 3,936 moviegoers could ogle Gloria Swanson in a splendor of pseudo-Renaissance gilt statues that would have made the Medici gasp—or perhaps gag? Where Listerine advertisements hinted ominously that halitosis could doom females to spinsterhood, men to social ostracism. Where Crane plumbing ads brought chic to the bathroom, and American Radiator's Ideal Type-A Heat Machine (*not* furnace!) was so clean and handsome the advertisements featured men in dinner jackets and women in evening gowns standing in the cellar eyeing the Ideal. Aimee Semple McPherson. Leopold and Loeb. Babe Ruth. Ruth Snyder. Ponzi, George Washington Hill, Sinclair Lewis, Alexander Woolcott, Wilson Mizner, Al Capone, Bobby Jones, Peaches Browning, Al Jolson.

They May Have Laughed When the Twenties Sat Down at the Piano—But When They Started to Play!

The first white men to set foot in the country were Spanish slavers in the early eighteenth century, and the whites were to cause a century of misery to the blacks before they departed. The slavers named the broad river that flowed from the distant mountains into the Atlantic the Río de Oro, not because they had discovered any gold in it but because they hoped they would; nonetheless the name stuck to the country. The slavers built a settlement at the mouth of the Río de Oro and slavery flourished, the chiefs of the Mandingo tribe furnishing the slaves from weaker tribes in the bush. In the early nineteenth century, the slave trade was officially abolished. The business continued, but on a much reduced scale and the Spaniards, grown weary of the inhospitable climate and reduced profits, lost interest in the settlement. It was then, in the 1840s, that several Abolitionist and missionary groups in America, taking their inspiration from the success of Liberia, raised $3,000,000 and offered the sum to the Spanish government for title to Río de Oro's thirty thousand square miles. The Spaniards, thoroughly sick of the place, accepted, and the Abolitionists then gave the country over to American blacks who might wish to settle there.

In the next twenty years, until the end of the Civil War and Emancipation, more than 100,000 exslaves or escaped slaves took up the offer and returned to the continent of their ancestors. However, Río de Oro was no promised land. Situated near the Ivory Coast at the southwestern tip of the western bulge of Africa, it had a climate that was steamily tropical, and the Americans, even those from the deep south, found it difficult to adjust to. Moreover, there was little opportunity, there being practically no industry, and the indigenous blacks resented this invasion of foreigners who, in turn, tended to disdain the Africans as primitives. The first years of Río de Oro were most difficult.

A republic was set up with a president, vice-president and elected assembly; essentially the government and court system were a reflection of those in the United States. Even the capital city at the mouth of the river was renamed Tylertown after President Tyler (ironically, considering he was a slave-owner from Virginia). However, the country was divided into two sections, and the American-modeled government in Tylertown, dominated by the ex-Americans, could hardly be called representative of the nation as a whole. In the up country, in the Nimba Mountains, the African tribes still governed themselves and fought jealously to safeguard their independence from the Tylertown regime.

Meanwhile trade was growing, slowly but steadily. Coconuts, pineapples (which grew wild in the forest), and rich iron deposits in the mountains generated revenue, and the second- and third-generation Río de Orians had adjusted to the climate, the searing Harmattan wind, and to the country itself so that life for the exslaves' grandchildren was much easier than it had been for the original settlers. By the twentieth century, Río de Oro was sleepy and capital-poor, but able to provide a decent life for most of its citizens; perhaps most important, it was still independent at a time when Europe's colonialism was at its peak.

The World War brought an end to this sleepy placidity by drying up most of the nation's trade, and the country was plunged into a severe depression. During the early Twenties, Río de Oro tried to pull itself out of the economic hole by inaugurating government work projects, mainly road building, which was much needed in this road-poor land, but these were only stop-gap measures. The country desperately needed capital, and investor interest in the backward, humid place was minimal. Trade did pick up somewhat, but not sufficiently to repair the damage of the depression. The country, under the leadership of an energetic young president named Arthur Chadwick, was trying to move out of the slough of poverty, but it was finding the going almost impossibly difficult.

This was the situation when, early in 1922, Sir Bruce Clark cabled Mark that a rubber plantation forty miles north of Tylertown was for sale, and that he thought Mark should investigate it. The plantation, consisting of 30,000 acres, was owned by an English planter wiped out by the American depression of 1921, and he was asking $100,000 for the entire spread. After his satisfying disposition of Franco, Mark had gone to London, then taken a slow, hot ship to Tylertown, where he inspected the property (the "sightseeing" as he'd put it to Big Johnnie). He took with him a London expert on rubber trees who confirmed to him that the trees were in fact in excellent shape although it was almost a year since the plantation had been abandoned. And though the buildings were run down and the place rapidly going to weed as the jungle began to reclaim territory that had once belonged to it, Mark saw that the plantation, known as Las Palmas, had the advantages of perfect rubber-tree climate (lying as it did almost exactly on the fifth parallel of northern latitude), good soil, access to a nearby port, Tylertown, and trees already producing latex. He decided to buy (thus initiating the "shopping" aspect of his trip as described to Big Johnnie in their last telephone conversation).

Mark had been given letters of introduction to the American ambassador (who doubled as consul) as well as to President Chadwick, and when he returned to Tylertown from Las Palmas it was to bathe and change at the embassy, where he was staying, then go with the ambassador, Jerome Muhlbach, to Government House to dine with the president. Tylertown was then a city of about 40,000, which straddled the wide Río de Oro, and it was laid out in a gridiron pattern, its streets mostly unpaved, the shacks and huts of the poor being in many instances adjacent to the pleasant brick houses of the well to do. Government House was a four-story stucco building in the center of town, across the street from the long, low Assembly Building. Each floor of Government House was an arcaded verandah, which provided much-needed ventilation, and the house inside was furnished with attractive, modest good taste.

President Chadwick was a tall, impressive man in his early forties whose skin was raven black. He had been educated in America and wore Western dress—on this evening, a well-cut, white dinner jacket. His wife, on the other hand, wore native dress, a beautifully dyed flowing cotton robe. Several other of the country's top black officials were present, as well as half a dozen members of Tylertown's small white community, and as the group sipped gin rickeys in the big, airy lounge prior to dinner, Mark was surprised at how unself-consciously the blacks and whites seemed to get along. Whatever his faults, Mark was a remarkably unprejudiced man for his time. He despised anti-Semitism and discouraged all bigotry in his factories—except that no black man ever rose above the level of janitor in the Manning Company. As with most of his white contemporaries, he took for granted that black men were not the same as whites. They were servants, cleaning help, farm hands—supernumeraries in that huge operatic production called America, who, with rare exception such as George Washington Carver, never managed a featured role. Now, however, he was being hosted by the top official of a country who was not only powerful but educated, charming and black. Moreover, most of the others present were equally as charming and well educated and equally as black. The experience constituted a genuine culture shock for Mark, but being flexible in all things, he rapidly adjusted to the circumstances. And at dinner, when he was seated at President Chadwick's right, in the place of honor, he found as he talked with the man that Chadwick was as ambitious as he, albeit the president's ambition was as much for his country as for himself. He

struck Mark as a genuine patriot, proud of his country's achieve-
ments, but by necessity aware of and disturbed by its inadequacies.
He went on at great length about the problems of a tiny black republic in a world dominated by huge white and Asiatic powers. "It
is capital," he said at one point, "always capital. We are held back
without money, and money is the one thing we cannot seem to get
our hands on."

Mark, who had done research on Río de Oro and was acquainted
with its problems, began to see an opportunity to ingratiate himself
with the president of the country to which he was about to commit
millions of his own company's money.

"How much capital would you like to have?" he asked casually,
forking the delicious chicken cooked in palm oil and smothered with
grated coconut, rice and the fiery hot peppers of the region.

President Chadwick smiled. "As much as I could get my hands on."

"Would $20,000,000 help?"

Chadwick's eyes narrowed behind his gold-rimmed glasses. "Of
course. It would be an enormous help. But who's going to give us
$20,000,000?"

"Well, I think the present administration in Washington might
consider loaning your country $20,000,000 if the right arguments
were used. I'm not without influence in Washington. I think I might
be able to make a very persuasive case for you, Mr. President, if you
could furnish me with a breakdown of how you would use the money."

President Chadwick drank half a glass of the excellent beer served
with the hot chicken, then asked, "Mr. Manning, I don't have to tell
you that anything you could do for my country would be highly
appreciated. But why are you offering to do it?"

"That's simple. I'm considering buying the Las Palmas plantation,
as you know. If I buy it, I'll expand it and commit a considerable
capital expense to your country. So it's to my benefit as well if the
United States invests in your country—not only to promote good will,
but those roads Uncle Sam would be loaning you the money to build
would come in handy for my people too. So everyone would benefit,
and that's the best of all possible worlds, isn't it?"

President Chadwick nodded enthusiastically. "The best, Mr. Manning. I need hardly tell you I'll be delighted—delighted!—if you can
manage it."

"Well, let's keep it to ourselves until I can get back to Washington.
But I think there's at least a reasonable chance . . ."

There was something else in Mark's mind, but he didn't want to
reveal it to the president until he had the loan in his pocket. He

spent four more days in Tylertown studying the local conditions, making inquiries about the native rubber gatherers and constructions facilities; then he took another slow and very hot boat to Marseilles, stopping at Dakar en route. From Marseilles he trained to Paris, then Le Havre, where he boarded a liner for New York. Within six months he had exerted enough pressure in Washington to elicit a promise from the administration to try to ease the $20,000,000 loan through Congress as a rider on a naval-defense bill, the reasoning being that the loan would be based on the Río de Oro government's providing docking and coaling facilities at Tylertown for U.S. naval vessels. Mark's argument, however, was much more to the point, and it was one that he was able to get backing for from the War Department. Rubber, he declared, was a priority item in the event of another war —as had been established in 1917 and 1918. It was generally agreed that one of Germany's major weaknesses during the war was its inability to get sufficient raw rubber. America, which consumed half the world's rubber supply, still was almost totally dependent on foreign powers for latex, and unless the American rubber industry could obtain its own supplies, the defense of the country would be as vulnerable as Germany's had been. His argument (plus another generous contribution to the Republican Party) prevailed, the death of President Harding in August proving only a temporary setback, as his successor, Mr. Calvin Coolidge, was equally as friendly to big business and, more to the point, to Mark personally. In November 1923 the naval bill passed Congress, and a thirty-year three-percent, $20,-000,000 loan was officially offered to the government of Río de Oro on the condition that a fifty-year agreement be signed between the two nations regarding the docking and coaling privileges.

Before the bill was passed, however, Mark made another trip to Tylertown, this time taking with him Melville Benny and Bill Bixby. The tea-drinking chemist Mark had hired almost twenty years before had become one of his most valued executives and had risen to a position in the company subordinate only to those of Harold Swenson and Mark himself. Melville was that genuine rarity—an inspired research man and a gifted administrator as well. He had been responsible for a number of valuable innovations, including the setting up of a reclaim division where old tires were purchased, treated and reclaimed to be used in the manufacture of new ones. And his most recent triumph had been the development of a "balloon" tire, a tire containing a much higher volume of air than the old ones, thus providing a much more comfortable and relatively bump-free ride. The balloon tire was launched with an expensive promotion campaign and quickly proved to be a best-selling item. Thus, Mark had ample reason to value Melville, whom he had rewarded with promotion to the title of senior vice-president (just below executive vice-president Harold Swenson) with a salary of $150,000 a year, which, along with stock bonuses, had made the serious and brilliant chemist a millionaire at the age of forty-three. Now Mark decided to put him in charge of the enormous and complex job of initiating the Las Palmas plantation project; there was no one else he trusted more or felt was as capable of getting the project moving.

Melville, however, had been somewhat reluctant to sign up for a two-year stint in a part of the world known as the "white man's grave." In 1921 Melville's wife of almost ten years, Elizabeth Benny, had died in a bizarre accident; while eating dinner at the Elkins Country Club, Elizabeth had choked on a fishbone and before help could be administered to her, had died. A few months after his wife's funeral, Melville began exhibiting signs of interest in the widow of Carter Lang, Lily Swenson Lang. Melville's interest in Lily Lang inevitably provoked amused gossip. Melville was notoriously shy, his first wife had been a rather mousy woman, and for Melville now to fall in love with the ebullient Lily, the unconventional, hard-drinking member of the country club set who had lovers? Why, it was unthinkable! Yet Melville had fallen desperately in love with the much-younger Lily and, as soon as he thought a decent interval had elapsed after his wife's death, had proposed to Lily. She had rejected him —Melville was hardly her type; skinny nearly to the point of emaciation, a teetotaler and, in Lily's blunt description, dreary. Melville persisted, however, and Lily's father, Harold Swenson, increasingly worried about his daughter's drinking habits and the stories that were circulating around the country club about her untidy morals, began to pressure Lily into accepting Melville's proposal. Finally Melville's persistence paid off, not so much because of Lily's change of heart as the shaky condition of Lily's finances—she had long since spent her way through Carter's insurance and he had left no estate to speak of—so Lily had been living on her parents' handouts. Melville was rich, and he held a position of power in the Manning Company, which especially appealed to Lily. So, finally, she said yes. It was at this point that Mark had asked Melville to take on the Las Palmas project, and Melville, after numerous delays, had finally accepted. He wasn't at all happy about it, though, nor was Lily. She refused point-blank to go to the goddamn jungle, as she put it, and a miserable Melville had finally arranged what he felt was a miserable compromise. They would be married after he returned from the exploratory trip to Tylertown with Mark and Bill Bixby. Then, when he returned to Río de Oro, Lily would stay in Elkins waiting for her new husband to finish his tour of duty in Africa. For obvious reasons, Melville didn't like this arrangement at all. Lily, however, saw certain definite advantages in it. After all, the last thing she wanted from her marriage with Melville was Melville.

This, then, was the situation when Mark, Melville and Bill Bixby disembarked at Tylertown in October of 1923. They were met by the ambassador, Mr. Muhlbach, as well as several high-ranking members of the government—Mark was now a very important person in Río de Oro's future. They then ensconced themselves at the embassy, where Mark handed out five grains of quinine hydrochloride to Benny and Bixby, informing them that there were three inviolable rules for whites in Río de Oro: (a) every day without fail take five grains of quinine, or malaria was inevitable; (b) every day from nine thirty to four thirty wear solar topees whether the sun was shining or not, for the "red rays" of the sun were so fierce this close to the equator that they could penetrate clouds; and (c) never drink water that was not boiled for at least a half hour. His two associates swallowed the quinine and the advice, then they all proceeded to Government House, where President Chadwick greeted them in his office.

"Mr. President," said Mark after they had taken chairs, "it appears the loan is going through. Congress will vote on the bill soon, and I'm told that it has every chance of passing."

President Chadwick, seated behind his big mahogany desk, beamed and nodded.

"My ambassador has told me the same thing, Mr. Manning. Río de Oro owes you a great debt for your efforts in our behalf."

Mark crossed his legs, trying to make himself comfortable, which was difficult as the temperature was ninety degrees and the humidity must have been one hundred percent. It was nearing the end of the rainy season, but the rain was presently thundering down outside the verandah beyond the president's desk. Everyone in the office was glistening with sweat despite the five electric fans.

"Mr. Benny here is going to be in charge of getting the project launched," Mark continued. "And Mr. Bixby, who in my opinion is one of the best architects and planners in America, is going to draw up what we consider a very ambitious construction plan for Las Palmas. We intend to expand the present plantation in a major way. Our present projection is to have a permanent administrative staff of one hundred living on the plantation. This will require building a small town with a school, a hospital and sanitary facilities. We also want to build our own electric plant, and Mr. Bixby will show your officials a proposal he's going to draw up for building a small dam and hydroelectric plant on one of the tributaries of the Río de Oro. All this is in addition to what we want to do for the workers. For them—and we're projecting that we'll ultimately be hiring almost 20,000 men—we want to put up a large infirmary and free educational facilities for their kids if they want it. So you can see that we're contemplating an extensive building program."

"I can appreciate that," said the president. "And I'm delighted that your company intends to get into the social and medical fields as well."

"We have to," replied Mark. "No plantation is going to produce anything if the staff and the workers are sick with malaria and blackwater fever and everything else that plagues this area. Now, we've bought 30,000 acres at Las Palmas, as you know. However, to make the expense we're going to undertake economically feasible, we need more land. In other words, the amount of rubber our 30,000 acres ultimately can produce isn't going to be worth it to us. So what we would like to get from your government is a commitment to lease to us on a ninety-nine year basis whatever additional lands our men determine would be suitable for planting."

President Arthur Chadwick was no fool. He was fully aware Mark Manning was a hard bargainer who would try to extract every advantage possible in return for the $20,000,000 loan he had arranged. Now, after the preliminary pleasantries, Río de Oro was about to hear the extent of the *quid* they would be obliged to put up to get their *quo*.

"But certainly you don't expect me to sign a blank check for you, Mr. Manning?" he said, smiling to cover his annoyance. "After all, you might try to take over the whole country!"

"Oh, nothing like that. There would be a limit, of course."

"How much?"

"A million acres. You would lease to us up to a million acres at a rental of five cents an acre per year for ninety-nine years."

Silence except for the dull roar of the rain and the whirring of the electric fans. The President pressed a buzzer on his desk and a male secretary appeared at the door. "Tell Mr. Simpson, Mr. Despard and Mr. Bartlet I'd like to see them at once."

"Yes, Mr. President."

The secretary closed the door and the President looked at his three white guests.

"I think," he said, "that my attorney general, my vice-president and my treasury secretary should hear the rest of this."

Mark nodded. "I understand."

What had begun as a welcome, ceremonial meeting had quickly become a tense bargaining session. They waited in silence until the three officials came into the president's office. Then they were introduced, chairs drawn up, and the president reiterated Mark's first demand. The officials looked surprised.

"A million acres?" said Mr. Simpson, the attorney general. "At five cents an acre? That strikes me, to say the least, as an excellent bargain for you, Mr. Manning."

"Yes, but remember we're going to be giving a lot of your people steady employment. But you'd better hear the entire package."

The officials and the President looked uncomfortable.

"Let's hear it," said Mr. Chadwick.

"All right, the first item is the land. The second item is our rights on the land. We want extraterritorial guarantees for all our company people. In other words, they will be immune from any interference from your government. If there is any civil or criminal dispute involving any of our personnel, the matter will be handled by us. In the case of litigation, that will be referred to Mr. Muhlbach, the ambassador, and the court action will be sent back to the States to go through the American courts."

"No!" Chadwick exclaimed angrily. "That's absolutely out of the question! You're asking us to give up our own sovereignty on our own territory!"

Mark nodded. "Exactly. But we feel it's necessary to protect our people. But as I said, you'd better hear the entire package."

The President nodded curtly.

"Third—we want a guarantee from your government that you will not interfere in any way with our work force. In other words, we hire and fire the workers as we please, we set the working conditions and salaries as we see fit, and we want a guarantee of no unions of any kind. On the other hand, we recognize the right of your government to inspect the plantation and working conditions at any time. We intend to treat the men well—I think you know my reputation in this area—but we want *no interference*."

Silence. Mr. Bartlet, the heavy-set secretary of the treasury, said, "What kind of salary are you planning to pay, Mr. Manning?"

"A shilling a day."

Río de Oro used the English currency system. The Secretary

smiled sarcastically. "You're very generous, sir. Would that include chop? Food?"

"That would include lunch. And free medical care and schooling, of course."

"Well," said the President, leaning back in his chair, "I don't think anyone's going to get rich working for you."

"The country will get rich, Mr. President," replied Mark, pleasantly. "Or at least rich-*er*."

"And yourself? I suspect you're going to end up quite a bit rich-*er* too, Mr. Manning."

"That's part of my business, Mr. President. I certainly could never justify to my stockholders the amount of money we intend to invest in Río de Oro unless I could show a reasonable profit on the venture. We've calculated that a shilling a day is the most we can offer the workers and still show a profit."

"Is *that* the entire package?"

"There's one more item. Of course, there will be a few more points that my lawyers can work out with you later on if we agree to go forward. But these are the main terms."

"And what is the last item?"

"Naturally, the huge investment we'll be making in Río de Oro is only as secure as the government itself, and I don't have to tell you gentlemen that politics is an uncertain profession. You, Mr. President, face a re-election in four years. I have no doubt you'll win, but we have to take the very long view. Someday someone else will be sitting in this office who might not be as statesmanlike as yourself, who might initiate government policies that would be—let's say—unhealthy for the country and for us as well. So for that reason we want a guarantee from your government that the manager of Las Palmas—Mr. Benny for the time being—will be kept informed of all government policies as they are being formulated—"

"*What?*"

"—all policies," went on Mark, undisturbed by the outburst, "domestic and foreign. All financial commitments, all treaties—"

"Never!"

"—anything, in short, of any importance that would affect the future stability of Río de Oro and our investment. We don't ask for a veto power—"

"How generous of you!"

"All we want is to be kept informed. And naturally, if the government is launching a venture that we think is unwise, we would hope that you would listen to our arguments against it. And I might add, the arguments of the United States government, which also will have a considerable vested interest in the stability of Río de Oro."

"Is that *all?*"

"That's all."

President Chadwick got up from his desk and walked to the door of the verandah. The others watched the big man whose six-foot-three height and imposing physique gave him a look of powerful dignity. He stared for a moment out at the rain. Then he turned and looked at Mark.

"Mr. Manning," he said quietly, "you are asking us to guarantee to you a million acres of our country at a laughable rental. Extra territorial rights over those acres that amount to annexation by a foreign power. Complete freedom to deal with our people as you see fit, with no interference from us, their elected officials. And what amounts to involvement in our government's policy making at the highest level. Why don't you simply raise an army and attack us?"

"I think you're somewhat overstating our position."

"No, sir, I'm not! You want what no government with any self-respect could agree to."

"We're simply trying to protect ourselves, Mr. President. We intend to create work for thousands of your people—work and health care and education. We intend to make Río de Oro one of the most important rubber-producing countries in the world. Through the government loan, we'll bring you capital you yourself said you must have to help your country build up its economy. Now, in light of all that, do you really think these requests are so unreasonable?"

"Yes, I do! You're asking us to give up our identity as a nation! Our national soul, if you will. Do you really think any nation can sell or trade off these things and survive? You must be either naïve, stupid or crazy if you do!"

Mark got to his feet. "I don't think I'm any of those things, Mr. President. However, our position is nonnegotiable. If you can't see your way to granting us these requests—"

"Demands! Not requests."

Mark shrugged. "Demands, then. We'll call off the whole thing. Including, naturally, the $20,000,000 loan. The last thing we want is to enter into a long-range project with bad feelings on either side."

The President spread his hands in a gesture of outraged frustration.

"But this is exploitation! Colonialism of the worst sort, because you're getting all the advantages of sovereign rule without any of the responsibilities!"

"That's not true! We *are* accepting responsibilities for the workers. I told you we'd give them excellent medical care, housing . . ."

"Only because you can't *afford* to let them get sick!"

"What the hell difference is the *reason?*" Mark was now angry himself. "The *effect* is what's important! You talk about your nation's soul and its honor and self-respect . . . Río de Oro is a backwater country. You know it! What good does self-respect do your people when they can't read, when they die of sleeping sickness and malaria, where there's no jobs for them? A man has self-respect when he has money in his pocket, food in his belly and reasonable security for his future."

"I've heard that argument from you whites *so* many times," said the President, dropping his voice. "*So* many times. It's your favorite tune because you know it's half true and it's seductive. But, Mr. Manning, it is only half true. The other half is that my people already have food in their bellies and they have security in a way of life that has kept them reasonably content for centuries. Why should they sell out all this for a shilling a day without full chop?"

"*Your* people?" said Mark. "But you're an American, Mr. President."

"On my father's side. My mother was from the Grebo tribe."

"Do you go your father's way, or your mother's? Do you enter the twentieth century or do you stay in the tenth? Maybe you're right. Maybe your country is better off just as it is. Maybe what we Americans consider progress wouldn't benefit Río de Oro. *I* don't believe it, but I can see how you might. In that case, it's better that we find this out now before the commitments are made, before Congress passes the loan agreement. On the other hand, I have an idea there are a lot of your people who are restless with the old ways, who want to try the new—no matter what it costs them. The decision is yours to make. I don't see any point in going on with this discussion until you and your government have decided what to do. Gentlemen?" He shook hands with the officials. Then he leaned across the desk and shook the President's hand.

"Think about it," said Mark. "The twentieth century or the tenth. Progress or stagnation."

President Chadwick glared at him with ill-disguised hostility. "You pose me a terrible dilemma, you know."

Mark smiled. "Mr. President, you'd be in the same dilemma even if you'd never met me. Sooner or later, you or one of your successors are going to have to make the choice. And come to think of it, I don't even believe you have much of a choice. No nation will be able to hide from progress much longer."

The President released his hand.

"*You* call it progress, Mr. Manning. I'm not so sure."

Mark nodded, turned to Benny and Bixby. "Let's go back to the embassy."

They left the office and walked past several uniformed guards until they reached the street. The rain had finally stopped. As they walked around the huge puddles, Melville Benny said, "You really put it to them."

"I guess I really did. I hope with both barrels."

"Do you think they'll buy?"

"They'll buy. Oh, there'll be some more talk about honor and independence to save face, and we may have to back down some, but in the end they'll go along."

"What makes you so sure?"

Mark jumped over a puddle.

"Because it's a damn good deal. We're offering money. They need it, and they need us. They need us a lot more than they need to save their souls."

He was right. After three days' deliberation, they agreed to Mark's conditions, though first extracting from Mark a penny a pound export duty on the raw rubber, which he was willing to give to get the rest of the package. Then he cabled his New York law firm to send out their experts to Tylertown to get the agreement down on paper, after which it would be presented to the assembly for passage. Meanwhile, he went over with Bixby and Melville Benny not only the plantation itself but all his plans for the place, plans that had been developing in his mind for months. "This isn't a pleasant place for white men to live," he told them. "We're going to have to do everything we can to *make* it pleasant so we can get good men to stay out here." And even though he felt plantation life was not for women, he said they should plan to build at least half the houses as family dwellings, "because until you get women and children in a community, you're not going to have any stability. And stability is what we have to design into this place. That's why I held out for those terms with the government—this place is going to supply Manning with raw rubber long after all of us are dead and buried. Las Palmas has got to be built *right*."

The problems were enormous, however. Not only living quarters for the staff had to be planned, but also a school and a hospital and a sewage-disposal plant; a firehouse; a chapel; a radio station; a shopping center, as well as a poultry and pig farm and a truck garden to supply fresh eggs, meat and vegetables (cattle, unfortunately, were subject to the dreaded tsetse fly, and they gave little milk in the heat anyway, so that fresh milk was virtually an impossibility to supply); guard houses and facilities for a police force; and a "palaver" hut to settle disputes with the native workers. ("Palaver" was a pidgin word for "talk," but, like most pidgin expressions, it had a latitude of meanings. "Mammy palaver" was a fight over women. "Kitchen palaver" or "chop palaver" could be a morning session to plan the day's menus. "Court palaver" was a lawsuit. Pidgin was the language used by the uneducated natives to communicate with the educated, the whites and, in the cases of tribal differences, each other). The three men threw themselves into the project, working day and night for two weeks until Mark felt most of the basic problems had been solved. Then he left Benny and Bixby to wait for the lawyers and took a boat for Marseilles for a month's vacation on the Riviera.

On his fifth night at the Negresco in Nice he was pleased to receive a cable from the Secretary of State in Washington informing him that the naval-defense bill had passed Congress and the loan had formally been accepted by President Chadwick.

During the following year, Mark devoted at least half his time to the Las Palmas project, hiring experts in tropical diseases from the Harvard Medical School to go to Río de Oro and set up the hospital, at the same time donating $100,000 of his own money to Harvard for further research in anopheles-mosquito control. Slowly, the construction proceeded, and by 1925, the plantation was in operation, almost 100,000 additional acres having been leased from the government for clearing and the planting of new bud-grafted trees. The impact of all this on Río de Oro was stunning. When the agreement with the Manning Company was introduced to the assembly by President Chadwick, the opposition put up strong arguments against it, claiming it was a "sell-out" to American dollar diplomacy. However, despite his private agreement with the criticism, Chadwick had committed himself to the venture, and he had no choice but to force the bill through. Ironically, he used Mark's own phrase in his speech to the assembly urging passage. He said, "Río de Oro must choose between progress and stagnation." Río de Oro—or at least the Tylertown government—opted for progress.

But in the up country, in the "Devil bush" of the Nimba Mountains, the tribal chiefs—descendants of the chiefs who had fought the "invasion" of the American slaves three generations earlier—thought differently about the American loan and the Las Palmas plantation project. To these men—leaders of the Krus, the Grebos, the Mandingos, the Vais—the agreements were further evidence of the treachery of the Tylertown regime. The chiefs saw it as nothing more than yet another invasion of their country, another annexation of their land.

And one of them, a young Kru prince named Tegai, decided to do something about it.

CHAPTER TWO

In June of 1926 Roger Boine, having already earned an A.B. from Amherst, was graduated third in his class at the University of Pennsylvania Medical School. Roger, now twenty-six, was a strapping, handsome young man who had impressed all his instructors at Amherst as well as at Penn with his pleasant personality, his intelligence and hard work. It didn't matter that the "sheiks" in his class thought him a grind, or that he never carried a hip flask to football games, or that he couldn't play the uke and, in fact, didn't even know all the words to "Lord Jeffrey Amherst." Most of his classmates still regarded him as a regular guy, even though he had a tendency to take life a bit seriously and didn't date much. But then, he was always hitting the books, so he didn't have much time for girls. His friends figured that one day poor easy pickings Roger would meet some knockout of a flapper and, because of his inexperience, be taken for a ride. This gave them a pleasant sense of sophisticated superiority that offset their envy of his spectacular grades. As a result Roger could be and was well liked despite his studiousness.

And now he was a doctor, and no parent watching the commencement exercises was prouder than Sheila Farr Boine Harrington. Sheila, indeed, had come a considerable distance since that night twenty-six years earlier when Roger had been conceived on the zinc-topped kitchen table in her mother's restaurant in Elkins, and Sheila's success in her own field was almost as remarkable as Mark's had been in his. She had cofounded the *American Woman* magazine with Calvin Harrington, now her husband, and after years of struggle, the little magazine had gradually grown in circulation until it was now one of the most successful of the slick women's biweeklies in the country. Calvin and Sheila had moved the company headquarters from Cleveland to New York, where, being majority stockholders in the magazine, they had become wealthy and influential publishers—more than gratifying Sheila's early dreams of becoming a reporter. She looked the successful career woman—smartly dressed, graying hair fashionably cut, and Roger, as he joined her to drive into Philadelphia for lunch at Bookbinders, was as proud of his mother as she was of her son. Calvin hadn't been able to make the graduation, confined to bed with a bad cold. After a fine meal, Sheila asked the question she had been holding back all day. "You haven't told me where you're going to take your internship, Roger."

"Well," he said, "the reason I haven't told you is that I don't think you're going to like what I'm considering."

"Oh, oh," she said, "this sounds dangerous. Let's see, you've fallen in love with a millionaire's daughter and she's got you a job at some Park Avenue hospital where you're going to have to compromise all your principles and become a specialist in rich women's neuroses."

Roger laughed. "Not exactly. I got a letter from Uncle Mark last week . . ." (Sheila winced; she hated to hear him call Mark "uncle," but it was a habit he'd fallen into years before at the Wooster School, and she had never been able to break him of it) ". . . and he's asked me if I'd like to take my internship at his hospital in Río de Oro. You know, at the Las Palmas plantation. I'm thinking of doing it."

"Africa?" she finally said. "But why would you want to go there? Of all the Godforsaken places—!"

"But that's what's exciting about it! It's different! It's a chance for me to see the world, or at least part of it, and the hospital's run by Dr. Vandeventer, who's got a great reputation, and . . . well, I'd just like to do it. I think it would be a great experience for me."

She told herself to stay calm. She knew he could be stubborn. He was, after all, Mark's son.

"Well, of course, if you *want* it . . . but with all the offers you've had here in the States—really excellent offers—I don't see why you'd want to go bury yourself in the jungle for two years."

"There's also a very practical reason. It will pay me a hundred dollars a month plus free lodging and food, and that's a lot more than

I can get here. Plus I'll be able to save most of that, which will come in handy later when I start my practice."

"But, darling, that's a short-sighted reason to throw away two years of your life! You know Calvin and I can lend you whatever you'll need to get started—"

"I want to do it on my own, mother. And I won't be throwing away two years of my life. I'll have a chance to treat a lot of diseases most doctors only read about in textbooks, and I should be able to get a good deal of surgical experience out there because the staff at Las Palmas is small and I'll have more responsibility than I would in a big hospital. Don't you see? It's that special opportunity that comes once in a lifetime—it doesn't even come once in most people's lifetimes—and, well, I want to grab it."

"I still think it would be a huge mistake. I've had such high hopes for you—you've done so well—and I just think going off on some crazy junket to Africa would be a crime—"

"If nothing else, I owe it to Uncle Mark."

"You don't owe him a thing," she said sharply.

"Oh, come on, mother, I know you don't like him because he's an evil conservative and you're a big New York liberal . . ."

"You don't have to be so flip about it!"

"I'm not. But you've always run him down, and I just don't think it's fair. He's doing a tremendous thing out there! He's bringing modern medicine to those natives, he's built them schools—"

"The one thing you've never understood about Uncle Mark is that he is, in fact, an evil man, though you may think that sounds melodramatic and like a big joke. He's an evil man who happens to be clever enough to make the evil he does *look* good. And you and most of this country swallow it."

"Oh, come on, what's so evil about building hospitals and schools for Africans? And look at all the things he's built in Elkins and what he's done for his workers. And there's the concert hall, the gym at Wooster—and let's not overlook the small fact that he paid for my education—"

"He lent me the money when I was broke, which you weren't supposed to know—and I'll never forgive him for telling you!" she said. "And I've tried dozens of times to get him to take the money back, which he's refused—just to spite me. So there's no reason to think you owe him a cent."

"But mother, the fact is he *did* give you the money when you needed it. And aside from the fact that I want to go to Las Palmas, to be honest with you, I repeat that I think I owe it to him to go."

She looked at him and knew she had lost. The realization intensified her bitterness, and the wild notion occurred to her that this was Mark's revenge—taking her son away from her to punish her for her unforgiving hatred of him. Or maybe it was because he was now laying claim to his property—and that's how he would think of Roger. It was damnable. She almost wished he had never come back into her life that afternoon back in 1913, except she had to admit Roger would never have had his superb education if he hadn't. The fact that she now was wealthy herself made it even that much worse—if she'd only had the money sooner! But she hadn't and Mark had been there. . . . Oh, God, how she hated him! And yet, to be fair—which was difficult—Roger *was* his son. He did have some claim on him, she supposed. But how she hated him for that claim . . .

"Mother," said Roger, reaching over to take her hand, "there's another reason I want to go. You see, I know."

She looked surprised. "You know what?"

"I know who Uncle Mark really is. I've known for years."

She was stunned. She couldn't speak for a moment.

"How did you . . . find out?" she finally said, trying her best not to make a fool of herself and cry.

"It wasn't too hard. Mostly, all I had to do was look in a mirror. Let's face it—no pun intended—I'm a carbon copy. Besides, why else was he paying for my education and coming down to see me all the time? So you see, I want to go to Las Palmas for him. Because he's my father, and he's offered me an opportunity."

Now the tears *were* coming down her cheeks and she couldn't help it. She wiped them with her napkin as she tried not to give way completely to her emotions. "I understand," she said, forcing a smile after she had wiped her cheeks. "I probably should have told you myself a long time ago, except that I was afraid it might hurt you, or you might think the less of me for it."

"You know I wouldn't have done that."

"A mother *never* knows what her son may think of her," she countered firmly. "Anyway, I suppose it's better this way and I *can* understand why you want to go out to Africa, but Roger . . ."

"Yes?"

She squeezed his hand and smiled. "I'm going to miss you terribly."

"And I'm going to miss you. And Calvin. But it's not as if I'm going away forever. I mean, it's only two years, after all."

"I suppose you're right," she sighed, releasing his hand and signaling the waiter for the check. Then she looked at her son again and said, quietly, "I'm so proud of you, darling."

It was a simple remark, but it said it all.

———————

The rich get richer, and that bromide was being well flogged by the fortunes of Mark Manning. By 1926, the Manning Rubber and Steel Corporation—as it had been renamed in 1925 when the steel-products division grossed over a hundred million in sales, making it difficult to ignore it any longer in the corporate title—was one of the fifty largest corporations in America, with annual sales of more than $500,000,000. The empire included sixteen rubber factories in America and abroad, five steel mills, two cotton mills, the cotton plantation in Texas and two more in Georgia, as well as the Las Palmas plantation in Africa and more than 1,200 dealerships around the world, most of which were at least partially owned by the parent company. The corporation also controlled three banks, each capitalized at over $100,-000,000, and a finance corporation called Manning Finance, which had originally been acquired to handle the time-purchase sales of the tire division but which had since branched out into the personal-loan business and now operated in twelve states.

Mark's holdings in this mammoth organization were worth $120,-000,000, but his other investments, notably in real estate and Acme Radio, had swollen his fortune to the $200,000,000 mark. In 1926 he filed one of the largest income-tax returns in America. His gross income for that year was just under $15,000,000. On that, after deductions, he paid total taxes of less than $500,000.

The rich got richer.

Since the death of Maxine Talbot and his divorce from Charlotte, Mark had become a loner and a drifter as well, spending a great deal of each year traveling. In the four years from 1922 through 1926, he visited most of the countries of the world, including in 1923 a trip to the Far East, where he opened a rubber-purchasing office in Singapore (despite his plans for Las Palmas, the company would still depend on the Malaysian rubber plantations for years to come), visited Saigon, Hong Kong, Shanghai, Peking, Tokyo and Manila and explored the considerable pleasure potential of each of those metropolises. Of all the places he visited, Spain captured his imagination the most, and he fell in love with that beautiful country, being enchanted by the Alhambra and overwhelmed by the austere magnificence of the

Escorial monastery and royal residence. That a farm boy from Ohio
would find his fancies realized in a place so utterly different as Spain
was not so unusual; postwar Europe was alive with Americans in
love with either Spain or France or Italy. But Mark had the where-
withal to do something about his new romance.

In 1926, after the collapse of the Florida real-estate boom, he took
a train to Palm Beach to see if he could pick up a land bargain.
There were few bargains; even the collapse of the boom failed to
affect prices in that stronghold of the superrich. But he was shown
four acres of superb beachfront in an area still comparatively empty,
which were going for a relatively bargain price. He bought them.
Hearing that the king of Palm Beach architects, Addison Mizner,
was not only expensive but also in the habit of leaving such useless
details out of his blueprints as doors and stairways, he hired his old
standby Bill Bixby, who had been made one of the more successful
architects in the Midwest by Mark's many commissions. "Bill," he
said, "I want to build a Spanish castle like the Escorial with a garden
like the Alhambra. Can you do it?" Bixby was a bit stunned by this
stylistic nightmare, but allowed as how he'd try. A month later he
came up with a design for a house that would be charitably referred
to as "unusual," whereas a more astringent verdict might be "vulgar."
It didn't matter—Mark was delighted by it. Undeterred by the estimate
of $3,000,000, he told Bill to go ahead. It was to be what many con-
sidered one of the grandest monuments to self-indulgence of the era,
an "epiphany of bad taste." Mark had a great deal of personal style
and surely was a man not without taste. But when it came to "Villa
del Mar," as the Spanish palace came to be known, his innate sense
of proportion lost out to his desire to build a lavish monument to
his success.

His interest in building Iberian mausolea was a new direction for
Mark, who up till now had shunned ostentation, or at least the more
obvious aspects of it. River Bend had been Charlotte's toy, and the
fact that he now spent as little time there as possible, having grown
to dislike the huge place except on those occasions when his children
were there, might have suggested that the last thing in this world that
he needed was an even bigger empty manse to rattle about in. The
opposite proved to be the case. His loneliness and increasing sense
of a lack of driving purpose had combined to give birth to a new
enthusiasm: acquisition. Not acquisition of new markets or more
money; that appetite had become, if not sated, dulled. He would
continue to invest, but he was too rich now to get much pleasure from
becoming richer. And the giant corporation he had fathered two

decades earlier was now, if not running itself, being run by Harold Swenson and the three dozen vice-presidents and hundreds of assistant vice-presidents, lawyers, accountants, salesmen and foremen under him—at least on a day-to-day basis. Mark made only major policy decisions, and this was not enough to keep his active mind busy. The answer for him was to plunge into the heady waters of acquisition, and, like so many rich men, he was bitten by the art bug. Rich men collected art, so there must be something to it. The only problem was, he knew nothing about it.

So, in his fashion, he decided to go to the best—the best art dealer in the world. At ten in the morning of the sixth day of October 1926 the discreet young male secretary of Sir Grigory Barjoonian came quietly into Sir Grigory's richly appointed office and said in his discreet upper-class English tones, "Mr. Manning is here."

Sir Grigory looked up from his ormolu desk. He had fierce Armenian eyes under fiercer bushy gray eyebrows that twisted upward, giving him a Mephistophelian look. His rich beard bristled aggressively, gray and black hairs springing out in all directions in contempt for the confines of manicuring. On his beaked nose perched an aristocratic gold pince-nez. His steel gray hair, the only part of his head that seemed tamed, was brushed back smoothly. His dark gray suit was impeccably tailored, his wing collar and dark blue polka-dot bow tie faultless; his hairy but expressive hands were, unlike his beard, carefully manicured. The man gave the impression of barbaric Armenian cunning encased in a Savile Row binding, which was precisely what he was. Grigory Barjoonian had come to London in the '80's a penniless Armenian emigrant. He got a job as stock boy at Christies and rapidly climbed the ladder. He learned a little about art, a lot about trading, and everything about the rich, and in 1906 he opened his own gallery in London. It was a success. Six years later, the newly knighted Sir Grigory bought an elegant townhouse on Sixty-second Street off Fifth Avenue and opened a New York branch; it became a fabulous success. When the superrich wanted to play the art game —to massage their egos by buying a piece of immortality, as it were— they came to Barjoonian and Co.

"Let him wait a bit," said Sir Grigory to his secretary. Sir Grigory's voice was an important part of his equipment. It could thunder; it could coo. It could bully; it could seduce. And all this with a thick *sui generis* Armenian-English accent that defied imitation.

"How long, Sir Grigory?"

"Oh . . ."—He smiled slyly—"until he gets hungry."

The secretary nodded and went back out to the gallery, where

Mark was looking at the dozen or so paintings hanging from the walls of the long rectangular room. "Sir Grigory will be with you shortly, Mr. Manning," said the secretary. Mark, who looked dapper himself in a Glen-plaid suit, nodded as the secretary returned to his French desk and sat down. The place was otherwise empty, and Mark thought it was something like a tomb. The long beige walls, devoid of any ornamentation except the silent paintings. The rich Persian rug on the marble floor. The occasional French chair by the walls, and the two padded leather benches in the middle of the room. Above, the long skylight. Silence. An odd place.

He wandered down the paintings, reading the brass labels. Vermeer. Titian. Fra Lippo Lippi. Velázquez. Frans Hals. Boucher. Mark recognized some of the names and admired some of the paintings, though most of them left him unmoved. But he knew enough to know that there was probably several million dollars worth of canvas in that quiet room.

He glanced at his watch. Ten fifteen. Where *was* the man?

He went down the other wall. Rubens. Van Dyke. Gainsborough. Ingres. Ingres? He stopped and looked at the large portrait of the plump woman in a brilliant blue dress standing in front of a big nineteenth-century mirror. The woman was hardly pretty, with her heavy-set face and massive arms, adorned with thick, gold bracelets and thin, gold rings. But there was something about her he liked. Ingres. In-grees? Who the hell was In-grees?

He went to the next painting, A Caravaggio. Never heard of him. Then a Rembrandt. *That* must cost a fortune! Kind of an ugly painting, though. Looks like an old peddler in a gold turban leaning on a stick with a yellow spotlight on him. What's the title? "Portrait of the Artist En Turque"? What did he do, dress up in a costume, then stand in front of a mirror and paint himself? Crazy. If you ask me, most artists are crazy. They *must* be to want to be artists. But there must be something I don't understand, because the big boys pay millions for these goddamn things. That In-grees was sort of pretty. I liked it.

Where the hell *is* this bird? It's ten twenty-five!

He went over to the desk.

"Would you tell Sir Grigory I'm a busy man and don't have all day to stand here and wait for him? What kind of place is this, anyway?"

"This is not a *place*, Mr. Manning," replied the secretary. "And Sir Grigory will be with you shortly."

"You said that half an hour ago!"

"When one is surrounded by the beauty of the ages," said the

Englishman, waving a thin, medieval hand in the direction of the paintings, "time takes on a new dimension."

They had the routine down beautifully, no doubt about it, Mark thought. He went back to the leather bench in the center of the room and sat down, toying with his hat. Ten minutes passed. He was about to jump up and tell the Englishman that he and the beauty of the ages might all go to hell when the door to Sir Grigory's office opened and Sir Grigory came out, polishing his pince-nez on a linen handkerchief. He came over to Mark, replaced his pince-nez on his nose, shoved his handkerchief into the breast pocket of his jacket and smiled through the bristling beard and moustache.

"Mr. Manning? I'm Sir Grigory Barjoonian. I hope I didn't keep you waiting? Mr. Mellon was on the phone."

He extended his hand. Mark started to say something, but changed his mind. Andrew *Mellon* . . .? He shook hands.

"Oh no." He shot a look at the smug-looking secretary as Sir Grigory led him into his office.

"Please sit down," Sir Grigory said, holding a rounded cane-back chair in front of the desk. Mark sat, glancing curiously at a large gold-framed painting of a Madonna standing on an easel in the corner of the room.

"Now, Mr. Manning," said Sir Grigory, sitting down at his desk and picking up a carved jade letter opener with which he toyed. "You are interested in art. But you know little about it, so you have come to me for guidance. Excellent. You have made a wise decision."

Mark cleared his throat. He felt vaguely uncomfortable, as if he had walked into a solid-gold trap.

"I hope so."

"We won't talk of aesthetics," continued Sir Grigory. "Aesthetics are a personal thing—*de gustibus*, as the Romans wisely said—and I prefer to talk to my clients about money because—let us be frank— this is a money game as well as an aesthetics game. My clients, most of whom are businessmen like yourself, understand this, as I'm sure you do."

Mark relaxed, feeling better.

"I understand money," he said. "I also think I understand you."

"I'm sure you do, Mr. Manning," smiled Sir Grigory. "But you manufacture tires. Tires have a definite use—a purpose. A painting has no use, of course. That's why it is so difficult to assess a painting's value. A tire? We know what a tire's worth. But this Madonna by Raphael?" He gestured at the painting on the easel. "The frame is probably worth five hundred dollars; it's a good one, beautifully carved. But the paint and canvas? I doubt if they'd fetch three dollars on Fourteenth Street. However, can you guess the price of the painting?"

Mark looked at the painting. "Two hundred thousand?"

"One million, Mr. Manning. One million dollars."

The farmer's son from Ohio stared at $1,000,000.

"So you see, Mr. Manning, we are dealing with the stuff of dreams, and dreams are misleading and tricky. That is why you are wise to come to a man who understands these dreams, who can guide you to wise investments and can help you build a collection that will carry your name down through the centuries. The Manning Rubber Company may be dust a hundred years from now. But the Manning *Collection?*" His eyes fairly glowed with fervor. "That will last a thousand years!"

"You have quite a line, Sir Grigory. I mean that both ways."

The Armenian smiled. "Thank you. Yes, it is a line. But it is also the truth. Now, my friend, to specifics. What do you want to buy? Paintings? Sculpture? Tapestries? Porcelains? What?"

"Paintings."

"I see. You want to start conservatively, of course. A minor investment—dip your toe in the water, so to speak."

Mark nodded. "Yes, that sounds all right. There's a painting out there . . ." He gestured toward the gallery. "The one of the woman in the blue dress standing in front of the mirror? The Ingrees?"

"Mr. Manning, if we're going to collect art, we ought to pronounce the artists' names correctly or people are going to laugh. *An*-gr. Jean Auguste Dominique Ingres, 1780 to 1867, a master of the French classical school. *An*-gr. The 'A' as in 'fat.' *An*-gr."

"*An*-gr." Which was what Mark felt, but decided to hell with it and to go along.

"Excellent. And that is one of his finest portraits, with an interesting provenance."

"Provenance?"

"Pedigree. The sitter is even more interesting. It is a portrait of the Duchesse de Choiseul-Praslin, painted in 1841. The duchess was a daughter of Maréchal Sebastiani, one of Napoleon's generals. She married one of the richest men in France, the duke, and bore him eleven children. Then, one day in 1847, he murdered her."

"The duke?"

"Correct. He hacked her to pieces. Apparently the duchess was a bit of a nag and the duke was having an *affaire* with his children's governess and he didn't enjoy his wife's nagging. It was a sensational crime, one of the most sensational crimes of the past century. And because the portrait is one of Ingres's best, that painting is of especial interest. But Mr. Manning, you want to start small. That would not be a small investment."

"How much?"

"Four hundred thousand dollars."

Mark looked shocked. He quickly shook his head. "No."

"Of course," said Sir Grigory, getting up from his desk. "We take baby steps before we take giant steps. Now, if you'll come with me, I'll take you to our first-floor gallery, our . . . bargain basement. There is an interesting little Corot down there you might like. Not sensational, of course, but, well, piquant. And a steal at $50,000!"

He led Mark out of his office past the secretary, down the gallery, chatting volubly about the virtues of slow beginnings. "Of course, when one buys prime art—the masters—one can never lose. It's like buying gold—pure gold; but baby steps first . . ."

"How much is that Rembrandt?" asked Mark. Sir Grigory had been pointing to the man in the gold turban.

"Ah, I'm afraid that's not for sale."

"Then why is it on display?"

"Well . . ." Sir Grigory looked torn. Then he smiled and whispered, "Well, I'll tell *you*, Mr. Manning, because I like you. Mr. Mellon is considering buying the Rembrandt. That's what I was talking to him about just now. He's *very* interested. And of course I could hardly afford to displease such an important man as Andrew Mellon by selling a painting out from under him, could I? You understand."

"How much is it?"

Sir Grigory looked at the painting a moment. "A million," he said casually. "I'm letting it go at a bargain price because it's Mr. Mellon. The painting is worth at least a hundred thousand more . . ."

Mark was staring at the Ingres two paintings away from the Rembrandt. He liked that painting, dammit. He liked the way it was painted—almost as real as a photograph—and the story of the husband murdering the wife . . . it was a good story. Why was he being so damned chintzy, going to the damn bargain basement? Who the hell did this Barjoonian think he was? He could buy the whole place if he wanted! The whole goddamn place! Maybe he was being conned . . . to hell with it . . .

"*I'll* buy it," he said aloud, almost startled by the sound of his voice.

"Buy what?" asked Sir Grigory.

"That. The duchess who got murdered. For four hundred thousand. Can you deliver it to Ohio?"

Sir Grigory shook his head sadly. "Mr. Manning, you don't understand. Ah, I suppose it's my fault. I didn't explain. The Ingres and the Rembrandt is a package deal with Mr. Mellon. He wants to buy them both, so neither is for sale. I'm sorry."

But now Barjoonian had gone one step too far. Mark, being neither a fool nor an amateur bargainer, was now quite certain he was being maneuvered. Barjoonian hadn't talked to Mellon—it was a trick, just as the package deal was a trick. Barjoonian's game was to insult his customer's ego by telling him to start "small," knowing that was the best way to excite his itch to buy "big." Then when the poor (rich) boob had made the plunge, as Mark had by offering to buy the Ingres, Barjoonian lured him into even deeper waters by saying it wasn't for sale unless it was bought with something else. It was an elegant shellgame, but a shellgame nonetheless. Mark decided it was time to call the man's bluff.

"I'll give you $1,300,000 for both paintings," he said. "And if you don't accept my offer, I'll walk out that door and give my business to Duveen." He smiled pleasantly. "Do we have a deal?"

Barjoonian eyed him. "Mr. Mellon will give me a million four for the paintings."

"Then sell them to Mr. Mellon."

He started toward the door.

"Ah . . . Mr. Manning?"

Barjoonian came over and extended his hand. "We have a deal."

"Good." He shook the dealer's hand, then walked over to the secretary's desk, pulling a checkbook from his coat pocket. "You," he said, pointing to the Englishman, "move so I can write your boss a check for $1,300,000. Is that right? Or do you charge for delivery?"

"We deliver free," said Sir Grigory, watching with pleasure as Mark sat down and opened his checkbook. Sir Grigory decided he had landed a big one.

Mark was amused by Sir Grigory's tactics, but he was genuinely excited by his purchase. In buying the Rembrandt and the Ingres, he had indeed bought a piece of eternity. When the paintings were delivered to Elkins in two weeks, he was going to open up River Bend for the first time in years and show the homefolks what Mark

Manning had bought. He was damn proud, and not afraid to admit it.

He returned to Ohio the next day and had Wilma Amstuts, his now middle-aged secretary of so many years, send out two hundred invitations to everyone who was anyone in the Elkins-Akron-Cleveland area inviting them to a buffet supper at River Bend on the evening of October 22, 1926. Then he instructed Peter, his butler, to have the house thoroughly cleaned, and he hired a caterer from Cleveland to bring in the food. He called a Detroit bootlegger with whom he had recently been doing business and ordered ten cases of Krug champagne to reinforce his private stock in the River Bend cellar. Next he instructed Marvin Senjak, his long-time chauffeur-bodyguard, to take whatever extra precautions would be needed to safeguard the security of the valuable paintings. Not that any thief in his right mind would try to steal anything from River Bend. Under Marvin's supervision, the guard force at the estate had become as efficient as the much larger security force for the Manning Company, a small army that now comprised more than five hundred men patroling and protecting the many Manning plants all over the country, and which was still under the direction of Jim Malloy. But while the exbank guard and now a high-ranking official of the company rarely saw Mark personally, the exprizefighter was in almost constant contact with Mark when he was in Ohio, and Marvin's fierce loyalty to his employer was by now widely known. He had married a local girl, and Mark had built him a comfortable home on the grounds of River Bend to house his family. Thus Marvin was always at work, in a manner of speaking, which was the way Mark wanted it.

Now, instead of guarding the Manning children from kidnapers—which had been what he was hired for originally—Marvin was to guard the embryo Manning art collection from thieves; the children were hardly ever in the enormous house any more. Marvin missed the children, having become almost a second father to them over the years, but he would guard the paintings with the same determination he had guarded David, Ellen, Richard and Christopher.

CHAPTER THREE

Lily Swenson Benny sat in front of her Art Deco vanity. As her colored maid Vera brushed her hair, Lily thought about the king, which had long been her private name for Mark.

The Bennys had built a big house in River Heights, which was the name the developer had given the most exclusive residential section in Elkins. River Heights was the hundred acres adjacent to River Bend, pretty land bordering the Matahoochi River, and just as the French court had swarmed to Versailles in the seventeenth and eighteenth centuries, the important Manning executives and local pooh-bahs had followed the lead of Lily's father, Harold Swenson, had bought land next to Elkins's Versailles and built their pseudo-Tudor, pseudocolonial, pseudo-Spanish-hacienda and sometimes charmingly authentic American houses. When Melville and Lily had been married in December 1923, the first thing they had done after returning from their honeymoon in Havana, Cuba, was to buy a five-acre plot of land in River Heights and plan a home. Except to Melville's dismay, Lily hadn't wanted pseudo-Tudor, colonial, Spanish or pseudo anything. Lily wanted *modern*. And she hired a smart young architect from Shaker Heights in Cleveland to design her the first modern home in Elkins—a curving, slick cement structure that Melville considered a monstrosity and everyone else in town considered the product of one of Lily's more vicious hangovers. But Lily liked it. She liked its round windows, its free-form lines, its fitting-in-with-the-landscape concept.

Most particularly, she liked it because everyone else hated it.

It wasn't finished until the end of 1925, thanks to building delays due mainly to Lily's continually changing her mind about the plans. When it was finally done, she decided to decorate it in the exciting new Art Deco style and filled it with all the latest furniture from New York and Chicago: jazzy chrome tables, aluminum chairs, beds with inlaid-wood Art Deco designs, huge round mirrors. Lily's taste was perhaps not flawless, but the place "worked," in what some said was a flashy way, which was also what she wanted. When everything was in place, she threw a huge open-house gin party. Then, promptly becoming bored with the place now that it was finished, she went back to her old way of life, spending entire days at the country club playing the slot machines and boozing and tooling around town in her jazzy Dagmar with its all-brass trim. Everyone said she was drinking herself into an early grave, but they were wrong. Lily drank because she was bored and frustrated, but she wasn't about to dig or water her own grave. She was merely waiting for The Call: the moment when she would suddenly see with dazzling clarity what her life's work was to be, the way her father had when Mark Manning hired him to come to work for the new Manning Company so many years before. Well, Lily was now thirty-two and she hadn't heard The Call yet, but she had no doubt some day it would happen. Lily believed in Destiny.

While the house was being built and Melville was away in Río de Oro, life had been fun for Lily. But then in 1926 Melville had finally come home and life had become restricted. Melville, dreary Melville, wanted children. His first wife had never conceived, and after two years in Africa he wanted to enjoy a normal home life. Lily didn't want children. Melville, dreary Melville, disapproved of drinking; he locked up the liquor and tried to force her onto the wagon. He even objected to her smoking! Melville was turning out to be more than Lily could take, and she was seriously considering chucking the whole thing and going off to Europe or somewhere, letting her lawyer arrange the divorce. The only thing that held her back, aside from her personal lack of money, was Bob Thompson, one of the new vice-presidents at Manning, who had come to Elkins the previous year. Bob was a bachelor, also good-looking and fun. He loved to drink, and Lily had been sleeping with him for the past ten months, arranging clandestine meetings in Bob's apartment which, eerily, was in the same apartment development near the Country Club, the Hampton Court, that poor Carter had lived in before they were married. That was sort of spooky, but Lily quickly got over her qualms. She liked Bob terrifically, and she loved having affairs. Melville had finally become suspicious (or could no longer avoid his suspicions) when one night, after he'd come back from the office, she wasn't home and in fact didn't show up until ten o'clock, reeling into the house after a session in Bob's apartment. He had been furious and accused her of sleeping with *some*one. "What gave you the clue, Sherlock?" she said, and went off to bed. Melville sulked for weeks, but avoided proving who her lover was. He was too ashamed and thought himself too much in love with her to divorce her, so he had buried himself in his office and tried to shut reality out of his mind. Lily had come out on top.

And then the invitation to River Bend had come in the mail and her whole life changed. River Bend! She hadn't been in it for years, and the whole Manning clan seemed to have passed out of her life, with the Manning children away at school or over in France with their mother, and the king traveling all over the world. But now the house was opening again, and the king was back, and everyone was talking about the million-dollar paintings he had bought in New York and the huge palace he was building in Palm Beach . . . Mark Manning. Forty-eight years old, but still handsome. She remembered that night in 1913 when Carter Lang had taken her to the ball at River Bend and Mark had been standing in the front hall greeting the guests and she had thought he was so wonderfully handsome and had wished he would kiss her . . . Mark Manning, whose life she had been envious of all her life while, at the same time, she rather passively longed for him—passively only because she had always assumed he was unobtainable and she had been involved with other men. The Carters, the Melvilles, the Bobs; the planets revolving around the sun. The king. And now, the invitation from the Sun King himself. The great Mark Manning, the man who had never remarried after his first wife left him, the man whose love life had become a mystery after the murder of Maxine Talbot (who, everybody whispered, had been his mistress). Mark Manning, who had always been Number One in Elkins and the Manning Company, while Lily's father, Harold, had always been Number Two.

Mark Manning. Suddenly, Lily knew she had received The Call.

"Ouch!" she yelled, as Vera's brush caught a snag in her hair.

"Sorry, Miss Lily," said Vera.

"For Christ sake, watch what you're *doing!*"

"I said I'm sorry!"

"Well, you should be."

She looked at her reflection. Despite the boozing, she decided she still looked terrific. She'd wear her sexy new Chanel dress with the bugle beads in the diamond design. Black-and-red and almost above the knees in front, a little lower in back. And naked, practically, on top. And her jazzy rhinestone pumps.

The king's eyes would pop out of their sockets.

Memories. They had swarmed through Mark's mind as the caterers moved into River Bend and the gardeners filled the giant vases with chrysanthemums from the greenhouse. Memories of Charlotte and the past and his youth, all of which he suddenly missed terribly. He became so depressed, he considered the idea of canceling the party. Instead, he went up to his bedroom and lay down on the bed to try to sleep.

Memories. Charlotte. He had been a fool to let her go. Charlotte had been the best thing in his life, but he had to lose her to realize it. She seemed like a ghost now—how long had it been since he had seen her? Five years? Was that possible? Several times he had started to have the Sargent portrait he had commissioned for their third anniversary taken down from above the fireplace, but then he had changed his mind. It haunted him, just as the house did, which was why he spent so little time in it. How ridiculous that all their differences had seemed to come down to some monumentally insipid word like "nice." He wasn't "nice." Anyone could be nice . . . oh, he knew it was more than that, knew that was only the feeble expression of the end. . . . She was apparently blissfully happy with her champagne-maker husband—at least judging from the secondhand reports he got from the children. He had secretly hoped the marriage would fail. It wasn't admirable, but it was human . . . But she was happy, and he was lonely. He missed Maxine too. But now, with River Bend being opened again after so long, it was Charlotte he ached for.

He rolled over on his stomach and cursed himself for being a sentimental fool. Charlotte was gone and Maxine was gone and he'd better accept it. He didn't need them or anyone . . . Life was a parade that moved along in sections, and once one section had passed, it was gone forever. The only constant thing was change— he remembered that from college. Some Greek had said it, and it was true. Everything passed and everything changed and all you had to hang onto was your own wits, your own guts, your own luck. Change. He was one of the most powerful men in the country. He owned a Rembrandt and an *An*-gr, he was a director of seven corporations, he was building a Spanish palace in Palm Beach . . . a Casa Encantade. . . . He thought of Carlos Innocente Flores—how many years ago had *that* been?—and it struck him as ironic that now it was *he* who was building the Viceroy's Outhouse, *he* who was leasing thousands of acres in another jungle to produce rubber, *he* who had killed . . . Was he becoming like Flores? Of course not. . . .

Change.

He thought of his oldest son. David was seventeen now and would be graduating from Lawrenceville the next June. He was a smart boy and a good son, but he had been a disappointment. To Mark, that is, not Charlotte. She adored him. Mark no longer thought she had turned David into a momma's boy, though she had tried. But the boy was still shy and sensitive. David would never build anything as his father had—he could only inherit and, perhaps, manage, though Mark wasn't sure he could do even that. David didn't have the drive. Of course, it was still early; he might develop. But so far, David had been a disappointment.

Ellen was not. She was turning into a beautiful young woman who, like David, was much like her mother physically, having even inherited Charlotte's musical talent. Ellen played the piano beautifully, she had a loving disposition, she was at Foxcroft, and Mark could hardly wait to see her during the Christmas holidays when all the children would be home—the arrangement he had made with Charlotte was that the children could spend their winter holidays with him and go to her in France during the summers. This gave Charlotte more time with them than he had, but it seemed to him the best way to divide their time, and she had agreed.

Richard, the third child, who was at Andover, was a good athlete and a fair student who showed promise of developing into a leader. But it was Christopher, the youngest, who had become Mark's favorite. Christopher was just like his father. He was red-haired, hot-tempered, and full of himself—no adolescent insecurities for Christopher! Something told Mark that someday it would be Christopher who would take over the management of the huge inheritance, not David or Richard. He was so fond of him that instead of sending him East to school like the others, he had put him in the nearby Wooster School, where he could drop down and see him. Wooster didn't have the prestige of Lawrenceville and Andover, of course, but Mark liked the school, had given money to it and felt at least one of his children—his legitimate children, that is—should be exposed to an Ohio education. But most importantly he liked having Christopher near him.

Roger Boine had gone to Wooster, had done well there—as he had at Amherst and the University of Pennsylvania Medical School—and Mark had been delighted when Roger accepted his offer to take his residency at Las Palmas. He had been out there four months now, and the reports Mark had gotten indicated Roger was doing a superlative job in the hospital. Roger did not know—nor did his mother, Sheila—that Mark had already willed him stock currently valued at almost $1,000,000 dollars. He wondered how the young doctor son of the ultraliberal mother and politically conservative father would use the money. It would be interesting to see. Except, of course, he wouldn't be around to see it.

Forty-eight years old. Almost half a century. And thinking about his will, his children, his past, their future. No wonder he was depressed! He was thinking like an old man, and he was far from old. He was healthy, fit, in the prime of life. He'd had a complete check-up only two months before, and the doctor told him he should live to be eighty. His sexuality was still that of a man half his age—the succession of girls he had bedded in the past four years would testify to that— so why was he feeling so blue? Damn it, he had everything to live for! Everything! He'd heard that men went through a sort of meno-pause—was it *possible* that was what was happening to him? He didn't know.

What he did know was that he needed a change.

She was playing it very cautiously.

She'd had only two glasses of the delicious champagne and was on her best behavior, staying close to her husband Melville through most of the party. Of course, she received the usual quota of hostile looks from the company wives (as well as lecherous looks from the hus-bands) but she was accustomed to that and, in fact, enjoyed it. Frumpy old bitches! Meanwhile, she was demureness itself, being very polite, tasting canapés, pausing to chat dutifully with her father and mother, making all the right moves in the tight little world of Elkins's upper stratum. And when she and Melville came up to Mark, she behaved even more cautiously. "I think the paintings are just fabulous, Mr. Manning," she said. "And how wonderful of you to let us all see them. It's just marvelous, the things you've done for this town. First the symphony, and now Rembrandt and Ingres!" (She pronounced it right, Mark noted.) "It's wonderful." Smile. Mark gave her an interested look, then began talking to Melville about business. Lily stood by, showing herself a woman careful not to intrude her-self on the hallowed ground of man talk, but she sensed she had scored her first point. Mark knew all about her, of course. He had heard the stories, her pressuring Carter Lang into marrying her, probably even about Bob Thompson. But she was the daughter of the Number Two man in the company and the wife of the Number Three man. He would be as cautious as she, perhaps even more so, and that was the problem. She might have to make the first move.

She toyed with the marquise diamond engagement ring Melville had given her and considered the situation. The first move . . . Well, if she were going to do it, she'd have to do it quickly. Mark Manning didn't spend much time in River Bend, and she had heard someone say he was leaving for Palm Beach in a few days to check on the progress of construction on his new house. She couldn't waste time.

She excused herself and made her way through the well-dressed crowd out of the huge living room into the big entrance hall. Servants were everywhere, as well as the private detective everyone could spot a mile off even though they wore dinner jackets. Those stony faces and watching, shifting eyes were a giveaway. Lily liked the idea of numberless servants and private detectives. She liked River Bend. She liked the deference everyone paid to the king. She liked the king. He was a sexy man, not only physically but in the sense of power that emanated from him. Power was sexy, and Mark Manning had power. Lily was attracted to it as a moth to a flame.

She went into the powder room and smiled at the colored maid in attendance.

"Isn't it a lovely party?" she said, opening her purse to remove her compact.

"Yes ma'am, it sure is."

Lily powdered her nose and retouched her lips. As she returned the lipstick case to her purse, she knocked the purse off the marble sink to the gray carpet.

"Oh honestly!" she said, surveying the spilled contents. "I'm so clumsy—"

"I'll get it, ma'am," said the maid, kneeling on the carpet to pick up the keys, compact, loose change, dollar bills and assorted junk Lily had crammed even into her smallish evening bag.

"Oh, thanks."

She watched as the maid retrieved the scattered objects. Then she removed her diamond engagement ring from her finger and hid it in her left hand while the maid got to her feet and handed her the purse. Lily took it, smiled, then took out a dollar bill which she gave to the maid.

"Thanks *so* much."

"Thank *you*, ma'am!" said the maid.

As Lily went out of the room, she dropped the diamond ring in her purse, snapped it shut.

Melville Benny was a genius chemist, an ambitious, hard-driving executive, and a man whose personality had never surfaced from his test tubes. He had absolutely no sense of humor, the Puritan work-ethic was an obsession with him; he had no vices, and despite his money, he was a chintz. His true passion was chemistry and his hobby was inventing things. He had no facility for small talk and was considered a bore. He struck people as timid and reserved. He was a first-class mind in a dour package.

He had, nonetheless, one very human trait. He was highly sexed, and his sexy wife never failed to excite him. At parties he had literally to concentrate his mind on other people for fear of thinking about Lily and suffering the embarrassment of an erection. If Lily had allowed him, he would have made love to her three or four times a night. The fact that this stringbean, apparent Caspar Milquetoast of a man had the sexual energy of a bull in heat never failed to amaze, and amuse, her.

Melville quite literally was crazy about Lily, which, of course, was why he put up with her. The thought of losing her panicked him to such an extent that he even put up with her lovers, though it racked him with jealousy. However, when Lily behaved as circumspectly as she had at River Bend, Melville was profoundly grateful. And as they drove home from the party, he couldn't stop telling her how wonderful she'd been.

"I was so *proud* of you! You acted like a real lady, said all the right things . . ."

Lily sighed. "What did you expect me to do? Pick my nose?"

"Lily! Anyway, you were wonderful, so don't spoil it. And beautiful too! Easily the most beautiful woman there!"

He reached over and put his hand on her knee.

"Both hands on the wheel, Melville. Safety first."

He withdrew his hand and stepped on the gas, in a hurry to get home and make love. He tore through River Heights and nearly through their garage door as well. Lily said irritably, "Come *on,* Melville. You're not going to explode."

"It's just that . . . that dress is so great on you . . ."

"Sure."

He parked in the driveway, leaned over to kiss her.

"The bedroom's not *that* far away, Melville. Don't you think we could wait?"

"Oh, I guess so." He got out to open the garage door. Lily knew by the way he walked that old faithful was up again.

Inside, Melville wasted no time getting out of his clothes. Lily dawdled in the living room. When she knew he was in bed, she called out, "Oh, Melville!"

"What's wrong?"

She hurried into the bedroom. "My engagement ring's gone!"

"Gone? You mean it's stolen?"

"How do I know? It's just *gone*. Oh, wait a minute . . . the bathroom . . ."

"Which bathroom?"

"The powder room at River Bend. I took the ring off when I washed my hands—you know I have a habit of doing that. I remember—I dropped it in my bag, then accidentally knocked the bag off the sink. The maid picked everything up, but she must have missed the ring . . ."

"Maybe she took it?"

"Oh, no. She wouldn't do that. It probably rolled in a corner . . . I'll run back to River Bend and get it. I'm sure it's there."

"Wait a minute. I'll go with you."

"Don't be silly. You stay ready and able in bed. I'll be back in half an hour."

She hurried out of the bedroom through the living and dining rooms to the kitchen, then into the garage. Opening the garage doors, she started to get in the car when Melville appeared in the kitchen door, a coat over his pajamas.

"I'm coming."

"*No!*" she said, getting into the car. "It's not necessary, see you soon . . ."

She started the car and backed out of the garage. Melville looked so miserable she almost felt sorry for him. She quickly pushed aside such sentimental diversions to concentrate on the far more important matter at hand.

When she reached River Bend, the lights were still on, although the caterers had cleaned up and left and most of the servants had gone to bed. Peter, the butler, answered the door, and she told him why she had come. He admitted her and she went into the powder room and searched the floor.

"It's not here!" she wailed after a minute. "But I *know* it must have fallen out . . ."

"Do you think someone might have picked it up, Miss Lily?" asked Peter.

She got to her feet.

"Well, I'd hate to think anyone would do that without telling Mr. Manning. Is he still up?"

"He's in his study."

"Maybe I should ask him?"

Peter led her through the big house to Mark's study, where he knocked on the door. Mark answered it, looking curiously at Lily.

"I'm very sorry to bother you, Mr. Manning," she said, "but I apparently dropped my engagement ring in the powder room and now I can't seem to find it. I wondered if anyone had possibly found it and told you?"

She wondered if he knew. She had a feeling, from the way he was looking at her, that he did.

"I'm afraid not," he said. "But why don't I help you look for it? Thank you, Peter. Why don't you call it a night?"

"Yes, Mr. Manning. Goodnight."

Peter walked off as Mark took in Lily with his eyes. She was a sexy woman, no doubt about that. A goddamn knockout. But he also knew she was a bitch. When Peter had gone, he said, "Why didn't Melville come with you?"

"He's already in bed. I was sure the ring was somewhere on the powder-room floor. You see, I took it off when I washed my hands . . ."

"Do you always take off rings when you wash your hands?"

"Matter of fact, I *do* . . ."

"I see. Well, before we start looking, why don't we have a drink? There's half a bottle of champagne in here. Would you like that?"

"Fine."

He held the door as she went into his study. She looked around the room. There was no champagne in view. She turned as he closed the door.

"Where's the champagne?"

"The same place your ring is."

She hesitated. Then she shrugged and pulled the ring out of her purse. Holding it up, she smiled. "Guess what I found?"

He came over and took her in his arms.

"I suppose I'll be able to find the champagne as easily."

As he kissed her, she reached her right hand behind her back and hastily undid the buttons of her Chanel dress.

CHAPTER FOUR

The body was found by the third rubber tree in the fourth row of Field B-18. It had been clawed to death. Dr. Roger Boine looked at the results of the savagery that had ripped open the man's chest, torn out one of his eyes, and slit his throat. It was the fifth such mutilation murder he had seen in two weeks. The horror still affected him.

"The Leopard Society," said Charlie Clark, the manager of Las Palmas. "How long has he been dead?"

"A few hours," Roger replied. He checked his watch. It was seven in the morning. "They must have killed him about five A.M., then brought the body here."

Charlie Clark nodded. He was a heavy-set man of forty-three who had lost fifty pounds since replacing Melville Benny as manager of the plantation the previous January. The heat still affected him, and even though it was still early enough to be relatively cool, the sweat was already running down his red face.

"Yeah, the drums. That was when they started, about five. Well, let's get him out of here and buried fast."

Roger used pidgin to direct his three hospital orderlies to take the body to the hospital, where it could be kept until the man's family was notified. The blacks were reluctant—they were literally shivering with fright—but they obeyed. Then Charlie and Roger started back to the main office. Neither spoke, both were thinking the same thing. Rumors had been drifting down from the up country for almost a year that there was a movement among the natives to attack the new rubber plantation, but no one had paid much attention to them. The Devil bush was something of a joke to the whites, although it was a joke tinged with certain respect. They might laugh at the mumbo jumbo and the witchdoctors, but no white would be foolish enough to go into the bush when the Big Devil was walking. "You see him, you finish," was what the natives said, and the old-time whites in Tylertown had corroborated the warning. They never went into the bush at Big Devil time, and they told the new whites at Las Palmas they shouldn't either. The new arrivals were skeptical, but they obeyed.

The Devil bush was an odd mixture of primitive religion and social organization that few people—white or black—who were not initiates truly understood. It was a secret society—actually a number of secret societies—presided over by priests. Certain sections of the bush or jungle were marked off as Devil bush, the territory of the societies. Anyone coming on a jungle trail marked by two crossed wands topped either with rags or feathers knew that should be the end of the trail for him—beyond the wands was Devil bush, and no man could enter Devil bush and depart alive. This was no idle threat. Every year at least a dozen or more natives would be found dead, and everyone knew how Devil bush killed. Sometimes four young trees were bent down, the man's arms and legs tied to the tops of the trees, then the restraining ropes were cut and the man was quartered alive as the trees sprang up. Sometimes the victims were poisoned by alligator gall or sasswood. Sometimes the Society of the Boh would "think" a man dead; whites joked about this, the natives did not. Perhaps the most horrifying death was pegging a man to the ground in the path of an oncoming army of driver ants. Millions of insects would move not over him but through him, cleaning him to his bones in minutes.

Whatever the method of execution, Devil bush killed, and the natives respected and feared it. The societies perpetuated themselves by recruiting boys and girls from the villages. These elect few could then be taken to poro bush for boys and gri-gri bush for girls, where thye would be initiated into the magic rites and taught useful handicrafts. Once in the Devil bush, no one left. It was a lifetime membership, a way of life. In normal times the Devil bush was a useful socioreligious organization, cementing the natives in an extra-tribal society that helped bring cohesion to the vast jungle. In abnormal times, the Devil bush could become an instrument of terror. And the arrival of the Manning Rubber and Steel Company of Elkins, Ohio, at Las Palmas plantation instituted abnormal times.

There was, in particular, the Leopard Society, which Roger had laughed at when he heard about it his first week at Las Palmas, but which quickly had ceased being a joke. The Leopard Society was an inner circle of the Devil bush, a secret society within a secret society. Only the bravest men were admitted to the Leopard Society, which was ruled by a high priest, a prince of the Kru tribe named Tegai, who was rumored to be seven feet tall and the strongest man in Africa. It was said he could tear a man's head off with his bare hands; whatever the truth of that, he was held in near religious awe by the natives, as was the Leopard Society itself. The society worshipped the leopard god, who, it claimed, could enter the body of a member at will, turn-

ing the man into a killer animal. This belief was carried out quite
literally. A society member would be dressed in a leopard suit
equipped with built-in iron claws attached to springs. When the man
attacked his victim, he activated the spring mechanism that would
release the iron claws. Then, using these ten, razor-sharp knives, he
would cut the victim to ribbons.

Roger had regarded all this as the wildest sort of Edgar Rice Bur-
roughs foolishness when he first came to Las Palmas . . . until the first
rubber worker had been found clawed to death. Within two weeks,
three more. And now this morning, the fifth body. And each murder
accompanied by the oppressive jungle drums, the bush telegraph that
spread the word throughout the country that the Leopard Society
had again done its work. They had had great difficulty keeping the
rubber workers from running off into the jungle after the first killing,
and after each successive one more of the men had vanished, despite
their efforts. Now, as they reached the office, a neat square building
raised on stilts and ventilated with wide-screened windows, Charlie
Clark was expecting the worst.

He got it.

"They've all gone," reported Phil Gates, the chief overseer. "Every
damn one of them. They heard the drums and they ran off."

Almost 9,000 rubber workers tapping and tending over 20,000 acres
of producing trees with an average of a hundred ten trees to the acre.
All vanished into the jungle. Charlie Clark sank into a canvas chair.

"What do we do now?" asked Phil Gates.

"We radio Elkins," Charlie said.

"And what do we tell them? That a bunch of black magic mumbo-
jumbo natives have scared away all the workers from the most modern
rubber plantation in the world?"

Charlie looked at him.

"Well, that's exactly what's happened, isn't it?"

––––––––––

Melville Benny was on the edge of nervous collapse.

He was certain his wife had a new lover, and he suspected it was
none other than the man he had worked for and admired for almost
twenty years. He told himself over and over again that he must be
wrong, that Mark would never do such a criminal thing to him—
such a foolish thing! He couldn't convince himself. Lily's maneuvering had started that night she had gone to River Bend to retrieve her
ring. She hadn't returned home until one thirty in the morning—she

told him they'd had to tear the house apart to find the ring, but Melville knew she'd been drinking and inevitably had been suspicious. And then Mark started behaving oddly. He canceled his trip to Palm Beach, at the same time Lily started making an unusual number of shopping trips to Cleveland. She said she was doing her Christmas shopping, but Melville thought it more than coincidence that Mark also began making side trips to Cleveland himself, his secretary explaining that Mark was "there on business." During the holidays, when Mark's children came home, the trips subsided, but shortly after New Year's Day of 1927, off Lily went to Cleveland again, this time to exchange presents, and Mark, it so happened, likewise was gone from his office the same day. (Business, as usual?) And when on the sixth of January Mark called him into his office, Melville was obliged to take four aspirin to kill the splitting headache that was torturing him. He wanted to blurt out his accusations and hope that somehow Mark could refute them. Except that he was afraid Mark would not and could not refute them.

Mark's office had been newly decorated. It was a far distance from the no-frills, spittoon-sporting office of the early days. Forty feet long and thirty feet wide, with a big window overlooking the seeming miles of factory below, it was paneled in light wood, with very contemporary darker-wood horizontal inlaid stripes adding a trim, tailored look. The furniture was the latest thing in executive styles, deep rounded chairs and a huge sofa that looked as if it had been pumped up with air like a tire. A blue carpet, handsome wooden lamps, autographed photos of the mighty of the land, including one of President and Mrs. Coolidge (the photo of President and Mrs. Harding had been retired after the Teapot Dome scandals), a recessed bar, several handsomely framed English landscape paintings. And, dominating everything, the imperial-sized desk with the green marble penholder, the Cartier clock, the multibuttoned phone, the Mark Cross leather blotter.

Behind this imposing massif sat Mark, and he didn't look happy.

"Sit down, Melville," he said, gesturing toward the huge chair opposite him. Melville sat. "Tell me everything you know about Tegai."

"Tegai? The head of the Leopard Society? I don't know that much about him. When I was at Las Palmas I heard about him, of course, and the Leopard Society. Except I didn't pay too much attention to it. Anyway, Tegai is the son of one of the Kru chiefs. He's called a prince and I guess his father claims the title of king."

"How old is he?"

"I'd say about thirty. He was taught by English missionaries so he learned English from them. But he turned away from Christianity when he was in his teens—well, that's misleading. It seems he went along with the missionaries to learn what they could teach him, then one day he told them he thought Christianity was a lot of white man's lies and that was that. They found out he'd been in the poro bush all along—you know, one of the secret societies. But then he surprised them again by getting accepted at Oxford. He went there for four years and got his degree."

Mark looked interested. "Isn't it unusual for a black man to go to Oxford?"

"Not if he's a prince, and a smart one to boot—and Tegai is smart, I'm told. As far as his attitude toward us, the story I got was that he thought President Chadwick had sold out to us and that we both should be run out of the country. He apparently has a lot of support among the natives. Why are you so interested in Tegai?"

Mark leaned back in his chair. "Because he's brought Las Palmas to a standstill."

"How?"

"By murdering five of the workers in two weeks. I haven't told you or anybody else about it because Harold and I decided to keep the news to ourselves and hope the trouble would go away. It hasn't. Three days ago Charlie Clark radioed us there'd been a fifth murder and every one of the rubber workers has taken off into the bush, scared out of their wits. It's a crazy situation! Here it is 1927 and here we are, one of the biggest corporations in America, and a plantation we've sunk thirty million into is brought to a dead stop by black magic out of the Dark Ages."

Melville nodded. "What are you planning to do?"

"Kill Tegai," Mark said. "And put the rest of the Leopard Society in jail. We can't afford not to. If the others think Tegai can get away with what he's done to us, then we're through in Río de Oro. But it's not going to be easy to catch him. Charlie Clark says the plantation police can't do it. Besides, he's worried Tegai may attack Las Palmas and try to burn it down. So I agreed with him to keep our men on the premises. I also radioed President Chadwick and tried to get him to send his militia into the bush after Tegai."

"Did he agree?"

"He weaseled. Oh, he'd like to get rid of Tegai—the man's a threat to him and the Tylertown government. But Chadwick's facing an election in four months and he's afraid that if he goes after Tegai the opposition will say that he's turning against his own countrymen, that he's a tool of Mark Manning. I can understand why the average citizen in Tylertown would not be too happy to see their own militia out after a man they probably consider a kind of romantic hero. Anyway, Chadwick weaseled and I let him off the hook. Personally I don't think his militia's that good and half of them are probably more rather than less sympathetic to Tegai. So with Chadwick out, I placed a call to the White House."

"Did you talk to the *President?*" asked Melville.

"Naturally," Mark said. "I told him the situation and explained that our whole investment out there is in jeopardy. He was very understanding and helpful. He discussed the situation with the secretary of the navy, and just a little while ago they both told me they're willing to put three navy gunboats at our disposal, with a hundred and fifty men. The gunboats are on maneuvers with part of the British fleet off Capetown right now, but they can be in Río de Oro in two weeks--they're under the command of a Lieutenant Commander Andrew Pritchard. Now, the only problem again is Chadwick. He's not going to be happy when he finds out Uncle Sam is sending in three gunboats to protect American property and hunt down a citizen of Río de Oro. It's going to make him look like a puppet, so he's going to have to be handled with soft kid gloves. Now as much as I like and trust Charlie Clark, I don't think he's got the tact to handle a thing like this. He's going to have to coordinate an operation involving the U.S. navy and the Tylertown government, and Charlie's just not right for the job. You are, and I want you to go out there and handle it."

"Me?" Melville sounded more surprised than he felt.

"You know the plantation, you know Chadwick and his government and they like and trust you. Besides, it will impress on everybody how seriously we're taking this if I send you out. I hate to ask you to go over there again, Melville, but you're the man for the job and I'd take it as a personal favor to me if you did it."

Melville said nothing. "A personal favor"—what a laugh! When Mark Manning "asked," it was an order. How convenient for Mark to get rid of the inconvenient husband for a few months! How damnably convenient! They wouldn't have to bother going to Cleveland any more. They could play their games in River Bend, now that the children were back in school and the husband was dispatched.

"Something the matter, Melville?"

"Oh, no, I was just thinking about Lily. She hates to be alone. So, if you wouldn't mind I'd like to take her along with me."

Was that a glint of annoyance in his eyes?

"Naturally you can take her if you want, and the company will, of course, pay her expenses. However, I hardly have to tell you Tylertown's not the best place in the world for a woman. But that's up to you. Anyway, I'll appreciate it if you can arrange to leave as soon as possible. I'll have Wilma make all the reservations for you, and you can tell her whether Lily's going or not."

Melville nodded, feeling a little better. At least Mark had put up no objections to his taking Lily, and if he really didn't care then maybe he wasn't . . .

Mark interrupted his thoughts, saying, "The line I want you to take with Chadwick is simple. He's got as much at stake as we have. If Tegai can shut us down, he can shut Tylertown down. If we're forced out of Río de Oro, Chadwick's as good as got his exit visa too. He may not like to hear that, but it's pretty much the truth. Naturally, you'll sugarcoat the pill."

"I understand."

"Good. Melville, I consider this above and beyond the call of duty, so to speak. I don't have to tell you how valuable you are to me—I think you know that already. The company owes a lot to you —hell, *I* owe a lot to you. As you know, Harold Swenson's developed a bad ticker. Nothing too bad, thank God, but he's worried about it, and I can't blame him. He's told me confidentially—and by the way, this isn't even for Lily to know—that he'd like to retire next year, and I couldn't very well say no, even though I'll hate to lose him. But as far as I'm concerned, when Harold retires you've got his job if you want it."

Melville was startled. Executive vice-president. Number Two. Annual salary, $200,000 plus stock options.

"Mark, I don't know what to say . . ."

"Then don't say anything." Mark got up and came around the massif. "I'd have given you the job even if you hadn't gone to Río de Oro for me, but now . . . well, I thought the news might make the trip more tolerable. We'll keep this to ourselves?"

He stuck out his hand and Melville stood to shake it.

"Yes, of course."

Mark escorted him out of his office mouthing pleasantries about keeping the Number Two job all in the *same* family, and how Harold would be pleased that his son-in-law would be replacing him and how Mark liked to think the whole company was one big happy family.

By the time Melville left the room he had almost forgotten his suspicions, almost . . .

"Go to Río de Oro? Melville, you must be kidding."

This was Lily's predictable reaction to the proposed trip that evening when Melville came home to ask her to go along. She was curled up on a chaise longue in her bedroom reading an article in the latest *Photoplay* hinting that Janet Gaynor and Charles Farrell were having a love affair on the set of *Seventh Heaven,* while, next to her, her bedroom radio gave forth with Ruth Etting singing "Shaking the Blues Away." Melville turned the radio off.

"I'm not kidding, and you're going with me. It's only for two months and it will be an interesting trip."

She angrily turned the radio back on. "To lovely, fashionable Tylertown? You know what I say to Tylertown?" She gave a loud raspberry.

"Lily, listen to me and be reasonable. There's trouble at Las Palmas, and Mark has asked me to go out and handle it for him. I don't want to go, for God's sake, but it would be a lot easier for me if you came along and it *would* be interesting. We can sail on the *Berengaria*—"

"No."

He clenched his teeth, sat down on the end of the chaise and compromised by turning the radio down but not off. "All right, would you go with me to London? You can stay there or go to Paris or wherever you want while I'm in Tylertown. Then we can meet on the Riviera or any place you say and take a nice vacation together before we come home. Now, you certainly can't say no to that. Two months in Europe during the winter?"

She put down *Photoplay* and looked at him.

"Melville, something tells me there's something buzzing around in that brain of yours. What's the matter? Are you afraid to leave me alone for two months in wicked old Elkins?"

Melville's saturnine face turned red with embarrassment. If there was anything he dreaded, it was to face the blunt truth.

"Well—"

"Oh, come on. Is that what's bothering you?"

"Lily, you know very well I love you more than anything—"

"That's very poetic."

"*Please* . . . I know I'm not exactly the most dashing man in the world"— He was miserable. To say it offended him to the soul—"I know there have been other men . . ."

"Oh, you do?"

He took a deep breath. "Are you having an affair with Mark?"

She stared at him. "Oh, Melville, that's *marvelous!* Oh God, I *love* it! Me and the king! I've underestimated you. You do have real imagination!"

"Lily, *are you?*"

"Uh huh, every night we rendezvous in the curing pits. Then we curl up inside a tire and just *steam* . . . Zingo!"

"Lily, tell me the truth . . ."

She stopped and looked at him contemptuously as she fiddled with the silver strap of her dress.

"You know Mark Manning's no fool. He needs you and he needs daddy. Now, do you honestly think he's going to upset his corporate applecart just to fool around with me? I mean, I'm attractive but I'm not Clara Bow, for God's sake. Use your head."

It was such an abrupt change of tone, so apparently and unexpectedly sensible that he believed it—which he was predisposed to do in any case if she would only give him some plausible argument. And now, to his delight, she had.

"Then it *isn't* true!"

"Of course not. I don't know how you could be *that* stupid. Besides, Melville, I may not be Elkins's most proper young married, but I'm hardly the company whore either."

He was relieved, and excited, as he leaned over on the chaise and began to kiss her, his sex pressing against her thigh.

She shoved him off.

"Melville, take it easy, you'll ruin my dress . . ."

"Damn it, Lily, I love you so much . . ."

Or at least want me, she thought. "Anyway," she said, "you go to Río de Oro. Lily will stay in Elkins and do her best to keep the home-fires burning."

If Melville had been surer of himself with women, he might have been able to cope with his wife more adroitly. But he had been raised in a strict Methodist family where sex was a proscribed subject and his first sexual encounter was not until he was twenty-three. It had been the classic visit to a brothel which had, also classically, been a traumatic experience for him, even compounding his already built-in fear of women—twenty-five minutes in a Columbus, Ohio, brothel with a fifty-year-old woman. His first wife had been so vapid she gave him no new understanding of women, though she did manage to abate his fear somewhat. By the time he had met and married Lily, he was past forty and too far along in life to have developed much finesse or understanding, although his need and capacity had hardly abated.

Melville also was no fool, and on the way to Africa, as time and distance separated him from his wife and his emotions cooled, his intelligence began to tell him he had allowed himself to be hood-winked. Of course Mark would not object to his wanting to bring Lily along on the trip. Mark would have known that Lily would refuse, which was exactly what had happened, and he had fallen for it with the collaboration of his ego, which made him want and need to believe them. It was the old David and Bathsheba story, the un-happy twist being that he, Melville, was Uriah being sent to the front. Heading now for Río de Oro on the slow, dirty ship from Southampton, he visualized them in all manner of erotic and exotic lovemaking throughout the dozens of bedrooms in the empty mansion at River Bend, no doubt joking about poor naïve Melville. He had no choice now but to go through with his mission and wait till he returned to Elkins. But then, for once, he would begin to act smart, he would trap them. And then what? He wasn't sure. But if his suspicions were true, he would somehow make them both pay for their treachery. . . .

The two militiamen sat in the corner watch tower smoking cigarettes and exchanging occasional sleepy remarks. They were Mandingo tribesmen recruited into the Río de Oro militia two years before and after basic training assigned to the permanent guard detachment at the national armory outside Ciba, the second largest city of the country, up river from Tylertown. They manned a German machine-gun, World War I surplus the government had picked up at a bargain price after the Armistice. The gun was clean and well oiled. The two men knew their business.

The armory was a square concrete building set in two acres of cleared land a mile from Ciba, surrounded by a high steel, barbed-wire-topped fence, at each of the four corners of which rose the thirty-foot wooden watch towers, each manned by two men and one machine-gun. The main gate to the compound centered on the east side and was guarded by a concrete pillbox with a machine-gun and a wooden guardhouse manned by two men. Similar security was pro-vided at the back gate on the west side. Beyond the barbed-wire fence the bush had been cleared for fifty feet. Then the jungle began, rising like a green, impenetrable wall on all four sides, except where the dirt road to Ciba breeched it on the east side and, at the rear, where a smaller road led to the guard barracks two hundred yards away. Four spotlights on top of the armory lazily swept the whole area, piercing the blackness of the night. It was 1:35 on the morning of January 12, 1927.

Agwe, one of the two guards in the southeast tower, had just lighted a cigarette when he saw the stars arching out of the jungle. What seemed like a thousand flames parabolaed up, then down, raining on the four wooden watch towers. Agwe involuntarily ducked as one landed next to his gun; Sam-Sam, his partner, cursed and grabbed the arrow tipped with the oil-soaked flaming rag, tossing it off the platform. After his initial shock, Agwe grabbed the gun and began firing into the black forest. Sam-Sam fed the cartridge belt as they heard the blastings of the other guns. Except that no one knew precisely what he was firing at.

The stars continued to shoot out of the forest, and Agwe saw one land on the corrugated-iron roof of the northeast tower and roll off. It bumped to the ground and started licking at the wooden stilts. He briefly remembered one of the officers sending complaining letters to Tylertown the year previously about the vulnerability of wooden watch towers. After months of bureaucratic delay, the answer had come back that budget requirements precluded the construction of steel towers.

Now the searchlights were out. Someone had cut the buried power cable, which meant that the warning siren could not be activated and the telephones would be dead. How could anyone have known where the cables were buried? The lights in the guardhouse and pillbox by the gate died too, and now the only illumination was from the shooting stars and the northeast tower, which was burning in two places—one pile was ablaze, lit by the torch that had bumped off the roof; and the platform itself was on fire from another arrow. Agwe shouted to Sam-Sam, "They'll hear the guns at the barracks!" Sam-Sam nodded and pulled another cartridge belt from the wooden case behind him. As he began to feed the new belt to the gun, a flaming arrow landed in the cartridge case. For a moment neither of the men noticed it. The arrow had come from behind them, and they were concentrating on the gun. Then Agwe smelled it. He turned, yelled, and reached for the fire, hurling the arrow off the platform. Sweating with fear, he saw the northeast tower now a flaming pyre; the two men stationed in it were scrambling down the wooden ladder.

They were halfway down when the flames exploded the ammunition. There was a loud noise as the tower turned into a fireball. Agwe winced as he saw the two men hurled from the ladder to the ground fifteen feet below.

Now a new noise could be heard above the chattering of the guns— a sustained, high-pitched sound from a thousand throats, which Agwe recognized as the battle cry of the Kru tribe. As he returned to his gun, they came out of the jungle wall like ants swarming out of a rotted tree trunk, running across the fifty foot clearing toward the east gate. The attack was accompanied and covered by a hail of arrows. Now that the shooting stars had stopped and the spotlights were out, Agwe no longer could see the arrows but he could hear them clanging as they hit the iron roof. Sweat poured down his forehead into his eyes as he fired the gun, sweeping back and forth across the clearing. He was killing them by the dozens. It was difficult to see in the dark, but of the hundreds of running shadows converging on the gate, at least half had fallen on the ground. Still they came, the high-pitched yell never lessening in pitch or intensity. "They got another tower!" called Sam-Sam, and Agwe turned quickly to see the southwest tower in flames.

Now he was panicked. "Why don't they send help from the barracks?"

Sam-Sam did not answer. An arrow had plunged into his chest. He grunted, grabbed the arrow with both hands in a feeble effort to pull it out of his khaki sleeveless shirt; then he slumped over, bumping his head against the wooden rail as he fell. Agwe stared at him a moment, aware that death now shared the guard tower with him. He returned to his firing.

Two thoughts swirled through his mind. How had they found the power and phone cables, and why did they storm the gates? They could burn the watch towers but they couldn't burn the concrete pillbox. He also doubted they could get through the steel fence—at least without modern tools to cut the strong chain. The answer was quickly forthcoming. He heard the yell burst with a new intensity and he saw what looked like two hundred more men come out of the jungle and rush toward the pillbox. A suicide force. The firing from the pillbox and from Agwe mowed the men down like scythed reeds, but there were so many of them that some inevitably managed to avoid the fire and reach the pillbox. Then, to Agwe's surprise, there were two loud explosions. The pillbox blew up, as did the gate. Somehow the tribesmen had gotten their hands on dynamite.

His was the only gun firing now, and he knew he was a dead man.

He fired the last bullets in his belt, then hurriedly reached in the wooden case for a new one.

The almost naked black man peeked over the flooring of the platform. He saw Agwe, black like himself although dressed in khaki shorts and shirt, crouching over his gun, his back toward him. The man silently climbed over the railing, his lithe body not making a noise as he moved up behind Agwe, then raised his machete over his head. With one slice he drove the blade down on the back of Agwe's neck. The head bumped on the floor. The tribesman picked it up by one ear, stared at the cascading blood for a second, then hurled it off the tower into the howling mass of men below.

By two o'clock it was all over. The iron doors of the armory were blown up by more dynamite and the men rushed inside. Within an hour 3,000 rifles, fifty cases of hand grenades, 100,000 rounds of rifle ammunition, thirty machine-guns with a hundred cases of belts, a dozen cases of dynamite, a French 155-mm. howitzer and two Austro-Hungarian 24-mm. howitzers were dragged off into the jungle. One-third of all the weaponry of the Río de Oro militia had been captured.

The reason the fifty sleeping men in the guard barracks had not heard the gunfire was that ten minutes before the attack on the armory the two guards on duty at the barracks had opened the gates to admit sixty tribesmen armed with spears. The guards were all dead within five minutes, except for the two who had opened the gates and told Tegai's lieutenants where the power and phone cables were buried.

They, of course, were both loyal members of the Leopard Society.

CHAPTER FIVE

When Melville reached Tylertown a week after the attack on the Armory, Río de Oro was in a state of civil war. President Chadwick, far from being upset at the idea of three U.S. gunboats coming to track down one of his countrymen, was besieging Jerome Muhlbach, the ambassador, with pleas for more assistance to suppress the revolt. Now it was no longer a question of a few shadowy Leopard Society members terrorizing rubber workers. Now Tegai had enough modern —or at least semimodern—weapons to outfit a small army. And Chadwick's information was that Tegai, bolstered by the prestige of his successful attack on the armory, was welding the up-country tribes into a unit with the purpose of taking on the militia, defeating it, then marching on Tylertown to take over the country. Tegai had used his father's tribe, the Krus, to attack the armory. Now by bringing in the Grebos, the Mandingos, the Vais and lesser tribes with the Krus, he could command a force estimated at anywhere from 10,000 to 30,000 men. The militia consisted of 8,000 men, and, as Mark had guessed, many of them were sympathetic to Tegai, particularly now that he seemed to be the winning side, so that the militia would hardly be a match for Tegai's army. It required no military genius to see that three gunboats with a hundred fifty sailors would not be much help either.

President Chadwick was asking Ambassador Muhlbach for 5,000 U.S. Marines. He had little hope of getting that many, but he thought that if he could get at least 2,000 and perhaps some aircraft assistance he could lead an attack into the up country against Tegai and wipe him out. The ambassador had forwarded the request to Washington. That was the situation when Melville arrived in Tylertown.

Melville immediately saw the inherent danger to the Manning interests. The Las Palmas plantation, though still bereft of its labor force, had so far been spared an attack by Tegai, who had been concentrating his efforts on bringing the tribes together. However, the plantation sat squarely in the middle of the two opposing forces, between Tylertown and the up country, and it was possible it might be destroyed when hostilities broke out. On the other hand there could be no doubt what would happen to it if Tegai in fact took over the country. Melville was forced into supporting Chadwick's request for the Marines, which he explained to Mark on the radio. Mark agreed with his reasoning; they had no choice but to back Chadwick, and he agreed to exert all the pressure he could in Washington to get the request accepted. He was as unhappy about the situation as Melville ("It's one thing to go after a few fanatics," he grumbled, "but now we're mixed up in a goddamn war.") But since it *was* war, he felt they should urge Washington to send enough men to do the job correctly. He would ask that Chadwick's request for 5,000 men be implemented; and rather than "some aircraft assistance," he would ask for an aircraft carrier to be sent to Tylertown so that whatever planes were needed would be on hand.

When Melville passed this information on to Chadwick, the president looked a bit taken aback—after all, an aircraft carrier!—but he quickly warmed to the idea. "Mr. Manning doesn't do things half way, does he?" he said with grudging admiration, remembering how Mark had pushed him to the wall four years previously.

"In no area," said Melville, thinking of Lily.

The gunboats arrived two days later, and the sight of the three American vessels in the Tylertown harbor rather miraculously boosted the morale of the pro-Chadwick portion of the population, which had become increasingly nervous after the attack on the armory. Morale shot even higher when, the day after the arrival of the gunboats, word was received that Washington was indeed sending 4,000 Marines on the aircraft carrier *Declaration of Independence* to Tylertown to be "at the disposal of the Government," as the diplomatic note phrased it.

American "intervention" in the affairs of foreign countries was nothing especially new. As early as 1909 U.S. Marines had been sent to Nicaragua to protect American "nationals" and American business interests, and from 1912 to 1933 a force of Marines was, with one brief exception, stationed in Managua to maintain a "friendly" government in office, supervise elections and train a constabulary. In 1914 President Wilson, an avowed noninterventionist, sent troops into Mexico, and two years later U.S. Marines literally took over Haiti (Franklin Delano Roosevelt, when running for the Vice-Presidency in 1920, publicly acknowledged that he had written the Haitian constitution while he was assistant secretary of the navy, adding, "it was a pretty darn good one, too!"). The Dominican Republic, Cuba and, of course, Panama were also subject to U.S. presence. However, by the Twenties the stated policy of the State Department was that the United States had no ambitions in or desire to interfere in its neighbors' domestic affairs, and public opinion was turning against the cruder displays of "dollar diplomacy." The Marines were removed from Nicaragua in 1925. However, a revolution immediately occurred, ousting the pro-American government, and in 1926 President Coolidge promptly sent the Marines back to restore the regime of Adolfo Diaz (a move that encouraged skeptics to question the sincerity of the State Department's noninterventionist position), and the Marines stayed on. Thus, when Mark brought pressure on President Coolidge to send help to Río de Oro to safeguard his own investment, the lives of the Americans at Las Palmas and the $20,000,000 investment of the U.S. Government as well as Chadwick's regime (which Mark—still exercising the political acumen, if on a grander scale, he had demonstrated some twenty-seven years earlier with a now long-forgotten obscure Ohio Congressman named Tutwiler—did not fail to point out was dominated by descendants of American slaves and which

America therefore had a "moral" commitment to support), President Coolidge, though by nature not avid for foreign adventures, was hard put not to respond.

Still another historical trend was playing into Mark's hands. In 1921 General Billy Mitchell, a World War ace who had become a public hero by flying the Atlantic in 1919 in the Curtiss NC-4 flying boat, staged a series of aerial bombings on target warships to prove to army and navy brass that air power would be the determining factor in future wars. With eight Martin bombers, he sank the *Ostfriesland,* an "unsinkable" German dreadnought, in twenty-five minutes. Despite this spectacular achievement, the brass remained unconvinced and hostile to Mitchell's campaign. And when Mitchell accused them of "incompetence and criminal negligence" after the *Shenandoah* dirigible tragedy of 1925, he was brought to trial in a well-publicized court martial that convicted him of insubordination. But though the brass had gotten rid of the "loud mouth" Mitchell, ironically his preaching had won converts. The navy had grudgingly come to concede the potential of air power and that carrier-based planes could greatly increase the fighting range of a fleet. Now it was actively looking for opportunities to rehearse air-land-sea operations. The Tylertown imbroglio provided an ideal opportunity; the chief of naval operations joined in bringing pressure on Coolidge to send out the *Declaration of Independence,* one of the two crude battleships-converted-into-carriers the navy at that time possessed. The pressure from Mark, one of his major campaign contributors, as well as from his own navy was more than enough to overcome whatever reluctance Coolidge felt; and on January 23, 1927, the *Declaration of Independence* left the naval base at Norfolk, Virginia, bound for arrival at Tylertown on the 8th with a complement on board of 2,000 Marines and twenty-six aircraft.

President Chadwick was delighted, if nervous.

Dr. Roger Boine was disgusted. For Roger, who had come to love the Africans, believed that the arrival of the Marines and the aircraft was to bring about a blood bath, the principal victims of which would be, as always, the innocent.

CHAPTER SIX

The three boys poised at the edge of the open window, one of them, the fifteen-year-old with flaming red hair tufting out from beneath his knitted snow hat, having one leg already over the sill ready to jump. It was midnight on January 24 in the year 1927.

"Chris, are you *sure* we should do this?" whispered the second boy, whose homely face had a light sprinkling of acne.

"Are you chicken?" said Chris.

Will Potter, the second boy, stiffened.

"Course not, but we could get in a lot of trouble if we're caught."

"We won't get caught. I *told* you, I've got it all worked out, come on."

Chris swung his other leg over the window sill, then looked down a moment. The drifting snow below looked clean and blue-white in the moonlight. He jumped. It was only three feet.

The other two boys, Will Potter and Barney Mundy, followed him out of the window of the Wooster School dormitory. Then, after carefully closing the window, the three roommates ran through the snow to the school garage, where Christopher Manning produced three keys from his pocket. One of them fitted the padlock of the garage door, which he opened. The three scooted inside the dark garage, and Christopher led them to the rear.

"Here's the truck," he whispered. "Barney, you open the garage door. I'll get the engine warmed up." Barney nodded as Chris and Will climbed in the front seat of the truck, Will shaking his head and mumbling, "I don't know, this seems awful dangerous to me. If Dr. Warner finds out, boy, are we in trouble!"

"Aw, pipe down," snapped Chris, inserting the second key he had stolen that afternoon into the truck's ignition and starting the engine. It was a new Ford, bought the previous summer by the school, and Chris reflected that it no doubt was equipped with Manning Snow-Gripper tires. He let the engine warm up as Barney climbed in alongside Will. There was no danger of being heard. The garage was a good thousand yards from any of the other school buildings, and the Wooster School had the most casual of security systems—no guards at all. It was going to be a snap.

When the engine was purring, Chris shifted gears and pulled out of the garage through the back door, taking the rear drive out to State Road 12, which led to the town of Hayesville, two miles away, a farming community named for Rutherford B. Hayes. The road was paved and it had been snow-plowed the previous day after the storm, so the ride was pleasant and as they tore down the empty road past the dark farmhouses and snow-drifted fields, even Will Potter's spirits rose a little.

"It's kind of exciting, isn't it?" he said uncertainly.

Chris and Barney laughed.

"See?" said Barney, who was the pudgy son of a Cleveland lawyer, "old Will's going to be a first-class criminal."

"Yeah, regular Al Capone, Junior," Chris said and laughed. "Don't worry, Will, if we get caught, the most we'll get is ten or twelve years."

Will's enthusiasm ebbed. "But you said we wouldn't be caught."

"Don't *worry*. Everything's jake. Leave it to me."

"Don't be a flat tire," Barney added.

Will sank back in the seat wondering what his father, a Columbus dentist, would say when he went to prison. He knew he was doomed. If he backed out now, Barney and Chris would know he was hopelessly chicken. On the other hand, if he went through with it and they weren't caught, the three of them would be bound together in the eternal bonds of co-conspiracy, and Will Potter's prestige among his classmates would soar. In particular, it would cement his friendship with Chris Manning, and Will wanted that desperately. His red-haired, good-looking, dashing roommate was everything Will wasn't but wished he were. Chris held no class office, having too many demerits to be included on the ballot, but if he had been on, there was no doubt he would be class president. Chris was the star—star pitcher on the baseball team, star swimmer, star quarterback, unofficial arbiter of all disputes, star mischief-maker, bravest boy in the class and the only one who everyone believed had *really* gone to bed with a girl (of course, everyone claimed that he had, but Chris was the only one the class tacitly agreed probably had actually achieved this summit). Chris Manning was Number One at Wooster, and to be Chris's pal meant to be really in. And Will Potter would risk almost anything for that.

Besides, Chris had dreamed up the whole plot just for Will, which made it doubly impossible for him to back out. Will had been warned not to buy anything at the Rosswell Sporting Goods Store in Hayesville. The whole school knew that Old Man Rosswell was a gypster

who loved nothing better than skinning the boys at Wooster, but
Will had gone in anyway the previous Saturday and bought the pair
of ice skates he'd seen in the window, because he wanted to learn
how to skate (as well as Chris did, naturally) and of course the
skates, which had cost twelve dollars (all that was left of his Christmas
money) had had a chip in the left blade that Will hadn't noticed, and
when he tried to get a refund an hour later Old Man Rosswell had
told him to go jump. Well, when Chris heard about that, he blew his
top. Rosswell had passed off a bad pair of skates on Will, and that was
the last straw. He'd gypped Wooster boys enough, and the only thing
to do was break into his store and steal a good pair of skates, leaving
the defective pair back in the window where Rosswell had stuck them
in the first place for display purposes. That was the plot, and Will
was the cause of it all, and he was stuck. But still and all, to break
into a store and *steal*—! As they neared Hayesville, Will began to feel
sick to his stomach.

"You know," he said lamely, "we *are* breaking the law."

Chris looked at him and laughed. "No kidding. Did you hear that,
Barney? Will's figured out we're breaking the law. Golly."

"How'd you figure that out, Will? That must have taken a lot of
thinking," Barney said.

"Aw come on, you guys."

Will sank even lower in the seat and briefly contemplated flight to
Mexico.

Chris slowed down as they hit Main Street. The town was deserted
—Hayesville's sidewalks rolled up at seven in the winter—but a number
of people lived on the main drag, in private houses as well as above
a few of the stores. It wouldn't do to wake them up. Chris turned
into the alley next to Rosswell Sporting Goods, drove down to the
back alley, then parked the truck by the service door. He pulled the
last key from his pocket and held it up. "This is the key to that door,"
he said proudly, nodding toward the steel service door. The two
boys looked impressed.

"How'd you get it, Chris?" Barney asked.

"Yeah—tell us," echoed Will, eager for any delay before action.

"Simple," said Chris, who'd been bursting to tell his brilliant idea
anyway. "I hitched a ride into town during lunch and came into the
store. I told Rosswell my father might be interested in setting up a
tire dealership in Hayesville and that he'd asked me to check out the
local merchants and would Mr. Rosswell be interested? Well, you
should've seen his face light up! He swallowed the whole thing and
showed me all around the store and told me what a solid businessman

he is and all that applesauce. And while we were back in the store-room, I saw the key hanging on a hook by the door. So I took it."

"Gee!" said Barney, "that took a lot of nerve!"

Chris shrugged nonchalantly. "Not particularly. Then I thanked him and hitched back to school. Anyway, here we are. Come on."

He opened the truck door and started to climb out.

"But . . ." said Will nervously, "wouldn't he miss the key?"

"Probably. But he'd never think *I* stole it. And even if he did, he wants my old man's dealership too much to say anything. We'll leave it on the hook when we leave and that'll be the end of it. Come on, let's go. It's cold! And don't slam the truck door."

The two other boys climbed out of the truck, carefully closing the doors as silently as possible, then followed Chris to the back of the store, Will staring nervously at the windowless brick rear walls of the Victorian buildings. Chris had brought a flashlight. Now he aimed the beam at the keyhole, inserted the key and turned it. The door opened. He hurried inside, waving the others in. Then he closed the door.

Silence. He ran the flashlight over the packing cases.

"Did you bring the skates, or did you leave 'em in the truck—you probably left 'em," whispered Chris.

"I've got 'em." Will was trembling. Sing Sing, Joliet, San Quentin . . .

"Okay, let's go in the front. And *this* time, pick out a good pair."

They tiptoed across the storeroom to the door that led to the front, which Chris pushed open. They went in, the front store being dimly illuminated by a street light.

"Take the flashlight," Chris whispered to Will, "and go pick out a new pair. I'll put the old ones back in the window—"

The store lights turned on. As the three boys blinked from the glare, Old Man Rosswell aimed his shotgun at them.

"I've been expecting you, Manning," he said.

Chris stared at the white-haired man in the plaid hunting coat standing behind the counter. Will and Barney sucked air.

"Oh, hello, Mr. Rosswell," he said casually as Will Potter started to moan. Chris kicked his shins. "We were just returning this lousy pair of skates you sold Will. I couldn't very well recommend to my father that he give you a franchise if I thought you sold inferior merchandise, could I?"

"You think you're so damn smart, don't you? Well, I knew who'd taken that key, and I've been waiting for you. You don't really think I believed that story about your father wanting to give me a tire franchise? I knew you was up to something, and I strung you along to see what it was. Well, now I know. Oh, a fine example you rich brats set—a fine example! You're nothing but a bunch of crooks!"

Chris looked at the barrel of the gun and wondered if he might shoot. Rosswell was furious, but Chris didn't think he was mad enough to do something that crazy. Still, he couldn't be sure. The uncertainty excited him.

"I don't know, Mr. Rosswell, that sounds like a pretty radical remark. And I think you *did* believe my story this afternoon. You're just saying you didn't now so you won't look so dumb."

"Don't give me any of your smart talk, Manning. Now the four of us is going to take a walk to the sheriff's office. Get moving!"

He waved the gun toward the front door. Will Potter started to cry. Chris squeezed his arm angrily. "Don't be a cry baby, dammit! That's just what he wants to see!"

Will nodded bravely as he could as Chris tossed the service door key on the glass counter top and started toward the front door, smiling at the man with the gun.

"You know, Mr. Rosswell, this is a really two-bit operation you've got here. Really hickey, you know?" He stopped by the door and frowned philosophically. "If you're going to do something, you ought to do it first class, Mr. Rosswell. Don't you think?"

Rosswell came around the counter, burning. "I think I ought to bash this gun butt right in your smart mouth—that's what I think!"

"But you won't."

He didn't.

Dr. Graham Warner sat at his desk looking at the well-dressed tycoon sitting across from him, and he cursed Chris Manning for putting him in this unenviable position. Dr. Warner was forty-two, a bright Harvard graduate who had written his doctorate on the novels of Stendhal. Fourteen years earlier he had been offered the headmastership of the small Wooster School, which he had eagerly accepted, bringing his attractive wife and two children from Andover, where he had been teaching English, to the challenging job out in the plains of Ohio. Energetic, ambitious for the school, an excellent teacher, he had built up the tiny school from near-nothing to near-something since his arrival, though it was still at least financially undistinguished compared to the Eastern schools he had left. Wooster, with an enrollment of a hundred boys, had an endowment of less than $1,000,000; and though Dr. Warner had been able to build the well-equipped new gymnasium (thanks mainly to Mark's contribution of $25,000) and raise faculty salaries to a level that would attract teachers of high quality, Wooster was nonetheless barely hanging on. Its undergraduates came mostly from middle- and a few upper-middle-class homes; their parents were hardly in a position to make the dramatic donations that the school desperately needed. Wooster's one multimillionaire, the one man interested in the school who could really help lift it out of the second rate, was, of course, Mark. Dr. Warner and Mark liked each other. Since the days of Roger Boine's attendance, they had been on a first-name basis; and Mark's enrolling his youngest son in the school had sent Dr. Warner's hopes soaring for a major contribution.

And now, Chris Manning had broken into the Rosswell Sporting Goods Store.

"Chris tells me this Mr. Rosswell had cheated the Potter boy," said Mark, who had driven down from Elkins the morning after the break-in to bail his son and his roommates out of the local jail.

"That's right. He's a sharp trader who's pulled fast ones on several of the boys."

"Well, then, isn't it conceivable he got what he deserved?"

Dr. Warner sighed. "Look, Mark, I'm sick about this whole thing. I'm not going to try and hide what I'm thinking. It's not only that I like Chris, which I do. But frankly, I hate to expel your son because I don't want to alienate your friendship to the school. Now if that sounds mercenary, I can't avoid it. Having Mark Manning send his son to Wooster means a lot to us. All right, along comes Chris who plans a neat little breaking and entering, apparently mitigated by the fact that Rosswell probably *did* deserve it. And Chris pulls it off in his dashing style—or almost pulls it off. Oh, that son of yours has got guts. But he also leaves the school during lunch without permission. He leaves his dormitory after lights out. He steals the keys to the school garage, then steals the school truck. And last but hardly least, he breaks into Rosswell's store to steal a pair of skates and ends up in jail. I have absolutely no choice. I must expel him and the others."

"I don't quite see it that way, Graham."

"I didn't think you would."

"I'm not denying that Chris broke the rules. But I've seen Rosswell.

I apologized to him and gave him a check for five hundred dollars to cover any damage to his peace of mind—his premises certainly seem intact—and he seemed to take a different view of the matter. He's not going to press charges. Now, if Rosswell is happy, I don't see that you have cause to be so upset. *Punish* the boys, naturally. That goes without saying. But expel them? That strikes me as a bit harsh."

"But Mark, they broke the law!"

Mark shrugged. "It was a schoolboy prank. You know that."

"But breaking into a store goes *beyond* a prank!"

Mark leaned forward. "All right, Graham, I won't argue semantics with you. I'll put it on a personal basis. I enrolled Chris here because I like you and the school, and because I wanted one of my children close to home. I'd like to keep him here, and I'd hate to see his scholastic record tarnished by an expulsion. Now, as a personal favor to me, will you please forget this idea of kicking them out?"

Dr. Warner shook his head slowly. "Mark, I can't. If I don't expel Chris, all the boys will know why. They're not fools. They know he's your son, and they know the school is strapped financially. They'd know it was favoritism, and it would undermine the whole disciplinary structure of the school. I just couldn't do it. Much as I hate to lose you and Chris, I have to expel him."

"I can't change your mind?"

"I'm afraid not. I hope there are no hard feelings?"

Mark laughed. "I'm not exactly full of affection for you right now, Graham, but I can see your point." He hesitated. "Still, it's a rather unrealistic, short-sighted attitude."

"What do you mean?"

"Just that you're being awfully naïve worrying about the boys' finding out there's such a thing as favoritism in this world—don't you think they know that already? And if they don't, hadn't they better be finding it out? Isn't that part of their education?"

"That's an awfully cynical attitude, Mark."

"It's the truth. Look, I think it's important that we have good schools in the Midwest as well as the East, and I've been considering making, as you would call it, a major contribution. To be specific, Chris has told me about the lab here—how it's so poorly equipped, and so on. These days the colleges are stressing science education, which I think they should, and I was considering funding not only a modern building for physics, biology and chemistry, but also establishing an endowment fund to pay for the instructors. I do blame Chris, of course. He's hot-headed and a little too smart for his own good. But I still feel you're overdoing it, and I think your worry about showing favoritism to Chris is going to hurt the school much more in the long run than whatever damage not expelling Chris might do to the boys' morale." He stood up and extended his hand. "Well, I've said my piece. I'm really sorry, Graham. And I appreciate your calling me this morning."

Dr. Warner was miserable as he looked at $200,000,000.

"You're not even going to shake my hand, Graham?"

"Sit down, Mark," the headmaster finally said.

Mark returned to his seat. Dr. Warner stared at his hands a moment. "All right. You made your point, and it's a legitimate one. Maybe I'm being too . . . fastidious."

Mark said nothing.

"Maybe another form of punishment might make more of an impression on the boys.

"For instance?"

Dr. Warner looked up shame-faced. "Something along the lines of kitchen work, scrubbing down floors, cleaning out bathrooms for a few months—demeaning work that might impress the other boys even more than expulsion, because the others would be able to see their humiliation over an extended period of time . . ."

Mark nodded. "That's an interesting approach. Of course, you wouldn't want to demean the boys *too* much—it might damage their spirit, but I can definitely see the value of their cleaning bathrooms for, say, a month."

Like father, like son, thought Dr. Warner. They both know what they want, and they take it.

"Then I take it you're changing your mind?"

Dr. Warner took a deep breath and nodded.

Again Mark stood up. "Graham, I think you've made a wise and humane decision."

Humane? Dr. Warner could hardly believe his ears. Mark picked up his Homburg from the desk. As Warner came around the desk, he put his hand on the headmaster's shoulder.

"Why don't we talk about that science building? I'll tell you what, I'm going to Palm Beach in a few days to take a look at my new place down there. I'll be there for a month. Why don't you line up a first-rate architect and make up some sketches. Then when I get back to Elkins in March, the two of you come up for dinner and we'll discuss the whole thing. Agreed?"

Dr. Warner nodded.

"Agreed." His voice was flat. It had hurt more than he thought it would.

Mark came out of the main school building and walked down the
snow-shoveled path to his maroon Packard limousine. It was a bright,
warm day and the sun was melting the snow. Marvin Senjak, looking
appropriately smart in his near-matching maroon chauffeur's uniform and shiny brown boots, was leaning against the car talking
through the open window to Chris in the back seat. It was noon. Mark
noticed about two dozen of the schoolboys ogling the shiny limousine
from the windows of the building.

When he reached the car he said, "Chris, come out here a minute."

Chris scrambled out of the car. He looked neither guilty nor apprehensive; rather, he was delighted to see his father. Chris hero-worshiped him as much as Will Potter hero-worshiped Chris.

"What did Doc Warner say?" he asked. "He's pretty hot under the
collar, isn't he?"

"He is, and so am I."

"Did you fix it for me?"

"I didn't fix it. Dr. Warner believes you didn't mean any harm,
and he's agreed to give you one more chance. But you and Will and
Barney are going to be on very familiar terms with the school toilets
for the next month."

"Toilets? Ah gee, dad—"

"You'll *do* it, young man, and I don't want to hear about you trying
to sneak out of your punishment. It's light enough as it is."

"Yes sir." A look of mischief came into Chris's blue eyes. He
lowered his voice. "How'd you do it, dad? All the guys are making
bets on how much it's going to cost you. How much *did* it cost?"

"You little devil, it's going to cost me plenty, but I don't intend
to buy your way out of trouble the rest of your life."

"Yes, sir."

"I mean it, Chris. You may think this whole thing's been a great
lark, but I warn you, don't let it happen again."

"Yes, sir."

"You don't feel one twinge of guilt, do you?"

"Oh, yes, I do, dad. Really."

Mark knew he was lying. He also knew he had to punish him.
Personally. Now. He was an easy mark for his children and most of
all for Chris; but he had to do something. He looked back at the
school building. At least twenty more boys had now joined the others
at the windows, viewing the meeting between their leader, Chris, and

his famous father. Mark turned back to his son.

"Chris, I want you to hit me."

"What?"

"Go on, hit me, now!"

"But why?"

"Just do what you're told."

"Aw, come on, dad! All the guys are watching!"

"That's the idea."

The look of confusion on Chris's face was replaced by one of intrigue.

"Well, okay. Can I hit you hard?"

"As hard as you can. I'll take my chances."

"You may be surprised, pop."

He sank his fist into Mark's stomach. His father almost lost his balance—the little bastard was stronger than he had thought.

Chris grinned at him as the boys in the windows stared in astonishment. Then Mark's open right hand moved through the air to his son's cheek, delivering so hard a slap that Chris, caught off balance, reeled back and fell into the snow, where he lay holding his jaw and staring up in amazement at his father. The boys in the windows were whispering excitedly to each other, "Geez, did you see *that*? Look at Chris—he really got shut up that time!"

Chris slowly got to his feet, trying to fight back the tears of pain and shock as he looked at his father.

"Why'd you do *that*?"

"To teach you three things. First, get rid of this idea that you can twist me around your finger. Understand?"

Chris nodded.

"Second, don't *ever* embarrass me or your family by doing anything dishonest. You have too many advantages other boys don't have, Chris. That doesn't mean you can break the rules. *Understand*?"

Chris nodded.

"Say, 'Yes, sir.' "

"Yes, sir."

"That's a little better."

He walked to the car. Marvin held the door for him as he got into the back seat. Marvin closed the door and got into the front seat to start the engine.

Chris came over to his father. Mark noticed that the hurt and resentment in his eyes had been replaced by anger. He was blazing mad.

He's just like me, he thought. Just like me.

"What's the third thing?" asked Chris sullenly.

"Never hit anyone bigger than you," replied his father. "Especially if he tells you to."

With that, the Packard pulled away, Chris watching after it as it moved down the driveway.

CHAPTER SEVEN

When Roger Boine first realized Mark Manning was his natural father, it came as a shock to him. But after a time, the shock wore off and he came to accept the situation—even to be intrigued by it. He pretended not to know, because it was so obvious that both his mother and Mark wished to preserve the fiction, but he wished he could end the pretense, at least with Mark, because he admired him extravagantly and had a natural desire to be recognized by his father as his son. He continued to play the game, out of shyness as well as deference to his parents' wishes, and his relationship with Mark remained a friendship only. Far from resenting Mark for not making him legitimate, Roger overcompensated for his lack of a real father by hero-worshiping the man who paid for his education. Roger followed Mark's career with avid interest, secretly delighting in his father's reflected glory. He saw nothing but good in the man, an attitude that was only re-enforced by his mother's continual criticism of Mark. Roger understood his mother's embittered feelings, but to him Mark represented all that was grand and, yes, heroic in American life. Mark had come from the bottom to build an industrial empire that was run with enlightened principles and which was an example to the whole world. Roger was proud Mark Manning was his father. And when the invitation to take his residency at Las Palmas had come, Roger had jumped at the chance—not only to show Mark his gratitude, as he had told his mother, but also because he wanted to be part of the Manning Rubber and Steel Company, if only for a few years. It was, after all, in a way partially his.

His first impressions of Las Palmas had been what he expected. The place was clean, attractive and efficiently run. The hospital was better than he expected and the health care given the staff and the workers was excellent. Here was American business's finest hour, bringing order and modern health care into the chaos of the jungle, helping the black man into the twentieth century, bringing him the benefits of American technology, giving him jobs. How wrong his mother was!

But he soon began noticing things that somewhat tarnished the glow. It was obvious, painfully obvious, that the white management lived by one set of rules and the black workers by another. Well, that was only to be suspected, he supposed; still, the Americans treated the blacks as if they ruled by divine right. For instance, one day two weeks after he arrived, Roger was assisting Dr. Vandeventer, the head of the hospital staff, in setting the broken leg of one of the black workers. It was a simple enough procedure. But when Miss Parsons, the head nurse, came in to tell Dr. Vandeventer that Mrs. Clark, the wife of the plantation manager, had just arrived complaining of a sore throat, Dr. Vandeventer turned the worker over to Roger to go attend Sally Clark. True, the worker was hardly *in extremis,* but Roger thought that Dr. Vandeventer's priorities were rather askew. There were other things. Nearly the entire white contingent referred privately to the blacks as "niggers." This was hardly any worse than the Belgians in the Belgian Congo referring to their blacks as *macaques,* or "apes," but still, the usage irritated Roger. He had come to like and admire the blacks he met, and he was fascinated by their culture—in which, incidentally, hardly any of his fellow whites exhibited the slightest interest. To call these people "niggers" was insulting and unfair. It smacked of the arrogant European attitude that Africans were backward children, and though Roger was aware that blacks in America hardly fared any better—what with the lynchings and the Klan in the South and the race riots in the North—still, it made him feel ashamed that Americans in Río de Oro would not behave better to their hosts.

Finally he began hearing the stories that complicated his feelings about the blacks because they dealt with the black government in Tylertown. President Chadwick, it was whispered, who had begun his administration a national hero, was now building up a private fortune, as were many of his subordinates. The stories varied, but the blacks to whom Roger talked—in particular, one of his orderlies, a highly intelligent young man named Toombe, who had become Roger's closest friend at Las Palmas—agreed that the money was coming either from the rental the Manning Company paid Río de Oro for the additional acreage it leased, or from the penny-a-pound export duty on the rubber. Apparently only a small proportion of this was finding its way into the national treasury; the rest was ending up in bureaucratic pockets. Roger had asked Charlie Clark about the stories; Clark's reply was a cynical shrug and smile. "How do you think Chadwick pays for his beach house?" he said. This doubly shocked Roger; not only was the Chadwick government cheating its own people, but the Manning management knew it and condoned it. Everyone knew the Manning Company had what amounted to a virtual veto power in the Tylertown regime; certainly if the company had wished to do something about this flagrant corruption—if nothing else, expose it—it could have.

Roger's mother Sheila and his "father" Calvin Harrington were considered liberal for their time—they had even gone so far as to espouse equality for Negroes, though admittedly they didn't dare put this in their magazine—and Roger tended to share this liberalism. Besides, he was young and idealistic, and his idealism was repulsed by what seemed the cynicism of his father's corporation. True, many of the Río de Orians shrugged off the corruption stories, much as Charlie Clark did; there was an established custom in the country of "gift giving" called "dash," and to many, President Chadwick's skimming was nothing more than the Manning Company's "dash" to the Tylertown regime. But many blacks, including Toombe, were angered by it, as was Roger. He told himself that if Mark knew what was going on, he would have taken steps to stop it, and several times Roger did sit down and write his father a letter explaining the situation. Each time, he tore the letter up. He wasn't sure why he did it, except that he was secretly afraid his father might not do anything. He didn't face the possibility quite that straightforwardly. After all, to do so would also be to accept the possibility that the idol he had admired for so many years might, if humanly, have clay feet.

Then had come the Leopard Society murders, the raid on the armory at Ciba and the gunboats' arrival in Tylertown harbor. The *Declaration of Independence* was on its way with Marines and aircraft, and Roger was disheartened to realize that the Manning Company—his father's company!—was not only tolerating graft and racism but now naked military force. From conversations Roger overheard in the company headquarters between Melville Benny and Charlie Clark, they were actually promoting it. He believed it was all wrong—completely, disastrously wrong—which he said to Toombe, who agreed with him. But now it was too late for letters to Mark. On the day before the scheduled arrival of the *Declaration of Independence,* Roger, after discussing with his friend Toombe what he was going to do, went to Melville Benny's house.

Melville had been given the guest house next door to Charlie Clark's residence, in what was known as the Number One Compound, the pleasantest area of Las Palmas, where six of the biggest houses were reserved for the top management of the plantation and their families. The houses were built around a small, square park planted with brilliant flowers; they were shaded with tall palms, and it was generally agreed that better living quarters were not to be found on any plantation in Africa.

It was seven thirty in the morning when Roger knocked on the screen door. He was admitted by the houseboy, who led him to the small dining room where Melville was eating fresh pineapple for breakfast.

"Mr. Benny, I'd like to talk to you for a minute."

Melville stood up and shook the young doctor's hand, thinking again, as he had when he first met him, that there was an amazing resemblance between him and Mark. Melville assumed it a coincidence, except that the thought had occurred to him that perhaps there was more to it than that.

"Of course, Roger. Take a seat. Some coffee?"

"Yes, thanks."

Roger was poured a cup of hot coffee. Then, when the houseboy returned to the kitchen, the young man said, "Mr. Benny, I'd like your permission to radio Mr. Manning in Elkins today."

"What for?"

"Well, sir, I'm convinced this whole operation against Tegai is a terrible mistake. A lot of people in this country admire Tegai, and if we bring in Marines and turn Río de Oro into a battlefield just to get rid of a troublemaker who is also a man the people look up to, well, I just believe it's stupid. More than that, it's wrong."

"Wrong? The man's a rebel."

"Why? Because he wants to kick out Chadwick? Everybody knows Chadwick's getting rich—"

Melville motioned to him to lower his voice, which he did, even though the houseboy was in the kitchen.

"He's pocketing money from what we pay the government. Can you deny that?"

"No, and I'm not happy about it either. Chadwick was an honest patriot when we first came here, but I'm afraid he's turned. Whether it was our pressuring him and his government that did it or whether the temptation was simply too much for him or any politician in power, I don't know. But it is true that he's making himself a very rich man and it's also true he's not being very cautious about it."

"And it's true we condone it, isn't it?"

"What do you suggest?"

"We certainly don't have to back him up with an aircraft carrier and Marines. We're playing into Tegai's hands! I mean, now when he says that Chadwick and the Manning Company ought to be kicked out together, it makes a lot more sense to more people. And I feel Mr. Manning doesn't realize this. If he did, he certainly wouldn't go along with what I'm afraid is going to turn into a blood bath."

Melville squirmed uncomfortably. The same thought had occurred to him, but he had dismissed it as being impractical.

"All right, Roger, but what's the alternative? We can't sit here and wait for Tegai to attack us, can we? He'll wipe us out."

"Why can't we send someone to talk to Tegai?" Roger countered.

"Talk to him about what?"

"Convince him that we're not necessarily married to Chadwick. Show him that we're interested in the country, not just one group of politicians. Tell him that we don't want a war, and maybe offer to mediate between him and Chadwick—"

"That's out of the question."

"Why?"

"Tegai doesn't want to mediate. He wants Chadwick's job!"

"All right, but why should *we* get involved in it? Why shouldn't we at least try to convince Tegai that we want to stay neutral? And that as long as he leaves us alone, we'll keep the Marines out of it? We certainly have some bargaining power with the *Declaration of Independence* here. I think Tegai would be more than anxious to make that kind of an arrangement with us. And that way, no matter who wins—Tegai or Chadwick—we won't be affected. Tegai *says* he wants to kick us out, but the country needs the good things we can do for it. And if we make a deal for at least neutrality with him now, he won't be forced to take reprisals against us later. That's plain common sense. More important, I don't think we have any right to take sides in an internal political fight, and we certainly don't have any right to support a government with force that the country doesn't want. Do you see my point?"

"Yes, I see your point, except I don't think it's quite that clearcut. We have a commitment to President Chadwick—"

"Why?"

"Because he has a commitment to us. We have a very nice arrangement with him, Roger, and if Tegai takes over the government, we have no guarantee that he won't want to start all over again. We have a lot at stake here—millions of dollars invested—and we have to take every means we can to protect it."

Roger said nothing for a moment. Then, "I'd still like to talk to

Mr. Manning. I think someone should point out an alternative to him before it's too late."

"But Roger, be practical. You're a young doctor here—why would Mark Manning listen to you?"

"I know Mr. Manning very well. He knows my mother, and he paid for my education. I think he'll listen to me."

Melville looked at the red hair and the striking facial resemblance and wondered again if it were possible . . .

"All right," he said, "I'll be making my daily report to Mr. Manning this afternoon. If you want to talk to him, be in the radio shack at one o'clock."

Roger smiled and stood up. "Thanks a lot, Mr. Benny. I really appreciate this."

"Well, don't be too surprised if Mr. Manning doesn't appreciate it. He's got a bad temper, you know, and something tells me he's not going to be overjoyed at being told how to run his company by a young intern."

"I'll take my chances."

Melville accompanied him to the front door of the house, then stopped. "Roger, may I ask you a personal question?"

"Sure."

Melville hesitated. "Are you related to Mr. Manning?"

The young man's face turned almost as red as his hair. Then he forced a smile.

"No, though a lot of people have asked me that. I guess there's a pretty unusual resemblance between us, isn't there?"

"There certainly is."

Roger shrugged. "It's just a coincidence, I guess." He pushed open the screen door. "Well, I'll see you at one."

Melville watched him as he walked down the path to the street. A most unadmirable thought had popped into his mind—so much so that it made him blush almost as deeply as Roger just had for even thinking it. He pushed the thought out of his mind, amazed that he was capable of thinking it.

It managed, however, to linger in his memory.

Mark did not lose his temper, as Melville had predicted, nor was he warmly responsive. When Roger told him his suggestion that afternoon on the shortwave radio, Mark listened, refraining from comment. When Roger had finished, there was a moment of static-filled silence. Then Mark said, "Roger, I invited you to go to Las Palmas to work with the sick, not to try and run my company. I appreciate your concern, but I'll ask you not to interfere with company policy. That's Mr. Benny's job and mine, not yours."

"But Uncle Mark, what you're doing is wrong! It's wrong and frankly, it's self-defeating. Why can't you at least send somebody to *talk* to Tegai? It couldn't hurt anything and it might work!"

"I said *no*." The voice was sharp. "Now, please put Mr. Benny back on."

Roger bit his lip, got up from the chair to let Melville sit down, then wandered out of the radio shack.

Mark talked to Melville a few more minutes, telling him he was taking the train that afternoon to Palm Beach, where he had chartered a yacht for a few weeks in which he would have a radio watch set up so he could keep in constant contact with the plantation. Then he said, "Is Roger there?"

"No, he left."

"Keep an eye on him, Melville. Don't let him do anything crazy. I don't want him to get into trouble."

"I'll watch him, Mark."

When he signed off, Melville left the radio shack, convinced now that the amazing resemblance between Roger Boine and Mark Manning was no mere coincidence, that Roger was probably the result of one of Mark's extracurricular romances. The "Uncle Mark" had done it, the way it had come out so naturally. An extracurricular romance like the one Uncle Mark was having with Lily?

The previous day he had received a letter from Lily saying she was going to Palm Beach for a few weeks where she would be staying at the Breakers. Too many coincidences too fast for even the most confirmed believer in the workings of capricious destiny.

Yes, Roger obviously was the result of the same kind of business now going on between Mark and his wife. Uriah at the front had finally gotten the word. Except Melville wasn't going to sit like Uriah and allow himself to be conveniently killed off. Melville would do something to strike back.

The same outrageous idea came back into his mind and again he rejected it. But its recurrence unnerved him so much that by the time he got back to his house he found he was sweating heavily—and this time not from the heat.

Early the next morning, Melville and Ambassador Muhlbach joined President and Mrs. Chadwick, General Mordecai Amberley, the commander of the national militia, and four top-ranking members of the Tylertown government in the presidential launch to meet the *Declaration of Independence*. The freshly painted ship seemed almost ludicrously large as it dropped anchor in the harbor, surrounded by dozens of native canoes, curious gnats nibbling at the hull of Leviathan. The launch carried the formally dressed official party to the accommodation ladder on the port side of the ship; then the president climbed up to the deck, followed by his wife and the others, where they were piped aboard and greeted by the carrier's commanding officer, Captain Matthias Strang, and by Rear Admiral Sylvester Ridgely, who had come along as an observer of the operation. A smart Marine band played the national anthems of the two countries. President Chadwick made a brief welcoming speech, and then the party retired to Captain Strang's cabin, where tea and punch (non-alcoholic!) were served and General Amberley briefed the Americans on the situation in Río de Oro. The situation was that nothing was happening—yet. But the latest information from the up country was that Tegai was gathering his army near Canning Landing, a trading post on the upper reaches of the Río de Oro that had been named after an English missionary. General Amberley and President Chadwick both urged that planes be sent to reconnoiter the area, at which point General Amberley's staff could plan a joint operation with the Americans. This was agreed upon, Captain Strang promising to send the planes out that afternoon. The presidential party then left the carrier and returned to Tylertown in the launch.

When Melville got back to the embassy with Ambassador Muhlbach, he was handed a message to call Charlie Clark at Las Palmas immediately, which he did.

"Roger Boine's disappeared," said Charlie.

"Disappeared?"

"Last night after he got off duty at the hospital. He took off into the bush with Toombe, one of his orderlies. Another orderly said he saw Toombe packing gear—"

"Wait a minute, why did he go?"

"The orderly thinks they're going to try and reach Tegai."

Melville felt sick. "Have you sent out someone to get them back?"

"Yes, but we didn't find out they were gone until this morning. They have an eight-hour head start. Any ideas why he'd want to see Tegai?"

"Yes, but I didn't think he'd be fool enough to do it. We've got to stop him before he gets there. The kid won't have a prayer if Tegai catches him."

"You're right. How about asking the navy to send out a few planes to try and spot them? I don't think there's much chance they can see anything in the jungle, but it's worth a try."

"Good idea. They're sending out reconnaisance planes this afternoon anyway. I'll tell them to keep an eye out for Roger. And I'll be at Las Palmas in about an hour."

Melville hung up, then asked Ambassador Muhlbach to send a messenger out to the carrier with the news. The terrible notion Melville had been flirting with had been to suggest to Roger that he make the effort to contact Tegai. What better way to strike back at Mark Manning than to send his natural son to what almost certainly would be his death? It had been a vicious thought, one that Melville had been shocked to discover he could even contemplate.

And now the crazy kid had done it on his own!

Somehow Melville almost felt that by thinking the unthinkable he had become personally responsible for Roger Boine's life. And if Roger succeeded in reaching Tegai, there wouldn't be much of him left to be responsible for.

In later years he would always remember it as a Twenties moon, this moon that hung like the storied yellow balloon in the Palm Beach sky, which would be a memento of one of the most delicious nights of his life, of a time in the late Twenties when despite the troubles in Río de Oro his world seemed peculiarly at peace with itself, secure in the prosperity of those special halcyon boom years. Of course Palm Beach was more secure than the rest of the world, its rich inhabitants girdled with the security of wealth, bolstered by the romance between their egos and their bank accounts.

Mark's love affair that moon-drenched January night in 1927 was more personal as he and Lily Benny wandered through his half-completed mansion on the beach—he was intrigued with life, entranced by the moon, but most particularly in love with Lily. She stood in the middle of the still roofless great hall of the house, her shingled light-blonde hair coiffing her in smart bangs, her lithe body encased in a skin-tight, white-silk taffeta evening gown that flared at her knees in a short burst of white tulle. She looked up toward the roof beams forty feet above, the moon shining down with effulgent splendor.

"Oh, Mark, it's the bee's knees!" she exclaimed.

"You like it?"

"*Like* it? It's fabulous! And this is going to be the entrance hall?"

"Well, a combination entrance hall and glorified living room. There'll be a balcony that runs around the second floor—very Spanish —and the place will be full of palms. Then over here's the dining room. It will seat fifty."

"Cozy." She followed him to yet another huge, roofless, ghostly room.

"We're having a mahogany dining room table made in Madrid," said Mark, his white dinner jacket glowing spectrally in the moonlight. "And there'll be fifty matching chairs upholstered in velvet that Bill Bixby tells me is some damn thing called claret-colored. Fancy?"

"Spectacular!"

She envisioned herself hostessing mammoth dinner parties.

He guided her through the rest of the house, stepping carefully over lumber and around sawhorses as he explained the layout. The house was shaped like a huge U facing the ocean, and in the big courtyard in the middle of the U would be a garden patio and a tiled pool. When they reached the side of the pool, which was half finished, Lily put her arms around him.

"I adore it," she said. "Except I wish the pool were finished. Then we could go in the nude and I'd *love* to do that with you."

He kissed her deeply, running his hands down her silk back, kneading her taut buttocks.

"There's always the ocean."

She giggled. "Do you think we dare? What if we get caught?"

In reply he took her hand and started running down the pool to the palm-fringed beach beyond. She hurried after him. They paused at the edge of the beach.

"Let's leave our clothes here," he said, starting to take off his jacket.

She kicked off her shoes, then began stripping off her dress.

"I can see the headlines now. 'Millionaire and Mystery Girlfriend Caught in Oceanside Love Nest.' Yum!"

"Lily, my love, you have the soul of a gossip columnist."

"Oh, I'm just a free spirit trying to express my creative true self in the moonlight." She stepped out of the dress and suddenly she was all silvery nakedness. Both naked, he took her hand again and they ran across the beach toward the surf, laughing like children. He did a running belly flop into the waves; she approached the water more cautiously, backing into it and squealing as a wave hit her, sending spray jetting toward the moon. Then she sank into the water and began swimming toward the lights of a distant ship on the black horizon.

"Race you to Cuba!" she called.

"How about Bermuda? It's closer."

"No, I want to go to Cuba."

He swam after her, his powerful strokes enabling him to catch her in short order. He grabbed her slippery ankle and pulled her beneath the water. She squirmed free and surfaced, running her hand over her wet hair. He came up in front of her and wrapped his legs around her thighs as he took her head in his hands.

"I love Lily!" he sang, feeling as ridiculously exuberant as a schoolboy. "I love her, I love her . . ."

"They'll hear you on the yacht," she said, laughing as she looked to the lights of their 150-foot power yacht, which was anchored a quarter of a mile up the beach.

"Who cares?"

She didn't. She loved the feeling of his legs on her skin, loved him loving her and saying so. He folded her body against his and began kissing her as they bobbed up and down in the swell, keeping afloat by lazily kicking their legs. Abruptly, she put her hands on top of his head and pushed him under. Then, laughing as she tried to evade his grasp, she started back to shore. Mark swam after her but she reached the beach first and ran out of the surf onto the sand, where she flopped down on her back. A moment later he joined her, lying beside her to catch his breath.

"You act like a ten-year-old." She smiled, lightly pushing the end of his nose with her finger.

"You *make* me feel like a ten-year-old."

"Well, you're not. You're forty-eight, and you should behave with dignity. Running around naked on the beach with someone half your age! For shame, Mr. Manning."

"You're not half my age. You're over thirty."

"Well, at least you're not a gentleman. Reminding a lady of her age—"

He put his hand on her left breast and squeezed it gently. The cool, wet skin seemed to have its own response to his touch; her red-brown nipple was hard and erect. He leaned over and kissed it. She smelled sweet and tasted of the sea. Lily was an ocean of sea-sweetness. He wanted to dive in and immerse himself in her. Now he was on top of her, kissing her again, his body aching for her.

"You have . . . no . . . respect for me . . . at all . . ." she murmured between kisses.

"You're damned right."

Then he was in her, thrusting with building excitement, and she was responding with small moans of delight, indifferent to the sand grating against her wet back and bottom and legs and hair. And the yellow moon began to swell and balloon until it exploded into a million pieces of brilliant colors and he shot into her as the wonder of their joined bodies performed its miracle.

Afterward, he lay beside her, breathing deeply, and they were quiet for a while.

"God, I feel like Eve," she said. "And you're Adam and here we are on a beach in Eden just screwing up a storm. Isn't it *keen?*"

"You're quite a romantic."

"Oh, but I am, really. You're the sexiest man I've ever met, which really is sort of odd. I mean, that you're older and everything. Even when I was a little girl I used to think you were dreamy. I think I was always meant to be your mistress."

He put his hands behind his head and stared at the moon.

"When's your birthday?" she asked.

"If I can't remind you of your age, you sure as hell can't remind me of mine."

"Oh, darling, I couldn't care less how old you are. I'm just curious about your sign. Let me guess—you're a Scorpio."

"My birthday's November fifth, whatever that is."

She sat up. "See? I was right! You *are* a Scorpio! God, isn't it fantastic?"

"Liar. You knew my birthday. Don't try and play games with me."

"Oh, all right. I *did* know. Anyway, you're an obvious Scorpio."

"What's an obvious Scorpio?"

"Oh, dynamic and very successful. And sort of cruel when you have to be, which I like. I mean, cruelty's very sexy, in a way. And you let absolutely nothing stand in your way when you want something. Am I right?"

"You are right."

"Scorpios make their own rules. I'm a Scorpio too. November eleventh."

"And you make your own rules? "

"Naturally. You know, you have the sexiest belly button . . . I'm just mad for it . . . and all that lovely golden-hair . . ."

"Would you like an autographed photo?"

"Yes, as a matter of fact, I'd love a photograph of all of you, jay-bird naked. Then I'd put it up on my wall and say to everyone, 'This beautiful man makes all the tires in the world, and he's screwed me all over the country.' Wouldn't that be darby?" She laughed and added, "Melville would love it. But screw Melville."

She leaned down and kissed his navel. Then she slowly brushed her lips up his stomach, kissing his skin softly until she reached his chest. Her mouth paused a moment, then moved to the right. He stirred slightly as he felt her lips over his nipple. She sucked it softly.

"You know too much," he whispered.

"Uh huh. A *lot*."

"Where'd you learn?"

She smiled. "Oh, with some of your vice-presidents. And I don't mean just Melville." She knew she was taking a chance talking this way, but she also decided the stakes were too high not to risk everything. And *now* was the time. It would never be this *right* again . . .

Silence for a moment. Then he said, "I'm crazy to fool around with you."

"I know."

"You're going to cause me an awful lot of trouble."

"I know. And you love it."

"Don't be so damned cocky."

She ran her fingers through his hair.

"That's your department. You want me, and what Scorpio wants he takes—to hell with whether it causes trouble or not."

He looked up at her.

"I'll care if it loses me Melville."

"You'd survive."

"Of course I'd survive. But I don't know if you're worth losing my righthand man for."

She smiled slightly. "Well, then I guess I'll have to prove to you I'm worth it."

"How?"

"Oh, well, for instance, I don't think Melville would do *this* for you. He might . . . but I don't *think* he would."

He felt her hand slide down his stomach until it rested on his penis. She rubbed it softly until it began to stiffen. Then she lowered herself down his body, rubbing her breasts across his skin until her mouth was at his midsection.

He closed his eyes. "You little bitch . . ."

When she was finished, she sat up and watched his face.

"Well?" she said.

His eyes were still closed.

"You disgust me."

"Liar."

He opened his eyes.

"Is that why you're so popular at the country club?"

She laughed, got to her feet and started back to the palm trees. He watched her silver body. How beautiful it was, and how corrupt on the inside. How completely different from Charlotte, who had early warned him about Lily and her blackmail threats against Carter Lang. And Maxine, she had at least been completely honest. Lily was the new generation. When he thought of her father, hard-working, old-fashioned Harold Swenson somehow spawning this bitch of a Lorelei . . . All right, face it, corrupt or not, even rotten and ruthless, he loved her. Loved? Obsessed, was more like it. But whatever it was, he had never felt this way about any other woman. Lily was sex. Incarnate and carnal. An old story? Maybe so.

She made him feel young again.

He got to his feet and started across the sand toward the house. Its naked roofbeams loomed above the palms, fingers ready to close over his Casa Encantada.

When he reached her, she was getting into her dress. He leaned his back against a tree and watched her a moment. Then he said, "Lily?"

"What?"

"Are you willing to divorce Melville?"

She reached down and picked up her shoes. Then she straightened and said, "Well, you might be able to talk me into it."

CHAPTER EIGHT

It had been Toombe's idea, not Roger's.

When Roger returned to the hospital from the radio shack, he had told his friend and orderly how Mark Manning had rejected his suggestion. Roger was bitter and angry. Toombe's reply caught him by surprise.

"Why don't *you* got to Tegai?" the young black had said casually.

"Me?"

He pointed out he had no official standing, didn't know how to reach Tegai—and at the same time began seriously considering the idea. In fact, why not? If he believed what he had said to his father—and he did—then why shouldn't he back up his words with action? And when, to his further surprise, Toombe told him that his older brother was an officer in Tegai's army and that he, Toombe, would be willing to lead Roger to the army and introduce him to his brother, who in turn would take him to Tegai, Roger made up his mind to do it. It was the right thing to do, it might avert war, and if nothing else would dramatize to his father the real folly of his policies. Last, but hardly least in Roger's mind, it would show his father that his son was not a man to be dismissed lightly. And Toombe's brother should reduce any potential danger in the trip. After all, he was one of them. . . .

They left the plantation that night and set out on the jungle trails for Canning Landing. Toombe knew the trails well, though Roger was rather surprised exactly *how* well he knew them. He seemed never to hesitate. They avoided open clearings during the day, Toombe having foreseen the possibility that planes might have been sent out to look for them, and, indeed, on their first day out they spotted two of the navy planes from the *Declaration of Independence*. They rested during the hottest period of the day, from eleven till four, and Toombe prepared good meals from the rice he had brought along and from pineapples, cassava roots and peppers he found in the bush. Roger wore the prescribed bush outfit for whites—riding breeches, knee boots, khaki shirt and solar topee. Toombe had left the plantation in his orderly uniform—white shorts and shirt—but a few miles from Las Palmas he took it off and put on a native breech clout, burying the white clothes under a rock. He told Roger the white could be too easily spotted, but Roger thought there was more to it than that: Toombe in the jungle discarded not only the white man's clothes but the white man's influences as well. At the time, it did not strike him as particularly ominous.

Toombe had told him the walk to Canning Landing would take four days, but on the second morning he led Roger onto a dark trail and they hadn't gone more than a hundred feet along it when they were stopped by two crossed sticks topped with white rags.

"Devil bush?" said Roger, awed.

Toombe nodded and started past the sticks.

"But should we go in there?"

"We'll be safe," replied his friend. Roger hesitated, then followed him down the trail. They had walked a few hundred feet more when two natives stepped out of the bush and confronted them. The natives held rifles, which they aimed at Roger and Toombe. Toombe seemed unconcerned. He spoke a few words in the Kru dialect, then one of the natives stationed himself to the rear and the other in the front, leading the party down the trail for a quarter of a mile until they reached a small clearing that contained half a dozen square mud huts with thatched roofs. The walls of the huts were decorated with herringbone-shaped stripes, which Roger recognized as typical of the Kru tribe. They were led to the center hut, which was guarded by two natives who motioned to them to enter. Roger removed his topee and ducked his head as he followed Toombe into the shadowy hut. Standing in the center of the room was a man about the same size as Toombe, though more powerfully built. His face was decorated with stripes of white paint, three on each cheek and two on his forehead, with one stripe diving down his nose and forking over the wide nostrils.

Toombe spoke a few words to the man, then turned to Roger and said, "This is my brother, Saafwe. He will take you to Tegai."

Roger moved forward, holding out his hand as a crashing blow in the middle of his back sent him sprawling on the dirt floor. He looked up at the guard, who had jammed his rifle butt between his shoulder blades. Then he got to his feet, back aching, and said to Toombe, "What's the idea?"

Toombe's face was expressionless.

"Toombe, why am I being treated this way?"

Silence.

"Am I a *prisoner*?"

Slowly Toombe nodded "yes" and walked out of the hut.

His hands were tied behind his back, then he was led outside the hut, where a wooden pole chair such as he had seen used by visiting Europeans on their trips into the bush was resting on the ground. One of the guards pointed to the seat and Roger climbed into it. He was blindfolded. "Toombe! Toombe, what the hell are they doing? Toombe!" No reply. Toombe had vanished, and the others spoke no English or pidgin—or if they did they weren't talking to Roger. He felt the chair being hoisted by four bearers; there was a brief conversation in Kru among the guards, then the chair began to bounce gently as they started off. Someone clapped his topee on his head and he heard several laughs. He imagined how ridiculous he must look, trussed and blindfolded like a white chicken, with his solar topee, the symbol of white authority in hat-conscious Africa, tipping over his forehead. His mind raced back over the past months, recalling his many talks with Toombe. Toombe was smart, he spoke better English than most of the natives, and Roger, more than somewhat lonely in this strange new country, had become his friend. It was Toombe who had quietly fed him most of the "inside" gossip of the country, who had told him of the corruption of Tylertown and the disillusionment of so much of the population with President Chadwick. That it was true was beside the point. Now Roger began strongly to suspect that Toombe had been softening him up, preparing him for that moment when he would casually suggest that Roger should seek out Tegai himself. But even if true, what was the point of it? Why encourage him to leave Las Palmas, then make him a prisoner? Obviously, Toombe belonged to the Devil bush, which explained why he wasn't afraid to go past the crossed wands. Obviously Toombe had gotten word to his brother where to meet them, either by a runner or, more likely, the bush telegraph—the drums. So it was a fairly elaborate plan, too elaborate to have no purpose.

After a while he decided he had been blindfolded to prevent him from remembering the route to Tegai's headquarters, which at least implied that they weren't going to kill him—why conceal the route if they were going to kill him? Besides, being carried in the chair was infinitely more comfortable than walking, despite the discomfort of having his hands tied behind his back. So he relaxed and began to listen to the jungle.

Visually, the jungle was not particularly beautiful. It was too dense, too monotonous; this part of Africa had few of the wildly beautiful tropical flowers. Besides, when he had been walking, his eyes had been too busy watching for snakes, insects and exposed roots to do much sightseeing. But now, sightless, he began to luxuriate in the sounds of the bush. The chattering of the monkeys, the occasional screech of a bird taking off from a tree top, the sudden crackling of branches as a startled animal ran into the bush. It was an eerily beautiful world, to which Roger had never really listened before. And as the hours dragged by, he found himself lulled and enchanted by it. His normal good spirits began to return.

The second day with Saafwe, Roger knew they were climbing into the hills. On several occasions he was taken out of the chair and led, still blindfolded, as the chairbearers scrambled up steep inclines. The humidity diminished, although as they left the jungle he could feel the sun beating on him and the searing Harmattan wind hardly made him feel more comfortable. The natives didn't bother him—no more gun-butt episodes. He was well-fed and given a canteen of water. However, on one occasion he heard excited talk and was rudely tugged out of the chair and pushed into what felt like the cleft of a rock. Immediately thereafter he heard the plane engines and realized that again the search parties were near. For a moment he contemplated running blindly out of his hiding place but decided against it. The natives would at the very least have knocked him out, and he doubted he would have much chance of being spotted in any case.

On the second evening, he knew they had reached their destination. The chair bumped to a stop and voices began chattering. He was helped out of the chair and, finally, to his relief, the blindfold was removed and his aching hands untied. They were on a plateau several hundred feet up the side of a mountain, and the crepuscular view, stretching to the south, was spectacular. To the north the mountain continued to rise. But in the hill was the mouth of a cave, bushes protecting it from observation from above. A number of armed natives dressed in khaki shorts and shirts were helping Saafwe's men take the chair into the cave. Then Saafwe led Roger in.

The cave's entrance was small but the interior of the cave was large, extending over a hundred feet back into the hill. Fresh air filtered in from several small airshafts that had been drilled up through the roof. Light was provided by a number of kerosene lamps on wooden desks that were stationed in neat, office-like rows in the front part of the cave, each desk manned by a uniformed native, most of whom were busy at paperwork. Roger was more than a little surprised by the calm, efficient, staff-headquarters atmosphere of the cave; it was almost like stumbling into a field office of some European army. There were even field telephones! He was led back through the desks to the rear of the cave, where a private office was partitioned off by large mats strung on wires. Saafwe ducked through the mat-door; a moment later he reappeared and beckoned Roger inside.

A tall man dressed like the others in an open-necked khaki shirt and khaki shorts was seated behind a desk. The man was impressive; he had presence. He looked about thirty. His face was rectangularly chiseled. His lips were full, his nose surprisingly narrow, almost aquiline; his eyes, set rather close together, were clear and intelligent. Altogether his face was more aristocratic than handsome, like a dark-skinned version of one of those long-faced British peers. To add to the Mayfair impression, the man was smoking a cigarette through a black Alfred Dunhill holder. He stood up to come around the desk, and Roger was amazed at how tall he was—at least six foot eight or nine. Rumors were that he could tear a man's head from his shoulders. When he extended his hand, Roger believed it. He had never seen a human hand or forearm of such size and obvious strength.

"I am Tegai," he said, shaking Roger's hand. "And you're Dr. Boine.

Welcome to our headquarters. I hope your trip was comfortable?"

He spoke excellent English with a British accent; Roger remembered
having heard that he had been taught by English missionaries and had
attended Oxford.

"As comfortable as anything can be when you're blindfolded and
your hands are tied."

"A regrettable but necessary precaution. But my men treated you
well?"

"Yes." Roger decided to overlook the gun butt in his shoulders.
Tegai apparently wanted to keep the meeting on an amicable basis,
and it seemed wise not to intrude a jarring note.

"Good. Would you like a beer?"

Roger said yes, and two beers were brought in by Saafwe as a chair
was offered the young doctor. Then Tegai returned to his desk as
Saafwe left the office. Roger sipped the refreshing beer. "This isn't
exactly when I expected."

"You mean our headquarters? Yes, it's not exactly what one would
imagine to find with an army of primitive bush fighters, is it? But
we're very well-organized, doctor. Our army is spread out in small,
easily maneuverable units that the American planes have been trying
to spot since the *Declaration of Independence* arrived on its Yankee
good-will mission." He smiled. "Most of our units are in communication by telephones we stole from the militia; phones aren't as convenient as drums, but unfortunately there are those in the militia who
can read the bush telegraph as well as we. So we decided to come into
the twentieth century. In fact, I think the Americans and Mr. Chadwick are going to be amazed at how modern we are. We've decided to
combine the best of our old, traditional fighting methods with the best
of the new. It should be an interesting war. Toombe tells me, through
his brother, that you wished to talk to me?"

Roger was surprised.

"Then you *know*—?"

"Of course. We've been kept informed of your dissatisfaction with
Mr. Manning's tactics, and we knew about your radio talk with Manning—if you can call it a talk. He seems to have cut you short. I
wouldn't think Mr. Manning would be interested in compromises
any more than I am, or President Chadwick, for that matter."

Roger's heart sank. "But you don't have a chance! All those Marines
and planes—you can't hold out against them! And thousands of people
are going to be killed for no purpose at all!"

Tegai inhaled from his holder. "I've heard you're a bit of an idealist,
and I see you are. I like that. I'm an idealist myself. But you're wrong

about there being no purpose to the killing. We want to govern our own country. We want to purge the corrupt Chadwick government and we want the profits from our rubber trees, which are now going, among other places, to Elkins, Ohio, U.S.A., to stay here and benefit us. If to achieve this we must take lives, the blood won't have been needlessly spilled. So you see, we have a purpose. I'm sorry, doctor, to crush your idealistic hope, but I'm in no mood for compromise. And I'm not afraid of the American Marines. We know the jungle, they don't. We have all the time in the world; they eventually will tire of this little adventure. In the long run, I should say the odds are on our side. But I didn't have you brought here to discuss politics or military tactics."

"Then you *did* have me brought here?"

"Yes. We had considered kidnapping you, but when Toombe told us of your, well, state of mind, we thought it would be easier to suggest you kidnap yourself." Again he smiled. "And you did."

Roger blanched with embarrassment and anger.

"But I hope you'll forgive us?"

"Why did you want to kidnap me?"

"That's simple. We not only need modern equipment and weapons, we need a modern doctor."

Roger was stunned. Of course. How obvious. So obvious it had never occurred to him.

"I realize," continued Tegai, "that ordinarily it would defy logic to expect a white man to change sides and work for us. But Toombe has told us of your dismay at the way the blacks are treated at Las Palmas—"

"Wait a minute. I never said that. I think the rubber workers have been treated pretty damn well, all things considered. And certainly none of us has ever clawed a worker to death the way your Leopard men did."

Tegai nodded. "True. The Leopard Society murders no doubt appear melodramatic in your eyes, but they have worked. They have frightened the workers away. They have achieved their purpose."

"You claim you're an idealist," Roger said, "but you use all this primitive mumbo jumbo for your own ends. You exploit native superstitions—"

The moment he said it, he wished he hadn't. Tegai's face froze.

"The primitive superstitions, or mumbo-jumbo as you call it, are our religions. Religions that are older and truer than the absurd fable you call Christianity. I *believe* in our religions. And, yes, I use them at the same time. They were *meant* to be used. No white man can ever understand our African religions, just as no white man can ever understand Africans. I may speak English, and I may appropriate some of your methods, doctor, but I am an African prince and a priest of the Leopard Society. I should advise you to speak of our religions with respect."

"I'm sorry," Roger said, "I didn't mean any lack of respect. But, damn it, the murders were horrible. All violence is horrible to me. It's hard for me to respect it."

"There are many kinds of violence," Tegai said quietly. "For example, a white man calling a black man *nigger*, as I was at Oxford many times. I was told you objected to the whites at Las Palmas calling the rubber workers niggers."

"I do. But I still say that's less evil than killing the men, as you did."

"You can kill a man and still respect him. To degrade a man is worse than killing him."

"I'm not so sure a dead man would agree. Killing someone doesn't seem to me a very good way to respect him."

"Then we've learned something about each other, haven't we? We've learned we have different philosophies. I respect you, doctor. I might also kill you."

The words, softly spoken, frightened Roger but he was determined not to show it. "Are you trying to say that if I don't agree to work for you, you'll kill me?"

"Of course not. I realize one cannot coerce a doctor to practice medicine. I also realize you are an American working for an American company, and presumably you wouldn't work for it unless you had a certain amount of respect for it. But I also understand that you have been dissatisfied with many of the practices at Las Palmas—dissatisfied enough to jeopardize your position in order to radio the owner of the company, dissatisfied enough to leave Las Palmas to seek me out—though, admittedly, we encouraged you toward that end. You are young, you are idealistic. *We* are the young and idealistic side in this conflict. I am hoping to be able to persuade you to help us, even though I realize that may not be possible. Frankly, we need you. There are few doctors in this part of the world—certainly few who would help us. The Tylertown doctors are all pro-Chadwick—that, of course, is where the fees are. We are going to have many casualties in this war, and our tribal medicine is not modern enough to suffice. *That* I'm willing to concede you. So I'm taking the calculated risk that I shall be able to convince you that our side is the right side, and the side worth working for. But don't worry, doctor, I'm not going to threaten you. If you say no, I'll have my men take you back—today, if you wish. That, of course, is why I had you blindfolded, so you wouldn't be able to reveal our location if you returned. If I *hadn't* had you blindfolded . . . *then* you might have had reason to be worried, as you no doubt realized at the time."

Roger nodded. "That seems fair, although I wish I could persuade you to see my side of it. I still think everybody's rushing into something foolish and unnecessary."

Tegai shook his head. "I see your point. I don't agree with it. You are wasting your breath."

Roger sighed. "Well, then I'll shut up, but you'll be wasting your breath trying to persuade me to work for you. And I can see *your* point. I mean, I can understand why you want to overthrow Chadwick and us as well. But I couldn't help you, not even if I wanted to. I have an obligation to the Manning Company, and even though I disagree with some of their politics, I couldn't just walk over to the other side."

"What is your obligation, doctor? Because you are on their payroll?"

Roger laughed. "If you knew my salary, you'd know *that's* not the obligation. No, Mr. Manning invited me to take my residency out here, which was a wonderful opportunity for me. Besides that, there are personal reasons why I couldn't even consider changing sides."

Tegai fitted a new cigarette into his holder and lighted it.

"I see. In other words, you're not quite the idealist I assumed you were?"

"That's not the point. I just couldn't walk out on Mr. Manning."

"Oh come now, doctor, be truthful. Isn't the real reason that you're an American? A *white* man? Who may make certain idealistic noises, who may say it's wrong to treat us Africans as niggers, but when it comes actually to committing yourself, you find your sympathies are essentially with your fellow whites? Isn't that the truth?"

He rushed on before Roger could do more than vehemently shake his head. "You're amused by my telephones and rifles and my taking on the modern Marine Corps. I'm just a nigger playing the white man's game—isn't that right?"

Roger held his temper with difficulty. "You're baiting me, Tegai. I've never thought that. I admire you, and I admire what you've done, to a point."

"Then why won't you help me?"

"Because I can't. I *told* you! I have an obligation to Mr. Manning!"

"Oh come now, what possible obligation could you have to a man like him? And what does he care about you? You're a mere pawn in his empire."

"That's not true!"

Tegai leaned forward, pounding his huge fist on the desk in a sudden explosion.

"It *has* to be true! What is this obligation to a multimillionaire *tire* manufacturer? The modern corporation is impersonal; I know that. The reason you won't help me is because your obligation is to your race—"

"Mark Manning is my father!" exclaimed Roger furiously. "He paid for my education! I am his bastard son! I am *not* a racist, and I don't approve of what he's doing to you, but I can't turn against my own father! Can't you see *that?*"

Tegai gave him a searching, disbelieving look.

"Is it true?" he said quietly.

"Do you think I would make it up? It's something I don't tell people. Needless to say I don't exactly enjoy being someone's illegitimate child. But it's true. And so even if I wanted to help you, I couldn't. And it has nothing to do with your being an African and my being an American or white. Believe me."

Tegai leaned back in his chair, still staring at the young red-haired man.

"I do believe you," he finally said. "I actually do." Then he called, "Saafwe," who quickly appeared. Tegai pointed to Roger and said something in the Kru dialect. Saafwe nodded and came over to Roger, grabbing his arm and jerking him to his feet.

"What are you doing?"

Tegai ground out his cigarette in his overflowing Cinzano ashtray.

"I'm sorry, doctor, but it looks as though you'll have to stay with us after all. I could hardly let Mark Manning's son—legitimate or not—walk out of here, could I? You're much too valuable."

"I *trusted* you!"

"Never trust a man in a position to kill you, Dr. Boine," said Tegai, sticking his holder in his shirt pocket. "Respect him, perhaps, but never trust him."

He gave an order to Saafwe, who dragged Roger through the mat-door out of the cave. Tegai watched them go, thoughtfully rubbing his beautifully molded square chin.

There was a worried look in his eyes.

CHAPTER NINE

The reason Mark had gone to Palm Beach—aside from wanting a vacation with Lily and wishing to inspect his new house—was his assumption that with Melville in Río de Oro and the *Declaration of Independence* in Tylertown the troubles in that country would be pretty well under control. That his assumption was wrong became abundantly clear when the day following his midnight gambol on the beach with Lily, he remembered to make contact with Melville via his chartered yacht's radio and learned that Roger had been gone for two days and that, so far, no one had been able to locate him. Mark erupted. He had *told* Melville to watch the kid. He had known he was about to do something crazy. "He's on his way to Tegai, isn't he?"

"Well, we *think* so . . ."

"Goddammit, you *know* that's where he's going! He wants to play hero. Melville, if something happens to that boy, I'll hold you personally responsible! You should have put a guard on him—anything!"

Melville, already feeling personally responsible, said, "Mark, we're trying everything. Search parties, planes . . . He's just vanished! We don't know what else we can do—"

"Attack Tegai before he gets there! What's the goddamn admiral waiting for, anyway? He's been there two days, hasn't he? Hell, he ought to have wiped out Tegai and be halfway back to Norfolk by now!"

"The fact is, no one knows where Tegai is either."

"What?"

"We thought his army was near Canning Landing, but they sent a detachment of Marines up river along with a dozen reconnaissance flights and so far they haven't seen a sign of Tegai *or* his army."

"Do you mean to tell me the U.S. Navy and the U.S. Marine Corps can't find a bunch of ignorant primitives—"

"They're not primitives, Mark. Tegai is a sophisticated guy, and he's got modern weapons. It's not going to be as easy as we all thought."

Mark, furious but realizing there was nothing more he could do, told Melville to redouble his efforts to find Roger, to put as much pressure on Admiral Ridgely as he could, and to keep him informed.

Then he signed off and went out of the radio shack to join Melville's wife on the fantail of the yacht.

The yacht Mark had chartered was a hundred-fifty-foot beauty called the *Windsweep II*. It had a crew of ten and could sleep eight in deluxe style, although currently it was sleeping only two—Mark and Lily. Lily, who had taken a suite at the Breakers to receive mail, was spending nearly all her time with Mark on the yacht, and was now sunbathing in a white wicker lounge chair on the fantail, sipping champagne supplied by a Cuban cabin boy named Félipe as the *Windsweep II* cruised lazily down the Florida coast. Mark, in a bathing suit with a tank top, joined her, sitting down in silence.

"How's Melville?" asked Lily, lazily.

"Not so good. The whole show over there's being messed up. Félipe, could you fix me a lemonade, please?"

"Yes sir."

Félipe headed into the saloon.

"What's wrong?"

"For one thing, they're all sitting on their rears because they can't locate Tegai's army. For another, Roger Boine has vanished."

"Who's he?"

"A young intern at the plantation hospital. He went off into the bush with a native. I think he's trying to reach Tegai."

"He took off with a native *girl?*" asked Lily, getting interested.

"No, for God's sake. A man."

"Oh. Well, I'm sure everything will work out. After all, what can a bunch of Hottentots do against the U.S. Navy?"

He gave her a look. "I'm afraid that's what I thought. Now I'm beginning to wonder if I haven't underestimated Tegai . . . Besides, it's Roger I'm really worried about."

"The intern? Why? Because he's off in the bush with a man?"

"God, is there ever anything decent in your mind? I'm worried about him because he happens to be my son."

Lily sat up. "Your *son?*"

Mark nodded. "My son. By a woman I knew when I was—what?— twenty-two. I didn't marry her because I thought she wouldn't be right for my *career*—what little career I had in those days."

"But, darling, how terrifically romantic! Is he a nice boy?"

"He's a fine boy. Or man, now. I put him through college and medical school and I offered him the job at Las Palmas. And now I'm afraid he's gotten himself into a real mess."

Lily reached over and put her hand on his arm. "How sweet. You're worried for him, aren't you?"

He looked at her. "Of course I'm worried. He's my son, for God's sake. And I'm sick and tired of not letting everybody know it. At one time I was convinced it would be bad for business. Mostly, though, it was his mother's wish. She really hates me, and I can't say I blame her. If anything happens to him now . . ."

"Well, don't worry. He'll be all right. You'll see. What's his birthday?"

"To tell the truth, I never knew."

"Well, I'll bet anything he's Virgo. A lot of doctors turn out to be Virgos—I don't know why. And you'd be amazed how Virgos manage to land on their feet, just like cats."

"Jesus, Lily, sometimes you really sound like the most stupid bitch—"

She removed her hand from his arm, her eyes turning cold. Then she laughed. "A bitch, darling. But not a stupid one. And here's your lemonade."

Félipe had emerged from the mahogany-and-glass saloon doors, adorned with sparkling brass hardware, carrying on a silver salver a tall frosted glass, which he offered Mark. Lily watched her Mark a moment, then got up and walked forward toward her cabin, telling Mark she'd be back in a moment. She motioned to Félipe, who came over to her. She whispered something in his ear; he nodded and went into the saloon as Lily hurried to her cabin door.

Mark was paying little attention to this as he sipped his lemonade and watched the placid blue Atlantic, on the other side of which a valuable part of his empire was in jeopardy—as well as his son. He was cursing himself for having sent Melville to Tylertown rather than going himself. Melville was a capable man, damn capable, but he wasn't the leader he, Mark, was. Mark wouldn't have allowed the situation to deteriorate as it had. But—if he were to be honest with himself—he had wanted to be with Lily. That was the real reason he had sent Melville. All this was Lily's fault, damn her. Self-centered Lily with her unbelievably supple and enterprising body . . .

Suddenly the tinny sound of recorded jazz blared from the saloon as Félipe put the phonograph needle on a record of George and Ira Gershwin's "Sweet and Low Down." Mark, who was hardly feeling in the mood for music, started to call in to turn it off. Lily emerged from her cabin. She wore a straw hat, silver pumps, and was carrying a cane. He watched as she came aft to the fantail. Then, as the music segued into the verse, she began to dance a smart soft-shoe, mouthing the words being sung on the record by Bertha "Chippie" Hill. Mark, despite himself, began to enjoy that impromptu show.

Lily's figure in its tight bathing suit was a delight to watch at any time, and she was expert at the strut. Now as the music went into the chorus of the jazz song, she raised the cane above her head on the long notes and moved her hips sensuously back and forth as she winked at her audience of one. Mark loved it. As she went into the last eight bars she stuck her cane under her arm, tipped her straw hat à la that Maurice Chevalier, and strutted around the fantail furniture.

Now the jazz band repeated the refrain, this time much more slowly in a heavy blues rhythm, and Lily changed her dance to match the beat, grinding in burlesque style, almost making love to one of the wicker chairs as she swung one of her legs over the top of it, planting her pump in the blue cushion as she ground her pelvis. Mark nearly felt inclined to whistle and clap. The beat picked up again for the last reprise, and Lily Charlestoned a wild finale, climaxing it by tossing her straw hat into the air. As it sailed down into the Atlantic, Mark called, "Encore!" She laughed, came over, dropped herself into his lap, put her arms around his neck and kissed him.

"Blues all gone?"

"Well, they're losing the fight," he admitted.

She squeezed the back of his neck gently, pleased with herself. Lily, he reflected, could be a witch as well as a bitch.

But the blues were to return.

Lily wanted to take the yacht to Havana for a few days, and Mark agreed. On the second of February they dropped anchor in Havana harbor, where twenty-nine years earlier the *Maine* had been sunk, and were met by Señor Antonio Lobo, owner of the Havana Manning franchise and scion of one of the wealthiest Cuban sugar families.

Lobo, an attractive man in his early forties, gave Mark and Lily a guided tour of the city—Lily had been there on her honeymoon with Melville, but Mark had never seen it—including a visit to Morro Castle on the east point of the harbor. He then invited them to his home for dinner, and they accepted. Señor Lobo's villa was in the section of the city called Vedado, to the west of the harbor and reached by the lovely, ocean-bordering Malecon, which was the enclave of Havana's rich. The house was sumptuous, as was the food. Neither Señor Lobo nor his chic French wife showed any reaction to the presence of Lily, and neither Mark nor Lily bothered to offer an explanation or cover—they were a *fait accompli*. Certainly their

Cuban host, who had an eye for women, could understand why Mark would have brought Lily along on his yacht. In her black bugle-bead cocktail dress and the thick diamond-and-ruby bracelet (purchased by her at Tiffany's two years earlier and charged to Melville), she looked young, vital and altogether delectable. The fact that she got high as a kite at dinner did embarrass her hosts and irritated Mark, but she at least kept the party bubbling with her barbed comments and outrageous stories—no matter how drunk Lily got, she was never maudlin nor slurred in her speech. In fact, her amusement quotient was often in direct ratio to her alcoholic intake, and Mark found it difficult to stay angry at her long. She simply made him laugh too much.

After dinner, even though it was nearly midnight, Lily insisted on returning to town to see a cockfight. The Lobos demurred, but made available their car and chauffeur. Off Mark and Lily went, back into Havana, where in an old section of town near the Ambos Mundos hotel they located the seedy restaurant Lily remembered from her honeymoon. They were led down to the smoke-filled basement, where in the cockpit at the center of the room two roosters with razors tied to their feet were butchering one another. The sight of the chicken blood excited Lily much more than Mark, who, after all, had seen and shed his share of the human variety. Indeed, Mark was nauseated by the barbaric sport and after two bouts insisted they return to the yacht. Lily didn't want to go to bed, but Mark insisted. They turned in, made love and went to sleep, Lily not bothering to return to her cabin. As far as either was concerned, by now they were in effect man and wife, except for the mostly forgotten detail of Lily's still being married to Melville.

The next morning Mark was wakened when Félipe knocked on his door. Tylertown was on the radio. Mark threw on a bathrobe and hurried to the radio shack. Melville was on the air, and he was excited.

"Great news! We've wiped out almost half of Tegai's army!"

"How?"

"We got ourselves an informer. One of Tegai's lower-echelon lieutenants who's had a grudge against the big man for some time because one of his wives' brothers was one of the men the Leopard Society killed at Las Palmas. He showed up at the plantation yesterday and said he knew where most of Tegai's units were and that he'd talk for five hundred dollars and protection for him and his family. Naturally, he was terrified but his anger was even stronger than his fear. We paid the money, of course, and gave him protection and he pinpointed the places on the maps. Captain Strang was worried it might be a trap—but General Amberley decided it was worth taking the chance, so at dawn this morning they raided eight of the encampments, including Tegai's headquarters, and caught them completely by surprise. They put up a good fight, all things considered. The count so far is about three hundred dead and wounded and they've rounded up over 3,000 prisoners that no one knows what to do with yet. Our side lost sixty-three men—only twelve Americans, thank God!—the rest were militia, and about a hundred wounded . . . Chadwick's so happy—"

"But what about Tegai? Did they get him?"

A pause. "Well, unfortunately, he wasn't at his headquarters. We think he was on his way to one of the encampments with members of his staff, we're not sure. And Mark, about his headquarters! Apparently it was in a cave about thirty miles west of Canning Landing, and it had telephones, desks, files—like a real army. General Amberley found the location of the other encampments in the files and sent out troops to attack them, but Tegai must have gotten the word because when the men got there they were deserted. But we've broken the main strength of the movement. Everyone agrees Tegai's finished now—it's just a matter of time. We got back more than half the weapons he stole from the armory including the artillery pieces—his people were having trouble figuring out how to work them . . . We heard a relic from the war, an Austro-Hungarian howitzer, blew up on them when they tried to fire it. Anyway, they were planning to bombard Tylertown when they got the guns working, but that's out now. In fact the whole thing's out. I guess it was a real show! The militia and the Marines and the planes were all well-coordinated, and the Admiral's as pleased as Chadwick—"

"Wait a minute. The estimate I heard of Tegai's strength was more like 8,000. If you took 3,000 prisoners and killed three hundred, he's still got over half his men, hasn't he?"

"Yes, but we figure they're demoralized. We got his best men and equipment and his headquarters—it's a mop-up operation now. The real question is what to do with the prisoners—where to put them, whether to try them for treason, or what. General Amberley wants to shoot them, but Chadwick's not for that. He wants to catch Tegai and the leaders, try them and then declare an amnesty, which I think is probably what will happen. Anyway, it's quite a day in Tylertown, believe me!"

"It seems to me that if you hadn't been lucky enough to get that informer, you'd still be nowhere."

"Well, I'll agree with that. But I'm not saying that to our military people."

"No, I agree . . . But what about Roger Boine?"

Another pause.

"Did you find him?"

"No, but he was there. At the headquarters. We found out Tegai had wanted to kidnap him to try and get him to set up a medical unit for his army, but Roger did the job for him by leaving Las Palmas to try and talk Tegai into a compromise. Tegai made him a prisoner."

"*Where is he?*"

"With Tegai. He took him with him."

"I don't like the sound of that."

"Why? Why would Tegai hurt a kid like Roger? Tegai's vulnerable, Mark, his back's to the wall. He's no fool, he knows he hasn't a chance for clemency if he hurts a young white doctor. I'm sure Roger's going to be all right."

Mark considered this. "I hope you're right, but I'll feel much better when we get Roger back."

"We'll get him back, Mark. Don't worry. And we'll get Tegai, too. I think we can all feel pretty good about the whole thing."

"Well, I'm glad to hear it. Send my congratulations to Strang and the admiral, and Amberley and Chadwick too."

"The latest I heard, Chadwick's planning a national celebration with a three-day holiday and fireworks and a big reception at Government House."

"Tell him not to buy the champagne until he's got Tegai locked up. Okay, Melville, keep me informed."

He left the radio shack and returned to his cabin. Lily was sitting up in bed nursing a hangover.

"What time is it?" She yawned.

"Early."

He sat down next to her, staring at his slippered feet.

"God, I feel *awful*," she said. "Like the Battle of the Marne was just fought somewhere on the back of my tongue."

"With that hogshead of booze you swilled last night, it's a miracle you're alive."

"It was fun, though, wasn't it? I like Tony Lobo. I'm mad for dark, Latin, lover types. Yum!" She yawned again. "What did Melville have to say?"

Mark told her.

"But that's marvelous! We won!"

"We?"

"You and me, darling. Mr. and Mrs. Mark Manning-to-be."

He shrugged.

"Sure, we won. Except I'm not so sure we really did." He was thinking of Roger.

They hoisted anchor an hour later and sailed out of Havana harbor heading northwest for Florida. The day was beautiful: cloudless blue skies, and the Straits of Florida were a turquoise mirror. Mark's personal barometer, however, was falling. As Lily watched him moving listlessly about the ship, or sitting slumped in the paneled saloon leafing absently through out-of-date magazines, she supposed he was still worried about his son. Except, after all, he wasn't his *real* son, and the kid wasn't in any particular danger that she could see.

The radio shack call came that afternoon at five thirty. Mark rushed to the shack. It was Melville. His tone, even through the static, conveyed trouble.

"Mark, a terrible thing has happened."

Mark closed his eyes a moment.

"Tell me."

"An hour ago a runner came to General Amberley's camp under a white flag—Amberley's taken over Tegai's former headquarters in the cave. The runner had a message from Tegai. It was addressed to you, and I've got a copy here. Shall I read it?"

"Go on."

"It's pretty strong stuff. In fact, it's an ultimatum. Here it is: 'Manning. You are a criminal. You have exploited my country's people and their resources. You have supported a puppet regime which has intrigued with you to fatten on corruption. You have brought foreign troops onto our soil and you have killed my people and taken them prisoner.'"

Melville hesitated; his voice was nervous.

"Go *on!*"

"'Thanks to the treachery of one of my men, our cause has suffered a temporary setback. But we are not defeated, nor will we ever be defeated. We will fight until you and yours, both white and black, have been driven from our soil. I cannot attack you personally, but it is in my power to attack someone of your own flesh. Your natural son, Dr. Roger Boine, is my prisoner. Proof of this is in the accompanying package—' "

"What package?"

"It . . . the runner brought it with the message. But I better finish."

"Hurry *up*!"

" 'I therefore present to you the following demands, knowing that the puppet Chadwick and the American invaders take their ultimate orders from you. (1) That within twenty-four hours of the receipt of this message, all my men taken prisoner by your forces be freed and allowed to return to me. (2) All weapons and ammunition stolen from my forces be returned. (3) All American forces brought in by the three U.S. Navy gunboats and the aircraft carrier *Declaration of Independence* be evacuated and returned to their ships which shall have set sail from Tylertown harbor by the end of the twenty-four hour period. (4) All support, financial or otherwise, by the Manning Company of the corrupt Chadwick regime be terminated immediately, and any existing treaties, loans, or agreements between the same be abrogated. (5) Title to the Manning rubber plantation at Las Palmas to be transferred back to the Republic of Río de Oro with the understanding that financial compensation will be adjudicated at a later date by the government that supersedes the Chadwick regime. (6) A written guarantee that all American personnel employed by you at the Las Palmas plantation shall have left this country on or before March 15, 1927.

" 'If, on that date, all of the above conditions have been satisfactorily met, your natural son, Dr. Roger Boine, will be returned to you alive. If, by the end of the twenty-four hour period, the first five of the above conditions have not been complied with, your natural son's life will be forfeit. Though I recognize he is innocent of your crimes, his death will be in a manner commensurate with the injustice practiced by you and those who have served you.

" 'Manning! Think of this innocent young man whom you brought into this world without even giving him the decency of your name! He has a long life ahead of him, a life rich with potential for the benefit of humanity. If you force me to kill him, you will be his murderer, not I. You stand to lose a small part of your empire. Your son will lose his life.

" 'If you entertain any doubts as to the strength of my determination, look at the contents of the accompanying package.'

"It's signed, 'Tegai, Hereditary Prince of the Kru Tribe.' "

"What," said Mark slowly, "is in the package?"

There was a protracted pause.

"*Tell* me, for God's sake!"

"A foot, cut off at the ankle. The skin's white with freckles and the top has red hair on it. There's no question that it's Roger's . . ."

Mark shut his eyes tight as tears started from beneath the lids. "Sweet Jesus," was all he could say.

He walked aft to the saloon of the yacht. For the first time in fifteen years, he poured himself a glass of whiskey, half of which he drained in the first gulp. The liquor hit his stomach and made him shudder. He finished the glass and refilled it.

Lily watched this, putting down her copy of *Vogue.*

"What's wrong?"

He slumped into one of the chintz-covered armchairs and slowly ran his hands over his eyes.

"My son," he said. "Tegai's threatening to kill him unless I get out of Río de Oro."

Lily got up and came over to him, sitting in the sofa next to his chair. "He's bluffing," she said. "It's got to be nothing but a desperate bluff."

He drank more of the whiskey. "He cut off Roger's foot . . ."

Lily's eyes widened. "My God, why . . . ?"

"As a promise of things to come. The man's a butcher . . ."

"But there must be *something* you can do! Half his army's been captured—can't they go in and get him?"

"Of course, they can. And the first one to die will be Roger. I can't even try to bluff or negotiate with him. He's holding Roger until March 15th. That's when I'm supposed to have all our people at the plantation out of the country and transfer title over to his government—"

"*What?*"

He told her the rest of the terms.

"You can't do it—just hand over the whole thing to a bunch of murderers. You've put so much into Las Palmas—all the time and effort and money—you *can't* give in to him!"

"Lily, it's my son—"

"He's not your son! Oh, God, Mark, I didn't mean to say that and I know you're upset . . . that was a horrible thing he did, but it still doesn't mean he isn't bluffing. He wouldn't dare actually kill your son . . . not if he expects to save his own neck . . ."

"Fanatics don't give a damn about their own necks . . ."

"Well, he brought this on himself, didn't he? Going off to see Tegai when you told him it was none of his business—"

Mark stared at her. "Do you realize what you're *saying*?"

"I'm saying no matter what you sometimes think of me, I care more about you and your life's work than this kid you hardly know and who's stuck his own neck in the noose—if that's what it really is. And what about your responsibility to your thousands of employees and stockholders? You know damn well what will happen if you give up Las Palmas. The stock will go down thirty points in a day—"

"Lily, he's my son! You're talking about a human life, not the goddamn Dow Jones Industrials!"

"I'm talking about the Manning Rubber and Steel Company," she said evenly, "which is more important than any single human life, including yours."

He gave her a curious look. "Do you *really* believe that?" he asked quietly.

"Yes, I do." Her answer was tinged with defiance. "And so do you."

"And what if it were *your* life?"

"I just answered that. But I would never be stupid enough to get myself in such a position."

He finished his drink, then got up and started toward the door.

"Where are you going?"

"Melville's standing by waiting for me to tell him what to do. I'm going to tell him to release the prisoners."

"You're giving in to him?"

He turned on her angrily. "Lily, for God's sake, I can't take the chance he's bluffing. Do you think I *want* to give in? Who knows better what we've put into Las Palmas! And who knows better what this means to me! We're going to have to start all over again somewhere else to get the rubber—"

"Somewhere else? Where some other Tegai is going to try the same thing on you! Don't you see, Mark? If you give in to them once, they're going to do it to you again! It's common sense. There'll be a hundred Tegais—a thousand of them—all after the same thing. *Your* power, *your* money, *your* resources. And they'll say they're doing it for patriotism or nationalism or their people or motherhood—it doesn't matter what. The point is, they're all just thieves—lazy, greedy thieves trying to steal what you've spent a life to build. And you are going to hand it over to them—"

"This is my *son!*"

Now she was out of her chair. "So *what?* It didn't bother you when those twelve Marines you didn't know were killed for you. Why should it bother you so much if an illegitimate son you hardly know gets killed? Assuming he will be killed . . ."

"Roger is my own flesh and blood!"

"And so is Las Palmas. Do you know why I love you, am *really* attracted to you? Oh, you're good-looking and you're rich and I'll admit all that appeals to me. But there are plenty of good-looking men in this world, and rich ones. What especially excites me about you is your power, and that you've *never* been afraid to use it. At least up to now. Scorpio, who makes his own rules, who is never weak, who never gives in to a lot of sentimental baloney. And now you're giving in." She pulled a cigarette from a box on a table and lighted it. "Talking about your son and your flesh and blood—he's not your son, he's your bastard. And even if he were your real son, it wouldn't matter. When any part of your world is attacked you ought to be willing to kill to protect it. And if you're not willing, you're going to lose it. This Tegai is through. Roger Boine is his last chip, and it's only worth as much as your lack of nerve lets it be worth. If you give him back his army and his weapons and pull out the Marines, then *we're* through. And if I have anything to say about it—I say again that one man's life, no matter *whose* it is, is not worth the price."

He looked at her a moment. "What do you think I am? What kind of *monster* do you think I am?"

"A beautiful, powerful animal who's clawed his way to the top of the heap. And now that you're there, the only way you're going to stay there is if you continue to be the kind of man that got there."

"That's *really* how you see me?"

"Yes. And I think I see you more clearly than you see yourself. Oh, you're a very civilized animal who covers his spoor by good works and charity, not only for protection but because I think part of you is also decent and feels guilty.'

She sat back down on the sofa and smiled. "Come to think of it, I've gotten all upset over nothing. If you were really going to sacrifice Las Palmas to save Roger, you wouldn't have come back here to think about it. You'd have done it. But you did come back here, hoping that maybe I'd screw up your courage for you. Well, I've done it, and you can blame it all on Lily. Cruel, hard-hearted Lily, who thinks corporations are more important than human life. Blame it on me; I don't care. But if I were a betting person, I'd bet a lot that when you go back to that radio shack to call Melville, you're not going to tell him to free those prisoners."

"You're wrong."

"Am I?"

Her smugness infuriated him; her perception chilled him. Shame ignited his rage like gasoline poured on a fire. Before he realized what he was doing, he was standing over her, slapping her face with all his strength. She cringed, tried to protect herself but didn't make a sound. He stopped, sank down on the sofa and buried his face in his hands. Slowly she sat up, her cheeks blazing red. She watched him, trying to hide the contempt she felt.

"Maybe I was wrong about you," she said. "Maybe you *are* no different than the rest of them."

He looked up. Tears were running freely down his face.

"You bitch, I'm crying because you're right."

Roger Boine was sick and he was afraid.

He had been kept prisoner in the steaming hut for two days now, ever since they had come with the axe and held him down and removed his boots and, with one blow, severed his left foot. He had fainted. When he revived and felt the searing pain in the stump where they had cauterized the wound with a burning torch and wrapped it in a crude bandage, he had fainted again from the new pain. He had no idea why they had done it. The guards had told him nothing. Why would Tegai have ordered this? It was crazy. The fever that had set in—Roger wondered whether it was a reaction to the amputation or malaria, or maybe something worse—the fever made him wonder if the whole thing was a wild nightmare.

And then on the evening of the second day, Tegai came into the hut. He was too weak to do anything but lie on the mat and watch as Tegai placed the kerosene lantern on the dirt floor and sat down, crossing his legs. Despite his hatred for the man—and fear of him— Roger couldn't help but notice that he looked troubled, nervous even. He had a pistol in his left hand. Now he placed it on the dirt beside him.

"I've come," he said, "to free you."

Roger forced himself to sit up. He looked at the gun.

"Why?"

"Because in spite of what I said to you that first day, I simply can't kill you. And I *should* kill you."

"Why should you kill me?" exclaimed Roger, his rage bursting out of him. "Why was I made a prisoner, and *why* in God's name did you hack off my foot? I thought you were *supposed* to be at least partly civilized—"

"If I *weren't,* you'd be a dead man. It is precisely my civilization—my weakness, my softness—that stops me from doing what I should do." He pulled out his cigarette holder and a crumpled pack of cigarettes, which he offered to Roger, who shook his head. Tegai fitted a cigarette in the holder, then lit it. "You see," he continued, "this was a simple and rather desperate gamble on my part to win a war I'm going to lose. I was betrayed by one of my men, and now they have taken half of my army. Everything I've worked years to build up was taken away in less than two hours. I was beaten, as I am now, and I knew it. But I had you. So I wrote a message to your father, trying to bargain with your life to induce him to leave Río de Oro. I had to show him I was serious. I sent your foot with the message. I thought it was the most expendable part of your anatomy. I could have cut off one of your hands, you know, as the Belgians used to do to the rubber workers in the Congo when they wanted to spur production, as they put it. But I hoped you would live, and a one-handed doctor would be somewhat at a disadvantage."

He took a drag on the cigarette.

"And my father," said Roger slowly, *"turned you down?"*

"Yes. He seems to think more of his rubber plantation than he does his own son. Now, the decision about your life is back in my hands. There is absolutely no doubt in my mind what I should do. My honor, not to mention the honor of my tribe and my country demands that I carry out my threat and kill you. Your father deserves your death. But I confess I like you. And unfortunately, you do *not* deserve your death. You are the innocent here. I've been struggling with this for hours. I cannot bring myself to kill you. The corruption of my education, I suppose," he added bitterly. "Before I went to Oxford, life seemed very simple and straightforward. Now life is less so. At any rate, you are free. My men will get you to Canning Landing and send you back to Tylertown by boat."

Roger was overwhelmed with feelings of relief and bitterness—relief that his life was being spared, bitterness at his father's willingness to sacrifice his own son . . .

"You know," he said, "for years my mother tried to convince me that my father was really some sort of an evil man—she used the word 'evil' and I used to laugh at her. Now it seems she was right after all."

"Oh, yes," said Tegai, tapping his cigarette ash on the floor, "it's easy to condemn your father. I've condemned him, and I'll continue to do it. But frankly, if I had been he, I very probably would have made the same decision."

Roger looked surprised. "You just said he deserves my death—"

"Yes, and I believe he does. But that doesn't mean I can't understand him. You see, in some ways I'm not so different from your father. We're both involved with power. And power is a jealous ruler. It doesn't like to compete with such sentiments as love or pity. It consumes."

Roger told himself he had better get out of the hut quickly and not tempt fate.

"Can you help me up?"

"Of course."

Tegai rose, then helped Roger up as he called outside the hut to Saafwe. The warrior appeared in the door with a crude crutch. He handed it to Roger, who fitted it under his arm and tried a few exploratory steps. "Not so bad," he said, "I think I might even get pretty good with this thing."

Tegai and Saafwe watched him but said nothing. Then Tegai nodded to Saafwe, who went to the door. Tegai picked up his gun from the floor, then came over to Roger.

"I'll bid you good-bye now," he said. I hope at least you will try to understand why I have done this thing to you. You're a very brave young man," he said. "And I respect you. Saafwe will take you to the chair."

Roger nodded and then took one last look at his jailer. Then he leaned on his crutch and hobbled to the doorway.

Tegai raised his gun and aimed at the back of the young man's head. Then he fired. Roger fell forward on his face; he was killed instantly.

Tegai walked over and stared down at the corpse. The blood was matting the reddish-gold hair on the back of its head. The Kru prince felt sick. He had had to do it. He had tried to make it as painless as possible for the young American. He had even lied to him to spare his knowing that he was about to be executed. Even so, he had killed him. He bent down and ran his hand gently over the hair, smearing his palm with the warm blood. It was almost a plea for forgiveness. Then he straightened and walked out of the hut into the darkness, leaving the lantern behind.

CHAPTER TEN

Letter from Hanson Mayberry to Madame Charlotte de Sibour at Château La Colline-sur-Marne, dated February 25, 1928.

Dear Charlotte:

Here is my private account of *the* wedding, as I promised to write when I was with you in Paris last month—and, by the way, again a thousand thanks for your charming hospitality and that of your delightful husband. But, to the wedding. Well, to lapse into the vulgate, it was *something*. In over twenty-five years of reporting the foibles and excesses of the rich, I must admit I've seen few foibles as excessive as this one. The second Mrs. Manning did it up brown, and even now, a week after the big event, I'm still not certain I'm recovered from the memory.

The house—named Villa del Mar, one of those house names that makes me bilious—is, after two years of construction, considered a wonder. I wonder how to describe it. Perhaps Palm Beach Paramount is the most descriptive name for the style, except you, who haven't been back to the States for so many years, may not know what that connotes, not having seen the Peoples' Palaces of our wondrous age, those Cheopsian piles of ostentation the movie people have built to dazzle the hoi polloi. It's huge; it's ocher; it has an orange-tile roof and a tower with white-coral Gothic arches in the top. It bristles with niches, pillars, statues and gewgaws all vaguely Iberian in flavor; it's surrounded by palm trees, wisteria, begonias and every gaudy flower in Mother Nature's catalogue. It has, in the "great hall," a $100,000 Louis XIV Gobelin tapestry that, when the Master pushes a button, glides up to reveal a *movie* screen. Its six-car garage is paneled in cork —I have no idea why, unless the Manning automobiles are, like the late Monsieur Proust, peculiarly sensitive to noise. Milady's bath is an incredible 45' by 25', overlooks the ocean, is made of pale green marble, has an 8'-by-10' sunken marble bathtub with silver swan faucets and an adjoining mirrored dressing room with closets big enough to hold the entire wardrobe of the Metropolitan Opera. Mr. Manning's personal towels are modestly embroidered with "Mark," and Mrs. M's have "Lily." Cozy? The sheets on their extravaganza-sized bed are pink silk, the tile pool in the patio garden facing the ocean is big enough to float several Roman galleys comfortably and the poolhouse has male and female marble footbaths so that the peasants won't spread what

I believe is inelegantly known as athlete's foot. The dining room, which seats fifty, has an enormous, breath-taking Rubens that Barjoonian sold Mr. M. for a reputed $800,000 and which swarms with pudgy goddesses being chased by—or are they chasing?—muscular satyrs. The library facing the patio is lined with impressive Moroccan bindings, but one wall of them hides an elaborate bar. Well, I could go on, but I hope by now you have the general idea. The whole thing cost a reputed $5,000,000. It's supposed to look something like the Escorial, but I'll be damned if I can see the resemblance and I doubt whether Philip II—dear old austere Félipe Segundo—would feel much at home there. I suppose a thousand years from now some archaeologist will stumble on the ruins of the Villa del Mar and marvel at the thing, wondering what strange American prince built this strange, vulgar monument to his own glory. *Sic transit* . . .

Well, into the midst of this Spanish phantasmagoria you place the sinuous Mrs. Manning and her doting, middle-aged magnate of a bridegroom who decide to celebrate their nuptials with a party lifted from the pages not of Spanish history—that would be too logical—but of French history, and we have a clash of culture that staggers the imagination. To wit, Mrs. Manning sent out 1,500 invitations to a ball to be held at Villa del Mar the night of their wedding (Mrs. Manning does things her own way. Actually, everyone knows that the newlyweds had long since plighted their troth, so privacy on their wedding night was not precisely what they were after. The wedding, for the record, was performed that morning by a humble justice of the peace in the library—not, as one might have expected from the look of the place, by the archbishop of Toledo). The ball was called *Les Plaisirs de l'Ile Enchantée ou les Fêtes et Divertissements du Roi* after the party Louis XIV gave at Versailles in 1664. Guests were instructed to come in costumes "from the French court of the period." Apparently all this was *Mrs.* Manning's idea—it seems she *likes* Louis XIV, and presumably she was trying to convey the idea that she had married a latter-day Sun King. (Judging from the record of mistresses *that* monarch achieved, Mrs. Manning had best not push the idea too far.) At any rate, out went the invitations to everyone who was anyone in Palm Beach, as well as New York, Chicago and various points west. Now, the new Mrs. Manning did not *know* all these people, though many of the husbands were business acquaintances of Mark. But the new Mrs. Manning is a very determined woman. She didn't care whether she knew them or not. Many of the Palm Beach old guard were turning noses upward at all this, but after all, it's difficult to ignore a man such as Mark Manning, who is currently a director in something like fifteen giant corporations, and it is *very* difficult not to wish to see the pleasures of an enchanted isle of the rich such as Villa del Mar. The upshot was, of course, everyone swallowed their snobbish predilections and accepted. Dressmakers and tailors were inundated with orders for costumes from the reign of the Grand Monarch, everyone vowing secretly to outdo everyone else in the plumage department.

Came the great night, which, luckily, was lovely and cool. Your faithful scribe, who was staying with the Robertson Peterboroughs, struggled into his rented courtier outfit (from which embarrassingly emanated the faint odor of theatrical mothballs) and proceeded to Versailles. The enchanted isle fairly glowed. Not with something so ordinary as paper lanterns, mind you, but with what best can be described as human torches. For stationed through the grounds and around the pool and along the beach were dozens of huge, immobile black gentlemen in silver turbans, silver Turkish pantaloons and nothing else, each holding a tall iron *torchère,* from the top of which burned a flame. This gesture, which must have provided employment for a goodly percentage of the colored population, if it did nothing else saved on the Mannings' electric bill. But it was only the beginning. In front of the garage, serenading the arriving guests, was the Manning Rubber Symphony Orchestra, playing *Eine Kleine Nachtmusik* and other 18th-century renditions, which one assumes no one had pointed out were written several years after Louis XIV had passed on to his heavenly reward. Never mind, it set the mood. Also establishing the mood were some two dozen big silver birdcages hanging from bushes and trees, each filled with exotic birds; an enormous circular stone fountain in front of the house, in which gamboled three luscious near-naked sea nymphs, representing—one can only guess!—the three great rivers of France? Or the Mississippi, the Missouri and the Monongahela? Or Chrysler, Ford and Chevrolet? I don't know. Anyway there thev were, looking gorgeous, and everyone ogled. But this wasn't all. The enchanted guests of the enchanted isle soon stumbled over (literally, in one hilarious case) wood nymphs as well, delectable young ballerinas who danced through the gardens in 17th-century ballet costumes, twirling through the palm trees to the pipes of Pan (or the Symphony, or the jazz band on the beach—it was difficult to tell which), as coy and coquettish as one could imagine.

Well, when one had absorbed this ambience, one went inside the house, which is overwhelming. Liveried footmen; orchids drooped from the iron chandeliers, and were indeed everywhere one could conceivably stick an orchid except, perhaps, in the hostess's ear; hundreds of guests milling around, all togged out in their costumes, the men in their perukes and high heels, the women in their heavy, bulging skirts and even heavier, bulging diamonds. Whatever else one may say about the reign of the Sun King, it was an awkward period of costume design. But we were to discover this was all part of the Plan, for when we trailed through the receiving line we found that our hostess, the beaming new Mrs. Manning, had decided to ignore her own party rules and showed herself off to the disadvantage of the other ladies present by wearing an 18th-century dress, a gorgeous silver-lamé gown strewn with pearls, giving her a very Madame du Barry look, which was twice as spectacular and feminine as anyone else's.

As you know, this is characteristic of our Lily. She is full of nerve, determined to be center stage and is already on everyone in Palm Beach's blacklist (which means, of course, she'll be "inadvertently" invited everywhere). I'll admit she's a stunning woman, though her face is a bit hard for my liking. The story is she went after Mark with net and trident; her husband, who was one of the top executives of the company, finally caught on but, to everyone's surprise, when he came back from Africa, instead of making the expected cuckold's noises, quietly accepted the situation, resigned from the company, and now has a top job with one of Mark's competitors—I think it's Goodyear. Anyway, neither of the lovebirds apparently felt much remorse— or if they did they're certainly not showing it. Lily is radiant. She's hit the jackpot with the Sun King, she knows it and she's not the least bit reticent about wearing her battle ribbons; on this evening they were a diamond necklace with pendant emeralds that evoked envious stares from even the Palm Beach regulars. She seems to have her husband wrapped about her finger, and she gives off the aura of a will of iron disguised in the proverbial velvet. You knew her when she was a young girl, and you've told me that even then she was someone to be reckoned with. Now I would say she is almost formidable. Gossip has it that she is interested in business, most particularly her husband's; one can only speculate as to what this will lead to. All I can say now is that she is as different from you as night from day.

Mark has changed. Not physically; he is still a handsome man who wears his years well, though the wrinkles are forming. But his personality seems oddly different. I never knew him well, of course; but I remember him vividly from that night, years ago, at your Christmas ball when he was shot by the lunatic Wobbly. Then he gave the impression of great confidence, strength and nerve—a man whom you might or might not like, but definitely a man to take seriously. Now something is missing, and I'd venture to say it's the confidence. Odd, isn't it? Then, when he was on the rise, he had an overabundance of it. Now that he's the Sun King, he seems somehow wary. Is that the word? Or guarded? I'm not sure, but there's something in his eyes— perhaps a sadness, even—that I didn't remember from before. You know, of course, of the tragedy that happened last year at his African plantation when his natural son was murdered by the outlaw chief, who was himself later shot by the authorities. Well, the rumors in New York are that Sheila Harrington, the boy's mother and co-publisher of the *American Woman*, is going to write a book about Mark, and that it's going to be quite a hatchet job. The Outraged Mother's

Revenge? Whether Mark's worried about the effect the book will have
on him, or whether he feels guilty about the boy's death or perhaps
something else, I can't tell. All I do know is that he seems a different
man, though, of course, still someone to command respect. He seems
even a rather lonely man, despite his new bride and all his gaudy
splendor.

But I digress—back to the party. There was an excellent jazz band
on the beach, and though doing the Charleston in farthingales presents definite problems, a few of the guests were trying it. Most, however, were standing about drinking, gossiping and fighting off the
boredom that is the plague of this resort. After years of social reporting, I have evolved a theory, which I now proclaim as Mayberry's
First Law of Inertia: the great crime of the American rich is not their
wealth, nor how they got it, nor how they spend it. The great crime
of the American Rich is that they are, as a class, incredibly, numb-
ingly dull. With all the hoopla that was going on, with all the wood
nymphs, liveried footmen, oceans of excellent champagne, music, et
cetera, surrounding them, the conversations, I could swear, never devi-
ated from (a) the market; (b) the newest chic place to go; (c) golf,
interchangeable with tennis, yachting or horses; and (d) whose wife
was seen with whom. The first category was subdivided into (a) The
boom will continue forever; (b) The bubble is about to burst, bringing Armageddon; and (c) No opinion. One would think art, politics,
philosophy, literature or wit had never been invented. Ah well, how
fortunate you are to live in France!

A mammoth dinner was served at midnight, with such supposedly
Louis XIV dishes as suckling pig, roast squabs, Egyptian quail and
so forth, all displayed on huge silver trays carried by the wigged footmen to the tables set up beneath gay Venetian tents; next a colossal
white wedding cake was unveiled by the pool and the first slice cut
by the unblushing bride—whether wedding cakes were contemporary
with Louis XIV no one bothered to ask. While all munched cake and
imbibed more champagne, the sea and wood nymphs, who had changed
to modern swim suits, put on a water ballet in the pool; this was
followed by a colored tap-dance act that I can swear was not contemporary with Louis XIV, but which was the hit of the evening.
Then tumblers and acrobats put on a show around the pool, while
fortune-tellers passed around the tables reading palms. Meanwhile,
in the huge ballroom, a casino was opened with chemin de fer, trente-
et-quarante, poker, craps and roulette. This proved exceedingly popular, and though play money was handed out by the croupiers, at
several tables the betting was real, and the Baroness Ilse von Fichtel-
Kasendorf reputedly dropped $12,000 at craps while a Patino from
Bolivia casually lost over $23,000 at chemmie. Easy come, and so forth.

By this time I was growing weary of the enchanted isle and was ready to call it a night. It was then that the best moment of the evening occurred. The host and hostess were dancing on the wooden floor set up just past the pool near the beach. I forgot to mention that Mark was decked out as the Sun King himself, with a dazzling gold-brocade suit and court shoes with the high heels painted red— as you may recall, Louis was the only one who could wear red heels, which was his royal prerogative. Well, one of those royal red heels came loose; Mark stumbled and fell flat on his face. There was a hush, followed by a few titters. He sat up and looked at his bride, who looked down at him. Then both of them broke into roars of laughter.

There may be hope for the world yet.

Yours from that other enchanted isle, Manhattan,

Fondly, Hanson

Excerpts from a review in the "Literary Digest," dated Feb. 5, 1932, of Sheila Harrington's book, *Mark's Millions*.

After five years of delays and exhaustive research, Mrs. Sheila Harrington, co-publisher of the *American Women,* has brought out her study of the Manning Rubber and Steel Company and its founder and chairman, Mark Manning. The book is worth the wait. It is a flawed masterpiece, a probing study of one of America's largest corporations and most prominent industrialists, a three dimensional portrait of a man who has acquired enormous power and managed to hang on to it.

It is made even more interesting by the fact that Mr. Manning was at one time Mrs. Harrington's lover and the father of her illegitimate son, the late Dr. Roger Boine. Admitting this publicly was, for a woman of Mrs. Harrington's position, an act of considerable bravery, but alas, while this adds a personal dimension to her portrait of Mr. Manning that is intriguing, it also contains the elements of my strongest criticism of this significant book. For Mrs. Harrington is biased. She admits it, but her bias against Mr. Manning is so strong that it distorts much of the book's material out of focus, with the result that the important ingredient in any scholarly work—objectivity—is missing, and we tend to grow skeptical. For instance, Mrs. Harrington baldly (and at some risk of legal action) accuses Mr. Manning of having caused the death of her son five years ago in Río de Oro. She insists Mr. Manning could have saved Dr. Boine's life—he had been working at the Manning plantation when he was captured by a native rebel leader—but failed to do so in order to protect his investment in Río de Oro. However, she offers no convincing proof to back up this charge, and the reader can't help but feel she is trying to forge rumor into fact, and that her credibility is seriously weakened by her

obvious dislike of Mr. Manning. She is on far safer ground when she
documents with exhaustive detail the role of the U.S. Navy and Marine
Corps in the Río de Oro imbroglio of five years back, and she asks
questions well worth asking—such as, is it to this country's advantage
to have its armed forces at the beck and call of its big businessmen
and political contributors? With the Depression forcing all of us to
take new and searching looks at our business leaders, Mrs. Harrington's book, with all its faults, is well worth reading. . . .

Excerpts from *Mark's Millions* by Sheila Harrington.

As I have tried to point out, Mr. Manning's approach to the problem
of being a tycoon in the 20th-century has been to appear publicly
benevolent while, privately, he operates the same way as his less hypocritical 19th-century forebears. Take the situation of the company
before the crash of '29. In August of that year, Manning stock had
reached an all-time high of 144. The net profits that year were a
record $18,000,000 on gross sales, from both the rubber and steel sec-
tors of the business, of over $175,000,000. The company employed a
total of 83,000 men; its share of the huge rubber industry was estimated at 17 percent, and its share of the car and truck tire market—
by far the most profitable part of the industry—was a whopping 27
percent. Its share of the nation's steel industry, though relatively
more modest, was still a substantial 6 percent. New factories had been
built in Los Angeles and England, and existing plants in Canada
and Massachusetts were expanded. New efficiency methods and improved
machinery, including power-driven, collapsible drums for building
the tires, had increased production. Though the company management,
under the new presidency of Harrison Starr, a dynamic young man
hand-picked by Mr. Manning, remained steadfastly antiunion, a company union set up by Mr. Manning in 1922 had achieved a remarkable record of labor harmony. It was claimed, apparently truthfully,
that every Manning employee owned stock in the company. Progressive
health insurance and pension plans were pacesetters for the industry.
Housing was offered to employees at favorable mortgage rates, a practice
that had been in force for years. Mr. Manning even built a country club
and golf course for his Elkins employees, surely the acme of management paternalism.

Thus, the picture was rosy in '29, and Mr. Manning's situation was
equally so. In 1927 Mr. Harold Swenson, the executive vice-president
since the founding of the company in 1905, retired for reasons of
health; the man slated to replace him, Mr. Melville Benny, resigned
for unspecified reasons (Mr. Benny's then wife divorced him shortly

after and is now married to Mr. Manning). Mr. Manning appointed himself chairman of the board and gave the presidency to the aforementioned Mr. Starr, formerly an up-and-coming executive at Goodyear. Mr. Benny, leaving Manning, became a top executive at Goodyear. Industrial musical chairs.

The reader may or may not recall that Mr. Manning achieved financial control of his company as long ago as 1915 by cornering the market in Henderson Steel stock, a daring maneuver favored by such 19th-century sharks as Jay Gould, which in 1915 was perfectly legal, though it is now frowned upon by the board of governors of the Exchange. The result of Mr. Manning's corner, aside from a still-unsolved murder of the man Mr. Manning cornered, was that Mr. Manning gained outright ownership (or control, since some of the stock was held in trust for the four Manning children) of 50 percent of the stock in his company. Since that time, there have been several recapitalizations and new stock offerings, one, in 1926, necessitated by the merger of Henderson Steel with Manning Rubber, which swelled Mr. Manning's stock position by 10 percent. However, since then Mr. Manning has reduced his position to a more modest, if still commanding, 41 percent of the total.

Now, throughout the boom years the benevolent Mr. Manning made repeated public statements lauding the free enterprise system and the stock market. In 1928, still reaffirming his faith in the market (and though it's hard to imagine now, at that time having faith in the market was the popular attitude), he sold all of his holdings in the Acme Radio Corporation, a transaction that netted him an astounding $83,000,000 (on, it was rumored, an initial investment of less than $50,000). Mr. Manning patriotically claimed he put the money back in the "economy," which everyone assumed meant the market. Actually, he invested all $83,000,000 in gilt-edged bonds. Had Mr. Manning received a tip from some of his knowing Palm Beach friends? He must have known *something*, because he proceeded to liquidate most of the rest of his bulging stock portfolio, including, ominously, a block of 150,000 shares of stock in his own company (reducing his ownership to the present 41 percent) and reinvested this sum, estimated at another $50,000,000, in more gilt-edged bonds, Manhattan and Los Angeles real estate and paintings by the Old Masters. What he left in the market—less than $1,000,000 in common stocks, aside from his Manning holdings—he later shifted to the short position, and in the crash reportedly tripled his money. Now, either Mr. Manning has the clairvoyant powers of a Nostradamus, or he was in that charmed circle of major industrialists who seemed to know something you and I and millions of other poor suckers didn't know. But at the very least, his private maneuvering casts serious doubts on his publicly professed love affair with the free-enterprise system.

All right, you say, so what? The man was a little smarter than the rest of us rubes. And if he did a little doubletalking along the way, is that so bad?

The facts continue.

In 1930 the Manning Company's profits dropped sharply. In 1931 the company reported the first loss in its history. Car production plummeted and with it, naturally went tires. This year of 1932 shapes up to be even worse. Now, what does our "progressive," benevolent tire magnate do? He does what everyone else is doing; he lays off workers, he cuts production, he trims to the bone to weather the storm. Fair enough—if you're willing to overlook the fact that one of the major causes of this mess we're in is that the majority of this nation's wealth is controlled by a handful of smart operators like Mr. Manning. But Mr. Manning was not content to do what other industrialists were doing. Presumably sensing that the mood of the country was ugly, he began touring his far-flung empire, making speeches to his workers, encouraging them to "hang on" (despite the fact that a fifth of them had been laid off and had precious little to hang on to), telling them that Father Manning had not forgotten them, that All Would Be Well. Accompanying him on this tour, which occurred in the fall of 1931, was Mrs. Lily Manning, an attractive woman in her midthirties who bore her husband a son in 1929. While Mr. Manning was delivering pep talks to the men, Mrs. Manning was touring the company housing projects talking to the wives and mothers of the workers, exchanging womanly talk about changing diapers and toilet training (despite the fact that Mrs. Manning has three nurses to relieve her of such tiresome chores), charming one and all with her sincere, winsome ways as a company photographer snapped photo after photo for national release. At the conclusion of each whistlestop, this team climaxed its act by announcing that all mortgage payments on company houses owned by men laid off would hereby be suspended until such time as economic conditions would allow their re-employment. Gasps of gratitude! Tears of joy! The homestead saved! A chorus of national praise went up for the Mannings the likes of which we've not heard since Lindy made his solo flight across the Atlantic. President Hoover went on the radio to praise Mr. Manning as an "enlightened" industrialist of whom "the entire country can be proud." (Lest we forget, Mr. Manning is one of the Republican Party's major campaign contributors.)

All right, again you say, so what? He could have stayed in his Palm Beach palace clipping his coupons. Instead, he's behaved rather magnanimously, all things considered.

But consider all things: the mortgages on these Manning Company houses are held by Manning Company banks. The company has nothing to gain by evicting the men because the houses are unsalable—who has the money to buy? And even if the company could sell them, their value has plummeted so far because of the deflation in prices, they'd be taking an enormous loss. Like those European war loans we've been hearing so much about these past years, if the loans can't be paid, what's the point of demanding payment? Far more sensible to declare a moratorium on the debts and hope that better times will enable the debtors to start paying up again later on. Similarly with the Manning mortgages.

And look what they have to gain by declaring the moratorium! An ocean of good will from men who otherwise might be picketing Manning factories. A resurgence of love for the Manning clan—these men might be on the dole, but Good Father Manning has kept a roof over their heads! And that sweet Mrs. Manning—why, she was here in my kitchen, talking about what formula is best for Junior! A cheap price to pay for labor harmony in these hard times, and a real bargain for worker loyalty. Again, the union movement—which is the one real hope for the Manning workers—has been undermined by the clever, hypocritical, double-dealing, Mr. Manning. . . .

PART

VIII

ELLEN IN LOVE; LILY IN ACTION

1933-1934

CHAPTER ONE

WHEN ELLEN Manning first met Leonard Hastings in the summer of 1931, she didn't think too much of him. He wasn't handsome, exactly, his face being what she thought of as "nice," or even worse, "cute." Certainly not the type that would bowl over a twenty-one-year-old girl. On the other hand, he had nice brown hair, rather greenish eyes, clear skin, and his body was well put together; he had that casually athletic animal grace of movement that she liked in men. But still, there was no great spark, no swelling Tchaikovskian melody when they met. He had been the roommate of Ellen's older brother their senior year at Princeton, and since Len's parents had just been transferred to Paris, where his father had become the new director of the Paris branch of the American National Bank, David Manning had invited his friend to the Château La Colline-sur-Marne for a weekend in July.

Several years before, Maurice de Sibour had built a small workshop-studio for himself, a short distance from the main house, and Charlotte had had a swimming pool put in near it. Since the weather was hot, Ellen, David, Len and the two other Manning children, Richard and Christopher, spent a good deal of time in the pool. Everyone got along well, there was the usual amount of horseplay in the water, but Ellen remained uninterested in Leonard, who struck her as rather immature in a typically Princeton way. She had just finished her junior year at Smith and was a somewhat reserved girl who dreamed of a career as a concert pianist, having inherited her mother's musical talent. However, her somewhat peripatetic life made her musical studies difficult. In the winter she took lessons from a teacher on the Smith faculty. During the summers, when in France visiting her mother and stepfather, she drove into Paris once a week for a lesson with a retired Russian pianist, Madame Olga Tashkoff. Madame Olga, as she was called by her pupils, was an excellent teacher; but studying with two different people was not a little confusing for Ellen. Besides, she realized that at twenty-one she was lagging far behind in her professional career. She had yet to give a debut, nor was she anywhere near ready for one. She tried to compensate for her tardiness by practicing harder, but she was beginning to recognize that the career she had dreamed of might be beyond her reach.

She was also interested in boys, though by no means "boy crazy." At Smith, she dated Yalies and Cornell boys, occasionally mixing in a few Harvards. It was all pretty casual. During the summers in France she went out with the sons of acquaintances of her parents. That summer of 1931 she had been seeing a good deal of a very serious young man named Valerian Grebert, whose family were friends of the de Sibours in Paris. She liked Valerian a lot—they shared a passion for Marcel Proust—but Valerian was another interruption in her piano studies. She felt that the last thing she needed was another man in her life to confuse things more. Even if she had been especially interested in Leonard Hastings, she would have been reluctant to get involved with him. And since she wasn't that interested, he dropped out of her life for two years and during that time she forgot all about him.

Ellen had always loved her true father, Mark, but since his remarriage to Lily in 1928 she had not felt as close to him as before. Her new stepmother seemed friendly enough, but Ellen felt, or perhaps believed, that the new Mrs. Manning was not overly anxious to expose her husband to his children by his former marriage, or, perhaps more accurately, she took pains when the children were there not to let them be alone with their father too much. Whether this was in Ellen's imagination or not, she wasn't sure, although her brothers privately agreed with her. None of them was too fond of Lily, and in the process, Mark had become less of a father and more of a father figure. On the other hand, she fell in love with her stepfather, Maurice de Sibour, almost as soon as she met him. So that gradually she had come to think of this gentle, pleasant Frenchman as her real father, and his pleasant château and elegant Paris apartment on the Avenue Kléber as her real home. Inevitably, she also came to think of herself as being at least as much French as American. She spoke French fluently, as did all the Manning children by this time, and France became, if not her country, much more her real home than either Palm Beach or Elkins.

Her mother, Charlotte, had also come to think of France as her home, but it had become her country as well. Charlotte occasionally missed the States; she occasionally even missed Mark, whose faults time had dimmed in her mind. But she had no real desire to return to America, even though she retained her American citizenship. She had found contentment in France, a country she had come to love deeply, and with Maurice, a man she adored. Their life in the country was pleasantly uncomplicated. They didn't entertain much, nor were they often entertained, Maurice's friends for the most part remaining rather cool to his new wife. This Charlotte accepted. She had heard that the more conservative circles of French society were chilly to outsiders, particularly Americans; besides, they had been friends of Maurice's first wife and were, Charlotte assumed, being rather naturally, if a bit stuffily, loyal to her memory. There was another reason for the aloofness that she suspected but never mentioned to Maurice. Her husband was aware of the coolness, but inasmuch as he tended to think of most of his country neighbors as more than a little boring and since it didn't seem to bother Charlotte, he most certainly would not allow it to bother him. It was, in fact, a bit of a relief. They both infinitely preferred the company of Maurice's Paris friends, who were much more interesting and who accepted Charlotte almost immediately.

Lack of social life in the country also took on a new advantage for the de Sibours. Curiously, what had begun with Maurice as a hobby— his detective-novel writing—had come to take more and more of his time. Throughout the Twenties, as he turned out ("churned out," some of his critics said) an average of three novels a year, his readership grew, until he had become one of the most popular writers of light fiction in France. His writing left little time for socializing in the country, even if they had wished it. It had, however, necessitated the building of the studio, where Maurice spent the mornings from eight till noon writing, and diverted more and more of his time and energies from the family champagne business. Charlotte had gradually come to fill in for her husband during his writing hours so that, in time, she grew to know as much about the business as Maurice. This was a happy arrangement, and provided another bond between them, further enriching their relationship. Whatever doubts Charlotte might have had about the institution of marriage from her first two unsuccessful tries had been dispelled by her third, gloriously successful one.

At the beginning of their marriage, Maurice had displayed little interest in politics. But during the upheavals of the Twenties his interest developed and intensified. By nature a tidy man—his novels were famous for their tight construction; no plot thread was ever misplaced or misused—he was dismayed by the untidyness of the Third Republic, which had been born in chaos and had grown to what many

Frenchmen considered a ripe immaturity dogged by constant turmoil. It had been founded in 1871 in the ashes of the collapse of Louis Napoleon's Second Empire when a national assembly was brought together to pull the nation out of its defeat by Bismarck's Germany. Four years later, after much wrangling, a constitution was finally passed that set up an assembly consisting of a senate elected indirectly by an electoral college and a popularly elected chamber of deputies. The president of the republic was elected by a majority vote of the senate and the chamber, which, fearing another Napoleon, tended to choose moderate, malleable men for the presidency. The president, in turn, picked a cabinet and a premier. In practice, however, the premier served more or less at the suffrance of the national assembly; and since the chamber of deputies was itself subject to an election only every four years, giving the deputies a good deal of security, and since the various national interests reflected themselves in a myriad of political parties, the mortal flaw of the Third Republic was that governments—meaning premiers—tended to come and go with astonishing rapidity, victims of the maneuvering for power always going on among the almost-omnipotent deputies.

Despite this, the Third Republic had managed to weather a number of serious storms, including the attempted royalist coup of General Boulanger in the Eighties, the tragic Dreyfus affair in the Nineties and early years of the 20th century, the painful divorce between the French state and the Catholic Church, and, last but hardly least, the trauma of World War I. This bloody conflict, in which most of the actual fighting had taken place on French soil, had cost France 134,000-000,000 gold francs' worth of goods and property and 1,500,000 dead. Yet France had emerged from it the strongest power in Europe. Its hated enemy since 1870, Germany, was totally defeated—its armies outlawed, its monarchy overthrown. France's former allies, Russia and England, were both seriously weakened, the former by the Bolshevik Revolution and the latter by the tremendous cost of the war; England was barely hanging on to its empire. France alone of the major European powers emerged from the war with a viable, though rather moribund, army, a self-sufficient agriculture, a potentially prosperous industry and a large and profitable empire in Africa and Indochina to bolster its prestige.

Yet the inherent weakness of its political structure continued to plague it. Premiers continued to come and go. And another well-entrenched habit of the French now reappeared to further bedevil this otherwise prosperous and reasonably contented nation: the hostility of the middle and upper classes toward taxes. The war damage had originally been intended to be paid for by reparations from Germany. However, Germany was broke; no reparations were paid. So to rebuild the industry and war-devastated regions of the country, the French government, its treasury drained by the war, had two choices—either to increase income taxes or float loans. Faced with the hostility of the moneyed classes toward any increase in taxes, the government chose the latter alternative. Loan after loan was floated. Finally in 1924 the treasury was empty again and the loan payments could not be met. The assembly grudgingly approved a 20-percent increase on all taxes, direct and indirect, although this still hurt the poor more than the rich, since the income taxes were riddled with loopholes, whereas no one could evade a sales tax. Still the well-to-do grumbled and sent their capital out of the country to foreign tax havens. Matters tottered from bad to worse; the franc fell in value. In the general election of that year, the country chose a radical chamber of deputies, which brought into power a socialist government under the premiership of Edouard Herriot. Herriot tried to solve the fiscal crisis by raising taxes; the following year, 1925, a conservative senate defeated a vote of confidence in the government and Herriot was out.

During the next fourteen months, six governments came and went; the franc fell to a ratio of fifty to the dollar; the nation faced bankruptcy. And all this, curiously, while the country's economy was booming and Paris was attracting thousands of tourists, drawn to what was universally considered the most charming and civilized city in the entire civilized world.

In this bleak government situation, the radical chamber of deputies switched direction to the right and brought in the conservative Poincaré, who had been president of the republic during the war and was known for his solid views on all manner of things. Poincaré did restore business confidence. Capital returned home and the franc firmed.

Through all this turbulence, Maurice de Sibour had become more and more disturbed by the weakness of the premiership and the presidency, by the whirling carousel of cabinets—by the chaos. He yearned for a strong leadership in government, a powerful president who could tame the stormy chamber of deputies rather than be its toady, who could bring calm and dignity to France. At the same time, as a wealthy businessman, he sided with the moneyed classes in their hostility to any increase in taxes. The accession to power of the conservative Poincaré caused Maurice to sigh with relief. But Poincaré was old and ill, with a prostate requiring surgery; in 1929 he resigned. The conservatives, elected to power the year before, continued to control the government. But the peaceful—or at least relatively peaceful—Twenties were drawing to a close, and the nightmare of the Thirties was on the horizon.

The Depression came to France late, not truly hitting the country until the collapse of the huge Kreditanstalt bank in Vienna in 1931 and the abandonment by England of the gold standard. Then the world-wide slump dug its heels into France, and it became evident that the conservatives would be turned out by the Socialists in the coming election of 1932. This alarmed Maurice, who foresaw a return to the political chaos of the mid-Twenties, as well as the threat of new taxes imposed on his already-suffering champagne business. For some years his friends in Paris had been urging him to translate his interest in politics into action by running for the chamber of deputies from his country district. He was, after all, a celebrity, known not only for his champagne but especially for his widely read mystery novels. He should have no trouble becoming elected, they assured him, and once in the chamber, his celebrity should help him become a voice to be reckoned with. Maurice tended to laugh off the suggestions, but in the winter of 1931, faced with the probable turn to the left in the spring elections, he changed his mind. After discussing it with Charlotte, who agreed, he decided to try for the Conservative-Nationalist candidacy in his district. It was a safe seat for the right, and the incumbent deputy had announced his retirement because of age. Further, the local chairman of the party was Maurice's old friend and fellow champagne producer, the Baron René de Courville.

Thus, one day in December of 1931, Maurice made an appointment with the baron, kissed Charlotte, got into his gorgeous white 1928 Hispano-Suiza "convertible victoria," with the graceful *Cigogne Volante* or flying stork hood emblem (Maurice had become a Hispano-Suiza devotee), and drove the seven kilometers to the château of the de Courvilles, where he was brought into the library to see the baron.

The de Courville family fortune had been founded in the reign of Louis XIII when, it was whispered, the young Captain Bérnard de Courville had become one of that sexually ambiguous king's male favorites. Given a title and estates for his services to the crown, the handsome captain had left the royal bedroom for the respectability of the landed gentry. Since that salacious beginning, the de Courvilles had been probity itself, surviving revolutions and wars to become one of the most solid pillars of the French establishment, intermarried with some of the noblest families in the country. The current bearer of the title was then in his earlier sixties, a small, rather delicate gentleman with white hair and a white moustache. He had perfect manners, and it was said he had never been known to raise his voice in anger. Notwithstanding this, the baron had a strong will. He was prominent in the Conservative-Nationalist Party, although he made no secret of his royalist sympathies and often spoke longingly in private of the day when the pretender to the throne of France, the Duc de Guise, would leave his exile in Brussels and return to Versailles to restore the palmy days of France's glory. In the early Thirties there were many royalist sympathizers in France and, indeed, the royalist newspaper, *L'Action Française,* was widely read and influential. A royalist-fascist movement, Action Française, had an organization of middle- and upper-class young men known as *Camelots du Roi,* who were, for all purposes, fascistlike storm troopers. Because of his prominence in the Conservative-Nationalist Party, the Baron de Courville did not openly align himself with Action Française, but his sympathies were with this odd and militant organization.

When Maurice came into the library, he was offered a cognac by the baron; then, snifters in hand, they both sat down.

"Now, Maurice, what is it you wanted to see me about?" asked the courtly older man, who was wearing an impeccably tailored tweed jacket.

"Politics," Maurice replied. "I want to offer myself as the Conservative-Nationalist candidate in the spring election."

The white eyebrows went up in surprise, which was not exactly the pleased reception Maurice had anticipated.

"My dear fellow, when did you become interested in politics?"

"I've been interested for a number of years, though I frankly never considered running for office until recently. René, the left is going to win this next election unless we fight them. They may win it anyway, but I want to be in on the fight. France needs strong leadership and men who are willing to support it in the assembly. We can't afford another mess such as we had in '25 and '26."

"Well, Maurice, I'm truly sorry to disappoint you," he said, "but we've already picked the candidate."

"May I ask who he is?"

"We'd rather not announce it just yet. There are a few minor matters to smooth out first. But you'll know soon enough. And I hope we'll be able to count on your support—"

"René, you're lying. You don't have a candidate. You're putting me off. What's wrong with me? *Why* don't you want me?"

At last, the smile faded. The baron sighed. "All right, Maurice, you force me to be blunt. We would be delighted to have you as our candidate. But there is a problem."

"*What* problem?"

"Your wife."

"Charlotte? But surely she'd be an asset! Unless—you mean because she's an American?"

"No. Because she's a Jewess."

Maurice was shocked. As a young man he had lived through the protracted and agonizing Dreyfus case that had torn France into two bitterly warring factions for more than ten years. In the fall of 1894 the French army had become aware that someone was selling military secrets to the Germans. After a hasty investigation a Captain Alfred Dreyfus, a Jew, was accused of the crime; a court martial, on the flimsiest of evidence, convicted him and sent him to Devil's Island for life. The case had evoked virulent anti-Semitism in France. Dreyfus was accused of being part of an international conspiracy of Jews to ruin the country; the army was hailed as the savior of the nation. Shortly afterward, new evidence came to light that led Major Georges Picquart, one of the war minister's official observers at Dreyfus' trial, to conclude that in fact Dreyfus was innocent, that the army had made a horrible blunder and to cover it up had railroaded Dreyfus, and that the real spy was a shadowy character named Major Count Ferdinand Walsin-Esterhazy. The fact that Major Esterhazy was connected to the noble Hungarian Esterhazy family while Dreyfus was a Jew had been a further convenience for the army, which tended to be dominated by arch-Catholic, anti-Semitic officers.

At risk of his own career and freedom, Major Picquart forced the new evidence into the public eye, and an aroused pro-Dreyfus faction began to demand a new trial. Finally, five years after Dreyfus had been sent to Devil's Island, a new trial was called, while the anti-Dreyfusards howled at the Dreyfusards and France was cleaved in two. The second trial again convicted Dreyfus of treason but reduced his sentence to ten years. The Dreyfusards redoubled the fury of their protests—either Dreyfus was guilty or innocent! The army was merely covering up its sins once again! To quiet the storm, the president of the republic pardoned Dreyfus, but it wasn't until 1906 that the man was finally vindicated, when the high court of appeals overturned the army's verdict on the grounds that the army had no evidence against Dreyfus at all.

At the beginning of the case, Maurice had sided with his parents who, like all their friends and, in fact, most of France, were violently anti-Dreyfusard. But as time passed and Dreyfus's innocence became apparent to anyone able to view the evidence with reasonably unprejudiced eyes, Maurice changed sides and became a pro-Dreyfusard, much to the dismay of his family, which continued to support the army and continued to mouth imprecations against Dreyfus and the Jews. The experience left permanent scars on Maurice's mind, as it did for many of his generation. When he met and fell in love with Charlotte, when she told him she was Jewish, while it surprised him (he told her he thought she was Episcopalian, which caused them both to laugh), it had made absolutely no difference to him. And through the years of their marriage, the fact of her Jewishness had receded in his mind so much that now, when the baron bluntly mentioned it, Maurice was genuinely amazed.

"What possible difference can that make?" he finally said.

"Oh come now, Maurice," replied the baron. "Don't be *naïf*. The French people don't like the Jews. For that matter, I don't either, though I confess I like Charlotte. But the point is, we can't afford to nominate a candidate who has any visible weakness. You're correct— the left is going to win this election and we're going to have a struggle to save this district for our side. Consequently, as much as I'd like to have you on the ticket, I must say no. Besides, you would hardly want to subject Charlotte to the possibility of personal abuse, would you? And the possibility definitely would exist."

Maurice said nothing for a moment, then stood up.

"I suppose I am *naïf*," he said. "It had never occurred to me that anyone could dislike my wife for anything, much less the fact that she is Jewish."

"Then you haven't used your good, French common sense. Charlotte's been married to you for over ten years. She's a charming, lovely woman. But in all that time, how many invitations have you had from your old friends? Few. Do you suppose the lack of invitations has been because we entertain less? Or haven't you noticed?"

"Of course I've noticed. As has Charlotte. I assumed it was because she was an American—"

"Oh really. If the heroes of your novels were as unobservant as you, they'd never solve your murders."

Maurice nodded. "Yes, I see your point. I've been very unobservant. Perhaps because I write about crime I don't notice it in my so-called friends."

The baron stood up. "Anti-Semitism isn't a crime, Maurice. It's a fact of life, a way to preserve the purity of the French nation." He held out his hand. "I hope there are no hard feelings?"

Maurice looked at the hand, turned and walked out of the room, saying nothing.

When he returned home Maurice told Charlotte that a candidate had already been selected, adding that in a way he was almost relieved. Running for office, he had come to realize through his talk with the baron, would be more of a strain than he had suspected.

He put on a cheerful face, but Charlotte wasn't fooled. She knew he was holding something back from her. And she was terribly afraid she knew what it was.

It was her first intimation of the gathering whirlwind and it chilled her. But the chill passed. Charlotte was not unaccustomed to anti-Semitism; it had been with her since her childhood in Ohio. Thanks, however, to her wealth and the fact that both her Gentile husbands, Mark and Maurice, had been happily free of it, she had always been spared the uglier manifestations of the disease. Being excluded from membership in certain clubs had never particularly bothered her—certainly exclusion from the Elkins Country Club had been a blessing; she felt a certain guilt because she had never been devout, and although all her children had been raised in the Jewish faith, none of them, at least at this stage of their lives, seemed particularly interested in any religion, being like most of their contemporaries secularly oriented. But aside from that and certain minor inconveniences, her Jewishness had never been a major element in her life. She was certainly not ashamed of it, nor was she trying to "pass" as a Gentile. It was just that her life style was secular. The fact that her neighbors in rural France were removing their masks and showing their naked faces was, while disturbing, certainly nothing to panic over. What did bother her, though, was that Maurice was being frustrated in his try for public office because of her. That was cruel and unfair, and though he pretended indifference, she could tell he was deeply upset by what had happened. The irony was that the insult to his wife bothered him more than it did Charlotte, at least insofar as her own feelings were concerned.

She considered speaking to him about it. But since he obviously hadn't wanted her to know what had happened—even though she had guessed—she decided to pretend ignorance for the time being. Several weeks passed. Then the Conservative-Nationalist candidate was announced, and Maurice's discontent visibly increased. The candidate was Georges Boildieu, a local lawyer whom Maurice considered a completely undistinguished retainer. The selection of Boildieu disturbed him so much that Charlotte finally decided to speak up.

She did so one evening as they were having their preprandial glass of champagne and dry biscuit in front of the big stone fireplace.

"Darling, don't you think it's time we talked about Boildieu?" she said.

They were sitting next to each other in two tall 17th-century chairs.

"I haven't anything to say about that idiot," replied Maurice sourly.

"Yes, you do. You've been brooding about him ever since they announced his candidacy. I hate to be left out of your broods, you know."

He laughed. "Well, to be honest, I've been figuring out different ways to assassinate Boildieu and get away with it, but I can't think of a method that's painful enough. I'd hate him to die without appropriate agony."

"How about poison?"

"I've thought about cyanide, but strychnine hurts more."

"Strychnine sounds lovely." She sipped her champagne. "Maurice?"

"What?"

"I know why René turned you down."

He looked over, startled.

"What do you mean?"

"It was because I'm Jewish, wasn't it?"

Pain spread across his face. He nodded.

"You could have told me."

"I thought you'd be terribly hurt. And I was ashamed for my own people."

They didn't speak for a few moments. They sat in their adjacent chairs watching the fire. Then he reached over and took her hand. She smiled at him, and they held hands like two young lovers, which indeed they were, though both were now in their fifties.

Finally he said, "I've made up my mind. I'm going to volunteer my services to Sarcy. As a speechwriter, or however he wishes to use me."

Phillipe Sarcy was the Socialist candidate.

"But Sarcy's attacking us in his campaign, isn't he? Not us personally, but the champagne producers. At least, that's what I've heard."

"I know. That's why having me on his side should help him that much more. To have one of the opposition defect should make an impression on the voters."

"Darling, you mustn't. I know you're angry at René, but you can't do this just to get back at him. There's too much at stake. It would make us absolute pariahs here and—"

"We're already pariahs," he said, "except I was too stupid to realize it or understand the reason for it. No, I've made up my mind. I don't agree with Sarcy's economics, but I hate René and *his* beliefs enough to help defeat Boildieu. And I'm going to do it." He saw tears forming in Charlotte's eyes. "Why are you crying?"

"Because I've gotten you into this terrible mess," she said.

He got up from his chair and came over to lean down and gently kiss her.

"There's nothing to cry about," he whispered, "because I love you so much."

That was all he said. But it was more than enough for Charlotte.

CHAPTER TWO

Lily Swenson Lang Benny Manning was furious.

She had been looking through the morning mail in her sitting room just off her bedroom on the second floor of River Bend. Nothing particularly interesting. Then she had picked up the new October 4, 1933 issue of *Collier's*, which had arrived with the mail, and leafed through it. When she saw the full-page advertisement she about exploded. Grabbing her white telephone (Lily was in her Jean Harlow period and, in fact, was wearing a white-satin negligée trimmed with white fox very much like the one she had seen Harlow wear in *Dinner at Eight*), she called her husband at his factory office. Before his new executive secretary, Miss Winslow, could put Lily through, she changed her mind, hung up, called for Vera, her maid, and proceeded to get dressed in a very sharp, brown Mainbocher suit. Slinging a mink coat around her shoulders, she grabbed the *Collier's*, hurried downstairs and got into her ivory-colored Model J Duesenberg roadster, then tore down the long driveway and roared out to the Number One Plant. When Lily was mad, she tore and roared, and to hell with the consequences.

Invading the executive reception room, she breezed by three vice-presidents waiting to see Mark and nodded briefly at Miss Winslow as she passed her desk (Wilma Amstuts having finally found romance at forty-eight and married a bald accountant, a grateful Mark gave her, aside from a generous pension, a new Chevrolet as a wedding present for her years of devoted secretarial services). "Oh, Mrs. Manning," exclaimed Miss Winslow, "Mr. Manning is in conference with Mr. Starr—"

"So what?" snapped Lily, and into the inner sanctum she went.

Mark was tilted back in his leather chair listening to the president of the company, Harrison Starr, a hefty, forty-one-year-old with curly hair and a fleshily pleasant face. Now they both stared as Lily swept up to the desk and stuck the *Collier's* in front of her husband.

"Look at *that*," she said, jabbing her finger at the offending page. "That's Melville's idea, the miserable little traitor!"

The full-page advertisement, taken out by the Premier Rubber Company, was bold in type and brassy in tone. It read:

WE CHALLENGE!

We at Premier Rubber are so convinced our new puncture-proof DYNA-RIDE TIRE is so superior to any other automobile tire on the market that we are offering a price of

$50,000

to the owner of any racing car equipped with tires of any other manufacturer which can beat Racing Champion STEVE RAYMOND, driving a re-worked, DYNARIDE-equipped, 221-cubic-inch Ford V-8 designed by the world-famous racing car genius Harry A. Miller, in a 300-mile endurance speed test to be held at BOCA RATON, FLORIDA

January 12, 1934

Elimination trials to be held the week of January 1 at Boca Raton. All entries to be submitted to Manager, DYNARIDE Race Contest, Premier Rubber Company, Sutterlee, Ohio, before December 15, 1933.

Other tire manufacturers claim they are the best.
Premier is ready to *prove* we are!

Mark and Harrison looked at the ad. Then Mark pushed the magazine away. "We know about it."

"Well? Are you going to do something?"

"We're thinking about it."

"What's there to think about? You can't let Melville get away with this! Accept his challenge! Get the best racer in the business and send him down there with a car that has Manning-Flow Tires on it and beat the nervy little bastard!"

Melville Benny had, in 1931, left Goodyear and bought up most of the stock of the small and Depression-bankrupted Premier Rubber Company, of which he made himself president. In little more than a year he had introduced a new tire on the market called the Dynaride, which he claimed was practically puncture-proof. Much to other tire manufacturers' surprise, unaggressive Melville had shrewdly gathered around him an aggressive management that had launched an equally aggressive sales and ad campaign for the Dynaride. Even more upsetting to the competition, Melville had arranged to sell the Dynaride through one of the biggest mail-order houses in the country, the C.W. Grayson Company, thus giving Premier at one stroke a huge marketing outlet for its products, with the added advantage of the hundreds of potential customers who subscribed to the Grayson mail-order catalogue. Sales of the Dynaride had leapt dramatically, painfully biting a large chunk out of the market. Even more painful to the competition, the Dynaride was gathering the most golden harvest of all: a word-of-mouth endorsement of the product from satisfied customers. People all over the country were telling their friends to buy the Dynaride. The damn thing really *didn't* blow out—or at least, it had a lot longer life than the other tires on the market.

And now, the ad.

Mark cleared his throat. "Look, Lily, I said we're thinking it over. And I don't appreciate you coming here telling me what I already know."

Lily pushed back her mink and stuck a defiant hand on her hip in the palm-and-finger-downward style she admired so much when she saw Ruth Chatterton do it in the movies.

"I happen to be on your side, you know."

"Yes, I assumed that. Now, Harrison and I are discussing some important—"

"What's more important than this race? Look, it's no news to anybody that I'm not just a dippy little housewife who takes a casual interest in hubby's business. I know a lot about what goes on here, and I *care!*"

"We care too, Lily—"

"It doesn't look like it! I can't imagine why you'd even *hesitate!* The Manning-Flow tire's the best in the country, and how dare Melville say that his crummy Dynaride piece of junk can beat ours? The nerve! I'd take out *two* full-page ads in *Collier's* and say we accept the challenge and that we'll pay the Premier Rubber Company a *hundred* thousand if they beat us!"

Mark and Harrison exchanged looks.

"Well?" said Lily.

"The fact is," replied her husband, "we're not sure we could win."

"Oh, come on."

"It's true. Melville's making a damned good tire, and there isn't any better driver in the business than Steve Raymond. If we accept the challenge and lose, we'll look like—"

Lily leaned on the desk. "—horses asses? So what? We're not exactly going to look like heroes of American industry if we don't accept the challenge, are we?"

Harrison Starr cleared *his* throat. "You've got a point, Mrs. Manning. And if we beat Benny's car, it would be a sweet deal for us. The Dynaride's been hurting our sales lately. It's been hurting a lot . . ."

Mark looked at his subordinate, as if to shut him up. Lily didn't miss it.

"What's so good about the Dynaride?" she asked.

"It's stronger," said Mark. "Melville's figured a way to strengthen the cording. Our lab's working on it, but they haven't found how he's doing it yet and, needless to say, Melville's not telling. In fact, it's one of the best-kept secrets in the tire industry."

"How much has he cut into our sales?" She knew he didn't like to admit bad news, especially to his wife and in front of subordinates.

"Well," he said, "the first half of this year it was something like 8 percent. But his sales are building. We think the last half of the year he may take as much as 20 percent of our business."

"*Twenty percent?* You've got to stop him!"

"I have every confidence our research people will solve the problem. Meanwhile, I think it may be smarter for us to lay low and not try to buck Melville. I still say if we get in this race and lose, it could hurt us more than not getting in. You have to take the long view—"

"But—"

"Lily, Harrison and I are *busy*."

She forced down her anger. "All right, I'm sorry I interrupted this way, but when I saw the ad I wanted to do *something*. And if either of you is interested in what I think, I say get in the race. But it's up to you men, of course." She smiled a moist smile at Harrison Starr, who looked slightly nervous. "I know you'll make the right decision. See you tonight, darling." Blowing her husband a kiss, she left the office, her mind working.

When Mark came home that evening, he found Lily in a pale-green, bare-backed satin evening gown, which from the sides also provided intriguing glimpses of her breasts. As had become her habit, she was already on her second martini and was dancing slowly around the giant living room to the strains of "You and the Night and the Music" emanating from the big Magnavox. Above the fireplace, Charlotte's portrait had long since been replaced by a magnificent Goya portrait of one of the Duchess of Alba's lovers.

On seeing Mark, she danced over to him, her arms outstretched, and foxtrotted into and against him.

"*Just* like Norma Shearer," she said, laughing and giving him a kiss. "How are you, darling?"

He removed her arms.

"I'm in no mood for dancing," he said, asking the butler to bring him a white-wine spritzer.

"Oh, oh, my husband is in a grouchy, grump mood. And a little bird tells me it's because Lily came to his office today. Is the little bird right?"

Mark sat down on his favorite sofa, facing the tall west window, and said nothing until Peter brought him the spritzer. When the butler had left, he said, "I'd appreciate your not pulling that crap in front of Peter."

"Sorry, darling," said Lily, sliding onto the sofa next to him. "But be honest. You *are* mad at me because I came to the office today, aren't you?"

"You know I don't like that. If you have something to tell me, Mr. Bell has invented a convenience called the telephone."

"Oh, all right, next time I'll call and I'm sorry. Aren't you going to kiss me? I put on your favorite dress."

He looked at the shimmery green satin that revealed so much of what even after five years of marriage was nearly irresistible to him. He kissed her and began to unwind.

"Well, I'll admit your visit shook things up," he said. "After you left, Harrison and I decided to look around for a good driver. If we can find one we think has a chance against Steve Raymond, we'll probably send a car down to Boca Raton."

Lily lighted up. "Good! Oh, God, I'd love to beat Melville—just *love* it! He's hoping you'll accept the challenge, you know. I'd bet a thousand dollars he thought up this race just to get back at us. Melville's so petty, so vindictive . . ."

"There's more to it than personal revenge. It's a damned good publicity stunt."

"Oh, I know. But he's never forgiven us, and this is his grandstand way of getting back. I know Melville. Beneath that meek mild exterior lies the heart of a Borgia."

She sipped more of the martini as her husband looked at her.

"You really do have a rather simple-minded view of human nature, don't you? All people are interested in is hurting other people and getting even when anybody hurts them."

"Well? It's true, isn't it?"

"No. Whether you or I like to admit it, there are a few people on this earth who aren't interested in hurting anyone."

"End of sermon, amen. Well, Melville's not one of them. I never did understand why he was so nice about everything when he came back from Africa. This is much more like the real Melville, believe me." She hesitated. "Are you sorry you married me, after all? I mean, if it hadn't been for me, Melville would still be working for you and you wouldn't have to worry about any of this."

"Skip it, Lily. I'm not sorry about anything . . ."

She entwined her arm in his. "That's what you'd *better* say. But if you're really not sorry, why are you dragging your heels about getting in the race? After all, he's really hurting us—I had no idea how much until today. If he's taken a fifth of the market—"

"Look, the reason is that I can't win that race no matter what. If Melville beats us, it's very damaging to the company. And if we beat Melville—well, to tell the truth, I won't exactly feel like celebrating."

"Because you feel guilty about what we did?"

"I don't know . . . maybe. I do know Melville made a lot of money for me. Not just from what he developed while he was working for me. He also put me onto Acme Radio when radios were just a toy. I made millions from that alone."

"But *you* took the risk, not Melville. You made the money legitimately. I don't see what you owe him. Besides, you made him a millionaire. He couldn't be doing what he's up to now if he hadn't had the money to buy out Premier. And you made him that money. So I don't see why you're going soft about Melville. Particularly when he's taking away so much business!"

"I'm not going soft about him. I just don't want to hurt him more than I already have."

Lily dropped the subject. She wasn't too surprised by Mark's attitude. In the five years of their marriage he had become an increasingly cautious man, a man who she knew was haunted by guilt —and not only guilt over what they had done to Melville. Though Lily had taken the blame for the decision that had cost Roger Boine his life, it was Mark who had made it, and to Lily's surprise—she had assumed he was basically a ruthless man and could always be such—it had left him a different person. Where previously he had been a decisive man, never afraid to take risks, he now shrank from the unorthodox and seemed intent on preserving his empire with as little controversy and public exposure as possible. He never talked about it to Lily in such blunt terms, but she sensed he wanted to square his accounts with life; that the sins he had committed in the past he wanted to redress by, at the very least, the avoidance of new ones. The murder of his own son had given him "religion," as she thought of it.

Furthermore, the passion he once had expended in building his mammoth corporation had now shifted to his huge collection of art. In the past five years he had spent an average of $2,000,000 a year acquiring paintings from Barjoonian and, in the process, had himself become a discriminating connoisseur. No longer was he the philistine novice who had bought the "In-grees" because he liked the way it was painted and was attracted by the story linked with the Duchesse de Choiseul-Praslin. Now he knew precisely what he was doing, and the daring he had once displayed in the business world was now evidenced in the art world, for Mark was buying Picassos and Cézannes as well as Old Masters. By the Thirties, buying Picassos was not exactly taking a fling, but for a conservative tycoon from Ohio it was unusual.

None of this meant that he had lost interest in business. Nor had "religion" softened or changed him in his basic political outlook. He still became near apoplectic at the idea of noncompany unions, and the election of Roosevelt with the innovative legislation of the first hundred days of his administration had infuriated Mark. But the death of Roger haunted him, and it had been Lily who goaded him into taking the tour in the fall of '31, Lily whose idea it was to declare a moratorium on the mortgage payments of the men Mark had been obliged to lay off, just as this day it was Lily who finally goaded him into accepting Melville Benny's challenge. If the fire and the daring and the powerlust had died down in Mark—who was, after all, now fifty-five—it was burning bright in his younger wife. Ironically, the same charge that had once been made against Mark by Charlotte was now most appropriate for Lily—she was more in love with the Manning Company than she was with Mark. It wasn't only the fantastic wealth the company put at her disposal (though actually the major part of Mark's fortune was now invested elsewhere, in bonds and real estate). Lily loved the limousines, the furs, the jewels, the big houses, the servants—the whole fairytale existence that she reveled in without a twinge of guilt or self-consciousness about the millions of her countrymen on the dole. The money, however, wasn't what intoxicated her. It was the power the company represented—the power of almost life and death over its thousands of employees, the power implicit in being a giant—a giant corporate "person." Melville's challenge enraged her because it was a challenge and a threat to the power.

Lily's love affair with her husband's company was not entirely self-gratifying. She was waging a silent struggle with Mark's past to win the inheritance for her four-year-old son by him, Evan Manning. A year after Evan's birth, Lily had developed a painful ovarian cyst that had necessitated a hysterectomy. Evan, then, was the last, as well as the first, child she would ever have. Lily was something less than a doting mother—she didn't particularly like "kids"—but she wanted her son to inherit the empire and Mark had been maddeningly cagey about his will. She knew he still respected his first wife, and though she loathed Charlotte she was too intelligent to talk against her to Mark or even to attempt to erase her memory (though she had, carefully, gradually, removed the more personal mementos of Charlotte from River Bend and was quietly redecorating the huge house a room at a time). The real problem was Mark's four children by Charlotte, and of the four, she felt the most serious threat to Evan was Christopher Manning, whom Mark adored. David, the oldest Manning son, was at Harvard Law School and had told his father he had no interest in the company. Richard, who was still at Princeton, was apparently a playboy and not particularly ambitious; even if he chose to go into the company, Lily privately discounted his ability to be a power in it. But Christopher, the youngest, was frank about what he wanted. He wanted someday to be what his father was.

And that was what Lily wanted for her own son. Even though Evan was extremely young to have his future mapped out for him, Lily was mapping it with intense care. The easiest way, of course, would be somehow to induce Mark to disinherit his other children, or at least leave a majority of the Manning stock to Evan; this she wanted to achieve eventually, but she wasn't at all sure to attempt it now wouldn't be premature. In any case, when and however she managed to do it, it was certainly of prime importance to preserve the company's front-rank position in the industry if Evan was ever to have anything worth inheriting. So that when Lily provoked Mark into action, she was not only doing it for herself but for her child as well. It was, for Lily, almost unselfish.

Given Mark's reluctance to take action against the threat posed to the Manning Company by Melville's Dynaride tire, as well as Lily's determination to maintain the Manning supremacy, it wasn't surprising that her mind had been hard at work ever since noting the ad in *Collier's* searching for a way to cripple Melville. Now, spurred by two martinis, Lily's mind rose to the challenge.

She knew what she had to do.

She was, in fact, looking forward to it.

CHAPTER THREE

Phillipe Sarcy had won the 1932 election against Boildieu, and the Socialist's victory was to a certain extent credited to Maurice de Sibour, who not only contributed his money to the campaign, but his writing talents as well. The defeat of the Conservative-Nationalist candidate was judged a defeat for the establishment as well as a stunning upset, since the seat had been held by the Conservative-Nationalists for years. The effect of Sarcy's victory on Maurice and Charlotte was not unexpected.

They were bitterly condemned by Baron de Courville and the other champagne producers as "turncoats" and "traitors." In fact, Maurice had managed to soften Sarcy's attacks on the champagne producers; the Socialists had initially wanted to call for a nationalization of the entire French wine industry, but Maurice had convinced Sarcy that this was too extreme and he retreated to a milder position, demanding higher wages for the wine workers. Nevertheless, Maurice's moderating influence was overlooked by his former friends, and where previously their attitude had been chilly, it now became glacial. This was expected. What was not expected was the hostility of many of the humbler residents of the area. The butcher who had provisioned the de Sibour family since before World War I bluntly told Maurice he was a Communist and he would no longer sell to him. Four of the house servants quit, refusing to work for "revolutionaries," and, most painful to Maurice, his *rémuer* of almost thirty years also resigned. Maurice was forced to observe to Charlotte that it seemed the last people to appreciate progress were those the progress was designed to benefit.

A local attempt to boycott de Sibour champagne was made, and for a while sales were down nationally as well, demonstrating that there were people all over France who objected to Maurice's apparent move to the left. His book sales dipped also, but in time people began to forget their resolutions as they hungered for the newest de Sibour mystery. Still, neither Maurice nor Charlotte was under any delusion about the memories of René de Courville and his friends. They would never forget, and Maurice was delighted about that.

Life gradually returned to something approaching normality, however, and in the fall of the next year, 1933, the main event in the de Sibour family was the concert debut of Ellen Manning. She had finally determined that she would never be satisfied until she had taken the plunge, and she had told her mother, who agreed with her, that if the debut went well she would continue her career, but if it went badly she would give it up. She worked feverishly preparing her program, practicing eight hours a day and seeing hardly anyone except her family and her teacher, Madame Olga. Finally the great night arrived. Because of her stepfather's celebrity—or, in some circles, notoriety—the concert was sold out and a fashionable and well-dressed crowd arrived at the historic Salle Pleyel. Ellen was so nervous she didn't think she could go on, and the fact that the hall was sold out only made her more nervous. But Madame Olga was on hand to keep her from falling apart, and Charlotte and Maurice hugged her, assuring her everything would go splendidly. The de Sibours then left her to take their seats in the fifth row. The house lights lowered. And finally Ellen came out on the stage.

She was now twenty-three and a beautiful young woman, with a slim figure flattered by the simple white dress she was wearing. The audience seemed to take to her immediately, and she received a warm welcoming applause. She curtsied by the piano, then sat down and addressed the keyboard. Her first selection was the Bach Chromatic Fantasy and Fugue. She attacked the opening run with vigor and precision. It seemed to be going well after all. Then, thirty seconds into the Fantasy, she had a memory lapse. She stopped playing, there was a painful silence in the hall. Charlotte felt her insides twist, she clutched Maurice's hand. Ellen began again at the beginning. This time she got all the way through the piece, but the memory lapse had taken its toll on her confidence. She played nervously and sloppily. The audience politely applauded, but everyone knew it would take a miracle to save her.

The miracle didn't occur. She played the rest of her program indifferently. By the time she got to the final number, the Chopin

Third Piano Sonata, her nerves were so raveled and her strength so expended she barely managed to get through the incredibly difficult finale. Chopin was connected in the public's mind with the Pleyel family, after whom the hall was named (the first three Nocturnes being dedicated to Mme. Camille Pleyel) and to mangle Chopin in the Salle Pleyel was a sin no audience, no matter how polite, could forgive. At the conclusion of the program the applause was scattered and perfunctory; there were even a few boos. Ellen made an awkward curtsy and hurried off the stage. By the time her parents reached her dressing room, she had finished crying. Trying to put on a brave face, she said to her mother as she kissed her, "Well, it looks as if I'm going to be a housewife."

Charlotte hugged her. "That's no disgrace, darling."

A party had been planned afterward at the de Sibour's apartment; under the circumstances it might have been more like a wake, except for Ellen's determination not to depress her friends with her own dejection. The guests, of course, lied and told her she had been wonderful. She didn't bother to correct them, but only continued to try to look cheerful, though twice she went off to her bedroom on the second floor of the duplex and gave way to her true feelings. Then, each time, she dried her eyes and came back out again.

It was after the second flight to the bedroom that a young American in a dark gray suit, someone she vaguely remembered from somewhere, came over to her and said, "How can you stand having all these people around? I'd think you'd want to be alone."

She was taken aback by his bluntness. "Why should I want to be alone?"

He gave her a curious look. "You mean you really believe what they're telling you?"

"That I was good?"

"Yes. I don't know much about music, but even *I* could tell you didn't play very well."

She started to get angry, then changed her mind and burst into laughter.

"What's so funny?" he said.

"You. I guess you're the only honest person here. I was really awful, wasn't I?"

"Lousy. Chopin must have been spinning in his grave."

"Not to mention Bach! Oh, when I forgot the notes it was the most horrible moment of my life! But I guess music will survive without me. It may survive better, in fact. Haven't we met before?"

"We have. At your place out in the country two summers ago.

I roomed with your brother David at Princeton. My name's Len Hastings."

"Oh, *sure,* I remember you now."

He smiled. "I guess I didn't make much of an impression, did I?"

"No impression at all. If you're going to be blunt with me, I'll be blunt with you. I thought you were immature and pretty dull."

He shrugged good-naturedly. "I was. Now I'm mature and fascinating."

"Oh, *well!* And modest, too!"

"Not very. H. L. Mencken says no healthy male is modest."

"Then I guess you're healthy."

"I hear David's trying to be a lawyer?"

"That's right. What are you trying to be, besides mature and fascinating?"

"A banker."

She made a face. "I don't think that's fascinating. I think that's dull."

He laughed. "Well, it has been so far. I'm hoping things pick up, though. I'm working for my father." He indicated a distinguished man talking to Charlotte. "He runs the American National Bank office on the Place Vendôme. I make the equivalent of sixty dollars a week, and if I look lean and hungry, it's because I am. That's why I crash parties like this one. I steal the canapés so that I don't have to buy groceries. Did you know that slightly stale caviar on toast makes an excellent breakfast?"

To prove his point, he pulled a handkerchief from his pocket and opened it to show her a half-dozen purloined, squashed caviar canapés. She took a look and sighed dramatically.

"*How romantic* your life must be! I can see it now. Your tiny garret—no heat, of course—and the starving Mr. Hastings dining on flat champagne and stolen stale caviar as his lean frame is racked with tubercular coughs. It sounds gorgeous!"

"Want to have dinner with me some night? I make the best spaghetti in Paris. Of course, don't expect any meat in the sauce."

She thought this over. "Do you promise to be mature and fascinating?"

"I'll dazzle you. How about tomorrow night?"

"Pushy, too. All right, I'm game."

"Good. I'll pick you up here at seven. And don't worry, my tiny garret at least has heat. Not only two space heaters and a fireplace. Me too."

"Oh, I see you're the great American lover as well. Spaghetti, no meat in the sauce, space heaters and King Kong. It sounds terrific. I'd better warn you, though, I carry a knife. If you attack I'll defend myself."

He lowered his voice. "If you butcher me the way you butchered poor Chopin, I'm a dead man."

"God, you are the *most* horrible man I've ever met!"

Which, of course, wasn't what she was thinking at all.

He lived not in a tiny garret but in a converted coachhouse on the grounds of his parents' rented villa in Neuilly. When he drove her through the Second Empire wrought-iron gates of the place in his rattling Citroën, he explained that she shouldn't get the wrong idea. He had to pay his father rent, so he really was "lean and hungry" and she really was getting only spaghetti, though he'd lifted a few bottles of a nice young Beaujolais from his old man's cellar—"What he doesn't know won't hurt him." The small coachhouse was set a good distance away from the main house and was cozily surrounded by shielding bushes. He parked the car and led her through the small front door next to the coach doors into a big, cheerful room that had once housed two carriages. The floor was brick, there were large windows, the walls were whitewashed stone and opposite the wide carriage doors was a stone fireplace, which Len explained had been put in before the war to warm up the antediluvian engines of the owner's prewar automobiles during the winter. A fire was burning in it now, its shadows dancing merrily on the brick floor, its light illuminating the two battered club chairs, the wooden table, the sagging cot and the innumerable travel and ski posters that had been taped to the walls. "Well, what do you think of it?" he asked as he took her tweed coat and tossed it on the bed. "It's not Versailles and it has none of the modern conveniences, like a john, but it's home."

"I like it," she said, sitting in one of the club chairs before the fire. "It's cozy. There's no kitchen?"

"Just a gas burner." He pointed to a shelf against the back wall which held the burner. On it stood a single big pot. "I get my water and everything else from the main house. But I manage, and it's private, which is nice. Would you like a drink?"

"A dry vermouth on the rocks, if you have it."

He went to the gas burner shelf, which also held a few cans, some liquor bottles, a salt shaker, a dilapidated ice bucket, and a few glasses.

"I do. The one thing I really miss is a kitchen. I like to cook and I'm pretty good at it but it's hard when you're doing it this primitively. I won't accept any complaints except my own though. You'll have to pretend to like it."

"I promise."

He brought her the drink, then pulled up the other club chair and sat next to her, a scotch in his own hand.

"You seem to have recovered from last night?" he said.

She nodded. "It wasn't all that unexpected, to tell the truth. I've had this private feeling all along I really wasn't good enough and, well, I was right. It's really almost a relief to have it over with. I'm lucky, because I have my mother as an example. She plays beautifully and she enjoys her music, and I'll always be able to enjoy my music privately. I think to have a public career you have to have a burning hunger for it, and I just don't have it. So it's probably better this way."

"That sounds pretty sensible."

"Oh, I'm always sensible. Or most of the time." She looked around at the posters. "Do you like to ski?"

"I love it. If I had my way, I'd do nothing but go from one slope to the next all year long. Do you ski?"

"A little. I'm not very good. Why don't you do it?"

"What?"

"Ski. I mean, if that's what you want to do, why be a banker?"

"Well, you see, we're not all heirs to millions like you." (Her cheeks stung.) "My father makes a decent salary from the bank and he gets a foreign-living allowance so he can hold up the bank's prestige, but otherwise we don't have any money. So I have to work. By the way, I didn't mean to attack you for your money. I think it's great you're rich. I'm hoping you'll find me so mature and fascinating you'll fall in love with me and keep me in the style I'd love to be kept in."

He said it so good-naturedly she couldn't take offense. "You *are* blunt, aren't you?" She laughed.

"Why not? Might as well say what you think. Do you see much of your father? Your real father, I mean?"

She looked into the vermouth.

"Not much anymore. Oh, I was over in the States last Christmas and saw him then. My stepmother and I don't get along too well. I mean, we don't *fight*, but I don't think she's exactly crazy about me or my brothers."

"The wicked stepmother?"

"Not 'wicked' exactly." She thought a moment, then smiled. "Well, maybe she is, a little."

"And is your father the 'wicked' tycoon that woman made him out to be in her book? What was its name? *Mark's Millions?*"

"Oh, *that* piece of trash. Did you read it?"

"No, but I heard people talking about it. I guess she really gave it to your old man."

"It was a pack of lies! From beginning to end. The woman was so obviously out to get daddy—I mean, my God, she called him a *murderer*! It was just ridiculous, the whole thing. Anyone who really knew father would know he couldn't hurt a flea and I think Mrs. Harrington is damned lucky daddy didn't sue her and her sleazy magazine for a million dollars!"

"Hey, wait a minute! Don't fly off the handle at *me*! I didn't write the book."

"Oh, I'm sorry." She sighed. "But I do get just a little bit emotional when anyone mentions that woman. Father has a hot temper, but he's really a very sweet man. He always has been to me . . . I love him very much and the idea that he could be the ruthless man she makes him out to be is really crazy."

Len smiled. "The sweet tycoon. Sounds nice. I think if I were a tycoon I'd do all sorts of good things and have everybody love me. Then I'd go off and ski. Except something tells me I'm never going to be a tycoon. I guess the water's boiling—I'll put the spaghetti in."

A few minutes later he announced that dinner was ready. She moved to the wooden table in the center of the room and waited while he served the steaming spaghetti. As she sat, she looked around the room again and wondered what it was she felt was missing. Then it occurred to her. There wasn't a single book in the place.

"I take it you don't waste much time reading?" she said as he sat down opposite her and poured the wine.

"Me? Oh, I read the Paris *Herald* and struggle through a few of the French magazines. My French doesn't exactly put me in the Voltaire class."

"But no books?"

He shrugged. "I read some books every once in a while. And I like H.L. Mencken. Aside from that, I'm not much of an intellectual. I live by my inconsiderable wits. Watch out—the spaghetti's hot."

Notwithstanding his own *caveat*, he dove into his mountain of sauce-doused pasta with hearty appetite. Ellen followed suit, finding that it was indeed tasty, if more American than Italian, and that the

Beaujolais was excellent. As the meal progressed, he kept up an easy running repertoire of amusing chatter. He was, in fact, no intellectual. Still, after dating so many intensely serious Frenchmen, she discovered that she enjoyed his somewhat hare-brained conversation. He was neither fascinating nor mature, contrary to his facetious claim; he was funny and immature. But whereas his immaturity, when she first met him, had left her cold, she now found it appealing. Perhaps it was the strain of the long preparation for her disastrous debut. She didn't want to think; she wanted to enjoy. And Len obviously enjoyed life in his slapdash way. He was a genuine grasshopper and made no bones about it. Rather to her surprise, Ellen was finding that the grasshopper's philosophy had its attractions.

After dinner he casually asked her if she wanted to go to bed with him.

"Well, I don't think so. Not quite yet," she replied, half-jokingly. "I think we should let our relationship ripen a bit, don't you?"

"You're not a virgin, I hope?" he asked rather nervously.

"Don't you think that's my business?"

"Hardly. That is, if we're going to keep seeing each other."

"Well, for your information, I'm not."

"That's a relief."

"But I don't sleep around casually, so don't get any ideas."

"Okay. I'm in no hurry. What'll we do tomorrow night?"

"I'm not sure I want to do anything with you tomorrow night."

"Do you have another date?"

"No, but maybe I'll want to stay home."

"How about a movie? American, not French. I can't follow the damn French dialogue. *Golddiggers of 1933* is playing at the Champs-Élysées."

She laughed. "Oh, God, you're terrible! You mean you'd really go to one of those awful musicals?"

He looked surprised. "I like them."

He was irresistible. She agreed to go with him. Then he took her back out to the car and kissed her. She found she enjoyed it, particularly as he wisely didn't try to go further. When he left her in front of her stepfather's apartment building, she decided she couldn't remember when she'd had a better time.

They went out five nights in a row, and by the end of that time she was desperately in love with him. He was the most uncomplicated person she had ever met in her life, and she adored his openness. On the fifth night they had made love on the sagging cot in the fire-lit coachhouse, and she adored that too. He was an animal. Not a crude animal—he was tender with her—but his lovemaking was as natural and vigorous and earthy as an animal's. Her two previous lovers, Valerian Grebert and a fellow piano student of Madame Olga's, approached the sex act as an intermission between interminable monologues on Life and Art and Politics. Not Len. For him the act of love was the show, not the intermission.

On the sixth night Charlotte, who wanted to learn more about this young American who had placed such stars in her daughter's eyes, asked him to the apartment for dinner. Len arrived in a rumpled dinner jacket and was his usual pleasant self. He ate a gargantuan amount of food (Ellen noticed with amusement that he managed to pocket his usual number of canapés) and was totally at ease the entire evening. After he had left Ellen hurried into the small library where her parents were having coffee. "Well?"

Charlotte and Maurice exchanged looks. Charlotte then said, "Ellen, I think he's the nicest twelve-year-old I've ever met."

"Oh, *mother!*"

"Well, darling, you have to admit he's a bit young for his age."

"He's just uncomplicated!"

"I suppose that's one way of putting it."

"I asked him who is favorite actress was," Maurice said, "and he said Ruby Keeler."

"Is there anything wrong with liking Ruby Keeler?"

"No, but she's hardly an *actress*. Of course, he's very pleasant but I'm surprised you'd be interested in someone so . . . superficial."

"But he's *not* superficial!" protested his stepdaughter. "Superficial implies phoniness, and Len isn't phony at all!"

"You mean he's honestly shallow?" suggested Charlotte.

"No! He's just open. He's what you see! Besides, he *is* smart, even if he's not an intellectual, and I don't think a man has to be an intellectual to be interesting. Valerian was an intellectual, but, my God, he was so gloomy! Len's a very happy human being, which I think is tremendously important in a person. He never gets upset at anything."

Maurice put down his demitasse.

"Ellen, neither your mother nor I has any business telling you whom to go out with, or not to go out with. You're an adult woman, and your friends are *your* business. We were only exposed to Mr. Hastings a few hours, so we are in no position to know him in any real sense. I admit it is superficial of *me* to say I found him superficial —he may be a genius. My only warning, if you wish to call it that, is that if it is true he has never been upset about anything, from my experience, I would suggest that is not much of a compliment. And with that, this old party is off to bed."

He got up, kissed his wife and stepdaughter, then left the room. When they were alone, Ellen turned to her mother and said, "I'm in love with him, momma. I hope you're not disappointed."

Her mother smiled and held open her arms. Ellen hugged her.

"Of course I'm not disappointed," said Charlotte. "I'm happy for you. And if you're in love with him, well, then there *must* be more to him than either Maurice or I was smart enough to see."

"Oh, there *is*, there really is."

But she wasn't to find out what it was for another month.

CHAPTER FOUR

It was on his return from Río de Oro in 1927 that Melville Benny had met on the *Berengaria* an attractive widow in her early forties named Lillian Shepherd. Lillian was from St. Louis. She had two married daughters by her late husband, who had died the previous year of a heart attack. She had been touring Europe. She was quiet, warm and understanding—just what Melville needed. Overcoming his customary initial shyness with women, he made friends with her and they began sharing the same table in the first-class dining room. In time Melville, who was longing to unburden himself, told Lillian his troubles. He told her of his certainty that his wife was having an affair with his long-time friend and employer, and of his rage at being sent to Africa to facilitate their affair. He also told her about his guilt from his role in the death of Roger Boine, admitting to Lillian that he'd had the awful thought of sending Roger to Tegai as a way to strike back at Mark. That Melville would admit all this to a near stranger was evidence of his misery as well as Lillian's ability to inspire confidence. She listened sympathetically to all of it. Then, on the third day of the voyage, she told him, "Do nothing. You're an intelligent man, you're a successful man, why are you making yourself miserable over a woman who obviously isn't worth the trouble?"

"But I still love her!"

"Do you?" she replied quietly.

By the time the ship docked in New York, he had come to the conclusion the charming widow was right. He wasn't in love with Lily, he was infatuated with her. The woman was a bitch, Mark was a bastard and to hell with both of them. Life was too short . . .

When he returned to Elkins—cured, so to speak—he was only too glad to withdraw from the whole situation. He also remembered Lillian Shepherd, and after going to work for Goodyear he wrote her a letter thanking her for her advice and telling her he was a better and happier man for it. She replied, they continued their correspondence and in the spring of 1929 they met at White Sulphur Springs for a two-week holiday. At the end of the first week Melville proposed and Lillian accepted. They were married the following month, and Lillian joined Melville in Akron, home of the Goodyear Company. They were both incredibly happy.

In 1931, after Melville's purchase of the Premier Rubber Company in Sutterlee, a small town a few miles south of Akron, he and Lillian bought a handsome Tudor-style brick home outside Sutterlee. The house had twelve acres and a kennel. Lillian loved dogs and bred schnauzers. They continued in their happiness, and Melville's faith in the female sex, nearly destroyed by his experience with Lily, was restored. He wondered how he could have been foolish enough ever to have seen *anything* in the new Mrs. Manning.

Then in the autumn of 1932 Lillian complained of pains in her abdomen. Melville took her to a Cleveland clinic, where she was examined. The doctors told Melville that his wife had stomach cancer, that it was too far advanced to operate and that she had, at most, a few months to live. Melville went into a near frenzy . . . they must be wrong . . . there had to be something they could do! There wasn't.

He went through the agony of trying to decide whether to tell Lillian or not, and couldn't bring himself to do it. He lied as cheerfully as he could and took her home to Sutterlee to wait for the inevitable. She soon guessed the truth, though, and told him she wasn't afraid. He was by her bedside when she died, and he knew it was true. She really wasn't afraid.

Once again Melville was deep in despair, except that this time the misery was even more acute because of the decency of the lovely woman who had given him so much in so short a time. He plunged himself into his business and at night buried himself in his house, trying to forget the memories that claimed him. His friends and business associates tried to interest him in other women. He would have none of it. Despite his awful loneliness (not to mention sexual frustration, for Melville, though now over fifty, had lost none of his strong need), he refused to see anyone. No woman could ever replace Lillian.

Such was his mood and despair when one cold evening in early November of 1933 Melville was surprised by the ringing of his door-chimes. He never entertained, and the number of times any person had dropped by his remote home since Lillian's death he could count on the fingers of one hand. He put aside the legal pad on which he had been writing notes and went to the door. When he opened it, surprise became astonishment. Standing there, wrapped in a rich, sable coat, was Lily.

"Hello, Melville," she said in a voice that seemed different from the one he remembered.

"What are *you* doing here?"

"I have to see you." Her voice had a subdued, almost pathetic tone to it. "I know what you must be thinking, but please let me talk to you for just a minute."

He stood aside and she came into the small entrance foyer. She looked around, glancing into the homey living room with the pale blue carpet and the rounded fireplace alive with a crackling fire. Melville closed the front door and looked at her.

"You're not welcome here," he said.

"I know. I'd be surprised if I were. But at least let me warm up in front of the fire. It's freezing out."

Before he could reply she had stepped down into the living room and gone over to stand in front of the fire. He trailed her, feeling tense and suspicious.

"Where's your *husband?*"

She turned. "We've separated. Just this afternoon. I'm driving to New York, and when I got here to Sutterlee I was so miserable and tired and I thought if I didn't have someone to talk to I'd *die*. So I came to see you. Please don't make me go yet, Melville. I know everything you feel about me and Mark, and you're absolutely right. But let me just stay a little while and talk. You don't even have to listen or say anything—I don't care. Just let me *talk* . . ."

She turned back to the mantel and stood quietly, her head bowed. She did not cry, just stood there. Then she straightened. "God, I feel like Stella Dallas. I don't suppose you'd have anything in this place to drink?"

He hesitated. "My wife drank sherry."

"That would be fine. Anything with alcohol. I heard about your wife. I'm truly sorry."

He said nothing and went into the dining room to fetch the bottle of sherry. When he returned, she had taken off her sable coat, draped it over the back of a chair in front of the fire. She had also removed her shoes and curled herself into the chair. He poured a glass of sherry and handed it to her.

"Thanks," she said, taking a large gulp. She closed her eyes a moment. He stood in front of her, watching her. She opened her eyes and looked up at him.

"Well, it's all turned out pretty funny, hasn't it? I mean, funny for me. I went after Mark, I got him, and I got the world's number-one bastard."

"Lily, you can stay a moment if you want to, but I won't have you using that kind of language in this house—"

"Sorry. Anyway, that's exactly what he is. Oh, the joke's on me, all right, and I suppose it belongs there. You know, I didn't mind his sleeping around—I expected that, after all. But when he started in with that secretary of his—"

"Wilma Amstuts?" said Melville disbelievingly.

"Oh, no, she got married a long time ago. This is Miss Winslow, a real knockout. Sweet little Miss Winslow, who must breakfast on rattlesnake meat for her daily ration of venom . . . Oh, *God,* I'm the laughing stock of Elkins, Melville. It's really mortifying."

Silence.

"I was the laughing stock of Elkins once."

"I know, and it was *my* fault. Well, I'm getting it back, if that's any satisfaction for you." She ran her hand wearily across her forehead. "Melville, do you believe in God?"

He was shocked by the question coming from her.

"Oh, you don't have to answer that. The point is, I never have, but I'm beginning to believe there's *someone* up there who pays us back. And then today . . . today he came home from the factory and we were supposed to go down to Palm Beach tomorrow and, well, he came in and told me he wouldn't be able to go until next week and that I should go on alone. . . . Well, I knew what he was up to—I ought to, we pulled that one on *you,* for God's sake!" She sipped more sherry. "So I told him I wasn't *budging* out of the house without him because I knew the moment I was out, *she'd* be in. At which point he slapped me and told me to get the hell out, it was *his* house and who did I think I was— It was a nightmare, a real nightmare. So I just ran out of the house and got in my car and started for New York . . . and here I am."

"What about your son? Did you just leave him? Or is he out in the car?"

"I left him, of course, which is another reason I'm so miserable.

Melville, I couldn't *think!* My whole world has just fallen apart and all I wanted to do was run! And now . . . now I don't know what to do. I don't know if running to New York is any good either. Maybe I should go back and fight him. And of course, Evan, my boy . . . I just can't leave him there with Mark. And what if he says I deserted him? Oh Melville, I'm so confused and tired . . ."

He watched her, saying nothing.

After a moment she laughed. "You know what the *real* joke was? On me, that is?"

He waited.

"Well, I assumed Mark Manning—big, powerful Mark Manning— would be such a terrific lover. Well, the report from the front is to the contrary. Maybe that's the real reason his first wife left him. I practically had to do handstands to get him interested. He was *nothing* compared to you. I guess I'm the classic case of not knowing when you're well off."

"If he's such a washout lover, why is he bothering with other women? Or they with him?"

"Oh, you know, he's Mark Manning and he has to pretend to the world he's Casanova, even if he really is a complete dud. I don't know *how* we ever had Evan. If you want to know the sad truth, I haven't been sexually satisfied for five years. I'm sure you couldn't care less, but if that information makes you feel any better, you're welcome to it." She put her head back on the chair and smiled. "Do you remember how I practically had to hold you off with a pitchfork? Well, those were the good old days, believe me."

"I would suppose," he said quietly, "you've had lovers. That used to be your style."

"Oh yes, it used to be. And you don't have to believe this, but I *have* been faithful to him. For Evan's sake, really. When you become a mother, you know, your attitude toward life somehow changes. You have a special responsibility. I don't know, maybe I've been wrong. Maybe the only to pay him back is to take a lover . . ."

"You shouldn't have any trouble in that department."

"I know, but it's different now. I'm older, and I'm Mrs. Mark Manning, and people are afraid of me, I suppose. I mean, they're afraid of Mark. So there's no reasonable prospect."

"I'm not afraid of Mark." He said it in a flat, even voice.

She looked at him, then smiled. "Oh, wouldn't that be marvelous? What a delicious way to pay him back!"

He nodded.

"But you're not serious, are you? I mean . . . *are* you?"

"I'm serious."

She sat up. "Oh, Melville, it's *too* perfect. Why didn't I think of it?"

"Didn't you?"

She blushed slightly. "Well, maybe it was a *little* thought in the back of my mind. But I didn't think I'd have a prayer, really. I mean, with you hating me the way you do . . ."

"It's Mark I hate, I never hated you. I understood your attraction to him, but I thought he'd at least try not to humiliate me."

Lily got out of her chair and came over to kneel on the carpet in front of Melville. She took his hand. "We *did* do a terrible thing to you, didn't we?" she said, softly. "Can you really forgive me?"

He looked down at her. "I can forgive *you*, Lily."

She kissed his hand. "Do you . . . still find me attractive, I mean the way you used to?"

"Yes, Lily."

"Do you want me?"

"Very much."

"Melville, I was wrong, so completely *wrong*."

"Let's go upstairs, Lily."

He stood up and helped her to her feet. She ran her hand over her marceled hair and smiled uncertainly.

"You *really* want me, Melville?"

He put his arms around her and kissed her.

"Darling, isn't it strange how we're back together again, after all these years?"

"Miraculous, Lily. Bring your drink and let's go up."

She looked at him, then went back to her chair and drained her glass. She set it down. "I don't want any more . . . You know, Melville, I really have been such a bitch all my life, maneuvering my way through husbands and lovers—for what? I really don't know any more. For a while I thought I did everything so I could one day be Mrs. Mark Manning. What a mistake *that* turned out to be. Now where have I left to go?"

He came over and took her hand. "To bed with me."

She smiled. "Maybe that's where I should have been all along. You know, I think I was really happy with you and didn't know it. I was so damn immature, so full of myself, so ambitious . . . I don't know how you could even *stand* me."

"I loved you, Lily," he said. "I thought you were the most beautiful and important thing in my life."

She put her other hand on his cheek. "You know, I even laughed at you. What a funny little man he is, I used to think. I enjoyed using you. And now . . . now here I am seeing for the first time the man you really are. Maybe I'm lucky after all, I mean, to have a second chance like this . . ."

He took her in his arms and kissed her again. Somehow it felt a bit mechanical and for a moment she wondered if for some reason he were leading *her* on. Then she felt Old Faithful press against her thigh, and she was sure that he wasn't.

For the third time, he said, "Let's go upstairs."

He led her across the room back to the entrance hall.

"What a charming house," she said.

"Nothing like River Bend or your place down in Palm Beach."

"Oh, those barns. You don't know how tired I am of them, Melville. They're so cold, so empty of any real human feeling. What are they, really, except monuments to Mark's ego, and who wants to live in monuments? Or with one? I'd much rather have a house like this one. You can tell someone has loved this house."

"You really have changed, Lily," he said, starting up the stairs.

"God, I hope so, Melville." She followed him up the stairs. "When I think of all the people I've hurt in my life, I get almost sick to my stomach. And for what? To be Mrs. Mark Manning and live in big, dead houses filled with big, dead paintings, God! Sometimes I wake up in the middle of the night and think I'm in the goddamn Louvre!"

They reached the upstairs hall and he turned on a lamp on a table. Then he opened the first door.

"We can use the guest bedroom," he said. "If you don't mind, I'd rather not use my . . . my wife's bed."

A look of real compassion seemed to come over her face. "Of course. Was she wonderful? Did she appreciate you, the way I never did?"

"Let's just not talk about it, if you don't mind." He led her into the room and turned on a light. It was a pleasant room with a four-poster bed and rose-splashed wallpaper. White ruffled curtains dipped across the big windows that looked out over the back fields.

"Oh, it reminds me of the room I had when I was a girl!"

Melville turned down the white chenille bedspread. "It's a colonial bed," he said. "I think you'll find it comfortable."

She smiled and came over and took his hands.

"But you make it sound so unromantic!" she said. "The way I feel now, I'd be happy on a park bench as long as you were on it with me."

"That's sweet of you, Lily."

"But I want *you* to be happy, darling. That's the important thing now."

He removed his hands from hers and took off his jacket.

"I'm very happy." He pulled down his striped tie and unbuttoned his collar. She said, rather uncertainly, "Maybe I should change in the bathroom?"

"Go ahead. I didn't realize you'd feel embarrassed."

She hesitated, looking at him. "Melville, are you *sure* you want me to . . . ?"

He smiled. "Of course I'm sure. I'm lonely, Lily. Very lonely. I haven't had a woman since my wife died last year, and you're still very attractive to me. And we both want to get back at Mark, don't we? So there's revenge in this, too."

"But I don't want it just to be an act of revenge for us, darling. I want . . . I want there to be some love. Does that sound foolish?'

"Maybe there still is some love between us, Lily. But let's start with revenge."

"I suppose you're right." She went into the bathroom, turned on the light, closed the door and began to undress. It wasn't working exactly as she had planned, but she was getting what she had come for, so she didn't really care. He was acting strangely, but for God's sake, what did she expect? Still, she was surprised at how quickly he had responded to the opening she'd given him, which she realized wasn't as subtle as it might have been. On the other hand, she had always excited him before and even though she might be older she was still attractive . . . she looked at herself in the mirror on the back of the door . . . and he had no doubt been celibate since his wife's death . . . poor bastard. Oh, she could still handle him all right. Maybe she had overdone the Stella Dallas business a little, but it seemed to have worked. And it would take only once to have him hooked all over again. Melville was like any cured drunk—one sip of the old booze and he'd be back on the bottle.

Feeling pleased with herself, she opened the bathroom door and walked into the bedroom. He was sitting on the edge of the bed, and she stared at his skinny white body. He held out his hands to her, and she came over and took them. Then he turned out the bed lamp, pulled her down on the bed and began kissing her. He certainly had lost none of the old steam, she reflected, as she whispered, "Oh, Melville, it's so damn good to be back in your arms."

"And it's good to have you back in them," he said as he moved on top of her, by now thoroughly worked up. "Just like old times . . ."

Afterward, he sat up and looked down at her. Her eyes were closed and she was smiling. "It was beautiful, darling. I'd forgotten how beautiful you make it seem."

"You can open your eyes now. And you can also get the hell out of here, you miserable bitch."

Her eyes blinked open as he turned on the bed lamp.

"Don't you think I know why you're here? You may have played me for a sucker for years, but I was never stupid then and I'm not stupid now."

"What are you *saying*, darling?"

'I'm saying you came here because you and Mark are afraid. Because for once that bastard has some real competition—me!—and now he's so worried he's sent you down here to do your act. One night, one time, and poor grateful Melville will tell irresistible Lily the secret of what makes the Dynaride a better tire than the Manning-Flow. Except it won't work any more, Lily. I've loved a *real* woman. I'll never forget the difference."

She sat up. "But you're *wrong* . . . I came here because Mark and I had a fight—"

"Oh, come on, Lily. Don't waste your time."

She dropped the mask. "You rotten . . . why did you lead me on? Couldn't you at least have been gentleman enough not to screw me?"

"*Gentleman?* What do you know about gentlemen? And I screwed you, as you, in your ladylike fashion, put it, for exactly the reason I said—revenge. And it was sweet, Lily. Damn sweet."

She got off the other side of the bed, walked around the foot of it and slammed into the bathroom. When she had dressed, she opened the door and came out again. He also was dressed and looked content.

"All right. One for Melville," she said. "I thought you were acting strangely but I didn't think you were a good enough actor to fool me. Well, I was wrong. Melville has learned and Lily has too—never underestimate the opposition, even if you think you own his soul." She shrugged. "It was still a good idea. By the way, you're wrong about Mark. He has no idea I came here tonight."

"Are you going to tell him?"

"That's my business."

Melville smiled. "I hope he beats the living hell out of you. That's what I should have done years ago. I'm glad I didn't, though."

"Why?"

"You might still be my wife."

"Fat chance." She started toward the door, then stopped and

turned back. "Oh, and for your information, Mark is a marvelous lover. Also for your information, you little creep, we're going to beat the bejesus out of you at Boca Raton."

"Get out of here," he said. "Get out of here before I get sick from the sight of you. Before I kill you."

He said it with such quiet intensity that it shook even her self-confidence.

"Good-bye, Melville," she said, going to the door. Then she gave him a final look. "You know, you really are a funny man."

And she was gone.

She had picked that night to see Melville because Mark had told her he would be at his office late—he wouldn't, in fact, be home for dinner since he, Harrison Starr and Stanley Wilmot, the pudgy vice-president in charge of advertising, would be meeting with representatives of their New York advertising agency, Simpson and Taine. In that case, Lily had told him, she would drive to Akron to do some pre-Palm Beach shopping and take in a movie. Now, as she drove up the driveway of River Bend at a quarter past midnight, she saw a number of cars parked in front of the big house and she assumed the meeting had transferred here from the office.

She pulled her Duesenberg into the garage, got out and walked to the front entrance. It was snowing lightly now and she hugged the sable around her, shivering from the wind. How odd it had been to see Melville after all those years, and how he had changed. And how badly she had miscalculated! It had seemed such a good idea and now it was turned around, pointed like a dagger against her. What if Mark found out? What if Melville should call him in the morning and tell him, out of spite? Why the hell had she told Melville that Mark hadn't sent her? Pride . . . pride of ownership of an idea that had backfired? Pride, like underestimating the opposition, was another luxury she could no longer afford. Mark had a violent temper, and God knew what he might do if he found out she had cheated on him—particularly with Melville, of all people—no matter what her motive. For a terrified moment, she wondered if her rash act might have cost her her husband. And then the terror subsided. She knew what she had to do, and quickly. She would have to tell Mark herself. Explain why. It wouldn't be pleasant but it was smarter than waiting for him to hear from Melville or somebody Melville would give the job to. When he understood why she had done it, when she convinced him how strong Melville had become, how committed to his own success and how fierce his hatred of the Mannings was, then he would have to forgive her for going to Sutterlee. At least, she hoped he would.

One thing she knew—some day she would pay Melville back for humiliating her. Some day, some way . . .

She let herself into the house, for the servants had gone to bed, then hung her sable in the coat closet and went through the living room to Mark's study, where she heard voices. She rapped on the door. Mark called "Come in" and she let herself into the room, where six years before he had first seduced her (or, more accurately, she had seduced him). She still could feel a tinge of remembered exhilaration when she went into that room, although this time it was subdued by the cloud of stale smoke in the air. Mark and four others were there, all in their shirtsleeves. In addition to Harrison Starr, Stanley Wilmot and Mark, she recognized the account executive for the multimillion-dollar Manning account, Richard Taine, and his top copy editor, Jerry de Yonge. The walls were lined with sketches of a new campaign that Mark had decided to launch to reinforce the sales of the Manning-Flow tire after his decision to enter the Boca Raton Challenge race. It had been a rush job—to get the ads in the Christmas issues of the national magazines had necessitated fast work, and on this night the group was making the final decision on which approach to favor. Lily could see from the tired faces that no decision had yet been reached.

"Oh, Lily," said Mark, who was sitting at his desk, "good; we need a fresh opinion."

She greeted Harrison and Stanley and the two men from New York, all of whom quickly got to their feet when the stunning woman— who, they knew, exerted great influence over her powerful husband —came into the room. Lily then glanced over at the more than twenty presentations propped against the walls and strewn about the room. Pudgy Stanley squatted back down on the floor in the middle of the sketches, puffing on a cigarette; Harrison wearily resumed his seat in a chair. The others watched Lily. The sketches were divided into two categories. One approach featured a happy housewife standing with her well-scrubbed children and handsome husband next to a pleasant suburban home. The poses varied, but in each a Manning-Flow tire was part of the family group, either in front of mom or being held by junior. The slogan was: "Our Family Will Never Tire of The Family Tire."

The other approach was very different. It featured five best-dressed-list society ladies endorsing the Manning-Flow tire, the most well known and sinuous of whom was Elizabeth, Countess of Manchester.

Lily had been aware that these were the two approaches being considered, and she had thought them both uninspired. Now as she looked at the presentations—with the image of the new and much more aggressive Melville fresh in her mind—she decided they were both flat tires.

"I think they all stink," she said.

Faces sagged.

Mark looked annoyed.

"None of them would persuade me to buy a Manning-Flow tire. Certainly this happy family pitch wouldn't. What does 'The Family Tire' mean?"

"It suggests dependability," said Harrison. "And loyalty. Also friendliness."

"Who needs a friendly tire? Besides, what if your family isn't dependable, loyal or friendly? I know a lot of families that hate each other's guts."

"Lily, that's not the point," Mark said. "People in families may get on each other's nerves, but most Americans still think of the family as a sacred institution, and any product that's a family product has an air of solid quality about it."

"That may be true, darling, but there's hundreds of so-called family products on the market, and they all can't be good. Besides, I still say that wouldn't get me to buy a Manning-Flow tire. It's just not peppy enough or different enough. It's *blah*."

Silence.

"What's wrong with the endorsements?" asked Stanley Wilmot.

"Well, I frankly couldn't care less what Betty Manchester thinks is a good tire. In the first place, you can't tell me that the Countess of Manchester knows anything about tires. All she knows about cars is how much they cost and are they flashy enough to impress people. In the second place, I know Betty Manchester personally, and believe me, she'd endorse toilet paper if the price were right."

"But the public doesn't know Betty personally," said Mark.

"But the public aren't idiots. Maybe society ladies' endorsements help sell cold cream, but I can't see how in the world they'd help sell tires."

"It gives the tire glamor and snob appeal," said Richard Taine, the account executive, who didn't look overly joyful about Lily's comments.

Lily shook her head. "Mr. Taine, it seems to me you've all made a basic mistake with both these campaigns, and the mistake is that you're assuming women have something to do with buying tires. It's simply not true. The husband buys the tires. And most American men are pretty lukewarm about snob appeal, at least this best-dressed-list kind of snob appeal. I'm really surprised at both these approaches— and frankly, I'm disappointed. With Premier's Dynaride tire hurting our sales the way it is, you're going to have to come up with something more original than this stuff to justify the money my husband is considering spending on this campaign."

The two agency men started talking all at once. Mark interrupted them.

"Wait a minute, gentlemen. Lily, Mr. Taine and Mr. de Yonge are two of the highest-paid men on Madison Avenue and, I'm told, two of the best. Society endorsements are apparently very popular right now, and the Family Tire idea is certainly a new approach for us and, I think, a valid one. We've been arguing all night which is better, and now you come in and tell us they're both no good. All right, what do you suggest?"

She looked around at the sketches again. Then she said, "Do you agree with me that men buy the tires?"

"Basically yes," said Richard Taine, "though new market surveys have shown that the housewife's influence is growing in this area. That's why we were aiming at the wife as well as the husband."

"But men still make the decision?"

"Yes," he admitted grudgingly.

"All right. What's the one thing that all men are interested in?"

"Money!" said Harrison Starr.

Lily laughed. "Speak for yourself, Mr. Starr. But the best things in life are free—at least most of the time. And most men, I would say, think the best thing in life is sex."

Silence.

"Sex?" said Richard Taine. "But you can't sell tires with sex!"

"Why not?"

"It would damage the product's reputation! You can sell lingerie with sex, and soap and cosmetics—but not something as basic as tires."

"What's more basic than sex?"

"That's not the issue. There are certain products, products linked with heavy industry, that are sexless products. No, I'm not phrasing that correctly. They are products the public thinks of as necessities. And if you link them in the public mind with something as controversial, as taboo as sex, you'll endanger the product's integrity."

"Mr. Taine," she said, "we obviously don't share the same attitude toward sex. I don't consider it either controversial or taboo. Frankly, I consider it a necessity." Harrison Starr winced. His superior's wife always made him feel rather squeamish. There was something off-color about her that made him uncomfortable. "I certainly consider it more necessary than the approval of the Countess of Manchester," she went on, "and I think it's definitely more eye-catching than a bunch of whey-faced, dull suburbanites. You ask me how I'd present the Manning-Flow tire? Well, I'd get one of the slickest artists in New York to paint me a big tire. And perched on top of that tire, looking directly out at me, the customer, would be this creamy-looking, gorgeous, nude girl—"

"Nude?" said Taine.

"Not a stitch. Of course, you'd fix her up. But there she'd be, appealing as all hell, and she'd be looking out at me with red lips and big blue eyes. And the slogan would say something like, 'I like rugged tires, and the rugged men that buy them.' And underneath that, in big letters, would be: MANNING-FLOW! THE RUGGED TIRE FOR RUGGED MEN! Now, I'm some underpaid city clerk with a three-year-old Chevy and a wife who's always picking on me and no one in the world thinks I'm worth much or very important or handsome—and certainly not rugged. And here's this dream of a girl looking out at me like I was Clark Gable, telling me all I have to do to be rugged is buy a Manning-Flow tire. And I'm going to forget all about whether the Dynaride gets more mileage, or Firestone has a better price, and I'm going to buy the Manning-Flow because that girl has gotten right through to what I care most about. Sex."

Silence. She looked around the room, but everyone had turned to Mark. His face was expressionless.

"Well," said Lily, "I guess I didn't win many converts."

"Mrs. Manning," said Taine, "it's a clever idea and if you were selling silk stockings . . . but—"

"If I were selling silk stockings, I'd have a naked man, not a woman."

"But these ads go in national, prestige publications! They won't accept, pardon me, vulgarity—"

"What's vulgar about sex? Besides, they'll print anything if you pay cash."

"But church groups! Women's clubs!"

"Churches don't buy tires!" she said angrily, "and neither do women! How many times do I have to repeat that?"

Richard Taine sighed and temporarily retired from the field. At which point Harrison Starr said, "Mrs. Manning, as president of the

Manning Company, I want to say that I'm proud of all the products we make. They are good products, fairly priced, with the backing of one of the largest corporations in America—a corporation, I might add, that has always stood for integrity. As a businessman, as a family man, and certainly as a Manning man, I would, frankly, be disturbed if I thought one of our major products was sold by exploiting the lowest levels of the public mind. I suggest it's beneath our dignity."

"What, might I ask, is less dignified than a product that doesn't sell? And if we're going to get basic about this, Mr. Starr, I might point out that as president of the Manning Company, it is your responsibility to see to it that we maintain our position as leader in the field of tire sales—a position we are *rapidly* losing! Melville Benny has a product that's taking one-fifth of our sales, and I don't give a damn *what* we do as long as we beat him out of that position. Gentlemen, I was once married to Mr. Benny and I can assure you, he is no fool. Perhaps a bit dull, but no fool. He's going to laugh when he sees this sort of advertising!" She waved at the sketches. "Family tire! Betty Manchester! Dignity! I say baloney. We're fighting to stay number one, and when you're fighting a war, you don't use powderpuffs."

Harrison Starr swabbed his forehead with a handkerchief. No one said a word. Lily turned to her husband.

"Well, you asked me what I thought, and I've told you. Now, what do *you* think, darling? After all, you're the boss."

Mark looked around the room.

"Gentlemen," he said quietly, "I'm sold on sex."

Lily might have struck out with Melville, but she was batting a thousand with her husband.

When the others had left River Bend, Mark opened a bottle of champagne and filled two glasses. He handed one to his wife and kissed her. "Lily, sometimes you aggravate the hell out of me, and sometimes you absolutely delight me. Tonight, you were magnificent. More than that, you were right. I knew something was wrong with those presentations, but I couldn't decide what it was. And along comes my wife and puts her finger right on it." He laughed. "Sex! Everyone's afraid to use it, and I bet we sell a million tires with it."

Lily had had what some might consider a strenuous evening but she didn't feel at all tired even though it was after one in the morning.

"I think it *will* sell tires," she said. "But I know what will sell more."

"What?"

"Winning at Boca Raton."

"Well, I've been thinking about that. Of course, we have an even chance now that we've got Roy Diamond driving for us." Harrison Starr had hired the famous driver, who earlier in his career had done some test-driving for the Manning Company before going on to win big purses at Le Mans and the Mille Miglia. Though he had never won the Indianapolis 500, Diamond was rated one of the top drivers in the country, and Mark was pleased to have gotten him. Admittedly, Diamond was ranked below Steve Raymond, who would be driving for Melville, but Diamond would be driving what Mark, as well as many others, considered the best racing car in America—the Stutz Super Bearcat. This was related by lineage to the venerable Stutz Bearcat of the late Teens and early Twenties, the Bearcat name having been revived for the roadster version of the magnificent Stutz DV-32, developed in 1929 and 1930. The DV-32 did not have thirty-two cylinders, as many erroneously inferred. Rather it had the straight-eight engine, though the chief Stutz engineer, Charles Greuter, had substituted double overhead cams for the single overhead and had added two more valves per cylinder, thus enormously increasing the power of the engine. The Super Bearcat was the 116-inch wheelbase lightweight version of the DV-32. And with Roy Diamond driving this fine machine, even Steve Raymond in his Miller-designed Ford V-8 was going to be given a run for his money.

The Manning Company had been sponsoring sports cars since 1911 when Mark, who had always been interested in racing and who was aware of its publicity value for his tires, had set up a "competition" division in the company, which concentrated on developing racing tires. Through the years, the Manning-sponsored cars had done well, though not spectacularly, winning the Indianapolis 500 a total of four times. The dependability of the tires being almost as important as the cars and the skill of the drivers, sports-car racing had been a natural magnet for all tire manufacturers, who had, over the years, invested millions in the various competitions. The entire package of Diamond and the Super Bearcat, plus mechanics and other expenses, was costing the Manning Company more than $50,000. However, the publicity the Premier Challenge—as the race was quickly named—had generated was so enormous that no one doubted the enormous profit increase a win would bring. Already twelve different tire manufacturers from Europe as well as America had announced entries.

The Premier Challenge was shaping up as a racing event of the first order.

Mark, however, after overcoming his initial reluctance to enter the race, was now having second thoughts about staying in, despite his understanding of the value of a win. "You know," he said, "even with Roy Diamond driving for us, we may have played this wrong. In the long run, it might pay us more to lose."

"Lose?" said Lily. "How could it pay for us to *lose?*"

"Because business is bad enough without companies going at each other's throats. I realize Melville has his private reasons for wanting to humiliate us, as I have mine for not wanting to humiliate him again. Melville has a damn good product. His Dynaride seems to be an improvement over our tire, and there's no question it's selling. On the other hand, compared to us, Melville's still small potatoes financially. I've been wondering if we couldn't bury the hatchet and arrange a merger. I know it wouldn't be easy, but I think in the long run it would benefit both of us so much that he might be able to forget the pa,t. And I certainly could make Melville a money offer he could hardl) pass up."

She shook her head. "He wouldn't accept if you offered him the mint.'

"How do we know? I know he wouldn't go for it at first. But if we made careful approaches to him, he might at least start thinking it over. Maybe the first step is for us to withdraw from the Challenge race."

"Withdraw? Are you out of your mind?"

'I don't think so. We have the best chance to beat Steve Raymond. So if we backed out, Melville would take it as a serious good will gesture."

She shook her head again.

"Mark, you couldn't be more wrong. If you want to buy Melville out, the best way is to win that race. It would be a blow to his prestige and profits and then he might *have* to consider a merger. Otherwise he's never going to consider it."

"What makes you so damn sure?"

"Because I saw Melville tonight."

He looked at her.

"Tonight?"

"Tonight. I drove down to Sutterlee, to his house."

"What the hell for?"

"To seduce him, except he seduced me."

"Lily, this is a very bad joke."

"Oh, it was a joke all right. A regular Marx Brothers howler. I thought if I could seduce Melville I eventually could get him to tell me the big secret of his Dynaride tires. Well, Melville played along and we went to bed—"

"Why, you incredible bitch!"

"Now, look, Mr. Mark Manning. I've never cheated on you and you know it. I never will cheat on you again, if for no better reason than that I *like* being Mrs. Mark Manning. I'm not exactly lusting after Melville's skinny white body. I did it tonight because you don't care any more, and *somebody's* got to keep this company from falling apart."

"What the hell do you mean, I don't care? My whole life's in this company!"

"Not any more. You're more interested in being Mark Manning the respected industrialist, the art collector, the benefactor of mankind. All right, that's your privilege. But let's be frank, darling, somebody's got to do the dirty work. Somebody has to do the sleeping around, if called for, and I thought it was called for tonight. Harrison Starr wouldn't do it! Pure Harrison, the family man who thinks sex is beneath our dignity, who no doubt *prays* on Sunday to God to keep the Manning Rubber Company on top! And you won't do it, because you've never gotten over what happened in Africa six years ago. So who's left? Lily. And Lily cares enough to do it—which she did."

"But why in hell would Melville go to bed with *you?*"

"Revenge, sweet and simple. To get back at you. All right, I made a mistake. He's smarter than I thought and when it was all over I knew he hated us more than ever—and that the dumbest thing to do would be to underestimate that hate or anything else about him. So get any idea you have that Melville will listen to sweet reason out of your head—he's out for our blood."

Mark got up and paced around the room. "I'm sure he is *now*. Of all the stupid damn tricks—he probably even thinks I sent you to do my dirty work . . ."

"He did, but I told him it was all my idea and I still say it was worth a try. Mark, I don't blame you for wanting to be the sainted figure of the industry. God knows, you've earned it. But frankly, darling, you've gotten complacent, and you've got a complacent management, and so you can't blame me for doing what I thought had to be done to keep this company on top for our son—"

"*And* Christopher!" he snapped, turning on her.

"Of course, and Christopher. But look at those idiots tonight. I'm no advertising genius, but you didn't have to be to see what was wrong. Those presentations were a joke—and God knows how much money you pay that agency! But did Harrison Starr see it—Harrison, who pulls down $200,000 a year just to watch out for stupid mistakes? No. Neither did Stanley Wilmot. And this whole business with Melville. I've had to nag like a fishwife to get you *in* the race, and now you're talking about getting *out* so we won't hurt Melville's feelings! You've spent thousands to have a chance to win the damned thing— which would be worth every penny—and I think it's crazy to even *think* about not doing everything in our power to win!"

He looked hard at her for a moment, then seemed to subside.

"All *right*," he said, "you've made your point. Maybe I have gotten a little complacent, and I'll admit that sometimes Harrison's not exactly a ball of fire. But Lily, I've done some things in my life . . . Roger . . . his mother . . . that review of her book about me—they couldn't believe what I'd done, but I did it and all the excuses to myself since that I thought Tegai was bluffing, that you drove me to it . . . they were all excuses. *I* did what I did, I'm responsible . . . for the good things *and* the rotten things. I'm tired, Lily. I'm tired of hurting people. It's been six years and I still haven't gotten over what I did to Roger. Before then I didn't really think much about what I did—I just did it. Since then it's been different." He paused and shrugged. "Maybe I'm getting mellow with old age. Or soft."

She came over to him and took his hand. "Then," she said, "let *me* do the bad things. I don't mind at all."

He looked at her. "No, you don't, do you? You're a winner, Lily —it takes one, like they say, to know one. I guess that's one reason we got together—and still are. You're what I used to be."

She kissed him. "But there's other reasons, aren't there? Besides, you're not *that* over the hill yet."

"You don't think so?"

"No. Thank God there's still some of the old Mark there, behind all that heavy respectability."

She made a "heavy respectable" face and looked dour. He laughed and took her in his arms. "Damn you, you're my resident devil. You know that?"

"I know. And you'll *never* get rid of me."

He kissed her hard and whispered, "Don't *ever* cheat on me again. Understand? Even if it's for the company—I don't give a damn what the reason is. You're mine, and I don't share what's mine, not with any man."

"Spoken like a true capitalist, darling."

"Seriously, Lily. I mean it."

"I won't. On one condition."

"No conditions."

"All right. But promise me you won't withdraw from the race."

"You never give up, do you?"

"Never. Promise?"

"All right, we'll stay in."

"And you'll do everything to make us win?"

"Yes."

"And to hell with Melville?"

"To hell with Melville."

She smiled, and kissed him. "I love you," she said intensely. "I love you because you're the biggest and best, and you don't ever have to worry about me again."

"As long as I stay biggest and best?"

"But you *will*, because, if necessary, Lily will nag and push and bother you into it. And if all that won't do it, why, Lily will just have to love you into it."

"I feel trapped."

"You are." She kissed him again. "Shall we go upstairs? And Lily will give you a nice back rub and a belly rub and a rubadubdub *all* over. Would you like that?"

"Sold."

"Good." She headed back to the sofa. "But let's finish our champagne first. I'm just the teensiest bit pooped."

He said nothing as he came over to refill her glass.

"How far are you willing to go?" she asked.

"What do you mean?"

"How far are you willing to go to make sure we win?"

He looked at her suspiciously. "What are you getting at?"

She picked up her glass and curled her legs under her on the sofa. "Just that races can be fixed, of course. Would you be willing to fix this one?"

He didn't answer.

"It could ruin Melville," she went on. "Absolutely ruin him. He'd be the laughing stock of the industry if he lost after those claims of his. And the public would find it pretty funny too. It's worth thinking about."

"I don't think you were listening to what I said. I told you I'm *tired* of hurting people."

"Do you know someone who could fix it?" she went on, as if not hearing his remark. "Someone you could make a phone call to? *That* wouldn't tire you. It should be as easy as writing a check to a university."

She sipped the champagne.

"You know goddamn well I know someone who could fix it," he said. "Don't play games."

She leaned back. "Well? How about it? Isn't it worth it?"

"No."

"Oh, come on, Mark. You told me you did a favor for Big Johnnie Marucca once, and all these years he's owed you one in return. Well, here's his chance. Johnnie could make sure Steve Raymond doesn't win, and you can't tell me it wouldn't be worth it. A simple, quiet fix is *always* worth it."

"I don't want to do it."

"I know you don't *want* to, but will you think about it? Please? That's all I'm asking."

He finished his champagne and set the glass down hard on the table.

"Let's go upstairs."

CHAPTER FIVE

Leonard Hastings was in love with Ellen Manning, but he was in love with her family too. It was strange that this scatterbrained, slap-dash, unintellectual young man would be so attracted to the de Sibours. There was a streak of the romantic in Len that was fascinated by the quietly elegant life Maurice and Charlotte lived, and as he spent more and more evenings in the lovely apartment on the Avenue Kléber, he fell even more deeply under the spell of the place and of Charlotte, who, in turn, overcame her initially unfavorable impression of the young American and became rather fond of him. His good humor was irresistible, his healthy animal openness was as attractive to her as it was to her daughter, and then, too, he was such a good audience! For Charlotte was aware that Len had come to admire her, and she was vain enough to be pleased by it. Only Maurice remained unconverted. He was pleasant to the young man, but he stayed unimpressed.

It wasn't the wealth of the de Sibours that appealed to Len; he wasn't all that dazzled by money, despite his joking remarks to Ellen about his being green with envy at her millions. In fact, the opposite was true. If anything, Ellen's father's fortune intimidated him. What did appeal to him was the quiet beauty that seemed to pervade the apartment and their lives. Neither Maurice nor Charlotte was frantically social, nor were they particularly chic. Neither dressed in the latest fashion, Maurice tending toward well-cut, conservative suits and Charlotte dressing in a timeless Chanel style that seemed somehow perfect for her. Her passion for interior decoration had dissipated with time, and while she occasionally went on antiquing forays, she had done little redecorating either of the château or the apartment, both of which remained rather old-fashioned and yet, like Charlotte, somehow exactly "right." Her fondness for elegant table settings had remained, however, and dinners at the de Sibours' were visual joys as well as epicurean delights—the crystal, china and silver were always lovely, and the food and wine superb—and though Len was no gourmet, despite his enjoyment of cooking, he appreciated fine food and, on occasion, demonstrated an overfondness for wine.

But what impressed him the most was the marriage itself.

Ellen had gone to the States to spend the Christmas holidays with her father and brothers in Palm Beach, and when she returned to Paris the first week in January of 1934, sporting a glorious tan, she immediately phoned Len. She had found that in her case absence had made the heart grow fonder and she was longing to see him. He picked her up at the apartment and took her to the coachhouse, where they made love, had dinner, then made love again. When he took her home, she made a date to go walking with him the next morning, a Saturday. And, though it looked like rain, he met her at ten and they strolled to the Luxembourg Gardens. By the time they arrived there, it had started to rain. Len liked walking in the rain and refused to carry an umbrella or wear a rainhat, maintaining that rainwater was tonic for the hair. Ellen wasn't convinced; she carried an umbrella, assuring him that a few more Paris winters would cure him of his passion for its rain. Now she opened it and they sat down on a park bench. It was then that Len brought up the subject of Maurice and Charlotte.

"You know," he said, "I really missed your parents while you were away."

"I hope you missed me too."

"Come on, you know I did. Don't fish for compliments. But I've really enjoyed knowing them—even your stepfather, though I'm not so sure he's all that happy knowing me. But they're interesting to watch. I've never met a couple as happy. They really are fantastically in love, aren't they?"

"Uh huh. It's as if they're on the same waves, almost."

"And they enjoy each other—that's the amazing thing to me. My parents get along all right, and they play bridge with their friends and all that, but I never have a feeling they get much of a kick out of each other. But I get that feeling with your parents. It's really wonderful."

"Well, *we* enjoy each other," said Ellen rather defensively. While she was pleased Len liked her family, she was, after all, more interested in his liking her.

"Oh, sure, but we're not married."

"But what if we were? Does that mean we wouldn't enjoy each other?"

An old man scurried by, holding his umbrella over his head.

"I don't know," replied Len thoughtfully. "Would you like to be married to me?"

"Is that a proposal?"

"Oh, no."

"Well, I don't think I'd mind it. Would you like to be married to me?"

"This is sort of a stupid conversation."

"I don't see why. *Would* you?"

"Oh, I think so. But there's no point in talking about it, because we're never going to get married."

"Why not?" she said quickly, just as quickly realizing she shouldn't have said it.

"Well, for one thing, I haven't proposed."

"I know that, silly. This is a . . . well, just a *general* conversation. I'm not going to pin you to the wall, if that's what's worrying you. But speaking *generally*, I don't see what's so impossible about our getting married."

"Then I'll tell you. One, I don't know what I want to do with my life, except I'm getting more sure every day I don't want to be a banker. Two, I haven't got any money. Three, I haven't even got much ambition—at least, I don't think I have. If I could ever figure out what I really wanted to do besides ski, maybe I'd have some, I don't know. But right now, I don't, I'm afraid, so I'd make a miserable husband and I like you too much to stick you with a bum like me. Does that answer your question?"

Despite the pessimistic tone of his remarks, she was glowing inwardly because he had at least admitted he "liked her too much." However, she concealed her pleasure as she watched the rain spatter off her umbrella onto her shoes.

"Well," she said, "I think you're being a little hard on yourself. Maybe when you figure out what you want to be, you'll be an absolute whizz at it."

"Maybe. I doubt it. I think I'm basically lazy. Besides, it wouldn't work for another reason."

"Now what?"

"Well, you're a very important person. I mean, your father's Mark Manning, and your stepfather's Maurice de Sibour, who doesn't think much of me—"

"That's not true!"

"Yes it is. I may be a bum, but I'm not such a dumb one. I know what he thinks. Anyway, I couldn't compete in that league."

"But you're marrying *me*, not my family!"

"I'm not even marrying you."

She mentally kicked herself.

"What I meant to say is, if we were really getting married, what difference would it make who my family is? After all, my father's a farmer's son . . ."

"Not any more. He's worth a couple of hundred million dollars and I make sixty bucks a week, and he'd sure as hell think I was after your money. So it wouldn't work."

Ellen seldom got mad, but she had inherited some of her father's temper. Now it exploded.

"What kind of man are you, anyway? If you really love me, what do you care what my father thinks? And who gives a damn if you *do* marry me for my money? I don't see anything wrong with that, as long as you love *me*! I happen to be a rich person. I can't help it. I'm not ashamed of it and I'm not proud of it. But whoever I marry is going to be marrying my money too, because I'm not about to give it away! So it really is a stupid argument and I don't want to discuss it any more. Besides, I'm getting sick and tired of sitting in this damned rain! Would you kindly walk me home or take me *somewhere* where it's dry?"

"Oh . . . sure," he said, rather startled by the outburst. They got up and began to walk toward the Rue Vaugirard to hail a taxi.

"Did you really mean all that?" he said after a while.

"Yes. And I don't want to talk about it any more."

He grinned. "Well, if you really mean it, why don't we get married?

I'm willing to sacrifice a point or two. And maybe in time I can come to love your money as much as I love you."

She stopped and looked at him.

"Are you serious?"

"Sure. Someone with as little character as I've got, it probably won't take me more than about a half hour to fall head over heels in love with your millions."

She threw her arms around him, narrowly averting banging his head with her umbrella.

"Oh Len, you idiot! And I accept before you have a chance to weasel out!"

They kissed in the rain for almost two minutes. An elderly Parisiénne passing by smiled, reassured that her city was, despite the headlines that morning, still the city of love.

They spent the rest of the day discussing their wedding plans and waiting for Maurice and Charlotte to return from a lunch in the country so they could spring the news on them first, although Len was a little nervous about Maurice's reaction. Ellen assured him all would go well, however; and when at three thirty that afternoon the de Sibours returned to the apartment, Len took a deep breath and told them. He had been right. Maurice received the news coldly, and it was apparent he was anything but pleased. Charlotte, however, after a moment's hesitation, kissed both of them and told them she was delighted and that they would celebrate the event that night at dinner. With that, Len rather gratefully excused himself to go home and change.

When he returned to the apartment at seven in his dinner jacket, Maurice seemed more pleasant, and Len guessed that while he had been gone both Ellen and Charlotte had worked on him to soften his objections. Certainly Ellen seemed relaxed and happy as her fiancé kissed her and she led him into the drawing room where the butler served cocktails. Charlotte, looking lovely in a black-chiffon evening gown, kept the conversation going, discussing where the wedding should be held, when they should get together with Len's parents, who should be on the guest list . . . Len eased his tension by having three martinis, which were two more than he should have had. By the time they went in to dinner, he was tight and Ellen was whispering to him to "be careful."

As dinner progressed, much champagne was served, Charlotte, out of preference as well as loyalty to her husband's product, serving nothing but champagne. Len, far from being "careful," kept his glass drained and Ellen watched him anxiously as the conversation drifted around to the subject that everyone in Paris was discussing that night —the Stavisky scandal.

Serge Alexander (Sacha) Stavisky was the son of Russian-Jewish parents who had migrated to Paris at the turn of the century. Young Sacha had early gotten into trouble with the police over a minor fraud, and by the Twenties he was an accomplished criminal who had tried his skilled hand at almost every crime, including drug peddling, forgery and even armed robbery—though after his first sentencing in 1912 he managed to avoid getting caught. In 1926, however, he was arrested for skinning some stockbrokers out of 7,000,000 francs; though he spent eighteen months in the Santé prison, he was finally released on provisional liberty, supposedly to face trial later on, a trial which kept getting miraculously postponed. By now, Sacha was a rich man, growing richer with each elaborate swindle. He owned two newspapers, a theater and a string of race horses and had friends in high places, including many prominent politicians. However, Sacha's most lucrative plum was proving to be the directorship of the municipal pawnshop (Mont-de-Piété) in the city of Bayonne.

In France there were no private pawnshops. Instead, every city had an official Mont-de-Piété backed by the bank of France and the credit of the Third Republic. People would bring valuables to the pawn-shop to hock, and since most of the people raising money in this fashion were hard up and already owed the money they received for their hocked goods, an amazing percentage of the pledges was never redeemed. Sacha, therefore, had a treasure chest of valuables at his disposal, which his flair for financial manipulation was quick to take advantage of. Using the jewels, furs, and other items deposited with him as collateral, he raised large private loans, the bankers not asking too many embarrassing questions about where the collateral was coming from, although they surely had a shrewd idea. With the Depression sending hundreds of people to the pawnshop, the supply of collateral was enormous, and Sacha's cup of gold was indeed run-ning over. With the loans, he financed several companies, sold stock, pyramided one company onto another and quickly spread his tentacles throughout French business. He also, through his connections, became the agent for floating municipal bonds, covering them with deposits of jewelry from the pawnshop, or with fancy techniques of ac-countancy.

Finally, on Christmas Eve of 1933, one of his friends in the Bayonne city government confessed that 239,000,000 francs' worth of bonds had been floated by being backed by Sacha's stolen jewelry. On January

3, 1934, *L'Action Française,* the rightist Paris newspaper, had published two letters written by a cabinet minister, recommending to insurance companies that they buy Stavisky's municipal bonds. The minister protested his innocence, but promptly resigned.

Now the fat was, indeed, in the fire.

In the election of 1932, the one that Maurice de Sibour had tried unsuccessfully to stand in as a deputy, the left had elected a majority to the chamber of deputies. However, this leftist majority could not agree on a program to keep France out of the trough of the Depression, and six governments had whirled in and out of office in less than two years. At the end of 1933, Camille Chautemps, a power in the Radical-Socialist Party (which was neither particularly radical nor socialist, despite its name) had become premier. Chautemps was in the embarrassing position of having as his brother-in-law the public prosecutor responsible for postponing the trial of Stavisky a remarkable grand total of nineteen times, not to mention the fact that his brother, Pierre Chautemps, was a lawyer for one of Stavisky's companies. This was a golden opportunity for the frustrated right to expose the leftist government as being infested with corruption, an opportunity that was not to be wasted. Furthermore, Stavisky had suddenly disappeared and it was said that the Sûreté itself had given him a passport, presumably to get him out of the country before he could talk. The newspapers howled for his blood, and on January 8, the very morning on which Len was proposing to Ellen in the Luxembourg Gardens, the Paris newspapers were announcing that the police had tracked Stavisky down to a châlet at Chamonix, where he had promptly committed suicide just as the police were breaking in the door. This was too much for the average Frenchman and Frenchwoman, most of whom assumed that, in fact, the police had shot Stavisky to shut him up permanently. And it was certainly too much for Maurice de Sibour, who, halfway through the turbot, was generating considerable heat about the entire mess.

"And the damnable thing is," he exclaimed, "I have no doubt the police *did* shoot him. If Stavisky had started talking, I know quite a few men who would be on their way out of the country on the first boat train, not the last of whom would be Jean Chiappe."

"Chiappe?" asked Charlotte. "The prefect of police?"

"Exactly. Chiappe was a friend of Stavisky's, and an even better friend of several of Stavisky's friends, some of whom are already in jail. And of course, let's not forget that Monsieur Chiappe was also hand in glove with more than a few leaders of the right, who are going to have such a good time attacking Chautemps in the next few days. Oh, it's a beautiful situation. Beautiful. And the people who are going to profit the most from it are our *friends,* René de Courville and his associates. I'll wager they're having a jolly time tonight."

He shook his head glumly. Len, who had a beatific alcohol-induced smile on his face and a glazed look in his eyes, said, "Well, after all, what do you expect from vermin like Stavisky?"

"It's not only Stavisky," Maurice said. "There have been crooks like him since the beginning of time, and there will continue to be crooks like him till the end. The tragedy is that the Government and the country are so cynical and greedy that crooks like Stavisky can get away with their miserable schemes."

"It's more than that," slurred Len, waving his hand in a boozy gesture dismissing that argument. "It's an international plot."

Maurice and Charlotte looked surprised.

"A plot of what?" asked Charlotte.

Len weaved slightly in his chair.

"Of Jews, of course!"

There was a deadly silence.

"The Jews are behind all this," he went on. "You don't think one man could pull off as much as Stavisky did without a lot of help? Course not. Stavisky's a Jew, and the Rothschilds and all the other big, rich kikes put him up to this just so they could bring down the government. That's what it's all about, believe me."

He looked across the table at Ellen, whose face had gone white. Then he looked at Charlotte, who was ice.

"I say something wrong?" He smiled weakly.

"Leonard," said Charlotte quietly, "I gather you don't know that I'm Jewish."

"Aw, come on. You? That's a laugh." Confusion came over his face. "You are? But you don't *look* it." He turned to Ellen. "But then . . . *you* must be Jewish too?"

"Yes, I am."

"Well, why didn't you ever tell me?"

"It never occurred to me you'd be interested."

Len shrugged. "Well, I really stuck my foot in my mouth, didn't I?"

Silence.

He wiped his mouth on his napkin, put it down, then got to his feet.

"I won't say I'm sorry," he said, hanging onto the back of his chair for support, "because how can I be sorry for something I didn't know? Except I *am* sorry, damn it. Sorry you're Jewish and sorry I didn't know it. See?" he said to Ellen, "I told you it wouldn't work out.

Should have listened to ol' Len!" He made a mock-polite bow to Charlotte, then one to Maurice; then he started toward the door. "Don't have to show me out," he said. "I know the way." He looked back at Ellen, a maudlin, drunken expression had come over his eyes. "And I was really in love with you!"

He weaved out of the room.

After he had gone, Ellen began to cry and her mother hurried from her chair to comfort her.

"Darling, I'm so sorry it happened this way," she said, putting her arm around her.

"Did you hear what he *said?* Did you *hear?* He's so sorry we're Jewish because he *had* been in love with me! As if there's something wrong with me now—"

"He was drunk . . ."

"Oh, don't make excuses for him!"

"You'd really never talked about it?" asked Maurice, wonderingly.

"No! You know Len, we never discuss anything serious for more than three seconds . . . I had no idea he was that way. . . ." She got out of her chair, tears running down her face. "God, I hate him!" she said, throwing down her napkin. "I *hate* him!"

She ran out of the room.

Maurice said sadly, "Well, if it had to happen, it's much better now than later. Frankly, I'm just as glad to be rid of him. But poor Ellen."

Charlotte nodded. "Yes, poor Ellen. The first man she ever loved. What rotten luck."

She was sick for an hour, alternately crying and running to her bathroom. Finally she calmed down. Maybe he hadn't really *meant* it. Maybe it was the champagne, maybe it was his idea of a stupid joke. Maybe in the morning he would come back and explain it all away, somehow. If it were possible to explain *that* away.

But he didn't call in the morning. And after two days, she admitted that she had been fooling herself. It hadn't been just a rotten joke. It had been rotten.

The first man she had wanted to marry was an anti-Semite.

CHAPTER SIX

The track at Boca Raton had been built in the Twenties, and was one of the biggest in the country, its lap distance being 2½ miles. It was situated a mile to the west of the city on flat land, a huge oval in the middle of what seemed nowhere, although at the south curve there was an abandoned ice-cream factory with a high water tower that sported a huge ice cream cone painted on its side, a peeling, forlorn memento of happier, pre-Depression days. The straightaways of the track were each almost a mile, and the two end curves were sharply banked. The track was paved with a tar-and-asphalt combination that was kept in excellent shape, and the consensus among drivers was that Boca, as it was called, was one of the best tracks in the world. The stands along the west side could seat almost ten thousand, and there was a small enclosed clubhouse at the top for dignitaries and track officials. The pit area was opposite the stands.

Behind the small garages was the paddock, where, at eleven fifteen on the morning of January 12, 1934, Lily and Mark were talking with their driver, Roy Diamond.

Diamond was in his early thirties, a wiry, intense man with a face that reminded Mark of one of those fierce Renaissance soldiers that appeared in the canvases of Italian paintings. It was a hawk face, long, and stamped with the determination that Diamond was famous for. The eyes, like all drivers' eyes, were embedded in wrinkles and pulled tight and sharp.

He looked dashing in his white overalls and red neckband, and Lily was pleased he was wearing the Manning corporate wheel on his right shoulder.

"Are you nervous?" she asked.

"Sure. A little. I'm always a little nervous. But it's a great day—we couldn't have asked for better weather—and that makes me less nervous. Rain would give me a real case of the jitters."

For days the cars had been worked on and repaired as faults showed up in the rigorous practice runs, and even now, forty-five minutes before the race was to start, the mechanics were going over the yellow Super Bearcat in the Manning garage, making every last possible check, while two Manning men from the competition division of the company fussed over the car's tires, four new S-14s—the dry-weather racing version of the Manning Flow.

A total of twenty-seven cars had entered the competition, but the track could safely accommodate no more than sixteen, so the practice trials had eliminated eleven of the entries. The remaining cars had had rigorous time trials to determine their position on the grid. Obviously, sixteen cars could not start a race abreast, so the practice trials, which set the starting positions, were almost as important as the race itself. The car clocking the best lap time got the post position, the position in the first row of three cars considered the one that would give the advantage on the first curve. This had gone to Steve Raymond, who had clocked a lap in the near-record time of 1 minute 24.32 seconds at a speed of 104 mph. Next to him in the first row would be the second-best lap time, clocked by Jerry Locke, an Englishman driving a green Bentley for Dunlop. The last position in the first row had gone to Roy Diamond. That the fastest cars and drivers got the best starting positions was an ironic fact of life in racing, but there was a good reason for it; nothing was more dangerous than slow cars and inept drivers, and it was to the safety advantage of everyone that the slowest be placed at the rear.

Mark and Lily shook Diamond's hand before leaving to go to the clubhouse. Then Lily leaned close to the driver and whispered, "If you win, there's a $3,000 bonus in it for you."

Diamond's eyes registered the unexpected surprise. Lily, as she walked out of the paddock, felt that if nothing else their driver was properly motivated.

Melville Benny was also motivated.

Not only had his driver, Steve Raymond, won the post position; not only was the weather near perfect for the race—a cloudless seventy-five degrees, with a gentle breeze from the ocean; not only was the crowd bigger than he had expected; but a veritable Who's Who of the rubber industry had arrived for the competition, and Melville, as host, felt that special glow of satisfaction that comes with having managed what appears to be a successful party. The guests he was most interested in were Mark and Lily Manning. He had been afraid they wouldn't show up for the occasion, assuming that Lily would not be anxious to run into him after her visit to his house in Sutterlee. Still, he had hoped they would, because this was to be his day of sweetest revenge. He had underestimated Lily's nerve. There they were, Mark dressed in a double-breasted, ice-cream-white suit and Panama hat, and Lily sporting a rather outrageous outfit—a fawn dress with a matching silver-fox-trimmed stole that swept almost to her ankles, an enormous wide-brimmed garden hat, and a huge diamond-spray brooch on her lapel. Lily was impossible to miss, and evidently not in the least apprehensive about running into Melville. They were in the clubhouse, mingling with friends and associates, nibbling canapés and sipping the wine punch Melville had provided for his guests.

He came over to them after they finished chatting with a member of the Firestone clan.

"Hello, Mark. Lily."

Mark turned to face his former friend he hadn't seen for so many years. Melville thought that on his face, at least, there was a trace of uncharacteristic tension . . . nervousness?

"Hello, Melville."

They didn't shake hands.

"What a lovely day for your race," Lily casually remarked.

"Yes, it is, isn't it?" An awkward pause. Melville stuck his hands in his pockets, to get them out of the way.

"I don't suppose you'd be interested in a side bet?" he said to Mark.

"No."

The answer came quickly, unequivocally, but Melville persisted.

"Oh, come on, now. Just a friendly bet for old times' sake? Say, $10,000? I'll admit my man's got the better starting position, but there are a lot of people saying your Stutz has got the edge over our Ford. How about it?"

"I have no interest in betting with you, Melville."

"Wait a minute, darling," Lily said. "Melville obviously is feeling very sure of himself, and it would be ungracious not to accept his little challenge. Except ten thousand is such chicken feed. If we're going to bet, let's make it worth while."

Melville was surprised at the angry look Mark gave her.

"I *don't* want to bet."

"But Melville does," persisted Lily. "And so do I. How about $100,-000, Melville? To make it interesting?"

A hundred thousand dollars! Melville was confident, but he wasn't sure he was that confident.

Lily smiled. "Too much for you, Melville?"

Mark's face was turning almost as red as his hair but he said nothing, and Melville marveled at Lily's persistence against his wishes.

"All right," he said. "A hundred thousand dollars that my man finishes ahead of yours."

"Wonderful," said Lily. "This should make the race worth watching. If we lose, I hope you'll accept our check? It won't bounce, I promise you."

"Oh, I'm sure," replied Melville. "The one *good* thing about both of you is your credit."

With that, he left them; Mark whispered to Lily, "That was a damn stupid thing to do."

"Why? He asked for it, so to hell with him. Besides, we're going to win. Shall we take our seats? The race is about to start."

The man wore an open-necked sports shirt, seersucker slacks, dark glasses and a white hat, and had a slight beer belly. Around his neck was slung a leather binoculars case. Aside from the leather case he was carrying in his hand, he might have passed for any one of the thousands of spectators at the race. Except that he wasn't in the grandstand. Rather, he had driven his Plymouth roadster with the Florida license plates into the weed-grown parking area by the abandoned Sunshine Ice Cream Company factory at the south end of the track. Now he got out of the car and looked around. Nothing. The factory had been for sale since the company went out of business in '32 and two years of neglect had taken their toll. Windows were broken, the stucco walls were cracked, and a lizard was sunning itself on the cement step in front of the boarded-up entrance. The ocean breeze stirred the weeds.

The man walked around the building to the water tower, tested the rusted steel ladder, then began to climb. In a few minutes he had reached the small wooden platform that girdled the circular tower. A few of the boards in the platform had rotted, and the man was careful as he edged around the tower until he came to the north side facing the south corner of the track. There, beneath the giant, peeling ice-cream cone—vanilla—he pulled out the binoculars and examined the pits more than a half mile away. The cars were being pushed out onto the track to take their starting positions in the grid. Despite the balmy weather, the midday sun had generated heat waves that made the distant cars shimmer slightly. Still, his height and his position give the man an excellent view.

He kneeled down, opened the leather case, and started to assemble the custom-built rifle with the telescopic lens. He had directed it numerous times previously against humans.

This time he had a much more prosaic target. A tire.

Steve Raymond was known by his peers as Lover Boy. He was not a handsome man, his gaunt, craggy face being decorated with a zigzag scar on his right cheek, which had been the result of a near-fatal accident three years before at Monza, outside Milan. But Steve had razzmatazz. He was a fashion plate, dressing like Fred Astaire when not driving, and the women swarmed after him. Most drivers liked to talk a big game, but they tended to be conservative by nature and were generally surprisingly uxorious. Steve was a bachelor and an exception. The girls chased him, he chased the girls, and by his lights it was an altogether wonderful and exciting life. Now, as he started around the track on the warm-up lap, he briefly thought of two things: girls— in this instance, Betty Terhune, whom he was taking to dinner that night—and death. Then he purposefully dismissed both thoughts from his mind and concentrated on the race. Like all drivers, while he was aware of the possibility of a fatal accident happening to him, he had long since learned to rationalize away the specter, to gauze it over with self-confidence and force the dread out of his mind with mental discipline. One could never win races if one were afraid to take chances. The best insurance was professionalism and technique, and Steve had more than his fair share of both.

He was the best in the business.

He had a plan for this race. The man to beat was Roy Diamond, even though Diamond had been just pushed out of second place in practice by the British driver, Locke. But Diamond was a better driver than Locke, in Steve's opinion; nor was he unaware of the intense rivalry between his sponsor, Melville Benny, and Diamond's sponsor, the Manning Company. Melville had made it clear to Steve that above all he wanted him to come in ahead of Roy Diamond. So Steve was acutely conscious of the yellow Super Bearcat two cars to his right.

Steve's plan was to take the lead early, try to maintain it as long as he could, but not to kill himself to keep it from Diamond until the very end of the race. Boca was what was known as a slipstreamer track. The long straightaways gave rise to the phenomenon known as slipstreaming, which was the partial vacuum created by the lead car as it reached the high speeds possible on the track. This vacuum created behind the lead car gave the second driver an advantage, for he could profit by the lack of air resistance to take the lead himself. But then he lost the advantage as his own car hit the air, in turn creating the new slipstream. So the trick was to take the lead only at the last possible moment. Steve was adept at this game, better at it than Roy Diamond, and he was confident his skill would win him the race today.

As he swung around the south curve in the lead on the warm-up lap, he glanced at the big ice cream cone on the water tower. It was a good luck sign to him, being connected in his mind with the Boca track, where he had won so many fat purses in the past. He noticed a small figure leaning on the rail of the platform and wondered why no one had ever thought of watching the races from there before, since it provided an ideal view. Then he dismissed that from his mind, as he had dismissed sex and death, and totally buckled down his mental hatches to concentrate on the race.

Mark did not watch the start of the race as the sixteen cars roared by the flag-waving marshal. Instead he was watching his wife sitting next to him, wondering if she had called Johnnie Marucca after all. Lily had pleaded with him for over a week to make the call that would fix the race and guarantee a win for the Manning-Flow tire, and, more importantly in her mind, a defeat for Melville. Mark had refused. Finally he had gone into a rage and ordered her to drop the idea, told her that he was not going to do it, and that if she persisted in bothering him about it he would ship her off to Hawaii until the race was over. This seemed to shut her up, and he assumed that, finally, she had realized she couldn't budge him.

And now she had accepted Melville's bet, raising the stakes tenfold to a hundred thousand dollars in the blink of an eye, despite his insistence they not bet at all. Mark was not that sure of their chances, particularly with Steve Raymond winning the post position, and he was not anxious to multiply his losses, as well as his mortification, by losing an enormous side bet. Moreover, Lily had done it so cooly and quickly that he was forced to wonder if *she* had fixed the race without his knowledge, if when he was so adamant in refusing to call Big Johnnie she had called him herself. The longer he thought about it, the more certain he became that she indeed had done it. He remembered how coldly she had urged him to sacrifice Roger Boine's life for the "good of the company." How much more motivation she had in this instance, when a guaranteed win would not only help the company—*her* company, as she seemed more and more to think of it—but humiliate her former husband as well. Mark had no illusions about her ability to make such a decision. He was perfectly aware that his beautiful wife had a marble heart.

She was watching the cars through her binoculars as they tore around the south curve on the first lap. Raymond's blue Ford had kept the lead, with the green Dunlop Bentley second and Roy Diamond's yellow Stutz a close third. As the roar of the cars diminished with distance, he leaned over and said in her ear, "You called Big Johnnie, didn't you?"

She kept her binoculars to her eyes. "Of course not. What makes you think such a thing?"

"The way you took Melville's bet."

"Don't be silly. I took Melville's bet because I thought we should. If we lose, I'll pay the hundred thousand myself. I'll sell some jewels or take in laundry or something."

"Don't be so damn flip!"

She lowered the binoculars and looked at him.

"I did not go behind your back. I wouldn't do such a thing. When I couldn't talk you into it, that was the *end* of it."

"You sure as hell would do such a thing. You already have when you went off to see Melville that night without telling me. You've got an obsession about winning this race—"

She frowned. "Oh, go to hell."

Then, seeing the wife of the president of Goodrich sitting on the other side of Mark give her a curious look, she smiled sweetly and said aloud, "Isn't it an exciting race?"

The wife of the president of Goodrich smiled uncertainly, and Lily put the binoculars back up to her eyes to watch the cars as they raced down the backstretch.

Mark waited until the plump woman on his right was talking with her husband. Then he leaned back to Lily and whispered, "You have not heard the end of this."

She ignored him, jumping to her feet. "Oh, look! Roy's taken second place!"

The yellow Stutz had passed the green Bentley on the north curve and was now solidly in second position. The crowd cheered as Lily smiled down triumphantly at her husband.

He told himself not to say anything more until he got her back home at Palm Beach. There was going to be a showdown, if she had done it. Whether she had been right or wrong about Roger Boine, his decision had cost a lifetime of guilt. Now, if she added still another life to his conscience, no matter how much it wrenched him, he would be through with her.

He was haunted by enough ghosts.

On the nineteenth lap, Roy Diamond had managed to take the lead from Steve Raymond. This didn't bother Raymond too much, since his strategy was to let Diamond take the lead near the completion of the race so that he could take advantage of Diamond's slipstream at the last moment. However, it was too early to give the lead to him permanently. There was always the possibility that the Stutz could attain too big a lead, as well as the danger of tipping his hand to Diamond if he appeared too unaggressive. So on the twenty-third lap, Steve decided to try to take the lead back.

As they roared down the northbound straightaway, Steve hit 104 mph. and maneuvered himself directly behind Diamond into his slipstream. Diamond was hugging the inside of the track, but he would swing further out to take the curve. Then Steve figured he could cut inside him and slipstream himself into the lead. It was a tricky maneuver, but one Steve had done often enough before. As the landscape blurred past, he kept his eyes fixed on the car in front of him. Then, just as they hit the north curve, Steve delayed braking for the split second that would give him the edge. Diamond's car swung out as Steve cut to the inside. The Ford seemed to teeter as it hit the sharp curve without braking, and for a second the car verged on losing control and going into a spin. But Steve's reflexes were near perfect. He braked just in time and zoomed past Diamond. As the two cars finished the curve and started down the southbound straightaway toward the stands with the Ford back in the lead, the crowd went wild with excitement.

The man on the water tower had assembled his rifle. Now as he watched the cars going south and toward him through his binoculars, and saw that Raymond had taken the lead again, he decided he would do it on the next lap.

Roy Diamond was well aware of what Steve Raymond was up to, Steve's hopes of surprising him nothwithstanding. Diamond had slipstreamed in his career, but today his strategy was basically simple:

to take the lead away from Raymond and maintain it to the end, hopefully putting enough distance between the cars so that Raymond couldn't recapture the lead on the last lap. Thus, the moment Steve retook the lead, Roy began concentrating on overtaking him. As they came out of the south curve and started the northbound straightaway, Roy gunned his Stutz. The interval between them narrowed slightly, and Roy maneuvered himself into Steve's slipstream. What had been Diamond's disadvantage on the last lap was now Raymond's—the Ford was now the car breaking the air resistance, and Raymond would have to swing out on the north curve, at which time Diamond hoped to cut inside and overtake him. They approached the north curve and Roy tensed himself for the maneuver. As the lead car braked for the curve, Roy started to cut inside him. Suddenly he heard a loud "pop"! The wheel jerked in his hand and the car swerved violently to the right, aiming directly at Steve Raymond. Adrenalin surging through his body, Roy Diamond tried to control the car, realizing one of his front tires had blown. The Stutz cut behind the Ford, missing it literally by inches, and roared up the steeply banked curve. Roy tugged the wheel to the left, but it was useless. The car crashed through the guard rail at 100 mph. and sailed into the air. Roy Diamond had a momentary sensation of floating, and time seemed to stand still in these last few seconds of his life. The sunny sky above him was drenched in blue, and it was cool and beautiful. The sun was a golden effulgence. Then the car hit the ground, flipped end over end and burst into flames.

He was killed instantly.

The crowd saw the tiny, distant car sail over the embankment and moaned as it leapt to its feet. Then, as they saw the flash of fire and the cloud of oily smoke roiling up, they screamed. Lily and Mark were on their feet too, Mark mumbling, "Oh, my God . . ." Then the sirens of the ambulance and the fire truck.

It's the wrong one, she was thinking. The wrong car and the wrong curve . . .

"Let's get downstairs," snapped Mark, moving past his neighbors to the aisle. Lily followed him, dazed and furious. The idiots! Could they possibly have made that enormous a mistake? They couldn't. It was incredible. Unless she'd been doublecrossed?

"I'm afraid he doesn't have a chance," said Mark as they hurried down the concrete steps. "His wife . . . Jesus."

The damn fools! Unless . . . was it possible Diamond simply had had an accident? No, an impossible coincidence. Something had gone horribly wrong. They had shot *her* tire, not *his* . . . Oh, the goddamn idiots! The stupid guineas . . .

At the same time, she thought there was at least one consolation. Now Mark could hardly blame her for going to Big Johnnie Marucca behind his back. After all, she had done it for *him,* couldn't he understand that? No, he wouldn't. He was getting worse and worse—or better and better, if you wanted to look at it that way. So pompous, so smug and unwilling to fight! She was getting damn sick of it. . . .

"I hope," she said, almost running to keep up with him as they rushed down the steps, "that you're going to apologize to me?"

"For what?"

"What you were accusing me of a while ago. Trying to fix the race. Unless you think I was fixing it for Melville?"

"All right, I apologize. Except we're still out a hundred thousand dollars, and a driver, a human being, who undoubtedly is dead."

They reached the bottom of the steps and pushed through the crowd milling around the hot dog stands to try to find someone who could tell them if by some miracle Roy Diamond had survived the accident.

When the man on the water tower saw Diamond's car go over the embankment, he was as confused as Lily. His instructions had been to put Steve Raymond out of the race so Diamond could win. But now Diamond couldn't possibly win, so what was he supposed to? Shoot out Raymond's front tire as he approached the southern curve, causing his car to shoot over the south embankment the same way Diamond's had sailed over the north? But that made no sense. If Big Johnnie had money riding on Diamond, he had already lost. There was no point putting Steve Raymond out of the race now.

The man began to disassemble his rifle. He was a professional. He did what he was paid for. In this case, he never had a chance to perform his service.

Steve Raymond won the race, but Melville refused to accept payment of the hundred thousand dollars from Mark. The bet, he said, had been that his man would beat Mark's, which hadn't really happened. Mark's man had been killed, and Roy Diamond's tragic death automatically canceled the bet. Besides, Steve Raymond had seen the blowout. Everyone knew Diamond had been killed because the Manning tires had not stood up to the test of the race. In Lily's opinion, Melville's cup of victory was more than sufficiently filled without taking the money, but she felt they should have forced payment on him anyway.

"There was something awfully arrogant about his not taking the $100,000," she said as she and her husband were driven back to Palm Beach by Marvin Senjak dressed in his white, Florida uniform. "Oh, he made it sound so noble, talking about the tragedy and so forth, but he still won the race and we lost. He could *afford* to be noble."

Mark was staring out the window as they drove along the ocean.

"You know," he said, "a man died today because of our tires. Or don't you give a damn?"

"Of course I do."

"You don't sound like it."

"What am I supposed to do? I'm not happy he died, I'm not happy about the whole rotten day. *Everything* went wrong! But the last thing I needed was having Melville go into his saint's act. That was really pouring salt in the wound."

He said nothing for a while as the white Cadillac limousine sped up Route 1 toward Delray Beach. Then he said, "Our tire wasn't good enough. It blew out, and it killed Roy. It was our fault."

"Oh, Mark, it was lousy, rotten luck, that's what it was. It could just as easily have been Melville's tire, or the Dunlop or the Goodyear."

"But it was ours."

That was all he said. She looked over at Mark and her previous annoyance at him softened as she realized how crushed he looked. His giant company that he had built up from a two-bit bicycle shop somewhere back in the Dark Ages, his empire he had nursed and pushed and watched swell to world-wide proportions had suddenly been punctured like an innertube, and deflated—humiliated. The S-14 Manning-Flow racing tire had blown out and caused a famous driver's death while the whole world looked on. It was rotten luck, yes, but it was also, as he had said, the inescapable fact that the tire wasn't good enough. Lily had connived to eliminate Steve Raymond— for which she felt no guilt—but she hadn't counted on their own tire blowing out first. Now she began to see her mistake. The problem wasn't so much to defeat Melville; that had been giving in to her own emotions, her own desire to humiliate the man who had humiliated her that night in Sutterlee. The problem was that the Manning Company was growing old. More accurately, Mark was growing old. Softer? Mellower? More interested now in respectability than forcing his company to stay in the leader's spot. Yes, that was all part of it. He made moral sounds and was upset, but what would he *do* about it? He was getting old. Oh, he was only fifty-six, true, but he was tired and too rich really to care any more, in spite of his denials. He no longer had either the energy or the desire to do what was becoming apparent had to be done—take a scalpel to the whole company and eliminate the fat and the fatheads from the whole upper echelon. That would take someone young. Someone who didn't gave a damn what the world thought as long as the Manning Company stayed number one.

Someone like herself.

She reflected on her situation. Over the years, she had insinuated herself more and more into the running of the company, but she had always done it as the power behind the power, being forced to influence and at times manipulate her husband through tricks and indirect pressure. But maybe she had been wrong. Maybe what was necsessary was that she assume the power herself—directly. Why should she be kept out of the head office, the corridors of real power, merely *because* she was the wife of the chairman of the board? If she had the better ideas—and certainly the success of the current sex-oriented ad campaign, which had been her brainchild, proved her ideas were not to be sneered at—if she had the better ideas and the energy and the desire, why shouldn't she have the power too? Of course, she knew the answer. She was a woman, and the back rooms of corporate power were traditional male preserves. It was a man's world, and no one believed that more firmly than Mark. But if the men—man—were not up to the job? . . .

She stopped her train of thought with a jolt. It wouldn't work. There was no way she could make it work. What could she do? Talk Mark into firing Harrison Starr and making her president in his place? Ridiculous. He'd never do it. And yet it would take something as revolutionary as that to enable her to achieve anything permanent and real.

Or would it?

What *was* power, after all? She began to consider it, to analyze it at its most prosaic level. Well, for a start, it meant having a desk and an office. That sounded ridiculous, but after all, without some physical place for her to be, to *sit,* she could do nothing. Mark controlled the company—or *half*-controlled it, these days—by sitting in his big office behind his massive desk and saying 'yes' and 'no,' 'do this,' 'do that.'

And people obeyed him because he was chairman of the board and majority stockholder and everyone knew that his massive desk in his big office was the power center. Well, that seemed simple enough. But she was his wife, and, thereby, an extension of him. What if *she* had an office and a desk—say, next to his office? What if, when those mealy-mouthed vice-presidents came skulking into his office to receive the Word, what if she were there with him? Conferring with him privately, attending his mind as well as his body, perhaps eventually taking over more and more of the decisions . . . She already did that on a limited scale, the limits being imposed by her never being physically at the power center. But at least if she had an office . . .

He would react against it at first, maybe even violently.

But if she seriously went to work on him . . .

By the time Marvin Senjak had driven the white Cadillac limousine through the elaborate gates of Villa del Mar, Lily had come to the decision it was definitely worth a try.

Even more important, she decided it was necessary.

CHAPTER SEVEN

In the month following the death of Sacha Stavisky in the villa at Chamonix, Paris boiled with excitement as scandal piled on scandal, revelation on revelation, all of which was to culminate in the bloodiest riot the city had seen since the Commune of 1871. The right-wing papers were shrilly denouncing the Radical-Socialist Chautemps government as being enmeshed in a network of Stavisky-inspired swindles, but they began denouncing almost as shrilly Maurice de Sibour who, a few days after Stavisky's suicide (or murder, depending on which theory one preferred) had volunteered his services to one of the moderate Paris newspapers to investigate the case independently and write a series of articles on it.

Maurice's reputation as a mystery and crime writer of the first rank gave him an authority the reading public respected, as well as a ready-made audience of his fans. And the dozen articles he wrote throughout that January brilliantly justified his readers' faith as, through his private investigations as well as his connections among politicians and the police, he exposed a number of fascinating clues that led the public through the labyrinth of the Stavisky affair writing accounts of Stavisky's muscular bodyguard, the improbably named Jo-Jo-the-Gray-Haired-Boy, and putting the spotlight of attention on innumerable individuals connected with the case. Maurice's motives for writing the articles were not to attract attention to himself. Rather, realizing that the left was under fire from the right because of the Chautemps government's involvement with Stavisky, he decided that it was vital to get Chautemps out as fast as possible so that a new leftist government could replace him before the right wing could come into power either by public demand or, more ominously, a coup d'état.

The possibility of a coup was growing daily. The rightist press, led by *L'Action Française,* was appealing to Parisians to march on the chamber of deputies, and on the evening of January 9 a crowd of 2,000 tried to attack the Palais Bourbon and was beaten back by the police. On the night of the 11th, another attempt was made, led by the right wing *Jeunesses Patriotes* and the royalist *Camelots du Roi;* this time the mobile guard and the fire department stopped them, the latter using fire hoses, but not before the demonstrators had inflicted considerable property damage and thrown up barricades on the streets—an all-too-familiar sign to Parisians. Still, Premier Chautemps delayed doing anything constructive about Stavisky. The riots continued. Finally, after a particularly severe riot on the 27th, Chautemps, presumably at last convinced the public meant business, resigned.

Throughout this time, Maurice's articles had been bringing added fire on Chautemps. But he had also aimed his literary guns at the right-wing prefect of police, Jean Chiappe, claiming Chiappe had also been involved with Stavisky. For this, Maurice, already detested by the right for his activities in the 1932 election, now earned their renewed hatred, even though he was as anti-Chautemps as they—if for other reasons. When the rightist press paused in its campaign against the government to catch its breath, it took up its cudgels to attack Maurice, calling him a literary hack, a turncoat, a bad reporter and, in one instance, a "tool of the Jews," reminding the public that his wife was "a rich American Jewess." It was not a time of either restraint or humanity.

On the resignation of Chautemps, the president of the republic appointed a new premier, another Radical-Socialist who was "clean" as far as the Stavisky scandal was concerned, a man named Édouard Daladier. Daladier then proceeded to take action, action that made questionable sense to many observers. Rather than firing the prefect of police, Chiappe, and the director of the Sûreté, Thomé, both of whom he and the public were now convinced had, at the very least, handled the Stavisky case badly, he promoted them upstairs, making Chiappe the resident-general in Morocco, and Thomé, astonishingly (or perhaps appropriately), the director of the Comédie Française. The latter promotion caused literate Paris to gasp—a policeman running the House of Molière? The former promotion provoked a new scandal, because the right wing promptly made Chiappe a martyr, claiming he had been fired to save face for the left. New calls were issued in the rightist press for the people to stage a massive demonstration against the government. Reports circulated that the government was bringing in black Senegalese troops with tanks and machine guns to "control" the populace, and this touched off *all* the newspapers, right, left, and center, who began publishing the cries of all factions to take to the streets. On the morning of February 6, the confusion was made complete when *L'Humanité*, the Communist daily, urged all Party members to take part in the demonstration planned for that night. And with the extreme left now joining the extreme right to bring about the downfall of the bourgeois government, Maurice also became alarmed. For though he detested the far right and had worked to prevent it carrying out a coup, he was, despite the attacks against him, far from being a Communist, and the threat of a far-left coup was equally as odious to him. He wanted *no* coup. He wanted reasonable reform and solid government.

It was too late for moderation. On the afternoon of the sixth, all the various elements and political or parapolitical leagues in the city began to converge on the Place de la Concorde, the elegant square confronting the chamber of deputies on the opposite side of the Seine, and by early evening several thousand demonstrators, many of them wielding razors strapped to sticks, were fighting with the mobile guard. Meanwhile, across the river, inside the chamber itself, the deputies were in session to ratify the new Daladier ministry, though the left and the right were causing pandemonium with cries of "Resign!" and repeated choruses of the "Marseillaise" and the "Internationale," all of which was making parliamentary procedure impossible. At around six thirty in the evening, the rioters, who were slashing at the legs of the horses of the mobile guard with their razors and beating those guards whose horses they brought down, were repulsed by a volley of shots; the shots were returned, and the melée was on in earnest. Into this fracas a new and explosive element was added when thousands of war veterans belonging to the powerful rightist and highly organized *Croix de Feu* flooded into the Place, while others marched down the Rue St. Honoré to attack the presidential Élysée Palace. Though the attack on the Élysée was thrown back, it soon became evident that the rioters had a better than even chance of storming the chamber of deputies, driving the politicians out (or, perhaps, even hanging them) and setting up a new government. The fighting was growing bloody and threatening to turn into a massacre. Finally, near midnight, Colonel Simon, the commander of the first legion of the gendarmerie, took charge of the situation, ordered up as many reinforcements as he could command, then led a charge on the Place. Quickly, and rather to everyone's amazement, he cleared the huge square of its thousands of demonstrators and the riot collapsed. The government was saved, though the deputies had long since decamped from their threatened building. The cost was high: out of some 40,000 rioters involved, sixteen were killed and six hundred fifty-five were injured. The police and guards suffered one death and over 1,600 injured.

More importantly, the faith of the French in their government and in the Third Republic itself was dealt a blow from which it was never to recover. (When six years later the Third Republic fell before the advancing Nazis, there were to be many Frenchmen who, though anguished by the way it had fallen, were nevertheless not heartbroken to see it go.)

Four mornings after the riot, the de Sibour butler answered the door of the Avenue Kléber apartment to find a young man in a familiar dark-gray suit and a herringbone overcoat standing outside. He asked, in bad French, if he could see Madame de Sibour, and the butler rather uncertainly admitted Leonard Hastings into the apartment, then went to the drawing room to inform his mistress of the presence of the young American. Charlotte was inspecting a new dress Ellen had bought for herself the previous afternoon at the Galeries Lafayette, which she was modeling for her mother. When the butler told them Len was outside, Ellen looked shocked.

"He wouldn't have the *nerve* to come here!"

Charlotte motioned to her to lower her voice. "Obviously, he does," she said, then, to the butler, "Show him in."

"No!"

"Ellen, don't act like a child. If you don't want to see him, then go upstairs. The young man's asked to see me, and I'm certainly not going to hide from him. Show him in," she repeated to the butler, who this time nodded and left the room. Ellen looked undecided for a moment. Then she sat down in the chair next to her mother, her face stone.

"Well, *I'm* certainly not going to hide from him either. In fact, I'll be glad to tell him what I think of him."

"Let him do the talking," cautioned her mother.

Just then the door to the room was reopened and Len came in. He had removed his overcoat, and now a sling was visible in which his right arm was resting. He closed the door, then looked at Charlotte and Ellen, who were sitting in front of the fireplace across the room. He walked slowly over to them. As Ellen watched him, she thought his face had an expression on it she had never seen before, an intense seriousness that certainly was new to him. He stopped in front of Charlotte, glanced at Ellen, then looked back into Charlotte's eyes.

"I've come to . . ." he began, then started over again. "I want to try to apologize for my behavior that night. I didn't remember too much the next morning, but I remembered enough. I've never been so ashamed of anything in my life. I don't expect you to excuse what I said. I . . . I loved this family, and I hurt it. I've hated myself since that night."

He had spoken with quiet conviction. Now Charlotte reached out and took his left hand. She smiled as she said warmly, "That took a good deal of courage, Leonard. Frankly, more than I expected you had. Of course, we accept your apology." A pleased look came over his face, and he started to say something when Ellen cut him off.

"I don't see what's so 'brave' about it. After all, it's been a month. And I don't see why we should accept his apology, either. He showed us what he really is that night, and I think it's detestable."

Len and Charlotte both looked at her.

"Well, let's say that *I* accept his apology, then," said Charlotte. "I think if Leonard had truly meant what he said that night, he wouldn't have come back to apologize, even after a month."

"Oh? You mean you can turn anti-Semitism on and off?" Ellen said bitterly. "Herr Hitler would be delighted to hear that, I'm sure."

"You can't turn it on and off," replied Len quietly, "but people can think. And they can learn. I've done a lot of thinking this past month—about myself and my life. And I've been reading the papers, what they've been saying about your stepfather. And you," he added to Charlotte. "And I've realized not only how ugly it is, but how stupid. Anyway, I've quit the job at the bank and I'm sailing for the States tomorrow. And before I left, I wanted to try and make up for a little of what I did."

"What happened to your arm?" Charlotte asked, releasing his hand as she indicated the sling.

"Oh, that. I was at the Concorde the other night, watching the riot. I wasn't doing any of the fighting, just watching. But I got a bullet in my elbow. It wasn't anything very serious but it sort of helped me . . . you know . . . *feel* the ugliness."

"Oh," said Ellen, getting out of her chair, "now he's a war hero as well as reformed bigot!"

"Ellen! You're behaving worse than Len did—"

"Worse? Have you forgotten what he said? He was in love with me! Until he found out I was Jewish, that is. Then suddenly he doesn't love me anymore! I'm dirt. And now he comes crawling back all filled with revelation and remorse, expecting us to tell him he's forgiven so he won't have a guilty conscience!"

"Ellen, I don't blame you for saying that," Len said. "I guess I was an anti-Semite. I never really thought about it that much. Fact is, I never really thought about anything that much, I guess, except skiing and you. But you're wrong about one thing. I didn't stop loving you that night. I was surprised and I was drunk and I, well, the worst of me came out. I'd like to think that now that it's out of me it's gone for good. I don't know, maybe I'm fooling myself. Anyway, the ironic thing is that now that I know you hate the sight of me, I love you more than ever."

She blushed slightly and said nothing. Then he nodded to both of them and said, "Well, good-bye." He paused, then added, "And thank you for seeing me again."

He took a last look at Ellen, then turned and started across the room toward the door. She started to say something, then changed her mind. She watched as he opened the door and went out, closing it behind him.

Her mother turned to her. "He meant it, you know."

"Well, what if he did? What am I supposed to do? Run after him and kiss him and tell him all is forgiven, Len darling, and I still love you?"

"Well? Do you?"

She hesitated. "Of course not," she finally said. "You can't love someone after you've been hurt like that. Love has to be based on respect."

Her mother picked up the *Herald*.

"I respect him for what he did. It's easy to make a fool of yourself, but it's very hard to apologize for it later. And as far as love is concerned, respect is part of it, of course. But I've never understood why people fall in love with each other, and I seriously doubt if you do either. All I know is, it's a rare item in this world and it seems to be getting rarer every day. So I wouldn't be quite so cavalier about it, if I were you."

She opened the paper and began reading as her daughter looked at the closed door.

That evening, as Len was packing his battered suitcase—a job not facilitated by his having only one hand to use—he heard a knock on the door of his coachhouse apartment. He went over and opened the door to see Ellen standing outside.

"Hello," she said, her breath frosting in the cold night air.

"Hello."

"May I come in?"

"Sure."

He held the door for her as she came in, took off her camel's hair coat, then went over to the fire to warm herself. She felt awkward and was searching for a way to say what she wanted. Len said nothing, not being much of a help. Finally, as he returned to his packing, she said, "What made you decide to quit the bank?"

"I was bored. I don't know, I just don't like banking. And I miss New York. So I'm going home and scrounge around for a job."

"Jobs are sort of hard to find now, aren't they?"

"I'll find something."

They said nothing for a while as he continued sticking things in the suitcase. Then she came over to the cot and said, "You're an awful packer. Let me do it."

She began rearranging the underwear and shirts he had shoved in the suitcase. Len sat down in one of the club chairs. Eventually she hit on a way to say what she wanted.

"Mother thinks I was rude to you this morning." He didn't say anything. "She was very impressed that you came to apologize."

"I was impressed too. Frankly, I was damned scared."

She gazed with amazement at his toothbrush, which she found inside a dirty sneaker, and took it out of the shoe to repack it in a more antiseptic side pouch of the bag. "Mother says love's in pretty short supply these days, and that I shouldn't have treated you so cavalierly, as she put it."

"I think your mother's a very wise woman."

She finished rearranging the contents of the bag, closed the scruffy lid and clamped it shut. Then she sat down on the cot and looked over at Len.

"Did you really mean it?" she said softly. "That you still love me?"

"Yes."

"Oh, Len, I'm so sorry it happened. I'm sorry about what you said, and I'm sorry that I was so nasty this morning. Do you really think we can start all over again?"

"No."

"What do you mean, 'no'?" she exclaimed, surprised.

"I mean I don't want to start all over again. I want to marry you, and I'd hate like hell to have to propose again. Proposing's a big bore."

She laughed. "Romantic as ever! Well, I insist you propose again. And as I remember, I did most of the proposing last time anyway. So come over here and get on your knees."

He obeyed.

"Ellen, you are very very lovely and much above me, a poor, humble character addicted to sloth and idleness. Still, when I'm close to you, I forget my basic worthlessness and am overwhelmed with the most embarrassing desires—"

"You nut!" She giggled.

"Shut up, I'm proposing. I get all sorts of embarrassing ideas, and, in sooth, I think I am desperately in love with you. Dare I hope my sentiment might be returned?"

"Yes, it *is* returned," she said, reaching out to take his hand. "And yes, I would be honored to be your wife."

"I didn't get to that part yet."

"It doesn't matter."

He got to his feet and brought her hand up to his lips. He kissed it, as well as each finger. Then he said, quite seriously, "And I'll be honored to be your husband."

There were tears in her eyes, but she had never felt happier in her life.

PART

IX

SCORPIO ASCENDANT

1937

CHAPTER ONE

$\mathbf{L}$ILY MANNING'S campaign to insinuate herself into the corridors of power had been remarkably unsuccessful. She had worked on her husband for almost a year, trying everything from gentle hints to outright pleading, but Mark had remained adamant. Lily could not have an office in the company, and no, Lily could not help run the damned business. He appreciated her interest, he wanted to hear her suggestions and ideas, he admitted she was often right; but it was his business, he had been perfectly capable of running it for over thirty years and he was perfectly capable of running it now.

Finally Lily give up trying. She recognized that she had discounted Mark too soon. In fact, the blow to the prestige of the Manning Company dealt by the tragedy at Boca Raton seemed to have galvanized Mark out of his cocoon of guilt and lethargy. Infuriated by the defeat, he fired the heads of both the competition and research divisions of the company, hiring a brilliant chemist named Paul Depew to head the research division, telling him to find out what was wrong with the S-14 and to fix it. Depew instead went to work on the Dynaride and finally broke Melville's secret. Oils and waxes were regularly combined with rubber as softeners. But Melville had developed a special oil that paradoxically, toughened the rubber. With this knowledge, and with new improvements devised by Depew, the Manning-Flow tire was enormously strengthened and rechristened the Manning Hercules Super-tire, it was relaunched on the market with a brand-new ad campaign.While Lily's nude was dropped from the ads, her notion of appealing to the American male's hunt for *machismo* was retained, and the Hercules Super-tire was pitched to the Manning Man, a rugged Mr. Super All-American, who preferred the Super-tire. It worked and the Hercules began to regain the percentage of the market the Manning-Flow had lost to the Dynaride. A further blow to Melville was a decision by the Federal Trade Com-

mission against selling tires through mail-order houses and which had
been giving their customers price reductions. Deprived of the facilities
of the C.W. Grayson Company, Melville's company lost a great advantage.

As the country slowly dragged itself out of the worst depression
in its history, Mark's own self-confidence and vigor seemed to feed
on the psychology of recovery. He proceeded to expand the company,
adding more than a hundred new franchise stores a year and building
six new plants. The products the company now made and sold were
so numerous, even Mark couldn't keep track of them; it made over
five hundred separate rubber articles for cars alone. To further di-
versify, in 1936 the Manning Company bought out a fledgling plastics
factory in Massachusetts and plunged into the new and exciting
plastics industry. During the early Thirties tractors and other farm
implements had begun to use rubber tires on a wide scale, and this
along with the huge expansion of the airlines industry added lucrative
new markets to the business. By 1936, although hard times still had
not vanished from the American scene, the Manning Company was
operating at more than 90 percent of capacity, and its profits for the
year amounted to a whopping $20,000,000. "The old man's not licked
yet," Mark crowed to his wife the night the profit figures were announced to the euphoric stockholders. And Lily had to admit that
perhaps she had buried him too soon.

She had other problems. Thanks to the growth of the company and
its increasing complexity, Mark had decided his sons could no longer
afford not to come into the corporation. Consequently, David Manning, who had taken his law degree and gone to work for a prestigious
Wall Street firm, was pressured by his father into working for him,
which in 1935 he had grudgingly agreed to. David had married
an attractive Park Avenue debutante named Amanda Shaw, and
David and Amanda moved to Elkins, building and moving into a
handsome home on the grounds of River Bend, where they promptly
began producing babies. David was made a vice-president in charge
of legal affairs. Lily disliked him intensely, considering him dull, pro-
Roosevelt and rather effeminate despite his spectacular ability to
spawn children. She also thought his wife was a snot. David and
Amanda heartily returned her dislike.

Richard Manning, who had enjoyed a short-lived career as a playboy in the fleshpots of Manhattan, was given an ultimatum by his
father in 1935. Either settle down and go to work or be disinherited.
Richard was twenty-three and a year out of college. Richard took the
long view, promptly removed to Elkins and went to work in the

steel plant, spending six months working in the factory itself, then going into a junior managerial position. He married Cynthia Fahnstock, a Chicago tractor heiress, built a house on the grounds of River Bend near David's, and, again like David, began to produce babies. Lily thought him handsome and stupid, and when it came to the brains department considered his wife, who was horsey and bucktoothed, on a level with the horses she so dearly loved. Richard and Cynthia returned her dislike. The River Bend estate, which was rapidly becoming a Manning family housing development, was also becoming a hotbed of intrafamily feuding.

Then there were Ellen and Len Hastings. To Ellen's surprise and Lily's horror, Mark took an immediate liking to the young and winning Mr. Hastings, amazing him with a wedding present of $100,000 —on the proviso he come to work for his new father-in-law. At least Len's job-hunting problems were resolved in spectacular fashion, and after a three-week honeymoon in Hawaii, in May 1934, Len and Ellen moved to Elkins, where they built a large house on the River Bend estate and they soon began producing heirs. Len went to work for six months in the curing pits, where he earned the respect of everyone; he was then brought into the sales department where, to Mark's delight, he proved to be full of ideas and an aggressive promoter.

Lily felt awash with Mannings.

And last, but hardly least, there was Mark's favorite, Christopher. He had been graduated by Princeton in 1934 and promptly went to work in the company, having all along expressed his desire and intent to work for his father. Christopher was strikingly handsome, still full of the devil, bright . . . and Lily detested him. He also detested Lily. Since Christopher was unmarried—though the rumors in Elkins were that he was "laying" every female in northern Ohio— he lived *in* River Bend itself, much to Lily's displeasure. The house was so huge and Christopher was home so infrequently that they confronted each other physically hardly at all. But when they did, they were barely civil to one another, and when Christopher was with his siblings, he referred to his attractive stepmother as Bitch Momma, a term of endearment that, when Lily heard about it from her maid, Vera, sent her right through the ceiling. She ranted for a full half hour at Mark, working off her spleen about all his children and their goddamn wives and demanding that he either make Chris respect her or—preferably—kick him out of the house. That night Mark talked to his son. Christopher promised to behave. He didn't. He continued to refer to Lily as Bitch Momma and when he was with her he replaced his thin civility with a contemptuous sort of Mother *dear*. She wanted to stick a knife through him.

All in all, life for Lily had definitely switched from being a bed of roses to a nightmare of Mannings. Far from taking over, as she had dreamed of a few years earlier, she now found herself in the position of being a sort of den mother for an estate full of step-children, all of whom she disliked and who disliked her, and all of whom—even worse—were gradually moving up the corporate ladder, while Lily's candidate, Evan, was only just entering the second grade. Furthermore, her husband, having apparently recharged his batteries, was running his empire with all the gusto of a thirty-year-old. By the end of 1936 and at age forty-two, Lily's future prospects for anything more challenging than a mother image for one of the nation's wealthiest industrial dynasties seemed gloomy indeed.

However, on New Year's Eve of 1936, her prospects took a remarkable turn for the better. That night, Mark held an open house for the family prior to his and Lily's departure for Palm Beach the next day. The entire clan gathered at River Bend in their evening clothes, and they made a handsome tableau indeed. The three Manning sons were striking in their white ties and tails, although David, the oldest, was too thin and had a rather owlish look that was accentuated by his thick horn-rimmed glasses—Lily referred to nearsighted David as Four Eyes. David's wife, Amanda, had a china-doll prettiness that was set off by a natural taste in clothes; even Lily admitted she dressed well. Cynthia Manning, Richard's wife, was definitely plain and had no taste in clothes at all. She was wearing a white evening dress with puffed sleeves that Lily considered more appropriate for a seedy fraternity dance. Ellen and Len looked blooming, Ellen being three months into her second pregnancy, and Christopher was dating a smashing-looking brunette from Cleveland named Rita Tweed, who was a born centerpiece. Nobody could overlook her, including Mark, which didn't endear Miss Tweed to Lily.

A big dinner was served, much champagne was poured by the efficient River Bend staff, everyone got high and went to the ballroom to dance to the combo Mark had imported from Akron, and Christopher and Miss Rita Tweed proceeded to show off by doing an energetic Big Apple. At eleven Mark took Lily aside and asked her to come to the library; he had something he wanted to talk to her about. When they were alone, he sat down behind his desk and told her to take a chair opposite him.

"This sounds like a business meeting," she said, taking the seat.

"It is, in a way. It's also my New Year's present to you."

Lily beamed. "Oh, darling, how nice. What is it?" A thought occurred to her: Christopher's getting married and moving out.

"Lily, what I want to talk to you about is my stock in the company." She was instantly attentive. "As you know, in the past few years I've transferred the majority of my bond holdings into municipals to cut down my tax load. This was recommended by my personal lawyer, Ben Dwyer, and I think it was a smart move. However, I'm still paying huge damn taxes on my Manning stock, and Ben has recommended that I get rid of it."

"Sell it?" exclaimed Lily, alarmed. "But darling, you can't do that!"

"No, no, not sell it. Transfer it into trusts for the children. I don't need the income—the income kicks my salary into such a high tax bracket it's more liability than asset. So Ben is setting up separate trusts for each of the five children, and the stock will be divided equally among them. However, I will still vote the stock, so nothing will be changed about running the company. Which brings me to you." He paused while she lighted a cigarette.

"I'm listening," she said, exhaling.

"I'd say, on the whole, our marriage has been a pretty successful one. You've done some things I haven't approved of, but then I've done things in the past that I haven't approved of either, so I'm not playing judge. And I'll say one thing about you, Lily—you're loyal. Maybe not so much loyal to me personally as loyal to the Company. You love it. Am I right?"

She looked at him. "Yes, I love it."

"Even more than you love me? Oh, don't worry, I won't take offense. Charlotte accused *me* of the same thing."

"You *are* the Manning Company, darling."

He smiled. "That's a nice diplomatic answer. All right, let's put our cards on the table. You've been after me for a say in running the company—oh, you've stopped lately, but I know you still want it. Well, I've kept you out of the company because I suppose I'm old-fashioned. I don't like the idea of women in business. That's not saying I don't think you've got the brains for it. You've got a damned sharp mind, Lily. If you'd been a man, you'd have been a big success in business."

"Well, thank you . . ."

"I also know you want Evan to take over the company some day. I suppose that's natural—he's your son and only child. And the other children are—well, I'll just say that I know what you think of them and what they think of you. It's unfortunate that this has happened, but it's not surprising. As for my preference, you know I've always had my eye on Christopher. In my opinion he's got the drive and energy and ambition needed to run a company like this. But it's still too early to say which one of them will turn out the best, and the one thing I'm really afraid of is that they may start fighting among themselves. They haven't started yet—at least not that I've noticed—but human nature being what it is and the stakes being as high as they are, one has to assume the worst, wouldn't you agree?"

"Definitely."

"I thought you would." He paused. "Now, no one likes to think about his own death, but I'll be fifty-nine this year and even though I'm still in good health, thank God, I have a responsibility to make arrangements for the future. So I want you to know what's in my will. It's pretty simple. If at my death you're still my wife—and I hope you will be—you'll inherit this house and the one in Palm Beach, plus all the furniture. You'll also receive $35,000,000 outright in bonds. The income from that ought to keep you off relief."

She took a deep breath.

"Yes, I think it should. Thank you, darling, but let's not talk about—"

He waved his hand. "Don't thank me, you deserve it. Now, the art collection, which Barjoonian figures is worth about $40,000,000, I'm giving to the public, either to one of the big museums, or maybe I'll build a museum of my own. I haven't decided on that yet. The rest of the estate will go equally to the children, although I'm giving about $10,000,000 to various charities and universities that I've supported in the past. You agree so far?"

"Of course."

"All right, this brings us back to the Manning stock. Now, if I die, the voting power will revert to a board of trustees, one of which is you, another Ben Dwyer, and the third the president of the company, whoever he is at the time of my death. The board will vote the stock for each of the children until each is thirty-five years old, at which point he, or she—in the case of Ellen—gets the voting power himself. By the time they're thirty-five, I figure they'll have fought out between themselves who's most capable of running the show. Maybe they won't, but I can't think of a better way of doing it. In the case of Evan, who's so much younger than the others, I've made an exception. He'll be able to vote his stock when he's twenty-one, and until that time you can vote it for him. You follow me so far?"

"Yes."

"All right. Now the other possibility—and this, I *hope*, is remote but we have to consider it—is that I don't die but become what the lawyers when they want to spare your feelings call incapacitated. I might have a stroke or lose my marbles or God knows what. Anyway, if that happens—if I'm incapable of making decisions—we've set it up that you will exercise my voting powers in the stock until I'm either back on my feet or in my grave. I do trust your loyalty and your business judgment. I also don't want the voting power—which means control of the company—out of my hands until I die. And I believe your hands, as much as anybody's, would be my hands."

"*That's* the best compliment you've ever paid me. You're right too."

"I hope so, Lily. Another reason I want you to have the power is that I don't want the children to have it while I'm still alive. Once again, I'm afraid they'd be at each other's throats, which could be a disaster. I don't need to tell you that this way they'd all be at *your* throat, but I think that better than having them fighting each other. Frankly, at this stage of the game at least, I think your judgment is better than theirs."

"Not to sound immodest, but I happen to agree."

He smiled and stood up. "Well, that's your New Year's present. It's not much of a present for *me*, but what the hell—I may outlive all of you."

She laughed as she came around the desk to kiss him. "I hope you do, darling. And *happy* 1937! The happy, happiest New Year of your whole life!"

"Have I made yours happy?"

"Well, I don't like all this gloomy talk of death, but I admit for the first time in my life I feel really rich! Thirty-five million dollars! How much is that a year? I'm terrible at numbers."

"No, you're not. And it's about a million, tax free."

"Mmmm. I'd be a very rich widow. I'll bet every gigolo in America would be chasing me."

"That's my Lily. Well, when they catch up with you, maybe at least every once in a while you'll take time out to think of me."

"Oh, Mark," she said softly, "I'd *never* forget you. *Never.*"

He looked at her. "Shall we go back and join the party?"

When they returned to the ballroom, Lily felt rhapsodic. Richard Manning and Len Hastings did not. They had gotten drunk and picked a fight about, of all things, who was the sexier woman, Marlene Dietrich in *Desire* or Jeanette MacDonald in *San Francisco,* Len hotly maintaining that anyone who thought Jeanette MacDonald was sexy had to be either crazy or blind. Mark calmed them down and ordered the musicians to play a waltz, as it was getting close to midnight. They swung into "Falling in Love with Love" and Mark led Lily out onto the floor, where he began a graceful waltz. His numerous children and in-laws watched from the sidelines as the still impressively handsome founder of the clan twirled around the floor with his stunning, younger wife, whom they all hated.

"She *is* beautiful," whispered Ellen to her sister-in-law Amanda.

"Yes, damn her," replied Amanda. "But give her five years and her figure will go literally to pot. That type always ages fast."

"Wishful thinking?"

"Maybe."

Lily's figure looked to be in good shape now, however, her white-satin gown showing it off to advantage. With the diamond-and-ruby earrings dangling from her ear lobes and the grand total of six thick diamond bracelets dangling from both wrists, she looked formidable and she knew it. As she waltzed around the floor with Mark, she felt on top of the world.

It was then that she noticed that Christopher and the fetching Miss Tweed had vanished.

They were in Christopher's bedroom on the other side of the house from the ballroom, and he was wrestling with her on top of his bed, trying to get her to take her clothes off.

"Chris, everyone will notice we're gone!" she said as she struggled to keep his hands off the zipper on the right side of her evening gown.

"So what?" he said, finally forcing the zipper down.

"So, I don't want your parents to think I'm a tramp!"

"Oh, cut it, will you? Come *on.*"

He pulled her shoulder straps down and tried to fold the top of the dress open. "How the hell do you get this thing off?"

"Oh, I'll do it."

She shoved him away and got off the bed, stepping out of the dress as he started taking off his pants. He was high but not drunk, and his face was flushed. He kicked off his patent-leather pumps and dropped his pants, then his shorts, though he kept on his starched shirt and white tie—too difficult to take the studs and cufflinks out and then put them back in again. Rita looked at him and giggled.

"You look funny."

"You don't."

He grabbed her hand and pulled her back down on the bed, kissing her hungrily as his hands fumbled with her bra. She put up little resistance. When he got the bra off, he tugged her panties down her round smooth hips and thighs and put his hand on her vagina, rubbing the pubic hair softly. She began to moan. He kissed her firm breasts for a while, then maneuvered himself on top of her and entered her. She let out a little gasp as he began thrusting himself, slowly at first, then with increasing fierceness. They were tonguing each other as she hungrily responded to him. They were at the moment of climax when the door opened.

Lily looked at them. "You *pig.*"

Christopher squeezed his eyes shut in anger and frustration.

"Get *out!*" he yelled, not looking around, recognizing Lily's harsh voice. Rita was panicking. She tried to shove Christopher off and out of her, staring with horror at Lily.

"No!"

"*Please!*"

"No. To hell with her—"

Lily came over to the bed. "How *dare* you do this to your father and me?" she said. "Do you think this house is a brothel?"

Christopher pulled himself out and sat up, covering himself with a pillow as Rita frantically hunched down under the bedspread.

"Yes, it *is* a brothel. Any house with you in it is a whorehouse."

She slapped him as hard as she could. He winced and put his hand to his cheek where one of the diamonds of her bracelet had cut him. He felt blood.

"Get dressed and get downstairs," she ordered. "Both of you. I won't say anything to your father because I don't want to ruin his New Year's Eve. But *you*"—She turned to Rita—"had better be out of here tomorrow morning before breakfast. And you?"—She turned to Christopher—"I don't care what you do away from River Bend. But when you're in my house, you'll behave like a gentleman."

"*Your* house? What happened to my father? And I happen to live here too."

She looked at him coldly. "Only as long as I let you."

Christopher grinned and stood up, tossing the pillow on the bed. Naked from the waist down, he walked over to Lily and tried to grab one of her wrists. Blood was still trickling down his cheek. "Hey, mother dear," he whispered. "How would you like to tumble with me? Huh? For a long time I've had a feeling that's what you'd really like to do, you know? So why not now? Rita wouldn't mind."

Lily glanced contemptuously at his midsection as she jerked her wrist free from his hand.

"You don't interest me," she said. "I already have the only Manning I want."

With a final look at the terrified Rita, she turned and walked out of the room.

CHAPTER TWO

In the middle of the following July, a heat wave settled over Ohio that seemed determined not to move. Day after sweltering day the temperature soared into the upper nineties and hundreds. The humidity drenched the air, and the citizens of Elkins sought relief by day in either the big municipal pool that Mark had built for the town in 1931 or the Matahoochi River, while during the steamy nights they tried to find sleep in their yards or front porches or, failing that, to drink enough beer or whiskey to besot their brains into slumber. The giant Manning factories, their huge chimneys spewing out smoke and the rubber stench that now became almost unbearable, were, despite their ventilating systems, almost impossible to work in. Management extended the lunch break an extra hour and provided salt tablets for the work force, but the sweat-drenched men considered this little more than a token gesture and grumbling swelled to major proportions. Still, work continued, as everyone watched the sky for a break in the weather and prayed for rain.

The town, which now boasted a population of almost 70,000, differed slightly from a thousand other industrial towns of the day. The classic limestone courthouse that had been built in 1912 was still considered the heart of the downtown section. The square that had been cleared when the courthouse was put up would never have won an award for architectural beauty, but it was pleasant enough, its elm trees providing shade for the cars parked along the curbs in front of the new parking meters that had been installed the year before, despite the howls of protest from the car owners. Gates's Department Store was holding a summer white sale, and two shops to the west, the Bon Ton Shoppe was pushing the latest California swimwear, hoping to cash in on the heat. On the corner, the Palace was featuring *Camille* and the manager wasn't sure whether it was Garbo, the escape inherent in the nineteenth-century Parisian setting of the story, or the fact that his theater was the coolest place in town that was drawing such crowds. The State Theater, too, was packing them in with a double feature consisting of *Dracula's Daughter* and a Johnny Mack Brown Western, along with chapter six of the popular Flash Gordon serial. Bank Night each Friday helped business too, though the manager wasn't too happy about his next feature, a rerelease of *Morocco*. Somehow, the Sahara wasn't such a good idea for a heat wave. The big Walgreen drug store was doing a booming business in ice-cream sodas, Woolworth's was selling electric fans in record numbers, and the Elkins Hotel on the east side of the square was featuring and doing record business with chicken salad for its businessmen's lunch, even though the businessmen usually preferred hot lunches.

A few of the more prosperous housewives had bought washing machines on "time," but the vast majority still did their laundry by hand and, with their families sweating through piles of shirts and underwear, they had their work cut out for them. Most of them owned refrigerators, though, so there was plenty of ice for iced tea, and almost all of them owned radios, so that in the humid afternoons they could escape their problems in the churning world of Mary Noble, Backstage Wife or Ma Perkins. At seven every evening during the week, an astonishing percentage of these radios would be tuned to the NBC Red Network to hear the latest adventure of Lightin' and Kingfish on "Amos 'n' Andy"; in Jackson Park, the Negro section, "Amos 'n' Andy" was also a must, the blacks ignoring—or unaware of—the fact that Amos and Andy were played by two whites (and that future, more-educated generations of blacks would consider the show a tasteless ethnic slur. The people in Jackson Park lived an ethnic slur).

After "Amos 'n' Andy," you could catch up with Father Barbour on "One Man's Family"—Wednesday at 8:00—or tune in "Fibber McGee and Molly" or George Burns and Gracie Allan. Jack Benny, of course, on Sundays; also on Sunday night, you could take in the Manning Symphony Orchestra on CBS, but that show didn't do well in Elkins. (Mark could never figure out whether it was that his fellow citizens had enough of the Mannings the rest of the week without hearing his radio program, or whether they didn't like classical music. Probably some of both.)

When the radio was off, talk during that July heat wave centered on the weather, of course; gossip, as always; and, much more frighteningly, the rumors of a savage outbreak of polio in Cleveland and elsewhere. Mothers and fathers shuddered at the mention of polio, which had the scare potential of the Black Death in the fourteenth century. Every summer there were a few cases; periodically there was an epidemic, and the memory was still vivid of the horrible summer of 1933 when, along with all the other problems of that miserable year, polio had swept through Elkins leaving in its wake nineteen deaths and two hundred permanently crippled children. When people mentioned the polio cases in Cleveland, they instinctively lowered their voices as if fearing that God, or the wind, or the fates, or whatever directed the course of the killer might overhear them and decide Elkins was the next place on its itinerary.

Otherwise, talk was of the heat, always the heat, the terrible Ohio midsummer heat that helped the corn but smothered the people. The heat and, of course, rumors of what was going on at the Manning factories. For everyone was aware that the CIO had sent one of its toughest organizers to Elkins to take on the Manning Company in a final do-or-die struggle to unionize the giant corporation, the "invisible empire," as one union spokesman had referred to it; no one quite understood what the phrase meant, but it had a catchy sound to it and seemed appropriately sinister. People sat around sipping their beer, ice tea or RC Cola and wondered lazily whether "Old Man Manning" would give in or fight. A lot of people were saying "Mr. David" Manning, the Harvard pinko (some said "fairy"), was urging his father to give in to the inevitable and accept the union. Others were saying "*that* woman," "the slut" or "Mrs. Manning" was ready to shoot "Mr. David" and had vowed she would blow the factories up before she'd allow the company to "go union." Everyone chuckled or smirked when they mentioned "Mr. Christopher." The whole town knew—or liked to think—he was too busy chasing girls to care whether the company unionized or not; for that reason, as well as the fact that "Mr. Christopher" was winningly informal and impossible not to like, the town had a soft spot in its heart for the youngest Manning son—the youngest, that is, of the *first* crop, the children of the "nice" Mrs. Manning. The rumor was that the *second* crop, Evan, was a spoiled monster.

At any rate, the Mannings, the family that had dominated the town for as long as anyone liked to remember, whether they were hated or loved, resented or respected, if nothing else gave the town a constant source of gossip. Even those Elkinsians who privately hated the clan admitted that if they ever packed up and moved out they'd probably be sorely missed. Not that anyone thought they would move out, even if they were forced into letting the CIO unionize the workers. They'd still be there in their beautiful homes, driving their beautiful cars, leading their beautiful, exciting lives, living almost like gods. No one thought the unions could ever change that. But forcing the unionization on them would bend their pride a little, and many Elkinsians cherished that thought. If nothing else, it promised to be a battle royal, almost a classic battle, some of the town philosophers thought. The old way against the new. Rugged individualism versus

modern collectivism. The few against the many. People in the town
who admired Mark Manning shook their heads and said that if men
like Mark were forced to give in to the union "rowdies," it was the
end of everything that had made America great. Mark's achievement,
after all, provided most of the town with employment, and who could
overlook what he had given the town? The new wing on the hospital,
the country club and golf course for the Manning employees and
their families, the municipal swimming pool, the Elkins concert hall,
the enormous gymnasium for the high school. Could the unions do as
much? In the last analysis, all men were not created equal. Only a
few had the ability to lead and achieve greatness, and it was the
special genius of America that these few were able to fulfill their
potential. Perhaps their motivation was not what was generally considered Christian or admirable. Lust for power, greed, egomania—
these weren't "nice" attributes, but they were, after all, what drove
men to build the economic empires that had made America the richest nation on earth. And if these men were restricted in their freedom,
if their power was diluted by the unions, if their wealth and incentive
were taxed away? Well, it would mean the end of personal initiative. . . .

The people in the town who hated Mark said all this was hogwash.
America wasn't that great—if it was so good, why was it in such a
mess? Why the Depression, why the widespread poverty? Why should
the Mannings have millions while the rest of the town sweated to
meet its time payments? All right, maybe at one point in the country's history rugged individuals were needed, but that day was past.
Now it was the little guy's turn, the pie should be sliced more equally
and the men in the factories who did the actual work should have as
much say in the running of the show as the men in Executive Row.
Maybe Mark Manning wasn't as bad as Sheila Harrington had said
in her book. There was no denying Mark had always treated his work
force well, and he'd done a lot for the town. But Mark had too much
—too much power, too much wealth. It was time he was forced to
give up a little of it.

So the argument went back and forth, and no one's mind was
changed from its original position. But at least it gave people something to talk about besides the heat.

Finally, on the thirteenth day of the heat wave, the weather broke.
The storm started building up at one in the afternoon, and by four-
thirty the sky had turned black as the huge thunderheads, which had
started piling their billows as far away as Montana, loomed forty to
fifty thousand feet in the air, poised, like giant black fists, ready to

smash down on the Ohio town. The air became as still as death. Lightning flashed silently to the west. Then a puff of wind, deliciously cool. A few raindrops spattered and hissed on the hot sidewalks as shoppers rushed to their cars and housewives hurried to take in the last few shirts off the clotheslines. At River Bend, the servants ran through the house closing windows as Lily, who was terrified of lightning, sought refuge in the basement with a gin rickey. At the country club, caddies and golfers hurried off the fairways to the locker room and, later, for the golfers, the bar. Two tables of ladies' bridge in the card room ordered new rounds of Cuba Libres and continued bidding. Someone put a quarter in the slot machine and hit bells.

And then the rain came. Heavy, pelting rain accompanied by strong winds and the wild lightning and booming thunder that was somehow never wilder or more booming anywhere else in the country than in the Midwest. The great summer storms of the great plains when Nature, as if wanting to remind the world of what she could do when she felt like it, sizzled and raged and blew and drenched in an awesome show of elemental fury. Proud oaks were struck and toppled like broken toothpicks. The round Victorian tower of the old Rosen house, which had been sold to the Elks years before, was struck, although the lightning rod prevented any damage. Two wooden picnic tables in Matahoochi Park were blown over, and a kitten fell in the river and was drowned. A high-tension power line was struck, and for twenty minutes the whole town was without electricity.

And then, an hour later, it was all over. The rain slowed to a halt, the lightning flashed its way east to bedevil Pennsylvania, the sky in the far west began to clear as a thin ribbon of brilliant yellow appeared on the horizon. The drooping leaves shed drops on the roofs of the Fords and Chevrolets, the windows and doors were opened and the people came out of their houses, shops and factories to fill their lungs with the clean, cool air. Everyone felt good again.

The heat wave was over.

Richard Manning and Len Hastings had become drinking buddies, and in the course of their frequent protracted boozing bouts in their homes (they alternated between Richard's study and Len's basement game room; the two houses were next to each other in the River Bend compound) they came to learn that they shared certain things in common. They both loved their wives and their children, but after several years of domestic tranquillity, they were both experiencing a certain amount of restlessness. Finally, Richard admitted to Len he was sleeping with a waitress at the country club, a young blonde named Josie Stevens. Very discreetly, of course, and Josie was safe and reliable, though prone to sulking at times. They'd go to her mother's house, where Josie had a room over the garage, and so far it had been working out all right, though Richard wasn't happy with the situation. There was always the chance he might be spotted coming or going—the damnable thing about being a Manning in Elkins was that everyone *knew* you—and if his wife, Cynthia, ever found out, there'd be hell to pay—not to mention what would happen if the old man ever found out!

Len, moved by his brother-in-law's confidence to one of his own, admitted he too was contemplating straying, though he felt miserably guilty about it. He loved Ellen very much, he adored his children, but . . . well, he'd been married three years now, and a man's eye begins to wander. And he'd met this knockout of a girl who was a clerk at Gates's Department Store. Her name was Irene Hayes, and she was really sweet, and of course while Len would never *do* anything with her—he would never do such a thing to Ellen, and besides he had no place to do it in; Irene was living with her parents who were very strict. . . . *Still,* he could *think* about it, couldn't he?

The result of these mutual revelations was that finally the two brothers-in-law decided to join forces. They rented a cottage on the banks of the Matahoochi River eight miles out of town, for the 1937 summer season. They told their wives they were going to use it as a fishing cabin, and when Cynthia and Ellen saw the primitive condition of the place, they were more than glad to let the men have it all to themselves. Len and Richard promptly bought a large ice cooler—the cabin had no electricity—then moved in with a case of scotch, two cases of White Rock, clean sheets and Josie and Irene for a summer idyll. For two months, they spent on the average of one night a week in the cabin. Neither of their wives suspected a thing. Josie and Irene were fun; Richard and Len could hardly believe their good fortune. They drowned their guilt in scotch and told each other that Josie and Irene had nothing to do with their love for their wives and children, that they were just for kicks.

Then, on the night of June 5, 1937, disaster of a sort struck. The four had been sitting on the front porch of the cabin, which overlooked the river, drinking since six that evening; by eight, they were all fairly well squiffed. It was then that Josie, who could be moody, began to complain that she was hungry and wanted dinner and that there were too many bugs on the porch. She kept it up, and Richard, who had a tendency to get surly when he was drinking, told her it was too early for dinner and would she please shut up? Words led to words, tempers flared, and Richard finally got up and slapped Josie with considerable force. She began screaming and crying and ran out of the cabin to Richard's car, her lover in pursuit, yelling at her to get back in the cabin. Richard stumbled and fell on his face, allowing Josie to scramble into his Buick. The keys were in the ignition, and she started the car and turned around. Then, as Len and Irene yelled after her to stop, she bumped down the rutted trail that led from the cabin through the surrounding clump of trees to the country road and turned onto the highway.

Richard, furious, went back to the cabin and poured himself another scotch, swearing that Josie had pulled her last stunt and that she could go to hell. Ten minutes later, a state patrol car pulled up to the cabin and parked. As Richard, Len and Irene watched nervously, a tall trooper got out and helped Josie out from the other side. Her forehead was cut and she was crying as the trooper led her back to the cabin.

"She went off the road," he drawled. His name was Don Burns, he was twenty-two and the son of a West Virginia hillbilly who had migrated to Elkins during the boom before the war and taken a job at the Manning plant. Trooper Burns still talked like a West Virginian. "The car's not too bad—just a smashed fender and broken windshield. Ah got her out and called a tow truck. She's shaken up, but she'll be all right. Afraid ah'll have to give her a ticket for drunken driving though, Mr. Manning, as well as make out a report."

Richard gulped when he heard his name. Then, as the trooper pulled a pad from his hip pocket, Richard said, "What kind of report?"

"Accident report. Ah see the car's registered in your name. And what's your name, miss?"

"Josephine Stevens," sniffed Josie, pushing back her unkempt blonde hair from her dirt-smudged face.

Richard and Len were exchanging panicked looks. Now Richard pulled his wallet from his back pants and looked inside. Twenty-five dollars. "Len, give me some money," he whispered. Len pulled out his wallet and took out all he had—forty-three dollars—which he gave his brother-in-law. The trooper was watching this.

"You gentlemen ain't figurin' on tryin' to *bribe* me, ah hope?" he said pleasantly.

"Look, uh . . . What's your name?" said Richard.

"Don Burns."

"Look, Don, this could be very embarrassing to me and this gentleman . . ."

"You mean Mr. Hastings?" said the trooper. Len turned pale at being recognized.

"You . . . know me?" he asked.

"Oh sure. Mah old man used to work at Plant One, so ah've been around, know all you folks. You remember Ralph Burns? He's retired on his pension now."

"Ralph Burns?" said Richard, pretending to remember. "Why sure I remember Ralph! And he's your old man?"

"That's right, Mr. Manning. Worked for your daddy twenty-five years."

"Good old Ralph! Why, Len, he was one of the best men in the company—father always used to say that! Say, it's a pleasure to meet his son." He grabbed the trooper's hand and shook it with both hands, trying to press the cash into his palm. "Well, now, look, Don," he said, in a lower voice, still holding his hand, "you understand how it is. Old Len here and I are having a little fun time, and if our wives found out . . . well, hell, if they found out, they wouldn't be very happy with us, you know what I mean?" He grinned and winked. "So, since no real harm's been done, why don't we just sort of pretend nothing's happened? Huh? Len, why don't you pour Don a scotch? This boy looks like he could use a drink."

"Oh, sure," said Len, hurrying to comply.

Richard released the trooper's hand. The young man stared down at the wad of bills left in his right hand, then looked up at Richard Manning, with his bloodshot eyes and nervous smile. Then at the two girls, who were very frightened. Then around the shabby, kerosene-lamp-lit shack. Then at the scotch Len Hastings was bringing him. He thought of his father, Ralph, who had worked for the Mannings most all his adult life, who had lost two fingers of his left hand to a swift, bias-slicing knife six years before, a month before he was laid off for a year at the bottom of the Depression. True, the Mannings had suspended mortgage payments on his company-built house, so Ralph and his family had kept their roof over their heads, and he had been one of the first to be hired back when production picked up. And now he was happy enough, retired and safe on his pension. But still, there were those two missing fingers and that year of near starvation and that lifetime working in those stinking Manning factories while the Mannings lived in River Bend and Palm Beach and

Europe and God knew where else. No, the score with the Mannings was still not quite balanced.

Trooper Burns put the cash on the table.

"Sorry, Mr. Manning," he said. "Ah don't take bribes, and ah don't drink on duty. Ah'm one of those dumb, honest troopers you hear about sometimes. There are *some* of us, you know."

He smiled, then proceeded to finish writing up his report as the sweat ran down Richard's temples and Len wondered what the chances of this getting back to Ellen were. He didn't like the thought of that happening.

He had gotten used to being a Manning, and he liked it.

Jim Malloy, the head of the Manning security force, had kept Mark informed of all the maneuvering going on in the Manning plants, so the sitdown strike had not come as a surprise. On August 4, 1937, George Bamford, the short, stocky, tough organizer sent in to Elkins by the c.i.o., had held a giant rally at the Green Lantern roller-skating rink, which a crowd, estimated at a staggering 6,000, had attended, filling the big rink and overflowing into the parking lot.

Bamford delivered a speech in which he asked for a "mandate" from the workers to present an ultimatum to the Manning management, the ultimatum to sign a contract with the c.i.o. as the only legitimate union representing all 85,000 Manning employees throughout the country, the dissolution of the "puppet" company union and an across-the-board raise of ten cents an hour. If the company did not accept the ultimatum, all the Manning plants would be struck indefinitely. The mandate was given Bamford with a roar of approval, and the next day Bamford presented his demands to Harrison Starr, the president of the company. Harrison came to Mark, who already knew the contents of the paper—not only had Jim Malloy had fifteen of his men at the Green Lantern skating rink the night before, but Rory Simpson, one of George Bamford's closest associates, was secretly on Jim Malloy's payroll and quietly passed him everything that went on in the union meetings. So Mark knew. He looked at the piece of paper Harrison Starr handed him. Then he put it down and said one word: "No." The next morning, the strike began.

Nineteen thirty-seven was not only the biggest strike year in American history, it was the year the sitdown strike became popular, and it was this tactic George Bamford chose to use against the Manning management. The workers in the plants moved into their factories with bedrolls and thermos jugs and took up residence. Again, Jim Malloy had warned Mark in advance that this was what would happen, and Jim wanted to prevent the workers from entering the plants by actual force. Jim's army was literally that; he had been stockpiling weapons for three years in anticipation of an ultimate showdown with the unions, and his arsenal (which, foresightedly, he kept in an isolated building outside the immediate area of the Manning factories) contained rifles, machine guns, tear gas, brass knuckles and even hand grenades. Jim didn't believe in pussyfooting. Nor did Lily, who had backed up Jim's recommendation, Lily being adamantly antiunion and believing wholeheartedly in the efficacy of force and Jim Malloy. David Manning had just as heatedly fought Jim and, incidentally, his stepmother. David had been strongly urging his father to go along with the unions and avoid the fight, stressing that the unions were not necessarily bad and that the company would be hurt much more in the long run by resisting what David believed was inevitable. David had managed to persuade his brothers to his way of thinking, so that the battle was shaping up along classic lines not only within the company but within the brick walls of the family compound at River Bend as well. The management of the company and a small minority of the workers were against the union; the vast majority of the workers were for it, having been sold on unionization by the efforts of George Bamford, reinforced by the temper of the times. At River Bend, Lily was against unionization, while her stepchildren were for it—their pro-union views being more than a little influenced by their dislike of their stepmother (as Amanda Manning observed, if Lily had suddenly become pro-union, she imagined a good many of the "junior" Mannings would just as quickly switch around to Jim Malloy's side).

Which left Mark, who had the final say. And while there was no question that Mark was as firmly antiunion as his wife, there was a basic difference between them. Lily wanted to use force to defeat the unions. Mark wouldn't. Everyone in the family knew why Lily was so strongly antiunion. She was not only a political conservative who had become more conservative with every New Deal measure; she wanted "the prize" (which had become the family's code name for the control of the empire) for her son, Evan, and she wanted it undiluted by union interference. The union had become in her mind a sort of monster intent on attacking her child, and all of Lily's considerable energies were concentrated on fending off this monster, and no tactic was considered too low to be used.

Unlike many of his fellow industrialists, Mark refused to use force, and his reasoning was a mixture of old-fashioned paternalism as well as his native shrewdness. He vividly remembered the night, twenty-four years before, when the band of would-be Wobblies had marched out to River Bend to confront them, and he could still "feel" in his mind the pain of Bill Sands's bullet tearing into his gut. Violence had its uses, and he had approved Jim Malloy's stockpiling of weapons on the grounds that, in case of a riot, they might be necessary. But violence could backfire; it was a dangerous weapon to use, and it was a bad tactic against his employees. Just as Bill Sands had emerged the villain after shooting Mark, Mark knew he would emerge the hated villain if he used Jim Malloy's army against the workers.

Mark believed his weapon was time. Let the workers sit down in the factories—he could outsit them in his office. He knew the union treasuries were drained by the series of strikes that had proliferated during the past few years. The CIO could not hold out forever, nor could his workers. He, on the other hand, could. And he fully intended to, until the union gave in. So he refused to unleash Jim Malloy when the workers "invaded" the factories with their bedrolls. Nor did he become either angry or upset by the invasion. Rather, he chose to ignore it, to pretend that everything was going on as usual. The morning following the strike, he had his usual breakfast at River Bend. He was just finishing his egg when a phone call came from Jim Malloy. The strikers had blocked the factory gate and were preventing everyone from entering. Jim wanted permission to clear them away. Mark told him not to do anything until he got there. Kissing Lily good-bye, he walked out of the house, said good morning to Marvin Senjak, who held the door of the Cadillac limousine as his employer of more than twenty years got into the back seat, and relaxed as Marvin got in the front and began the drive to Plant One.

Marvin knew from long experience that Mark preferred to ride in silence, but this morning was different. After all, Marvin was not only Mark's chauffeur, he was his personal bodyguard. So he said into the brass speaking tube, "Mr. Manning, what do you want me to do if there's any trouble at the gate?"

Mark picked up his end of the speaking tube. "When we get there, let me out of the car. I want to talk to Jim Malloy. You stay in the car."

"Yes, sir."

There was trouble. When the black car reached the big steel gates of Plant One, there were at least fifty men sitting in front of them, some crosslegged, some stretching out on the brick pavement. Marvin stopped the car and Mark got out as Jim Malloy came over to him.

"Mark," he said, "we can't let them just squat there. Let me clear them away."

Mark looked at the men. "How do you plan doing it? With a steam shovel?"

"Hell, we can drag them away from the gate. I can get the sheriff to arrest 'em for trespassing."

Mark shook his head.

"Forget it. If we're going to start arresting them for trespassing, we'll have to arrest everyone in the factories, and there aren't enough jails in the goddamn country to hold them all. No, don't do anything. I'll go over and talk to them."

Jim looked disgusted at this, but he waited by the car as his boss walked over to the strikers.

"I want through," he said quietly.

"We're not going to let you," replied a young man sprawled on his side in front of him. He was wearing a brown cap and a dirty seersucker suit, and Mark recognized him as one of the union organizers.

"Aren't you Perry Griswold?" he said.

"That's right."

"Look, Griswold, this is my company, and I have a right to go to my office, strike or no strike. So tell these men to get out of the way."

"No one's coming in or going out of this factory until you give us a contract. So you might as well get right back in your fancy car and go home, Mr. Manning, because we're not moving."

There was an insolent edge to Griswold's voice that dug the knife in even deeper, and Mark fought to keep his temper down. Again, he remembered the night of the Wobbly ball at River Bend so many years before. Then, the workers had been outside the gates of his home wanting to come in, and he had cleverly let them in—and he had always considered his decision to admit them a smart one, even though it resulted in his being shot. Now the tables were turned. He was outside the gate to his second home, his office, and they were refusing him admittance. He looked around the crowd for a familar face, but somewhat to his surprise he didn't see anyone he recognized.

"Are all you men working for me?" he called out.

"We *were*," came one reply. "Nobody's workin' now. We're just settin'."

"Do you agree with Griswold? Do you think a man should be kept out of his own office?"

"Yes!" came a chorus, intermingled with "damn right!" and even stronger expletives.

Perry Griswold said, "Give us a contract and we'll move."

"Yeah, give us a contract!"

"We've gone without a union long enough!"

After a while the shouting died down. Mark knew he was at a tremendous disadvantage, and that the wise course would probably be to get back in his car and go home. And yet, perhaps the wiser course was to turn his disadvantage into an advantage. Perhaps if he forced their hand now, he could deal a body blow to the union's prestige. He seriously doubted if any of these men would have the nerve to actually lay a hand on him if he took the simplest, boldest way to get to his office—namely, to step over them and through them to get to the gate. It should take them by surprise, and if they did rough him up, then wouldn't the sympathies of the workers and the town and the nation be with him? And wouldn't the union look despicable if its organizers watched a crowd attack a fifty-nine-year-old, defenseless man? Of course. It would be the same as when Bill Sands shot him that night in 1913. The bullet Sands had fired into his body had helped buy him twenty-four years of labor peace; now he was being presented with a similar opportunity a second time—without the danger of a half-crazed man with a gun. And if they didn't touch him? Then he would have faced down the union and made them look like an empty threat. Either way he would win, and the worst he could get out of it was a roughing up. It was the kind of no-lose, clear-cut situation that appealed to him.

To Perry Griswold's surprise, Mark stepped over him.

"Hey—!"

Griswold bolted upright and grabbed for Mark's right leg; but Mark had already stepped past the man behind Griswold and was out of reach.

"Stop him!" yelled Griswold.

The squatters didn't move. They were watching incredulously as the multimillionaire in the white suit, the legendary Mark Manning who had dominated their lives for so long, calmly stepped through the sitting strikers, making his way to safety on the other side.

"Goddammit, *stop* him!" called Griswold. "Don't let him get to the gate!"

No one moved. Mark was exhilarated. It was working! They didn't have the nerve to touch him, and Griswold was looking more like an ass every second. Just two more men to step over, and then he was at the gate—

Suddenly, something hit the back of his head and a fierce pain exploded in his skull and everything went black. He toppled forward on top of the two men still sitting between him and the gate. They caught him as he fell. He was unconscious.

Perry Griswold had picked up a rock and thrown it. Perry Griswold was a good pitcher, and the rock had hit its target.

Marvin Senjak was out of the Cadillac racing for Griswold, his face contorted with rage. When he reached the organizer, he grabbed him and smashed his fist into the man's face. Griswold stumbled backward and fell. Marvin dived on top of him and began punching him. Jim Malloy waved his arm at two of his men inside the gate. They blew whistles, and guards started converging on the scene. Meanwhile, some of the strikers had gotten to their feet and were trying to separate Marvin Senjak and Perry Griswold, while others had stretched Mark out on the pavement, loosening his tie and pillowing his head with his jacket. He was still unconscious.

Within minutes the scene was a melée as the factory guards spilled out of the gates and waded into the crowd of strikers, swinging at them with clubs. The strikers fought for a while, but then began to give ground as still more of Malloy's guards arrived. In ten minutes, most of the strikers had taken off on the run and the guards were in control of the gate. Marvin Senjak, blood spilling out of his nose from a direct hit by Perry Griswold, was kneeling beside his employer.

"He'll be all right," said Jim Malloy. "He just got a bad knock on the back of his head. Let's take him to his office."

Marvin picked him up gently as a baby and carried him back to the Cadillac, Mark's hundred and seventy-five pounds being no burden to the exprizefighter. He deposited him in the back seat, then got in the front and drove the limousine through the gates to the entrance of the executive wing. Then he and one of the guards carried Mark into his office and laid him on a couch.

"Do you think we should get a doctor?" asked Marvin nervously.

"Nah, he'll be all right."

Marvin didn't look convinced. And after ten minutes had passed and Mark was still unconscious, he knew something was wrong and called the hospital. Five minutes later an ambulance shrieked its way through the factory gates and parked in front of the executive wing. Dr. Roy Carson hurried into the building with two assistants and went to Mark's office, where he took a look at the unconscious man, then checked his pulse.

"It's been almost a half hour now," said Marvin. "Shouldn't he be waking up?"

"I'd think so," said the doctor, ordering his assistants to get Mark into the ambulance. As they transferred him to a litter, Marvin said, "What do you think's the matter? A concussion?"

"Possibly," said Dr. Carson. "And possibly it's something else."

When they got him to the hospital, they found out it was something else.

CHAPTER THREE

Rita Tweed sat on the edge of her father's swimming pool in Shaker Heights, Cleveland, and watched the young man poised on the diving board. The hot noon sun was turning his already tan skin almost black and his red-gold hair the color of wheat, and Rita loved the color combination as she loved the body it decorated—that beautifully put together, muscular body of Christopher Manning. Then he was up on his toes; he sprang, soaring into the air like a graceful bird; then a perfect jackknife, from which he straightened just in time to slice cleanly into the water. When he surfaced a moment later, he called out, "How was that?"

"*Magnifico*," said Rita. Her father owned a 50,000-acre cattle ranch in the northern Mexican state of Chihuahua, where she spent a lot of time, and she sometimes dropped Spanish words into her conversation.

Christopher swam over and splashed out of the pool, sitting next to her. He pointed to the solitaire diamond ring on her finger. "It's getting bigger," he said.

She smiled at the engagement ring he'd given her the night before when she'd accepted his proposal.

"Isn't it? I think it's grown a carat since breakfast."

He put his arm around her and kissed her hard on the mouth. After a while, he took his mouth away from hers. "Haven't changed your mind, have you?"

She laughed. "After all the trouble I went to to catch you? Not on your life."

"I thought it was the other way around—that you were playing hard to get."

"That's because I wanted you to think that," she replied.

"Uh huh. Anyway, have you decided where we're going on our honeymoon yet?"

"Of course not. Decisions like that take time."

"Then I'll decide for you. First, we'll go to Paris so you can meet my mother—although she'll probably come to the wedding. At least I hope she comes. Anyway, you'll like her. She's beautiful and not a bit like Bitch Momma."

Rita laughed as she rubbed her left leg.

"You really are nuts about your stepmother, aren't you?"

"*Crazy* for her. Anyway, my stepfather's got this neat château on the Marne, so we could spend a few days there. It's, you know, sixteenth-century, I think, and very romantic and has a resident ghost and the works."

"A real ghost?"

"Well, no one's ever seen it that I know of, but that's the story. One of my stepfather's ancestors died in her wedding bed or something like that, and she walks through the halls at midnight moaning about how she missed out on all the fun. Anyway, why are you rubbing your legs?"

"Oh, they've kind of been aching this morning. Like growing pains."

"That's because you smoke too much. You really ought to quit. It's a disgusting habit."

"Oh, Mr. Clean Liver talking!" In defiance, she pulled a Lucky Strike from its green package and lit it.

"My father's never smoked in his whole life," said Christopher, "and neither have I. And when we get married, neither will my wife."

"We'll see. Anyway, where will we go after we leave the château?"

"How about Austria?"

"That sounds fun. Then maybe we could go to Italy and see if the trains really do run on time."

Christopher jutted out his jaw in an Il Duce pose, then stuck his arm out in a Fascist salute. "Hey, you dumba trains, you runna on time or I *shoota* you!"

Rita giggled as her father's butler came out of the garden room overlooking the pool terrace. "Mr. Manning, there's a phone call for you."

"Oh, thanks."

Christopher got to his feet and went into the house as Rita finished her cigarette by the pool, thinking of what a wonderful three days she'd had with her fiancé. There had been that great pool party at the Watsons the first evening, which had been lucky because it had been sweltering. Then Christopher had taken her out to dinner last night and popped the big question . . . Rita wondered how Bitch Momma was going to take the news after that nasty little scene in the River Bend bedroom the previous New Year's Eve. But then, Christopher had said his stepmother was so eager to get him married and out of the house, she probably wouldn't have minded if he'd married a Hottentot, which wasn't exactly complimentary to Rita, but she got the point . . . Anyway, she was dseperately in love with him and she couldn't be happier, although she *did* wish her legs would stop aching. . . .

As Christopher came out of the house, she could tell something was very wrong from the look on his face. He came over and said, "I have to go home right away. Something's happened to my father."

"What?" she asked, getting to her feet.

"There was a sort of skirmish, I guess, at Plant One this morning and he got hit on the head with a rock. My brother says they think he may have had a cerebral hemorrhage."

"Oh, Chris, I'm sorry . . ."

He kissed her and forced a smile, though she knew he was frightened. She knew how he worshiped Mark Manning. Then, after getting dressed and piling his suitcase in his yellow Dodge convertible, he told her he'd call her that night and let her know how things were going. He got into the car and started the engine. He leaned out the window and kissed her, then said, "Next time I see you, remind me to tell you how crazy I am about you."

"You wonderful nut." She sighed. "I saw that movie with you— don't you remember? And Fred MacMurray gives that line to Frances Farmer."

"Well, anyway, I *am* crazy about you." He looked at her, and she knew he meant it.

Then he pulled out of the driveway and headed south for Elkins.

The family of the founder of the Manning Rubber and Steel Corporation gathered around the hospital bed in the new Mark Manning wing of the Elkins Hospital and stared in disbelief at the silent, apparently sleeping figure before them. The room was big—the best room in the wing, of course—but the big man in the bed looked remarkably small. The top of his head had been shaved and the famous red-gold hair replaced with surgical dressing. Lily looked deeply upset, but Christopher was sure she was faking. Ellen Hastings wasn't so sure. No one said anything as they waited for the specialist from Cleveland,

Dr. Ashton, the neurosurgeon Roy Carson had called in as a con-
sultant.

Finally the two doctors came into the room. Carson in his late
thirties, inclining to fat as his brown hair inclined to thin, Ashton in
his fifties, seemingly in excellent trim. Dr. Ashton nodded at the
famous family, then said, "Mr. Manning has suffered a contusion of
the brain surface and a slight cerebral hemorrhage. Now, this is not
unusual, and I think I can safely say that Mr. Manning's chances for
recovery are excellent, bearing in mind that he is a man of almost
sixty years of age. With Dr. Carson, I took a series of X-rays of the
skull . . . we considered taking a spinal tap too, but decided it wasn't
necessary. Then we took a ventriculogram—"

"A what?" interrupted Lily.

"We drilled a series of burr holes in the skull on either side of the
midline. Then we inserted long needles into the four ventricles, the
hollows inside the brain. These ventricles are normally prevented
from showing up in an X-ray because they are filled with cerebro-
spinal fluid that appears the same as the brain tissue on the plates. So
we replaced a certain amount of the fluid with air, then took X-rays.
The air allows the ventricles to show up. The result was that we got
an excellent picture of what has happened to Mr. Manning's brain.
The shock from the blow of the rock has caused it to swell, and the
pressure inside it is abnormally high. This is preventing him from
regaining consciousness."

He paused and David Manning said, "What will happen, doctor?"

"We were able to remove some of the blood that had hemorrhaged,
and what is left I don't think will cause any permanent paralysis.
However, that can't be determined definitely until later. What will
happen now is that we will wait and hope and, perhaps, pray. The
brain is an enormously sensitive instrument, and Mr. Manning's has
suffered a severe trauma. But it should begin to heal itself in time.
Eventually the pressure should subside and the brain will return to
normal size. As it does so, consciousness will begin gradually to return
to Mr. Manning. I would hope we would begin to see signs of consciousness appearing within two weeks, and if it is much longer than
that, well, then I think to be honest with you that we should be prepared for the worst. However, I am being purposely gloomy to prepare you for the worst. Actually, I have no reason to think that he
won't come out of the coma within two weeks—three at the most.

"When you say consciousness will return gradually," said Christopher, "exactly what do you mean?"

"That his brain will begin to function again bit by bit. As he comes out of the deep coma, he will go into what I call a gray area where he will be partially with us, so to speak. This transition period can last for a month, and often complete recovery may not come for many months. We should also be prepared for partial paralysis—perhaps even general paralysis. But again, this should only be temporary. Then, little by little all of his normal mental functions will come back to him, his memory should be restored—again, bit by bit—and eventually we can hope for a complete recovery. In the meantime, as I said, the best we can do is sit and wait."

"Is there any reason," said Lily, "why he has to stay here in the hospital? I mean, after a few days couldn't I have him brought home —assuming, naturally, that I arrange for round-the-clock nurses?"

The doctor considered this.

"I don't see why not. I would prefer to wait four or five days—say a week—to make sure there is no unforeseen complication. But then, yes, I would say you could take him home."

"Good. Dr. Carson, perhaps you'd be kind enough to make the arrangements for me, and to hire the nurses? Naturally, I will want women best qualified in the field."

"Of course, Mrs. Manning."

"Well, then." Lily looked around at her stepchildren. "I think we all understand the situation. Do any of you have any questions?"

Christopher bristled at the rather school-principal, top-sergeant tone she had assumed, as did Ellen, who changed her mind about the possible genuineness of Lily's upset expression. But no one had any questions. Lily came over to shake the two physicians' hands.

"Then I want to thank both of you. I feel so relieved to know my husband has the best men taking care of him."

The doctors thanked her, then she left the room, followed by the rest of the family. By the time David Manning came out into the corridor, his stepmother was already halfway down the hall to the elevator. She didn't wait for her stepchildren, but rather caught the elevator as its doors were closing and squeezed inside.

David wondered why she was in such a hurry.

———————————

Marvin Senjak had gone back to River Bend after his employer had been taken to the hospital. Marvin felt strongly about always preserving the Manning image of class and dignity, and with his bloody nose and dirty uniform, that image, he felt, was being tarnished. So he hurried back to wash up and change into a clean uniform; then he had driven Lily to the hospital, where she had spent the next six hours waiting for the tests on her husband to be finished. Now, at four thirty in the afternoon, Marvin jumped out of the limousine as he saw Lily hurrying down the front steps of the hospital.

"Is he going to be all right, Mrs. Manning?" he asked as he opened the door for her.

"Yes, thank God. And Marvin, I can't tell you how much I appreciate what you did for him. Thank heavens you had the sense to call the hospital!" She placed her hand on his sleeve and smiled warmly. "It's in times of stress, like this, that one really appreciates loyalty so much. I do thank you."

He was surprised by this effusion of gratitude. This Mrs. Manning, like the first Mrs. Manning, had always treated her husband's body-guard-chauffeur with, at best, diffidence, at worst, thinly concealed hostility. For some reason, both women had resented his closeness to their husband, as if Marvin were an intrusion on their privacy. Marvin worshiped the man who had given him life-long security, as well as a lovely rent-free home for his wife and family, and perhaps both the Mrs. Mannings had sensed this worship and been rather jealous of it. He didn't know. At any rate, he had never been at all popular with this Mrs. Manning, and her sudden rush of affection put him on guard. It was out of character.

He thanked her, then got in the car and asked if she wanted to go home.

"I want to go to Plant One."

"Yes, m'am."

He started the engine and began the drive back to the factory complex. As he drove, he adjusted his rearview mirror slightly so he could look at his passenger. She was wearing a white summer suit with a blue polka-dot silk blouse, and on her slickly coiffed white-blonde hair was a small, chic white hat set at a smart tilt. Her face was beautiful but hard, which was about as usual. But, Marvin thought, there was a strange fierceness in her green eyes as she stared out the window that he had never seen before.

Ben Dwyer, Mark's personal lawyer for the past thirteen years, was a soft-spoken Clevelander with silvery-white hair and a bearing and look of such distinction that any Hollywood producer would surely have been delighted to cast him as either a senator or clergyman. In fact, he had the mentality of a pirate. Ben was considered one of

the sharpest tax lawyers in the country, and with the sudden inflation of taxes brought about by the New Deal, tax lawyers had become
very important men in the lives of people rich enough to need them.
At ten that morning Ben had received a phone call from Lily Manning in his Cleveland office. After lunch he had been driven down to
Elkins by his chauffeur—after all, Mark Manning was his most important client. At five that afternoon Mark's wife came into the office
of Harrison Starr, the company president, where Ben had been instructed to wait for her (the gates having been cleared of the strikers
that morning, the executives had been able to reach their offices, although they had little to do. Now it was not only the workers who
were sitting.).

"Lily," Ben said, coming over to take her hand in both of his, "I'm
so shocked to hear about this. How is Mark? Is he going to be all
right?"

"We hope so," she said, nodding curtly at Harrison Starr. Then
she took a seat in front of Harrison's desk and pulled a cigarette from
her purse, which Ben lit for her.

"Thank you," she said. "Did you bring the papers?"

"Yes," Ben said.

"Then perhaps you'll explain everything to Harrison."

"Of course."

Ben went back to his chair to get his briefcase, from which he
pulled a sheaf of papers. He placed them in front of a confused Harrison Starr.

"What this boils down to, Harrison, is that Mark had foresightedly
made a provision for just this sort of situation—in which he would
be temporarily out of commission, so to speak. And as you can see
from this document, Mark's voting power in his stock is to be exercised by Lily until such time as Lily and myself and two qualified
doctors—one to be picked by Lily and the other to be picked by Mark's
children—all agree that Mark is ready to resume voting his stock himself. Now, obviously, Mark is out of commission, so for the time
being, Lily will be representing his stock position."

"What Ben means," Lily said pleasantly, "is that from now on you
will be taking orders from me."

Harrison glanced uncertainly at Ben, who nodded.

"Yes, that's what I mean."

"I see." Harrison looked at Lily, who was watching him closely.
He knew he didn't rate high in her book. "Well," he said, "is there
anything in particular you wanted done right now?"

"Yes. Ask Jim Malloy to come in here."

Harrison issued a quiet order to his secretary over the intercom. Then he sat back and waited. Lily said nothing, merely smoking as she gazed out the window that overlooked the factory two floors below. He wondered what the hell she was thinking.

When Jim Malloy came into the office, he told Lily how sorry he was about what had happened to Mark. She said, "Jim, what's happened to the man who threw the rock at him?"

"Griswold's been arrested for assault. The union got him out on bail."

"As far as you can tell, what's the general reaction of the workers to what happened? I mean, do they feel Mark was victimized? Is there any sympathy for him and resentment at Griswold?"

Jim shrugged. "That's hard to say. Oh, some of the men don't like what happened—I'd say there's probably a general sympathy for Mark —after all, he's hurt and he's in the hospital. But no one's about to call off the strike, if that's what you're getting at."

"I see." She thought a moment, then asked, "Could your men clear the strikers out of the factories?"

Jim looked surprised. "Well now, hold on. It's one thing to stop them from coming in, and I tried to get Mark to let me but he wouldn't. But hell, I don't know if we can get them out now that they're in. I mean, we *could*, but—"

"But what?"

"It might get pretty rough."

"But the point is, the men are trespassing on private property," Lily said. "They have no right to do what they're doing. We have every right to force them out—"

"But Mrs. Manning," interrupted Harrison, "it was Mark's policy not to interfere with the strikers—"

"He interfered with them this morning, didn't he?"

"Yes, but he told me several times he wanted to avoid any violence, that he wanted to outwait them—"

"*They* are the ones who started the violence by hitting my husband's head with a rock, Mr. Starr. And I'm sorry to see that I need to remind you that *I* am making the decisions here now. Mark wanted it that way, and I'm truly surprised you'd question his wishes."

Harrison's face turned red, but he said nothing. Lily turned to Jim Malloy.

"You have tear gas, don't you?"

"Yes."

"Can't you use it to force them out of the buildings?"

"Sure, but there's bound to be a fight once they're out."

"That's your job, your responsibility. Tomorrow morning at eight, tell all the factories that the men have one hour to return to work or vacate the buildings. If by nine o'clock they haven't done either one, then force them out." She stood up. "And don't be afraid to use everything you've got. The one thing these union goons understand is muscle, and I expect you to show them how much muscle the Manning Company has. Gentlemen?"

She nodded at the men and walked out of the office. When she was gone, Harrison Starr said to Ben Dwyer, "This is crazy!"

Ben picked up his briefcase. "Maybe so," he said, "but she happens to have the law—and Mark's will—on her side."

Christopher Manning was lying on his bed thinking about his father, and his fiancée, when he heard a knock on his bedroom door.

"Come in," he called, sitting up. The door opened and his stepmother entered.

"May I talk to you for a moment, Christopher?" she asked in a subdued, almost humble tone that made her youngest stepson wary.

"Why not?"

She quietly closed the door, then came over to the bed. He sat on the edge of the bed, not giving her the courtesy of standing up. She didn't seem to take offense. Rather, she looked as if she were trying to search for words, something the normally outspoken Lily was not accustomed to. Finally she said, "Christopher, I know what you think of me."

"Oh? How'd you possibly guess?"

"It hasn't been hard, and I suppose I can't really blame you. A stepmother is a difficult person to accept under the best of circumstances, and I won't deny that I've not been the most lovable stepmother of all time—mainly, and you don't have to believe this, but mainly because I've felt very much on the defensive. I mean, for an outsider to come into the Manning family is, well, it's a bit of a challenge. And I'm afraid it's a challenge I haven't met too well."

"Why," he said suspiciously, "are you saying this now?"

"Because of what happened this morning. It came to me as such a shock—you don't know how much I depend on your father, how important he is to *my* life! and now . . ." She walked over to the window and looked out over the swimming pool. Then she turned back to her stepson. "What I'm trying to say is, now that this terrible thing has happened to Mark, I would like it so much if we could all for-get the past and come together as a family—as a family united with love, or at least tolerance, instead of tearing at each other. Is that possible, Christopher? Or do you all hate me too much?"

He looked a little embarrassed. "Oh, I don't think we hate you, exactly. It's just that . . . I don't know, you did sort of move in and he's always seemed closer to you than to us, and—"

"But isn't that natural? I'm his wife, after all."

"I guess, I don't know . . . anyway, I'm willing to try to bury the hatchet if you are. At least until father's well again."

She came over to him, took hold of both his hands, and squeezed them.

"Oh, thank you, Chris. And I think your father would want us to pull together."

"Yeah, I guess so."

She released his hands. "Well, I hope when Mark's well again we can go right on being friends instead of back to the way things were. It's silly for families to quarrel, don't you think?"

He nodded.

"Of course it is. And, Chris, I honestly hope this is the beginning of a much better feeling among all of us." She started toward the door, but halfway there stopped and turned around. "Oh, there's something else . . ."

"What?"

"Well, this is rather awkward to say, and I know that you're going to think I'm trying to get rid of you like I have in the past, but it really isn't that . . ."

"You want me to move out?"

She nodded. "Just until your father gets better. You see, because I'm not *that* much older than you, well . . . I'm just afraid people might talk if we were both here alone in the house. People can be so vicious, particularly about us—you know that, Chris. Would you mind terribly? I mean, you could move into David's house, or Ellen's . . ."

"But we wouldn't be here alone!" he said. "There's all the servants—"

"That's not the same, I'm afraid. They wouldn't stop gossip."

"All right, but I thought you were bringing father home from the hospital next week . . ."

"But he'll be unconscious! Oh, I know it's an imposition and I know I'm probably being overly sensitive, but people have talked about me for *so* many years in this town and it would just kill me if now, of all times, they began to say things. . . . Would you do it for me, Chris? I honestly would appreciate it *so* much."

"Well," he finally said, feeling somehow trapped, "sure, if you're *that* nervous about it."

"I'm afraid I am."

"Besides, I'll be moving out anyway in a while. Rita and I are engaged."

She looked surprised and started to say something, then changed her mind. "How very nice. I'm really terribly pleased for both of you."

As she left the room, Christopher's suspicions were reawakened.

Unknown to Mark Manning, his eldest son had undergone psychoanalysis while he was living in New York. After six months of four sessions a week, the analyst, Dr. Rubin, told David Manning there was nothing basically wrong with him but that, like many sons of powerful men he felt overshadowed by his father and he resented him, a resentment that went back to his childhood—a resentment that was not one-sided. Among many incidents David had lured out of his memory while on Dr. Rubin's couch was his father's thirty-ninth birthday party for which David had written the poem that had brought him such a sharp rebuke from Mark. Dr. Rubin found that incident most significant. Not only was David overshadowed by Mark, but Mark, perhaps unconsciously, had tried to emasculate his oldest son by making him feel inferior and effeminate, and at any sign of rebellion from David—even as slight a sign as the poem—Mark would attack. Why? Because David was a potential challenge to Mark, as any son is to any father. Mark knew some day his sons would inherit what he had built, and inwardly he resented it. He tried to stave off the inevitable by weakening his children, by making them feel inferior and insignificant and unmanly. Especially David, the oldest and therefore symbolically the most threatening—no matter what he was really like.

How accurate this analysis was David wasn't sure, but it made him feel better and he believed there was some truth in it. At any rate, he was no longer in awe of his father, nor had Mark continued to treat his eldest son with the harshness of which Charlotte had complained so bitterly to Amelia Clark. Mark and David got along well now—or well enough. David, though, still didn't like him.

It had been David's dislike of his father, as well as an ideological dislike of what he considered the outmoded nineteenth-century unbridled individualism of which his father was such a blatant example and proponent that had led David to try to make a career for himself outside the enormous Manning empire. And though he had given in to Mark's urgings and finally joined the company, there were still times when David wished he had stayed out. The power that his father thrived on and his stepmother lusted after held no appeal for him. In fact, he thought the continual jockeying for position, the sycophantic adulation of Mark that so many of the Manning executives wallowed in, was offensive. As head of the company's legal division, he knew that the Manning Company was as honest as most giant corporations. It didn't knowingly cheat or defraud, but the company pushed legality up to the limit to achieve an advantage. And while David was not privy to his father's personal affairs, this being the jealously guarded domain of Ben Dwyer, he was intelligent enough to surmise that legality was probably a bit manhandled again to lighten Mark's tax load. All of this was offensive to David, who was acutely sensitive to the plight of the poor in America, who was genuinely agonized by the victims of the Dust Bowl making their impoverished pilgrimage to the promised land of California. And that his father would deny his thousands of employees the right to unionize was, to David, an outrage as well as a stupid resistance to the thrust of the times. He, of course, condemned Perry Griswold's braining Mark with a rock, but he did feel it was a stupid thing that never should have happened—if Mark had been more reasonable about the union.

None of his father's failings, however, prepared David for what he witnessed the morning following Griswold's attack. The Manning sons, all living within walking distance of each other on the grounds of their father's estate, had formed a car pool to take themselves to work, and that morning David, Richard, Len Hastings and Christopher (who had moved into David's house the night before) had all piled into David's limousine to be driven to Plant One by David's chauffeur. However, when they arrived at the factory, they were blocked from entering, this time not by the strikers, but by Jim Malloy's security men.

"What's this all about?" David asked the blue-uniformed guard.

"Sorry, Mr. Manning, but we've sent in an ultimatum to the strikers. They've got till nine o'clock to leave the buildings. No one's being let through the gate until we get the strikers out."

David looked at his brothers, then turned back to the security man.

"Whose order is this?"

"Mr. Malloy's."

"Where is he?"

The security man pointed to a Packard parked a half block away. David got out and walked over to the Packard, where Jim Malloy and Harrison Starr were standing. "Jim, what's the idea of giving this ultimatum?" David asked.

"Didn't you know?"

"Know what?"

"I mean, didn't your stepmother tell you?"

"Tell me *what?*"

"Mrs. Manning ordered this," said Harrison Starr, with obvious bitterness. "According to Ben Dwyer, she now controls Mark's stock. She came to my office yesterday afternoon and told Jim to get the strikers out of the plants."

"Which," said Jim, checking his watch, "in about five minutes I'm going to do."

"Jim's going to fire tear gas into the factories if the strikers don't come out voluntarily."

"You mean," David said, "my stepmother claims *she* controls my father's stock . . . ?"

"She doesn't just claim it," Harrison told him. "Your father gave her control in case of an incapacitating illness. It's all down on paper, signed and witnessed and legal as hell. And I know what you're thinking, David, but forget it. There's nothing you or I can do. This is what she wants, and this is what she's going to get."

David returned to his car in a daze. His brothers had gotten out of the limousine. He told them what he'd just learned.

"She can't do that!" said Christopher angrily.

"She not only can, she *has,*" replied David. Just then there was a series of distant *pops,* and the Mannings turned toward the factories. Jim Malloy had given the signal and tear-gas pellets had been fired through the windows of the enormous buildings. Men with rifles were stationed on the roofs, and through the steel fence could be seen dozens of the security men who had taken positions on the grounds. Smoke began roiling out of the broken windows, and soon the workers were streaming out of the buildings, coughing and gasping for fresh air. Men with megaphones shouted at them to leave the factory grounds peaceably, but the workers were in no mood for peace. In their anger, they attacked the security men who, though being outnumbered by the hundreds of workers, had the advantage of having weapons. And they had been told to use them. The rifles on the roofs began firing; a number of the workers were hit; others panicked. They ran for the gate, pushing through into the street. It had all happened so quickly that David and his brothers weren't aware of their own vulnerability. Now some of the workers spotted them and began running toward them.

"Christ, they're after *us!*" Richard said.

"Get back in the car—"

The three Manning sons and Len Hastings pushed their way back into the limousine, slamming and locking the doors as David yelled at his chauffeur to get moving. The driver needed little prompting. He began to turn the big car around, but the very length of the limousine prevented him from executing a U-turn without stopping and backing once, and this enabled the workers to catch up with the car before it could get away. For a moment, David Manning feared for their lives as the men surrounded the car, banging it with their naked fists, their tear-streaked, and in a few cases bloody, faces pressed against the windows as they yelled at the Mannings trapped inside like so many goldfish in their chauffeured bowl. Just as somebody broke a window with a brick, the chauffeur gunned the car, preventing the man who had broken the window from reaching through and unlocking the door, which he obviously intended doing. Instead, he and the others had to jump back as the car gained speed.

But not before David and his brothers heard what the man yelled.

"You bastards. Every Manning is a killer! Every damn one of you!"

CHAPTER FOUR

Four strikers were killed and more than two dozen wounded in the skirmish, which hit the headlines all over the country. But as far as Lily was concerned, the fight had achieved its purpose—the strikers were out of the buildings. And though picket lines were immediately formed and although the union organizers held new rallies denouncing the company's "bloodlust," Lily was convinced she had done the right thing. The company had shown itself master in its own house, and the union had been intimidated. The strike would go on, but the advantage had shifted to the company.

Two days after the battle Harrison Starr received a letter from

Lily asking for his resignation and offering him a year's salary as
severance pay. Harrison complained bitterly to David that Lily was
trying to make him a scapegoat for the slaughter, which he had opposed all along. David tried to calm him, recommending he submit
his resignation with an explanation. "Lily's hanging herself," David
insisted. "When father comes out of the coma, he's going to fire *her*
and rehire you. You know that, Harrison. So for the time being,
play her game and go on record."

"Well, maybe you're right, David. Except how in the hell you can
take all this so calmly is beyond me. You've been against fighting
the union all along! And when your stepmother orders out the goddamn guns—"

"And you were the one who said there was nothing I could do!
Do you think I'm happy about all this? Except I say the best thing
to do is play along until father is well again, at which point Lily is
going to be in one hell of a mess, believe me."

Harrison gave in, but the family was even more up in arms than
Harrison. That night, all the junior Mannings gathered in the taste-
fully decorated living room of David and Amanda Manning for a
council of war. Present were Christopher, Ellen and Len Hastings,
Richard and Cynthia Manning and of course David and Amanda.
Notably absent were Lily and her son, Evan. David stood up in front
of the mantel and took charge of the gathering because of his seniority.
"Now, I know you're all worried about what's happening—"

"Worried?" interrupted Ellen. "That's a beautiful, lawyer's under-
statement if I've ever heard one! I'm frantic."

"Yes, all right; but there's no need for us to go off half cocked—"

"Come on, David," Christopher said, "she's fired Harrison Starr,
for God's sake! I'd like to know where she gets the right to do that!"

"I'll tell you if you'll keep quiet. Father, as chairman of the board
and majority stockholder, has the power to fire all executives. So
Lily, legally exercising father's stock—"

"We *know* that," snapped Christopher, "but she hasn't become
chairman of the board, has she? So how does she get away with firing
Harrison?"

David nodded. "Right, she hasn't become chairman of the board,
exactly. I mean, it is certainly a fuzzy distinction, and I'm sure if we
wanted to take a stand on the issue, there would be a legitimate fight.
But I'm telling all of you what I told Harrison this afternoon. We
should not make a fight on this issue; we should let Harrison resign.
Because when father regains consciousness, all of our objections to
what Lily's doing will become academic. Frankly, I think she must

have lost her mind, taking over this way. She knows what father's going to say when he comes out of his coma."

"But what if he doesn't come out of it?" said Richard, finally saying the unthinkable.

David took a deep breath. "Well, that's what we should really discuss this evening. As you all know, the stock we inherited from our grandfather Rosen, which had been held in trust for us, is now ours, but father asked Dick, Chris and Ellen to give him their proxies until he thought Dick and Chris and Len had been with the company long enough' to make them directors. He made me a director last year, so I can vote my stock. But your proxies extend till the next directors' meeting, which is three months from now. So until then your stock is pretty well useless to us. However, if it looks as if father *isn't* going to come out of the coma, I can start sounding out the other directors, and at the next meeting I can force a showdown with Lily. Admittedly, her clout is big, with father's stock behind her. But I seriously doubt she would want to buck all of us as well as the other directors and risk the possibility of a total, all-out, proxy war, which she might lose. So I think, in the long run, our position is good."

"But it's pretty rotten in the short run!" snapped Ellen. "Besides, how do you know she'd lose an all-out proxy war? Don't underestimate that bitch! She'll do anything to get the prize for Evan, including going out and buttering up enough of the individual stockholders to get a majority of the proxies! I think you're being too optimistic, David. Besides, I'm not so sure she's even worried about what father will say if he does come out of the coma. She's got him so wrapped around her finger—didn't he give her the voting rights in his stock? He certainly didn't give it to any of us! She's obviously poisoned him against us, and meanwhile we sit around twiddling our thumbs while she steals away what's rightfully ours!"

There was a silence after Ellen's outburst, as if her verbalizing what many of them were thinking had revealed ugly truths no one wanted to face.

"Well, Ellen," David said, "I think you're overstating the case a bit. Lily undoubtedly influences father—none of us would deny that. But on the other hand, she has so blatantly gone against his wishes by letting the security men fire on the workers that I can't imagine when he comes out of the coma . . ."

"*If* he comes out," interrupted Christopher.

David frowned at the interruption. "Yes, we're all aware of the if, Chris."

"But have you thought of this angle to it?"

"What angle?"

The youngest Manning came into the center of the circle. "Let's look at what Lily's done and what she's said she's going to do. She said she's going to take father out of the hospital and bring him to River Bend next week—right?"

"Right."

"Now, the other night she came into my room at River Bend just sweet as maple syrup and gave me a lot of bull about wanting the family to pull together. Well, we all know what she thinks of me, don't we?"

Ellen laughed. "She hates you almost more than she hates me and Len."

"Oh, I get the Lily Hates Medal, for what that's worth. Okay. So she's sugar-sweet to me, which I begin to swallow and start to feel ashamed and think that maybe we've misjudged her and all that junk, when she pulls this will I please move out of the house stuff to save her reputation . . . which, like a sap, I did."

"We all know this, Chris," David said.

"The point is, why does she want to get me out of River Bend just before she brings father *in?* Think about it. There's no one in the house except Lily, father—who's helpless—Evan and the servants and private nurses. None of us is in there, now that she's got me out. Doesn't it sound like a, well, a golden opportunity . . . ?"

"For *what?*"

Christopher looked around the room. "What's the one thing that could most benefit Lily?"

Silence.

"Then I'll tell you—that father *never* wakes up. And I for one think Lily means to make sure he doesn't."

A stunned silence.

"Oh, come on, Chris," said David, "that's going too far. She's not going to murder him, for God's sake!"

"Why not? If it insures her the control of the corporation until Evan is old enough to take over, why wouldn't she do it? And don't tell me you think that Lily is above killing?"

"But we don't know what's in father's will. Maybe it's not even to her advantage—"

"Maybe. But *she* knows what's in his will, I'll bet. And I'll bet if it *is* to her advantage to have father out of the way, then she sure as hell wouldn't think twice about doing it, one way or the other. And the trouble is, we wouldn't know for sure until it was done. So to protect father's life, I think we have to assume the worst."

Richard Manning shook his handsome, not overly bright head.

"I don't believe it, Chris. I just don't believe she'd try murder. She doesn't want to end up in the electric chair."

"You only get that if you get *caught*," said Christopher. "And I'll bet she's working it out so she won't get caught. After all, it's easy to arrange the death of an invalid. It probably happens all the time, except no one ever hears about it because the people don't get caught."

Amanda said, "Really, Christopher, I honestly think you're being a bit melodramatic. I'll grant you Lily's capable of murdering someone —God knows, I'd certainly hate to be in a dark room alone with her— but I just don't think she's going to do your father in. I don't think she'd be willing to take the risk."

"Nor do I," added Len Hastings.

"But don't you think there's *enough* of a reasonable possibility that we ought to take countersteps?" said Christopher.

"Like what?"

"Well, show her we suspect her. Maybe I should try to move back in. If our father's life is really at stake, which I think it is. And can any of you think of a better idea?"

"Yes," David said. "I think you're being overly alarmist, Chris, but I'll grant you there's the possibility Lily might be considering something drastic against father. So I think I should talk to Marvin Senjak. He's father's bodyguard, he's fanatically loyal to him, and if I quietly suggest he keep an eye on father when they bring him to River Bend from the hospital, well, between Marvin and the private nurses, I think it would be extremely difficult for Lily to try anything —if that's what's going on in her mind. Does that meet with everyone's approval?"

He looked around the room, and the others nodded.

"Good. Now, as to Lily's firing Harrison Starr, I still maintain that our best course is to sit tight and wait to see if father comes out of the coma. And if he doesn't, as I said, then I think we start lining up the directors. I realize this is the cautious, lawyer's way of going about it, but I think it's the wise way too. Are there any objections?"

There weren't, and the meeting broke up. As Christopher was talking with Len over a highball, he was called to the phone. To Christopher's surprise, Rita's mother was on the line, and she was in tears. "Christopher," she said, "something terrible has happened."

"What?" he asked in an alarmed voice.

"It's Rita. She has polio."

For a moment he couldn't say anything. All he could think of was that beautiful body and those beautiful legs. In his mind's eye, they slowly withered and became encased in steel braces.

———————

The party was being held in the formal gardens of the Château de Bray, near Fontainebleau to the southeast of Paris, and a fair sampling of the cream of French Jewish society was there in all its elegance, standing around smooth, green lawns beneath the clear sky, most of them having interrupted their August holiday to come to Fontainebleau for the occasion. They were lured not only by the social and financial prestige of their hosts, the Baron and Baronne Gustave Weil, but by the importance of the cause. The party was to raise money to finance the emigration of Jews from Nazi Germany, and there were few Jews left in France who held any illusions about the plight of their brethren on the other side of the Rhine. There was no raffle, no hoopla, to raise money. The guests were expected to slip a sealed envelope into a large Ming dynasty vase, the envelope containing either a check or a pledge; then they were free to mingle with the other guests. No pressure was exerted. That would have been ill bred.

Maurice and Charlotte de Sibour had donated 115,000 francs apiece, the equivalent of $5,000 each, the franc then having fallen to 23 to the dollar, and many of the guests contributed much more. Some gave less, for the French Jews were not one hundred percent anti-Hitler, even at this late date, even with the anti-Semitism then rampant in Germany. Some of the wealthiest Jews actually sided with their Gentile peers in preferring the stability of fascism, even with its attendant anti-Semitism, to the chaos of democratic France. But few of these were at the party, and the Baron Weil was to take out of his Ming vase more than 4,600,000 francs for the German Jews. For this, he was providing excellent champagne and caviar as well as the legendary beauty of his Château de Bray, which had been built in the 1550s by Diane de Poitiers, the duchess of Valentinois and mistress of Henry II. It was a gorgeous setting for a party, whatever the reason; the inherent worth of the cause made it only that much more enjoyable to Charlotte de Sibour.

She was chatting with Hermine Perrata, the chic wife of a textile manufacturer, when she spotted a ghost from the past. Standing beneath a tree a few feet away was a thin man who looked close to seventy. He was wearing a very elegantly cut light-gray suit and was holding a glass of champagne, staring at Charlotte. It was Sydney Fine.

Oddly, she felt nothing but curiosity. Excusing herself, she left Madame Perrata and walked over to her first husband, whom she hadn't seen for thirty-two years. She knew, of course, that he lived in Paris; she knew Richard Goldmark had died of vague causes three years before; there were mutual acquaintances who would periodically convey a scrap of news. But she had never run into him. Now, on this lovely late-August day, so far in distance and time from that evening in 1905 when he had humiliated her in front of her guests at their Fifth Avenue townhouse, they were meeting again. She held out her gloved hand and said in English, "Hello, Sydney," as if they had lunched the previous day. He replied, also in English, "Hello, Charlottes," as if he had just come home from the office. It was eerie; a conversation with a ghost.

"You haven't changed much," she said tentatively.

"Please don't lie," he replied rather cooly. "I'm a wreck, a Morro Castle of a human being, and I know it and I'm not in the least sensitive about it. So you may say that I look like a badly preserved prune, or an Egyptian antiquity, and I won't take offense. But you look much younger than I would have expected. I know that you're fifty-nine and will be sixty next month on the tenth—you see, I forget nothing. But you could pass for forty-five. Congratulations."

She nodded her head slightly in bemused acceptance of his compliment.

"Have you met my husband?" she went on.

"No, and I don't think that I want to. That would be awkward, I think. However, I know who he is, of course. I've read his articles, which are excellent—though they aren't calculated to make him very popular with the right, are they?"

"Hardly."

"You're happily married, I take it."

"Extremely."

"Good. You've had two very successful marriages after a first one that, shall we say, didn't turn out quite as expected. Although I have a feeling, looking at you, that you forgave me a long time ago. Am I right?"

"Yes. I forgave and, frankly, I forgot. That world is dead now."

The remark seemed to affect him strongly. His slight chilliness melted and his wrinkled face became sad.

"Yes, it is," he said. "It was a beautiful world, wasn't it?"

"I thought so. You apparently weren't so sure."

He shot her a look. "I see you haven't forgotten everything."

She smiled. "It doesn't matter. It's all over with. I was sorry to hear about Richard's death."

"Thank you."

There was a long silence, as if neither was sure whether to continue the conversation, and, if so, how to do it. Then he said, "I'm thinking of returning to America. After all these years. I'm afraid it will be a strain on me, since I haven't been back, even once. Of course, I've seen photos. New York is totally different from what I remember . . . horses and carriages."

"Are you staying long?"

"Oh, it won't be a visit. I'm going back permanently. You should think about it, too. Do you still have your American citizenship?"

"Yes . . ."

"Then you're lucky. I gave mine up years ago. I may have trouble about that, but I have cousins in the State Department."

"But why are you going back?"

He looked at her curiously, surprised she even asked.

"The war," he said. "The Nazis. There's going to be a war—surely you realize that? And the Nazis are going to invade France, just the way they did last time. Except this time I imagine they'll do a better job of it. France is not going to be a comfortable place for us Jews— even us American Jews. You certainly should consider going home."

"This is my home," replied Charlotte.

He shrugged. "Have it your way."

"I would never leave my husband," she added.

"I heard you left your second one?"

"I did. But this one I love. It *is* the most important thing in the long run, isn't it, Sydney? Love, I mean."

He thought about this. Then he said, "Perhaps."

A handsome young man came up to him and gave Charlotte a curious look. Then he said to Sydney, in French, "I'm bored. Let's go."

Sydney nodded and extended his hand to Charlotte.

"Good-bye, Charlotte. I doubt we'll see each other again. At least," —he smiled—"in this world," and gestured around him.

"I'm afraid you may be right."

They shook hands, then he turned to leave.

"Sydney?" she said.

He stopped and looked back.

"Yes?"

"Have you been at all happy?"

He considered this.

"As much as any of us has a right to expect, I'd say."

Then he turned and walked away.

CHAPTER FIVE

There are three types of polio—spinal, bulbar (which affects centers in the bulb of the brain), and the rare and very serious combination of the two, bulbospinal. It was this last variety that Rita Tweed had contracted. And while the possibility of her dying was great, the doctors consoled her parents and Christopher Manning with the promise that if she did survive, her chances of a complete recovery were very high. For one of the perversities of this peculiar disease was that while a milder variety might not endanger the patient's life, it could leave him permanently crippled, as had been the case with the nation's most famous polio victim, President Roosevelt. Yet the most dangerous variety might leave the patient—if he survived—unscathed.

Rita's problem was compounded by an assault of the virus on her breathing centers—the intercostal and phrenic nerves—so that the diaphragm in her chest partially "froze" and her breathing was becoming shallow and labored. This, along with a rapid pulse, sweating, and a flushed face due to excess accumulation of carbon dioxide in her system, prompted the doctor to put her in an iron lung. Christopher, who had moved in with Rita's parents during the ordeal, felt a sense of empathetic, claustrophobic terror as he watched the nurses place Rita on the wheeled cot with the steel headboard, through which her head pierced a sponge-rubber collar. Then the cot was swiftly wheeled inside the cylindrical tank, the headboard forming the seal at the end of the cylinder, and the motor operating the rubber bellows underneath the tank was turned on. The *swish, swosh, bing, bang* sound of the bellows was one never to be forgotten by a victim or a loved one of a victim.

The machine had been invented in 1927 by a young scientist named Philip Drinker who was doing inhalation experiments with a cat sealed from the neck down in a vacuum box. The thought occurred to Drinker that the process might be reversed—rather than the cat breathing in the partial vacuum, why couldn't the vacuum be made to "breathe" for the cat? The result was the first iron lung, which worked on the simple principle that nature abhors a vacuum. When the rubber bellows opened, air was gently suctioned out of the tank and Rita's body was surrounded by a partial vacuum, which caused her chest to rise and forced her to inhale. Then, when the bellows closed, air poured back into the tank and out through a trap valve, destroying the partial vacuum, permitting Rita's chest to fall and forcing her to exhale. It was an ingenious invention that saved hundreds of lives. But as Christopher watched his fiancée's body being sealed in the shiny steel cylinder with the eight sponge-rubber "armports" on the side to allow the nurses to reach in and adjust, move or stimulate Rita's immobilized body, it seemed to him like some hideous medieval instrument of torture.

Rita looked into the tilted mirror above her and saw the strained faces of Chris and her parents watching her. She was as terrified as they, but she forced herself to smile.

At least she was alive.

A week after Christopher left for Cleveland to be with Rita, Lily Manning announced the appointment of herself as president of the Manning Rubber and Steel Corporation, an announcement that caused reverberations around the country. The Manning stock, which had already slipped fourteen points because of the strike and Mark's serious injury, now plummeted another nine points in one trading session, and the influx of sell orders was so great that trading was suspended for two hours on the Exchange. David Manning, as senior member of the family, was swamped with calls from outraged directors, all of whom demanded to know what right Lily had to appoint herself president. "A woman can't run a huge company like Manning!" said Ardley Bennet, eldest son and heir of Frank Bennet, who had inherited his father's directorship in the company after Frank's death the previous year. "Why, it's ridiculous! The whole country's laughing, and look what's happening to the stock! My God!"

"I know, I know . . ." mumbled David.

"Well, what are you going to *do* about it?" demanded Ardley, and since the giant Bennet Motor Company was still Manning's biggest individual customer, this was a question that could hardly be put off for long. But David managed to deflect it momentarily with vague promises of "taking some sort of decisive action" and his by now time-worn reminder that Lily's self-appointment would only be good until Mark came out of his coma. Then he ordered his car to meet him at the entrance of the executive wing, where he got in and told his chauffeur to drive him to Cleveland.

Two hours later he was admitted to the carpeted office of Ben Dwyer, who shook his hand and offered him a chair. Twelve Victorian judges and Q.C.'s, sketched by Spy, looked down at the two lawyers as they sat down. Then Ben said, "I think I have an idea why you're here. It's Lily naming herself president?"

"Yes, that's exactly what it is! I've got every director of the company at my throat demanding—and I don't use the word lightly—to know how she's getting away with this, and how can anyone who's not in a loony bin expect her to run a company as big as this, and Ben, I don't have an answer for them!"

"Well, as far as the legality of what she's done is concerned, it states in the incorporating by-laws that the chairman of the board—or his duly appointed representative—and I quote, has the power to appoint all executives of the company, with the proviso that the appointment be approved by a majority of the directors at the next regularly scheduled directors' meeting. So Lily has the power to make herself president."

David nodded impatiently.

"All right, I knew you were going to say that. But let's forget the directors and the incorporating by-laws for a while and get to the real issue. I've been putting everyone off, including myself, by saying wait for father to come out of his coma, but he hasn't come out yet—this is the beginning of his third week—and I'm beginning to face what will happen if he dies. I mean, Lily as president for a few days is bad enough; but Lily as president for a long time is a disaster. Now, Ben, I realize what I'm going to ask you to do is totally unethical, but I'm asking anyway. Can you tell me—at least generally—the terms of father's will?"

Ben frowned. "Come now, David, you're a lawyer. You know I can't break a client's trust."

"Of course I know it, but Ben, this is different. I'm worried about Lily. Provoking that bloodbath at the factories was bad enough, but firing Harrison Starr and now naming herself president of the company—! I mean, we have to do something to stop her, Ben. Can't you see that? I simply can't believe she'd do these things if she thought father was going to get well."

Ben looked at him sharply. "What are you implying?"

David shifted nervously in his chair. "Christopher mentioned it first, and I felt I had to put him off. But I'm not so sure he wasn't right. Chris thinks Lily is acting this way because she *knows* father is never going to come out of his coma . . ."

Ben leaned back in his padded chair. "That's a terrible accusation to make, David."

"I'm making it. Now can you see why it's important to us to know what's in father's will?"

"Yes . . ."

"Let me put it this way, Ben. Is there anything in father's will that would make it, shall we say, advantageous to Lily to kill him?"

"Well, Lily will be an extremely wealthy widow. But I hardly think that would induce her to commit murder. She's much wealthier as Mark's wife."

"No, I realize that. It's not the money she's after, anyway. It's the company. Is there anything in the will that would make it convenient for her to have father out of the way? What I'm pussyfooting around trying to say is, does she get father's stock?"

Ben took a deep breath, then gave in.

"No."

David looked relieved. "Thank God. That takes a lot off my mind. Ben—I can't tell you how much I appreciate your telling me—"

"Well, since I've gone this far, I might as well go a little further, David. Don't get *too* relieved."

"What does that mean?"

"David, I would never tell you this if it weren't for my long friend-ship with your father. But with all these extraordinary circumstances —well, I think now it probably is better that you know what's in the will. When your father and I worked out the details of it several years ago, you were just starting in the business, Mark wasn't sure what Richard would do, Ellen was still in Paris and—well, to put it right on the line, he was very undecided—and unhappy, I might add—about all of you as far as your interest in the company was concerned. Lily, on the other hand, had always been, to put it mildly, interested in the company, and Mark admired her business sense. For that reason, while he left his stock in the corporation equally in trust to all of the five children, we set it up so that the stock is to be voted by a trust com-mittee until the trusts are dissolved. I might add that if any one of you dies, that stock goes to his heirs, or in case he has none, is divided equally among the other children."

"Who makes up the committee that votes the stock?"

"Myself, Lily and the president of the company."

"So that's why she's made herself president!"

"I wouldn't rush to any conclusions, David, but I'll admit that might possibly be in her mind. I'm sure Mark never thought that she would try to make herself president. She couldn't have under ordinary circumstances. I mean, if Mark had died. What's caused all this is that Mark *hasn't* died, that he's at least temporarily out of the picture, which gives all his power to her . . . temporarily. Now, as president of the company, she would constitute two-thirds of the trust committee and she could outvote me. So if Mark died now, I confess she'd be in a unique position."

"How long do the trusts run?"

"Until each child is thirty-five."

"My God."

"With the exception of Evan. Because he's so much younger than the rest of you, Mark terminated his trust when he reaches twenty-one."

David looked suddenly haggard.

"It's almost beautiful in its structure," he said softly. "Beautiful for Lily, I mean. If father dies, she can run the company almost singlehanded for the next *seven* years! I won't be thirty-five until 1944. Ellen is a year younger than I am, so Lily can vote her stock until 1945, Richard's until 1946 and Chris's until 1947—God, it's *ten* years, really! Plus, she'll have Evan's stock to vote too! She'll be able to set the company up any way she wants in that time. She'll be able to load the board of directors with her patsies, make all the top executives her yes men and make it damned hard for any of us ever to get back in the picture. For that matter, she could *fire* all of us—myself and Dick and Len and Chris . . . and even if we challenged her in a proxy fight, she'd have so much on her side, being president, that I have serious doubt about how well we'd do. Plus, of course, a proxy fight would tear the company to pieces . . ."

"But hold on, David," Ben Dwyer said. "All this is *possible,* but is it probable? You have to assume Lily really would do it, which we really don't know."

"Oh, I'm afraid we do," David said with a bitterness that was unusual for him.

"Mark did tell me she eventually wants Evan to run the company."

"Yes, there's Evan, she wants it for him. But she wants it for herself, too, Ben. I'll admit I don't like Lily, so I'm biased against her. But, Ben, I've met women like her before, women over forty who've gotten power hungry, just like they once were sex hungry. Lily works very quietly behind the scenes and you hardly know she's there, or what she's up to until suddenly, whammo! You see the whole thing, just the way I'm seeing it now. Oh, there's no question. Lily wants the prize for herself as much as for Evan."

"I'd agree with what you said, David, except you left something out."

"What's that?"

"You talked about power-hungry women, as if it's a disease limited to the fair sex. For every power-hungry woman around, there's a hundred equally voracious men."

David neither could, nor would, argue that point. After all, in his opinion his stepmother wasn't all that different from his father. She just operated differently. And more to the point, she was operating against him.

What he said to Ben was, "Maybe that's what's wrong with the world."

Things were going well for Lily Manning.

As she sat behind her husband's huge desk in his enormous office, her eyes followed the dark wood horizontal stripe around the paneled walls until it struck the big window behind her. Then she turned completely around and looked out over the factories below. She thought of her father, dead of a heart attack two years before in his Florida retirement home. Harold Swenson had done well for a Swedish emigrant, but he had always been Number Two.

His daughter had become Number One.

As far as she knew, she was the first woman ever to take over a giant corporation, and Miss Winslow had been swamped with phone calls from reporters wishing to interview the new president of the Manning Rubber and Steel Corporation. That very afternoon she was to be interviewed and photographed for *Life,* and the New York *Times* was sending out one of its reporters to write her up. The women's magazines were ecstatic, and there had been hints that the *Ladies' Home Journal* wanted to put her on its cover. It was all exciting and very heady to Lily.

She felt almost fulfilled.

Miss Winslow came in to announce the Honorable Seymour Ruggles, mayor of Elkins. Lily told her to show him in. Mayor Ruggles, an expansive, beamish man who was very influential in the local Elks and was a real-estate salesman in what he called "real life" (indicating that he shared his critics' appraisal of his political career as having a certain fantasylike quality to it), came into the big office, crossed the yards of carpet to Lily's desk. She smiled at her distinguished visitor and told him to sit down.

"I understand," said Lily, "that you're running for reelection next year?"

"That's right, Mrs. Manning. The voters seem to think they can stomach two more years of me, and if they're willing, I'm willing." He laughed wholeheartedly.

"Well, I'd like to make a personal contribution to your campaign." She pulled an envelope from her desk drawer and tossed it across the desk to him. "Open it."

He needed little prompting. Opening the flap, he looked inside at the packet of hundred dollar bills. "Why, Mrs. Manning, you're being *very* generous!"

"There are fifty hundreds in the packet, your honor. Don't bother counting. It's an expression of my warm admiration for your administration."

"Why, I . . . I'm overwhelmed . . ."

"Don't be."

He didn't miss her tone. Tucking the envelope in his jacket pocket, he lowered his voice.

"I take it that, because this is a cash donation, you don't want, that is, you'd prefer to remain anonymous?"

Lily nodded. "You take it right."

"Well, it will be our little secret, Mrs. Manning. No one will ever hear a peep out of me, believe me. Now, what can I do for you?"

Lily nearly laughed in his face. It was so damned easy when you had the power! That's what most people would never believe, how really *easy* it was . . . like a marvelous game, really. Here was this boob politician not even bothering to conceal his corruption! It was truly delicious.

"Well, your honor, I've become very concerned about polio."

"Oh yes, it's terrible. And I'm so sorry to hear about your stepson's fiancée."

"Yes, isn't that a shame? But others are catching it too, and it seems to me this town should *do* something about it."

"Well, we've closed down the municipal swimming pool—the one Mr. Manning gave the town—and we're talking about shutting the movie thee-a-turs."

"I know, but I think we should do more. I think the Board of Health should ban all meetings of over five people for the duration of the emergency. I think that not only the theaters should be closed, but the Green Lantern skating rink and the churches too. Do you see what I mean?"

He saw. He was a boob, not an idiot.

"Yes, I do. Of course, that would mean breaking up the picket lines around the factories, wouldn't it?"

"I'm afraid it would."

"As well as any meeting the union might try to hold?"

"Exactly."

The mayor looked nervous. "That might not sit too well with a lot of people in town, you know."

"I never thought it would be popular, even though it is for the town's safety. That's why I contributed $5,000 to your campaign chest, your honor—because I know that you're a man of integrity who is not afraid to do the unpopular thing."

The mayor thought about this, not looking too happy. He sighed. "Well, it has to be done, that's all there is to it. The union may yell its head off, but it's my clear duty as mayor to protect the children of this town from infantile paralysis."

"It certainly is."

His honor stood up. "After all, kids' lives are more important than a union contract, aren't they?"

"They certainly are."

His honor reached over to shake Lily's hand. "Mrs. Manning, it's as good as done."

She smiled. "I knew I could count on you."

The mayor started toward the door. Halfway across the office, he stopped and turned back to the big desk. "By the way," he said, "since we've become colleagues, if that's the right word, maybe you'd be interested in some information I don't think you know."

Lily said nothing, waited.

He returned to the desk. "A little over two months ago your stepson, Richard, came to my office and put pressure on me to get a police report out of the files for him. I told him I had no influence with the state police, but he kept insisting and, well, to make a long story short, I managed to get the report for him."

"What was it?"

"Well, it seems that Richard and Mr. Hastings, Miss Ellen's husband, rented a fishing shack last spring . . ."

"I remember. What about it?"

"They weren't fishing there, Mrs. Manning. At least, not for fish. They had Josie Stevens, that little waitress at the country club, and Irene Hayes, who works at Gates's, out there and they were having themselves a little old ball. And one night last June, the Stevens girl went off in Richard's car and put it in a ditch. Well, she was picked up by a state trooper, who took her back to the cabin, and there they

all were. They tried to bribe the trooper, but he filed his report anyway, and that was when Mr. Richard came to me. But I figured you
might want to know about it. Something tells me Mr. Richard wasn't
planning on telling you."

Lily smiled her prettiest smile.

"Your honor," she said, "I think we're going to get along just fine."

It was a half hour later, at quarter to eleven, that Miss Winslow
put through a call to Lily from Miss Hogan, the morning nurse at
River Bend. Miss Hogan was extremely excited. "Mrs. Manning!" she
said. "He's awake! Your husband is awake, and he's talking to me!"

Lily's face was expressionless.

"I'll be right over," she said. Then she hung up.

Mark had been put in his bedroom on the second floor of River
Bend, which was separated from his wife's newly decorated bedroom
by a single door. The private nurses hired to care for him had had
little to do except force-feed him vitamins, move him every hour to
prevent bedsores, empty the bedpan and try to keep him clean as
possible under the circumstances. However, they had not tried to
shave him, so that now he displayed a twenty-two-day growth of red-
gold beard, and it was this that seemed to confuse him the most as
Lily stood beside his bed.

"Why a beard?" he said weakly, his eyes mostly shut, though they
would sometimes open. He thrashed around spasmodically, as if his
brain, like an engine that had lain idle for too long, was having difficulty warming up.

"It's been over three weeks, darling," said Lily. Dr. Carson was
standing next to her, watching his patient. "Actually, twenty-two days.
We didn't shave you."

"Charlotte," he whispered, "I *didn't* have anything to do with
Sylvia . . . Baker . . . I really didn't . . ."

Lily looked at Dr. Carson. The doctor whispered, "His memory's
coming back in bits and pieces, not always in context."

"Why don't you believe me? . . . I love you, Charlotte, I wouldn't
cheat on you . . ." His eyes opened again and he stared in confusion
at Lily and Dr. Carson. "You're not Charlotte . . ."

"No, I'm Lily, darling, and this is Dr. Carson. You remember Dr.

Carson, don't you?"

He looked blankly at the doctor. "No."

"You've had a serious accident, Mr. Manning," said Dr. Carson. "You were hit on the back of the head with a rock, and you've been unconscious for twenty-two days. It looks, though, as if you're going to be all right."

Mark remained in confusion. "Bill Sands . . . crazy Bill . . . he shot me, didn't he?"

"Yes, darling, but that was a long time ago. *Years* ago."

"Years?" He looked even more confused. Then, as if giving up, he closed his eyes again.

"He'll be this way for some time," said the doctor. "Waking up then going to sleep again. His brain's adjusting now, but I think we'll all be surprised how quickly he begins to focus. I'd say the worst is over now. If he'd remained unconscious much longer, I'd have started to worry, but this is very encouraging."

"Well, I'm terribly relieved, needless to say. Is there anything special or different we should do for him?"

"No, just the same routine, except it should become easier. I think he'll start feeding himself from now on, and I think in a few days we can give him a better diet. We'll see how he progresses." She accompanied him out to the hallway and thanked him; then she went back into the bedroom and stood next to the bed, looking down at her husband.

He was sleeping now, and he looked peaceful.

Lily thanked Miss Hogan for calling her and left the room.

When Christopher Manning was told over the phone by his sister, Ellen, the latest development in Lily's career, he blew his stack.

"She's shut the union out on account of *polio?*"

"Yes. The town's closed down tight and it looks as if the strike's broken, at least for the time being. Of course, everyone knows Lily's behind it. Everyone saw Mayor Ruggles—that ass!—cross the picket line to go into the executive wing, and then this afternoon the Board of Health bans all meetings? Well, no one's fooled. But it worked, Chris. The union's holed up, licking its wounds."

"But Ellen, look at the price we pay! It's so rotten cynical to *use* an epidemic like she's doing! My God, Rita's in an iron lung fighting for her life, and my stepmother is *using* the disease to maneuver a union? This town's going to *really* hate us . . ."

"I know, Chris. Good Lord, I'm not blind!"

"Then why doesn't somebody do something? Why doesn't David *move*, for once in his life?"

"Now calm down, Chris. David finally *has* moved. Father started to come out of his coma this morning—"

"*Thank God!* How is he?"

"Pretty foggy and confused, and he's only awake for five or ten minutes at a time, then goes back to sleep again. But anyway he *is* coming out of it, and Dr. Carson is very encouraged."

For a moment Chris said nothing. He was almost at the end of his string, having the two people he loved most in the world both in critical condition—Rita and his father. Now the news that his father at least was showing signs of recovery was a tremendous relief.

"Of course," continued Ellen, "the problem now isn't so much father's brain as dear old Lily."

"What do you mean?"

"We had a family meeting a little while ago, and for once David was quite forceful. He went to see Ben Dwyer about father's will and Chris, you were right—if father were to die, Lily's in charge. We get all the stock in trust, but until we're thirty-five Lily controls it, as father's widow and now as president of the company. So David thinks there's a chance, now that father's started to recover, that Lily might try something. And we're all going over to River Bend at six this evening for a face-to-face with our sainted stepmother."

"And what are you going to tell her?"

"That from now on, one of us is going to be in the room with father twenty-four hours a day, along with the nurse. She's not going to like it, but that's too bad. Because David says—and he's right, I think— that our only chance now is father. We've *got* to protect him, not only to save him but to save ourselves. It should be a charming scene."

"That's for sure! And would I love to be there to watch her. I'm glad David's finally doing the right thing. We've got to show her we mean business."

"Yes, I think so. Anyway, that's the situation as of now and I'll keep you posted. How's Rita?"

"Hanging on." He sounded depressed, then forced himself to cheer up. "But the doctor says the fact she's still alive is an encouraging sign."

Ellen sighed. "Like it was with father . . . doctors have such a lovely way of putting things, don't they? Well, darling, all our thoughts are with you and Rita."

"Thanks, Ellen, and I'll keep my fingers crossed for all of you."

"Yes, wish us luck. We'll need it."

Lily was waiting for them in the living room of River Bend, seated in front of the big west window. She was wearing a pink-and-white striped Norell gown she'd bought two years before, and its simple, summery lines were most flattering to her. She wore no jewelry except the enormous cabochon-emerald ring Mark had given her for their fifth anniversary, and Ellen, who thought her stepmother's taste was suspect and that she tended to overdress, had to admit as she and her husband and her brothers and their wives were led into the room by the butler, Peter, that for once Lily looked quietly chic. Moreover, she didn't seem at all intimidated or apprehensive at this invasion by her numerous stepchildren. She sat smoking a cigarette and sipping a martini, watching them as they told Peter their drinks. She chatted pleasantly until the cocktails were served. There was a silence when the servants had left the room. David, who had grown up in this house and had loved it, wondered at how inhospitable it now seemed to him.

"All right," said Lily pleasantly, "what's this all about?"

David cleared his throat. "It's about father."

"And what about him?"

"Now that he's coming out of the coma, we'd like to be with him."

"You're perfectly free to go upstairs and see him."

"We mean, we want to sit with him. Around the clock."

Lily's green eyes narrowed slightly as she glanced at Ellen, Len, Richard, Amanda, and Cynthia. Then back to David.

"I see."

"Ellen," went on David, "has volunteered to take the days, eight A.M. to four P.M. Richard and I will alternate the four to midnight shift. And Marvin Senjak has agreed to take from midnight to eight.

Lily looked amused. "Oh, it's wonderful," she said. "You're really afraid I'm going to do something to him, aren't you?"

The others looked taken aback by her bluntness. She stood up and went behind her chair to lean against its back. "But you're all so obvious! Didn't you think I'd guess? The children standing guard duty so that wicked stepmomma won't sneak in and smother father with a pillow or whatever?" She laughed. "But you're all so damn stupid! Why do you think I'd want to kill Mark?"

"We didn't say that—"

"You don't have to, Richard. It's written all over your faces. Now, if we're through with the preliminaries, let's get down to it. It's all in the family, after all. Why would I kill the husband I adore? Because I'm afraid he'll be furious at the things I've done since he's been in his coma? Is that it?"

"That's partly it," David said. "When father finds out about that slaughter you ordered at the factories, not to mention this underhanded business with the mayor—"

"Do you know anything at all about your father's career? Do you?" She looked around at them.

"Of course we know," said Richard. "He started with a bicycle shop—"

"And he jes' grew, like Topsy? Jes' grew into one of the twenty biggest corporations in America? Why, you damn naïve fools, you're his flesh and blood and you've bought the official story, the Horatio Alger story of Mark Manning, farm boy become empire builder, philanthropist and art collector. How do you think empires get built, and how do you think they stay in power? By muscle, by violence if necessary, and, yes, by deceit. Do you know how Mark got the Bennet account, the one that made him? Oh, he's told me *this* one a thousand times. He caught Frank Bennet in a Detroit whorehouse and *blackmailed* him! And you call *me* underhanded?"

"This has nothing to do with why we're here!" said Ellen.

"It has everything to do with why you're here! You're accusing me of wanting to *murder* my husband for fear that he'll—what? Divorce me, I suppose, when he finds out that I've used deceit and violence to save his company for him. Well, I'm telling you that it was deceit and violence that built this goddamn company in the first place! And I mean *violence*—bloodshed, murder. It was all there in Sheila Harrington's book, except none of you would believe it because you didn't *want* to believe it!"

"That book was full of lies!" Ellen said angrily.

"Oh, was it? Well, darling, I happened to be on that yacht ten years ago when Mark radioed the Las Palmas plantation and, in effect, ordered the death of Roger Boine to save that plantation. I heard him, so don't tell *me* that book's a lie! She was a lot closer to the truth than even *she* knew. And don't give me any of this nonsense that Mark's going to hate me for what I've done since he's been in the coma. Mark Manning is going to love me even more than he already does— because I *saved* his company, never matter how." She looked at them with contempt. "So go ahead, stand guard over daddy but you're wasting your time. I can hardly wait till Mark wakes up! Because what you smug little idiots can't understand is, he's going to *approve* my appointment as president of the company—because there's nobody

628 THE MANNINGS

better equipped for the job."

"I don't believe it—any of it!" Ellen said. "I can believe *you* would commit murder—God knows what you might do! But never in a million years could my father do it! One of your least-attractive qualities, Lily—and my God you do have your share of them—is that you try to drag everyone else down to your gutter level!"

"Oh, how touching," Lily said. "How loyal, true blue—and wonderfully observant. Yes, Ellen, you're an extraordinarily observant woman who sees everything about her father, just as she sees everything about her husband. And you, Cynthia, I suppose you share this opinion of the Mannings? Mark, noble captain of industry? Young Richard, loyal husband? Richard and Len, why don't you tell the ladies all about your little fishing shack, and all those wonderful evenings you spent out there with—let's see, was it Barbara Hutton? Doris Duke? Oh no, how stupid of me, we were being so democratic last spring . . . it was that sweet Josie Stevens who serves such a neat martini at the country club, and the young Hayes girl, who sells lingerie, I believe, at Gates's? Wasn't that it, *gentlemen?* Did you tell your wives about the evening Josie got tipsy and drove your Buick into the ditch? And that state trooper who wouldn't take the bribe, and wrote up the accident report? Why ladies, you look surprised! You mean you didn't know?"

"Would you shut up?"

Lily laughed. "Well, Richard, I surely didn't mean to cause any embarrassment among you dear sweet people. Except I think it is *so* important that we Mannings see each other just as we are. All of us. *Without* exception. We are, definitely, not saints. Wouldn't you say?"

Ellen was staring at Len. "Is this true?" she said in a low voice. He glanced miserably at Richard, then nodded.

"I'm sorry, but it's true."

Deep hurt came over Ellen's face but she said nothing. Cynthia was looking at Richard, who refused to look back at his wife. He got to his feet. "Lily, we're not perfect, we have skeletons in our closet—so what? The point is you're trying to take over this company that rightfully belongs to us, not to mention the stockholders and—"

"Calm down, Richard," said David, who had remained seated. Everyone turned to him. He said quietly, "I don't deny much of what you said, Lily, but I think there's one thing you don't understand—father has changed. Don't misunderstand, I don't particularly like him. I never have and I may be unfair to him but I doubt if he changed so much because of any desire on his part to become noble and good. He's changed, at least partly, because he's smart enough to see he has to. The old days of pure rugged individualism are gone.

The days of company unions are gone. The days of bullying the little guy are gone. Father may not have accepted the union idea yet, but when he finds out that you're responsible for the death of four strikers, you're fooling yourself if you think he's going to approve of what you've done—no matter how you try to justify it. All he'll have to do is look at what the stock's dropped to and he'll realize how bankrupt your policies have been and how stupid any attempts to strong-arm labor is in the year 1937." He stood up. "So at least now we have it all out in the open. Maybe we're wrong to think you intend any harm to our father. Frankly I still have my suspicions. And so from now on he's going to be guarded. If you'll excuse me, I'm going upstairs right now to take the first shift." He turned to his wife. "Amanda, please arrange for my dinner to be sent up?"

"Of course, darling." She turned to Lily. "I just wanted to add that everything David has said I back up one hundred percent."

"Me, too," said Ellen.

"And me," said Richard.

"Count me in," said Len.

Cynthia said likewise.

Lily looked around at them, and Ellen had to admit she had never looked more excitingly beautiful. It was as if the challenge made her radiate.

"So it's open war?" she finally said in a soft voice. "I couldn't be more pleased. You don't know how loathesome it's been to have had to pretend even to be able to *stand* any of you."

David signaled to the others. They put down their drinks and started across the room to the door. No one spoke. David was the last to file out. As he looked back at his stepmother, she was still standing in front of the great west window, her slim figure bathed in the shimmering oranges and yellows of the setting sun.

Then he left the room and went up to his father.

As she left the front door of River Bend, Ellen Manning Hastings said to her husband in a low voice, "I don't ever want to discuss this again, Len. But I want to make my position clear right now. I married you because I loved you and I thought you loved me—"

"Ellen—"

"Wait a minute. I'm old-fashioned. I think love implies fidelity."

"It was just a stupid little fling."

"All right, you're entitled to one, which you've had. I could add

you might have shown a little more taste but I'm not going to get
into *that*. Anyway, if I ever find out about another one, I'm through.
Clear?"

He nodded, looking guilty and ashamed. She took his hand, kissed
his cheek, and hoped against hope he wasn't acting.

Cynthia Fahnstock Manning said nothing as Richard drove her
to their home from River Bend. Once inside the house, she ran to
their study, slammed the door, threw herself into a chair and began
crying. Richard came into the room and looked at her. "That bitch,"
he said, going over to the bar. "I don't know how she found out
about it, but she had one giant-sized nerve saying anything."

"*She* had nerve? What about you?"

Richard poured himself a scotch from the crystal decanter, then
squirted in a shot of soda from the silver-and-crystal siphon. He
looked at his wife. "Cynthia," he said, taking a sip of the whiskey,
"I'll be damned if I'll be a hypocrite. Josie Stevens was neither the
first nor the last. You know that. You heard Lily say my father wasn't
exactly a paragon in his climb to the top. I never made an empire, but
I guess in some ways I'm my father's son. If I were you, I wouldn't
expect too much change. I don't know if I'm worse than most men
but I'm sure not much better. There are no medals on this one. You
let me know what you decide to do."

Cynthia watched as the large, handsome man she adored went
out of the study and closed the door behind him. She told herself she
should make a scene, threaten a divorce. She did none of these things.
She, too, in her way, was honest. She simply couldn't stand the idea
of losing him. Maybe they both were weak. He was her weakness.
He'd at least been honest with her. She'd try to be the same with
herself. They might not be the ideal couple, but in a way they were
ideally suited. Josie? Who the hell was Josie? Did it matter? Cynthia
Manning? She knew who *that* was. So did everybody else.

Cynthia Manning. She'd settle for that.

On the afternoon of August 27, 1937, five days after the guard
watch was instituted in Mark's bedroom, a premature hint of autumn
swept over northern Ohio as a Canadian air mass dropped southward,

bringing with it chilly winds and rain. The rain began as a drizzle, but by nightfall it had turned into a steady downpour that turned scorched lawns into squishy bogs and dried brooks into small rivers. After so much hot, dry weather the rain was welcome, but its unseasonable chilliness sent housewives into their closets and chests to drag out blankets for the night.

At River Bend, Lily Manning ate alone in the big dining room Then after a light supper she went into the living room, where she had coffee and a cigarette, standing before the west window and watching the rain teardrop down its panes, giving the impression that the huge house was weeping. At nine o'clock she walked through the long corridors of River Bend until she reached the first-floor bedroom of her eight-year-old son, Evan, which was directly below her own bedroom on the second floor. Evan had already been put to bed by his governess, Mrs. Simpkins, and was waiting for his mother to kiss him good night, as was her custom. Mrs. Simpkins left the room to retire to her own bedroom in the opposite wing of the house. (Lily had moved her away from Evan after his sixth birthday. She didn't want him to become too dependent on anyone but herself.) Alone with her son, Lily talked with him awhile. Despite the way the other Mannings complained about his character, this youngest of the second generation was a beautiful child, and the intelligence in his calm blue eyes suggested he had gotten more than a fair share of both his parents' brains. When Lily was finished talking to him, he nodded. Then she kissed him, turned out the light and left the room. Going upstairs, she looked in on Mark. He was asleep, being watched by a drowsy Richard Manning and Mrs. Albright, the evening nurse.

"Is everything all right?" asked Lily.

"Oh, yes, Mrs. Manning," whispered Mrs. Albright. "He was awake for several hours and ate a big dinner. He seemed in good spirits, and was talking with his son. It's remarkable progress."

"Good," said Lily. She nodded at Richard, who cooly nodded back; they were hardly speaking to one another. Lily then bade Mrs. Albright good night and went through the adjoining door to her bedroom, closing the door behind her as she turned on the lights.

She had recently had the bedroom redecorated, and it was done almost entirely in pale blue: blue watered-silk walls with matching curtains; a blue silk canopy on the fourposter bed; pale blue carpet; even pale blue shades on the twenty-odd lights of the big crystal chandelier. She kicked off her shoes and summoned Vera, her maid, who helped her undress. After changing into her pale blue satin nightgown, she dismissed Vera and crawled between her blue silk sheets to read another chapter of *Gone With the Wind* and smoke a final cigarette. Stubbing the butt out in a blue-marble ashtray, she exhaled a cloud of smoke, tossed the heavy book on the floor, took one last look around her lovely blue room, and turned out the lights.

As she lay her head back on the pillow, she listened to the steady drumming of the rain on the roof of the huge house that had been built in 1913 by her predecessor, the house that was the heart of the Manning empire.

The sound of the rain never slacked in its tempo. It, too, seemed to be pale blue.

It was twenty past two the next morning when Marvin Senjak first smelled the smoke. A second later, he and Miss Sweeney, the night nurse, heard a cry from Lily's bedroom. Then the door opened and Lily ran in, struggling with her peignoir. "Evan's room's on fire! The smoke's pouring into my room and I can see flames from his window . . . we've got to get him out!"

Her bedroom was filled with a thin haze, and Marvin lost no time running to the hall door. "Call the fire department!" he yelled as he raced into the upstairs corridor and headed toward the distant stairway. With amazing speed for a man in his late forties, he charged past the pipe organ at the head of the stairs, then, grabbing the elaborate wrought-iron balustrade, almost slid down the marble steps to the entrance hall. Slapping on a light switch, he headed down the matching first floor corridor toward Evan's room. The door was closed, but smoke was billowing out from under it, and when Marvin grabbed the brass handle, it was almost too hot to touch, let alone grasp firmly. Taking a deep breath, he pushed open the door to confront a crackling inferno—the room was filled with flames. He backed away, throwing up his arm to protect his face from the blast of heat. It was impossible to save Evan; by now the kid would have been finished. Coughing from the smoke, Marvin started back toward the entrance hall, where he ran into a frightened Peter, who had thrown a raincoat over his pajamas and was barefoot. "I saw the fire from my house and ran over! It's Mr. Evan's room?"

"Yeah, and it's too late to save him. Come on. Help me get Mr. Manning out."

The two men started up the stairs, almost colliding with Miss Sweeney, who was running down them.

"His room's on fire!" she screamed. "I phoned the fire department and when I came back his room was on fire!"

"Jesus, already?"

Redoubling his efforts, Marvin leaped up the remaining stairs and started down the long corridor, which was filling with smoke. The door to Mark's bedroom was open, and the room was indeed on fire, though it was not the inferno Evan's room was. As Marvin plunged into the smoke, he noticed that Lily's bedroom was a blazing furnace.

Mark was unconscious, but he had been trying to get out of his bed when he passed out. One foot was on the floor. Flames were licking at the wooden headboard and the sheets on the right side of the bed were burning as Marvin picked him up and started carrying him out of the room, zigzagging around the fires now chewing the carpet. He lost his breath and was forced to fill his lungs with smoke, which nauseated him and sent him into a coughing fit that almost made him drop Mark. But he made it to the hall. Laying Mark on the floor, he leaned against the wall and gasped for air. When he had partially cleared out his lungs, he began dragging Mark down the hall by his arms, being too exhausted to pick him up. Halfway to the stair, Peter joined him and the two men were able to lift and carry Mark down the stairway to the hall and out into the rain, where the distant whine of the fire-engine sirens could already be heard.

The servants were all awake and outside by now, and Peter yelled at them to save the paintings as Marvin ran to the garage to get a car. With admirable presence of mind, the old butler organized the servants into teams, and by the time the fire engines clanged up in front of the house, a half dozen Old Masters had already been transported to the stables for safekeeping. The firemen rigged a pump and a hose in the swimming pool and ran another down to the Matahoochi as they turned the nozzles on the section of the house that was blazing. By now the flames seemed to be licking the rain clouds, and the other Mannings, awakened by the noise, had come from their homes and were helping the servants get the irreplaceable works of art out of the house. Ellen helped Marvin get Mark into the car he had brought from the garage. Then together they drove him to David's house, where he was put to bed, still unconscious but apparently not otherwise seriously harmed. Leaving him in Amanda's care, Ellen and Marvin hurried back to River Bend, where the rain and the firemen were beginning to get the flames under control.

"Where did it start?" she yelled over the noise to Marvin as they got out of the car.

"In Evan's bedroom."

"Oh, God," she said, feeling a rush of guilt for all the snide remarks she'd made about her young stepbrother. "Is he . . . dead?"

"I'm afraid so, Miss Ellen."

But when they reached the brick courtyard in front of the main entrance to the house, which was thronged with firemen, servants and Mannings, there, holding his mother's hand, was Evan.

"How did he—" Marvin started to say, pointing to the boy in the raincoat.

"He climbed out his window," said Lily. "Thank God!"

Marvin looked at the boy's feet. Something was wrong.

Evan's feet were warmly encased in rubber boots, and each of the four buckles of each boot had been neatly clasped.

Marvin knew that Evan Manning hated wearing boots.

Marvin didn't have to tell Mark. He knew.

He had been awakened by the smoke and the yelling. He had seen Lily splashing the gasoline out of the five-gallon can from the garage, pouring the stuff around the carpet near his bed. At first he had thought it was some bizarre nightmare. Then the reality hit him, but by then it was too late. She had run out of the room, the gasoline had whooshed into flames, the heat and the smoke had assaulted him, and as he tried to get out of the bed, he had lost consciousness. So the next morning when Marvin stood by his bed in David's house and told him, in guarded tones, his suspicions that Mrs. Manning had started the fire in Evan's bedroom—first making sure that Evan had climbed out the window, even going so far as to have him put on his boots so as not to get his feet wet (which had been her motherly if stupid and unLilylike mistake)—Mark had needed no persuading to believe the accusation. He knew that the woman he had been obsessed with for ten years—the woman he had trusted even more than his own children—had tried to murder him.

Now the problem was, what should he do about it? Oddly enough, as enraged as he was at her, in a way he understood why she had done it. Mark Manning understood her awful itch for power. It had, after all, driven him most of his life. What she had done in the weeks he had been unconscious, he had no idea, but he knew that, having tasted power, the temptation to hold onto it had been great enough to overcome her natural caution and drive her to this one incredibly desperate act.

Again—what should he do about it?

Prosecution was out of the question. The publicity was anathema to him, and bad for the company.

There was really only one sensible course to take. He took it.

Lily sat in the club car of the Seaboard Express, bound from New York to Miami, nursing a highball as she considered such matters as love and power and money and death . . . and the goddamn Mannings. She was learning to live with herself again, but oh, God, how she regretted what she had done, although it had seemed so clearcut, so simple and *necessary* at the time.

Actually, the most stupid thing, as in so many matters, was to have tried and not succeeded.

She had, of course, come out of it rather well. A $5,000,000 divorce settlement and custody of Evan six months out of every year—all on the proviso that she keep her mouth shut and stay out of Elkins. It wasn't the same as being president of the Manning Company, but things could certainly be worse. Mark had been so anxious to cover everything over, to keep the truth out of the papers, to keep the precious Manning reputation unblemished.

At first, knowing his hatred of bad publicity, she had challenged him, told him he wouldn't dare claim his *wife* actually tried to murder him. Besides, he couldn't *prove* anything and Evan would back her up. He had listened, then told her that ordinarily she might be right. But not this time. If she refused to take his settlement and get out, quietly and with no fuss, he would indeed accuse her, risk anything involved. She would *not* get away with what she'd done, and she knew that when it came down to it, they would believe him. She knew something about the power of the Manning name . . .

In the end she took the realistic way. She took the best she could get. It had been a long and exhilarating ride, being Mrs. Mark Manning. All right, it was over. But not necessarily everything else . . .

"Excuse me, aren't you Mrs. Mark Manning?"

She looked at the man sitting next to her who, up to now, she had been vaguely aware had been staring at her. Blond, about thirty-five, she thought, not so bad looking, well-dressed.

"Yes," she said, at the same time thinking she wouldn't be much longer.

"I thought you looked familiar. I'm from Cleveland, and I've seen your picture in the *Plain Dealer.* "My name's Jerry Hawkins."

"Hello, Jerry Hawkins."

"Isn't it a little early for Palm Beach?"

"I'm going to Miami."

"Oh? I thought you had a home in Palm Beach?"

She finished her drink.

"I am getting a divorce."

"Oh. I see. Sorry to hear that."

Clickety-clack, clickety-clack. The train wheels moving toward the sun and a new life. Away from Mark. The king. The Sun King. And she had been the Queen—and in more than name only . . .

"Waiter, I'll have another, please."

"Yes, ma'am."

He took her glass on his tray and headed for the bar. Jerry Hawkins offered her a Chesterfield.

"Thanks."

He lit it for her, she blew out the smoke.

"I'm going to Miami, too. I'm the new golf pro at the Mirador."

"Oh? That's nice."

He smiled, not put off by her tone.

"Do you play golf?"

"I hate golf."

"That's only because you've never been taught by a good pro."

"I assume you're a good pro?"

"The best. If you drop by the Mirador, I'll give you a lesson on the house."

She drew in a lungful of smoke. "I don't think I want to do that."

"Why not? You might enjoy it."

"Look, Jerry Hawkins, or whatever your name is, I'm feeling rather depressed just now, as you may imagine, and I really don't want to do anything except just sit by myself. Alone. Without small, pushy people trying to get themselves into my life. Is any of that clear?"

He didn't bat an eye—she rather admired his nerve.

"There's nothing like new faces to beat away the blues," he said cheerfully. "Why don't you think about it?"

By the time the waiter brought her the fresh drink, Lily had decided that Jerry Hawkins's face wasn't the best-looking nor the youngest nor the most interesting she'd ever seen. It was, however, the newest. It was immediately available.

And now that she was a middle-aged, wealthy divorcée exiled to the resorts of the world, perhaps it was time she took up golf.

As he walked toward the room he had turned over to his father until River Bend was rebuilt, David Manning wondered what his father was going to say to him. The last week had been, to put it mildly, a strain. First there had been the newspaper stories about the fire, which David had disliked. What with the tension in the town because of the strike, any publicity about the Mannings was even more unwelcome than usual. Then had come the shock of the news of his father's decision to divorce Lily. Not that he hadn't been delighted to hear it—all of them had been delighted. But it had come as a surprise. And then Richard had started the rumor. Normally unobservant Richard, who had seen Evan outside the burning house and had noticed he had his boots on. Richard had asked the same question Marvin Senjak had asked—would anyone waking up in his bed to find the room on fire put his boots on before getting out? The answer was obvious. Richard began saying Lily must have started the fire to kill Mark, and Mark had found out about it some way and divorced her. Although Mark was saying nothing, nor was his lawyer —nor Lily—this was what everyone in the family believed.

In any case, they couldn't have been happier about the outcome— it had finally gotten rid of Lily.

David opened the door and walked into his father's bedroom. Mark was shaved now and gaining strength every day, though no one, including himself, pretended he would ever be the same as before. The experience had made him, suddenly, an old man. The long coma had left him twenty-eight pounds lighter, and the skin on his face was now hanging slightly and the wrinkles were deep. Where he had always looked younger than his age before, he now looked older. But his mind was coming back. And he had been intensely concerned to find out what Lily had done to the business, to learn of the state of the strike, the still descending price of the stock, who was running the show and what was left of it to run.

Now he was sitting in a chair before a window reading the *Wall Street Journal*, wearing a plaid bathrobe over his pajamas. As David entered the room, he lowered the paper and looked at his eldest son, the son he had formerly liked the least.

"You wanted to see me, father?"

"Yes, David. Pull up a chair."

He did so, as Mark folded the paper and put it on a table. Then he said, "David, I haven't said much to any of you about Lily. I'd prefer leaving that a closed chapter, so to speak. But I will admit to you that I was wrong about her, and I think you know I don't like to admit being wrong."

"Yes, sir, I know that."

"I suppose I was so much taken with her, I couldn't or wouldn't see her faults. I knew, of course, that she was smart and ambitious, but just *how* ambitious . . . Well, let's say I made a very bad mistake." He paused. "I've made a mistake about you, too. Frankly, I'd always thought you were the least likely of my children to take over the company. But from what I've heard from Ben Dwyer and Ellen and Marvin, you did your best to hold the company together under what were pretty fierce circumstances. And of course, you showed initiative and courage trying to protect me from Lily. I appreciate it, and I want to thank you."

David's face suddenly had the look of an eight-year-old being given, for the first time in his life, the love and appreciation of his father.

"I . . . I tried to do my best, father."

"You not only tried, you showed you have a lot of guts. David, I've decided to make you the new president of the company. I'll remain chairman, but I'm not going to be very active from now on. I'm not only getting old, I'm feeling old and pretty damn tired. And there are other things I want to do in the time that's left. So you'll be running the show very much on your own from now on. You're a young man for such a responsibility, but I'm willing to take the gamble on you. You think you're up to it?"

"Yes, sir, I do. But I have to tell you something first."

"What's that?"

"The first thing I'm going to do as president is offer the union a contract, and one that's just about on their own terms."

Mark smiled an old man's smile. "Don't you think I know that?"

David stood up. As he clasped his father's outstretched hand, he was embarrassed to find he was crying like that eight-year-old boy.

After all these years, his father had finally recognized that his son David could be a whizz at something after all.

"Take care of the company, David," Mark said quietly, still holding his hand. "I know there's a lot of bitterness against us now because of what's happened. Well, that's understandable. But I hope you can get rid of most of it and make the company something this family can be proud of again."

"I'll try like hell, sir."

Mark squeezed his hand affectionately, then slowly let it go. As

David left the room, he wondered what his mother would think when she heard the news.

Knowing Charlotte's opinion of the Manning Rubber and Steel Company, David decided she would have mixed emotions about her favorite son becoming the head of the gigantic concern her father had helped found thirty-two years before.

PART

X

FINISHING SCHOOL

1940–1942

WHICH WAS not true. Charlotte was delighted that her eldest son had won the leadership of the empire, for she had long since removed herself emotionally from the company. It no longer influenced her life one way or the other, though she recognized that it loomed very large in the lives of her children and grandchildren. That the shy, sensitive David she had loved so much as a boy had grown up to replace his unshy, insensitive—as she tended to think of him—father struck her as ironic, but she was glad for David's sake.

In June 1938 Charlotte and Maurice sailed on the beautiful *Normandie* for New York to attend Christopher Manning's wedding in Shaker Heights to Rita Tweed. Rita, who had been one of the fortunate victims of bulbospinal polio to survive, had recovered completely. She made a beautiful bride. Christopher was a handsome groom, and Charlotte felt more than a little proud as she looked at all her handsome children and her—at that time—grand total of ten grandchildren. Mark, whom she hadn't seen since Richard's wedding, looked shockingly older to her. But he, too, was pleased to see the swelling tribe of Mannings, and he was touchingly delighted to see Charlotte again. He asked her and Maurice to come to River Bend for a visit. Charlotte was tempted but declined, telling her former husband that she and Maurice were going on to California, which Maurice had never seen, to take a look at some of the wineries there and they really shouldn't break their schedule. "However, I'd like to see it again, in a way," she told Mark. "I hear you've had it rebuilt since the fire?"

"Yes, it's completely restored. We were very lucky with the paintings, too. We only lost a Renoir and a small Greuze. Of course they are real losses but considering the extent of the fire, I think we were very fortunate."

"I understand you're thinking of building a museum for the town?"

Mark nodded. "And believe me, it'll be fireproof," he added. Also, he thought, Lilyproof. And timeproof.

Before Charlotte and Maurice left for California, Mark repeated his invitation to River Bend, but Charlotte shook her head. "It would bring back too many memories," she said. "And at my age, some memories are better avoided."

"I know what you mean," replied Mark. "It was always your house," he added. "It's never been the same since you left."

She kissed his cheek, touched by the remark. She thought how time makes one forget the unpleasant things about people one has known well, and remember mostly the pleasant. As she boarded the train, she was surprised how many truly pleasant things she remembered about her second husband.

It was the last time she was ever to see him or any of their children.

It is one of the freakish twists of history that France's darkest hour occurred during the loveliest, balmiest spring and early summer anyone could remember since the World War. In May, June and July of 1940, the Third Republic collapsed like a house of cards and the highly respected French army went down to total defeat. Through this holocaust the weather remained perversely blissful. With a swiftness that stunned the French as well as the world, France fell apart as the nation was invaded by the Germans. On June 12, the Maginot Line—that great fortification that the nation had banked on to insure its defense—was abandoned by General Weygand, and millions of Parisians started fleeing the capital to the south. On June 14 the German armies entered Paris and the French government fled to Bordeaux. On June 22, in the forest of Compiègne north of Paris, on the same spot where the Germans had signed an armistice in 1918, the French gave up. A few weeks later, on July 10, at Vichy, the Third Republic in effect committed suicide and the dictatorship of the aged Marshal Pétain was established. France was cut in two.

On June 13 Charlotte and Maurice de Sibour sat in the drawing room of the Château La Colline-sur-Marne and asked Gaspard, their butler, who was now over ninety, to bring them each a glass of champagne with their habitual dry biscuit. Gaspard, his eyes filling with tears, went off to fetch the drinks as Charlotte and her husband walked out to the formal garden terraces that stretched in front of the château down to the Marne. It was a warm, lovely afternoon, and the countryside looked deceptively peaceful. Both knew, however, that a German colonel was on his way to arrest them.

When the invasion had become imminent, Maurice had pleaded with his wife to return to America. She still retained her American citizenship, and he knew that he was high on the Nazis' list of "undesirables" because of the strong antifascist stand he had taken in his articles over recent years, as well as being high on René de Courville's list—the French right was not going to lose the opportunity to settle old scores with its opponents. He was certain to be arrested, and he told Charlotte that if she stayed she would undoubtedly be arrested, too, despite her American citizenship, and that, being Jewish, she might have a worse time of it than he. To all his arguments and entreaties, Charlotte maintained one position. If he went to America with her, she would go. If he stayed in France, she would stay with him. France was her home, and her husband was her life. She would not abandon either of them.

A miserable Maurice had told her he couldn't leave France. He was too well known for his anti-Nazi views, and if he deserted France just at the time the French people desperately needed some show of strength, he could never live with himself again. He had even contemplated hiding out and starting an underground newspaper, but he thought that would not be as useful at the time as a visible show of defiance. "I'm not eager to become a martyr," he told Charlotte. "But I think perhaps France is going to need a few in the next couple of weeks."

"Then France can add one more to the list," she said, "because if you stay, I stay."

They stayed.

Gaspard came out to the terrace and set the silver tray with the two tulip glasses on the white iron table with the gaily striped umbrella above it. Charlotte and Maurice were seated in the umbrella's shade, she in a soft yellow-chiffon dress with a matching picture hat, he in a striped blazer and white ducks. They could have been posing for a de Sibour champagne ad, or some lovely Twenties conversation piece, which was the effect they intended. It would be their best weapon against the Nazis who were on their way. And if they were to go, they told each other, they at least would go with style.

Gaspard popped the cork, then, with trembling hands, tilted the tulip glass and slowly poured in the golden champagne. Charlotte smiled and took his gnarled hand and squeezed it gently. "We'll be back, Gaspard," she said. "Perhaps sooner than any of us think."

He nodded. "Oh, I know, madame. I'm sure. The Boches are stupid, but why should they arrest either of you? It makes no sense, does it?"

"Of course not. That's why we'll be back soon."

This seemed to cheer the old man up somewhat, and he moved slowly back into the château. Charlotte whispered, "You *did* leave him enough money, so he'll be all right?"

"Oh yes. In cash. I gave it to his daughter."

They took their glasses and raised them and looked into each other's eyes for a while. They both knew each other's thoughts. Finally Maurice said, "It's been nineteen beautiful, happy years, my darling. I've been the luckiest man in France."

"And I the luckiest woman. I've loved you since that first day you brought me here to lunch, and I love you even more today. You've made my life beautiful, Maurice. Thank you."

They touched their glasses and sipped the champagne. They said nothing more about the past or the future. They chatted about the house, the business and the vines until they saw the olive-drab Mercedes staff car heading up the drive. Then Charlotte reached over and took her husband's hand.

When the German colonel walked onto the terrace, he thought he had never seen such a handsome couple. Or two people more in love.

On April 11, 1942, a crowd of distinguished guests assembled in the marble entrance hall of the Charlotte Manning Gallery of Art for the dedication ceremonies of the beautiful new building set in a five-acre park next to the concert hall Mark had built for Elkins in the Twenties. The guests included the governor and senior senator of Ohio, a sprinkling of state senators from Columbus, representatives of some of the leading industrial dynasties of the Midwest, and a crowd of Mannings. David and Amanda with their five children; Len and Ellen Hastings with their four children, Len now a lieutenant commander in the navy; thirteen-year-old Evan Manning, who was being raised by his "Aunt" Ellen, and who was home from Lawrenceville on Easter vacation; Richard and Cynthia Manning and their six children (including a set of twins), Richard being embarrassingly 4-F because of flat feet and an ulcer; Chris and Rita Manning and their three children, Chris being a second lieutenant in the air force. And Mark Manning.

Mark had had a serious heart attack the year before and everyone had tried to prevent him from coming to the ceremony. He had, of course, insisted. He had "paid for the goddamn building," he said, "and all the paintings in it," so he had a right to see it christened, didn't he? Besides, he wanted to be there for Charlotte's sake. No one had had the heart to say no, so Mark was there in a blue suit, looking thinner and gaunter and older than ever, his red-gold hair having turned a sandy gray, his private nurse, Miss Lindstrom, sitting next to him on the dais.

The Elkins High School Band was there in its blue-and-green uniforms, and they played a medley of patriotic songs as the guests were arriving, including "Let's Remember Pearl Harbor," the new Frank Loesser hit, "Praise the Lord and Pass the Ammunition," and

"When the Lights Go on Again All Over the World." The band was hitting a lot of sour notes, but since half the Manning Symphony had been drafted, the band was all that was left, and everyone thought the "kids" were making a good show of it.

The building itself, designed by a New York architect in a coolly restrained classical style, was, everyone agreed, magnificent. It wasn't joltingly modern—Mark thought "modern" architecture was too "faddy" for his one hundred and twenty-seven canvases. He wanted something permanent and lasting. "Think of it as my mausoleum," he had remarked to the architect in an offhand moment, "except don't make it *look* like one. I want people to enjoy the place." A happy mausoleum was a difficult assignment for any architect, but this one had come up with a compromise between classic Greek and modern that, surprisingly, worked. The long marble galleries lined with Titians, Rembrandts, Ingres, Picassos, Renoirs, Watteaus, Matisses and Gainsboroughs the Ohio farmer's son had collected through the years were perfect settings for the masterpieces, and the fountain in the center of the tall entrance hall of the building was the perfect adornment. If the museum was to be a monument to Mark's image, or the image he wanted to hand down through the ages, it was one of taste and dignity. He had gotten his money's worth, and putting Charlotte's name on it had seemed to him somehow perfect. He liked the idea of his memory linked with hers. It was a comforting thought for eternity.

The band played "The Star-Spangled Banner" and everyone rose to sing the national anthem. Then, after they had taken their seats again, David Manning stepped up to the podium and fiddled with the microphone. David was now thirty-five and had proved to be an excellent choice to head the corporation. The war had forced the company to strain its resources as it had never done before, and everyone agreed David had risen to the challenge magnificently. When the Japanese took over the Malaysian and Sumatran rubber plantations that supplied so much of the nation's raw rubber, rubber had become a priority item, and the once-bloodied Manning plantation at Las Palmas in Río de Oro had become so important to the country that, again, U.S. Marines were dispatched to the African continent, this time to guard the plantation from attack, not from the natives but from the Germans. Furthermore, the Manning research division was working twenty-four hours a day trying to perfect the manufacture of synthetic rubber, something in which the Germans were well ahead of the Americans, the I.G. Farben Company having developed a working process in the Thirties. However, David Manning was getting encouraging reports from his chemists, and he had told the desperate War Department that a breakthrough was imminent.

But now, on this cool April day, the business of war was temporarily forgotten as David and his brothers and sister gathered to honor their mother.

"Ladies and gentlemen," David said, adjusting his horn-rimmed glasses, "several years ago, when my father began making plans for this gallery, none of us gave much thought to what we were going to name it. And then, two months ago, my brothers and my sister and I received word through the International Red Cross that our mother, Madame Charlotte de Sibour, had died in a concentration camp in Germany named Ravensbruck. We don't know how she died. The camp commander said she had caught the flu, but there seems to be some question as to the truth of this. At any rate, when we learned of mother's death, our father told us he wished to name this gallery in her honor, which we gratefully agreed to." (Mark's mind was wandering. He was looking at the High School Band and he was hearing "Columbia, the Gem of the Ocean" being played by another band, far away and long ago, on that Fourth of July back at the beginning of time. . . .)

"Our mother was born and raised here in Elkins. Perhaps some of the older citizens here may remember her father, Samuel Rosen, who emigrated to this country from Germany in the last century . . ." (There she was, seated at the Bechstein in the front parlor, turning half around looking at him, her delicate left hand still resting on the keyboard, her auburn hair pinned carelessly in a chignon like the Gibson Girls. He had seen Charlotte Rosen from a distance, riding through town in her father's carriage. Now, up close, she took his breath away. . . .) "Our mother lived many years in this town. But after the last war, she married our stepfather and moved to France . . ." ("Oh, I've seen pictures of his château, and he really slaved his ass off to get that, too, didn't he? Well, I don't make good tires, Charlotte. I make the *best* tires. And I built this whole thing up myself . . ." "Oh, is that all there is to life? Building up a big company, making money, seeing your name on tires all over the world? And besides, you *didn't* do it all by yourself. You had just a little bit of help from my father!" "Your father never even thought about getting into the business until I came to him!" "Oh Mark, why should we hurt each other? Does it make any sense? Let's just let go of each other . . .") ". . . where, in June of 1940, she and our stepfather were arrested by the Germans. The charge against our stepfather was that he was anti-Nazi. The only charge against our mother was that she was Jewish." (Ellen remembered the night on the Avenue Kléber when she told her mother she was in love with Len, and now she felt suddenly old. She wasn't so sure she was in love with Len any more. She had heard the rumors about a second "little fling," and if the rumors were true, should she carry out her threat and divorce him? Or should she try to save what was left of their marriage? What had her mother said that day in Paris, so long ago? "I've never under-stood why people fall in love with each other. . . . All I know is, love's a rare commodity in this world, and it seems to be getting rarer every day. . . .")

David paused to clear his throat. He was feeling older, too, and he missed his mother. He missed her terribly. She had always been so beautiful, so tender and good to him . . .

"And now," he continued, "she's dead. And all that we, her children, can hope is that the irrational hatred that caused her arrest and her death half a world away will not be allowed to last much longer on the face of the earth."

There was muted applause. In Ohio, the war was not being fought for the Jews. It was being fought against the Nazis and the Japs and the "forces of evil," as the newsreels called "the enemy." But the audience knew when it was expected to clap.

David stepped to the back of the dais, where two white curtains were hung against the tall marble wall. Taking hold of a pullcord, he said loudly, "I now dedicate this gallery to the memory of Charlotte Rosen Manning de Sibour." Then he pulled the cord, and the curtains slowly and gracefully parted, revealing the big Sargent portrait of Charlotte painted in 1910. Beneath the gilt frame, her name and dates, 1878–1941, were chiseled in the marble wall.

Mark turned to look up at the graceful portrait, and the impact of her death struck him with renewed force. He felt a savage pain in his chest, and for a moment he was frightened—he was too smart not to know what was happening to him—but a moment later, he accepted it. He was too smart not to. Miss Lindstrom reached out to steady him as he leaned over, holding his chest. She wasn't as quick as he to realize what was happening. As his vision began to blur, he took a last look up at the youthful Charlotte and wondered what they would put on his tombstone. Mark Manning—conniver, adulterer, murderer? Or Mark Manning—industrialist, entrepreneur, philan-thropist? Oh, undoubtedly the latter, though the truth was a mixture of both. If nothing else, he'd be remembered for a while.

And in Elkins, he was.